The Complete Classical Wisdom Collection (Vol. 2)

Letters from a Stoic, On the Shortness of Life &
As a Man Thinketh
— Timeless Lessons in Resilience and Self-
Mastery

A Modern Translation

Adapted for the Contemporary Reader

Seneca | Aristotle | James Allen

Translated by Tim Zengerink

Table of Contents

Preface - Message to the Reader

What If You Could Help Rebuild the Greatest Library in Human History?

Thousands of years ago, the Library of Alexandria stood as the crown jewel of human achievement — a sanctuary where the collected wisdom of every known civilization was gathered, preserved, and shared freely.

And then, it was lost.

Through fire, conquest, and the slow erosion of time, humanity lost not just books — but ideas, dreams, discoveries, and stories that could have changed the world forever.

Today, the Library of Alexandria lives again — and you are invited to be a part of its restoration.

Our mission is simple yet profound:

To rebuild the greatest library the world has ever known, and to translate all timeless works into every language and dialect, so that no seeker of knowledge is ever left behind again.

By joining our movement to rebuild the modern Library of Alexandria, you become part of an unprecedented mission:

- **Unlimited Access to the Greatest Audiobooks & eBooks Ever Written:**

  Instantly explore thousands of legendary works—Plato, Shakespeare, Jane Austen, Leo Tolstoy, and countless more. All instantly available to read or listen, placing a complete literary universe at your fingertips.

- **Beautiful Paperback & Deluxe Editions at Printing Cost**

  Own any title as an elegant paperback, deluxe hardcover, or stunning collectible boxset—offered to you at true printing cost, delivered straight to your door. Build your personal Library of Alexandria, crafted for beauty, built for durability, and worthy of proud display.

- **Fresh Translations for Modern Readers—in Every Language & Dialect**

  Enjoy timeless masterpieces reimagined in clear, contemporary language—no more outdated phrases or obscure references. Alongside the original versions, we're tirelessly translating these classics into every language and dialect imaginable, ensuring accessibility and understanding across cultures and generations.

- **Join a Global Renaissance of Literature & Knowledge**

  You directly support expanding our library, publishing deluxe editions at true cost, translating works into all global languages, and bringing humanity's greatest stories to people everywhere. By joining today, you're not just preserving a legacy of masterpieces; you set in motion a powerful wave of literary accessibility.

Become a Torchbearer of Knowledge.

Join us for free now at **LibraryofAlexandria.com**

Together, we will ensure that the light of human wisdom never fades again.

With gratitude and a shared love of knowledge,
The Modern Library of Alexandria Team

Visit:

www.libraryofalexandria.com

Or scan the code below:

Introduction

Endurance, Insight, and Inner Power:
The Stoic and Moral Philosophy of Resilience

Human history is full of turbulence—wars, plagues, betrayal, grief, poverty, and the ever-present awareness of death. Yet across these trials, there have always been individuals who discovered a way to live with calm, courage, and dignity amid the chaos. These are the voices of classical wisdom—those who taught that true strength is not found in conquest or wealth, but in the mastery of one's own mind.

The Complete Classical Wisdom Collection (Vol. 2) brings together three such voices: Lucius Annaeus Seneca, the Roman Stoic philosopher and statesman; and James Allen, a modern moral thinker whose quietly revolutionary insights helped shape the foundations of personal development. This volume contains Seneca's Letters from a Stoic and On the Shortness of Life, alongside Allen's brief but powerful As a Man Thinketh. Though separated by nearly two millennia, these works speak to the same fundamental concern: How can we live with resilience, clarity, and purpose, even in the face of adversity?

These authors do not promise comfort. They promise awakening. They do not teach us how to avoid difficulty, but how to face it with grace. They do not advocate escape from life's demands, but a deeper engagement with what truly matters. Their wisdom is not a luxury for the elite or the idle—it is an essential toolset for every person striving to meet life as it is, with strength drawn from within.

This introduction explores the core themes and practical value of the three works included in this volume. We will begin with Seneca's Stoic letters and reflections, then turn to James Allen's inwardly-focused moral philosophy. What binds them together is a shared belief in the power of thought, the importance of discipline, and the pursuit of an inner life rooted in virtue.

Seneca:
The Practice of Stoic Fortitude

Seneca (c. 4 BCE – 65 CE) was one of Rome's most celebrated intellectuals and a leading figure in the Stoic school of philosophy. Trained in rhetoric and philosophy, he rose to prominence as a tutor and later advisor to the emperor Nero, though his political career was marked by contradiction and tragedy. His writings, especially his letters and essays, are not theoretical treatises but practical meditations—offered as guidance to those navigating the challenges of ambition, suffering, and the fleeting nature of time.

In Letters from a Stoic, we find Seneca in a deeply personal mode. The letters are addressed to his friend Lucilius, but they are intended for all readers who seek wisdom. Seneca writes on everything from death and illness to anger, friendship, wealth, and the importance of solitude. He insists that the key to peace lies in mastering the passions, disciplining the will, and living in accordance with nature and reason.

Stoicism, for Seneca, is not an abstract set of doctrines—it is a lifelong training. He urges the reader to examine their judgments, root out toxic desires, and live each day as if it were their last. Time, he says, is not something to be spent recklessly. It is our most precious possession. "We are not given a short life," he writes, "but we make it short by wasting it."

This message is amplified in On the Shortness of Life, a brilliant and urgent essay that challenges the reader to reflect on how they use their days. Seneca observes that most people are preoccupied with trivial pursuits—business, pleasure, social obligation—and postpone living until it is too late. The truly wise, he argues, devote their lives to philosophy, not as a retreat from the world but as a deeper way of inhabiting it.

What makes Seneca so powerful is his combination of philosophical clarity and literary force. He writes with moral urgency and poetic elegance, calling us not just to think differently but to live differently. His Stoicism is not austere or detached—it is fierce, compassionate, and profoundly human. He acknowledges the messiness of life, but insists that within it lies the opportunity for greatness through moral resolve.

For modern readers overwhelmed by distraction, anxiety, and noise, Seneca's voice is a call to return to the center—to take responsibility for our time, our thoughts, and our souls. His Stoicism is not about withdrawal from the world, but about cultivating an unshakable core amid its storms.

James Allen:
The Mind as the Master of Destiny

James Allen (1864–1912) lived in a different age and context, but his insights are no less profound. A self-educated English writer who drew inspiration from Christian ethics, Stoic thought, and Eastern philosophy, Allen became one of the earliest figures in the self-help and personal development movement. His most famous work, As a Man Thinketh, remains a cornerstone of inspirational literature and a testament to the transformative power of thought.

In just a few short chapters, Allen unfolds a complete vision of human potential. He begins with the premise that "mind is the master-weaver" of our fate—that the conditions of our lives reflect the quality of our thoughts. He does not mean this in a naïve or magical sense, but in a moral and psychological one. What we dwell upon, we become. Our habits of thinking shape our character, and our character shapes our destiny.

Allen insists that personal power lies not in external conditions, but in internal transformation. Prosperity, health, peace, and success are not ends in themselves, but by-products of self-mastery. The man who learns to govern his thoughts becomes strong, steady, and serene—unmoved by hardship, generous in prosperity, and free from fear.

There is a deep ethical dimension to Allen's philosophy. He does not advocate selfish ambition or materialism. Rather, he teaches that the highest good is inner peace, and that peace arises from purity, kindness, and purpose. He invites the reader to become both architect and gardener of their inner life—to plant good thoughts, uproot the weeds of fear and anger, and cultivate the fruit of virtue.

In As a Man Thinketh, we hear echoes of both Eastern non-attachment and Stoic self-control. But Allen's tone is uniquely his own—gentle, encouraging, and quietly revolutionary. His message is not one of harsh discipline, but of quiet conviction: you are not a victim of fate, but a participant in its unfolding. You can choose who you become.

For readers seeking a path to freedom—not through rebellion, but through responsibility—Allen offers a roadmap. His wisdom is accessible, but not simplistic. It challenges us to face our own minds with honesty and courage. It affirms that no change is possible without inward change—and that such change is always possible.

Living Deliberately:
Ancient Roots and Modern Relevance

Bringing together Seneca and James Allen in a single volume may seem unusual at first. One is a Roman statesman writing in the age of emperors; the other, a modest Englishman writing in the age of steam and industry. Yet their union reveals something essential about classical wisdom: it transcends time. It is not limited to any culture, era, or creed. It is rooted in universal truths about human nature, the mind, and the soul.

Both writers teach:

- That we are not in control of circumstances, but always in control of how we respond.
- That discipline is not repression, but liberation.
- That time is fleeting, and must be used with purpose.
- That peace comes not from avoiding difficulty, but from mastering our own reactions.
- That happiness is not something we find, but something we create through right thought and right action.

These are not just ideas. They are practices. They must be lived. And that is why these texts endure—not as artifacts of a past age, but as guides for the present moment.

In a culture obsessed with consumption, Seneca and Allen remind us to simplify. In a world addicted to distraction, they call us back to clarity. In a time of external noise, they teach us to listen to the still, small voice within. Their teachings offer a philosophy of inner strength, a compass for navigating hardship, and a quiet assurance that self-mastery is not only possible, but essential.

Welcome to The Complete Classical Wisdom Collection (Vol. 2). May these pages offer not only wisdom, but transformation. May they awaken in you the resolve to live more deliberately, to think more clearly, and to become, day by day, the person you are capable of being.

Letters from a Stoic

Seneca

Introduction

I. Biography of Seneca

Lucius Annaeus Seneca, commonly known as Seneca the Younger, was born into a prominent Roman family around 4 BC in Corduba, Hispania (modern-day Córdoba, Spain). His father, Seneca the Elder, was a distinguished rhetorician and writer known for his work on declamations and rhetoric, a critical part of Roman education. This intellectual environment greatly influenced Seneca from an early age and gave him a foundation in rhetoric and literature.

Seneca's family moved to Rome during his childhood to ensure he received a comprehensive education. Rome, the epicenter of the empire, offered a thriving intellectual atmosphere where Seneca could develop his talents. In Rome, young Seneca was educated under the guidance of prominent Stoic philosophers such as Attalus, who taught him the importance of virtue and self-control, and Sotion, who introduced him to Pythagorean thought. These early influences shaped Seneca's philosophical outlook, instilling in him the Stoic principles that would define his later work.

His education was comprehensive, covering philosophy, rhetoric, literature, and science. He excelled in his studies, gaining a reputation for his eloquence and intellectual prowess. These formative experiences laid the foundation for his future contributions as a philosopher and statesman, preparing him to navigate Rome's complex political and social landscapes.

Political career and role in Roman society

Seneca's political career was as remarkable as it was tumultuous, reflecting his intellectual brilliance and the volatile nature of Roman politics. He rose to prominence during the reign of Emperor Caligula, whose unpredictable and often tyrannical rule created a challenging environment for those in positions of power. The fact that this philosopher maintained his oratorical skills and philosophical acumen despite the dangers earned him respect and influence within the imperial court.

In 31 AD, Seneca became involved in politics when he was appointed quaestor, a public office that marked the beginning of his political career. His reputation as an eloquent speaker grew, and he became known for his philosophical discourses. His rising influence drew the ire of Emperor Caligula, who reportedly saw him as a threat and considered having him executed. According to some accounts, Caligula only spared Seneca's life because he believed he was ill and would not live much longer.

Seneca's fortunes improved during the reign of Emperor Claudius, who succeeded Caligula. In 41 AD, he became a tutor to the young Lucius Domitius Ahenobarbus, who would later become Emperor Nero. This position placed him in a pivotal role, as he was responsible for shaping the education and character of the future emperor. Under Claudius, Seneca also served as a senator and became one of the most influential figures in Roman politics, using his position to advocate for Stoic governance principles.

Seneca's influence peaked when Nero ascended to the throne in 54 AD. As one of Nero's closest advisors, he worked alongside Sextus Afranius Burrus, the prefect of the Praetorian Guard, to guide the young emperor's early rule. During this period, often referred to as the Quinquennium Neronis or the "Five Good Years" of Nero's reign, Seneca and Burrus implemented policies that promoted justice, reduced corruption, and fostered stability within the empire.

Despite his efforts to steer Nero toward enlightened rule, this exceptional thinker faced mounting challenges as Nero's reign progressed. The emperor's increasingly erratic behavior and indulgence in personal excesses strained their relationship. Seneca attempted to retire from public life around 62 AD, but Nero refused to allow him to leave the court, citing his continued need for this consummate rhetorician's guidance.

Political intrigue and conspiracies precipitated Seneca's eventual fall from grace within the court. Although evidence of his involvement was dubious, Seneca was implicated in the Pisonian Conspiracy, a plot to assassinate Nero and replace him with Gaius Calpurnius Piso. The accusations were enough for Nero to demand Seneca's death, and in 65 AD, he committed suicide, a fate he met with Stoic calmness and dignity, drinking hemlock and bleeding to death in his bathtub. His demise was consistent with the philosophical ideals he had espoused throughout his life.

Historical context

During the lifetime of Lucius Annaeus Seneca, the Roman Empire was at the zenith of its power and cultural influence. Spanning from Britain in the west to Egypt in the east, the empire was a vast and diverse conglomeration of peoples, cultures, and economies, all governed from the epicenter of Rome. This period was characterized by significant territorial expansion, economic prosperity, and an unparalleled flourishing of arts and literature.

Rome was a marvel of engineering and architecture, with grand structures such as the Colosseum and the Pantheon exemplifying Roman innovation. This cultural richness contributed to the vibrant intellectual climate in which Seneca lived and wrote, influencing his philosophical development and the content of his letters.

However, the empire was plagued by deep-seated social and political issues. The vast expanse of the empire presented challenges in governance, communication, and maintaining order. The political landscape was marred by corruption, and the consolidation of power in the hands of a few elites. The Senate had largely become a ceremonial body, with real power concentrated in the hands of the emperor.

Key events and challenges faced during his life

Seneca's life spanned the reigns of four Roman emperors, each of whom left a distinct mark on the empire and Seneca's fortunes.

Tiberius (14-37 AD): Seneca was born during the reign of Tiberius, who ruled with an iron fist and maintained a reclusive lifestyle. A climate of fear and suspicion marked Tiberius's later years as political purges and executions became commonplace. This environment of distrust and paranoia shaped the political landscape that Seneca would later experience.

Caligula (37-41 AD): Caligula's reign was brief but notorious for its extravagance and cruelty. His erratic behavior and tyrannical rule led to widespread unrest and his eventual assassination. During Caligula's rule, Seneca began his career in the public eye, gaining recognition for his rhetorical skills, although he narrowly escaped death due to the emperor's acknowledgment of Seneca's poor health.

Claudius (41-54 AD): Seneca's fortunes improved significantly under Claudius. He was appointed as a tutor to Nero, placing him at the heart of the imperial court. Claudius' reign was more stable, characterized by administrative reforms and territorial expansion. However, it was also plagued by court intrigues and the influence of powerful freedmen and women, such as the notorious Messalina and Agrippina the Younger.

Nero (54-68 AD): Nero's ascension marked the peak of Seneca's influence as one of the emperor's principal advisors. The early years of Nero's reign were relatively stable and prosperous, guided by Seneca and the Praetorian Prefect Burrus. This scholar's Stoic principles initially influenced Nero's policies, but their relationship soured as Nero grew more autocratic. Seneca eventually sought to retire from public life, but the political environment became increasingly perilous.

Exile: In 41 AD, Seneca was accused of involvement in a conspiracy against Emperor Claudius and exiled to the island of Corsica. This period of exile lasted eight years and was a time of reflection and writing for him . He used this opportunity to delve deeper into Stoic philosophy, producing works that emphasized the importance of virtue and accepting fate.

Return to power: With the intervention of Agrippina, Claudius's wife, who recalled him, Seneca returned from exile to tutor her son Nero. This role brought Seneca immense power and influence, allowing him to implement policies that reflected his Stoic ideals, such as reducing taxes and promoting public welfare.

Fall from grace and forced suicide: Seneca's influence waned as Nero's rule became more tyrannical and erratic. Accusations of complicity in the Pisonian Conspiracy, a plot to assassinate Nero, led to Seneca's downfall. Although the evidence against him was circumstantial, Nero demanded his death. In 65 AD, Seneca committed suicide, leaving behind a legacy of philosophical writings that continue to inspire readers.

II. The Duality of Seneca

Philosopher and statesman

Lucius Annaeus Seneca was a figure of remarkable duality, embodying the complex interplay between philosophical ideals and political realities. As a Stoic philosopher, Seneca devoted himself to pursuing wisdom, virtue, and ethical living. Yet, as a prominent statesman in the Roman Empire, he operated within a corrupt political landscape

Both Seneca's philosophical pursuits and his political responsibilities were a defining aspect of his life. His role as an advisor to Emperor Nero placed him at the epicenter of Roman power, where he wielded significant influence over imperial policy and governance. This position allowed him to implement Stoic principles on a grand scale, yet it also subjected him to the moral complexities of imperial politics.

Seneca's writings reflect his struggle to maintain his Stoic ideals while fulfilling his public duties. He believed in the Stoic ideals of virtue, rationality, and living in accordance with nature, which he sought to apply in his guidance of Nero and his administration.

Seneca advocated for policies that promoted justice, temperance, and the welfare of the Roman people, striving to steer Nero's reign toward stability and benevolence.

Nonetheless, the realities of political life often demanded that he make pragmatic compromises. Seneca found himself entangled in the power dynamics of the Roman court, where ambition and self-interest frequently overshadowed moral considerations. As Nero's advisor, Seneca was involved in decisions that tested his philosophical integrity, such as dealing with court conspiracies and the machinations of influential figures like Agrippina the Younger.

Seneca's Letters often grapple with his ethical challenges, exploring themes of power, ambition, and the limits of personal influence. He reflects on the difficulty of maintaining virtue in a corrupt system, acknowledging the tension between his philosophical ideals and the compromises required by political life. These reflections offer valuable insights into the complexities of ethical leadership, illustrating the perennial struggle to reconcile moral principles with the demands of governance.

Seneca's dual role as a public figure and private philosopher highlights the discrepancies between his teachings and actions. While his philosophical writings advocate for simplicity, self-discipline, and ethical living, his position in the imperial court necessitated a lifestyle that often conflicted with these values.

This philosopher's wealth and status as an imperial advisor often contradicted his Stoic teachings, which emphasized the importance of detachment from material possessions and external success. Critics of Seneca pointed to these inconsistencies, questioning the authenticity of his philosophical convictions.

Still, Seneca addressed these criticisms directly in his writings, acknowledging the challenges of living up to Stoic ideals while operating within the constraints of political life. He argued that wealth and power were indifferent, neither inherently good nor bad, and that their moral value depended on their use. Seneca sought to use his influence and resources to promote the public good, even as he wrestled with the tension between his public role and private beliefs.

Seneca remained committed to the core principles of Stoicism, striving to reconcile his philosophical ideals with the realities of his political duties. He was a man deeply engaged in self-examination, using Stoic practices such as reflection, meditation, and ethical reasoning to navigate the complexities of his life.

Seneca's writings encourage readers to consider the interplay between personal values and public responsibilities, offering guidance on maintaining integrity and purpose when facing external pressures. By candidly exploring the discrepancies between his ideals and actions, Seneca provides a nuanced perspective on the human struggle for ethical consistency.

Ultimately, Seneca's duality as a philosopher and a statesman underscores the timeless challenge of balancing ethical aspirations with practical realities. His reflections offer a valuable framework for understanding the complexities of leadership and the pursuit of virtue, inspiring readers to engage in thoughtful introspection and strive for moral excellence in their own lives.

III. Philosophical Background

Stoicism is a Hellenistic philosophy founded in the early 3rd century BC by Zeno of Citium. It emerged in Athens and quickly gained prominence as a school of thought that offered practical guidance for living a virtuous life. Stoicism emphasizes the development of self-control and fortitude as a means of overcoming destructive emotions. It is a philosophy designed for action, helping individuals navigate the complexities of life with wisdom and resilience.

Stoicism teaches that the path to true happiness lies in living in accordance with nature and reason, which involves understanding the natural order of the universe and our place within it. We must recognize that we cannot control external events, but we can control our reactions to them. By cultivating a rational mindset and focusing on what is within our control, Stoics seek to achieve tranquility and inner peace.

Core principles of Stoicism

Three main pillars characterize Stoicism: ethics, logic, and natural philosophy. Each component is crucial in shaping the Stoic worldview and guiding individuals toward a virtuous life.

- Ethics: The Stoic approach to ethics revolves around living a life of virtue, which they see as the only true good. Four cardinal qualities define virtue: wisdom, courage, justice, and temperance. For the Stoics, the ultimate goal is to achieve moral excellence by aligning one's actions with these virtues. They believe that external goods, such as wealth or fame, are inconsequential and do not contribute to true happiness.
- Logic: Logic is essential to Stoicism as it provides the framework for clear thinking and rational decision-making. Stoics emphasize the importance of developing a disciplined mind capable of distinguishing between true and false judgments. This logical approach helps individuals avoid errors in reasoning and maintain clarity in their thoughts and actions.
- Natural philosophy: Stoics view the universe as a rational and interconnected whole, governed by the principle of "Logos," or divine reason. Understanding the laws of nature and accepting the inevitability of change is fundamental to Stoic philosophy. By recognizing that everything in the universe is subject to the natural order, Stoics cultivate an attitude of acceptance and adaptability.

The pursuit of virtue and living in accordance with nature

Stoics believe that by aligning one's actions with nature, individuals can achieve a state of inner tranquility and contentment. Living in accordance with nature means acknowledging the limits of human control and accepting life's transient nature. Stoics teach that true freedom and happiness come from understanding what is within our power and what is not. By focusing on internal virtues rather than external circumstances, individuals can cultivate a sense of equanimity and resilience in the face of life's challenges.

Stoic philosophy deeply influenced Seneca, permeating his writings and personal life. He demonstrates his commitment to Stoic ideals, offering practical guidance on applying these principles to everyday life.

Seneca's integration of Stoic philosophy into his writings reflects his belief in the transformative power of Stoicism. His Letters explore a wide range of topics, from the nature of happiness and the management of emotions to the ethical dilemmas of power and wealth. Throughout his correspondence, Seneca emphasizes the importance of virtue, rationality, and self-discipline as tools for achieving a fulfilling life.

In his personal life, he endeavored to embody Stoic principles, striving to maintain composure and clarity amidst the pressures of political life. His philosophical reflections reveal a deep engagement with Stoic exercises, which he used to explore the moral complexities and challenges he faced as a statesman.

Key figures and texts that influenced his thoughts

A rich tradition of Stoic thought and interactions with contemporary thinkers shaped Seneca's philosophical outlook. This section explores the key figures and texts that influenced Seneca's development as a Stoic philosopher and how these influences manifest in his writings.

The Stoic tradition that this figure inherited built on the foundational teachings of earlier philosophers who laid the groundwork for the school's principles and practices. These early Stoics provided the intellectual framework that Seneca would later expand upon in his Letters.

- Zeno of Citium: Zeno of Citium, the founder of Stoicism, established the school in Athens around the early 3rd century BC. Zeno's teachings emphasized living in accordance with nature, the importance of virtue as the highest good, and the development of self-control to achieve a tranquil life. Zeno's vision of Stoicism was one of practical philosophy, designed to help individuals live better lives through the cultivation of wisdom and virtue. Zeno's foundational ideas influenced Seneca, particularly the concept of living in harmony with nature. Zeno's emphasis on rationality and self-discipline is evident in Seneca's commitment to these principles.

- Chrysippus: Chrysippus, a successor of Zeno, is often credited with systematizing Stoic philosophy and expanding its theoretical foundations. He greatly contributed to Stoic logic, ethics, and physics, solidifying the school's reputation as a major philosophical force. Chrysippus' work on logic, particularly his development of propositional logic, laid the groundwork for later philosophical inquiry. Seneca drew inspiration from Chrysippus' rigorous approach to Stoic doctrine, incorporating his logical precision and ethical insights into his writings. The emphasis on reason and the importance of clear thinking in Stoicism owes much to Chrysippus' influence. Seneca's letters reflect this intellectual rigor, as he encourages readers to cultivate a disciplined mind capable of distinguishing between true and false judgments.

- Posidonius: Posidonius was a later Stoic philosopher who integrated Stoicism with elements of Platonism and Aristotelianism. His work expanded the scope of Stoic philosophy to include topics such as natural science, ethics, and the psychology of emotions. Posidonius was known for his interest in the cosmos' interconnectedness and the individual's role within it. Posidonius' holistic approach to philosophy, which combined scientific inquiry with ethical reflection, inspired Seneca. This impact is evident in Seneca's discussions on the nature of the universe, the importance of understanding human emotions, and the pursuit of knowledge as a means to live a virtuous life. Seneca admired Posidonius' ability to synthesize diverse philosophical traditions, which resonated with his own efforts to apply Stoic principles to a wide range of topics.

IV. The Letters from a Stoic

Seneca's Letters from a Stoic is a collection of personal letters that provides an intimate glimpse into the application of Stoic philosophy in everyday life. Unlike a traditional philosophical treatise that systematically explores theoretical concepts, these letters are practical, direct, and deeply personal. Written as a series of correspondences with Lucilius Junior, a young Roman official and friend, the Letters aim to offer guidance and insight into living a virtuous life grounded in Stoic principles.

The format of the Letters is key to understanding their unique character. Seneca wrote these letters to Lucilius not as abstract discourses, but as personal reflections and advice meant to address specific issues and challenges faced by his correspondent. This epistolary form allows Seneca to discuss philosophy in a relatable and accessible manner, drawing on personal anecdotes, current events, and practical examples to illustrate his points.

The conversational tone of the Letters creates a sense of intimacy and immediacy that engages the reader. Seneca uses this to explore a wide range of topics, from the nature of happiness and the importance of self-discipline to the management of emotions and the acceptance of mortality. By framing his philosophical reflections as personal advice, Seneca invites us to reflect on our own lives and consider how we can apply Stoic principles to our circumstances.

This approach emphasizes the practical application of Stoicism, encouraging us to actively engage with philosophical ideas rather than passively absorb them.

Written as correspondence with Lucilius Junior

Lucilius Junior, the primary recipient of Seneca's Letters, was a Roman official with aspirations toward philosophical understanding and personal growth. Through his correspondence with Lucilius, Seneca seeks to mentor and guide him in the pursuit of wisdom and virtue. The Letters address Lucilius's specific concerns and questions, offering practical advice on navigating life's challenges with a Stoic mindset.

From discussions on the nature of friendship and the value of time to meditations on death and the fleeting nature of life, Seneca provides Lucilius with a comprehensive guide to ethical living. This personalized approach allows Seneca to address the complexities of human experience, offering insights that remain relevant and applicable to modern readers.

While the Letters are addressed to Lucilius, Seneca clearly intended them for a broader audience. Through his correspondence, Seneca aims to educate and inspire readers from all walks of life, encouraging them to embrace Stoic philosophy as a means of achieving personal growth and fulfillment. He designs the Letters as a resource for anyone seeking to cultivate inner peace, resilience, and ethical integrity. These are an educational tool, offering readers a thorough introduction to Stoic philosophy and its practical applications. He presents Stoicism as a pathway to self-improvement, urging readers to examine their beliefs, attitudes, and behaviors in light of Stoic principles. By providing concrete examples and actionable advice, Seneca empowers readers to take charge of their own development, fostering a sense of autonomy and purpose.

Seneca's eloquent and persuasive writing encourages readers to aspire to greatness, not through external achievements but through the cultivation of a virtuous character. His reflections challenge readers to rethink their priorities and embrace a life of simplicity, humility, and integrity.

Seneca's primary aim is to encourage readers to apply Stoic philosophy to the challenges of everyday life. He emphasizes the importance of practical wisdom, teaching that philosophy should be a guide to action rather than mere theoretical speculation. Through his Letters, Seneca demonstrates how Stoic principles can be used to confront adversity, manage emotions, and find meaning in even the most difficult circumstances.

By addressing real-life issues and providing concrete strategies for dealing with them, Seneca offers readers a powerful toolkit for personal transformation. His Letters inspire confidence in the ability to overcome obstacles and lead a life of purpose and fulfillment, grounded in the timeless wisdom of Stoic philosophy.

Therefore, Letters from a Stoic is a masterful exploration of Stoic philosophy, presented in a personal and profound format. Seneca's letters continue to resonate with readers, offering valuable insights into the art of living well and the pursuit of a virtuous life.

Structure and style

Seneca's Letters from a Stoic is a collection of 124 letters that cover a wide range of topics, each shedding light on different aspects of Stoic philosophy and its application to everyday life.

The structure of the Letters allows Seneca to discuss various philosophical themes. Each letter stands alone as an independent piece of writing, addressing specific issues or questions raised by Lucilius or inspired by Seneca's own reflections. This enables readers to engage with the text at their own pace, selecting what resonates with their personal interests or current challenges.

The Letters cover an array of philosophical topics, including:

- Ethics: Seneca delves into the nature of virtue and the importance of living a morally upright life. He discusses the qualities that define a virtuous person, such as wisdom, courage, justice, and temperance, and provides guidance on cultivating these virtues in oneself.

- Friendship: Seneca reflects on the value of friendship and the qualities that make for meaningful and lasting relationships. He emphasizes the importance of mutual respect, trust, and support, highlighting how friendship can be a source of strength and personal growth.

- Death: The Letters frequently address the theme of mortality, encouraging readers to confront the inevitability of death with equanimity and acceptance. Seneca explores how an awareness of mortality can inspire a more purposeful and deliberate approach to life.

- The nature of happiness: Seneca examines the concept of happiness from a Stoic perspective, arguing that true happiness is found not in external possessions or achievements but in living a life aligned with one's values and principles. He offers insights into how individuals can find contentment and fulfillment through the pursuit of virtue and self-mastery.

This thematic diversity makes the Letters a valuable resource for anyone seeking to understand and apply Stoic philosophy in their own life. Each letter provides a unique perspective on the challenges and opportunities of human experience, offering timeless wisdom that remains relevant in the modern world.

Literary style and use of language

Seneca's written language is accessible and engaging, making complex philosophical ideas understandable and relevant to a broad audience. Seneca adopts a direct and conversational tone throughout his Letters, creating a sense of intimacy and immediacy that draws readers into the text. This approach allows him to communicate his ideas in an approachable and compelling manner, breaking down complex philosophical concepts into clear, relatable insights.

The conversational and dialectical style of the Letters reflects Seneca's belief that philosophy should be practical and applicable to daily life. He writes to guide and mentor Lucilius, using straightforward yet profound language. Seneca employs a variety of rhetorical devices to enhance the impact of his writing and convey his ideas more effectively. He uses analogies, metaphors, and rhetorical questions to illustrate his points, making abstract concepts more tangible and memorable. These devices help clarify complex ideas and encourage readers to reflect on their own experiences and beliefs.

In addition to rhetorical devices, Seneca frequently incorporates personal anecdotes and historical examples into his Letters. He draws on his own life experiences and observations to provide concrete illustrations of Stoic principles in action. By sharing his personal reflections and challenges, Seneca offers readers a window into his own philosophical journey, making his teachings more authentic.

The personal anecdotes also serve to humanize Seneca, highlighting his struggles and successes in applying Stoic philosophy to his own life. This transparency fosters a sense of connection and empathy with readers, who may find inspiration and guidance in Seneca's candid exploration of his thoughts and experiences.

Overall, the structure and style of these Letters contribute to their enduring appeal and effectiveness as a philosophical guide. Seneca's ability to communicate complex ideas with clarity and elegance ensures that his reflections continue to resonate with readers seeking wisdom and guidance in the pursuit of a virtuous life.

V. Themes and content of Letters from a Stoic

Seneca's Letters from a Stoic provide a profound exploration of the human condition, offering guidance on navigating life's challenges with wisdom, resilience, and integrity. This section examines some of the key themes in the letters, which continue to resonate with readers seeking personal growth and fulfillment.

Key themes

The pursuit of virtue and self-improvement

One of the central themes in these Letters is the pursuit of virtue and the continuous effort toward self-improvement. Seneca emphasizes that true happiness and fulfillment are achieved not through external achievements but through the cultivation of inner virtue. He encourages readers to engage in self-examination and moral development, urging them to reflect on their actions, intentions, and character.

Seneca believes that self-improvement is a lifelong journey requiring constant vigilance and effort. He suggests to practice introspection, identify their strengths and weaknesses, and strive to align their lives with Stoic ideals. Individuals can develop a strong moral character that serves as the foundation for a meaningful life by cultivating virtues such as wisdom, courage, justice, and temperance.

According to Seneca, the pursuit of virtue involves the disciplined practice of ethical principles, leading to a state of inner harmony and contentment. He tells readers to focus on what is within their control, letting go of concerns about external circumstances and societal expectations. Through his Letters, Seneca provides a roadmap for achieving personal excellence and living a life of purpose and integrity.

The nature of death and impermanence

Seneca frequently addresses the theme of death and impermanence, inviting us to confront the inevitability of mortality with acceptance and equanimity. He argues that an awareness of death is essential for living a meaningful life, as it encourages us to prioritize what truly matters and make the most of the present moment. Our scholar believes we can achieve a sense of peace and wisdom by accepting the transient nature of life. He advises readers to view death not as something to be feared but as a natural part of the human experience. This perspective allows one to let go of anxiety and focus on living virtuously, free from the fear of the unknown.

Seneca's reflections on mortality are intended to inspire a sense of urgency and purpose, advising readers to live each day with intention and gratitude. By embracing the impermanence of life, individuals can cultivate a deeper appreciation for the present and foster a more profound connection to their values and priorities.

The insignificance of wealth and status

A recurring theme in these Letters is Seneca's critique of materialism and the pursuit of external validation. He challenges the notion that wealth, fame, and social status are essential for happiness, arguing that true fulfillment comes from within. Seneca emphasizes that material possessions and societal recognition are fleeting and do not contribute to genuine well-being.

Seneca encourages readers to question the societal emphasis on wealth and status, advocating for a life of simplicity and self-sufficiency. He believes the relentless pursuit of material goods can lead to dissatisfaction and distraction from what truly matters. Instead, he advises individuals to focus on cultivating inner virtues and developing a sense of contentment independent of external circumstances. By rejecting the allure of materialism, Seneca invites readers to find fulfillment through personal growth and ethical living. His Letters encourage people to reevaluate their priorities and seek meaning through character development and the pursuit of wisdom.

Dealing with emotions and maintaining composure

Seneca acknowledges the complexity of human emotions, such as anger, fear, and desire, and offers strategies for managing these emotions through reason and self-discipline. He advises readers to cultivate a rational mindset, using reason as a tool to navigate emotional turbulence and maintain inner peace. He capitalizes the importance of self-awareness, encouraging individuals to recognize and examine their emotional responses. By understanding the root causes of their emotions, people can develop strategies for managing them effectively.

Seneca also advocates mindfulness, encouraging readers to remain present and focused in the moment. Individuals can respond to challenges with clarity and composure by cultivating awareness and detachment, protecting themselves from the influence of irrational impulses.

Through his Letters, Seneca provides practical guidance on harnessing the power of reason to achieve emotional resilience and stability. His teachings help readers to develop the skills needed to face the complexities of life with grace and poise, fostering a sense of tranquility and balance.

Stoic practices and exercises for personal growth

Seneca teaches us the importance of integrating Stoic principles into daily life through practical application, encouraging readers to engage actively with philosophy as a means of self-improvement and emotional mastery. Seneca's Letters contain exercises aimed at cultivating resilience and emotional control. These practices are designed to help us develop the mental fortitude necessary to navigate life's challenges with equanimity and composure.

Practical exercises for developing resilience and emotional control

- Negative visualization (premeditatio malorum): One of the key exercises that Seneca advocates is negative visualization, or premeditatio malorum. This practice involves mentally rehearsing potential challenges and adversities before they occur. By envisioning worst-case scenarios, people can prepare themselves emotionally and mentally for difficulties, reducing their impact when they arise. This exercise is intended to build resilience by familiarizing oneself with the possibility of setbacks, thereby diminishing the fear and anxiety associated with them. By confronting potential challenges in advance, we can develop strategies for coping and remain composed when faced with unexpected events.

- Journaling and reflection: Seneca places great emphasis on the practice of daily journaling and reflection as a tool for self-examination. Writing about one's thoughts, actions, and emotions allows people to gain insight into their behavior and identify areas for improvement. This practice encourages self-awareness and fosters a deeper understanding of one's motivations and values. Through reflection, people can assess their adherence to Stoic principles, recognizing successes and acknowledging areas where they have fallen short. This ongoing process of introspection promotes continuous growth and self-improvement, helping people align their actions with their philosophical ideals.

- Mindfulness and presence: Seneca encourages the cultivation of mindfulness and presence to maintain focus and clarity in the present moment. By practicing mindfulness, we can become more attuned to our thoughts and emotions, allowing them to respond thoughtfully rather than react impulsively. This exercise helps people cultivate emotional control by fostering a sense of detachment from external events and distractions. By remaining grounded in the present, we can make more deliberate choices and maintain a sense of inner peace, even amidst the chaos of daily life.

- Acceptance and amor fati: A central tenet of Stoicism that Seneca advocates is the acceptance of fate, or amor fati. This practice involves embracing the unfolding of events as part of the natural order and accepting what cannot be changed. By adopting an attitude of acceptance, people can free themselves from the burden of resistance and cultivate a sense of tranquility and contentment. Seneca encourages readers to focus on what is within their control and let go of concerns about external circumstances. This exercise promotes resilience by helping us develop the mental flexibility to adapt to changing conditions and find meaning in every experience.

Reflection on past actions and future intentions as a means of self-improvement

Seneca recognizes the importance of reflecting on past actions and setting future intentions as a pathway to self-improvement. This practice encourages people to learn from their experiences, drawing lessons from successes and failures.

- Reviewing past actions: By reflecting on past actions, we can gain insight into behaviors and identify patterns that may hinder our growth. Seneca encourages readers to consider their responses to past challenges and evaluate their adherence to Stoic principles. This reflection fosters accountability and encourages us to take responsibility for our actions.

- Setting future intentions: Seneca advises readers to set clear intentions for the future, aligning their goals and actions with their core values and principles. By establishing a vision for personal growth, people can create a roadmap for achieving their aspirations while focusing on what truly matters. Setting future intentions helps people prioritize their efforts and make deliberate choices that contribute to their overall well-being and fulfillment. This exercise empowers us to take control of our personal development and pursue a life of purpose and virtue.

Through these practices and exercises, Seneca provides readers with practical tools for cultivating resilience, emotional control, and self-awareness. His Letters offer a blueprint for integrating Stoic philosophy into everyday life, inspiring individuals to pursue continuous growth and self-improvement.

VI. The Legacy of Seneca

Seneca's contributions to philosophy and culture have left an indelible mark on the intellectual landscape, with his writings continuing to resonate across centuries. His profound insights into human nature and ethical living have inspired countless thinkers and remain deeply relevant today. This section explores the lasting impact of Seneca's work, highlighting its influence on subsequent generations and its continued significance in the modern world.

Impact on philosophy and culture

Seneca's writings, particularly his Letters, have profoundly influenced the development of Western philosophy and literature. His ability to articulate Stoic principles in a relatable and accessible manner has ensured that his ideas have been passed down through the ages, shaping the thoughts and writings of many influential figures.

- Legacy in Western philosophy and literature: Seneca's philosophical reflections have inspired many philosophers and writers throughout history. His emphasis on virtue, rationality, and ethical living resonated with early Christian thinkers who found common ground between Stoic and Christian ideals. Seneca's moral teachings influenced figures such as Augustine and Thomas Aquinas, prompting them to incorporate aspects of his thought into their own theological frameworks.

  During the Renaissance, a period marked by a revival of interest in classical texts, Seneca's works experienced renewed popularity. Humanists such as Erasmus of Rotterdam and Montaigne admired Seneca for his eloquent expression of Stoic ideals and his practical approach to philosophy. Montaigne, in particular, drew heavily on Seneca's writings in his own essays, praising his wisdom and insight into the human condition.

  In addition to his influence on philosophy, Seneca's writings have impacted literature and drama. His tragedies, characterized by their exploration of moral and existential themes, were a major influence on playwrights such as William Shakespeare and Jean Racine. Seneca's ability to capture the complexities of human emotion and the moral dilemmas of life has left a lasting legacy in the world of literature.

- Influence on later Stoics and Renaissance Humanists: Seneca's work served as a bridge between ancient Stoicism and later philosophical developments. His integration of Stoic principles with a focus on personal experience and practical application laid the groundwork for the continued evolution of Stoic thought.

Seneca's writings inspired the revival of Stoicism during the Renaissance. His emphasis on self-examination, moral integrity, and the pursuit of wisdom resonated with the humanist ideals of individual potential and personal development.

Seneca's influence extended to the Enlightenment, where thinkers such as Voltaire and Diderot, admired his commitment to reason and his critique of superstition and dogma. His writings on ethics and the nature of happiness contributed to the development of modern philosophical thought, inspiring a commitment to rational inquiry and the exploration of human potential.

Continuing relevance and appeal of his thoughts in modern times

Seneca's reflections on the human experience and the nature of virtue remain relevant for contemporary readers, offering timeless insights into personal development and ethical living. His ability to address universal themes with clarity and eloquence ensures that his ideas remain pertinent in addressing modern challenges.

Seneca's exploration of human nature and the pursuit of virtue provides valuable guidance for individuals seeking to navigate the complexities of modern life. His teachings on the importance of self-discipline, resilience, and ethical integrity offer a framework for personal growth and self-improvement. By emphasizing the cultivation of inner virtues over external achievements, Seneca encourages readers to find fulfillment through the development of character and the pursuit of wisdom.

His reflections on the nature of happiness and the role of emotions continue to resonate with readers seeking to achieve a balanced and meaningful life. Seneca's insights into managing emotions and maintaining composure in the face of adversity are particularly relevant in today's fast-paced and often chaotic world, where the ability to navigate stress and uncertainty is more important than ever.

Seneca's Stoic principles offer practical solutions to many of the challenges faced by individuals and society today. His emphasis on rationality, self-control, and the acceptance of fate provides a foundation for developing resilience in the face of life's uncertainties.

His critique of materialism and the pursuit of external validation offers a valuable perspective on prioritizing inner values over superficial success.

Seneca's Letters also provide insights into ethical leadership and the responsibilities of those in positions of power. His reflections on the challenges of maintaining integrity and virtue in the face of political and social pressures offer guidance for leaders seeking to navigate the complexities of governance with wisdom and fairness.

Thus, Seneca's legacy is one of enduring wisdom and relevance. His writings continue to inspire and challenge readers, offering timeless insights into the pursuit of a virtuous and meaningful life. By engaging with Seneca's reflections, contemporary readers can find guidance and inspiration for navigating the complexities of modern existence and striving for personal and ethical excellence.

VII. Conclusion

Seneca's philosophical journey is a testament to the enduring struggle between theory and practice, a tension he navigated throughout his life. As a statesman and philosopher, Seneca found himself at the intersection of public duty and personal conviction, often grappling with the complexities of applying Stoic principles in a world of moral ambiguity and political intrigue. Throughout these Letters, Seneca offers a candid exploration of his attempts to reconcile his philosophical ideals with the demands of his public responsibilities. His writings reveal a man deeply committed to the pursuit of wisdom and virtue yet acutely aware of the challenges posed by the realities of Roman political life. Seneca's Letters illuminate his philosophical evolution, illustrating his commitment to self-examination and moral development. He candidly addresses his shortcomings and aspirations, offering readers a nuanced perspective on the human condition. Our philospopher's willingness to engage with the contradictions of his life and the limitations of his ideals makes his writings both relatable and profound, providing valuable insights into the complexities of ethical living.

Furthermore, Seneca's Letters invite readers to embark on their own journey of personal and ethical growth, offering guidance and inspiration for enduring the challenges of modern life. Through his reflections, Seneca encourages readers to engage actively with Stoic philosophy, exploring its potential to transform their lives and enhance their understanding of themselves and the world around them.

These Letters provide a rich source of wisdom for individuals seeking to cultivate virtue and resilience in the face of life's uncertainties. Seneca's emphasis on self-examination, rationality, and emotional control offers practical tools for personal growth, empowering readers to take charge of their development and strive for excellence in all areas of life. Seneca encourages readers to reflect on their actions and intentions, fostering a deeper awareness of their values and priorities. By engaging with the text, people can gain insights into their behavior and motivations, enabling them to make more deliberate and purposeful choices. Seneca's teachings inspire a commitment to continuous self-improvement, encouraging readers to pursue a life of integrity and meaning.

Lastly, Seneca's Letters from a Stoic continues to be a powerful source of guidance and inspiration, offering timeless insights into the art of living well. By engaging with these Letters, readers can embark on a transformative journey of personal growth, discovering the enduring relevance of Stoic philosophy in shaping a life of purpose, virtue, and fulfillment.

Letter 1 - On Saving Time

Greetings from Seneca to his friend Lucilius.

Keep doing what you're doing, my dear Lucilius—set yourself free for your own sake. Take back and save your time, which until recently has been taken from you, stolen away, or has simply slipped from your hands. Make yourself believe what I'm saying—that some moments are torn from us, that some are gently taken away, and that others quietly slip out of our reach. The most disgraceful kind of loss, however, is the one that happens because of carelessness. Furthermore, if you pay close attention to this problem, you will find that the largest part of our life passes while we are doing wrong, a good portion while we are doing nothing, and all our time while we are doing things that aren't important. What person can you show me who truly values their time, who understands the worth of each day, who realizes that they are dying a little every day? For we are mistaken when we think of death as something in the future; the biggest part of death has already passed. Whatever years lie behind us are already in death's hands.

So, Lucilius, do as you told me you are doing: hold on to every hour. Take care of today's task, and you won't have to depend so much on tomorrow. While we are delaying, life speeds by. Nothing, Lucilius, truly belongs to us except time. Nature gave us ownership of this one thing, but it's so fleeting and slippery that anyone who wants to can take it away from us. How foolish people are! They allow the cheapest and most useless things, which can easily be replaced, to be accounted for, after they have gotten them; but they never think of themselves as in debt when they receive some of that precious thing—time! And yet time is the one loan that even a grateful person cannot repay.

You might wonder how I, who preach to you so freely, practice what I'm saying. I'll be honest with you: my expenses balance out, as you would expect from someone who is generous but careful. I can't say that I waste nothing, but I can at least tell you what I am wasting, and the reason and manner of the loss; I can explain why I am a poor man. My situation, however, is like that of many people who are reduced to having little through no fault of their own: everyone forgives them, but no one helps them.

So what is the situation, then? It is this: I don't consider a person poor if the little they have is enough for them. I advise you, however, to hold on to what is really yours; and you cannot start too early. For, as our ancestors believed, it's too late to save when you reach the dregs of the cask. What remains at the bottom is small in amount, and poor in quality. Farewell.

Letter 2 - On discursiveness in reading

Based on what you write to me and what I hear, I'm forming a positive opinion about your future. You don't run from place to place, distracting yourself by constantly changing where you live; because such restlessness is a sign of a troubled mind. To me, the first sign of a well-organized mind is a person's ability to stay in one place and enjoy their own company.

However, be careful that this habit of reading many different authors and books doesn't make you scattered and unsteady. You should spend time with a limited number of great thinkers and deeply absorb their works if you want to gain ideas that will firmly take root in your mind. Being everywhere means being nowhere. When a person spends all their time traveling to foreign places, they end up with many acquaintances but no real friends. The same applies to people who don't get to know any one author well but rush through many of them.

Food does no good and isn't digested into the body if it leaves the stomach as soon as it's eaten; nothing hinders a cure more than constantly changing medicine; no wound will heal if one ointment is applied after another; and a plant that is often moved can never grow strong. There is nothing so effective that it can help you if it's constantly being changed. Reading too many books causes the same kind of distraction.

So, since you can't read all the books you may own, it's enough to own only as many books as you can actually read. You might say, "But I want to dip into one book and then another." I tell you that it's a sign of a picky appetite to play with many dishes; when they are numerous and varied, they satisfy your curiosity but don't truly nourish you. So you should always read works by respected authors; and when you crave something different, go back to those you've read before. Each day, learn something that will strengthen you against poverty, against death, and even against other misfortunes; and after you've gone through many thoughts, pick one to fully digest that day.

This is what I do myself; from the many things I've read, I choose one part for myself. The thought for today is one that I found in Epicurus; because I'm used to visiting even the enemy's camp—not as a deserter, but as a scout. He says: "Satisfied poverty is an honorable state." Indeed, if it's satisfied, it's not poverty at all. It's not the person who has too little, but the one who craves more, who is truly poor. What does it matter how much money a person has in their safe or in their warehouse, how large their flocks are, or how much they earn in dividends, if they covet their neighbor's property and count not what they have already gained, but what they hope to gain in the future? Do you ask what is the proper limit to wealth? It is, first, to have what is necessary, and second, to have what is enough. Farewell.

Letter 3 - On true and false friendship

You have sent a letter to me through someone you call a "friend." But in the very next sentence, you warn me not to discuss all your matters with him, saying that even you don't usually do this yourself. In other words, in the same letter, you've both confirmed and denied that he is your friend.

Now, if you used the word "friend" in the usual way, like when we call all candidates "honorable gentlemen," or when we greet people casually with "my dear sir" if we momentarily forget their names, that's one thing. But if you consider someone a friend whom you don't trust as much as you trust yourself, you're making a big mistake and don't fully understand what true friendship means. I believe you should discuss everything with a friend; but first, you must discuss the person himself. Once friendship is established, you must trust; before forming a friendship, you must judge. Some people get this backward—they trust someone first and only judge them later, which is a mistake according to Theophrastus. Think carefully and for a long time before you decide to let someone into your circle of friends; but once you've made that decision, welcome them with all your heart. Speak as freely with them as you would with yourself.

As for yourself, even though you should live in such a way that you wouldn't mind if even an enemy knew your secrets, there are still some things that social norms require us to keep private. However, you should at least share all your worries and thoughts with a friend. If you trust him as being loyal, you will make him loyal. Some people, by being afraid of being deceived, have actually taught others to deceive them; their suspicions give their friend a reason to do wrong. Why should I hold back anything when I'm with my friend? Why shouldn't I feel like I'm alone when I'm with him?

There are some people who share with anyone they meet things that should only be shared with friends, dumping all their troubles on whoever will listen. Others are too afraid to confide in even their closest friends; if they could, they wouldn't even trust themselves, hiding their secrets deep in their hearts. But we should avoid both extremes. It's just as wrong to trust everyone as it is to trust no one. Yet, if I had to choose, I'd say it's more innocent to trust too much, though it's safer to trust too little.

In the same way, you should criticize both those who are always restless and those who are always idle. Loving busyness doesn't mean you're being productive—it's just a sign of a mind that's being hunted by its own thoughts. And true rest doesn't mean rejecting all activity as bothersome; that kind of rest is just laziness and stagnation.

So, remember this saying that I found in my reading of Pomponius: "Some people hide in dark corners so much that they see darkness even during the day." No, people should combine both tendencies—those who rest should also take action, and those who take action should also find time to rest. Talk to Nature about it; she will tell you that she created both day and night. Farewell.

Letter 4 - On the terrors of death

Keep going as you have started, and hurry as much as you can, so that you can enjoy an improved mind for a longer time, one that is at peace with itself. Of course, you will enjoy yourself while you're improving your mind and bringing it to peace; but the pleasure you'll feel when your mind is completely free from every stain and shines is very different.

You remember the joy you felt when you put aside the clothes of boyhood and put on the toga of manhood, and were led to the forum. But you can look forward to an even greater joy when you set aside the mind of a boy and when wisdom considers you a man. Because what stays with us isn't boyhood, but something worse—childishness.

This is even more serious because we have the authority of old age combined with the foolishness of childhood, and even the foolishness of infancy. Boys fear little things, children fear shadows, and we fear both.

All you need to do is move forward, and you'll realize that some things are less scary simply because they cause us great fear. No evil is great if it's the last evil of all. Death comes; it would be something to dread if it could stay with you. But death must either not come at all, or else it must come and pass away.

"It's difficult," you might say, "to bring the mind to a point where it can look down on life." But don't you see what little reasons make people scorn life? One person hangs himself in front of his lover's door; another jumps off a roof because he can't stand the insults of a bad-tempered master; a third, to avoid being caught after running away, stabs himself with a sword. Don't you think that virtue can be as effective as excessive fear? No one can live a peaceful life if they think too much about trying to live longer, or believe that living through many years is a great blessing.

Think about this every day, so that you can leave life peacefully; many people cling to life like those who are swept away by a rushing stream, grabbing onto briars and sharp rocks. Most people are stuck in misery, constantly wavering between the fear of death and the struggles of life; they don't want to live, but they also don't know how to die.

For this reason, make your whole life enjoyable by getting rid of all worries about it. No good thing can make its owner happy unless their mind is at peace with the idea of losing it; and nothing is easier to lose with less discomfort than something that, when lost, cannot be missed. So, strengthen and toughen your spirit against the misfortunes that can happen to even the most powerful people.

For example, Pompey's fate was decided by a boy and a eunuch, and Crassus's fate by a cruel and arrogant Parthian. Gaius Caesar ordered Lepidus to offer his neck to the axe of the tribune Dexter, and he himself offered his own throat to Chaerea. No one has ever been so favored by Fortune that she didn't threaten them as much as she had previously rewarded them. Don't trust her apparent calm; in a moment, the sea can be stirred to its depths. The very day ships have shown off in games, they can be swallowed by the sea.

Remember that a robber or an enemy could cut your throat; and even though they aren't your master, any slave has the power of life and death over you. So, I say to you: the person who doesn't care about their own life is the master of yours. Think of those who have died because of plots in their own homes, killed either openly or secretly; you'll see that just as many people have been killed by angry slaves as by angry kings. So why does it matter how powerful the person you fear is, when everyone has the power that causes your fear?

"But," you might say, "if you fall into the hands of the enemy, the conqueror will order you to be taken away"—yes, but only where you are already being led. Why do you deceive yourself and need to be told for the first time what fate you've been living under all along? Believe me: from the day you were born, you have been moving toward this end. We must think about this, and similar thoughts, if we want to be calm as we wait for that last hour, the fear of which makes all the earlier hours uneasy.

But I must end my letter. Let me share with you the saying that pleased me today. It's also taken from another man's teachings: "Poverty, when it aligns with the law of nature, is great wealth." Do you know what limits that law of nature sets for us? Just enough to avoid hunger, thirst, and cold. To get rid of hunger and thirst, you don't need to bow down to the wealthy or submit to their harsh looks or their humiliating kindness; nor do you need to sail the seas or go to war; nature's needs are easy to meet and close at hand.

It's the unnecessary things that make people sweat—the unnecessary things that wear out our clothes, that force us to grow old in the military, that send us to foreign lands. What is enough is within our reach. The person who has made peace with poverty is rich. Farewell.

Letter 5 - On the philosopher's mean

I praise you and am happy that you are staying committed to your studies, and that you make it your goal each day to become a better person, putting everything else aside. I don't just encourage you to keep it up; I actually beg you to do so. However, I must warn you not to behave like those who want to be noticed rather than to improve, by doing things that draw attention, like how you dress or how you live.

Avoid wearing unattractive clothes, having messy hair, an unkempt beard, openly despising silver dishes, sleeping on the bare ground, and any other strange forms of showing off. The name "philosophy," even when practiced quietly, already draws enough criticism; and what would happen if we started separating ourselves from the customs of our fellow people? On the inside, we should be different in every way, but on the outside, we should fit in with society.

Don't wear a toga that's too fancy, but also not one that's too shabby. You don't need silver plates covered in gold; but we shouldn't think that not having silver and gold proves we live a simple life. We should try to live better than the average person, but not in a way that's completely different; otherwise, we will scare away and push away the very people we are trying to help improve. We might also cause them to be unwilling to imitate us in anything because they're afraid they might have to imitate us in everything.

The first thing philosophy aims to give is a connection with all people; in other words, kindness and sociability. We go against this goal if we make ourselves too different from others. We must make sure that the things we do to try to gain admiration are not ridiculous and unpleasant. Our motto, as you know, is "Live according to Nature"; but it is completely against nature to torture the body, to dislike simple elegance, to be dirty on purpose, or to eat food that is not only plain but disgusting and unappealing.

Just as it's a sign of luxury to seek out fancy foods, it's also madness to avoid what is normal and easy to get at a low cost. Philosophy calls for simple living, but not for punishment; and we can be simple and neat at the same time. This is the balance I support; our lives should find a happy middle ground between the ways of a wise person and the ways of the world at large; everyone should admire it, but they should also be able to understand it.

"Well then, should we act just like everyone else? Should there be no difference between us and the rest of the world?" Yes, a very big difference; let people see that we are different from the average person, but only if they look closely. If they visit us at home, they should admire us, not our belongings. He is a great person who uses earthenware dishes as if they were silver; but he is equally great who uses silver as if it were earthenware. It's a sign of a weak mind not to be able to handle wealth.

But I want to share with you today's lesson. I found in the writings of our Hecato that controlling our desires also helps to cure our fears: "Stop hoping," he says, "and you will stop fearing." "But how," you might reply, "can two things so different be connected?" Here's how, my dear Lucilius: even though they seem different, they are actually linked. Just like the same chain binds both the prisoner and the soldier who guards him, hope and fear, as different as they are, go hand in hand; fear follows hope.

I'm not surprised that they work this way; both belong to a mind that is uncertain, a mind that is stressed by looking ahead to the future. But the main cause of both these problems is that we don't focus on the present, but instead send our thoughts far ahead. And so, foresight, which is supposed to be the greatest gift of the human race, becomes twisted.

Animals avoid the dangers they can see, and once they escape, they are free from worry; but we humans torment ourselves over what is to come as well as what is past. Many of our blessings turn into curses for us; because memory brings back the pains of fear, while foresight anticipates them. The present alone cannot make anyone miserable. Farewell.

Letter 6 - On sharing knowledge

I feel, my dear Lucilius, that I am not just being improved but completely transformed. However, I don't yet allow myself to believe or hope that there are no more things in me that need to be changed. Of course, there are still many things that need to be tightened, made lighter, or brought out more clearly. In fact, the very fact that I can see my own faults, which I was unaware of before, shows that my spirit has changed for the better. In some cases, sick people are congratulated because they have recognized that they are sick.

So I want to share with you this sudden change in myself; that way, I can begin to trust our friendship more securely—the true friendship that cannot be broken by hope, fear, or self-interest, the kind of friendship where people would even face death for each other. I can show you many people who lacked not a friend, but true friendship; however, this cannot happen when souls are brought together by similar values and shared honorable desires. And why can't this happen? Because in such cases, people know that they share everything, especially their troubles.

You wouldn't believe the clear progress I see in myself each day. And when you say, "Share with me these things that you've found so helpful," I reply that I am eager to share all these benefits with you, and that I'm glad to learn so that I can teach. Nothing will ever please me, no matter how excellent or beneficial, if I have to keep it to myself. And if wisdom were given to me with the condition that I must keep it hidden and not share it, I would refuse it. No good thing is enjoyable to possess without friends to share it with.

So I will send you the actual books; and to save you time searching here and there for the best parts, I will mark certain passages so that you can go straight to the ones I admire and approve. But, of course, the living voice and the closeness of a shared life will help you more than written words. You must come to where the action is, first, because people trust their eyes more than their ears, and second, because the journey is long if you follow instructions, but short and helpful if you follow examples.

Cleanthes couldn't have become the true image of Zeno if he had only listened to his lectures; he shared in his life, understood his hidden intentions, and observed whether he lived according to his own rules. Plato, Aristotle, and all the other wise men who later went their separate ways, gained more from the character of Socrates than from his words. It wasn't Epicurus's classroom but living together under the same roof that made great men out of Metrodorus, Hermarchus, and Polyaenus.

So I invite you to my home, not just so you can gain something, but so you can also give something back; because we can help each other greatly.

Meanwhile, I owe you my small daily offering; today, I was pleased by something I read in the writings of Hecato. He said: "What progress have I made? I have begun to be a friend to myself." That is indeed a great achievement; such a person can never be lonely. You can be sure that someone like that is a friend to all people. Farewell.

Letter 7 - On crowds

Do you ask me what you should especially avoid? I say, crowds; because right now, you can't trust yourself to be around them safely. I'll admit my own weakness: I never come back home with the same character that I took with me when I went out. Something in me that I had calmed down gets disturbed; some of the bad habits that I had overcome start coming back. It's like a sick person who has been weak for a long time and isn't strong enough to leave the house without getting worse again. We are like that when our souls are still recovering from a long-lasting illness.

Being around crowds is harmful; there's no one who doesn't either attract us to some bad habit, make it seem okay, or infect us with it without us even realizing it. The larger the crowd we mix with, the greater the danger. But nothing harms good character more than spending time at the games, because that's when bad behavior sneaks in through the pleasure we feel.

What do I mean by that? I mean that I come home more greedy, more ambitious, more indulgent, and even more cruel and inhuman—because I have been among human beings. By chance, I attended a midday show, expecting to enjoy some fun, wit, and relaxation—a show where people's eyes get a break from watching others kill each other. But it was quite the opposite. The earlier fights seemed compassionate in comparison; now all the playing around is gone, and it's pure killing.

The men have no armor to protect them. They are completely exposed to blows, and no one ever misses. Many people prefer this type of show to the usual pairs and matches. Of course they do; there's no helmet or shield to block the weapon. What's the point of armor or skill? All those do is delay death. In the morning, they throw men to the lions and bears; at noon, they throw them to the spectators. The crowd demands that the killer face the man who will kill him in turn, and they always save the last winner for another slaughter. The outcome of every fight is death, and the methods are fire and sword. This goes on even when the arena is empty.

You might say, "But he was a highway robber; he killed someone!" So what? Even if, as a murderer, he deserved this punishment, what did you do wrong, poor fellow, that you deserve to sit and watch this show? In the morning, the crowd yells, "Kill him! Whip him! Burn him! Why is he so cowardly when he meets the sword? Why does he fight so weakly? Why doesn't he die bravely? Whip him to face his wounds! Let them strike blow for blow, with chests bare and open to the sword!" And when the games stop for a break, they announce, "A little throat-cutting in the meantime, so there's still something happening!"

Come on, don't you understand even this simple truth, that a bad example affects the person who sets it? Thank the immortal gods that you're teaching cruelty to someone who can't learn to be cruel. The young character, which can't hold on to righteousness, must be saved from the crowd; it's too easy to go along with the majority. Even Socrates, Cato, and Laelius might have had their moral strength shaken by a crowd that was different from them; it's true that none of us, no matter how much we work on our abilities, can stand strong against the faults that approach with so much support.

A single case of indulgence or greed can do a lot of harm; a close friend, if he is indulgent, weakens and softens us without us realizing it; a neighbor, if he is rich, stirs up our greed; a companion, if he is a gossip, spreads his bad habits to us, even if we are pure and sincere. So what do you think the effect will be on our character when the whole world assaults it? You must either imitate or despise the world.

But both of those choices should be avoided; you shouldn't copy the bad just because there are many of them, and you shouldn't hate the many just because they are different from you. Withdraw into yourself as much as you can. Associate with those who will make you a better person. Welcome those whom you can help improve. The process is mutual; people learn while they teach.

There's no reason why the desire to show off your abilities should lure you into the public eye, making you want to recite or speak in front of a large crowd. I'd be okay with you doing that if you had something that suited such a crowd; as it is, not one of them can understand you. One or two individuals might come your way, but even they will have to be shaped and trained by you to understand you. You may ask, "What was the point of learning all these things?"

But don't worry that you've wasted your efforts; you learned them for yourself.

However, so that I haven't learned something today just for myself, I'll share with you three excellent sayings that I came across, which all have a similar meaning. This letter will give you one of them as payment for my debt; the other two you can take as a gift in advance. Democritus says: "One man means as much to me as a crowd, and a crowd only as much as one man." Another wise person, whose name is uncertain, was asked what the purpose was of all his studies in an art that would reach very few people. He replied, "I am content with few, content with one, content with none at all." The third saying, which is also noteworthy, comes from Epicurus, who wrote to one of his study partners: "I write this not for the many, but for you; each of us is enough of an audience for the other."

Take these words to heart, Lucilius, so that you may learn to ignore the pleasure that comes from the applause of the majority. Many people may praise you, but do you have any reason to be pleased with yourself if you are a person whom the majority can understand? Your good qualities should be directed inward. Farewell.

Letter 8 - On the philosopher's seclusion

"Do you tell me," you ask, "to avoid the crowd, to withdraw from people, and to be content with my own thoughts? What about the teachings of your school, which tell us that a person should die while actively working?" The course of action I seem to be suggesting to you, now and then, is that I shut myself away and lock the door so that I can help a greater number of people. I never spend a day doing nothing; I even use part of the night for study. I don't allow myself time for sleep; I only give in to it when I absolutely must, and when my eyes are too tired to stay open, I still push them to keep working.

I have withdrawn not only from people but also from my own personal affairs; I am working for future generations, writing down some ideas that may help them. There are some wise teachings, like prescriptions for useful medicine, that I am putting into writing because they have helped heal my own wounds. These wounds may not be completely cured, but at least they've stopped getting worse.

I point others to the right path, which I found late in life, after being tired from wandering. I call out to them, "Avoid whatever pleases the crowd; avoid the gifts of Fortune! Be cautious and doubtful of every good thing that Chance brings you, because it's the dumb animals and fish that are tricked by tempting bait. Do you call these things the 'gifts' of Fortune? They are traps. Any of you who want to live safely should avoid, as much as possible, these traps of Fortune, by which we humans—most unfortunate in this respect— are deceived. We think we are holding them, but they are holding us.

Such a path leads us to dangerous heights, and living on such heights eventually leads to a fall. Moreover, we can't even stand up to good fortune when it starts to push us in the wrong direction; nor can we go down gracefully or all at once. Fortune doesn't just knock us over; she plunges us headfirst and smashes us on the rocks.

So, hold on to this sound and healthy rule of life: indulge the body only as much as is necessary for good health. The body should be treated strictly so that it doesn't disobey the mind. Eat only to satisfy your hunger; drink only to quench your thirst; dress only to keep warm; and live in a house only to protect yourself from discomfort. It doesn't matter whether the house is made of simple turf or fancy imported marble; understand that a person is sheltered just as well by a thatched roof as by a roof of gold. Despise everything that is created by useless labor as an ornament or object of beauty. And remember that nothing except the soul is truly worthy of admiration; because to the soul, if it is great, nothing else is great."

When I talk to myself and future generations like this, don't you think I am doing more good than when I act as a lawyer in court, put my seal on a will, or help a candidate in the senate by word or action? Believe me, those who seem to be busy with nothing are actually busy with the most important tasks; they are dealing with both mortal and immortal things.

But I must stop now and pay my usual contribution to balance out this letter. The payment won't come from my own thoughts today, as I am still reading Epicurus. Today, I read this sentence in his works: "If you want to enjoy real freedom, you must become a slave to Philosophy." The person who submits and surrenders to her doesn't have to wait; he is freed immediately. Because the very service of Philosophy is freedom.

You might ask me why I quote so many of Epicurus's wise sayings instead of quotes from our own school. But is there any reason why you should think of them as sayings of Epicurus and not as common wisdom? How many poets express ideas that have been, or could be, spoken by philosophers! I don't need to mention the tragedians and our writers of national drama; because even they are somewhat serious and stand between comedy and tragedy. How many wise verses are hidden in the mime! How many lines from Publilius are worthy of being spoken by actors in serious plays as well as in lighter ones!

I'll quote one verse of his that relates to philosophy, and particularly to the topic we were discussing a moment ago, in which he says that the gifts of Chance shouldn't be considered our true possessions: "Still alien is whatever you have gained by coveting."

I remember that you yourself expressed this idea much more effectively and briefly: "What Chance has made yours is not really yours."

And a third saying, spoken by you even more wisely, should not be left out: "The good that could be given can be taken away."

I won't count this as part of the expense, because I've given it to you from your own thoughts. Farewell.

Letter 9 - On philosophy and friendship

You want to know if Epicurus is right when, in one of his letters, he criticizes those who believe that a wise person is self-sufficient and therefore doesn't need friends. This is the criticism Epicurus makes against Stilbo and others who think that the highest good is a soul that doesn't feel anything.

We run into a problem if we try to translate the Greek term "lack of feeling" with just one word in Latin, like "impatientia." People might understand it in a way that's opposite to what we mean. We want to say that it's a soul that rejects any sensation of evil, but people might think we mean a soul that can't endure any evil. So, maybe it's better to say "a soul that cannot be harmed" or "a soul completely beyond suffering."

There's a difference between our philosophy and the other school: our ideal wise person feels their troubles but overcomes them; their wise person doesn't feel them at all. But both schools agree that the wise person is self-sufficient. Even so, the wise person still wants friends, neighbors, and companions, no matter how self-sufficient they are.

And notice how self-sufficient they are; because in certain situations, they can be content with just a part of themselves. If they lose a hand due to illness or war, or if an accident causes them to lose one or both of their eyes, they will be satisfied with what's left, taking as much joy in their impaired and injured body as they did when it was whole. But while they don't long for these parts if they lose them, they would prefer not to lose them.

In this way, the wise person is self-sufficient, meaning they can do without friends, not that they want to do without them. When I say "can," I mean they can handle the loss of a friend calmly. But they don't have to be without friends because it's within their power to make new ones quickly. Just as Phidias, if he loses a statue, can carve another right away, our master in the art of friendship can replace a lost friend just as quickly.

If you ask how someone can make a friend quickly, I'll tell you, as long as we agree that this can count as me paying my debt to you in this letter. Hecato says, "I can show you a love potion made without any drugs, herbs, or spells: 'If you want to be loved, love.'" There's great joy not only in keeping old, established friendships but also in starting and building new ones.

There's a difference between making a new friend and already having one, just as there's a difference between the farmer who sows seeds and the farmer who reaps the harvest. The philosopher Attalus used to say, "It's more enjoyable to make a friend than to keep one, just as it's more enjoyable for an artist to paint than to admire the finished painting." When you're busy and absorbed in your work, the work itself brings great pleasure; but when you've finished, the pleasure isn't as strong. In the case of our children, their young adulthood may bring greater rewards, but their childhood was sweeter.

Let's get back to the question. The wise person, I say, is self-sufficient, but still desires friends, if only to practice friendship, so that their noble qualities don't go unused. Not for the reason Epicurus mentions in the letter I quoted earlier: "So that there's someone to sit by them when they're sick, to help them when they're in prison or in need." But rather, so that they have someone whose sickbed they can sit by, someone who is a prisoner that they can free. If someone seeks friendships only for their own benefit, they're making a mistake. Such friendships will end just like they began: someone who became your friend because it benefited them will leave you as soon as it stops benefiting them.

These are what we call "fair-weather" friendships; a friend chosen for usefulness will only be a friend as long as they are useful. That's why successful people are surrounded by crowds of friends, but those who fail are left all alone, their friends fleeing when they're needed most. We often see people who, out of fear, betray or abandon others.

The way a friendship starts will determine how it ends. A person who becomes your friend because of what they can gain will stop being your friend when the gain is gone. A person who is attracted to friendship for anything other than friendship itself will be drawn by some reward, not true loyalty.

So why do I make friends? To have someone I can die for, someone I can follow into exile, someone whose death I would risk my own life to prevent. The kind of friendship you describe is more like a business deal, not true friendship; it's based on convenience and looks only at the results.

Without a doubt, the feeling of a lover is something like friendship; you could call it friendship driven mad. But even though that's true, does anyone love for the sake of profit, or advancement, or fame? Pure love, indifferent to everything else, fills the soul with desire for the beautiful, not without hope that the affection will be returned. So, can a more honorable cause lead to a less noble passion?

You might say, "We're not discussing whether friendship should be pursued for its own sake." But that's exactly what needs to be proven. If friendship is to be sought for its own sake, then even someone who is self-sufficient should seek it. "How then," you ask, "does he seek it?" He seeks it just as he seeks an object of great beauty, not driven by desire for gain, nor deterred by the instability of Fortune. A person who seeks friendship for favorable conditions takes away all its nobility.

"The wise person is self-sufficient." This phrase, my dear Lucilius, is often misunderstood; people think it means the wise person withdraws from the world and lives entirely within themselves. But we must be careful to understand what this phrase really means and how far it applies. The wise person is self-sufficient for a happy life, but not for mere existence. They need many things for everyday life, but for happiness, they need only a sound and upright soul, one that despises Fortune.

I'd like to share with you a distinction made by Chrysippus, who said that the wise person wants for nothing but still needs many things. On the other hand, he says, "The fool needs nothing because he doesn't know how to use anything, but he wants everything." The wise person needs hands, eyes, and many other things necessary for daily life, but he doesn't want anything. "Want" implies necessity, and nothing is necessary to the wise person.

So, even though the wise person is self-sufficient, he still needs friends. He desires as many friends as possible, but not because he needs them to be happy, because he will live happily even without friends. The highest good doesn't rely on anything external; it's developed within and arises entirely from itself. If the good needs anything from outside, it becomes subject to Fortune.

People might say, "But what kind of life will the wise person have if he is left friendless when he is thrown in prison, stranded in a foreign land, delayed on a long voyage, or trapped on a deserted shore?" His life will be like that of Jupiter, who, during the dissolution of the world, when the gods are confused and Nature takes a break, can retreat into himself and focus on his own thoughts. In a similar way, the wise person will retreat into himself and live with themselves.

As long as he's allowed to live according to his own judgment, he is self-sufficient—yet he married a wife, raised children, and cannot live without the company of others. Natural instincts, not personal needs, draw him into friendships. Just as other things attract us naturally, so does friendship. We hate being alone and crave companionship, so Nature draws people together, and this desire leads us to friendship.

Nevertheless, even though the wise person may love their friends dearly, often valuing them as much as or even more than himself, all the good they possess will still be contained within his own being. He will speak the words once spoken by Stilbo, the same Stilbo whom Epicurus criticized in his letter. After Stilbo's city was captured and his wife and children lost, he emerged from the destruction alone but happy, and when Demetrius, known as the Sacker of Cities, asked him if he had lost anything, Stilbo replied, "I have all my goods with me!"

There's a brave and strong-hearted man for you! The enemy may have conquered, but Stilbo conquered his conqueror. "I have lost nothing!" He made Demetrius wonder if he had truly won after all. "My goods are all with me!" In other words, Stilbo considered nothing that could be taken from him to be a true possession.

We marvel at certain animals that can pass through fire unharmed; but how much more remarkable is a person who has walked through fire, sword, and devastation without being harmed! Do you see now how much easier it is to conquer a whole tribe than to conquer one person? Stilbo's statement aligns with Stoicism; the Stoic can carry their goods, undamaged, through cities that have been burned to the ground because they are self-sufficient. These are the limits the Stoic sets on their happiness.

But don't think that our school is the only one that can speak noble words; Epicurus himself, who criticized Stilbo, said something similar. Count this as something I'm adding to my account, even though I've already settled my debt for today. He says: "Whoever doesn't see what they have as the greatest wealth is unhappy, even if they are the master of the whole world." Or, if you prefer a different phrasing—since we should try to capture the meaning, not just the words—"A person may rule the world and still be unhappy if they don't feel supremely happy."

To show you that these ideas are universal and come naturally to us, you'll find a similar thought in one of the comic poets: "Unblest is he who thinks himself unblest." What does it matter what your condition is if you think it's bad?

You may say, "But what if a man, rich by dishonest means and a master of many but a slave to even more, calls himself happy—does that make him truly happy?" It doesn't matter what one says, but what one feels; and not just how one feels on a particular day, but how they feel at all times. However, you don't need to worry that this great privilege of happiness will fall into unworthy hands; only the wise person is pleased with what they have. Foolishness is always troubled with dissatisfaction. Farewell.

Letter 10 - On living to oneself

Yes, I still hold my opinion: avoid large crowds, avoid small groups, and even avoid being alone with just one person. I don't know anyone I would want you to share your time with, and this shows how much trust I have in you, because I dare to trust you with yourself. Crates, a student of Stilbo, whom I mentioned in a previous letter, once saw a young man walking by himself and asked him what he was doing alone. "I am spending time with myself," the young man replied. "Be careful," said Crates, "and take good heed; you are spending time with a dangerous person!"

When people are grieving or scared, we often keep an eye on them to stop them from making bad decisions while they are alone. No careless person should be left alone; in such cases, they only end up planning foolish things and setting themselves or others up for future trouble. They give in to their base desires; their mind reveals what fear or shame usually keeps hidden. It sharpens their recklessness, stirs their passions, and fuels their anger. In the end, even the one benefit that solitude might offer—the habit of trusting no one and fearing no witnesses—is lost to the fool because they betray themselves.

So, consider what my hopes are for you—or rather, what I am promising myself, since hope is just the name of an uncertain blessing. I don't know anyone I'd rather have you spend time with than yourself. I remember how powerfully you expressed certain thoughts, and how strong they were! I immediately congratulated myself and thought, "These words didn't just come from the surface; they have a solid foundation. This man is not like the others; he truly cares about his own well-being."

Speak and live in this way; make sure nothing holds you back. As for your past prayers, you can release the gods from answering them; offer new prayers instead. Pray for a sound mind and good health, first for your soul and then for your body. And, of course, you should offer these prayers often. Call upon God with confidence; you won't be asking for something that belongs to someone else.

But as usual, I must send a little gift along with this letter. Here's a wise saying I found in Athenodorus: "You know you are free from all desires when you reach the point where you can pray to God for nothing except what you could pray for openly." But how foolish people are today! They whisper the most shameful prayers to heaven, but if anyone is around to hear, they go silent. They tell God things they would never want other people to know. Don't you think this advice would be helpful to you: "Live among people as if God is watching you; speak with God as if everyone is listening"? Farewell.

Letter 11 - On the blush of modesty

Your friend and I had a conversation. He is a talented person; his very first words showed the spirit and understanding he has and the progress he has already made. He gave me a glimpse of his potential, and I'm sure he will live up to it. He spoke not with preparation but was caught off guard. When he tried to collect himself, he could hardly hide his blush, which is a good sign in a young man. The blush that spread over his face seemed to come from deep within. I am sure this habit of blushing will stay with him even after he has strengthened his character, removed all his faults, and become wise. No amount of wisdom can remove the natural tendencies of the body. What is inborn can be toned down by training but not completely overcome.

Even the most confident speaker often breaks into a sweat in public, as if he has overexerted himself; some people's knees tremble when they rise to speak; I know of some whose teeth chatter, whose tongues falter, and whose lips quiver. Training and experience can never fully remove this habit; nature shows her power and makes herself known even to the strongest through such a weakness. I know that blushing, too, is a habit like this, suddenly spreading over the faces of even the most dignified people. It is more common in youth because of the warmer blood and sensitive skin, but both experienced and older people are affected by it. Some people are at their most dangerous when they blush, as if all their shame is leaving them.

Sulla, for example, was in his fiercest mood when his cheeks reddened. Pompey had a very sensitive face; he always blushed when he was in front of a crowd, especially at public gatherings. I also remember Fabianus blushing when he appeared as a witness before the senate, and his embarrassment suited him very well. This habit is not due to weakness of mind but to the novelty of the situation; an inexperienced person is not necessarily confused, but they are usually affected because this habit comes from the body's natural tendencies. Just as some people are full-blooded, others have quick and active blood that rushes to their faces instantly.

As I mentioned, wisdom can never completely remove this habit; if it could erase all our faults, it would rule the universe. Whatever is given to us by birth and by the makeup of our bodies will stay with us, no matter how hard or long the soul may try to control itself. We cannot stop these feelings any more than we can summon them. Actors in the theater, who imitate emotions like fear and nervousness or sorrow, try to imitate bashfulness by hanging their heads, lowering their voices, and keeping their eyes on the ground. But they cannot make themselves blush; blushing cannot be controlled or forced. Wisdom won't provide a remedy or help against it; it comes and goes on its own, and we have no control over it.

But my letter needs a closing thought. Listen to and remember this useful and wise advice: "Admire someone of high character, and keep them always in your mind, living as if they are watching you, and guiding all your actions as if they see them." This, my dear Lucilius, is the advice of Epicurus; he has wisely given us a guardian and a guide. We can avoid most mistakes if we imagine we have a witness with us when we are tempted to do wrong. The soul should have someone it respects—someone whose authority makes even its inner thoughts more honorable. Happy is the person who can make others better, not only when they are together but even when they are in their thoughts! And happy also is the one who respects someone enough to calm and guide themselves by remembering them! A person who can respect another will soon be worthy of respect themselves.

So, choose a role model like Cato; or, if Cato seems too strict, choose Laelius, who had a gentler spirit. Choose someone whose life, conversation, and expression have impressed you; picture them always as your protector or your guide. For we all need someone by whom we can shape our character; you can never straighten something that is crooked unless you use a ruler. Farewell.

Letter 12 - On old age

Wherever I look, I see signs that I'm getting older. I recently visited my country house and complained about the money being spent on fixing the old building. My caretaker defended himself, saying that the damage wasn't due to his carelessness; he was doing everything he could, but the house was just old. And this is the house that was built during my lifetime! What does the future hold for me if things that are as old as I am are already falling apart?

I got angry and took the first chance to vent my frustration in front of the caretaker. "It's obvious," I said, "that these plane trees are being neglected; they have no leaves. Their branches are twisted and shriveled, and their trunks are rough and unkempt! This wouldn't happen if someone loosened the soil around them and watered them." The caretaker swore by my guardian deity that he was doing everything possible and never stopped trying, but the trees were just old. The truth is, I had planted those trees myself, and I remember seeing them when they first sprouted leaves.

Then I turned to the door and asked, "Who is that old, broken-down man? You did well to put him by the entrance because he looks like he's ready to leave this world. Where did you find him? Why did you bother to bring someone else's dead back to life?" But the servant said, "Don't you recognize me, sir? I'm Felicio; you used to bring me little toys. My father was Philositus the steward, and I was your favorite slave."

I thought, "The man is crazy. Has my favorite slave become a little boy again? But I guess it's possible; his teeth are just now falling out."

It was at my country house that I realized how old I was, no matter where I looked. We should appreciate and love old age because it's full of pleasure if you know how to use it. Fruits are most delicious when they're almost overripe; youth is most charming at its close; the last drink delights the drinker—the one that finally makes him fully drunk. Each pleasure saves the best for last. Life is most enjoyable when it's on the downward slope but hasn't yet reached the steep decline. I believe that the time of life that stands on the edge of the roof, so to speak, has its own pleasures. Or maybe the very fact that we no longer crave pleasures has taken the place of the pleasures themselves. It's comforting to be free of desires and to have done with them!

"But," you might say, "it's a nuisance to be constantly facing death!" Death, however, should be faced by both young and old alike. We aren't summoned to die according to our age on the census list. Besides, no one is so old that it would be wrong for them to hope for another day of life. And remember, each day is a step on life's journey.

Our life is divided into parts; it's made up of large circles enclosing smaller ones. One circle covers our whole life, from birth to death. Another circle limits our young adulthood. A third circle contains our childhood. Then there is the year, which has its own divisions of time, and these add up to our entire life. The month is contained within an even smaller circle. The smallest circle of all is the day, but even a day has its beginning and its ending, its sunrise and its sunset.

That's why Heraclitus, known for his obscure style, said, "One day is equal to every day." People have interpreted this saying in different ways. Some think it means that all days have the same number of hours, which is true if by "day" we mean a 24-hour period, where the night makes up for what the day loses. Others believe that one day is equal to all days because every long span of time contains the same elements found in a single day—namely, light and darkness. Even in eternity, the difference is not in what happens but in how many times it happens.

So, every day should be lived as if it's the last in our life, as if it rounds out and completes our existence. Pacuvius, who ruled Syria for a long time, used to hold a mock funeral for himself every day. He would have a burial feast with wine and all the usual ceremonies, and then he would have himself carried from the dining room to his bedroom while eunuchs applauded and sang in Greek, "He has lived his life, he has lived his life!"

Pacuvius had himself carried out to burial every day. But we should do the same thing with a good motive, not a foolish one. Let's go to sleep with joy and gladness, saying, "I have lived; the course that Fortune set for me is finished." And if God is pleased to give us another day, we should welcome it with happy hearts. The happiest person is the one who can face tomorrow without fear. When a person can say, "I have lived," every morning they wake up, they receive a bonus.

But now I should close my letter. "What?" you ask, "Will it come to me without any little gift?" Don't worry; it brings something—actually, it brings a lot. For what is more valuable than this saying, which I'm sending with this letter: "It is wrong to live under constraint; but no one is forced to live under constraint." Of course not. There are many easy and simple paths to freedom all around us, and let's thank God that no one can be kept alive against their will. We can reject the very things that hold us.

"But," you might say, "Epicurus said those words. Why are you using someone else's thoughts?" I believe that any truth is my own property. And I'll keep sharing quotes from Epicurus with you so that all those who value the speaker more than the words may understand that the best ideas belong to everyone. Farewell.

Letter 13 - On groundless fears

I know you have plenty of spirit; even before you started filling your mind with wise sayings that help you overcome obstacles, you were proud of your fight with Fortune. And now that you've confronted Fortune and tested your strength, this is even more true. We can't truly trust our abilities until we've faced many difficulties and sometimes even been beaten by them. It's only in these moments that our true strength can be tested—the strength that refuses to be controlled by things outside of ourselves.

This is the true test of such a spirit. No fighter can enter the ring with confidence if they've never been bruised and bloodied. The only one who can confidently face a challenge is the person who has seen their own blood, felt their teeth rattle under an opponent's punch, been knocked down, and yet gets back up with even more determination. In the same way, Fortune has often gotten the upper hand on you, but you've never given up; instead, you've jumped up and fought back even harder. For courage grows stronger when it's challenged.

However, if you agree, let me offer some additional advice to help you strengthen yourself.

There are more things likely to scare us than there are to actually harm us; we suffer more in our imagination than in reality. I'm not speaking to you in a strict Stoic way but in a gentler tone. The Stoic way is to dismiss everything that causes cries and groans as unimportant and not worth noticing. But you and I should set aside such grand words, even though they are true. What I suggest is that you avoid being unhappy before the crisis actually arrives. It may be that the dangers you feared won't come to pass; they haven't happened yet, at least.

So, some things torment us more than they should; some torment us before they should; and some torment us when they shouldn't torment us at all. We often exaggerate, imagine, or anticipate sorrow.

The first of these three faults can be set aside for now because we're still discussing the issue, and the case is still open, so to speak. What I might call trivial, you might consider very serious. I know that some people can laugh while being flogged, while others wince at a mere slap. We can talk later about whether these evils have power because of their own strength or because of our weakness.

Do me a favor: when people surround you and try to convince you that you're unhappy, don't focus on what they say, but on what you feel. Take advice from your own feelings and ask yourself honestly, because you know your own situation better than anyone else. Ask yourself: "Is there any reason why these people should pity me? Why should they be worried or afraid, as if my troubles could spread to them? Is there any real evil here, or is it just bad rumors, not actual harm?" Ask yourself, "Am I being tormented without good reason? Am I turning something that isn't an evil into something that is?"

You might ask, "How do I know if my sufferings are real or just imagined?" Here's the rule for that: We're troubled either by things happening now, things that might happen in the future, or both. When it comes to the present, it's easy to decide. If your body is free and healthy, and you're not suffering any immediate harm, then for now, everything is fine. As for what might happen in the future, we'll deal with that later.

"But," you say, "something bad might happen." First, consider if your fears of future trouble are certain. More often than not, we're troubled by our fears, and we're fooled by rumors, which often create fear in people. Yes, my dear Lucilius, we're too quick to believe what others say. We don't test the things that scare us; we don't examine them; we just panic and run away like soldiers fleeing from a dust cloud raised by stampeding cattle or from some unfounded rumor.

Somehow, it's the baseless rumors that disturb us the most. Truth has clear limits, but uncertainty is left to wild guesses and the reckless imagination of a frightened mind. That's why no fear is as destructive and uncontrollable as panic. Other fears may be unfounded, but panic is senseless.

So, let's look closely at the matter. It's possible that some troubles may come our way, but they aren't here yet. How often has the unexpected happened? How often has the expected never occurred? Even if it is destined to happen, what good does it do to rush out to meet your suffering? You'll suffer soon enough when it arrives, so in the meantime, hope for better things.

What do you gain by doing this? Time. Many things can happen in the meantime that might delay, end, or shift the trials that are near or even right in front of you. A fire might open up a way to escape. People have been gently let down by a disaster. Sometimes, the sword is stopped even at the victim's throat. Some have survived their own executioners. Even bad luck is unpredictable. Maybe it will come, maybe it won't; in the meantime, it's not here yet. So, look forward to better things.

The mind sometimes creates false fears when there are no real signs of danger. It misinterprets a vague word or imagines a small grudge to be more serious than it is, focusing not on how angry someone is but on what they might do if they stay angry. But life isn't worth living if we allow our fears to grow to their fullest extent; in this case, let wisdom guide you, and face your fears with a strong spirit, even when they seem very real. If you can't do this, then balance your fear with hope. There's nothing so certain among the things we fear that it isn't even more certain that our fears often fade into nothing and our hopes are often misleading.

So, weigh your hopes and fears carefully, and when everything is uncertain, choose to believe what you prefer. And if fear still seems stronger, lean toward hope anyway, and stop tormenting your soul. Remember that most people, even when no trouble is actually present or certain to happen in the future, still get excited and anxious. No one stops themselves when they start to panic; no one measures their fear against the truth. No one says, "The person who started this rumor is foolish, and the person who believed it is foolish too." We let ourselves be blown around by every breeze; we're frightened by uncertainties as if they were certainties. We don't know how to be moderate. The smallest thing can tip the scales and throw us into a panic.

But I'm almost ashamed to either scold you harshly or try to comfort you with mild remedies. Let someone else say, "Maybe the worst won't happen." You should say to yourself, "So what if it does happen? Let's see who wins! Maybe it will turn out to be the best thing for me; maybe this kind of death will bring honor to my life." Socrates was honored by the cup of hemlock he drank. If you take away Cato's sword, which defended his freedom, you take away a large part of his glory.

I've gone on far too long, considering that you need reminding rather than lecturing. The path I'm leading you on is no different from the one your nature already leads you on; you were born to live the way I'm describing. That's all the more reason why you should grow and perfect the good qualities you already have.

Now, to close my letter, I'll leave you with a final thought, as usual—a wise saying for you to reflect on: "The fool, with all his other faults, also has this one—he is always getting ready to live." Think about what this means, my dear Lucilius, and you'll see how absurd it is that people keep laying new foundations for their lives every day, building up fresh hopes even when they're on the brink of the grave.

Look into your own mind for examples; you'll find old men who are just now preparing themselves for a political career, or for travel, or for business. And what could be more ridiculous than getting ready to live when you're already old? I wouldn't mention the author of this saying, except that it's not very well-known and isn't one of those popular sayings by Epicurus that I've praised and shared with you. Farewell.

Letter 14 - On the reasons for withdrawing from the world

I admit that we all naturally care about our bodies; I admit that we are responsible for taking care of them. I don't say that we should ignore our bodies completely, but I do say that we shouldn't become slaves to them. If you let your body control you, if you're too afraid for its safety, or if you judge everything based on your body, you'll end up with many masters.

We should live not as if our only goal is to take care of the body, but as if we simply cannot live without it. Loving the body too much makes us anxious with fears, burdens us with worries, and opens us up to insults. A person who values their body too highly will think too little of virtue. We should take great care of our bodies, but we should also be ready, when reason, self-respect, and duty require it, to give up our bodies even to the flames.

However, as much as possible, we should avoid discomforts and dangers, and protect ourselves by constantly thinking about how to avoid what we fear. If I'm not mistaken, there are three main things we fear: we fear poverty, we fear sickness, and we fear the troubles that come from others who are more powerful. Of these, the fear that affects us most is the fear of those who have power over us because it comes with a lot of noise and commotion. But the natural fears of poverty and sickness creep up on us quietly, without the same shock to our senses. The other kind of fear comes with a big show, like a parade of horrors. It's surrounded by swords, fire, chains, and wild animals ready to tear apart people.

Imagine a prison, a cross, a rack, a hook, and a stake that they push straight through a person until it sticks out of their throat. Think about human limbs being torn apart by chariots driving in opposite directions, about the terrible shirt covered with flammable materials, and about all the other cruel inventions people have created, besides the ones I've already mentioned. It's not surprising, then, that our greatest fear is of this kind of fate; it comes in many forms, and the things that go with it are terrifying. Just like how a torturer does more harm by showing off more tools – the sight alone can break the spirit of those who might have patiently endured the pain – in the same way, the things that control and overpower our minds the most are the ones that make a big display. Those other troubles are, of course, no less serious; I mean things like hunger, thirst, stomach ulcers, and fevers that burn us from the inside. However, these problems are hidden; they don't make a big show or announce themselves loudly. But the visible, large displays, like massive armies, win because of their showiness and their equipment.

Therefore, we should make sure to avoid causing offense. Sometimes we should fear the people around us, or sometimes a group of powerful leaders in the Senate, if the government is run in such a way that these leaders have most of the control. Other times, we should be wary of individuals who have been given power by the people and against the people. It's exhausting to try to keep the friendship of all these people; it's enough not to make them your enemies. So the wise person will never provoke those in power; they will even change their course, just as they would steer a ship away from a storm.

When you traveled to Sicily, you crossed the Straits. The reckless captain ignored the dangerous South Wind, the wind that churns up the Sicilian Sea and creates rough currents. He aimed not for the shore on the left but for the coast near where Charybdis churns the waters. A more careful captain, however, asks those who know the area about the tides and the meaning of the clouds. He steers far away from the region known for its dangerous whirlpools. Our wise person does the same; they avoid a powerful person who could harm them, making sure not to seem like they are avoiding them, because part of staying safe is not making it obvious that you're trying to stay safe. What you avoid, you condemn.

We should, therefore, look around and see how we can protect ourselves from the masses. First of all, we should have no desires like theirs because rivalry leads to conflict. Also, we should own nothing that can be taken from us to the great benefit of someone plotting against us. Keep as little valuable property on you as possible. No one sets out to kill someone just for the sake of killing—at least very few do. Most murderers are after a profit, not just driven by hate. If you're empty-handed, the highwayman will pass you by; even on a dangerous road, the poor can travel in peace.

Next, we must follow the old saying and avoid three things with special care: hatred, jealousy, and scorn. Only wisdom can show you how to do this. It's hard to find the right balance; we must be careful not to let the fear of jealousy make us into objects of scorn. We should be cautious, not to crush others, but also not let them think they can crush us. The power to make others afraid has caused many to live in fear themselves.

We should withdraw in every way possible; it's just as harmful to be scorned as it is to be admired.

One must therefore take refuge in philosophy. This pursuit, in the eyes of both good people and those who are only moderately bad, is a kind of protective emblem. Public speaking, or any other activity that draws public attention, wins enemies for a person, but philosophy is peaceful and minds its own business. People can't scorn it; every profession honors it, even the lowest among them. Evil can never grow so strong, and nobility of character can never be so attacked, that the name of philosophy will stop being respected and sacred.

Philosophy itself, however, should be practiced with calmness and moderation. "Very well," you might say, "but do you consider Marcus Cato's philosophy to be moderate? Cato's voice tried to stop a civil war. Cato stepped in between leaders mad with power. When some attacked Pompey and others attacked Caesar, Cato stood up to both sides at once!"

But one might question whether, at that time, a wise person should have taken any part in public affairs, and ask, "What are you doing, Marcus Cato? This isn't about freedom anymore; freedom was lost long ago. The question is, who will control the state, Caesar or Pompey? Why should you take sides in that fight? It's not your business; a tyrant is being chosen. What does it matter to you who wins? The better man might win, but the winner will still be a tyrant." I'm referring to Cato's final actions, but even in earlier years, the wise person shouldn't have gotten involved in the plundering of the state. What could Cato do except raise his voice and speak in vain? At one time, he was attacked by the mob, spat on, forcibly removed from the forum, and marked for exile. At another time, he was taken straight to prison from the Senate chamber.

However, we'll discuss later whether the wise person should get involved in politics. For now, I ask you to think about those Stoics who, shut out from public life, have withdrawn into privacy to improve people's lives and create laws for humanity without upsetting those in power. The wise person won't disturb the customs of the people, nor will they draw attention to themselves by living in any strange way.

"What then?" you might ask. "Can someone who follows this plan be safe in any situation?" I can't guarantee you this any more than I can guarantee good health to a person who lives moderately, although, in fact, good health often results from moderation. Sometimes a ship sinks even in the harbor; but what do you think happens out on the open sea? And how much more dangerous would it be for a person who isn't even safe in their leisure if they were busy with many things! Innocent people sometimes die; who would deny that? But the guilty die more often. A soldier's skill isn't at fault if he's killed despite his armor.

Finally, the wise person looks at the reason for all their actions, not the results. The beginning is within our control; fortune decides the outcome, but I don't allow her to judge me. You might say, "But she can cause me to suffer." The highwayman doesn't judge when he kills.

Now you're reaching out for your daily gift. It will be a golden gift with which I'll load you; and since we're talking about gold, let me tell you how to use and enjoy it to bring you greater pleasure: "He who needs riches least, enjoys riches most." You might ask, "Who said that?" To show you how generous I am, I intend to praise the sayings of other schools of thought. This saying belongs to Epicurus, or Metrodorus, or someone from that school. But what difference does it make who said it? It was said for the benefit of everyone. He who craves riches is afraid because of them. No one, however, enjoys a blessing that brings anxiety; they're always trying to get a little more. While they worry about increasing their wealth, they forget how to use it. They spend their time counting their money, pacing the floor in the marketplace, and checking their ledgers. In short, he stops being the master and becomes the slave. Farewell.

Letter 15 - On brawn and brains

The old Romans had a custom that continued even into my lifetime. They would start their letters with: "If you are well, it is well; I am also well." People like us would do better to say, "If you are studying philosophy, it is well." Because being well really means being engaged in philosophy. Without philosophy, the mind is sickly, and even if the body is strong, it's only strong in the way that a madman or lunatic might be strong.

This kind of health—the health of the mind—is what you should focus on first. The health of the body is secondary and requires little effort if you want to stay well physically. It's foolish, my dear Lucilius, and unbecoming for a thoughtful person, to work hard on developing muscles, broadening shoulders, and strengthening the lungs. Even if heavy eating makes your muscles solid, you will never be as strong as a top-class bull. Besides, by overloading the body with food, you stifle the soul and make it less active. So, keep the body in check as much as possible and give more freedom to the spirit.

There are many downsides to those who dedicate themselves to such physical pursuits. First, they have to engage in exercises that drain their energy and make them less fit for real challenges or more serious studies. Second, their sharpness is dulled by overeating. Moreover, they end up taking orders from the lowest of people—those who spend their day alternating between the oil flask and the wine bottle, thinking their day is a success if they've worked up a good sweat and then drink huge amounts to replace what they lost due to their fasting. Drinking and sweating—it's the life of someone with digestive problems!

There are short and simple exercises that tire the body quickly and save us time, and time is something we should always value. These exercises include running, lifting weights, and jumping—whether high-jumping, broad-jumping, or what I call "the priest's dance," or, in a less flattering way, "the laundryman's jump." Pick any one of these exercises, and you'll find it straightforward and easy. But whatever you do, return quickly from focusing on the body to focusing on the mind. The mind needs exercise both day and night because it is nourished by moderate effort, and this kind of exercise isn't hindered by cold or hot weather, or even by old age. Cultivate the good that improves with time.

Of course, I'm not saying you should always be hunched over books and writing materials; the mind needs a change, but a change that relaxes it without weakening it. Riding in a carriage shakes up the body without interfering with study; you can read, dictate, converse, or listen to someone else. Even walking doesn't stop you from doing any of these things.

You don't need to disregard voice training, but I forbid you to practice raising and lowering your voice with scales and specific tones. What's next, will you take lessons in how to walk? If you consult someone who has learned tricks from hunger, you'll find someone to monitor your steps, watch every bite you take, and push their boundaries as far as you let them. You might ask, "So should I start by shouting and straining my lungs to the limit?" No, the natural way is to build up gradually, just like people who start arguing in a normal tone of voice and only gradually start shouting. No speaker starts by yelling "Help me, citizens!" at the beginning of a speech.

So, whenever your spirit moves you, make noise, sometimes louder, sometimes softer, as your voice and your spirit guide you. Then, when you bring your voice back to a normal level, let it come down gently, not abruptly. It should taper off smoothly and not drop suddenly like a countryman's loud bellowing. Our goal is not to give the voice exercise but to let it give us exercise.

As you can see, I've saved you from a lot of trouble, and I'll also add a little extra gift—it's a Greek proverb, and a good one: "The fool's life is empty of gratitude and full of fears; it's all about the future." You might ask, "Who said that?" The same writer I mentioned before. And what kind of life do you think is meant by the fool's life? That of someone like Baba or Isio? No, it means our own lives because we're driven by blind desires into actions that harm us and never satisfy us. If we could be satisfied with anything, we would have been satisfied long ago. We don't realize how pleasant it is to want nothing and how noble it is to be content and not depend on fortune.

So, always remind yourself, Lucilius, of how many ambitions you've already achieved. When you see many people ahead of you, think of how many are behind you! If you want to thank the gods and be grateful for your life, you should consider how many people you've surpassed. But what does it matter about others? You've surpassed yourself.

Set a limit that you won't even want to exceed, even if you could. Finally, get rid of all these deceptive goods! They look better to those who hope for them than to those who have them. If there were anything truly valuable in them, they would eventually satisfy you; instead, they only make you thirstier, like a drinker who can't get enough. Get rid of these showy things that only serve for display! As for what the future holds, why should I ask Fortune to give me more rather than ask myself not to want more? And why should I want more? Should I pile up more wealth and forget that life is fleeting? Why should I work so hard? Look, today could be my last; if not, it's close. Farewell.

Letter 16 - On philosophy, the guide of life

I'm sure you understand, Lucilius, that no one can live a truly happy life, or even a bearable one, without studying philosophy. You also know that a happy life is reached when we fully develop our philosophy, but life is still manageable even when we're just starting to learn. However, even though this idea is clear, it must be reinforced and deeply ingrained through daily reflection. It's more important for you to keep the resolutions you've already made than to constantly come up with new ones. You must keep going, building new strength through continuous study, until what is now just a good intention becomes a firmly settled purpose.

So, you don't need to come to me with lots of words and promises; I know you've made great progress. I understand your feelings and know that your words are sincere. Still, I'll tell you what I think—I have hopes for you, but not yet complete trust. I hope you take the same attitude toward yourself; there's no reason to trust yourself too quickly and easily. Examine yourself, watch yourself closely, and especially see whether you've made progress in philosophy or just in life itself.

Philosophy is not a show for the public; it's not something done for appearances. It's about actions, not just words. Philosophy isn't meant to fill the day with amusement or to relieve the boredom of our free time. It shapes and builds the soul, directs our lives, guides our actions, and shows us what we should do and what we should avoid. It steers our course when we're uncertain. Without philosophy, no one can live without fear or have peace of mind. Many things happen every day that require advice, and that advice should come from philosophy.

Someone might say, "How can philosophy help me if Fate controls everything? What good is it if God rules the universe? What good is it if Chance governs everything? If everything is predetermined, we can't change it, and if everything is random, we can't plan for it." Whether Fate, God, or Chance is in control, we still need philosophy. Philosophy will encourage us to obey God cheerfully and defy Fortune with courage. It will teach us to follow God's lead and endure whatever Chance throws at us.

But I don't want to get into a debate about what's within our control—whether everything is predetermined, or if events drag us along, or if sudden, unexpected things rule our lives. Instead, I return to my advice: don't let the fire in your spirit weaken or grow cold. Hold onto it and make it strong, so that what is now just a spark becomes a lasting flame in your mind.

If I know you well, you've probably been trying to figure out from the start what little piece of wisdom this letter offers. Look closely, and you'll find it. Don't be too impressed with my skill; for now, I'm mostly sharing the philosophy of others. But why say "others"? Anything well said by anyone is mine. Here's something from Epicurus: "If you live according to nature, you will never be poor; if you live according to opinion, you will never be rich."

Nature's needs are simple, but the demands of opinion are endless. Suppose you own the wealth of many millionaires. Imagine that fortune grants you more wealth than any private person could need, covers you in gold, clothes you in fine garments, and gives you so much luxury and wealth that you could cover the earth with marble floors, so that you not only possess riches but walk on them. Add statues, paintings, and everything else that luxury demands, and you'll only learn to crave more.

Natural desires have limits, but desires based on false opinions know no bounds. The false has no end. When you're on a road, there must be a destination; but when you're lost, your wandering has no limit. So, turn back from chasing after meaningless things, and whenever you're unsure if what you want is based on natural desire or a misleading one, ask yourself if it has a clear end. If you find that after traveling far, there's always another goal in sight, you can be sure this pursuit goes against nature. Farewell.

Letter 17 - On philosophy and riches

If you are wise, you should get rid of anything that holds you back; actually, you should do it so that you can become wise. Focus all your energy and effort on having a healthy mind. If something is stopping you, either untangle it or cut it loose. You might say, "But my property is slowing me down; I want to make sure I have enough so that when I retire, I won't be burdened by poverty, or be a burden to others."

When you say this, it seems like you don't fully understand how powerful and valuable philosophy really is. You do understand that philosophy is incredibly important and beneficial, but you don't yet see all the ways it can help you in every aspect of life. To put it in Cicero's words, philosophy helps us not only in big matters but also in small ones. Take my advice: consult wisdom; she will tell you not to spend all your time on financial matters.

You're probably thinking that by delaying your studies, you're making sure you won't have to worry about poverty. But what if poverty is actually something to be desired? Riches have kept many people from gaining wisdom, while poverty frees you from many worries. When the alarm sounds, the poor man knows that no one is targeting him; when there's a shout of "Fire," he only needs to find a way out and doesn't worry about saving his possessions.

If a poor man has to go to sea, the harbor isn't crowded with his followers, nor are the docks bustling with people serving just him. A poor man isn't surrounded by a crowd of slaves—slaves whose mouths the master must feed with crops from faraway lands. It's easy to fill a few stomachs when they are trained to only want food. Hunger is cheap; being picky is expensive. Poverty is satisfied with just meeting basic needs.

So why should you reject philosophy as a companion? Even rich people try to live like philosophers when they are thinking clearly. If you want to have free time to think, you should either be poor or live like you are poor. Studying can't help you unless you make an effort to live simply, and living simply is like choosing to be poor. So stop making excuses like, "I don't have enough yet; once I have enough, then I'll focus entirely on philosophy." But actually, this goal you're putting off and treating as less important should come first; you should start with it.

You might reply, "But I want to make sure I have something to live on." Yes, but learn while you're doing that; because if something stops you from living a noble life, nothing can stop you from dying nobly. Poverty shouldn't pull us away from philosophy, and neither should extreme need. When you're chasing after wisdom, you should be willing to endure even hunger. People have endured hunger when their cities were under siege, and what did they get as a reward? They avoided falling into the hands of the enemy.

How much greater is the reward of gaining everlasting freedom and knowing that you don't have to fear either God or man! Even if we're starving, we must reach that goal. Armies have endured all kinds of hardships, living on roots and eating food so terrible we don't even want to talk about it. They went through all that to win a kingdom, and what's even more amazing, to win a kingdom that would end up belonging to someone else. So will anyone hesitate to endure poverty to free their mind from madness?

Therefore, you shouldn't aim to get rich first; you can reach philosophy without needing money for the journey. That's true. After you have gained everything else, will you then wish to gain wisdom too? Should philosophy be the last thing you think about in life, like an afterthought? No, your plan should be this: be a philosopher now, whether you have anything or not—because if you do have something, how do you know you don't already have too much? But if you have nothing, seek understanding first, before anything else.

You might say, "But I won't have the necessities of life." First of all, you can't really lack them, because nature requires so little, and a wise person adjusts their needs to match what nature requires. But if the worst comes to worst, the wise person will quickly leave life behind and stop being a burden to themselves. However, if what they have is small and barely enough, they will make the best of it without worrying or stressing about anything beyond the basics. They will take care of their basic needs and, with a free and happy spirit, laugh at the rush and fuss of rich people who are always chasing after wealth.

They might say, "Why are you putting off your real life and waiting for some future time? Are you going to wait for some interest payment, some profit from your trade, or for a spot in the will of some rich old man, when you can be rich right now? Wisdom offers wealth immediately and gives it to those who have learned to see wealth as unnecessary." These words apply to others, but you are closer to being rich. If you change the time you live in, you already have too much. But in every time, what is enough stays the same.

I could end my letter here if I hadn't gotten you into the habit of expecting more. One can't visit Parthian royalty without bringing a gift; in your case, I can't say goodbye without giving something extra. So what should I do? I'll borrow from Epicurus: "For many people, gaining wealth has not been an end to their troubles, but just a change in them."

I'm not surprised. The problem isn't the wealth itself but the mind. The same thing that made poverty a burden now makes wealth a burden too. It doesn't matter much if you put a sick person on a wooden bed or a golden one; wherever you move them, they will still carry their illness with them. In the same way, it doesn't matter whether a troubled mind is in wealth or poverty; the trouble stays with the person. Farewell.

Letter 18 - On festivals and fasting

It's December, and yet the city is buzzing with activity. People are getting ready to celebrate, as if the Saturnalia is any different from an ordinary day! It's so true that there's no real difference that someone once said, "December used to be a month; now it's like a whole year."

If you were here with me, I'd be glad to ask your advice on what we should do—whether we should stick to our regular routine or if we should join in the festivities and dress more casually. As it stands now, we Romans have changed our clothes for the sake of pleasure and celebration, even though in the past we only did this when the state was in trouble and facing hard times.

I think, knowing you as I do, that you would suggest finding a balance. You'd probably want us not to be exactly like the partying crowd, but also not completely different from them. Maybe this is the right time to test our own self-discipline by avoiding pleasures while everyone else is indulging. This would be the best way to prove our inner strength—by not seeking out things that tempt us to luxury and by not being led into them.

It takes more courage to stay sober and in control when everyone around you is drunk and losing themselves. But it takes even more self-control to not withdraw and to do what the crowd is doing, but in your own way—without standing out and without completely blending in. You can still enjoy a holiday without going overboard.

I'm so determined to test your willpower that I want to give you a challenge based on the teachings of great philosophers: Set aside a few days where you only eat the simplest, cheapest food and wear rough, plain clothing. During this time, keep asking yourself, "Is this what I was so afraid of?"

It's exactly when life is easy that we should prepare ourselves for harder times. When Fortune is kind to us, we should strengthen ourselves against the possibility of bad times. Soldiers practice maneuvers and build fortifications even when there's no enemy in sight so that they're ready when real trouble comes. If you don't want someone to panic in a crisis, you have to train them before the crisis hits. That's what those wise people did when they practiced living in poverty every month—they did this so that if they ever faced real poverty, they wouldn't be afraid.

Don't think I'm talking about the kind of meals that rich people sometimes try out for fun, or those fake "poor man's" huts they build to amuse themselves. No, I mean real hardship—sleeping on a rough bed, wearing coarse clothing, and eating hard, unappetizing bread. Do this for three or four days, or even longer, so that it becomes a real test of your endurance, not just a hobby. Then, I promise you, my dear Lucilius, you'll feel a great sense of joy when a small amount of food fills you up, and you'll realize that peace of mind doesn't depend on Fortune. Even when she's angry, she still gives us enough to survive.

But don't think you're doing something extraordinary; after all, many slaves and poor people live like this every day. But you can take pride in the fact that you're doing it voluntarily, and that you could endure it permanently if you had to, not just as an experiment. Let's practice with this "dummy" of poverty so that Fortune won't catch us off guard. We'll enjoy our wealth more comfortably if we learn that poverty isn't really such a burden.

Even Epicurus, the philosopher who taught about pleasure, used to set aside certain times to eat very frugally. He wanted to see if he was any less happy when he did this, and if so, how much less happy, and whether that small amount of happiness was worth all the extra effort. He mentioned this in a famous letter to Polyaenus during the time of the archon Charinus. In fact, he bragged that he lived on less than a penny a day, though Metrodorus, who wasn't as advanced, needed a whole penny.

Do you think you can feel full on such a small amount of food? Yes, and there's pleasure in it too—not the kind of pleasure that fades quickly and needs constant refreshing, but a steady, reliable pleasure. While water, barley meal, and barley bread might not seem like a fun diet, it's the highest form of pleasure to be able to enjoy this kind of food and to reduce your needs to something so small that no misfortune can take it away.

Even prisoners awaiting execution get more generous meals, and those condemned to death aren't fed so poorly by the people who are about to execute them. So what kind of noble spirit must one have to willingly choose a diet that even the condemned don't have to fear? This is truly preparing yourself for the worst that Fortune can throw at you.

So, my dear Lucilius, start following the example of these men, and set aside certain days where you step away from your regular life and make do with the bare minimum. Get to know poverty as if you're doing business with it.

Dare, my friend, to turn away from the sight of wealth, And shape yourself to be close to the divine.

For only the person who has scorned wealth is close to God. Of course, I'm not saying you can't own wealth, but I want you to reach a point where you own it without fear. You can only do this by convincing yourself that you can live just as happily without it as you do with it, and by always remembering that wealth can slip away at any moment.

But now I need to wrap up this letter. "Settle your debts first," you might say. So here's a payment from Epicurus: "Uncontrolled anger leads to madness." You know how true this is, especially if you've ever had slaves or enemies.

But really, this emotion can flare up against anyone; it can come from love as much as from hate, and it can show itself in both serious matters and in jokes. And it doesn't matter how big the reason for your anger is; what matters is the kind of person it affects. It's like fire—it doesn't matter how big the flame is; what matters is what it lands on. Strong, solid wood can resist even a large fire, while dry, flammable stuff can turn the smallest spark into a huge blaze. It's the same with anger, my dear Lucilius; the result of great anger is madness, so we should avoid anger—not just to avoid going too far, but to keep our minds healthy. Farewell.

Letter 19 - On worldliness and retirement

I feel really happy whenever I get letters from you because they fill me with hope. These letters are no longer just updates about you; they're promises. I beg you to keep going on this path because what better request could I make to a friend than one that's for his own good? If possible, try to get away from all the business you mentioned; and if you can't do that, force yourself to leave it behind. We've already wasted enough time; now that we're getting older, it's time to start packing up.

No one should begrudge us this decision. We've spent our lives sailing on rough seas; let's make sure we die in a safe harbor. I'm not suggesting that you should seek fame by retiring. Your retirement shouldn't be flaunted or hidden. I don't want you to think that I'm urging you to consider everyone else as crazy and then hide yourself away in obscurity. Instead, try to live quietly without drawing too much attention, even though your retirement should still be noticeable.

On the other hand, while some people have the freedom to choose whether they want to live a quiet life, you don't have that option. Your talent and energy have pushed you into the public eye, and so have your writing skills and friendships with famous people. Fame has already claimed you. Even if you try to hide yourself completely, your past actions will still reveal who you are. You can't stay in the shadows because some of the light from your previous achievements will follow you wherever you go.

You can find peace without making anyone dislike you, without feeling like you're losing something, and without feeling guilty. After all, what would you leave behind that you'd really miss? Your clients? But they're not interested in you for who you are; they're just interested in what they can get from you. People used to seek out friends, but now they're just after money. If an old man changes his will, the morning visitors simply move on to someone else's door. You can't buy important things with small amounts; so think about whether it's better to leave behind your true self or just some of your possessions.

I wish you had grown old in the simple circumstances of your origins, without fortune raising you to such heights! Your quick rise to success, your position in the province, your role as procurator, and everything that comes with it has taken you far away from a healthy way of living. Next, you'll take on even more important duties, and then even more after that. And what will happen then? Why wait until there's nothing left for you to desire? That time will never come.

Just as we believe there's a chain of causes that creates fate, you can be sure that there's a chain of desires too—each one begins where the last one ends. You've been pulled into a life that will never bring an end to your misery and servitude. Free your neck from the yoke; it's better to cut it off once and for all than to keep suffering forever.

If you retreat to a private life, everything will be on a smaller scale, but you'll find plenty of satisfaction. However, in your current situation, there's no real satisfaction in the abundance that surrounds you. Would you rather be poor and content or rich and always wanting more? Prosperity is not only greedy, but it also makes you a target for the greed of others. And as long as you're never satisfied, you won't be able to satisfy others.

You might ask, "But how do I step away from all this?" Any way you like. Think about how many risks you've taken for money and how much work you've put in for a title! You need to be just as brave in pursuing a life of leisure—or else grow old in the constant worries of procuratorships abroad and civil duties at home, living in a state of turmoil with never-ending responsibilities. No one has ever managed to avoid these responsibilities by living quietly or withdrawing from public life. It doesn't matter if you personally want a quiet life; your position in the world demands the opposite! And what if, even now, you let your position grow even bigger? Everything you add to your successes will only add to your fears.

At this point, I want to quote something Maecenas said when he was at the height of his power: "There's thunder even on the highest peaks." If you're wondering where these words come from, they're in a book called Prometheus. He meant that the highest places are also surrounded by storms. But is any amount of power worth the price of adopting such a corrupt lifestyle to get it? Maecenas was a talented man who could have left a great legacy for Roman oratory, but his good fortune made him weak—no, it emasculated him! You'll face the same fate unless you immediately shorten your sails and, unlike Maecenas who waited too long, steer close to the shore!

This saying from Maecenas could have been enough to finish my letter, but knowing you, I'm sure you won't let me get away with such a simple and low-quality response. So, I'll turn to the teachings of Epicurus instead. He said, "You must think carefully about who you eat and drink with, rather than what you eat and drink. For a meal of meat without the company of a friend is like the life of a lion or a wolf."

You won't have this privilege unless you withdraw from the world; otherwise, your dinner guests will only be those whom your secretary selects from the crowd of visitors. But it's a mistake to choose your friends in the reception hall or test them at the dinner table. The worst thing for a busy man overwhelmed by his possessions is that he thinks people are his friends when he isn't really a friend to them, and he believes that his favors can win friends, even though some people only hate him more the more they owe him. A small debt makes someone your debtor; a large one makes them your enemy.

You might ask, "Don't acts of kindness create friendships?" They do, if you've had the chance to choose who receives them and if they're given wisely, not just scattered randomly. So, as you start to reclaim your mind, apply this wise saying: Consider that it's more important who receives a gift than what the gift is. Farewell.

Letter 20 - On practicing what you preach

If you're feeling healthy and believe you're finally ready to take control of your own life, I'm happy for you. I'll be proud if I can help you escape from the difficulties you've been struggling with, where it seemed like there was no way out. But, my dear Lucilius, I ask and beg you to let wisdom truly sink into your soul. Test your progress not by what you say or write, but by how strong your heart is and by how much less you desire things. Prove your words by your actions.

The goals of those who make speeches and seek the approval of a crowd are very different from those who try to impress young people and idlers with clever arguments. Philosophy teaches us to act, not just to speak. It demands that each person lives according to their own values, that their life should be in harmony with their words, and that their inner life should match all their actions. This, I believe, is the highest duty and the greatest proof of wisdom—to ensure that actions and words are in sync and that a person remains true to themselves in all situations.

You might say, "But who can keep up this standard?" Very few, of course, but some can. It's certainly a tough challenge, and I'm not saying that a philosopher can always keep the same pace. But they can always stay on the same path.

So, examine yourself and see if your lifestyle is consistent. Are you living in a way that shows harmony between your words and actions? Do you treat yourself lavishly while being stingy with your family? Do you eat simple meals but live in luxurious homes? You should choose one way to live and follow that standard in everything you do. Some people act modestly at home but show off in public. This inconsistency is a flaw and shows a mind that is still unsteady and can't find its balance.

I can also tell you where this inconsistency comes from: It happens because people don't really decide what they want. Even if they do make a decision, they don't stick with it—they change their minds and go back to what they've abandoned. So, to simplify the ancient definitions of wisdom and apply them to everyday life, I'd say wisdom is always wanting the same things and always rejecting the same things. You might not need to add the condition that what you want should be right because no one can consistently want the same thing unless it's the right thing.

This is why people often don't know what they want, except at the moment they're wanting it. No one ever decides once and for all what to desire or reject. Their judgment changes day by day, making many people live their lives like a game. So, keep going as you've started; maybe you'll reach perfection, or at least get to a point where you know you're close.

You might wonder, "But what will happen to my household if I stop supporting it with my income?" If you stop providing for that crowd, they will take care of themselves. Or maybe you'll learn through poverty what you couldn't learn through wealth. Poverty will show you who your true friends are; you'll be rid of those who were only seeking you for what you had. Isn't it true that you should love poverty, if only because it shows you who truly loves you? Oh, when will that time come when no one flatters you with lies?

So, focus your thoughts, efforts, and desires on being content with yourself and the things that come from within. Leave all your other prayers to God's care. What happiness could be closer to you than that? Bring yourself down to a humble life from which you can't be thrown out. To help you do this more eagerly, I'll share a piece of advice in this letter right away.

Although you might be skeptical, Epicurus once again provides the answer: "Believe me, your words will have more power if you sleep on a simple bed and wear plain clothes. That way, you won't just be saying them; you'll be living them." I, for one, listen to our friend Demetrius differently after seeing him lying on a bed without even a cloak to cover him, and without rugs to lie on. He isn't just a teacher of truth; he's a living example of it.

You might ask, "Can't someone still despise wealth even if they have it in their pocket?" Of course, they can. A great person can see riches all around them and, after thinking long and hard about how they came to have them, can smile and know that they belong to them only in name. It means a lot not to be spoiled by wealth. A truly great person can remain poor even when surrounded by riches.

You might say, "But how will this person handle sudden poverty if it comes?" And I might ask, Epicurus, how would a poor person handle sudden riches? In both cases, it's the mind that needs to be examined. We need to see whether the rich person can enjoy their poverty and whether the poor person would be unhappy with sudden wealth. Otherwise, sleeping on a simple bed and wearing rags doesn't really prove anything unless it's clear that the person is enduring these conditions by choice, not because they have to.

However, it's the sign of a noble spirit not to rush into these hardships just because they seem better, but to practice them so that they become easier to handle. And they are easy to handle, Lucilius; when you've prepared for them through practice, they can even be pleasant because they bring a sense of freedom from worry—and without that, nothing is truly enjoyable.

That's why I believe it's important, as I've told you in a previous letter, to set aside a few days where we can prepare ourselves for real poverty by pretending to be poor. There's even more reason to do this because we've become so used to luxury that we see all duties as hard and burdensome. Let the soul be awakened from its sleep and reminded that nature requires very little from us. No one is born rich. Everyone, when they first see the light of day, is expected to be content with milk and rags. That's how we all start, yet even kingdoms become too small for us! Farewell.

Letter 21 - On the renown which my writings will bring you

Are you having trouble with the people you wrote to me about? Your biggest problem is with yourself because you're the one getting in your own way. You don't really know what you want. You're better at approving the right path than actually following it. You see where true happiness lies, but you don't have the courage to go after it. Let me tell you what's holding you back since you can't see it yourself.

You think that the life you're considering leaving is important, and even though you've decided to seek a more peaceful state, you're still drawn to the shiny aspects of your current life, as if moving on would mean sinking into something dirty and dark. This is a mistake, Lucilius; leaving your current life behind would actually be a step up. The difference between these two lives is like the difference between a mere reflection and real light; the real light has a source within itself, while the reflection only shines because it's borrowed from somewhere else. The reflection can easily be blocked by anything that comes between it and the light, but the true light glows from within.

Your studies and dedication will make you shine and stand out. Let me give you an example from Epicurus. He once wrote to Idomeneus, trying to convince him to leave behind a flashy life in exchange for true and lasting fame. At that time, Idomeneus was a high-ranking official with a lot of power and responsibilities. Epicurus told him, "If you're seeking fame, my letters will make you more famous than all the things you currently cherish." And Epicurus wasn't lying. Who would have remembered Idomeneus if the philosopher hadn't written about him in his letters? All the other powerful people of that time, even the king himself, are now forgotten, but Idomeneus is still remembered.

Cicero's letters have kept the name of his friend Atticus alive. It wouldn't have mattered if Atticus had important family connections like having Agrippa as a son-in-law, Tiberius as a grandson-in-law, and Drusus Caesar as a great-grandson. Without Cicero's writings, his name would have been lost among those big names. A few great men will manage to rise above the waves of time, and although they'll eventually disappear into the silence of history, they'll fight against being forgotten for as long as they can.

What Epicurus could promise his friend, I can promise you, Lucilius. I'll be remembered by future generations, and I can take your name along with mine. Our poet Vergil promised eternal fame to two heroes, and he kept that promise:

"Blessed heroes, if my song has power,
Your names shall never be erased from the book of Time,
As long as Aeneas' tribe holds the Capitol,
And Romans rule the empire."

Whenever people are pushed forward by luck, whenever they become part of someone else's power, they are well-liked and their homes are full of visitors. But this lasts only as long as they stay in that position. When they lose it, they are quickly forgotten. But for those with natural talent, the respect people have for them only grows.

Not only do they earn honor for themselves, but everything connected to their memory is passed on to others.

To make sure Idomeneus isn't mentioned here for free, let him repay the favor with some wisdom from his own account. Epicurus once told him something famous, urging him to make Pythocles wealthy—but not in the usual sense. He said, "If you want to make Pythocles rich, don't add to his money, but take away from his desires." This idea is clear enough on its own and clever enough that it doesn't need further explanation.

But there's one thing I want to warn you about—don't think this advice only applies to money. It's just as valuable no matter how you use it. "If you want to make Pythocles honorable, don't add to his honors, but take away from his desires." "If you want Pythocles to have lasting pleasure, don't add to his pleasures, but take away from his desires." "If you want to make Pythocles live a full life, don't add years to his life, but take away from his desires."

There's no reason to think these words belong only to Epicurus; they're for everyone. In philosophy, we should do what they do in the Senate: when someone makes a motion that I agree with, I ask them to split it into parts, and I vote for the part I approve of. I'm all the more happy to repeat Epicurus' wise words to show those who follow him for the wrong reasons—thinking they can use his teachings to excuse their own faults—that they must live honorably, no matter what school of thought they follow.

Go to his Garden and read the motto carved there: "Stranger, you'll do well to stay here; our highest good is pleasure." The caretaker of that place, a kind host, will be ready to welcome you with barley-meal and plenty of water, saying, "Haven't you been well taken care of?" He'll add, "This garden doesn't make you hungry; it satisfies your hunger. It doesn't make you thirstier with every drink; it quenches your thirst with a natural remedy—one that costs nothing. This is the 'pleasure' I've grown old enjoying."

When I talk to you, however, I'm referring to those desires that can't be satisfied, that have to be bribed to stop. For those desires that can be postponed or controlled, I have just one thought to share with you: pleasures like these are natural but not necessary; you owe them nothing. Whatever you spend on them is a free gift. The belly, however, won't listen to reason; it makes demands and keeps pestering you. But it's not a difficult creditor to satisfy; you can send it away with a small payment, as long as you give it what you owe, not everything you can give. Farewell.

Letter 22 - On the futility of half-way measures

You understand by now that you need to distance yourself from those flashy and corrupt pursuits, but you still want to know how to do it. Some things can only be pointed out by someone who is there with you. A doctor can't prescribe the exact time to eat or bathe through a letter; he needs to check your pulse in person. There's an old saying about gladiators—that they plan their fight in the ring. As they watch closely, something in the opponent's eyes, a movement of his hand, or even a slight shift in his body gives them a warning.

We can set general rules and write them down, explaining what usually happens or what should be done. This advice can be given not just to friends who are far away, but to future generations as well. But when it comes to the specific question of when or how to carry out your plan, no one can give you advice from a distance; we need to be present in the actual situation. You must be not only physically present but also mentally alert if you want to take advantage of the fleeting opportunity.

So, look around you for that opportunity; if you see it, seize it, and with all your energy and strength, focus on freeing yourself from those business duties.

Now listen carefully to my advice: I believe you should either withdraw from that kind of life or from life altogether. But I also think you should take a gentle approach, loosening the knot you've tied rather than cutting it—unless, of course, there's no other way to untie it, in which case you may need to cut it. No one is so weak that they would prefer to stay in suspense forever rather than face a final end.

Meanwhile—and this is the most important thing—don't burden yourself further. Be content with the business you've already taken on, or, as you might prefer others to think, the business you've stumbled into. There's no need to push further; if you do, you'll lose all excuses, and people will see that it wasn't an accident. The usual excuse people give is wrong: "I was forced to do it. Even though I didn't want to, I had no choice." But no one is forced to chase prosperity at full speed; it means something to stop, even if you don't resist, instead of eagerly pursuing good fortune.

Will you be upset if I not only give you advice but also bring in wiser people than myself to help you? Read this letter from Epicurus that relates to this matter; it's addressed to Idomeneus. Epicurus urges him to retreat as quickly as possible before a stronger force comes between him and takes away his chance to withdraw. But he also adds that we shouldn't attempt anything unless the time is right. When the long-awaited opportunity comes, we must act. Epicurus warns us not to be lazy when planning our escape; he tells us to hope for a safe release even from the hardest situations, as long as we're not too hasty before the time is right or too slow when it finally arrives.

Now, I suppose you're looking for a Stoic motto as well. There's no reason for anyone to accuse the Stoics of being reckless; in fact, they're more cautious than they are brave. You might expect them to say things like this: "It's shameful to flinch under a burden. Face the duties you've taken on. No one is brave and dedicated if they avoid danger, if their spirit doesn't grow stronger with the difficulty of the task." Words like these will indeed be spoken to you, but only if your perseverance has a worthy goal and you don't have to do or endure anything unworthy of a good person. A good person won't waste their energy on low and discreditable work or stay busy just for the sake of being busy. Nor will they, as you might think, get so caught up in ambitious plans that they have to constantly deal with their ups and downs. No, when they see the dangers, uncertainties, and risks they used to face, they will gradually pull back to a safer position, not by turning their back to the enemy, but by slowly retreating to safety.

It's easy to escape from business, my dear Lucilius, if only you stop valuing the rewards it offers. We're held back and kept from leaving by thoughts like these: "What then? Should I leave behind these great prospects? Should I walk away just as I'm about to reap the rewards? Should I give up having slaves at my side, a grand entourage, or a crowded reception room?" That's why people leave these advantages so reluctantly; they love the rewards of their hard work but hate the work itself. People complain about their ambitions just like they complain about their lovers—in other words, if you look closely at their true feelings, you'll find not hatred but bickering. If you examine the minds of those who criticize what they once desired and talk about escaping from things they can't live without, you'll see that they're staying in that situation by choice, even though they say it's hard and miserable.

It's true, my dear Lucilius; a few people are trapped by slavery, but many more cling to it themselves. If you truly want to be free from this slavery, if freedom genuinely appeals to you, and if you're seeking advice on how to achieve it without constant trouble, how could all the Stoic philosophers fail to support your decision? Zeno, Chrysippus, and all their followers would give you advice that is moderate, honorable, and appropriate. But if you keep looking back to see how much you can take with you, how much money you can keep to support your life of leisure, you'll never find a way out. No one can swim to shore while carrying their baggage with them. Rise to a higher life with the help of the gods, but don't seek the kind of favor the gods sometimes give—when they, with kind faces, bestow great misfortunes that end up causing irritation and suffering, all because they were granted in response to prayers.

I was just about to seal this letter, but I'll reopen it to include its usual contribution—some wise words. Here's one that comes to mind; I'm not sure if its truth or its eloquence is greater. "Who said it?" you ask. Epicurus, of course; I'm still borrowing from others. The words are: "Everyone leaves life just as if they had only just entered it." Catch anyone off guard—whether young, old, or middle-aged—and you'll find that they're all equally afraid of death and equally ignorant of life. No one has anything completed because we keep putting off all our tasks for the future.

The part of this quote that I like most is how it points out that old men are like infants. "No one," he says, "leaves this world any differently than someone who has just been born." But that's not entirely true; we're actually worse off when we die than when we were born, but that's our fault, not Nature's. Nature should scold us, saying, "What's the meaning of this? I brought you into the world without desires or fears, free from superstition, betrayal, and other curses. Now leave as you were when you entered!"

A person has truly grasped wisdom if they can die as free from worry as they were at birth. But as it is, we become agitated as the dreaded end approaches. Our courage fails, our faces turn pale, and our tears fall, even though they're useless. But what could be more shameful than to worry at the very moment when peace is within reach?

The reason for this is that we've lost everything valuable; we've thrown overboard the cargo of life and are now in distress because nothing has been saved. People don't care about living nobly; they only care about living long. Yet it's within every person's power to live nobly, but within no one's power to live long. Farewell.

Letter 23 - On the true joy which comes from philosophy

Do you think I'm going to write to you about how mild and short the winter has been, or how unpleasant the spring is with its unexpected cold? And all the other small talk people write about when they can't think of anything else? No, I want to share something that can help both you and me. And what would that be, if not some advice on how to have a healthy mind? You ask what the foundation of a healthy mind is? It's not finding joy in useless things. I said it was the foundation, but it's really the highest point. We've reached the top if we know what truly makes us happy and if we haven't placed our happiness in the hands of external things. The person who is driven by hope for anything, even if it's within reach, even if it's easy to get, and even if their dreams have never let them down, is still troubled and unsure of themselves.

Above all, my dear Lucilius, make it your priority to learn how to feel real joy. Do you think I'm taking away many of your pleasures by trying to steer you away from the gifts of chance, by advising you to avoid hope, which is often considered the sweetest thing that brightens our hearts? Quite the opposite; I don't want you to ever be without joy. I want it to be born in your own home, and it will be if it comes from within you. Other things that bring happiness don't fill a person's heart; they only smooth their brow and are unpredictable—unless you think that someone who laughs is truly joyful. Real joy must come from deep within and be steady, rising above all circumstances.

Real joy, believe me, is serious business. Can someone truly despise death with a carefree attitude, or with a "light and happy" expression, as some young people like to say? Can someone welcome poverty, control their desires, or face the endurance of pain with ease? The person who thinks deeply about these things in their heart is indeed full of joy, but it's not a shallow, cheerful joy. This is the kind of joy I want you to have because once you find its source, it will never leave you.

The shallow joy from trivial things is like the surface of poor mines—only a thin layer of pleasure. The real treasure lies deep, and those who dig deeper will find richer rewards. Similarly, the little joys that please the common crowd are only superficial, like a thin coating, and every joy that's only skin-deep lacks a solid foundation. But the joy I'm talking about, the one I'm trying to lead you to, is something solid, revealing more of itself as you go deeper into it.

So, my dear Lucilius, I urge you to do the one thing that can make you truly happy: cast aside and trample underfoot all those things that glitter on the outside and are offered to you by someone else or seem to be obtainable from others. Look toward the true good and find joy only in what comes from within you. And what do I mean by "within you"? I mean the best part of you, your very self. The frail body, even though we can't do anything without it, should be seen as necessary rather than important. It drags us into pointless pleasures, which are short-lived and soon regretted. Unless they are controlled by strong self-discipline, these pleasures can quickly turn into their opposites—sorrow and pain.

But it's hard to control something you believe to be good. The real good can be desired safely. Do you ask me what this real good is and where it comes from? I'll tell you: it comes from a good conscience, from honorable purposes, from right actions, from not caring about the gifts of chance, and from living a steady and calm life that follows one consistent path. People who constantly jump from one goal to another, or are just carried along by chance, how can they ever possess any good that is stable and lasting?

Only a few people control themselves and their lives by a clear purpose; the rest don't progress—they're just swept along like objects floating in a river. And of these objects, some are held back by slow-moving water and drift gently; others are swept along by a stronger current. Some, which are closest to the shore, are left behind as the current slows; others are carried out to sea by the rushing stream. That's why we should decide what we want and stick to that decision.

Now it's time for me to share something of value with you. I can give you a saying from your friend Epicurus and clear this letter of its obligation: "It's troublesome to always be starting life over." Or another, which might express it better: "They live poorly who are always beginning to live."

You're right to ask why; this saying does need some explanation. It's because the life of such people is always incomplete. But a person cannot be ready for death if they've only just begun to live. We must aim to have already lived long enough. No one thinks they've done so if they're still in the process of planning their life.

Don't think that there are only a few people like this; almost everyone is like this. Some people only start living when it's time for them to stop living. And if this surprises you, I'll add something that will surprise you even more: some people stop living before they even begin. Farewell.

Letter 24 - On despising death

You wrote to me that you're worried about the outcome of a lawsuit, where an angry opponent is threatening you. You probably expect me to tell you to imagine a better outcome and to take comfort in hope. But why should we invite trouble that will come soon enough anyway, or spoil the present by fearing the future? It's silly to be unhappy now just because you might be unhappy later.

Instead, I'll guide you to peace of mind in a different way: if you want to stop worrying, assume that what you fear will definitely happen. Whatever the trouble may be, think about it in your mind and measure how much it really scares you. This way, you'll understand that what you fear is either small or won't last long.

You don't need to spend much time finding examples to strengthen yourself; every time in history has them. Look back at any period in Roman or foreign history, and you'll find many examples of people who faced challenges with courage. If you lose this case, what could happen that's worse than being exiled or imprisoned? Is there anything more frightening than being burned or killed? List these penalties one by one and think of the people who have faced them bravely; it's not hard to find them, just a matter of choosing.

Rutilius accepted his unjust conviction as if the unfairness was the only thing that bothered him. Metellus faced exile with courage, and Rutilius even with happiness. Metellus returned only because his country called him back, but Rutilius refused to return when Sulla summoned him—and no one said "no" to Sulla! Socrates spoke wisely in prison and refused to escape when given the chance. He stayed there to free people from the fear of two of the most dreaded things: death and imprisonment.

Mucius put his hand in the fire. It's painful to be burned, but how much more painful to do it to yourself! Mucius was not a learned man, prepared by wisdom to face death and pain, but just a soldier with courage. He punished himself for his failed attempt by letting his hand burn away on the enemy's brazier, not pulling it back until his enemy removed the fire. He might have achieved something more successful in that camp, but never anything braver. Notice how much more eager a brave person is to face danger than a cruel person is to inflict it: Porsenna was quicker to forgive Mucius for trying to kill him than Mucius was to forgive himself for failing.

You might say, "Oh, those stories have been told over and over in schools; next, you'll tell me about Cato when talking about despising death." But why shouldn't I tell you about Cato? How he read Plato's book on his last glorious night, with a sword beside his bed. He had prepared these two things for his final moments—the will to die and the means to do it. He put his affairs in order as best he could in a world that was falling apart, and made sure no one could either kill or save Cato. Drawing the sword, which he had kept unstained by blood until the last day, he said, "Fortune, you've achieved nothing by resisting all my efforts. I've fought for my country's freedom, not for my own. I didn't strive so hard to be free, but only to live among free people. Now, since humanity's future is hopeless, let Cato be saved."

With those words, he inflicted a mortal wound on himself. After the doctors patched him up, Cato had less blood and strength but no less courage. Angry not only at Caesar but also at himself, he used his hands to reopen his wound and forced out, rather than let go, his noble soul that had defied all worldly power.

I'm not bringing up these examples to show off my wit but to encourage you to face what is often seen as the most terrifying thing—death. And I'll do this more easily by showing that not only the strong have faced the moment of death with courage, but even some who were otherwise weak have shown bravery in this regard. Take Scipio, the father-in-law of Gnaeus Pompeius, for example. When a headwind drove his ship back to the African coast, and he saw it was in enemy hands, he pierced his body with a sword. When asked where the commander was, he replied, "All is well with the commander."

These words brought him up to the level of his ancestors and kept the glory that fate gave to the Scipios in Africa intact. It was a great deed to conquer Carthage, but an even greater deed to conquer death. "All is well with the commander!" How else should a general die, especially one of Cato's generals?

I won't refer you to history or gather examples of people who have despised death throughout the ages because there are many. Look at our own times, which are often criticized for being weak and overly refined; even now, you'll find people of every rank, life situation, and age who have ended their troubles through death.

Believe me, Lucilius, death is so little to be feared that because of it, nothing else should be feared. So when your enemy threatens you, listen calmly. Even if your conscience gives you confidence, remember that many things can affect the outcome, things beyond your control. Hope for complete justice, but also prepare yourself for the worst injustice. But above all, strip away all the things that disturb and confuse you, and see what each thing really is at its core; you'll realize that nothing is truly scary except fear itself.

What happens to boys happens to us too—we're just slightly bigger boys. When someone they love and play with every day appears wearing a mask, they're terrified. We should take the mask off not just people but also things and see them for what they really are.

"Why do you scare me with swords, fires, and a crowd of executioners? Take away all that useless show, behind which you hide and scare fools! You are nothing but Death, whom even my servant and maid did not fear yesterday! Why do you try to frighten me with whips, racks, and all the other tools for tearing a person apart? Get rid of all this stuff that makes us freeze in terror! And silence the groans, cries, and bitter screams of the victim on the rack! You are just Pain, scorned by the man with gout, endured by the person with indigestion, and bravely borne by the woman in labor. You are small if I can bear you, and short if I cannot!"

Think about these words, which you've heard and said many times. Then, prove by your actions whether what you've heard and said is true. Our philosophy is often criticized for focusing on words rather than actions, which is a shameful accusation.

What, did you just now realize that death is always hanging over your head, that exile or grief could happen at any moment? You were born into these dangers. Let's think of everything that could happen as something that will happen.

I know you've already done what I'm advising you to do; now I'm warning you not to let these little worries overwhelm your soul. If you do, your soul will be dulled and won't have enough strength left when the time comes for it to rise. Focus on the bigger picture, not just your personal case. Remind yourself that our bodies are mortal and fragile; pain can come from many sources, not just from injustice or the power of others. Even our pleasures can become torment; feasts lead to indigestion, parties to muscle paralysis, and bad habits affect our bodies in many painful ways.

I may become poor; I will then be one among many. I may be exiled; I will then consider myself born in the place I'm sent to. They may put me in chains. What of it? Am I free from bonds now? Look at this heavy burden of a body that nature has chained me to! "I shall die," you say; you mean to say, "I shall stop risking sickness, imprisonment, and death."

I'm not so foolish as to repeat the arguments Epicurus always uses, saying that the terrors of the underworld are baseless—that Ixion doesn't spin on his wheel, Sisyphus doesn't push his stone uphill, and no one's insides are eaten and restored every day. No one is so childish as to fear Cerberus, ghosts, or skeletons. Death either frees us or ends us. If we are released, the better part of us remains after the burden is lifted; if we are ended, nothing remains—good and bad alike disappear.

Let me quote a verse of yours here, reminding you that when you wrote it, you meant it for yourself just as much as for others. It's shameful to say one thing and mean another; and even more shameful to write one thing and mean another. I remember one day you were discussing the common idea that we don't suddenly fall into death but move towards it gradually; we die every day.

Every day, a little of our life is taken from us; even as we grow, our life is shrinking. We lose our childhood, then our boyhood, and then our youth. Even yesterday is lost time; the day we're living now is shared between us and death. It's not the last drop that empties the water-clock but all the drops that came before it. Similarly, the final hour when we stop living doesn't bring death on its own; it simply completes the process. We reach death at that moment, but we've been moving towards it for a long time.

When describing this, you said in your usual style (which is always impressive but especially powerful when you're speaking the truth):

"Death doesn't come just once; the death that takes us away is simply the last of all."

I'd rather you read your own words than my letter; that way, you'll see that the death we fear is the last, but not the only death.

I see what you're looking for; you want to know what wise saying I've included in this letter, what useful advice I've packed in. So I'll give you something that ties into what we've been discussing. Epicurus criticizes those who both crave and fear death: "It's absurd," he says, "to run towards death because you're tired of life when it's the way you've lived that makes you run towards death." And in another passage: "What could be more absurd than seeking death when your fear of death has robbed your life of peace?" You might also consider this third statement: "People are so thoughtless, even mad, that some force themselves to die out of fear of death."

Whichever of these ideas you focus on, you'll strengthen your mind to face both death and life. We need to be warned and strengthened in both directions—not to love or hate life too much. Even when reason tells us it's time to end it, we shouldn't act impulsively or recklessly.

The brave and wise person shouldn't rush to leave life but should exit in a dignified manner. Above all, they should avoid the weakness that has taken hold of so many—the desire for death. Just as the mind can drift towards other things without thinking, it can also drift towards death. This happens to both noble and spirited people as well as the cowardly and despicable. The former despise life; the latter find it unbearable.

Some people are also driven by boredom with doing and seeing the same things, not so much by a hatred of life but because they're tired of it. We slip into this state while philosophy itself pushes us on, and we say, "How long must I endure the same things? Shall I continue to wake and sleep, be hungry and full, shiver and sweat? Nothing ever ends; everything is connected in a kind of circle; things flee and are pursued. Night follows day, day follows night; summer ends in autumn, winter rushes after autumn, and winter melts into spring; all of nature passes, only to return. I do nothing new; I see nothing new; sooner or later, I'll get tired of this too." Many people don't find living painful but just unnecessary. Farewell.

Letter 25 - On reformation

When dealing with these two friends of ours, we have to take different approaches. One friend's faults should be corrected, while the other's faults need to be completely eliminated. I will be very direct because I don't truly care for this friend if I'm not willing to hurt his feelings. You might ask, "Do you plan to keep guiding a man who is already forty years old? Think about his age; he's already set in his ways and hard to change!" It's true that it's difficult to reshape someone like this; only young minds are easily molded. I'm not sure if I will succeed, but I would rather try and fail than not try at all. You shouldn't give up on curing someone who is sick, even when the illness is serious, as long as you stand firm against their excesses and force them to do things they don't want to do. As for our other friend, I'm not entirely confident either, except for the fact that he still feels shame when he sins. This sense of shame should be encouraged because as long as it lasts, there is hope. But for this older friend of yours, I think we should be more careful so that he doesn't lose hope in himself.

There's no better time to approach him than now, when he has some peace and seems like he's trying to correct his faults. Others may have been fooled by this brief period of good behavior, but I'm not fooled. I'm certain these faults will come back even stronger because right now, they are just hidden, not gone. I will spend some time on this and try to see if anything can be done.

But you, as you've already been doing, need to show me that you are strong-hearted; lighten your load for the journey ahead. None of our possessions are truly necessary. Let's go back to living by nature's laws because then we will have true wealth. The things we really need are either free or very cheap; nature only requires bread and water. No one is poor by this standard, and when a person limits their desires to these needs, they can even rival the happiness of the god Jupiter, as Epicurus says. I must include one or two more of his sayings in this letter:

"Do everything as if Epicurus were watching you." It's good for a person to have someone to look up to, someone who they think is always watching them, even in their thoughts. It's much better to live as though a good person is always by your side, but I'm happy if you just act as though someone, anyone, is watching you because being alone often leads us to do wrong. And when you've made enough progress that you respect yourself, you can let go of this guardian. But until then, place yourself under the authority of some great man, like Cato, Scipio, or Laelius—someone whose presence would make even the worst people behave. In the meantime, you should work on becoming the kind of person you wouldn't dare misbehave around. Once you've achieved this and start to respect yourself, I will slowly allow you to follow what Epicurus suggests in another passage: "The time when you should withdraw into yourself the most is when you are forced to be in a crowd."

You should aim to be different from the crowd. So, while it's not yet safe to withdraw into complete solitude, seek out a few good people to be around because everyone is better off with some company, no matter who, than being alone. "The time when you should withdraw into yourself the most is when you are forced to be in a crowd." Yes, but only if you are a good, calm, and self-controlled person; otherwise, it's better to be in a crowd to escape from yourself. When you're alone, you are too close to the troublemaker within you. Farewell.

Letter 26 - On old age and death

Not long ago, I told you that I was getting close to old age. Now, I'm afraid I might have already entered into it. Maybe another word better describes my years now—or at least my body—since old age usually means a time of life that is tired but not completely worn out. You could say I'm in the group of those who are worn out and nearing the end.

Still, I'm thankful to myself, and you can be my witness, because I feel like age hasn't hurt my mind, even though it has affected my body. Only my bad habits and the things that go with them have gotten old; my mind is strong and happy that it doesn't have much connection to my body anymore. It has let go of most of its burdens. It's alert and even challenges me about old age, saying that this is its time to flourish. So, I'll trust it and let it make the most of the benefits it has. My mind tells me to think about how much of this peace and balanced character I owe to wisdom and how much to my age. It asks me to carefully consider what I can't do anymore versus what I don't want to do.

Why should anyone complain or see it as a bad thing if abilities that are supposed to fade away have lessened? But you might say it's a big problem to be worn out and fade away, or, if I can be literal, to slowly waste away! We aren't suddenly struck down; we gradually lose our abilities day by day.

But is there a better way to end life than to smoothly glide into rest when nature decides it's time to let go? Not that there's anything painful about a sudden and unexpected departure from life; it's just that this slow withdrawal is easier. For me, it's like the final test is near, and the day has come to see what all my years have amounted to. So, I watch over myself and reflect on this:

All the progress we've made so far, in words or deeds, doesn't really amount to much. It's all just a small and misleading sign of our spirit, wrapped in a lot of pretense. I'll leave it to Death to determine how far I've come. So, with a brave heart, I get ready for the day when I'll put aside all pretenses and judge myself honestly—whether I'm just talking big or if I really believe what I say, whether all the bold things I've said against fate are true or just an act. Forget about public opinion; it always changes and takes both sides. Forget about the studies you've done all your life; Death will deliver the final judgment. Here's what I mean: your debates and deep discussions, your wise sayings, your thoughtful conversations—all of these don't really prove how strong your soul is. Even the most timid person can give a bold speech. What you've done in the past will only be truly revealed when you take your last breath. I accept these terms; I don't shy away from this judgment.

This is what I tell myself, but I hope you understand that I'm also saying it to you. You're younger, but so what? There's no set number of years we're guaranteed to live. You don't know where death is waiting for you, so be ready for it everywhere.

I was about to finish, and my hand was ready to write the closing words, but there's still a bit more to say, and I need to give the letter something to take with it. And just pretend I'm not telling you where I plan to borrow what I need to finish this letter; you already know whose wisdom I rely on. Wait a moment, and I'll give you something from my own thoughts; in the meantime, Epicurus will help out with these words: "Think about death," or, if you prefer, "Think about going to heaven."

The meaning is clear—it's important to thoroughly learn how to die. You might think it's unnecessary to learn something you'll only do once, but that's exactly why we should think about it. When we can never be sure if we've truly learned something, we must always keep learning it. "Think about death." By saying this, he's really telling us to think about freedom. The person who has learned how to die has also learned how to live freely; they are above any external power or at least beyond its reach. What do prisons, chains, and bars matter to them? They know they have a way out. Only one thing keeps us tied to life: our love of life. We may not be able to throw this off, but we can wear it down so that when the time comes, nothing will stop us from doing what we must eventually do anyway. Farewell.

Letter 27 - On the good which abides

You might be thinking, "Why are you giving me advice? Have you already fixed all your own problems? Is that why you have time to help others?" No, I'm not so shameless that I'd try to fix others when I'm still struggling myself. But I'm talking to you about issues we both deal with, and I'm sharing the solution with you, just like we're both sick in the same hospital. So listen to me as if I'm talking to myself. I'm letting you in on my deepest thoughts, and I'm really just working things out for myself, using you as my excuse.

I keep telling myself: "Count your years, and you'll be ashamed to still want and chase the same things you did when you were young. Make sure of this one thing before you die—let your faults die before you do. Get rid of those wild pleasures that come at a high cost; it's not just the ones in the future that hurt me, but also the ones that have already happened. Just like crimes, even if they aren't caught at the time, still cause anxiety later, guilty pleasures leave regret even after they're over. They aren't real, they aren't trustworthy; even if they don't hurt us, they don't last.

Instead, look for something good that will last. But there can't be any lasting good unless the soul finds it within itself. Only virtue brings lasting and peaceful joy. Even if something gets in the way, it's like a cloud passing in front of the sun—it never really blocks it."

When will you finally reach this kind of joy? You haven't been lazy, but you need to speed up. There's still a lot of work to do, and you have to put in all your time and effort if you want to achieve it. This isn't something you can ask someone else to do for you.

Other kinds of work can be done with help from others. For example, there was a rich man named Calvisius Sabinus, who had a lot of money but not much intelligence. I've never seen anyone whose good luck was a bigger insult to common sense. His memory was so bad that he would sometimes forget the names of famous people like Ulysses, Achilles, or Priam—names everyone knows as well as their own servants' names. No elderly butler, who mixes up people's names in his old age, ever messed up his master's guests' names as badly as Sabinus did with the heroes of Troy and Greece. But still, he wanted to seem smart.

So he came up with this shortcut to learning: he bought expensive slaves—one who knew Homer's works by heart, another who knew Hesiod's works, and one for each of the nine lyric poets. You shouldn't be surprised that he paid a lot for these slaves; if he couldn't find them ready-made, he had them specially trained. After gathering this group, he made life miserable for his guests by asking these slaves to recite verses while he tried to repeat them, often messing up halfway through a word.

A man named Satellius Quadratus, who liked to flatter rich fools and mock them at the same time, suggested that Sabinus should hire some scholars to correct his mistakes. Sabinus said that each slave cost him a hundred thousand sesterces, and Satellius replied, "You could have bought as many bookcases for less." But Sabinus believed that whatever his slaves knew, he knew too.

This same Satellius advised Sabinus to start taking wrestling lessons, even though Sabinus was sickly, pale, and weak. Sabinus replied, "How can I? I can barely stay alive now." Satellius responded, "Don't say that! Think about how many healthy slaves you have!" No one can borrow or buy a sound mind; in fact, even if sound minds were for sale, I doubt anyone would buy them. But twisted minds are bought and sold every day.

But let me finish up and say goodbye with this thought: "Real wealth is living in harmony with nature, even if that means living in poverty." Epicurus said this in different ways, but it's worth repeating often because it's something we need to keep learning. For some people, the remedy should just be suggested; for others, it should be forced upon them. Farewell.

Letter 28 - On travel as a cure for discontent

Do you think you're the only one who's felt this way? Are you surprised that after traveling so far and seeing so many new places, you still can't shake off the sadness and heaviness in your mind? What you need is a change in your soul, not just a change of scenery. Even if you cross vast oceans, like our poet Vergil says, "Lands and cities are left behind," your problems will follow you wherever you go.

Socrates said something similar to someone who was complaining:

"Why are you surprised that traveling doesn't help you when you always take yourself with you? The reason you're running away is always right there with you."

What's the point of seeing new places or visiting famous cities? All this rushing around is pointless. Do you wonder why running away doesn't help? It's because you're running away with yourself. You must put aside the burdens in your mind; until you do this, no place will make you feel satisfied. Think about how you are acting now—it's like the prophetess that Vergil describes: she is filled with excitement and driven into a frenzy, carrying within her a lot of inspiration that isn't her own. The priestess raves, hoping she can shake the great god from her heart. You move from place to place, trying to get rid of the burden that weighs on you, but it only gets heavier because of your restlessness. Just like in a ship, when the cargo stays in one place, it doesn't cause any trouble, but when it shifts from side to side, it makes the ship tilt more quickly in the direction where the cargo has settled. Everything you do ends up working against you, and you hurt yourself with your own unrest; it's like you are shaking up a sick person.

Once you remove that trouble, every change of scenery will become enjoyable; even if you are driven to the farthest ends of the earth, wherever you find yourself, no matter how wild or harsh, that place will feel welcoming to you. The person you are matters more than the place you go; for this reason, we should not allow our minds to become slaves to any one place. Live with this belief:

"I am not born for any one corner of the universe; the whole world is my home."

If you saw this clearly, you wouldn't be surprised that you don't feel better when you move to new places just because you're tired of the old ones. The first place would have pleased you if you had truly believed it was yours. But as it is, you're not really traveling; you're just drifting and being driven from one place to another, even though the thing you're looking for—how to live well—can be found anywhere. Can there be any place as full of confusion as the Forum? Yet you can live quietly even there, if you have to. Of course, if I could choose, I would stay far away from even the sight or neighborhood of the Forum. Just like unhealthy places can make even a strong person sick, there are some places that aren't good for a healthy mind that is still recovering from its troubles.

I disagree with those who throw themselves into the middle of life's struggles, welcoming a stormy life, and wrestling every day with life's problems. The wise person can endure all that but wouldn't choose it; they would prefer to be at peace rather than at war. It doesn't help much to get rid of your own faults if you have to constantly fight against the faults of others. Some people say, "There were thirty tyrants surrounding Socrates, and yet they couldn't break his spirit," but what does it matter how many masters a person has? "Slavery" has no plural, and the person who has scorned it is free, no matter how many masters are around them.

It's time to stop, but not before I fulfill my duty to share wisdom. "The knowledge of sin is the beginning of salvation." This saying of Epicurus seems noble to me. For the person who doesn't know they have sinned doesn't want to be corrected; you must realize you are in the wrong before you can fix yourself. Some people even boast about their faults. Do you think a person who counts their vices as virtues is thinking about changing their ways? So, as much as possible, prove yourself guilty, bring charges against yourself; play the roles of accuser, judge, and finally, defender. At times, be strict with yourself. Farewell.

Letter 29 - On the critical condition of Marcellinus

You've been asking about our friend Marcellinus, and you want to know how he's doing. He doesn't visit me often, and that's because he's afraid of hearing the truth. Right now, he's safe from hearing it because you shouldn't talk to someone unless they're willing to listen. That's why people sometimes question whether philosophers like Diogenes and other Cynics, who gave advice to everyone they met, should have done so.

For example, what's the point of scolding someone who's deaf or who can't speak because they were born that way or because of illness? But you might say, "Why should I hold back my words? They don't cost anything. I don't know if I'll help the person I'm advising, but I know that if I advise many people, I'll help someone. I have to spread my advice widely. It's impossible to keep trying without succeeding at least once."

But this, my dear Lucilius, is exactly what a great person shouldn't do. Their influence becomes weaker; it doesn't have as much impact on the people it could have helped if it hadn't been used so carelessly. A skilled archer shouldn't only hit the target sometimes; they should miss only occasionally. If something works by chance, it's not a skill. Wisdom is a skill, and it should have a clear goal, helping only those who will make progress and stepping back from those who seem hopeless—but not giving up too soon. Only when it's clear that someone can't be helped should you try stronger measures.

As for our friend Marcellinus, I haven't given up hope yet. He can still be saved, but we need to help him soon. There's a risk he might drag his helper down with him because he has a strong character that's already leaning toward bad behavior. But I'll take that risk and boldly show him his faults.

He'll do what he usually does—he'll use his wit, which can make people smile even when they're sad. He'll joke, first about himself and then about me. He'll make fun of our philosophical systems, accusing philosophers of taking money, having mistresses, and giving in to their desires. He'll point out one philosopher caught in an affair, another who hangs out in cafes, and another who spends time in court.

He'll even mention Aristo, the philosopher of Marcus Lepidus, who used to hold discussions in his carriage. Aristo would edit his work while riding, so Scaurus joked that Aristo wasn't one of the "Walking Philosophers." Julius Graecinus, a respected man, was asked the same thing and replied, "I can't tell you because I don't know what he does when he's off his horse," as if Aristo were like a chariot-racing gladiator.

These kinds of philosophers, who would have been better off leaving philosophy alone than using it to their advantage, are the ones Marcellinus will throw in my face. But I've decided to endure the teasing. He may make me laugh, but maybe I'll make him cry, or if he keeps joking, I'll find some happiness in his foolishness. But that kind of humor doesn't last long. Watch these people, and you'll see that they laugh too much and get angry too much in a short time.

My plan is to approach him and show him how much more valuable he was when people thought he was less important. Even if I can't completely get rid of his faults, I'll slow them down. They might not stop, but they'll take a break, and maybe they'll stop for good if they get used to taking breaks. This isn't something to ignore because, for people who are seriously struggling, getting some relief is almost like being healed.

So while I get ready to help Marcellinus, you, in the meantime, should work on improving yourself since you know where you've come from and where you're going, and because of that, you understand how far you still have to go. Strengthen your character, build your courage, and stand firm against the things that scare you. Don't worry about how many people threaten you. Wouldn't you think it was silly to be afraid of a crowd in a place where only one person could pass at a time? In the same way, there aren't many who can actually kill you, even if many threaten you with death. Nature has arranged it so that just as only one person gave you life, only one person can take it away.

If you had any shame, you would have let me off the hook for this final piece of advice. But I won't hold back; I'll give you what I still owe: "I've never wanted to please the crowd because they don't appreciate what I know, and I don't know what they like."

You're asking, "Who said this?" as if you don't know whose wisdom I'm using; it's Epicurus. But you can hear this same message from any philosophical school—whether it's Peripatetic, Academic, Stoic, or Cynic. For who that loves virtue can also please the crowd? You need to use tricks to win their approval, and you must make yourself like them. They won't approve of you if they don't see you as one of them. But what you think of yourself is much more important than what others think of you. The favor of unworthy people can only be won by unworthy means.

So, what's the benefit of the philosophy we praise so highly and are told to value above all else? It will make you prefer to please yourself rather than the crowd. It will make you weigh people's opinions instead of just counting them. It will help you live without fear of gods or men, and it will help you either overcome difficulties or put an end to them. Otherwise, if I see you being cheered by the crowd, if your appearance is met with applause and praise—the kind of attention that's fit only for actors—if the whole city, even women and children, sing your praises, how can I not feel sorry for you? Because I know what path leads to such popularity. Farewell.

Letter 30 - On conquering the conqueror

I have seen Aufidius Bassus, a noble man, struggling with his health and getting older. But now, age has weighed him down so much that he can't stand up anymore; old age has come upon him heavily, with its full weight. You know that his body was always weak and lacked energy. For a long time, he managed to hold himself together, or rather, he managed to keep himself going; suddenly, he has collapsed. Just like on a ship that springs a leak, you can always patch the first or second hole, but when many holes appear and let water in, the ship can't be saved. In the same way, in an old person's body, there is a limit to how much you can support its weakness. But when it becomes like an old, worn-out building—where every joint starts to fall apart, and while one part is being fixed, another part breaks down—then it's time for a person to think about how they might peacefully exit life.

But the mind of our friend Bassus is still active. Philosophy gives us this gift: it makes us happy even when facing death, strong and brave no matter how weak our body is, cheerful and steady even when our body fails us. A great captain can still sail a ship even when the sails are torn; if his ship is damaged, he can still fix what's left and keep it on course. This is what our friend Bassus is doing; he looks at his own end with courage and calmness, which you might think is too indifferent if you saw someone looking at another person's death in the same way.

This is a big achievement, Lucilius, and it takes a lot of practice to learn how to leave this world calmly when the time comes. Other kinds of death have a bit of hope in them: a disease might end; a fire might be put out; falling houses might safely let go of those they seemed sure to crush; the sea might push ashore people it pulled under, using the same force that dragged them down; a soldier might pull his sword back from the neck of his enemy at the last moment. But those whom old age is leading toward death have nothing to hope for; old age is the one thing that gives no second chances. No end is more painless, but none takes longer.

Our friend Bassus seemed to me to be attending his own funeral, laying out his own body for burial, and living almost as if he had already survived his own death, bearing with wise acceptance the sorrow of his own passing. For he talks openly about death, trying hard to convince us that if this process has any discomfort or fear, it's the fault of the person dying, not of death itself. He also says that there is no more discomfort at the moment of death than there is after it's over. "And it's just as foolish," he adds, "for a person to fear what won't happen to them, as it is to fear what they won't feel if it does happen." Or does anyone think it's possible that the thing that removes feeling can itself be felt? "Therefore," says Bassus, "death is so far beyond all evil that it's beyond the fear of all evils."

I know that all this has been said many times and should be said many more times, but when I read these ideas, they didn't affect me as much, nor did they when I heard them from people who were far from the fear of the things they said shouldn't be feared. But this old man had a huge impact on me when he talked about death and it was close. For I have to tell you what I think: I believe that a person is braver at the moment of death than when they are approaching death. For death, when it's near, gives even inexperienced people the courage to face what can't be avoided. Just like a gladiator who might have been scared throughout the fight but still offers his throat to his opponent and directs the blade to the right spot. But an end that is near and certain calls for a strong courage of soul; this is a rarer thing, and only the wise can show it.

So, I listened to Bassus with deep pleasure; he was sharing his thoughts on death and showing what it's like when observed up close. I suppose you would trust someone more and believe them if they had come back to life and said from experience that there is no evil in death. And so, when it comes to the approach of death, those who can tell you best about the fears it brings are the ones who have stood close to it, seen it coming, and welcomed it. Bassus is one of these people; he had no wish to deceive us. He says it's as foolish to fear death as it is to fear old age, because death follows old age just like old age follows youth. If someone doesn't want to die, they can't have really wanted to live. Life is given to us with the condition that we will die; this is where our path leads. So, how foolish it is to fear it, since people only wait for what is certain, but fear only what is uncertain! Death has a fixed rule—fair and unavoidable. Who can complain when we are governed by rules that apply to everyone? The main part of fairness, though, is equality.

But it's not necessary to argue in favor of Nature right now, because she wants our laws to match her own. She only breaks down what she has put together and puts back together what she has broken down. Also, if any person is lucky enough to be gently led away by old age—not suddenly taken from life, but slowly removed—they should thank the gods because, after they've had their fill, they are moved to a rest that is meant for everyone, a rest that is welcome to those who are tired. You might see some people who crave death more eagerly than others beg for life. And I'm not sure which people give us more courage—the ones who call for death, or the ones who face it cheerfully and calmly—for the first attitude might be driven by madness or sudden anger, while the second comes from a calm, thoughtful decision. Before now, some people have gone to meet death in a rage; but when death comes to meet them, no one welcomes it cheerfully except the person who has long since prepared themselves for it.

So, I admit that I visited this dear friend of mine more often, using different excuses, but really to see if he was always the same and if his mental strength was perhaps weakening along with his body. But it was actually growing stronger, just like a charioteer's joy becomes clearer when he is on the seventh lap of the race and getting closer to the prize. Indeed, he often said, agreeing with the teachings of Epicurus: "I hope, first of all, that there is no pain at the moment a person takes their last breath; but if there is, one can find comfort in how short it will be. For no great pain lasts long. And at the very least, a person will find relief at the moment when the soul and body are being separated, even if it's very painful, in the thought that once this pain is over, they can't feel any more pain. I'm sure, though, that an old person's soul is right on the edge, and that it only takes a little push to separate it from the body. A fire that has caught hold of something that keeps it burning needs water to put it out, or sometimes the destruction of the building itself; but a fire that has no more fuel to burn dies out on its own."

I'm glad to hear such words, my dear Lucilius—not because they are new to me, but because they bring me face-to-face with reality. And what then? Haven't I seen many people die? I have indeed seen such people; but those who have the most impact on me are the ones who approach death without any hatred for life, letting death in, so to speak, and not rushing toward it. Bassus kept saying: "It's our own fault that we feel this pain, because we only fear dying when we think our end is near." But who isn't near death? It's always ready for us, everywhere and at all times. "Let's think," he continued, "when some form of death seems close, how much closer are other forms of death that we don't fear." A person is threatened with death by an enemy, but this type of death could be preceded by an upset stomach. And if we're willing to look closely at the things we fear, we'll find that some are real, and others just seem to be. We don't fear death; we fear the thought of death. For death itself is always the same distance from us; so, if it's to be feared at all, it should be feared all the time. For what part of our life is free from death?

But what I should really worry about is that you might hate this long letter more than death itself, so I'll stop here. However, you should always think about death so that you'll never fear it. Farewell.

Letter 31 - On siren songs

Now I can see the real you, Lucilius! You're starting to show the character you've always had inside. Keep following the urge that led you to aim for the best things, ignoring what the crowd approves of. I don't want you to become greater or better than you planned because your foundation is already strong and wide. Just finish what you started and work on the plans you have in mind.

In short, you'll become wise if you close your ears to distractions. But it's not enough to block them with wax; you need something thicker than what Ulysses used for his friends. The song he feared was tempting but came from only one direction. The song you must fear comes from all around the world. So, don't just sail past one place you're wary of because of its false pleasures, but past every city. Ignore even those who love you most, because they often wish bad things for you with good intentions. And if you want to be happy, ask the gods that none of their well-meaning wishes for you come true.

What they want for you isn't really good. There's only one true good, the foundation of a happy life: trust in yourself. But you can't have this unless you learn to dismiss hard work and see it as neither good nor bad. Because something can't be bad at one time and good at another, sometimes easy and sometimes something to fear. Work is not a good thing. Then what is good? I say, it's looking down on work. That's why I should criticize people who work for no purpose. But when a person is striving for honorable things, the more they work, and the less they let themselves be beaten or slow down, the more I'll praise them and cheer them on, saying, "You're getting better! Keep going, take a deep breath, and try to climb that hill in one go!"

Work is what feeds noble minds. So, there's no reason for you to pick and choose what kind of luck you want or what you should pray for, just because your parents made an old vow. Besides, it's shameful for a person who's already reached the highest honors to still be begging the gods. Why make vows? Make yourself happy through your own efforts. You can do this if you understand that anything connected with virtue is good and anything connected with vice is bad. Just like nothing shines without light, nothing is black unless it has darkness, and nothing is hot without fire, and nothing is cold without air. In the same way, it's the connection with virtue or vice that makes things honorable or disgraceful.

So, what is good? The knowledge of things. What is evil? The lack of knowledge of things. A wise person, who is also skilled, will choose or reject things based on the situation, but they won't fear what they reject, nor will they admire what they choose, as long as they have a strong and unbreakable spirit. I tell you not to be discouraged or sad. It's not enough to just not avoid work; you should ask for it.

"But," you might say, "isn't pointless work, or work done for the wrong reasons, a bad thing?" No, it's not any worse than work done for noble goals because the very spirit that endures hard work and pushes itself to overcome challenges is the one that says, "Why are you getting lazy? It's not manly to be afraid of sweating."

Besides, for virtue to be complete, there needs to be a balanced and consistent way of life, and this can't happen without knowledge of things and the skill to understand human and divine matters. That's the greatest good. If you grasp this, you begin to be like the gods, not just someone who asks them for help.

"But how," you ask, "does someone reach that goal?" You don't need to cross the Pennine or Graian mountains, or travel through the Candavian wilderness, or face the Syrtes, or Scylla, or Charybdis, even though you've traveled through all these places for a small government job. The journey nature has prepared for you is safe and pleasant. She has given you gifts that, if you don't betray them, will help you rise to the level of God.

But your money won't make you equal to God because God owns nothing. Your fancy clothes won't do it either because God doesn't wear clothes. Neither will your reputation, your public image, or the fact that people all over the world know your name because no one really knows God. Many people even disrespect Him and don't suffer for it. The crowd of slaves carrying your litter through city streets and foreign places won't help you either because this God I'm talking about, who is the highest and most powerful being, carries everything on His own shoulders. Neither beauty nor strength can make you blessed because none of these can resist old age.

So, what should we seek? That which doesn't get more and more controlled by something stronger every day. And what is this? It's the soul—but the soul that is upright, good, and great. What else could you call such a soul but a god living as a guest in a human body? A soul like this can be found in a Roman knight, a freedman's son, or even a slave. Because what is a Roman knight, a freedman's son, or a slave? They are just titles, created by ambition or injustice. You can reach heaven even from the slums. Just rise and shape yourself to be like your God.

This shaping won't be done in gold or silver; an image that's to be like God can't be made of such materials. Remember that when the gods were kind to humans, they were molded out of clay. Farewell.

Letter 32 - On progress

I've been asking about you and talking to everyone who comes from your area, asking what you're doing, where you're spending your time, and who you're with. You can't fool me because I'm with you in spirit. Live as if I'm sure to hear news of your actions, or even as if I'm there to see them. And if you're wondering what news about you makes me happiest, it's that I hear nothing at all, that most of the people I ask don't know what you're up to.

This is a good habit—to stay away from people who have different values and goals than you. I'm sure that you can't be easily influenced, that you'll stick to your path even if the crowd around you tries to distract you. So, what's on my mind? I'm not worried that they'll change you, but I do worry that they might slow down your progress. Even someone who just holds you back can do a lot of harm, especially since life is so short; and we make it even shorter by being inconsistent, by starting our lives over and over again, now

118

doing one thing, and then immediately switching to another. We break life into small pieces and waste it away.

So hurry forward, my dear Lucilius, and think about how much faster you'd move if you knew an enemy was right behind you or if you thought the cavalry was coming up fast, pressing hard as you fled. It's true—the enemy is indeed close behind you. You should, therefore, quicken your pace, escape to a safe place, and keep in mind how noble it is to complete your life's work before death arrives, and then wait in peace for the rest of your time, asking for nothing more, since you already have a happy life. A life like this isn't made any better by being longer.

Oh, when will you see the day when you realize that time doesn't matter to you, when you'll be calm and peaceful, not worried about tomorrow because you're fully enjoying your life today? Do you know what makes people greedy for the future? It's because no one has really found themselves yet. Your parents, of course, wished for other blessings for you, but I pray that you may come to despise all those things that your parents wanted for you in abundance. Their prayers take away from others just to give to you. Whatever they give you has to be taken from someone else.

I pray that you gain such control over yourself that your mind, which is now unsettled by wandering thoughts, may finally find peace and become steady, that it may be content with itself, and, having understood what things are truly good—and they are in our possession as soon as we know this—that it may not need extra years. A person has finally moved beyond all necessities—has earned an honorable discharge and is truly free—when they keep on living even after their life's work is done. Farewell.

Letter 33 - On the futility of learning maxims

You want me to end these letters with some quotes from the leaders of our philosophy, just like I did with my previous letters. But they didn't focus on clever sayings; their whole work is full of strength. You see, it's uneven when some things stand out more than others. A single tree isn't special if the whole forest is the same height. Poetry and history are full of these kinds of sayings. That's why I don't want you to think these sayings belong only to Epicurus: they are common to all of us, and they're especially ours. However, they stand out more in Epicurus's work because they appear rarely and unexpectedly, and because it's surprising to hear brave words from a man who was known for being soft. That's what most people think. But in my opinion, Epicurus was actually a brave man, even though he wore long sleeves. Strength, energy, and readiness for battle can be found among the Persians, just as much as among people who wear their clothes high.

So, you don't need to ask me for quotes and sayings; the thoughts that other philosophers sprinkle here and there throughout their work run all through ours. That's why we don't have any "display goods," and we don't trick people into thinking there's nothing else behind what's in the window. We let customers take samples from anywhere they want.

If we were to pick out each saying from the general stock, who would we credit them to? Zeno, Cleanthes, Chrysippus, Panaetius, or Posidonius? We Stoics aren't ruled by a single leader: each of us claims our own freedom. But in other schools of thought, whatever Hermarchus or Metrodorus says is credited to one source. In that group, everything anyone says is spoken under the leadership and authority of one person. But in our philosophy, no matter how hard we try, we can't pick out anything from such a large collection of equally good ideas.

Only a poor man counts his flock. Wherever you look, you'll find something that might stand out if it weren't surrounded by equally notable context.

So stop thinking that you can understand the wisdom of great people by just skimming through summaries. Look at their wisdom as a whole; study it as a whole. They're working on a plan, weaving together, line by line, a masterpiece, from which nothing can be removed without damaging the whole. You can examine the separate parts if you want, but only as parts of the whole person. A woman isn't considered beautiful because of her ankle or arm, but because her overall appearance makes you forget to admire just one part of her.

However, if you insist, I won't be stingy with you, but generous; there are plenty of these sayings. They're scattered everywhere, not needing to be gathered, just picked up. They don't just drip out occasionally; they flow continuously. They are unbroken and closely connected. They might be helpful to those who are still beginners and learning from the outside because single sayings are easier to understand when they're short and separate, like a line of poetry. That's why we give children proverbs or short sayings, like the Greeks call Chria, to memorize; this type of thing is easier for a young mind to grasp, which can't yet hold onto more. But for someone who has made real progress, to chase after select sayings and rely on well-known and brief quotes to support their weakness and depend on their memory is disgraceful. It's time for that person to rely on themselves. They should create such sayings, not memorize them. It's shameful for an old person, or someone approaching old age, to only have knowledge that comes from a notebook. "This is what Zeno said." But what have you said? "This is Cleanthes' opinion." But what is your own opinion? How long will you march under someone else's orders? Take command, and say something that people will remember in the future. Bring out something from your own store.

That's why I believe there's nothing great in people who never create anything themselves but always stay in the shadow of others, playing the role of interpreters, never daring to put into practice what they've spent so long learning. They've trained their memories on other people's material. But remembering is one thing, knowing is another. Remembering is just holding onto something stored in memory; knowing means making everything your own. It means not depending on the copy and not always looking back at the teacher.

"This is what Zeno said, and this is what Cleanthes said, indeed!" Let there be a difference between you and your book! How long will you be a student? From now on, be a teacher too! "But why," someone might ask, "should I keep listening to lectures on what I can read?" "The spoken word," someone else replies, "is a great help." Maybe, but not a voice that only repeats someone else's words and just serves as a reporter.

Think about this too. Those who have never gained their own mental independence start by following the leader even when everyone else has left him. Then, they follow him even in matters where the truth is still being figured out. But the truth will never be discovered if we're satisfied with what's already been found. Besides, someone who only follows another discovers nothing and isn't even searching.

So what then? Should I not follow in the footsteps of those who came before me? I will indeed use the old road, but if I find a shorter and smoother path, I'll open a new road. The people who made these discoveries before us aren't our masters, but our guides. Truth is open to everyone; it hasn't been completely taken over. And there's plenty left for future generations to discover. Farewell.

Letter 34 - On a promising pupil

I feel my spirit lift, and I am filled with joy, shaking off my years, and my blood feels warm again whenever I see, from your actions and your letters, how much you have surpassed yourself. As for the ordinary man, you left him behind long ago. If a farmer is pleased when his tree grows strong and bears fruit, if a shepherd takes joy in the increase of his flock, if every teacher feels pride when they see their student showing signs of growth—then imagine how those who have shaped a mind and nurtured a young idea must feel when they see it suddenly mature.

I consider you my own; you are my creation. When I saw your potential, I took you under my wing. I encouraged you, pushed you forward, and didn't let you slow down, but kept urging you on. And now, I continue to do the same, but at this point, I'm cheering on someone who is already in the race and, in turn, cheers me on.

"What more do you want from me?" you ask. "I still have the will to continue." Well, in this case, having the will is almost everything, and not just half, as the saying goes, "A task once begun is half done." It's more than half because the matter we're talking about is determined by the soul. That's why the greater part of becoming good is the desire to be good. Do you know what I mean by a good person? It's someone who is complete and fully developed, someone who no pressure or need can make bad.

I see that kind of person in you, as long as you keep moving forward, commit to your task, and make sure that all your actions and words align and match each other, and are shaped by the same principles. If a person's actions don't match, it means their soul is crooked. Farewell.

Letter 35 - On the friendship of kindred minds

When I urge you so strongly to continue your studies, it's actually in my own interest; I want your friendship, and I can't truly have it unless you keep working on improving yourself as you've started. Right now, even though you love me, you're not yet really my friend. "But," you might ask, "aren't love and friendship the same?" No, they are quite different in meaning. A friend does love you, of course; but someone who loves you is not always your friend. Friendship is always beneficial, but love can sometimes even cause harm. So, try to perfect yourself, if for no other reason, to learn how to love properly.

Hurry in your self-improvement so that, while you're perfecting yourself for my benefit, you don't end up doing it for someone else instead. I'm already feeling some benefit by imagining that we will be of one mind and that whatever strength I've lost with age will return to me through your strength, even though there isn't a big difference in our ages. But still, I want to actually see this happen and rejoice in it. We feel joy for those we love, even when we're apart from them, but that kind of joy is light and doesn't last long. Seeing someone, being with them, and interacting with them gives a deeper pleasure. This is especially true if we not only see the person we desire but see them become the person we want them to be. So, give yourself to me as a valuable gift, and to motivate yourself, remember that you are mortal, and I am getting old.

Hurry to find me, but first, hurry to find yourself. Make progress, and above all, try to be consistent with yourself. When you want to know if you've accomplished anything, think about whether you desire the same things today that you desired yesterday. A change in your desires shows that your mind is unsettled, moving in different directions like a ship at sea, swayed by the wind. But what is steady and solid doesn't move from its place. This is the fortunate state of the completely wise person, and also, to some extent, of the person who is progressing and making some headway. Now, what is the difference between these two types of people? The one is in motion, but doesn't change position; they simply move up and down in the same place, while the other doesn't move at all. Farewell.

Letter 36 - On the value of retirement

Encourage your friend to bravely ignore those who criticize him for choosing a quieter life and stepping away from a career of honors. Even though he could have achieved more, he has chosen peace over all of that. Let him show these critics every day how wisely he has taken care of his own well-being. Those who are envied by others will continue to move forward; some will be pushed aside, and others will fall. Success can be a wild and restless thing; it troubles the mind in many ways, pushing people toward different goals—some toward power, others toward a life of luxury. Some people get puffed up by it, while others become lazy and weak.

"But," someone might say, "so-and-so handles his success well." Yes, just like someone who handles their liquor well. So don't let this kind of person convince you that someone surrounded by crowds is happy; people rush to them like crowds rush to a pool of water, making it muddy while they drink from it. But you say, "People call our friend a fool and a lazy person." There are people, you know, who use the wrong words for things. They called him happy; so what? Was he really happy?

Even the fact that some people think he is rough and gloomy doesn't bother me. Aristo used to say that he preferred a young person with a serious nature to one who was just a fun and agreeable person for the crowd. "Because," he said, "wine that tastes harsh and sour when it's new becomes good wine with time, but wine that tastes good right from the start doesn't age well." So let them call him stern and uninterested in his own success. It's this seriousness that will serve him well as he grows older, as long as he keeps valuing virtue and deeply absorbing the studies that lead to true wisdom—not just sprinkling a little knowledge on himself, but soaking his mind in it.

Now is the time to learn. "What? Is there ever a time when a person shouldn't learn?" Of course not; but just as it's good for every age to study, it's not good for every age to be starting from scratch. An old man learning his ABCs is a sad and silly sight; the young man should gather knowledge, and the old man should use it. So, you'll be doing something very helpful for yourself if you make this friend of yours as good a person as possible. They say that the best acts of kindness are the ones that benefit both the giver and the receiver, and this is undoubtedly true.

Finally, he no longer has a choice in the matter; he has given his word. And it's less shameful to settle a debt with a creditor than to settle for less than your potential. To pay off a money debt, a businessperson needs a successful journey, and a farmer needs good crops and favorable weather. But the debt your friend owes can be paid off with nothing more than goodwill. Fortune has no control over a person's character. Let him shape his character so that, in perfect peace, he can fully develop the spirit within him—a spirit that neither loss nor gain can change, but that remains steady no matter what happens. A spirit like this, if it's surrounded by wealth, rises above it; and if, on the other hand, chance takes away part of his wealth, or even all of it, his spirit remains strong.

If your friend had been born in Parthia, he would have started learning to use a bow as a child; if in Germany, he would have been brandishing a slender spear. If he had been born in the days of our ancestors, he would have learned to ride a horse and fight his enemy in hand-to-hand combat. These are the activities that each culture encourages its people to pursue—yes, even demands of them. So what should your friend focus on? I say, let him learn something that's useful against all kinds of weapons and enemies—contempt for death. No one doubts that death has something terrifying in it, something that shocks even our souls, which are naturally inclined to love life. Otherwise, there would be no need to prepare ourselves or to strengthen our courage to face something we should approach willingly, just as all people naturally strive to preserve their lives.

No one learns something just so they can lie down calmly on a bed of roses if the need arises. Instead, they toughen up so they won't betray their commitment, even if they have to endure torture, and so they can hold their ground in the trenches, even if they're wounded, without leaning on their spear. Because leaning on anything might make them fall asleep, which is dangerous in battle.

There is nothing harmful in death because there has to be something for it to harm. Yet, if you have a strong desire for a longer life, remember that nothing truly vanishes when it disappears from our sight. Everything that fades away is absorbed back into the world it came from, only to return again. Death, which we fear and shy away from, merely interrupts life; it doesn't take it away. The time will come when we'll return to the light of day, and many people would object to this if they weren't brought back without memories of the past.

But I'll explain this to you in more detail later, that everything that seems to disappear is only changing form. Since you're destined to return, you should leave with a calm mind. Notice how the universe repeats its cycle; you'll see that no star in the sky is ever truly extinguished. They all set and rise in turn. Summer is gone, but another year will bring it back; winter has laid low, but it will return in its proper months. Night has overtaken the sun, but day will soon push the night away again. The wandering stars retrace their paths; part of the sky is always rising, and part is always sinking.

One last thing, and then I'll stop: infants, young children, and people who have lost their minds have no fear of death, and it's a shame if reason can't give us the peace of mind that their lack of understanding does. Farewell.

Letter 37 - On allegiance to virtue

You have promised to be a good person; you have committed to this under oath, and that is the strongest bond that will keep you on the path to wisdom. Anyone would be wrong to tell you that this is an easy and gentle kind of commitment. I don't want you to be misled. The words of this honorable promise are the same as those in the most difficult promises, which say: "Through fire, imprisonment, or death by the sword."

For those who sell their strength for the arena, who eat and drink at the cost of their blood, there is a guarantee that they will face such trials, even if they do so unwillingly. But for you, the guarantee is that you will face them willingly and eagerly. The gladiator may lower his weapon and try to get mercy from the crowd, but you must not lower your weapon or beg for life. You must face death standing tall and unyielding. Besides, what good is it to gain a few extra days or years? From the moment we are born, there is no way out.

"So how can I free myself?" you ask. You can't escape the necessities of life, but you can overcome them. A way is made by force. And this way will be shown to you by philosophy. Turn to philosophy if you want to be safe, calm, happy, and most importantly, if you want to be truly free. There is no other way to achieve this.

Foolishness is low, miserable, weak, and controlled by many of the most painful emotions. These emotions, which are harsh rulers, sometimes taking turns and sometimes working together, can be driven away by wisdom, which is the only true freedom. There is only one path leading to this freedom, and it is a straight path; you will not get lost. Walk steadily on this path, and if you want to have control over everything, put yourself under the control of reason. If reason becomes your guide, you will become the master of many things. You will learn from reason what you should do and how to do it; you won't stumble into things by accident.

You can't show me anyone who knows how they started wanting the things they want. They didn't get there through careful thought; they were driven there by impulse. Fortune attacks us as often as we try to seize Fortune. It is shameful to be swept along by events instead of moving forward with purpose, and then, in the middle of all the chaos, to suddenly ask in confusion, "How did I end up in this situation?" Farewell.

Letter 38 - On quiet conversation

You are right when you say that we should write to each other more often. But the greatest benefit comes from talking face-to-face, because conversation slowly seeps into the soul. Lectures that are prepared in advance and delivered to a large audience may have more noise, but they lack the personal touch. Philosophy is like giving good advice, and no one can give advice by shouting. Of course, sometimes we need to use speeches like these, if I can call them that, when someone who is uncertain needs a push. But when the goal is to make someone truly learn, not just to make them want to learn, we need to use the quiet, calm words of a conversation. These words enter the mind more easily and stick in the memory; we don't need many words, but rather, effective ones.

Words should be scattered like seeds; no matter how small the seed may be, if it lands on fertile ground, it will grow strong, spreading from something small to something great. Reason works in the same way; it might not look like much at first, but it grows as it is used. Few words are spoken, but if the mind truly grasps them, they will gain strength and take root. Yes, advice and seeds have the same quality; they produce a lot, even though they are small. But as I said, the mind must be ready and willing to take them in and make them its own. Then, the mind itself will produce even more in return, giving back more than it received. Farewell.

Letter 39 - On noble aspirations

I will definitely organize and simplify the notes you asked for. But think about whether you might learn more from the usual method than from what people now call a "breviary," which in the old days when real Latin was spoken, was called a "summary." The usual method is more useful for someone who is still learning a subject, while the summary is better for someone who already knows it and just needs a reminder. But I'll make sure you have plenty of opportunities for both. Someone like you shouldn't need to ask me for proof or references; a person who has to rely on someone else's authority shows that they are not well-known themselves.

So, I will write exactly what you want, but I'll do it in my own way. In the meantime, you have many other authors whose works will help you keep your thoughts organized. Just looking at the list of philosophers will make you want to wake up and get to work when you see how many people have been working to benefit you. You will feel eager to become one of them yourself. This is one of the best qualities of a noble soul—it can be inspired to do great things. No person with high abilities is satisfied with low and trivial things; the vision of great achievements calls to them and lifts them up.

Just as a flame rises straight into the air and cannot be contained or kept down, our soul is always in motion, and the more passionate it is, the greater its energy and activity. But lucky is the person who has given their soul this drive toward better things! They will rise above the control of fate; they will wisely manage success, they will lessen adversity, and they will look down on what others admire.

It is the mark of a great soul to look down on great things and to prefer what is simple rather than what is too grand. The simple things are useful and life-giving, but the grand things can be harmful because they are excessive. In the same way, soil that is too rich makes crops fall over, branches break under too heavy a load, and too much productivity prevents fruit from ripening properly. The same thing happens to the soul; it is ruined by uncontrolled success, which harms not only others but also itself.

What enemy has ever been as insulting to an opponent as pleasures are to certain people? The only excuse we can give for the lack of self-control and wild desires of these people is that they suffer from the same evils they inflict on others. And they are rightly tormented by this madness because desire needs endless room to roam if it goes beyond what is natural. Nature has limits, but reckless actions and the desires that come from willful lust have no boundaries.

Practical needs are measured by what is useful, but how can you measure what is unnecessary? That's why people get lost in pleasures, and once they are used to them, they can't live without them. This is why they are so miserable because they have reached a point where what was once extra has now become essential. So, they become slaves to their pleasures instead of enjoying them; they even love their own problems—and that's the worst problem of all! The height of unhappiness is reached when people are not only drawn to but even find joy in shameful things, and when there is no longer any chance of a cure, because what was once a vice has now become a habit. Farewell.

Letter 40 - On the proper style for a philosopher's discourse

I'm grateful that you write to me so often because it's the only way you can really show me who you are. Whenever I receive a letter from you, it's like you're right here with me. If we find comfort in pictures of our absent friends, even though they only help us remember and ease our longing a little, how much more comforting is a letter, which brings us real traces and real evidence of a friend who is far away! The sweetest part of meeting in person is found in the recognition we feel when we see the familiar handwriting of a friend in a letter.

You wrote to me that you heard a lecture by the philosopher Serapio when he arrived at the place where you're staying. You said, "He tends to speak very quickly, and he doesn't let his words come out one by one, but instead, they rush and collide with each other. The words come out so fast that one voice can hardly keep up." I don't approve of this in a philosopher; his speech, like his life, should be calm and composed, and nothing that rushes and hurries can be well-organized. That's why, in Homer's writings, the fast-paced style, which flows like a heavy snowfall, is given to the younger speaker, while the older man speaks more gently, with words that are sweeter than honey.

So, take note of what I'm saying; that forceful and rapid way of speaking is better suited to a showman than to someone who is discussing and teaching important and serious subjects. But I also don't think it's good for someone to speak too slowly and drag out their words, because that can make the audience lose interest. Even though the word that is waited for longer can stick in the mind better than one that flies past quickly, speech that is too slow can make listeners tired and less attentive. Finally, people talk about "handing down" teachings to their students, but you can't "hand down" something that slips away before it can be grasped.

Besides, speech that deals with the truth should be plain and simple. The flashy style that tries to impress the crowd and captivate unthinking listeners with its speed doesn't belong in philosophy; it doesn't invite discussion but instead tries to avoid it. But how can that kind of speech lead others if it can't even control itself? May I also point out that speech meant to heal our minds should sink in deeply? Just like medicine won't work unless it stays in the body, words won't help us unless they stay with us.

Also, this type of speech is often full of emptiness; it has more noise than substance. My fears should be calmed, my anger soothed, my false beliefs shaken off, my indulgences checked, and my greed corrected. And which of these things can be done in a hurry? What doctor can heal a patient with a quick visit? Let me add that this kind of confusing and poorly chosen speech doesn't even bring pleasure. No; just like you might be satisfied to see through a magic trick you thought was impossible, hearing these fast-talking performers once is more than enough. What could anyone want to learn or imitate from them? What can you think of their minds when their speech is so chaotic and out of control?

Just like when you run downhill and can't stop at the place you planned because your momentum carries you further, this kind of fast speech has no control over itself, and it's not suitable for philosophy. Philosophy should carefully place its words, not throw them out recklessly, and should proceed step by step.

"What then?" you might ask. "Shouldn't philosophy sometimes speak with more passion?" Of course, but it should still maintain dignity, which is lost when speech becomes too violent and forceful. Philosophy should have great power but keep it under control; let its ideas flow steadily, but not like a rushing torrent. I wouldn't even recommend this rapid style to an orator, who needs to be understood by judges who might be inexperienced and untrained. Even when an orator is carried away by emotion or the desire to show off, they still shouldn't speak faster than their audience can follow.

So, you'll be doing the right thing if you don't admire those who focus more on how much they say rather than how they say it. And if you had to choose, it would be better to speak slowly like Publius Vinicius, who was known for his slow speech. When someone asked Asellius how Vinicius spoke, he replied, "Gradually!" (By the way, it was Geminus Varius who said, "I don't see how you can call that man 'eloquent'; he can't even get out three words together.") So why not choose to speak as Vinicius did?

Though, of course, you might encounter someone like the person who jokingly asked Vinicius, as he dragged out his words as if he were dictating, "Say, don't you have anything to say?" Yet that would still be a better choice because the rapid speech of Quintus Haterius, the most famous orator of his time, is something I think a sensible person should avoid. Haterius never hesitated, never paused; he started speaking once and didn't stop until he was finished.

However, I suppose that certain styles of speech suit different cultures. With a Greek, you can tolerate a more unrestrained style, but we Romans, even when writing, have learned to separate our words carefully. And our fellow Roman, Cicero, who brought Roman oratory to prominence, was also known for his measured pace. The Roman language is more inclined to be thoughtful, to weigh its words, and to offer something worth considering.

Fabianus, a man known for his virtuous life, his knowledge, and, less importantly, his eloquence, used to discuss topics with quickness but not haste; you might call it ease rather than speed. I approve of this quality in a wise person, but I don't demand it; I only ask that their speech flows freely, though I prefer that it be delivered thoughtfully rather than hastily.

However, I have one more reason to warn you against this fast-paced style of speech: you can only succeed in it by losing your sense of modesty. You would have to get rid of all shame and refuse to hear yourself speak. That reckless flow of words will carry with it many things you might later wish to criticize. And, as I said, you can't master this style without losing your sense of shame. Moreover, you would need to practice it every day, shifting your focus from the content of your speech to the words themselves. But even if the words come to you easily and flow without effort, they would still need to be controlled. Just as a philosopher should have a modest way of walking, so should their speech be restrained and far from boldness. So, the main point of my advice is this: I urge you to speak slowly. Farewell.

Letter 41 - On the god within us

You are doing something excellent, something that will be very good for you, if, as you say in your letter, you are continuing your efforts to gain a sound understanding. It is foolish to pray for this when you can achieve it yourself. We don't need to raise our hands toward heaven or beg the keeper of a temple to let us get close to an idol's ear, as if our prayers would be more likely to be heard that way. God is near you, He is with you, He is within you.

This is what I mean, Lucilius: there is a holy spirit within us, one that observes our good and bad deeds and acts as our guardian. As we treat this spirit, so are we treated by it. Indeed, no one can be truly good without the help of God. Can anyone rise above the challenges of life unless God helps him? It is He who gives noble and upright counsel. In every good person, a god dwells, but we do not know which god.

If you have ever come across a grove filled with ancient trees that have grown to an unusual height, blocking out the sky with a thick canopy of intertwined branches, then the majesty of the forest, the seclusion of the spot, and your amazement at the deep, unbroken shade in the midst of open spaces will make you feel the presence of a divine power. Or if you find a cave, created by the deep crumbling of rocks, holding up a mountain on its arch—a place not built by human hands but formed into a spacious cavern by natural forces—your soul will be deeply moved by a certain sense of the existence of God. We worship the sources of mighty rivers, we build altars at places where great streams suddenly burst from hidden springs, we revere hot springs as divine, and we consecrate certain pools because of their dark waters or their immeasurable depth.

If you see a person who is unafraid in the face of danger, untouched by desires, happy even in adversity, calm amid the storm, who looks down on others from a higher plane and views the gods as equals, won't you feel a sense of reverence for him? Won't you say, "This quality is too great and too lofty to be just a part of this small human body where it lives? A divine power has entered that person."

When a soul rises above other souls, when it is controlled and calm, when it passes through every experience as if it were of little importance, when it smiles at our fears and our prayers, it is driven by a force from heaven. Something like this cannot stand tall unless it is supported by the divine. Therefore, a greater part of it stays in the place from where it came down to earth. Just as the rays of the sun touch the earth but still remain at their source, so too does the great and hallowed soul, which has come down to earth so that we may have a closer knowledge of divinity, associate with us but still stay connected to its origin. It depends on that source, turns its gaze toward it, strives to return to it, and only concerns itself with our doings as something higher than ourselves.

So, what is such a soul? It is one that shines with its own inner goodness, not with anything external. For what could be more foolish than to praise a person for qualities that come from outside? And what could be more ridiculous than to admire things that could, at any moment, belong to someone else? A golden bit doesn't make a better horse. The lion with a gilded mane, trained and worn out to endure the decoration, is sent into the arena very differently from the wild lion whose spirit remains untamed. The wild lion, bold in its attack as nature intended, impressive because of its wild appearance—and it is his glory that no one can look upon him without fear—is preferred over the other lion, who is merely a tired, gilded creature.

No one should take pride in anything except what truly belongs to them. We praise a vine if it produces many shoots and bends the poles with its heavy fruit. Would anyone prefer a vine with golden grapes and leaves hanging down? The virtue of a vine is its fertility; in a person, we should praise what is truly theirs. Suppose someone has a retinue of handsome slaves, a beautiful house, a large farm, and a big income—none of these things are truly part of the person; they are all external.

Praise the quality in them that cannot be given or taken away, the quality that is uniquely theirs. Do you want to know what this is? It is the soul and reason perfected in the soul. For a person is a reasoning creature. Therefore, a person's highest good is achieved when they fulfill the purpose for which nature designed them at birth. And what does this reason demand of them? The easiest thing in the world— to live in accordance with their own nature. But this has become a hard task because of the general madness of humanity; we push each other into vice. And how can a person be saved when no one is holding them back, and everyone is urging them on? Farewell.

Letter 42 - On values

Has that friend of yours already convinced you that he is a good person? Yet, it's impossible for someone to become truly good or be recognized as good in such a short time. Do you know what kind of person I mean when I talk about "a good person"? I'm talking about someone of the second rank, like your friend. Someone of the highest rank, like a true sage, perhaps only comes into existence once in five hundred years, like the mythical phoenix. It's not surprising that true greatness only develops at long intervals; Fortune often creates average people who are meant to please the crowd, but she makes extraordinary people rare, so they stand out even more.

However, the person you spoke of is still far from the level he claims to have reached. And if he really knew what it meant to be "a good person," he wouldn't believe he was one yet; he might even doubt whether he could ever become truly good. "But," you say, "he thinks poorly of bad people." Well, so do bad people themselves, and there is no worse punishment for vice than being unhappy with yourself and with others who share your faults.

"But he hates those who misuse great power when they suddenly acquire it." I would argue that he will do the same thing as soon as he gains that kind of power. For many people, their vices go unnoticed because they don't have the opportunity to show them. But as soon as these people feel confident in their own strength, their vices will be just as bold as those that prosperity has already revealed in others. These people simply lack the means to fully express their wickedness. It's like handling a poisonous snake that's stiff with cold; the poison is still there, but it's temporarily inactive. In many people, their cruelty, ambition, and indulgence are just waiting for the right circumstances to make them dare to commit the worst crimes. You'll quickly see that their desires are the same as those who have already shown their vices, just give them the power to act on their wishes.

Do you remember how, when you told me that a certain person was under your influence, I said that he was fickle and unreliable, and that you held him not by the foot but only by a wing? Was I wrong? You only held onto a feather; he left it in your hand and escaped. You know how he behaved afterward, how many of the things he tried ended up backfiring on him. He didn't realize that in trying to harm others, he was setting himself up for a fall. He didn't consider how burdensome the things he was chasing after would be, even if they weren't unnecessary.

So, when it comes to the things we pursue and strive for with great effort, we should recognize this truth: either they aren't truly desirable, or the undesirable aspects outweigh the benefits. Some things are unnecessary; others aren't worth the price we pay for them. But we don't see this clearly, and we think of things as free gifts when they actually cost us a great deal.

Our foolishness is obvious in the fact that we think "buying" only refers to things we pay money for, and we consider things we spend our time and energy on as free. We would refuse to buy these things if we had to pay for them with our houses or valuable property, but we eagerly go after them at the cost of our peace of mind, safety, honor, freedom, and time. It's true that each person values themselves less than anything else.

So, in all our plans and actions, let's act like we do when we approach a vendor selling goods; let's see how much we have to pay for what we desire. Often, the things that seem free end up costing us the most. I can show you many things that, in the quest to acquire them, have taken away our freedom. We would truly belong to ourselves if only these things didn't belong to us.

I would also like you to think this way not only when it comes to gaining things but also when it comes to losing them. "This item is bound to be lost." Yes, it was just an extra; you'll live without it just as easily as you did before. If you've had it for a long time, you lose it after you've had your fill of it; if you haven't had it long, then you lose it before you've become too attached to it. "You'll have less money." Yes, and less trouble. "Less influence." Yes, and less envy. Look around and notice the things that drive us crazy and make us cry when we lose them; you'll see that it's not the actual loss that bothers us, but the idea of losing them. No one truly feels that they've lost something, but their mind tells them they have. A person who owns themselves has lost nothing. But how few people are truly in control of themselves! Farewell.

Letter 43 - On the relativity of fame

You ask how I found out, and who told me, that you were considering this idea, even though you hadn't mentioned it to anyone? It was that most well-informed person—gossip. "What," you say, "am I so important that I can stir up gossip?" Now, there's no need for you to measure yourself based on the world at large; instead, think about the place where you live.

Any point that rises above those around it seems large at that spot. Greatness isn't absolute; it grows or shrinks in comparison to what's nearby. A ship that looks big on a river seems small on the ocean. A rudder that's big for one ship is small for another.

So in your region, you're actually quite important, even if you don't think so. People are asking what you do, how you eat, and how you sleep, and they're finding out, too; so you have all the more reason to live carefully. But don't consider yourself truly happy until you can live openly, until your walls protect you but don't hide you. We tend to think that walls are there not just to keep us safe but to let us sin in secret.

Let me share something that will help you understand a person's character: you'll hardly find anyone who can live with their door wide open. It's our conscience, not our pride, that has put doorkeepers at our doors; we live in such a way that being suddenly exposed feels like being caught in the act. But what good is it to hide away and avoid the eyes and ears of others?

A good conscience welcomes the crowd, but a bad conscience is disturbed and troubled even when alone. If your actions are honorable, let everyone know about them; if they're shameful, what does it matter if no one else knows, as long as you know yourself? How miserable you must be if you despise such an important witness! Farewell.

Letter 44 - On philosophy and pedigrees

You keep telling me that you feel like a nobody and that both nature and fortune have treated you unfairly. But remember, you have the power to set yourself apart from the crowd and reach the highest level of happiness! If there is any good in philosophy, it's this: it doesn't care about your family background. All people, if you trace them back far enough, come from the gods.

You are a Roman knight, and your hard work got you to this level; but there are many who can't even reach the fourteen rows reserved for knights in the theater. Not everyone can enter the Senate, and the army is very selective about who it allows to face toil and danger. But a noble mind is available to everyone; by this measure, we can all stand out. Philosophy neither rejects nor favors anyone; its light shines for all.

Socrates wasn't born into a noble family. Cleanthes worked at a well and served as a hired hand watering a garden. Philosophy didn't find Plato as a nobleman; it made him one. So why should you doubt that you can rank with men like these? They are all your ancestors if you live in a way that honors them. And you will do so if you convince yourself from the start that no one surpasses you in true nobility.

We all have the same number of ancestors; there is no one whose origins don't go beyond memory. Plato says, "Every king has slaves among his ancestors, and every slave has kings among his ancestors." The passage of time, with its ups and downs, has mixed everything together, and Fortune has turned things upside down.

So, who is truly well-born? The one who is naturally suited for virtue. That is the only thing that matters; otherwise, if you look back far enough, everyone's ancestry goes back to a time when there was nothing. From the very beginning of the universe to now, we have all come from origins that have alternated between being noble and common. A hall full of smoke-stained busts doesn't make someone noble. No life lived in the past can give us glory, and what happened before us is not ours; only the soul makes us noble, and it can rise above Fortune from any previous condition, no matter what that condition was.

Suppose, then, that you weren't a Roman knight but a freed slave. You could still, through your own efforts, become the only truly free person among a crowd of gentlemen. "How?" you ask. By simply learning to tell the difference between good and bad things without copying the opinions of the crowd. You should focus not on where these things come from, but on where they lead.

If there is anything that can make life happy, it is good on its own merits because it can't turn into something bad. So where do people go wrong, since everyone wants a happy life? The mistake is that they think the things that lead to happiness are the same as happiness itself. While they seek happiness, they are actually running away from it. The essence of a happy life is freedom from worry, and the key to that freedom is unshakable confidence. Yet people gather the very things that cause worry, and while traveling life's uncertain road, they not only carry burdens but even add more burdens to themselves. As a result, they move farther and farther away from what they seek. The more effort they put in, the more they get in their own way and fall behind. This is what happens when you rush through a maze; the faster you go, the more tangled up you get. Farewell.

Letter 45 - On sophistical argumentation

You're complaining that there aren't many books available where you live. But it's not the quantity of books that matters; it's the quality. A short list of good books is beneficial, while a large variety of them just brings pleasure. If you want to reach your goal, you need to follow one path and not wander down many. What you're suggesting isn't really traveling; it's just wandering around aimlessly.

"But," you say, "I would rather have your advice than books." I'm still willing to send you all the books I have, to search through my entire collection. If it were possible, I would come to you myself. If I didn't believe you would finish your term of office soon, I would have made this journey, even though I'm an old man. No Scylla or Charybdis, or any of those dangerous straits from the myths, could have scared me away. I would not only have crossed over, but I would have been willing to swim across those waters, just to greet you and see in person how much you've grown in spirit.

Your request for me to send you my own writings doesn't make me think of myself as learned, any more than someone asking for my picture would make me think of myself as handsome. I know it's because of your kindness rather than your judgment. And even if it's because of your judgment, it's your kindness that influenced your judgment.

But whatever the quality of my work may be, read it as if I were still searching for the truth and hadn't found it yet, but was stubbornly seeking it. I haven't sold myself to anyone; I don't follow any one master. I respect the opinions of great thinkers, but I also have my own thoughts. These thinkers didn't leave us absolute truths but problems that still need solutions. Maybe they would have discovered the essentials if they hadn't also sought out the unnecessary.

They wasted a lot of time arguing about words and engaging in tricky debates that don't really accomplish anything. We tie words into knots and give them double meanings, only to try to untie them again. Do we really have time for this? Do we already know how to live or die? We should be focusing our whole efforts on making sure that things, as well as words, don't deceive us.

Why, I ask, do you argue about similar words when no one is ever misled by them, except during the discussion itself? It's things, not words, that lead us astray. We must distinguish between things, not just words. We embrace evil instead of good; we pray for something that's the opposite of what we've prayed for in the past. Our prayers contradict each other, and our plans conflict with our other plans.

How closely flattery resembles friendship! It doesn't just mimic friendship; it often outdoes it. Flattery is welcomed with open ears and sinks deep into the heart, pleasing us even as it does harm. Show me how I can see through this deception! An enemy might approach me full of compliments, pretending to be a friend. Vices creep into our hearts disguised as virtues: recklessness is called bravery, laziness is called moderation, and cowardice is seen as prudence. There's great danger if we go astray in these matters, so we must label them clearly.

Then, consider this: the person who is asked if he has horns on his head isn't such a fool that he'll reach up to feel for them, nor is he so silly that you can convince him through subtle arguments that he doesn't know the facts. These tricky debates are as harmlessly deceptive as a magician's tricks with cups and dice, where it's the very trickery that amuses us. But if you show me how the trick is done, I lose interest. I feel the same way about these tricky word games; what else can we call them but sophistries? Not knowing them doesn't hurt us, and mastering them doesn't help us.

If you want to analyze the meanings of words, teach us instead that the happy person isn't the one the crowd thinks is happy— someone whose coffers are full of money—but rather the one whose true wealth is in his soul. He is upright, confident, and rejects inconsistency. He doesn't wish to trade places with anyone, values people for who they are, learns from Nature, follows her laws, and lives as she commands. No force can take away his true possessions, and he turns evil into good. He is firm in his judgment, unshaken, unafraid, and while he may be affected by force, he's never thrown into confusion. When Fortune throws her deadliest weapons at him, they might graze him but never wound him. Fortune's other weapons, which defeat most people, simply bounce off him, like hail on a roof that does no harm to those inside and then melts away.

Why do you bother me with what you yourself call the "liar" fallacy, about which so many books have been written? Come now, let's suppose my whole life is a lie. Prove that to be wrong, and if you're clever enough, bring me back to the truth. Right now, life holds as essential many things that are actually unnecessary. And even those things that aren't unnecessary don't necessarily make one fortunate or blessed. Just because something is necessary doesn't mean it's good. Otherwise, we'd be lowering the meaning of "good" if we applied it to basic things like bread or porridge, or other essentials without which we can't live.

Goodness must always be necessary, but what's necessary isn't always good, since even the most trivial things can be necessary. No one is so ignorant of the noble meaning of the word "good" as to bring it down to the level of these everyday necessities.

So, shouldn't you focus instead on making it clear to everyone that searching for unnecessary things wastes a lot of time, and that many people go through life just accumulating tools for living? Look at individuals, observe people in general; there isn't a single person whose life isn't focused on the future.

"What's wrong with that?" you ask. There's a lot wrong with it. Such people aren't living; they're just preparing to live. They put everything off. Even if we were paying close attention, life would still pass us by quickly. But as we are now, life finds us lingering and leaves us behind, as if it belonged to someone else. And even though life officially ends on the final day, we lose a bit of it every day.

But I shouldn't go beyond the limits of a letter, which shouldn't be so long that it fills the reader's left hand. So I'll save our discussion about these overly clever thinkers who make arguments more important than anything else for another day. Farewell.

Letter 46 - On a new book by Lucilius

I received the book you promised me. I opened it quickly, thinking I would just skim through it later, as I planned only to take a quick look at it. But the book itself was so engaging that it made me read more than I intended. You can tell from this how well-written it was; it had a smooth style and didn't seem like something either you or I would write. At first glance, it could have been written by someone like Titus Livius or Epicurus. I was so impressed and captivated by its charm that I finished it without taking a break. Even though the sunlight was fading, I was getting hungry, and the clouds were gathering, I read the book from beginning to end.

I wasn't just pleased—I was thrilled. It was full of wit and spirit! I would have said it had "force," but that would imply there were moments of calm or that it only had energy in parts. But what I found was a steady flow—a style that was strong and pure. Still, I noticed your sweetness from time to time and your gentle touch here and there. Your style is high and noble, and I want you to stick with this approach. Your choice of topic also helped; that's why you should pick subjects that grab the mind and stir it.

I'll give you a more detailed review after I read the book a second time; for now, my thoughts are still a bit uncertain, as if I had heard it read aloud rather than read it myself. You'll have to let me go through it again. Don't worry; I'll tell you the truth. You're lucky that being so far away keeps people from lying to you! Unless, of course, we've gotten so used to lying that we do it even when there's no reason to! Farewell.

Letter 47 - On master and slave

I'm happy to hear from those who visit you that you treat your slaves like friends. This is exactly how a sensible and well-educated person like you should act. People might say, "But they're just slaves." No, they're humans. "Slaves!" No, they're companions. "Slaves!" No, they're humble friends. "Slaves!" No, they're fellow servants, because Fortune has the same control over both slaves and free people.

That's why I find it funny when people think it's beneath them to eat with their slaves. But why do they think that? It's only because the rich and powerful surround themselves with a crowd of standing slaves at dinner. The master eats more than he can handle, stuffing himself until his belly is stretched to the limit and can't function properly, so that he struggles more to get rid of all the food than he did to eat it.

Meanwhile, the poor slaves aren't even allowed to move their lips to speak. Even the slightest sound—like a cough, a sneeze, or a hiccup—is punished with a beating. There's a severe penalty for breaking the silence. All night long, they have to stand around, hungry and silent.

The result is that these slaves, who can't talk in their master's presence, end up talking about him behind his back. But in the old days, slaves were allowed to speak not only in front of their master but even with him. Their mouths weren't sewn shut, and they were ready to risk their lives to protect their master. They would talk at the feast but stay silent under torture.

Finally, the saying became popular: "As many enemies as you have slaves." They weren't enemies when we first acquired them; we made them into enemies. I won't go into other cruel and inhumane ways we treat them, but we often treat them not as humans but as beasts of burden. When we recline at a banquet, one slave cleans up the vomited food, another crouches under the table to gather the leftovers from the drunken guests.

Another slave carves the expensive game birds, cutting precise pieces from the breast or rump with skilled hands. Poor guy, his whole purpose in life is to carve fat capons correctly—unless, of course, the person who teaches this skill for fun is even more pitiful than the one who has to learn it because he must.

Another slave, who serves the wine, has to dress like a woman and fight against aging. He can't escape his boyhood; he's forced to stay young. Even though his body is already like a soldier's, he's kept beardless by having his hair smoothed or plucked out, and he has to stay awake all night, splitting his time between his master's drunkenness and his lust; he has to be a man in the bedroom but a boy at the feast.

Another slave's job is to judge the guests and watch who flatters or acts shamefully, either by overeating or by talking too much, so they know who will be invited back tomorrow. Think also of the poor slaves who prepare the food, who know their master's tastes so well, who understand what flavors will excite their appetite, what will please their eyes, what new dishes will revive their tired stomachs, what food will disgust them because they're sick of it, and what will make them hungry again that day. Yet, with all these slaves, the master won't dine with them; he thinks it's beneath him to eat at the same table with a slave! Heaven forbid!

But how many masters is he creating in these very slaves! I've seen the former master of Callistus waiting in line outside Callistus's door. I've seen that same master shut out while others were welcomed— the master who once put a "For Sale" sign on Callistus and sold him with the other worthless slaves. But now that slave has paid back his master, who once put him in the first group of slaves to be auctioned off. The slave has now removed his former master's name from the guest list and judged him unworthy to enter his house. The master sold Callistus, but how much has Callistus made his master pay!

Remember that the person you call your slave comes from the same human stock as you, is under the same sky, and breathes, lives, and dies just like you. It's just as possible for you to see a free man in him as for him to see a slave in you. After the massacres during the time of Marius, many men of noble birth, who were just starting their path to senatorial rank through military service, were brought low by fortune, becoming shepherds or caretakers of a country house. So, despise them if you dare, even though you might one day find yourself in their position, even as you look down on them.

I don't want to get into too big of a topic and discuss how we Romans are often too proud, cruel, and insulting to our slaves. But here's my main advice: Treat those below you the way you would want to be treated by those above you. And whenever you think about how much power you have over a slave, remember that your master has just as much power over you.

"But I have no master," you say. You're still young; maybe one day you will. Do you know how old Hecuba was when she became a captive? Or Croesus? Or the mother of Darius? Or Plato? Or Diogenes?

Be kind and even friendly with your slaves; let them talk with you, plan with you, live with you. I know some people will be shocked by this and say, "There's nothing more degrading or shameful than this." But these are the same people I sometimes catch kissing the hands of other men's slaves.

Don't you see how our ancestors removed everything hateful from being a master and everything insulting from being a slave? They called the master "father of the household" and the slaves "members of the household," a custom still kept alive in plays. They even created a holiday when masters and slaves would eat together— not just as a special day, but because it was required on that day. They allowed slaves to hold honors in the household and make judgments; they saw the household as a small community.

"Are you saying," someone might ask, "that I should invite all my slaves to my table?" No, not any more than you should invite all free men to it. You're mistaken if you think I would exclude certain slaves whose jobs are more humble, like a mule driver or a herdsman; I suggest valuing them for their character, not their duties. Each person builds their character, but chance decides their job. Invite some to your table because they deserve it, and others so they can learn to deserve it. If any of their lower behavior comes from their low position, it will fade away by spending time with more refined people.

You don't need to search for friends only in the forum or the Senate; if you're careful and observant, you'll find them at home too. Good potential often goes to waste without someone to bring it out; try it, and you'll see. It's foolish to judge a horse by its saddle and bridle rather than its qualities, and it's doubly foolish to judge a person by their clothes or rank, which are just like a robe we wear.

"He's a slave." But his soul might be that of a free man. "He's a slave." But should that hold him back? Show me a person who isn't a slave; one is a slave to lust, another to greed, another to ambition, and everyone is a slave to fear. I could name an ex-consul who's a slave to an old woman, a millionaire who's a slave to a maidservant; I could show you young nobles enslaved to actors! No servitude is more disgraceful than the kind we bring upon ourselves.

So don't let these snobbish people stop you from being friendly and approachable with your slaves; they should respect you, not fear you. Some may argue that I'm giving slaves too much freedom and lowering masters from their high position because I tell slaves to respect their masters instead of fearing them. They say, "He clearly means that slaves should act like clients or morning callers!" But anyone who thinks this way forgets that if respect is enough for a god, it's certainly enough for a master. Respect means love, and love and fear don't go together.

So I believe you're absolutely right not to want your slaves to fear you and to discipline them only with words. Only dumb animals need to be whipped.

What annoys us doesn't necessarily hurt us; but our luxurious lives make us so quick to anger that anything that doesn't go our way makes us furious. We take on the temper of kings. They, too, forget their own strength and the weakness of others and become furious as if they've been wronged, even though their high position protects them from such harm. They know this is true, but by finding fault, they create opportunities to do harm; they claim they've been wronged just so they can inflict injuries.

I don't want to keep you any longer because you don't need more advice. One sign of good character is that it forms its own judgments and sticks to them, while bad character is fickle and constantly changing—not for the better, but just for something different. Farewell.

Letter 48 - On quibbling as unworthy of the philosopher

I received the letter you wrote while you were traveling, – a letter as long as the journey itself, and I'll reply to it later. I need to take some time alone to think carefully about the advice I should give you. You took a long time to decide whether to ask me for advice, so I should take even more time to think about what to say, especially because giving good advice requires more thought than asking for it. This is even more important when what is good for you might be different from what is good for me. Am I starting to sound like an Epicurean again? But the truth is, what's good for you is also good for me. I'm not truly your friend unless I care about what happens to you as much as I care about what happens to me. Friendship means sharing everything that matters to us. There's no such thing as good or bad fortune for just one person; we share it all. No one can be happy if they only think about themselves and turn everything into a question of their own benefit. You have to live for others if you want to truly live for yourself.

This shared life, carefully maintained, which makes us connect with other people and reminds us that all humans have certain rights in common, also helps us to value close friendships, which I started talking about earlier. For when you share a lot with another person, you will share everything with a friend.

Now, my dear Lucilius, I wish those clever philosophers of yours would advise me on how to help a friend or a fellow human being, instead of just telling me how many different ways the word "friend" can be used or how many meanings the word "man" has. Wisdom and foolishness are taking opposite sides—who should I join? Which side do you want me to follow? On one side, a "man" is the same as a "friend," while on the other side, a "friend" is not the same as a "man." One side wants a friend for their own benefit, while the other side wants to be a benefit to their friend. What you're offering me is just playing with words and splitting hairs.

It's clear that unless I come up with some tricky arguments and use false logic, I won't be able to tell the difference between what's good and what's bad. I'm embarrassed! We are old men dealing with serious problems, and yet we're turning it into a game!

"'Mouse' is a syllable. A mouse eats cheese; therefore, a syllable eats cheese." If I can't solve this problem, see what danger I'm in because of such ignorance! What a mess I'll be in! Obviously, I need to be careful, or one day I'll be catching syllables in a mousetrap, or if I'm not careful, a book might eat my cheese! Unless, of course, the following argument is even smarter: "'Mouse' is a syllable. A syllable does not eat cheese. Therefore, a mouse does not eat cheese."

What childish nonsense! Are we really wasting our time on these kind of problems? Do we grow our beards long for this? Is this what we teach with serious faces?

If you really want to know what philosophy offers to humanity, it offers advice. Death takes one person away, and poverty troubles another; someone else is worried about their neighbor's wealth or even their own. Some people fear bad luck, while others want to escape their own good fortune. Some are mistreated by other people, while others feel wronged by the gods.

So why are you making these silly games for me? This is not the time for jokes; you are supposed to be helping unhappy people. You promised to help those in danger at sea, those in captivity, the sick and needy, and those whose lives are at risk. Where are you going? What are you doing?

Your friend, who you're joking with, is actually afraid. Help him, and take away the thing that's making him feel so scared, like taking a noose from around his neck. People all around you are reaching out, asking for your help. Their lifes are either ruined or in danger of being ruined, and they're begging for some kind of support. They're hoping that you can save them from their worries and show them the clear truth, especially since they feel lost and confused.

Tell them what nature says is truly necessary and what is just extra. Show them how simple the rules that nature has given us really are. Life can be enjoyable and easy if we follow these natural rules. But if people trust opinions instead of following what nature tells us, life becomes bitter and confusing.

I would think your logic games were helpful if you could first show me how they help people with their real problems. What part of these games will help someone overcome their desires? Or control them? I wish I could say that they were just useless, but they're actually harmful. I can show you clearly, whenever you want, that a noble spirit gets weaker when it gets involved in such trivialities. I'm ashamed to say what weak weapons they give to people who are supposed to fight against life's challenges, and how poorly they prepare them!

Is this the path to the greatest good? Is philosophy supposed to work through tricks and arguments that would even be embarrassing for lawyers? What else are you doing when you trap the person you're questioning with tricky words, making it look like they've lost their case on a technicality? But just as a judge can reinstate someone who has lost a case this way, philosophy has restored these victims of trickery to their original state.

Why do you abandon your grand promises, and after telling me in fancy words that you will make me strong enough to not be dazzled by gold or afraid of a sword, you go back to the basics of schoolroom debates? What is your answer? Is this the path to heaven?

Because that's exactly what philosophy promises me, that I will be made equal to God. For this, I have been called; for this purpose, I have come. Philosophy, keep your promise!

So, my dear Lucilius, stay away from these tricks and arguments of so-called philosophers. Honesty and simplicity are the true marks of goodness. Even if you had many years left, you would need to use them wisely to have enough time for the important things. But as it is, when your time is so short, it's foolish to waste it on unnecessary things. Farewell.

Letter 49 - On the shortness of life

A person is indeed truly lazy and careless, my dear Lucilius, if he only remembers a friend when he sees a place that reminds him of that friend. But sometimes, familiar places bring back a feeling of loss that we've kept hidden inside. They don't just bring back dead memories but wake them up from where they've been sleeping, like how seeing a lost friend's favorite slave, cloak, or house can renew the sadness, even if time has made it softer.

Now, look at Campania, especially Naples and your beloved Pompeii. When I saw them, they made me miss you a lot. I can picture you clearly in my mind, like I'm about to say goodbye to you. I see you trying hard to hold back your tears but not being able to stop the emotions that rise up just when you try to control them. It feels like I lost you just a moment ago because, when we use our memory, everything feels like it happened just a short while ago.

It seems like just a moment ago that I was a young boy sitting in the philosopher Sotion's school, just a moment ago that I started working as a lawyer, just a moment ago that I lost the desire to practice law, and just a moment ago that I lost the ability to do it. Time flies incredibly fast, especially when we look back at it. When we're focused on what's happening now, we don't notice how fast time is passing because it moves so gently and quickly.

Do you wonder why? All the time that has passed is in the same place; it all looks the same to us, like it's all mixed together. Everything slips into the same emptiness. Also, something that is so short can't have long periods within it. The time we spend living is just a tiny point, or even smaller than a point. But this tiny bit of time, short as it is, nature has tricked us into thinking it's longer than it really is. She has divided it into parts like infancy, childhood, youth, the gradual slope from youth to old age, and old age itself is yet another part. How many steps there are for such a short climb!

It feels like just a moment ago that I saw you off on your journey, and yet this "moment ago" makes up a good part of our existence. This existence is so brief that we should remember it will soon end altogether. In other years, time didn't seem to go by so quickly; now, it seems to fly by faster than I can believe, maybe because I feel that the end is getting closer, or maybe because I've started to notice and count my losses.

For this reason, I'm even more upset that some people spend most of this short time on things that don't matter—time that, no matter how carefully we protect it, isn't enough even for the important things. Cicero said that even if he had twice as many days to live, he wouldn't have time to read the lyric poets. You could say the same thing about people who study complicated arguments, but they are foolish in a sadder way. The lyric poets admit that they are writing for fun, but these people think they're doing something serious.

I'm not saying you shouldn't look at these complex arguments, but you should only glance at them, like saying a quick hello at the door, just to avoid being tricked into thinking they're really valuable. Why stress yourself out and lose weight over some problem that it's smarter to ignore than to solve? When a soldier is relaxed and traveling at his own pace, he can stop to look at small things along the way, but when the enemy is close behind and the order is given to speed up, he has to throw away everything he picked up during peaceful times.

I don't have time to figure out the tricky details of words or to show off how clever I am with them. Look at the enemy gathering, the gates locked tight, and weapons ready for battle. I need a strong heart to listen to this noise of battle all around me without flinching.

Everyone would rightly think I was crazy if, while the older men and women were piling up rocks for the walls, and the young men in armor inside the gates were waiting or even asking for the order to attack, and the enemy's spears were shaking our gates, and the ground was trembling with mines and tunnels, I sat there doing nothing, asking silly questions like, "What you haven't lost, you still have. But you haven't lost any horns. So, you must have horns," or other nonsense like that.

And yet, you might think I'm just as crazy if I spend my energy on that kind of thing, because even now, I'm under siege. But in the first case, the danger would only be from the outside, with a wall between me and the enemy; but now, the danger of death is right here with me. I don't have time for such foolishness; I have a big task ahead of me. What should I do? Death is close behind me, and life is slipping away.

Teach me something to help me face these troubles. Help me stop trying to run away from death, and help me stop letting life slip through my fingers. Give me the courage to face hardships; make me calm in the face of what I can't avoid. Help me make the most of the short time I have. Show me that the value of life doesn't depend on how long it is, but on how well I use it. Also, show me that it's possible, or even common, for someone who has lived a long life to have actually lived very little. Tell me when I lie down to sleep, "You might not wake up again!" And when I wake up, "You might not go to sleep again!" Tell me when I leave my house, "You might not come back!" And when I come back, "You might not leave again!"

You're wrong if you think that there's only a thin line between life and death on a sea voyage. No, that line is just as thin everywhere. It's just that we don't always see death so close by, but he's always just as near.

Take away these shadowy fears, and then it will be easier for you to teach me the lessons I'm ready to learn. When we were born, nature made us capable of learning, and she gave us reason, not perfect, but capable of being perfected.

Teach me about justice, duty, self-discipline, and the two types of purity—one that keeps us from harming others and one that keeps us true to ourselves. If you don't lead me down the wrong paths, I'll reach my goal more easily. As the tragic poet says: "The language of truth is simple." So we shouldn't make that language complicated; nothing is less suitable for a person with great goals than tricky cleverness. Farewell.

Letter 50 - On our blindness and its cure

I got your letter many months after you sent it, so I thought it would be useless to ask the person who delivered it what you were doing at that time. He would need an especially good memory to remember that! But I hope that by now, you are living in a way that I can be sure of what you are doing, no matter where you are. After all, what else could you be doing but improving yourself every day, getting rid of some mistakes, and realizing that the faults you blame on circumstances are really within you? We often blame certain problems on where we are or when something happens, but those problems will follow us no matter where we go.

You remember Harpasté, my wife's female clown; she stayed in my house as a burden I inherited. I really disapprove of these kinds of jokers; whenever I want to laugh at something silly, I don't need to look far—I can laugh at myself. Now, this clown suddenly went blind. It sounds unbelievable, but it's true: she doesn't know that she's blind. She keeps asking her helper to move her to a different room; she says her current rooms are too dark.

You can clearly see that what makes us laugh about Harpasté happens to all of us; no one realizes they are greedy, or that they are selfish. But unlike the blind, who ask for a guide, we wander around without one, saying things like: "I'm not selfish, but you can't live in Rome any other way. I'm not extravagant, but living in the city costs a lot. It's not my fault that I get angry easily, or that I haven't settled on a specific life plan; it's just because I'm young."

Why do we fool ourselves? The problem that hurts us isn't outside; it's inside us, deep in our core. That's why it's so hard to get better, because we don't even know that we're sick. Imagine we've started to heal; when will we finally get rid of these diseases with all their strength? Right now, we don't even go to the doctor, whose job would be easier if he were called when the illness was just starting. Young and inexperienced minds would follow his advice if he pointed out the right way.

No one finds it hard to return to a natural way of living, except for the person who has turned away from nature. We feel ashamed to receive lessons in common sense, but honestly, if we think it's too embarrassing to seek out a teacher for this, we should also give up hoping that we could somehow learn such a great thing by chance. No, we must work on it. To be honest, the work isn't even that hard if, as I said, we start to shape and rebuild our minds before they become hardened by bad habits. But I don't lose hope even for someone who has already become set in their bad ways.

There's nothing that won't give in to persistent effort, careful attention, and focus; no matter how bent the wood is, you can straighten it out again. Heat can straighten curved beams, and wood that grew in a different shape can be made to fit our needs. So how much easier should it be to shape the mind, which is flexible and more moldable than any liquid! After all, what is the mind but air in a certain state? And you see that air is more adaptable than any other material because it is lighter and more fluid.

There's nothing, Lucilius, that should stop you from having good hopes for us, just because we are still struggling with bad things, or because we've been stuck with them for a long time. No one starts out with a good mind; it's always the bad mind that takes hold of us first. Learning virtue means unlearning vice.

We should be even more determined to free ourselves from our faults because, once we gain what is good, it stays with us forever; virtue cannot be unlearned. Things that don't belong together find it hard to stay together, so they can be pushed out and gotten rid of; but things that naturally belong together stay faithfully. Virtue is natural; vice is against nature and hostile to it.

But even though virtues, once accepted, cannot leave and are easy to keep, the first steps toward them are difficult because it's natural for a weak and sick mind to fear what it doesn't know. That's why the mind must be forced to take the first step; after that, the cure doesn't seem so bad, because as soon as it starts healing us, it also starts to feel good. Most cures are only enjoyable after we've recovered, but the medicine of philosophy is both healing and pleasant at the same time. Farewell.

Letter 51 - On Baiae and morals

Everyone does the best they can, my dear Lucilius! You have Mount Etna, that tall and famous mountain in Sicily (though I'm not sure why Messala—or maybe it was Valgius? I've been reading both—called it "unique," since many places have volcanoes, not just the tall ones where it's more common because fire tends to rise high, but also in lower areas). As for me, I've had to settle for Baiae. I left it the day after I got there because Baiae is a place to avoid. Even though it has some natural benefits, luxury has taken it over.

You might ask, "Should any place be avoided completely?" Not really. But just like a wise and honest person might prefer one style of clothing over another—not because they hate a particular color, but because some colors don't suit someone who lives simply—there are also places that a wise person, or someone trying to be wise, will avoid because they don't fit with good morals. So, if someone is thinking about withdrawing from the world, they wouldn't choose Canopus (even though Canopus doesn't stop anyone from living simply) or Baiae either, because both places have become centers of vice. In Canopus, people indulge in luxury to the max; in Baiae, they're even more relaxed about it, as if the place itself encourages a certain amount of bad behavior.

We should choose places that are healthy not just for our bodies but also for our character. Just like I wouldn't want to live in a place that feels like torture, I also wouldn't want to live in a place that feels like a party all the time. Seeing people wandering drunk along the beach, hearing the wild partying of people on boats, the lakes filled with loud songs, and all the other ways that luxury, when it's freed from the rules, not only sins but shows off those sins—why would I want to see all that?

We should make sure to get as far away as possible from things that tempt us to do wrong. We need to toughen our minds and keep them far from the attractions of pleasure. Just one winter in Campania softened Hannibal, weakening the hero who had triumphed over the snowy Alps. He won with his weapons, but was defeated by his vices.

We also have a war to fight—a kind of war where there is no rest or break. The first things we have to conquer are pleasures, which, as you can see, have even overtaken the strongest of people. If someone understands how big the challenge is that they've taken on, they'll see that there's no room for laziness or softness. What do I have to do with those hot baths or steam rooms where they trap in the dry heat to sap your strength? Sweat should come after hard work.

Imagine we did what Hannibal did—stopped fighting and started pampering ourselves. Everyone would rightly blame us for being lazy at the wrong time, which is dangerous even for someone who has already won, let alone someone who is still fighting to win. And we have even less right to do this than those who followed the

Carthaginian flag, because our danger is greater if we slow down, and our work is harder even if we push ahead.

Fortune is fighting against me, but I won't follow her orders. I refuse to submit to her control; in fact, I'm shaking off the yoke she's put on me, which takes even more courage. The soul shouldn't be pampered; giving in to pleasure means giving in to pain, to hard work, to poverty. Ambition and anger will demand the same power over me as pleasure, and I'll be torn apart, or rather, pulled in different directions by all these conflicting desires.

I've set my sights on freedom, and that's the reward I'm working for. And what is freedom, you ask? It means not being a slave to any situation, any pressure, any random chance; it means forcing Fortune to meet me on equal terms. And on the day I know I have the upper hand, her power will mean nothing. When I control my own fate, should I still take orders from her?

So, someone who is thinking about these things should choose a simple and pure place to live. The spirit gets weakened by surroundings that are too comfortable, and without a doubt, where you live can make you weaker. Animals whose hooves get toughened on rough ground can travel any road; but when they are fattened on soft, marshy meadows, their hooves wear out quickly. The bravest soldier comes from rugged areas, but those raised in towns or pampered at home are slow to act. The hand that goes from plowing the fields to wielding a sword never complains about hard work; but the smooth and well-dressed man shrinks from the first cloud of dust.

Being trained in a tough environment builds character and prepares it for great deeds. It was more honorable for Scipio to spend his exile at Liternum than at Baiae; his fall didn't need a setting so soft. Even those who first took control of Rome's wealth—Gaius Marius, Gnaeus Pompey, and Caesar—did build villas near Baiae, but they placed them on the highest mountains. This seemed more fitting for soldiers, to look down from a high point on the lands spread out below. Look at the location, position, and type of buildings they chose; you'll see that they weren't country houses—they were like camps.

Do you think Cato would ever have lived in a pleasure palace, counting the passing boats full of immoral women, looking at the many types of brightly painted boats, smelling the roses floating on the lake, or listening to the late-night songs of rowdy partiers? Wouldn't he have preferred to stay in the shelter of a trench he dug himself, just for one night? Wouldn't any real man rather be woken by a war trumpet than by a chorus of singers?

But I've talked against Baiae long enough, though I could never talk enough against vice. Vice, Lucilius, is what I want you to fight against, without stopping. Because vice has no limit and no end. If any vice tears at your heart, throw it away from you; and if you can't get rid of it any other way, tear out your heart too. Above all, get pleasures out of your sight. Hate them more than anything else, because they're like those robbers the Egyptians call "lovers," who embrace us only to strangle us. Farewell.

Letter 52 - On choosing our teachers

What is this force, Lucilius, that pulls us one way when we want to go another, pushing us toward the very place we're trying to avoid? What is it that battles with our spirit and stops us from sticking to our decisions? We constantly change our plans. None of our wishes are free, none are definite, none last very long.

"But it's only a fool," you might say, "who can't make up his mind and keeps changing it." But how, or when, can we pull ourselves away from this foolishness? No one has enough strength on their own to rise above it; they need a helping hand, someone to pull them out.

Epicurus mentions that some people have found the truth without anyone's help, carving out their own path. He praises these people especially because their drive came from within, and they pushed forward by themselves. He also says there are others who need help from outside, who won't move forward unless someone leads the way, but who will follow faithfully. Metrodorus was one of these people. This type of person is also great, but they belong to the second level. We aren't in that first class either; we'll be lucky if we make it into the second. And you shouldn't look down on someone who can only be saved with the help of others; just wanting to be saved is a big deal too.

You'll find another type of person—not to be dismissed—who can be pushed and driven towards doing the right thing. They don't need a guide as much as they need someone to encourage them and push them forward. This is the third type. If you ask for an example of this type, Epicurus tells us that Hermarchus was like this. Of the last two types, he is more ready to congratulate the one who follows easily, but he has more respect for the one who needs pushing; because even though both reach the same goal, it's more impressive to achieve it with more challenging material to work with.

Imagine two buildings have been constructed, each different in their foundations but equal in height and grandeur. One is built on solid ground, so the building goes up smoothly. The other is built on soft, shifting ground, so the foundations took up much of the building materials, and a lot of effort was spent just reaching the solid rock. When you look at both, you can clearly see the progress of the first, but the harder, more difficult work on the second is hidden.

It's the same with people's dispositions; some are easy to guide, while others require a lot of hard work, as if they're being shaped by hand and are entirely focused on building their own foundations. I'd consider the person who never struggled with themselves more fortunate; but the one who has fought against their own nature and has won, who hasn't gently led themselves but wrestled their way to wisdom, has earned even more respect from themselves.

You can be sure that this stubborn nature, which demands so much effort, is within us. There are obstacles in our way, so let's fight them and call for some help. "Who should I call on?" you ask. "This person or that one?" There's another option too; you can go to the wisdom of the past because they have the time to help you. We can get help not only from the living but also from those who have passed away.

But let's choose our guides from the living, not those who speak with the greatest ease, turning out common sayings and holding what feels like their own little shows—not those, but people who teach us by their lives. These are the ones who show us what we should do and then prove it by their actions, who show us what we should avoid, and then are never caught doing what they told us not to.

Choose a guide whom you'll admire more for what they do than for what they say. Of course, I wouldn't stop you from listening to those philosophers who hold public talks and discussions, as long as they do it to improve themselves and others, and not for self-promotion. Because what's more disgraceful than a philosopher seeking applause? Does a sick person praise the doctor while he's operating? No, they submit to the treatment in silence and with respect.

Even if you applaud, I'll listen to it as if you were groaning when your wounds were touched. Do you want to show that you're paying attention, that you're moved by the importance of the topic? You can do this at the right time; I'll allow you to judge and vote on the best course. Pythagoras made his students stay silent for five years; do you think that gave them the right to suddenly burst into applause?

How foolish is it to leave a lecture happy just because of applause from people who don't even know what they're clapping for? Why do you enjoy being praised by people you wouldn't praise yourself? Fabianus used to give public talks, but his audience listened with self-control. Occasionally, loud praise would burst out, but it was driven by the greatness of his subject, not by the pleasant sound of his words.

There should be a difference between applause in a theater and applause in a school, and there's a certain dignity even in giving praise. If you look closely, all actions mean something, and you can judge a person's character even by the smallest signs. A lustful person reveals themselves by their walk, a gesture, sometimes just by a single answer, by touching their head with a finger, or by the shift of their eyes. A scoundrel shows himself by his laugh; a madman by his face and general appearance. These traits are known by certain signs; but you can tell a person's character by how they give and receive praise.

The philosopher's audience stretches out their hands in admiration, and sometimes they almost lean over the speaker's head. But if you really understand, that's not praise; it's just applause. These outbursts should be saved for the arts that aim to please the crowd; let philosophy be respected in silence. Young people might need to let out their impulses sometimes, but it should only be when they can't help it. Such praise encourages the listeners themselves and acts as motivation for young minds. But let them be stirred by the content, not the style; otherwise, eloquence does them harm by making them love the way things are said instead of the ideas themselves.

I'll save this topic for later; it needs a longer and more focused discussion on how the public should be addressed, what freedoms should be allowed to a speaker in public, and what should be allowed to the audience. There's no doubt that philosophy has lost something now that it's being sold to the highest bidder. But it can still be found in its purest form if the person presenting it is a true teacher, not just a seller. Farewell.

Letter 53 - On the faults of the spirit

You can talk me into almost anything right now because I recently got talked into traveling by sea. We set sail when the sea was calm, but the sky was heavy with dark clouds, the kind that usually bring rain or storms. Still, I thought the short trip from Puteoli to your beloved Parthenope wouldn't take long, even with the uncertain weather. So, to make the journey quicker, I headed straight out to sea towards Nesis, planning to skip all the bays and inlets.

But when we were far enough out that it didn't matter if we turned back or not, the calm weather that had lured me in disappeared. The storm hadn't hit yet, but the waves were starting to pick up, coming in faster. I asked the pilot to get me to shore somewhere, but he said the coast was rough and dangerous, especially in a storm. He feared a dangerous shore more than anything else.

But I was feeling too awful to care about the danger. I was hit with a slow, miserable seasickness that didn't even bring any relief, the kind that makes you feel sick without actually throwing up. So, I insisted that the pilot head for the shore, no matter what. When we got close, I didn't wait for the boat to be properly turned or anchored, as the poet Vergil would have advised. I remembered my old habit of jumping into cold water and, still wearing my cloak, I plunged into the sea like a true cold-water bather.

What do you think I felt, scrambling over the rocks, trying to find a path or make one myself? I finally understood why sailors are so afraid of land. It's hard to describe what I went through when I couldn't even stand myself. Now I understand why Ulysses got shipwrecked so many times—it wasn't just because the sea god was angry with him; he probably got seasick like I did. From now on, if I have to travel by sea, I'll probably only reach my destination in twenty years.

After I finally settled my stomach (because you know seasickness doesn't just go away once you get off the sea) and refreshed myself, I started thinking about how we often forget or ignore our own flaws, even the ones affecting our bodies that constantly remind us they're there—let alone the more serious flaws that are hidden inside us.

A slight fever might not seem like much, but when it gets worse and turns into a real illness, even the toughest person has to admit they're sick. If there's pain in our foot or a tingling in our joints, we might ignore it at first, saying we just sprained something or we're tired from too much exercise. But when it gets worse, and our ankles start swelling, we finally admit we have gout.

The same thing happens with our minds. The worse off we are, the less we realize it. But you shouldn't be surprised, my dear Lucilius. A person who sleeps lightly might have dreams and sometimes even knows they're dreaming. But deep sleep wipes out even dreams, sinking the mind so deep that it loses all awareness.

So why won't anyone admit their faults? Because they're still trapped by them. Only someone who's awake can talk about their dreams, and only someone with a clear mind can confess their sins.

Let's wake up so we can fix our mistakes. Philosophy is the only thing that can wake us up and shake us out of our deep sleep. Dedicate yourself entirely to philosophy. You are worthy of it, and it is worthy of you. Embrace it fully. Say goodbye to all other distractions with courage and honesty. Don't just study philosophy in your spare time.

If you were seriously sick, you would stop worrying about your personal affairs and forget about your business. You wouldn't think any client was important enough to handle their case while you were feeling even a little better. You would do everything you could to get better as quickly as possible. So, what are you waiting for now? Throw aside all distractions and give all your time to getting a sound mind because no one can achieve it if they're distracted by other things. Philosophy has its own authority; it sets its own schedule and doesn't allow others to decide when to pay attention to it. It's not something to be done just occasionally but something to practice every day. Philosophy is the master, and it demands our full attention.

Alexander, when a city offered him part of their land and half their wealth, replied, "I came to conquer Asia, not to accept what you might give, but to let you keep what I might leave behind." Philosophy says the same thing to all other pursuits: "I'm not here to accept whatever time you have left over; I'll let you keep whatever time I leave behind."

So turn to philosophy with all your heart, stay close to it, and cherish it. You'll find yourself far ahead of other people, and even the gods won't be far ahead of you. What's the difference between you and the gods? They live longer. But it's a sign of a great artist to capture a full likeness in a small space. The wise person's life covers as much ground as all eternity does for a god.

In one way, the sage has an advantage over the god; the god is free from fear because of nature's gift, while the wise person is free from fear because of their own effort. What a wonderful thing it is to have the weaknesses of a human but the calmness of a god! The power of philosophy to soften the blows of fate is beyond belief. Nothing can penetrate her defenses. She deflects some blows and pushes others aside with such force that they bounce back to where they came from. Farewell.

Letter 54 - On asthma and death

I had been feeling better for a long time, but suddenly my illness came back. You might wonder what kind of illness I'm talking about. Well, I've had many kinds of health problems, but there's one in particular that keeps bothering me. I don't know why I should use the Greek name for it, so I'll just call it what it is: shortness of breath. When it hits, it's like a sudden storm at sea—it usually lasts less than an hour. After all, who could struggle to breathe for too long?

I've dealt with many illnesses and physical challenges, but nothing seems worse than this. And that makes sense because most illnesses can be called just that—illnesses. But this one feels more like a constant struggle to catch my last breath. That's why doctors say it's like practicing how to die, because one day, the breath that's always been difficult will finally succeed in stopping altogether.

You might think I'm writing this with a light heart because I've recovered, but it would be silly to be happy about getting better as if I've won something. It's like a person thinking they've won a court case just because the trial got postponed. Still, even in the middle of struggling to breathe, I kept my mind calm and strong.

I told myself, "Does death keep testing me? Let it! I've been testing death for a long time." When, you ask? Before I was born. Death is just non-existence, and I already know what that's like. What was true before I was born will happen again after I die. If there's any pain in that state, it must have been there before we were born too, but we didn't feel anything then.

Think about it—wouldn't it be foolish to think that a lamp is worse off when it's blown out than it was before it was ever lit? We humans are like lamps—we get lit, we burn, and then we get blown out. There's suffering in between, but on either side of life, there's deep peace. I think we make a mistake by thinking that death only comes at the end. In reality, death was there before us, and it will be there after us too. Whatever state we were in before we were born— that's death. What difference does it make if you never start or if you stop, since the result is the same: not existing?

I kept encouraging myself with thoughts like these, quietly, of course, because I couldn't speak. Eventually, my shortness of breath started to come less frequently, slowed down, and finally stopped. Even now, though I'm not gasping anymore, my breathing isn't completely normal. There's still some hesitation and delay. But that's okay, as long as my soul isn't sighing.

You can trust me on this: I'll never be afraid when the final hour comes. I'm already prepared and don't plan too far ahead. But you should admire and follow the example of someone who isn't bothered by the idea of dying, even though they enjoy living. After all, what's the point of going willingly when you're being pushed out? But there's even some virtue in that: I may be pushed out, but I'll act as if I'm leaving willingly. That's why a wise person can never really be forced out, because they don't leave a place unwillingly. The wise person does nothing against their will. They avoid being forced because they choose to do what life is about to force on them anyway. Farewell.

Letter 55 - On Vatia's villa

I have just come back from a ride in my litter, and I am as tired as if I had walked the whole way instead of being carried. Even being carried for a long time can be exhausting, maybe even more so because it's not something we are naturally meant to do. Nature gave us legs so we could walk, and eyes so we could see for ourselves. But because we indulge in luxuries, we have become weak; we've stopped being able to do things for ourselves because we've chosen not to do them for so long.

Still, I found it necessary to shake up my body a bit. I thought it might help get rid of the bile that had gathered in my throat, or maybe it would make my breathing easier if it had become too thick for some reason. So, I insisted on being carried for longer than usual, along a beautiful beach that curves between Cumae and Servilius Vatia's villa. The beach is squeezed between the sea on one side and the lake on the other, like a narrow path. The sand was packed down firm because of a recent storm, as you know, when waves crash hard against the beach, they press the sand down; but when the weather stays calm, the sand becomes loose because it dries out and loses its moisture.

As usual, I began looking around for something that might be useful to me when I saw the villa that used to belong to Vatia. This is where that famous praetorian millionaire spent his old age! He was famous for nothing but living a quiet life, and people thought he was lucky because of that. Whenever others were ruined by being friends with Asinius Gallus, or by hating Sejanus, and later by being close to him—since it was just as dangerous to offend him as it was to be friends with him—people used to say, "Oh, Vatia, you alone know how to live!"

But Vatia didn't really know how to live; he only knew how to hide. And there is a big difference between living a quiet life and just being idle. So every time I passed his villa while he was still alive, I would say to myself, "Here lies Vatia!"

But, my dear Lucilius, philosophy is something sacred, something to be honored, so much so that even a fake version of it can seem pleasing. Most people think that someone who has withdrawn from society, is free from worries, and lives for himself is truly living. But only a wise person can really enjoy these things. Can someone who is constantly worried know how to live for himself? Does he even know how to live at all?

The person who has run away from responsibilities and other people, who hides away because his desires have made him unhappy, isn't living for himself. He's living for his stomach, his sleep, and his pleasures, and that's the most shameful way to live. Just because someone doesn't live for anyone else doesn't mean he's truly living for himself.

Still, there is something to be said for being steadfast and sticking to one's purpose. Even laziness, if it's consistent, can seem to have a kind of authority.

I can't describe the villa in detail because I've only seen the front and the parts that are visible to anyone passing by. There are two large man-made caves, as big as the biggest hall, one that never gets sunlight and another that keeps the sunlight until it sets. There's also a stream running through a grove of plane trees, fed by both the sea and Lake Acheron. It flows through the grove like a water channel, and it's big enough to hold fish, although the water is constantly being drawn off. When the sea is calm, they don't use the stream and only rely on it when storms keep the fishermen from working.

The best thing about the villa is that it's close to Baiae. It doesn't have the problems of that resort but still enjoys its pleasures. I understand the appeal of this place, and I think it's a villa suitable for any season. It faces the west wind and blocks it so that Baiae doesn't get it. So, it seems Vatia wasn't foolish when he chose this place to spend his last years.

But really, the place where you live doesn't do much to make you peaceful. It's your mind that has to make everything pleasant for you. I've seen people miserable in beautiful villas, and I've seen them busy as ever in the middle of nowhere. So don't think your life is any worse just because you're not in Campania. And why aren't you there? Just let your thoughts wander, even to this place.

You can connect with your friends even when they're far away, as often as you want, and for as long as you want. We actually enjoy our friends' company more when we're apart from them. When we're together, we take it for granted because we can talk or sit together anytime we want. But when we're apart, we appreciate our friends more.

We should be happy even when we're apart from our friends because, even when we're together, we're often apart for different reasons—like nighttime, different responsibilities, private studies, or trips to the countryside. So, being apart doesn't take much away from our friendship.

A friend should always be in your thoughts, and that way, they're never really absent. You can see anyone you want every day, in your mind.

So, I want you to share your studies, meals, and walks with me. Our thoughts should have no limits. I see you, my dear Lucilius, and at this moment, I hear you. I'm with you so much that I'm wondering if I should start sending you short notes instead of letters. Farewell.

Letter 56 - On quiet and study

I swear there's nothing more important for someone who isolates themselves to study than silence! Imagine the variety of noises that fill my ears! I have a room right above a public bathhouse. So picture all the sounds that are loud enough to make me wish I couldn't hear at all! For example, when someone is working out with heavy weights, straining themselves, or at least pretending to, I can hear them grunt;

and whenever they let out their breath, I can hear them panting in a wheezy, high-pitched tone. Or maybe I notice someone lazy, just getting a cheap massage, and I hear the sound of the masseur's hands hitting his shoulder, making different noises depending on how the hands land—sometimes flat, sometimes hollow. Then, maybe a professional athlete comes along, shouting out scores; that's the final touch.

Add to this the occasional arrest of a drunk or a pickpocket, the noise of the person who always loves to hear his own voice in the bath, or the overly enthusiastic guy who jumps into the swimming pool with way too much noise and splashing. And then there are people who, even if their voices aren't any good, imagine the hair-plucker with his sharp, shrill voice—shouting to advertise his services—and never stopping, except when he's pulling out hairs and making his customer scream instead.

So you might say: "You must have nerves of steel or be half-deaf if you can stand all these noises—so many different and clashing sounds—when our friend Chrysippus couldn't even stand the constant greetings of 'good morning'!" But honestly, this racket means no more to me than the sound of waves or a waterfall, although you might remind me that some people once moved their city just because they couldn't stand the noise of a waterfall.

Words distract me more than noises because words demand attention, but noises just fill the ears and beat against them. Among the sounds that don't bother me, I include passing carriages, a machinist in the same building, a saw-sharpener nearby, or some guy demonstrating flutes and pipes at the Trickling Fountain, shouting rather than singing.

Furthermore, sudden noises bother me more than constant ones. But by now, I've toughened myself against all that, so I can even endure a boatswain shouting orders to his crew. I force my mind to concentrate and not wander to things outside of itself; the world outside can be chaotic, as long as there's no disturbance within me, as long as fear isn't fighting with desire inside my chest, and as long as stinginess and wastefulness aren't battling each other, each causing trouble. What good is a quiet neighborhood if our emotions are in chaos?

It was night, and the whole world was calm. But that's not true; there's no real rest unless our mind is at peace. Night doesn't get rid of our troubles; it just changes them. Even when we try to sleep, our sleepless moments can be just as stressful as during the day. Real peace is what comes when a clear and balanced mind is relaxed.

Think of the poor person who tries to find sleep by making his whole house silent, who demands that everyone around him be quiet and walk on tiptoe so as not to disturb his ears; yet he tosses and turns, trying to find sleep amid his worries! He complains that he's heard noises when he hasn't heard anything at all. Why? Because his mind is in turmoil; it needs to be calmed, and its restless murmuring needs to be quieted. Just because the body is still doesn't mean the mind is at peace. Sometimes, quiet means unrest.

So, we need to wake ourselves up and get busy with good activities whenever we're stuck in a lazy, uncontrollable mood. Great generals, when they see their troops getting restless, keep them in line by giving them some work or by sending them on small missions. Busy people don't have time for mischief, and it's a common saying that the troubles of idleness can be shaken off by hard work. Even though people might think I sought seclusion because I was fed up with politics and regretted my unlucky and ungrateful position, in the retreat that fear and exhaustion drove me to, my ambition sometimes comes back to life. It's not that my ambition was rooted out; it just got tired or maybe even frustrated by its failures.

The same goes for luxury, which sometimes seems to have left us. But then, even after we've claimed to live simply, it starts to bother us again, and in the midst of our frugality, it searches for the pleasures we've only left behind, not condemned. And the quieter it comes, the stronger it is. All open vices are less dangerous; a disease is also closer to being cured when it shows itself and reveals its strength. The same is true for greed, ambition, and other evils of the mind—believe me, they do the most harm when they're hiding behind a pretense of health.

People think we're in retirement, but we're not. Because if we've truly retired, if we've truly signaled our retreat, and if we've scorned external distractions, then, as I said before, no external noise will distract us; no music from people or birds can interrupt good thoughts once they're firm and strong.

The mind that flinches at words or sudden sounds is unstable and hasn't yet retreated into itself; it carries within it some anxiety and deep-seated fear, which makes it vulnerable to worry, as our Vergil says:

"I, who once never flinched at the spear or the clashing armor of the crowded enemy, now tremble at every sound, fearing both for my child and the burden I carry."

This man in his first state is wise; he doesn't fear the brandished spear, the clashing armor, or the noise of a city under attack. This man in his second state is ignorant; he fears for his own concerns and turns pale at every sound; any noise seems like a battle cry and throws him into panic; the slightest disturbance makes him breathless with fear. It's the burden that makes him afraid.

So, pick anyone you like from among Fortune's favorites, those who are burdened with many responsibilities and loads, and you'll see a picture of Vergil's hero, "fearing both for his child and the burden he carries."

You can be sure you're at peace with yourself when no noise reaches you, when no word shakes you out of yourself, whether it's flattery, a threat, or just meaningless noise buzzing around you.

"What then?" you might ask. "Isn't it sometimes easier to just avoid the noise?" I agree. So, I'll change where I'm staying. I just wanted to test myself and practice. Why should I be tormented any longer when Ulysses found such a simple cure for his comrades, even against the songs of the Sirens? Farewell.

Letter 57 - On the trials of travel

When it was time for me to go back to Naples from Baiae, I quickly convinced myself that a storm was coming so I could avoid another sea trip. However, the road was so muddy all the way that it felt like I was on a voyage anyway. On that day, I felt like I had gone through everything an athlete endures; I started with the oiling up (like athletes do), and then got covered in dust while going through the Naples tunnel.

No place could feel longer than that tunnel; nothing could be dimmer than those torches, which didn't really help us see in the darkness but just showed us how dark it was. Even if there was light in the tunnel, the dust, which is already annoying in the open air, would have ruined it; imagine how much worse it was in that tunnel where the dust swirled around and blew back into the faces of those who stirred it up! So we had to deal with two problems at the same time that were complete opposites: we fought with both mud and dust on the same road and on the same day.

The darkness made me think, and I felt a kind of mental thrill, not from fear, but from the strangeness and unpleasantness of the situation. Of course, I'm not talking about myself here, because I'm far from being perfect or even average; I'm talking about someone who fortune has no control over. Even a person like that would feel a thrill and their face might change color.

There are some emotions, my dear Lucilius, that even the bravest person cannot avoid; nature reminds courage of how fragile it is. So, even the bravest person might frown when facing something scary, might shiver at sudden sights, or feel dizzy when standing on the edge of a high cliff and looking down. This isn't fear; it's a natural feeling that reason cannot completely get rid of.

That's why some brave people, who are willing to shed their own blood, can't stand to see the blood of others. Some people faint at the sight of a fresh wound; others react the same way when they see an old wound that's festering. And some people would rather take a sword hit themselves than watch one happen to someone else.

So, like I said, I felt a certain change in myself, though it wasn't exactly confusion. Then, as soon as I saw daylight again, my good spirits came back without me even thinking about it. I started to wonder how foolish we are to fear some things more or less than others, when they all end the same way. After all, what difference does it make whether a watchtower or a mountain falls on us? You'll find there's no difference at all. But still, some people fear one more than the other, even though both would be just as deadly; it shows that fear isn't about the result, but the cause.

Do you think I'm talking about the Stoics now, who say that if a man is crushed by something heavy, his soul can't survive and just scatters because it didn't have a clear way to escape? That's not what I mean; I think those who believe that are wrong.

Just like fire can't be crushed because it finds a way out around the edges of whatever is trying to smother it; just like air can't be hurt by slaps or blows or even cut, but just moves around whatever's in its way; in the same way, the soul, which is made of the finest particles, can't be trapped or destroyed inside the body. Instead, because it's so delicate, it will find a way out through whatever's crushing it. Just like lightning can strike and flash over a wide area but still finds a way back through a small opening, the soul, which is even more delicate than fire, can escape through any part of the body.

So, this brings us to the question: can the soul be immortal? But know this: if the soul survives after the body is crushed, then it can't be crushed out, because it doesn't die; for something that's immortal can't be harmed, and nothing can hurt what lasts forever. Farewell.

Letter 58 - On being

Today, I realized how limited and poor our language is. We were talking about Plato, and many topics came up that needed names but didn't have any, and there were other things that once had names but have lost them because we were too picky about using them. But who can afford to be picky when language is so limited?

There's an insect the Greeks call oestrus that drives cattle wild and scatters them all over the fields; it used to be called asilus in our language, as you can see from Vergil's writing:

"Near the groves of Silarus and the shades of green-clad Alburnus,

Flits an insect, named Asilus by the Romans; in Greek,

The word is rendered oestrus. With a rough

And strident sound, it buzzes and drives wild

The terror-stricken herds throughout the woods."

This shows that the word asilus has gone out of use. And, not to keep you waiting too long, there were some simple words that used to be common, like cernere ferro inter se, as Vergil also shows:

"Great heroes, born in various lands, had come

To settle matters mutually with the sword."

This "settling matters" we now say as decernere. The simple word has become outdated.

The ancients used to say iusso instead of iussero in conditional sentences. You don't have to take my word for it; you can check Vergil again:

"The other soldiers shall conduct the fight

With me, where I shall bid."

I'm not trying to show how much time I've spent studying language with these examples; I just want you to understand how many words that were common in the works of Ennius and Accius have become old and unused. Even in Vergil's works, which people read every day, some words have been lost to us.

You might ask, "What's the point of this introduction?" I won't keep it a secret; I want to use the word essentia with your approval. If I can't get that, I'll use it anyway, even if it annoys you. I have Cicero as my authority for using this word, and I consider him a strong authority. If you want a more recent example, I'll cite Fabianus, who was careful with his speech, refined, and polished in style, making him suitable even for our picky tastes. But what can we do, dear Lucilius? How else can we find a word for what the Greeks call ousia, something essential, something that is the basic substance of everything? So, please, allow me to use the word essentia. However, I'll try to use this privilege sparingly; maybe I'll just be happy knowing I have the right to use it.

But what good will your permission do me if, despite it all, I can't express in Latin the meaning of the word that led me to complain about the poverty of our language? You'll find our Roman language even more limited when you discover that there's a one-syllable word I can't translate. "What's this word?" you ask. It's the word on. You might think I'm lacking in skill; you might think the word could easily be translated as quod est. But I notice a big difference; you're forcing me to turn a noun into a verb.

But if I have to, I'll translate it as quod est. Plato, according to a learned friend of ours, expressed this idea in six different ways, as he told me today. I'll explain them all to you, but first, let me point out that there's something called genus and something called species.

Right now, we're looking for the primary idea of genus, on which all the others, the different species, depend, which is the source of all classification, the term under which universal ideas are included. We can reach the idea of genus if we start by going back from the specific examples, because that's how we'll be led back to the primary concept.

Now, "man" is a species, as Aristotle says; so is "horse," and so is "dog." So, we must find a common link for all these terms, one that includes them all and holds them under itself. And what is this link? It's "animal." And so, we begin to have a genus "animal," which includes all these terms: "man," "horse," and "dog."

But there are some things that have life (anima) but are not "animals." For example, plants and trees are considered to have life, which is why we say they live and die. So, the term "living things" will be higher up, because both animals and plants fall into this category. However, some things lack life, like rocks. So, we need another term that takes precedence over "living things," and that's "substance." I would classify "substance" by saying that all substances are either animate or inanimate.

But there's still something superior to "substance," because we speak of certain things as having substance and others as lacking substance. So, what's the term from which these things come? It's what we recently gave an inaccurate name, "that which exists." By using this term, we can divide things into species, so that we can say: that which exists either has or lacks substance.

This is what genus is: the primary, original, and (to play with the word) "general." Of course, there are other genera, but they are "special" genera: for example, "man" is a genus. For "man" includes species: by nations, such as Greek, Roman, Parthian; by colors, such as white, black, yellow. The term also includes individuals: Cato, Cicero, Lucretius. So, "man" falls into the genus category, as it includes many kinds; but as it's subordinate to another term, it falls into the species category. But the genus "that which exists" is general and has no term superior to it. It's the first term in the classification of things, and all things are included under it.

The Stoics would put another genus ahead of this, even more primary; I'll discuss that shortly after proving that the genus we've talked about should rightly be placed first, as it can include everything.

So, I divide "that which exists" into these two species: things with, and things without, substance. There's no third category. And how do I divide "substance"? By saying it's either animate or inanimate. And how do I divide the "animate"? By saying: "Certain things have a mind, while others have only life." Or I could say it like this: "Certain things can move, progress, and change position, while others are rooted in the ground; they're fed and grow only through their roots." Again, how do I divide "animals"? They're either perishable or imperishable.

Some Stoics consider the primary genus to be "something." I'll add their reasoning for this belief; they say: "In the order of nature, some things exist, and other things do not. And even the things that do not exist are still part of nature. These could be things like centaurs, giants, and other figments of the imagination, which have begun to take shape, even though they have no real substance."

But now I return to the subject I promised to discuss with you: how Plato divides all existing things into six different categories. The first class of "that which exists" cannot be grasped by sight, touch, or any of the senses; it can only be grasped by thought. Any generic concept, such as the idea of "man," is not something the eyes can see; but a specific man, like Cicero or Cato, is visible. The term "animal" is not seen; it's only understood by thought. However, a particular animal, like a horse or a dog, can be seen.

The second class of "things that exist," according to Plato, is that which stands out and is superior to everything else; this, he says, exists in the highest degree. The word "poet" is used broadly for all writers of verse, but among the Greeks, it's come to specifically mean one person. You know that when people say "the poet," they mean Homer. So, what is this supreme being? It's God, who is greater and more powerful than anyone else.

The third class is made up of things that exist in the proper sense of the word; they are countless in number but are beyond our sight. "What are these?" you ask. They are what Plato calls "ideas," and from these all visible things are created, and everything is fashioned according to their pattern. They are immortal, unchangeable, and inviolable.

And this "idea," or rather, Plato's concept of it, is as follows: "The 'idea' is the eternal pattern of things created by nature." I'll explain this definition so you can understand it better: Suppose I want to make a picture of you; I use your appearance as the pattern for the picture, and this is what my mind uses as a guide in creating the artwork. That outward appearance, which guides me, is the "idea." Nature has infinite numbers of such patterns: of men, fish, trees, according to which everything in nature is created.

In the fourth place, we'll put "form." And if you want to know what "form" means, you'll need to pay close attention, and you can blame Plato, not me, for the difficulty of understanding it. However, we can't make fine distinctions without facing challenges. A moment ago, I used the artist as an example. When the artist wants to paint Vergil, he looks at Vergil himself. The "idea" is Vergil's outward appearance, and that's the pattern the artist intends to capture. The thing the artist draws from this "idea" and includes in his work is the "form."

Do you ask what the difference is? The former is the pattern, while the latter is the shape taken from the pattern and embodied in the work. The artist follows one but creates the other. A statue has a certain outward appearance; this appearance of the statue is the "form." And the pattern itself has a certain appearance, which the sculptor gazes upon to fashion his statue; this is the "idea." If you want another distinction, I'll say that the "form" is in the artist's work, and the "idea" is outside his work, not only outside it but before it.

The fifth class is made up of things that exist in the usual sense of the word. These things are the first that have to do with us: here we have all things like men, cattle, and objects. The sixth class includes all that has a fictional existence, like void or time.

Plato doesn't include things that can be seen or touched among the things he believes truly exist. These things are the first that have to do with us: here we have all things like men, cattle, and objects. Because they're always changing, constantly growing or shrinking. None of us is the same person in old age as we were in youth, nor the same person tomorrow as we were yesterday. Our bodies flow like water in a river; every visible thing passes with time; nothing we see stays the same. Even I, as I comment on this change, am changing myself.

This is what Heraclitus says: "We go down twice into the same river, and yet into a different river." The river keeps the same name, but the water has already flowed by. Of course, this is more obvious with rivers than with people. But we humans also move along just as quickly; and it makes me wonder at our foolishness in becoming so attached to something as fleeting as the body, and in fearing that we might one day die, when every moment means the death of our previous condition. Won't you stop fearing that something will happen once that really happens every day?

So much for people—a substance that flows and falls, exposed to every influence; but the universe, too, immortal and enduring as it is, changes and never stays the same. Even though it has everything within itself, it has it differently now than it had before; it keeps changing its arrangement.

"Very well," you say, "but what good do I get from all this reasoning?" None, if you want me to answer your question honestly. However, just as an engraver rests his eyes after a long, tiring work and enjoys a break, so we should sometimes give our minds a rest and refresh them with some kind of entertainment. But let even your entertainment be work; and if you're careful, you might find something useful in even the most unlikely places.

That's what I do, Lucilius: I try to find and use something helpful from every field of thought, no matter how far it seems from philosophy. Now, what could be less likely to improve character than the subjects we've been discussing? And how can Plato's "ideas" make me a better person? What can I take from them that will help me control my desires? Maybe just the thought that all these things that appeal to our senses and excite us are, according to Plato, not even real.

These things are therefore imaginary, and although they seem to be something real for the moment, they're neither permanent nor substantial; yet we crave them as if they were eternal, or as if we would always possess them. We are weak, fragile beings standing among unrealities; therefore, let us turn our minds to things that are everlasting. Let us look up to the ideal forms of all things that float above and to the God who moves among them, planning how to protect from death that which he couldn't make immortal because of its substance, and overcoming the body's weaknesses through reason.

For all things endure, not because they are everlasting, but because they are protected by the care of the one who governs everything; but that which is imperishable would need no guardian. The Creator keeps them safe, overcoming their weakness with His power. Let us despise everything so worthless that it makes us doubt whether it even exists at all.

At the same time, let us reflect that just as Providence protects the world from its dangers, even though the world is as mortal as we are, to some extent, we can also keep our frail bodies on earth a little longer through our own efforts if we learn to control and limit those pleasures that cause the downfall of most people.

Plato himself reached old age by taking care of himself. Of course, he was lucky to have a strong and healthy body (his very name was given to him because of his broad chest); but his strength was worn down by sea voyages and dangerous adventures. Yet, by living frugally, by setting limits on his desires, and by taking careful care of himself, he reached a long life despite many challenges.

You probably know that Plato had the good fortune, thanks to his careful living, to die on his birthday, after exactly completing his eighty-first year. Because of this, wise men from the East, who happened to be in Athens at the time, sacrificed to him after his death, believing that his long life was too perfect for a mortal man, since he had completed the perfect number of nine times nine. I don't doubt that he would have been quite willing to give up a few days from this total, as well as the sacrifice.

Frugal living can bring one to old age; and to me, old age is not something to avoid, nor is it something to crave. There is a pleasure in being with oneself as long as possible when one has made oneself worth enjoying. So the question we have to answer is whether one should avoid extreme old age and hurry the end, or wait for it to come naturally. A man who sluggishly waits for his fate is almost a coward, just like someone who drinks a jar dry and even drinks the dregs is overly fond of wine.

But we should also ask this question: "Is the end of life the dregs, or is it the clearest and purest part, as long as the mind is unimpaired, the senses are still sharp, and the body is not worn out and dying before its time?" Because it makes a big difference whether a man is lengthening his life or his death.

But if the body is no longer useful, why shouldn't one free the struggling soul? Maybe one should do this a little before the end comes, in case, when it's time, he can't do it anymore. And since the danger of living in misery is greater than the danger of dying soon, he is a fool who refuses to risk a little time for a chance at great gain.

Few have lived through extreme old age without losing their abilities, and many have lain useless, unable to do anything. How much more cruel, then, do you think it is to have lost part of your life than to have lost the right to end that life?

Don't take this personally, but consider what I'm saying. It's this: I won't abandon old age if old age keeps me whole and intact, especially in my mind, which is the best part of me; but if old age begins to break down my mind and tear apart its various faculties, if it leaves me not life but only the breath of life, I'll rush out of a house that's crumbling and falling apart.

I won't avoid illness by seeking death, as long as the illness can be cured and doesn't hinder my soul. I won't take my own life just because I'm in pain; because dying in such circumstances is defeat. But if I find out that the pain will never go away, I'll leave, not because of the pain, but because it will stop me from living for the reasons I value. Someone who dies just because of pain is weak, a coward; but someone who lives just to endure pain is a fool.

But I'm going on too long, and there's enough here to fill a whole day. How can a man end his life if he can't even end a letter? So farewell. You'll probably read this last word with more pleasure than all my talk about death. Farewell.

Letter 59 - On pleasure and joy

I really enjoyed your letter; let me use the word "enjoyed" in the way people usually do, without worrying about the strict Stoic meaning. As Stoics, we believe that pleasure is something bad. Maybe it is, but we often use the word "pleasure" when we want to talk about feeling happy. I know that if we stick to our Stoic rules, even "pleasure" would be considered bad, and only truly wise people can feel real joy. For us, "joy" is a feeling of deep happiness that comes from believing in the goodness and truth of what we have. But most people talk about feeling "joy" when a friend becomes a leader, gets married, or has a child; but these things often lead to future sadness. Real joy never stops and never turns into something bad.

That's why when our poet Vergil talks about "The evil joys of the mind," he uses fancy language, but it's not really accurate. No real "joy" can be evil. He used the word "joy" to mean "pleasures" and was trying to show how people can take pleasure in things that are bad for them. Still, I wasn't wrong when I said I got a lot of "pleasure" from your letter. Even though a person who doesn't know better might feel "joy" from something good, that feeling can change quickly, so I call it "pleasure" because it's based on a wrong idea of what's good, and it often goes too far.

But back to what I was saying, let me tell you what made me happy about your letter. You have control over your words. You don't let your language carry you away or take you beyond the limits you've set. Many writers get tempted by some fancy phrase and end up talking about something completely different from what they started. But that didn't happen with you; all your words are focused and fit the subject perfectly. You say everything you want to, and you even imply more than you say. This shows that what you're writing about is important and that your mind, like your words, has nothing unnecessary or over-the-top.

However, I do notice some metaphors in your writing—not wild ones, but those that have been used often and are accepted. I also see some comparisons. Now, if someone says we shouldn't use comparisons, claiming that only poets can do that, it seems they haven't read any of our older prose writers who didn't try to show off with fancy language. These early writers, who focused on getting their point across, used plenty of comparisons; and I think they are necessary, not for the same reason poets use them, but because they help us explain things more clearly, making both the speaker and listener understand the topic better.

For example, I'm currently reading Sextius; he's a sharp thinker and a philosopher who, even though he writes in Greek, follows Roman principles. One of his comparisons struck me: he describes an army marching in formation in a place where the enemy could attack from any direction. "This," he says, "is how the wise person should be—ready for battle on all sides, so that no matter where the attack comes from, he can respond immediately and without confusion." We see this in armies led by great generals; the soldiers instantly understand their leader's orders because they are arranged in a way that allows a signal to reach both the cavalry and infantry at the same time.

Sextius says this is even more important for people like us; soldiers often fear the enemy for no reason, and what they think is the most dangerous part of the march might actually be the safest. But foolishness never finds peace; it is haunted by fear at the front, rear, and sides of the column. Foolishness is always in danger, facing threats from all directions. It panics at everything and isn't prepared for anything. It even gets scared of its own allies. But the wise person is ready for any challenge; he stays alert and doesn't back down in the face of poverty, sorrow, disgrace, or pain. He walks confidently, whether he's facing these challenges or surrounded by them.

We humans are tied down and weakened by many bad habits; we've been stuck in them for a long time, and it's hard to clean ourselves of them. We're not just dirty; we're stained by them. But instead of jumping from one idea to another, I want to ask a question that I often think about: why does foolishness hold on to us so tightly? First, it's because we don't fight it hard enough; we don't struggle for our own salvation with all our strength. Second, it's because we don't trust the wisdom of the wise enough, and we don't fully take in their teachings with open hearts; we approach this big problem with too little seriousness.

But how can someone learn enough to fight against their bad habits if the time they spend learning is just the leftover time they have after indulging in those bad habits? None of us goes deep into the matter. We only skim the surface, and we think the little bit of time we spend searching for wisdom is more than enough for someone as busy as we are.

What holds us back the most is that we're too easily pleased with ourselves. If someone calls us good, sensible, or holy, we believe them. We don't just settle for moderate praise; we take in every bit of flattery, no matter how exaggerated, as if we deserve it. We agree with people who say we're the best and wisest, even though we know they often lie. And we're so full of ourselves that we want praise for things when we're actually doing the exact opposite. A person might hear themselves called "most gentle" while they're torturing someone, "most generous" while they're stealing, or "most temperate" while they're drunk and indulging in lust. This is why we don't want to change—we think we're already the best.

Alexander the Great traveled as far as India, attacking tribes that were barely known to their neighbors. During the siege of a certain city, while scouting the walls for weaknesses, he was wounded by an arrow. Even so, he continued the siege, determined to finish what he started. But as the wound began to dry up and the blood stopped flowing, the pain increased. His leg gradually went numb as he sat on his horse, and finally, when he had to withdraw, he exclaimed, "Everyone says I'm the son of Jupiter, but this wound proves I'm mortal."

We should do the same. Each of us, in our own way, is fooled by flattery. We should say to those who flatter us, "You call me wise, but I know how many of the things I desire are useless, and how many of the things I want will harm me. I don't even have the basic knowledge that animals have about how much food or drink is enough. I don't even know how much I can handle."

Now, I'll show you how you can tell if you're not wise. The wise person is joyful, happy, calm, and unshaken; he lives on the same level as the gods. Now, ask yourself: if you're never sad, if your mind isn't troubled by worries about the future, if your soul remains steady and content day and night, then you've achieved the greatest good that humans can possess. But if you're constantly chasing after all kinds of pleasures, you should know that you're as far from wisdom as you are from true joy. Joy is what you want, but you're off track if you think you can find it while you're surrounded by wealth and titles—in other words, if you're looking for joy in the midst of worries. The things you're striving for so eagerly, thinking they'll bring you happiness and pleasure, are really just sources of sorrow.

I believe that all people like this are chasing after joy, but they don't know where to find joy that's both deep and lasting. Some look for it in feasting and indulgence; others, in seeking honors and being surrounded by followers; others, in their lovers; and still others, in showing off their knowledge and in literature that doesn't help them grow. All these people are led astray by pleasures that are misleading and short-lived—like drunkenness, which gives an hour of wild happiness but is followed by days of sickness, or like applause and popularity, which are gained and paid for with great mental unrest.

So think about this: the result of wisdom is joy that's unbroken and continuous. The mind of the wise person is like the sky above the moon—eternal calm fills that region. So, you have a reason to want to be wise if the wise person is never without joy. This joy comes only from knowing that you possess virtues. Only the brave, the just, and the self-restrained can truly rejoice.

And when you ask, "What do you mean? Don't foolish and wicked people also rejoice?" I'll answer, no more than lions who have caught their prey. When people wear themselves out with wine and lust, when the night ends before they're done with their revelry, when the pleasures they've piled onto a body too small to hold them start to rot, that's when they miserably cry out those lines from Vergil: "You know how, amid false-glittering joys, we spent that last night."

Pleasure-seekers spend every night amid false-glittering joys, just as if it were their last. But the joy that belongs to the gods, and to those who imitate the gods, isn't interrupted, nor does it end; and it would end if it came from outside. Just because it doesn't come from anyone else, it's not at the mercy of someone else's whims. What Fortune didn't give, she can't take away. Farewell.

Letter 60 - On harmful prayers

I am filing a complaint, taking this to court, and I am angry. Do you still want what your nurse, your guardian, or your mother prayed for on your behalf? Don't you realize yet how harmful their prayers were? Oh, how much harm the wishes of our loved ones can bring us! And the more completely their wishes are fulfilled, the more harmful they are. At my age, it's no surprise that nothing but trouble has followed us since our early youth; we have grown up surrounded by the curses that our parents called down on us. And may the gods hear our cry as well, a cry that asks for no favors!

How long will we continue to make demands on the gods, as if we still can't take care of ourselves? How long will we keep filling the marketplaces of our great cities with food? How long must we have others gather it for us? How long will many ships carry the supplies for just one meal, bringing them from all over the seas? The bull is satisfied when it feeds over a few acres; and one forest is big enough for a herd of elephants. However, humans take their food from both the earth and the sea.

So, did nature give us bellies so insatiable, even though she gave us such small bodies, that we should outdo even the biggest and most voracious animals in greed? Not at all. How small is the amount that will satisfy nature? A very little will make her content. It's not the natural hunger of our stomachs that costs us so much, but our endless cravings.

Therefore, those who, as Sallust puts it, "listen to their stomachs," should be counted among the animals, and not among men; and some men, indeed, should not even be counted among the animals, but among the dead. The person who really lives is the one who is useful to many; the person who really lives is the one who makes use of themselves. But those men who hide away and grow sluggish are no better off in their homes than if they were in their graves. Right there on the marble door of such a man's house, you could inscribe his name, for he has died before he is dead. Farewell.

Letter 61 - On meeting death cheerfully

Let's stop wanting the things we've always wanted. At least, I'm trying to do this: now that I'm older, I've stopped wanting the things I wanted when I was younger. My days and nights are focused on one goal: to get rid of my long-lasting troubles. I'm trying to live each day as if it were a full, complete life. I'm not grabbing at life as if it were my last day, but I do treat it like it could be my last.

I'm writing this letter to you with that thought in mind, as if death might take me away while I'm still writing. I'm ready to go, and I enjoy life because I'm not overly worried about when I'll leave. Before I grew old, I tried to live well; now that I'm old, I'm trying to die well. But dying well means dying with a positive attitude. Make sure you never do anything unwillingly.

If you're forced to do something, it feels like a burden. But if you choose to do it, then it's not really a burden. This is what I mean: the person who willingly accepts what they have to do avoids the worst part of being forced into something—doing what they don't want to do. The person who does things because they have to isn't miserable; the person who does things against their will is. So let's train our minds to want whatever life demands of us, and especially to think about our death without sadness.

We should prepare for death even before we prepare for life. Life gives us enough, but we always seem to want more; there always seems to be something missing, and there always will be. Living long enough doesn't depend on how many years or days we have, but on our state of mind. I have lived long enough, my dear friend Lucilius. I am satisfied; I'm ready for death. Farewell.

Letter 62 - On good company

We are tricked by people who try to convince us that they're too busy to study or learn. They pretend to be occupied with many tasks, but really, they're just keeping themselves busy with unimportant things. As for me, Lucilius, my time is my own; it truly is, and no matter where I am, I am in control of myself. I don't let my tasks take over my life; instead, I just lend myself to them. I don't make excuses for wasting time. And wherever I am, I think about important ideas and keep my mind focused on something good.

When I spend time with my friends, I don't stop being with myself. I don't spend time with people just because of some event or work-related duty. Instead, I spend my time with the best people, even if they lived in different places or different times. I let my thoughts reach out to them.

For example, I often think of Demetrius, who is one of the best people I know. I prefer to spend time in my thoughts with him, even though he dresses simply, rather than with people who wear fancy clothes. Why wouldn't I respect him? I've learned that he doesn't need anything. Anyone can learn to look down on material things, but no one can have everything. The quickest way to be rich is to stop wanting riches. Our friend Demetrius doesn't just act like he has given up material things—he actually lives as though he has given them away for others to own. Farewell.

Letter 63 - On grief for lost friends

I am saddened to hear that your friend Flaccus has died, but I hope you won't grieve more than is necessary. I won't insist that you shouldn't mourn at all, even though I know that's the better way. But who can be so strong and steady in spirit unless they've already risen above what life throws at them? Even a person like that will feel a sting from an event like this, but it will only be a small sting. However, we can be forgiven for crying as long as our tears don't go too far, and we manage to control them. Don't let your eyes stay dry when you've lost a friend, but don't let them overflow either. We can cry, but we shouldn't wail.

Do you think the advice I'm giving you is harsh when even the greatest Greek poet said that crying should only last one day, as in the story where even Niobe eventually thought of food? Do you want to know why people cry and mourn too much? It's because they seek proof of their loss through their tears, and they don't truly let themselves feel the sorrow but instead put on a show of it. No one mourns just for themselves. It's embarrassing how we act foolishly at the wrong times! There's even a bit of selfishness in our sorrow.

You might say, "What? Should I forget my friend?" But if your memory of him only lasts as long as your grief, it's not much of a memory. Soon enough, something will make you smile or laugh, even if it's just something small. I'm only asking you to let your sadness fade away in time, to calm even the deepest sorrow. Once you stop focusing on your own suffering, the picture of grief you've held onto will fade. Right now, you're watching over your own pain, but even while you're watching, it's slipping away, and the sharper the pain, the faster it fades.

Let's try to remember those we've lost with a smile. No one enjoys thinking about something that only brings pain. So, it's natural that when we think of the names of those we've loved and lost, it might sting a little, but there's also a strange pleasure in that sting. As my friend Attalus used to say, "Remembering lost friends is like tasting fruit that's pleasantly sour or enjoying the bitterness of very old wine. In time, the pain fades, and we're left with the sweetness."

If we listen to Attalus, he says, "Thinking of living friends is like enjoying a meal of cakes and honey. Remembering friends who have passed away brings a pleasure that's a bit bittersweet. But who can deny that even these bittersweet things can help to stir the appetite?" For me, I don't quite agree with him. To me, thinking about my dead friends is sweet and comforting. I had them knowing that one day I might lose them, and I've lost them as if I still have them.

So, Lucilius, act with the calmness you possess and stop seeing Fortune's gifts in the wrong way. Fortune has taken away, but

Fortune has also given. Let's enjoy our friends eagerly because we don't know how long we'll have them. Let's remember how often we've been apart from them on distant trips or even when we're in the same place but still don't see each other. We'll realize that we've missed too much of their time while they were alive.

But how can you stand people who don't care much for their friends while they're alive but mourn them excessively when they're gone? They don't truly love anyone until they've lost them. The reason they mourn so loudly is that they're afraid people will doubt that they really loved them. Too late, they try to prove their feelings.

If we have other friends, it's wrong to think so little of them that they don't comfort us after losing one. But if we have no other friends, we've done more harm to ourselves than Fortune has done to us; Fortune took one friend, but we've deprived ourselves of any new friends we could have made. Also, someone who can only love one person hasn't really loved even that one enough. If a man who loses his only coat to a thief spends his time complaining instead of finding a way to stay warm, wouldn't you think he was foolish?

You've lost someone you loved; now look for someone new to love. It's better to find a new friend than to keep crying over the one you lost. What I'm about to say is common, but I won't skip it just because it's often repeated: Time will end your grief even if you don't want it to. But it's shameful for a wise person to let time heal their sorrow instead of ending it themselves. I'd rather you let go of your grief than have your grief let go of you; and you should stop grieving as soon as you can, because even if you try to hold onto it, you won't be able to for long.

Our ancestors decided that women should mourn for a year, not because they needed to grieve for that long, but so that they wouldn't grieve any longer. Men, however, have no such rules because it's not considered honorable for them to mourn at all. But still, show me a woman who cried so much over a loss that she couldn't be dragged away from the funeral, and I'll show you someone whose tears didn't last a whole month. Nothing becomes annoying faster than grief; when it's fresh, people offer comfort and sympathy, but when it drags on, it becomes a joke, and rightly so. Long-lasting grief is either fake or foolish.

The one writing these words to you is none other than me, who cried so much for my dear friend Annaeus Serenus that, despite my best efforts, I became one of those who let grief overpower them. But today, I regret that, and I understand that the reason I grieved so much was that I never imagined he could die before me. I only thought about how much younger he was, as if the Fates care about the order of our ages!

So, let's always remember not just that everything is mortal, but that death follows no set rules. Whatever can happen at any time can happen today. So let's think, my dear Lucilius, that soon enough we'll reach the same place our friend has gone to, which makes us sad now. And maybe, if the wise people are right and there is a place that welcomes us after death, then the friend we think we've lost has only gone ahead to wait for us. Farewell.

Letter 64 - On the philosopher's task

Yesterday you were with us. You might be upset if I just said "yesterday," so I added "with us." For me, you are always with me in spirit. Some friends came over, and because of that, we made the fire a bit brighter—not the kind of fire that rich people have that can cause a lot of smoke and trouble, but a nice, moderate fire that shows we have guests. Our conversation moved across different topics, as usually happens at dinner; it didn't stick to one subject but jumped from one idea to another. We also read a book by Quintus Sextius the Elder.

He is an amazing person, if you trust my opinion, and truly a Stoic, even though he doesn't claim to be one. Wow, what strength and energy you find in his work! This isn't true for all philosophers; some have famous names but their writings lack energy. They make rules, argue, and split hairs, but they don't inspire because they lack spirit themselves. But when you read Sextius, you will say: "He is full of life; he is strong; he is free; he is more than just a man; he fills me with great confidence even before I finish his book."

I'll admit to you how I feel when I read his works: I want to take on every challenge; I want to shout: "Why are you making me wait, Fortune? Bring it on! I'm ready for you!" I feel like a person who is eager to find a way to test themselves, a way to show their worth, like someone who is restless among peaceful sheep and prays that a wild boar or a fierce lion will cross their path.

I want something to overcome, something to test my endurance. This is another remarkable thing about Sextius: he shows you how great a happy life can be, but he doesn't make you feel like it's out of reach; you will understand that it's high up, but that it's possible to reach it if you really want to.

Virtue itself will have the same effect on you—it will make you admire it and also hope to achieve it. For me, just thinking about wisdom takes up a lot of my time; I look at it with wonder, just like I sometimes gaze at the sky as if I'm seeing it for the first time.

This is why I admire the discoveries of wisdom and those who discovered them; it's a joy to inherit the knowledge passed down by many who came before us. They saved this treasure for us; they worked hard for our benefit. But we should act like responsible homeowners; we should add to what we have inherited. This inheritance should pass from me to those who come after me, larger than it was before.

There is still much to do, and there always will be, and someone born a thousand years from now will still have a chance to add something new. Even if the old masters have discovered everything, there will always be something new—the way we apply, study, and classify the discoveries made by others. Think about how doctors have given us treatments for eye problems; there's no need for me to look for new ones, but I do need to know how to adapt these treatments to specific diseases and stages of those diseases. Use this treatment to heal inflamed eyelids, that one to reduce swelling, this one to stop sudden pain or tears, and that one to improve vision. Then combine these different treatments, figure out the right time to use them, and apply the right treatment in each case.

The cures for the soul were also discovered by the ancient thinkers; but it's our job to learn how and when to apply them. Our predecessors made great improvements, but they didn't solve everything. They deserve our respect, and they should be honored with almost a divine reverence. Why shouldn't I keep statues of great men to inspire me and celebrate their birthdays? Why shouldn't I always show them respect and honor? The reverence I owe to my own teachers is the same respect I owe to those who have taught the human race, the source of such great blessings.

If I meet a consul or a praetor (important officials), I will pay him all the respect that his position deserves: I will get off my horse, take off my hat, and give him the right of way. So, what then? Should I welcome into my soul with any less respect Marcus Cato, the Elder and the Younger, Laelius the Wise, Socrates and Plato, Zeno and Cleanthes? I truly honor them and always rise to show my respect for such noble names. Farewell.

Letter 65 - On the first cause

Yesterday, I spent my time dealing with an illness; it took up the whole morning, but in the afternoon, I got some time back. So, I first tested my mind by reading. When I found that reading was possible, I decided to push myself further, or maybe I should say, I allowed myself to do more. I wrote a little, and I was even more focused than usual because I'm working on a difficult subject, and I don't want to be defeated by it. In the middle of this, some friends came to visit me, intending to stop me, as if I were a sick man doing too much. So, instead of writing, we talked. And from this conversation, I'll share with you the topic that we're still debating, because we've chosen you to decide who's right. You have more of a task than you might think, because the argument has three parts.

Our Stoic philosophers, as you know, say that there are two things in the universe that are the source of everything: cause and matter. Matter is inactive, just sitting there, ready to be used for anything, but it will remain unused unless someone moves it. Cause, which we also call reason, shapes matter and directs it wherever it needs to go, producing various results. So, for everything that exists, there has to be something it's made from, and there has to be something that makes it. The first is its material, and the second is its cause.

All art is just an imitation of nature; so, let me apply these general ideas to things made by people. For example, a statue needed material to work with and an artist to shape that material. So, in the case of the statue, the material was bronze, and the cause was the artist. And it's the same with everything—they consist of what they're made of and the one who makes them. The Stoics believe in only one cause— the maker. But Aristotle thinks that the word "cause" can be used in three ways: "The first cause," he says, "is the actual material, without which nothing can be made. The second is the artist. The third is the form, which is the shape given to the work—a statue, for example." Aristotle calls this form the idos.

He also says there's a fourth cause—the purpose of the work as a whole. Now I'll explain what this last cause means. Bronze is the "first cause" of the statue because it couldn't have been made without something to mold. The "second cause" is the artist, because without the skilled hands of a workman, the bronze couldn't be shaped into the statue. The "third cause" is the form, because our statue couldn't be called The Lance-Bearer or The Boy Binding his Hair without this specific shape. The "fourth cause" is the purpose of the work. If this purpose hadn't existed, the statue wouldn't have been made.

Now, what is this purpose? It's what motivated the artist, what he was aiming for when he made the statue. It might have been money if he made it to sell, or fame if he worked for recognition, or religion if he made it as a gift for a temple. So, this is also a cause that contributes to the making of the statue. Or do you think we should ignore something that, without it, the statue wouldn't have been made?

Plato adds a fifth cause—the pattern, which he calls the "idea." This is what the artist looked at when he created the work he wanted to make. It doesn't matter if this pattern was outside of him so that he could look at it, or inside his mind, created by himself. God has within Himself the patterns of all things, and His mind understands the order and structure of everything that needs to be made. He is full of these shapes, which Plato calls the "ideas"—unchanging, everlasting, and not subject to decay. So, even though men die, humanity itself, or the idea of man, according to which men are made, continues, and even though men work and perish, this idea doesn't change.

So, as Plato says, there are five causes: the material, the agent, the makeup, the model, and the goal. The last is the result of all these. Just as with the statue, to go back to the example we started with, the material is the bronze, the agent is the artist, the makeup is the form given to the material, the model is the pattern the artist copied, the goal is the purpose in the maker's mind, and finally, the result of all these is the statue itself. The universe, according to Plato, also has all these elements. The agent is God; the source is matter; the form is the shape and arrangement of the visible world. The model is the pattern God used to create this great and beautiful world. The purpose is His reason for doing it. Do you ask what God's purpose is? It is goodness. Plato says, "What was God's reason for creating the world? God is good, and no good person holds back anything that is good. So, God made it the best world possible." Now, give your opinion, O judge; say who you think is closest to the truth, not who is absolutely right. Because understanding the full truth is as far beyond us as the truth itself.

This group of causes, as described by Aristotle and Plato, either includes too much or too little. Because if they call everything a "cause" that's needed to make something, they haven't named enough. Time must also be included as a cause, because nothing can be made without time. They also need to include place, because if there's no place where something can be made, it won't be made. And motion too; nothing is made or destroyed without motion. There is no art without motion, no change of any kind.

Now, I'm searching for the first, the general cause; this must be simple, just as matter is simple. Do we ask what cause is? It's surely Creative Reason—in other words, God. Because those elements you mentioned are not a great number of independent causes; they all depend on one alone, and that's the creative cause. Do you think that form is a cause? That's just what the artist impresses on his work; it's part of a cause, but not the cause. Neither is the pattern a cause, but it's a necessary tool for the cause. The pattern is as necessary to the artist as the chisel or the file; without these, art can't move forward. But even so, these things are neither parts of the art nor causes of it.

Then, you might say, "The purpose of the artist, the reason he decided to create something, is the cause." It may be a cause, but it's not the main cause, just an additional one. But there are countless additional causes; what we're discussing is the general cause. Now, what Plato and Aristotle said doesn't match their usual deep thinking when they say that the whole universe, this perfectly crafted work, is a cause. Because there's a big difference between a work and the cause of a work.

Either give your opinion, or, as is easier in these kinds of cases, say that the matter isn't clear and ask for another discussion. But you might ask: "What pleasure do you get from spending your time on these problems that don't take away any of your emotions or stop any of your desires?" As for me, I treat and discuss these things because I believe they help calm the mind, and I search myself first, and then the world around me. And even now, as you might think, I'm not wasting my time. Because all these questions, as long as they aren't overcomplicated and broken down into useless details, lift and lighten the soul, which is weighed down by a heavy burden and wants to be free and return to the elements it was once a part of. Because this body of ours is a weight on the soul and its punishment. As the load presses down, the soul is crushed and enslaved unless philosophy comes to help it and encourages it by thinking about the universe, turning it from earthly things to divine things. There, the soul finds its freedom; there, it can wander freely; in the meantime, it escapes the prison where it's kept and renews its life in heaven.

Just like skilled workers who have been focused on delicate work that tires their eyes if the light they have is poor or uncertain, they go outside into the open air and enjoy the bright light of day in a park. In the same way, the soul, trapped in this gloomy and dark body, seeks the open sky whenever it can, and finds rest in thinking about the universe.

The wise person, the one seeking wisdom, is closely connected to their body, but in their better self, they are absent, concentrating on higher things. Bound, so to speak, by an oath of loyalty, they see life as their term of service. They are trained not to love or hate life; they endure the mortal condition, knowing that a greater fate awaits them.

Do you forbid me from thinking about the universe? Do you force me to pull away from the whole and focus only on a part? Can't I ask what the beginnings of all things are, who shaped the universe, who took the chaotic and mixed-up mass of inactive matter and separated it into its parts? Can't I inquire who is the Master-Builder of this universe, how the huge mass was brought under control by law and order, who gathered the scattered atoms, who separated the chaotic elements and gave form to what was once a shapeless mass? Or where did all the light come from? And is it fire, or something even brighter than fire?

Can't I ask these questions? Do I have to stay ignorant of the heights I came from? Will I see this world only once, or will I be born many times? What happens to me afterward? Where will my soul go when it's freed from the laws of slavery among humans? Do you forbid me to take part in the heavens? In other words, do you tell me to live with my head bowed down?

No, I am above such a life; I was born for a greater destiny than to be just a slave to my body, and I see this body as nothing more than a chain that holds back my freedom. So, I offer it as a kind of shield to protect me from fortune, and I won't let any wound reach my soul. Because my body is the only part of me that can be hurt. In this house, which is open to danger, my soul lives free. My body will never make me feel fear, or force me to pretend to be something that's not worthy of a good person. I will never lie to honor this small body. When the time seems right, I will break my connection with it. And for now, while we're still together, our alliance will not be equal; the soul will bring all disputes before its own court. To despise our bodies is true freedom.

To go back to our main topic; this freedom will be greatly helped by the kind of thinking we were just discussing. All things are made up of matter and of God. God controls matter, which surrounds Him and follows Him as its guide and leader. And that which creates, in other words, God, is more powerful and valuable than matter, which is acted upon by God.

God's role in the universe is like the soul's role in a person. World-matter is like our mortal body; so, the lower should serve the higher. Let us be brave in the face of dangers. Let us not fear wrongs, or wounds, or chains, or poverty. And what is death? It is either the end or a process of change. I don't fear ceasing to exist; it's the same as not having begun. Nor do I fear changing into another state, because under no circumstances will I be as restricted as I am now. Farewell.

Letter 66 - On various aspects of virtue

I recently saw my old school friend Claranus for the first time in many years. You don't need me to tell you that he is an old man, but I assure you that I found him strong in spirit and determined, even though his body is weak and frail. It seems unfair that Nature gave him a weak body to house such a remarkable soul, or maybe it was to show us that a truly strong and happy mind can exist in any body. Either way, Claranus overcomes all these obstacles, and by disregarding his own body, he has reached a point where he can disregard other things as well.

The poet who said, "Virtue looks better in a beautiful form," in my opinion, is mistaken. Virtue doesn't need anything to make it shine; it is its own great glory, and it makes the body it inhabits special. I've begun to see Claranus in a different light; he seems handsome to me, and his body is as strong as his mind. A great person can come from a humble background, just as a beautiful and great soul can come from an ugly and insignificant body. For this reason, Nature seems to produce certain people like Claranus to prove that virtue can be born anywhere. If it were possible for Nature to create souls by themselves, without bodies, she would have done so. But instead, she does something even greater by producing people who, despite their weak bodies, break through the limitations.

I believe Claranus was created as an example to show us that the soul is not made ugly by an unattractive body, but rather, the body is made beautiful by the goodness of the soul.

Although Claranus and I have only spent a few days together, we've had many deep conversations, which I'll share with you now. On the first day, we explored this problem: how can good things be equal if they come in three kinds? According to our philosophical beliefs, some goods are primary, like joy, peace, and the well-being of one's country. Others are of the second order, formed from difficult experiences, like enduring suffering and showing self-control during serious illness. We pray for the goods of the first kind outright, but for the second kind, we pray only if the need arises. There is also a third type, like having a modest walk, a calm and honest face, and a demeanor that suits a wise person.

Now, how can these things be equal when compared, if we believe we should pray for one kind and avoid the other? If we make distinctions among them, we should go back to the First Good and consider what it truly is: it's the soul that understands truth, that knows what to seek and what to avoid, setting standards based on nature, not opinion. This soul sees the whole world and looks carefully at all its aspects, focusing equally on thoughts and actions, remaining great and strong, rising above hardships and pleasures, not letting either good fortune or bad fortune affect it. This soul is absolutely beautiful, perfectly balanced with grace and strength, healthy and resilient, calm and fearless, unbroken by violence, and unmoved by chance. A soul like this is virtue itself.

There you have its appearance, if it could ever be seen all at once in its complete form. But there are many aspects of it. These aspects unfold as life changes and as actions differ, but virtue itself does not become smaller or greater. The Supreme Good cannot decrease, nor can virtue go backward; rather, it transforms, taking on different qualities as needed, shaping itself according to the role it needs to play.

Whatever virtue touches, it makes similar to itself and colors with its own character. It enhances our actions, our friendships, and sometimes even whole households that it enters and puts in order. Whatever virtue handles, it immediately makes lovable, notable, and admirable.

Therefore, the power and greatness of virtue cannot rise any higher because nothing can be added to something that is already as great as it can be. You will find nothing straighter than the straight, nothing truer than the truth, and nothing more moderate than that which is moderate. Every virtue is limitless; limits depend on specific measurements. Steadfastness cannot be improved, just as fidelity, truthfulness, or loyalty cannot be improved. What can be added to something that is perfect? Nothing else can be added to something perfect, because if something is added, it wasn't perfect to begin with. Nor can anything be added to virtue, because if something can be added to it, it must have had a flaw. Honor also allows no addition, for it is honorable because of the qualities I've mentioned.

What then? Do you think that propriety, justice, and lawfulness don't also belong to the same category and are not kept within fixed limits? The ability to increase is proof that something is still imperfect.

The good, in every instance, is subject to these same laws. The well-being of the state and the individual are connected; it is as impossible to separate them as it is to separate what is commendable from what is desirable. Therefore, virtues are mutually equal, and so are the works of virtue and all men who are fortunate enough to possess these virtues.

But since the virtues of plants and animals are perishable, they are also fragile, fleeting, and uncertain. They come and go, and for this reason, they are not valued the same way. But human virtues are governed by one rule alone. Right reason is single and of one kind. Nothing is more divine than the divine, or more heavenly than the heavenly.

Mortal things decay, fall, wear out, grow, exhaust, and replenish. So, in their case, because of their uncertain nature, there is inequality. But things divine have a single nature. Reason, however, is nothing else but a part of the divine spirit placed in a human body. If reason is divine, and the good never lacks reason, then the good in every case is divine. And furthermore, there is no distinction between things divine, so there is none between goods either.

Therefore, it follows that joy and a brave endurance of torture are equal goods, for both involve the same greatness of soul—relaxed and cheerful in one case, combative and ready for action in the other. What? Do you not think that the virtue of someone who bravely storms the enemy's stronghold is equal to that of someone who endures a siege with the utmost patience? Scipio is great when he surrounds Numantia and forces the hands of an enemy he cannot defeat to destroy themselves. But the souls of the defenders are also great—men who know that as long as the path to death is open, the blockade is not complete, and who die in the arms of freedom.

In the same way, other virtues are also equal when compared with each other: tranquility, simplicity, generosity, constancy, equanimity, and endurance. For underneath them all is a single virtue—the one that keeps the soul straight and steady.

"What then," you might ask, "is there no difference between joy and enduring pain?" None at all when it comes to the virtues themselves; however, there is a great difference in the situations where these virtues are displayed. In one case, there is a natural relaxation and loosening of the soul; in the other, there is unnatural pain. So, while there is a great difference in these situations, which belong to the category of indifferent things, the virtue shown in each case is equal.

Virtue is not changed by the difficulty of the situation it deals with; if the situation is hard and stubborn, it doesn't make the virtue worse; if pleasant and joyous, it doesn't make it better. Therefore, virtue necessarily remains equal. In each case, what is done is done with equal uprightness, with equal wisdom, and with equal honor. So, the states of goodness involved are equal, and it is impossible for a person to be better in these states of goodness, whether in joy or suffering. And two goods, neither of which can be better, are equal.

For if things outside of virtue can either diminish or increase virtue, then what is honorable ceases to be the only good. If you grant this, honor has completely disappeared. And why? Let me tell you: it's because no act is honorable if it's done unwillingly or under compulsion. Every honorable act is voluntary. If you mix reluctance, complaints, cowardice, or fear into it, it loses its best quality—self-approval. That which is not free cannot be honorable, for fear means slavery.

The honorable is completely free from anxiety and is calm. If it ever objects, complains, or considers anything evil, it becomes disturbed and begins to flounder in confusion. For on one side, the appearance of what is right calls to it, while on the other side, the suspicion of evil pulls it back. Therefore, when a person is about to do something honorable, they should not consider any obstacles as evil, even if they see them as inconvenient. They should choose to do the deed willingly. For every honorable act is done without commands or compulsion; it is pure and has no mixture of evil.

I know what you might say in response: "Are you trying to convince us that it doesn't matter whether a person feels joy or is lying on the rack being tortured?" I might answer: "Epicurus also says that the wise man, even when being tortured, will say, 'This is pleasant and doesn't concern me at all.'" Why should you be surprised if I say that the person enjoying a banquet and the one enduring torture possess equal goods when Epicurus claims something even harder to believe, namely, that it's pleasant to be tortured?

But my actual response is that there is a great difference between joy and pain. If I'm asked to choose, I will seek the former and avoid the latter. The former is in line with nature, the latter is against it. As long as we judge them by this standard, there is a great difference between them. But when it comes to the virtue involved, the virtue in each case is the same, whether it comes through joy or through suffering.

Vexation, pain, and other inconveniences don't matter because they are overcome by virtue. Just as the brightness of the sun outshines all lesser lights, so virtue, by its own greatness, overpowers all pains, annoyances, and wrongs. Wherever its radiance reaches, all other lights, which shine without the help of virtue, are extinguished, and inconveniences, when they come in contact with virtue, are no more important than a storm cloud at sea.

This can be proven by the fact that a good person will hasten unhesitatingly to any noble deed; even if confronted by executioners, torturers, and the stake, they will persist, focusing not on what they must suffer but on what they must do. They will trust themselves to an honorable deed as readily as they would trust themselves to a good person. They will consider it beneficial, safe, and favorable. And they will have the same attitude toward an honorable deed, even if it involves sorrow and hardship, as they would toward a good person who is poor or suffering in exile.

Now, compare a good person who is wealthy with one who has nothing but who has everything within himself. They will be equally good, even though they experience different fortunes. This same standard applies to things as well as to people. Virtue is just as praiseworthy if it exists in a healthy and free body as in one that is sickly or in bondage.

Therefore, regarding your own virtue, you will not praise it more if fortune has favored you with a healthy body than if fortune has given you a body with a physical disability. Doing so would be like rating a master lower because he is dressed like a slave. For all those things over which chance holds power—money, appearance, position—are weak, unstable, prone to perish, and of uncertain possession. On the other hand, the works of virtue are free and unrestrained, neither more worthy to be sought when fortune treats them kindly nor less worthy when any adversity weighs upon them.

Now, friendship among people corresponds to desirability in things. You wouldn't love a good person more if they were rich than if they were poor, nor would you love someone who is strong and muscular more than someone who is slender and delicate. So, you won't seek or love a good thing that is joyful and peaceful more than one that is full of challenges and hard work.

If you do, you might as well care more for a good person who is neat and well-groomed than for one who is dirty and unkempt, and you would care more for someone who has long, curly hair than for someone who is bald, even if both are equally just and wise. Whenever the virtue in each person is equal, any inequality in their other attributes is not noticeable. For all other things are not parts of the person but mere accessories.

Would any father judge his children so unfairly as to care more for a healthy son than for a sickly one, or for a tall child more than one who is short or of average height? Wild animals don't show favoritism among their offspring; they lie down to nurse them all equally. Birds divide their food fairly among their young. Ulysses hurried back to the rocky shores of Ithaca just as eagerly as Agamemnon hurried to the royal walls of Mycenae. No one loves their homeland because it is great; they love it because it is theirs.

And what is the point of all this? It's to show you that virtue values all her works equally, as if they were her children, showing the same kindness to all and even more care to those that face hardships. Just as parents often show more affection to the children they pity, virtue, too, may not necessarily love her works more when they are in trouble and under heavy burdens, but like good parents, she gives them more of her attention.

Why is no good greater than any other good? It's because nothing can be more fitting than what is fitting, and nothing can be more level than what is level. You can't say that one thing is more equal to another; similarly, nothing is more honorable than what is honorable.

So, if all virtues are by nature equal, then the three types of goods are also equal. This means that there is an equality between feeling joy with self-control and enduring pain with self-control. The joy in one case does not surpass the steadfastness of soul in the other case when the victim remains strong even while being tortured. Goods of the first kind are desirable, while those of the second kind are admirable. And in both cases, they are equal because any inconvenience in the latter is balanced by the greatness of the good.

Anyone who believes they are unequal is focusing on external appearances and not on the virtues themselves. True goods have the same weight and importance. The false ones, on the other hand, are full of emptiness. So, when they are weighed, they fall short, even though they may look impressive on the surface.

Yes, my dear Lucilius, the good that true reason approves is solid and lasting. It strengthens and uplifts the spirit so that it will always stay on the heights. But those things that are carelessly praised as goods by the masses only fill us with empty joy. And those things that are feared as evils only make people anxious because they are disturbed by the appearance of danger, just like animals are. So, it is without reason that both these things—pleasures and pains—trouble and sting the spirit. One is not worthy of joy, and the other is not worthy of fear.

It is reason alone that remains unchanged and firm in its decisions because reason is not a servant to the senses but a ruler over them. Reason is equal to reason, just as one straight line is equal to another; therefore, virtue is also equal to virtue. Virtue is nothing else but right reason. All virtues are based on reason. Reasons are equal if they are right reasons. If they are right, they are also equal.

As reason is, so also are actions; therefore, all actions are equal. Since they are based on reason, they also resemble each other. Moreover, I believe that actions are equal to each other in so far as they are honorable and right actions. Of course, there will be significant differences depending on the situation—some actions are broader, others narrower; some are glorious, others lowly; some have wide-ranging effects, others are limited. However, the best part of all these actions is equal: they are all honorable.

In the same way, all good people are equal in so far as they are good. There are differences in age—one person may be older, another younger; in appearance—one may be handsome, another unattractive; in fortune—one may be rich, another poor, one may be influential and well-known, while another is unknown and obscure. But all are equal in what makes them good.

The senses do not decide what is good and evil; they do not know what is useful and what is not. They can only judge what is in front of them; they cannot see into the future or remember the past, and they do not understand cause and effect. But it is from such knowledge that a sequence of actions is created, leading to a unified life—a life that will follow a straight path.

Reason, therefore, is the judge of good and evil; it considers anything foreign and external to be unimportant and regards what is neither good nor evil as merely secondary, insignificant, and trivial. All its good is found in the soul.

But there are certain goods that reason considers primary and directly pursues, like victory, good children, and the welfare of one's country. Other goods are secondary and only become apparent in adversity, like showing calmness in severe illness or exile. Some goods are indifferent; these are neither in line with nature nor against it, like having a calm and composed walk or sitting in a dignified manner. Sitting is no less natural than standing or walking.

The two higher kinds of goods are different. The primary ones are in line with nature, like the joy that comes from the dutiful behavior of one's children or the well-being of one's country. The secondary ones are against nature, like the strength to resist torture or endure thirst during illness.

"What then," you might ask, "can something against nature be a good?" Of course not. But the situation in which this good arises is sometimes against nature. For example, being wounded, wasting away in a fire, or suffering from poor health are against nature, but it is in line with nature for a person to maintain an unyielding soul in these situations.

To put it simply, the situation in which a good occurs may be against nature, but the good itself never is, because no good lacks reason, and reason is in line with nature.

"What then," you ask, "is reason?" It is following nature's example. "And what," you ask, "is the greatest good that a person can possess?" It is to live according to what nature intends.

"There's no doubt," the skeptic says, "that peace is more enjoyable when it hasn't been disturbed than when it has been restored after a great battle." "There's also no doubt," they continue, "that health is more enjoyable when it hasn't been harmed than when it's been restored through great effort and after suffering serious illnesses that threatened life itself. Similarly, there will be no doubt that joy is a greater good than enduring the torments of wounds or being burned at the stake."

Not at all. Things that result from chance allow for wide differences because they are valued based on their usefulness to those who experience them. But when it comes to goods, the only thing to consider is that they are in line with nature, and this is true for all goods. In a Senate meeting, when we vote in favor of someone's motion, it cannot be said that one person agrees with the motion more than another. Everyone votes for the same motion. The same is true for virtues—they are all in line with nature. The same is true for goods—they are all in line with nature.

One person dies young, another in old age, and another in infancy, having experienced nothing more than a brief glimpse of life. They have all been equally subject to death, even though one was allowed to live longer, another was cut off in their prime, and the third had their life ended just as it began.

Some people die peacefully at the dinner table. Others pass from sleep into the sleep of death. Some die in the midst of excess. Now compare these with those who have been killed by the sword, bitten to death by snakes, crushed by falling buildings, or tortured to death by the twisting of their muscles. Some of these deaths may seem better or worse, but the act of dying is the same in all cases. The methods of dying differ, but the end is the same. Death has no degrees of more or less; it has the same finality in all cases—the end of life.

The same is true for goods; you will find one in a situation of pure pleasure, another in sorrow and bitterness. One controls fortune's favors; the other overcomes her attacks. Each is equally good, even though one walks a smooth and easy path, while the other travels a rough road. But the end of both is the same: they are goods, they are worthy of praise, and they accompany virtue and reason. Virtue makes all things it acknowledges equal to one another.

Don't be surprised that this is one of our principles; even Epicurus mentions two goods in his teachings, which together make up his Supreme Good, or blessedness: a body free from pain and a soul free from disturbance. These goods, when complete, do not increase, because how can something that is complete increase? If the body is free from pain, what can be added to this absence of pain? If the soul is composed and calm, what can be added to this tranquility?

Just as perfectly clear weather cannot become clearer, so when a person takes care of both their body and soul, weaving their good from both, their condition is perfect, and they have achieved their highest goal if there is no commotion in their soul or pain in their body. Whatever additional pleasures they experience do not increase their Supreme Good; they simply enhance it, adding spice to it. The ultimate good for human nature is satisfied with peace in the body and peace in the soul.

I can show you right now in the writings of Epicurus a list of goods very similar to those of our own school. He states that there are some things he prefers to have, like bodily rest free from all discomfort and a soul that delights in contemplating its own goods. And there are other things, which he would prefer not to experience but still praises and approves of, like the kind of resilience in times of illness and severe suffering that I mentioned earlier, which Epicurus himself displayed on the last and most blessed day of his life. He tells us that he endured excruciating pain from a diseased bladder and an ulcerated stomach—so severe that it could not become any worse. "And yet," he says, "that day was still happy." And no one can spend such a day in happiness unless they possess the Supreme Good.

So, even Epicurus mentions goods that one would prefer not to experience, but which, because circumstances demand it, must be embraced and valued as equal to the greatest goods. We cannot say that the good which completed a happy life, the good for which Epicurus gave thanks in his final words, is not equal to the greatest.

Allow me, excellent Lucilius, to say something even bolder: if any goods could be greater than others, I would prefer those that seem harsh to those that are mild and pleasing, and I would consider them greater. It is a greater achievement to overcome difficulties than to keep joy within bounds.

It requires the same use of reason, I fully understand, for a person to handle prosperity well and to endure misfortune bravely. A person may be just as brave who sleeps outside the camp walls without fear when no enemy is attacking as the one who, with his legs' tendons severed, holds himself up on his knees and does not drop his weapons. But it is to the blood-stained soldier returning from the battlefield that people cry, "Well done, hero!" And so I would give greater praise to those goods that have been tested, shown courage, and fought against fortune.

Should I hesitate to give greater praise to the maimed and shriveled hand of Mucius than to the uninjured hand of the bravest person in the world? There stood Mucius, disregarding the enemy and the fire, watching his hand as it dripped blood over the fire on his enemy's altar until Porsenna, envious of the hero's fame, ordered the fire to be removed, despite the victim's will.

Why shouldn't I consider this good among the primary goods and deem it greater than those other goods that come without danger and have not been tested by fortune, just as it is a rarer thing to overcome an enemy with a lost hand than with an armed one? "What then," you ask, "would you desire this good for yourself?" Of course, I would. Because this is something a person cannot achieve unless they also desire it.

Should I instead desire to stretch out my limbs for my slaves to massage or to have someone, whether a woman or a man transformed into the likeness of a woman, pull my fingers? I can't help but think that Mucius was all the luckier because he handled the flames as calmly as if he were holding out his hand to a masseur. He erased all his previous mistakes; he ended the war unarmed and maimed, and with that stump of a hand, he conquered two kings. Farewell.

Letter 67 - On ill-health and endurance of suffering

If I may start with a common saying, spring is slowly revealing itself. But even though it's heading toward summer, when you'd expect warmer weather, it has stayed rather cool, and you still can't be sure if it will stay that way. Often, it slides back into winter weather. Do you want to know how unpredictable it still is? I'm not yet ready to take a completely cold bath; even now, I warm it up a bit. You might say that this doesn't show much endurance for either heat or cold. You're right, dear Lucilius, but at my age, I'm content with the natural chill of my body. I can hardly warm up even in the middle of summer. So, I spend most of the time bundled up, and I thank old age for keeping me close to my bed. Why shouldn't I thank old age for this? I no longer have the ability to do things I shouldn't wish to do. Most of my time is spent with books. Whenever your letters arrive, I imagine that I'm with you, and I feel like I'm speaking my response rather than writing it. So, let's explore your problem together, just as if we were talking face to face.

You ask me whether every good thing is worth wanting. You say, "If it's good to be brave under torture, to face death with courage, and to endure illness with patience, then these things must be worth wanting. But I don't see that anyone would pray for these things. I've never heard of anyone making a vow after being beaten, twisted by gout, or stretched on the rack." My dear Lucilius, you need to make a distinction in these cases; then you'll see that there is something worth wanting in them. I would prefer not to face torture, but if it must happen, I would want to face it with bravery, honor, and courage. Of course, I'd rather avoid war, but if war comes, I'd want to endure the wounds, starvation, and everything else it brings with nobility. I'm not so foolish as to wish for illness, but if I must suffer through it, I'd want to behave with self-control and dignity. The point is not that hardships are desirable, but that the virtue which allows us to endure them is desirable.

Some of our school believe that, of all these qualities, strong endurance isn't something to be desired—though it shouldn't be rejected either—because we should only pray for things that are purely good, peaceful, and free from trouble. Personally, I don't agree with them. And why? First, because it's impossible for something to be good without also being desirable. Secondly, because if virtue is desirable, and if nothing good lacks virtue, then everything good must be desirable. And finally, because enduring hardships bravely, even under torture, is desirable.

Now, I ask you: Isn't bravery desirable? Yet bravery means facing and even challenging danger. The most admirable part of bravery is that it doesn't shy away from the stake, faces wounds head-on, and sometimes even meets the spear with an opposing chest. If bravery is desirable, then so is patiently enduring torture because it's a part of bravery. You just need to examine these things closely, as I've suggested; then there will be nothing to mislead you. It's not just enduring torture that's desirable, but enduring it bravely. That's why I desire "brave" endurance, and that's virtue.

"But," you might say, "who would ever wish for something like that for themselves?" Some prayers are direct, where the requests are made specifically, while others are indirect, where many requests are included under one title. For example, I wish for a life of honor. Now, a life of honor includes various kinds of actions; it might include the chest in which Regulus was confined, or the wound Cato inflicted on himself, or the exile of Rutilius, or the cup of poison that sent Socrates from prison to heaven. So, in wishing for a life of honor, I've also wished for those things without which, in some cases, life can't be honorable.

"Often praised and blessed are those who died under Troy's towering walls, meeting a noble death before their parents' eyes!" What difference does it make whether you wish this for someone specific or admit that it was desirable in the past? Decius sacrificed himself for the State; he spurred his horse and charged into the enemy, seeking death. The second Decius, matching his father's bravery, repeated the words that had already become sacred, rushed into the thick of the fight, caring only that his sacrifice would bring victory, and saw a noble death as something to be desired. Do you still doubt whether it's best to die gloriously while performing a brave act?

When someone endures torture bravely, they are using all the virtues. Endurance might be the most visible virtue in such a situation, but bravery is there too, along with patience, and long-suffering. Foresight is also present because no plan can be made without it; foresight advises us to bear what we cannot avoid as bravely as possible. Steadfastness is there too, which cannot be shaken from its purpose by any force. The whole group of virtues is present together; every honorable act is the work of one virtue, but it's supported by the judgment of all the virtues. And anything approved by all the virtues, even if it seems to be the work of just one, is desirable.

What? Do you think only those things are desirable which come to us with pleasure and ease, which we decorate our homes to welcome? There are some goods whose appearances are harsh. There are some prayers offered by people who aren't joyful but are humble and worshipful. Don't you think Regulus prayed like this as he made his way to Carthage? Put on a hero's courage and step away for a moment from the opinions of ordinary people. Imagine virtue as it truly is—a thing of incredible beauty and greatness; this image isn't something to be worshipped with incense or flowers, but with sweat and blood.

Look at Marcus Cato, placing his clean hands on his wounded chest and tearing apart the wounds that hadn't gone deep enough to kill him! What should you say to him? "I hope everything goes well" or "Good luck with your mission"?

In this connection, I think of our friend Demetrius, who calls an easy life, free from Fortune's attacks, a "Dead Sea." If you have nothing to stir you up and make you act, nothing that tests your resolve with threats and dangers; if you live in constant comfort, it's not true peace; it's just a calm that leads nowhere. The Stoic Attalus used to say: "I'd rather have Fortune keep me in her camp than in the lap of luxury. If I'm tortured but bear it bravely, all is well; if I die but die bravely, that is also well." Listen to Epicurus; he'll tell you that it's actually pleasant. I, however, will never use a soft word for something so honorable and tough. If I go to the stake, I'll go undefeated.

Why shouldn't I see this as desirable—not because the fire burns me, but because it doesn't overcome me? Nothing is more excellent or more beautiful than virtue; whatever we do under its guidance is both good and desirable. Farewell.

Letter 68 - On wisdom and retirement

I agree with your plan; withdraw and find peace in rest. But also keep your withdrawal a secret. By doing this, you can be sure that you are following the Stoics' example, even if not their exact teachings. But you will also be following their teachings; this way, you will satisfy both yourself and any Stoic you encounter.

We Stoics do not push everyone to take part in public life in every situation, or at all times, or without any exceptions. Also, when we give our wise person a role in public life, we mean the entire universe, not just a small part of it. So, even if the wise person withdraws from public life, they are not truly apart from it. In fact, they may have only left a small corner of the world and moved on to larger and wider areas. And when they are in the heavens, they understand how lowly the place was where they once sat, even if it was in a high position like a magistrate's chair. Remember this: the wise person is never more involved in life than when they can see both divine and human matters.

Now, I return to the advice I wanted to give you: keep your withdrawal in the background. You don't need to hang a sign on yourself that says, "Philosopher and Recluse." Call your withdrawal something else; say it is due to poor health, physical weakness, or just laziness. To brag about our withdrawal is simply seeking attention.

Some animals hide themselves by confusing their tracks near their homes. You should do the same. Otherwise, someone will always be following your tracks. Many people overlook what is visible and instead look for things that are hidden; a locked room invites a thief. Things that are out in the open seem cheap; the burglar ignores what is in plain sight. This is how the world works, and how all ignorant people think: they want to uncover hidden things. So, it's best not to brag about your withdrawal. However, it is also a kind of bragging to make too much of your hiding and withdrawal from the public eye.

Someone might say, "So-and-so has gone into hiding in Tarentum," or "Another man has locked himself up in Naples," or "This third person hasn't stepped outside his house in years." To announce your withdrawal is to attract a crowd.

When you withdraw from the world, your goal should be to talk to yourself, not to have others talk about you. But what should you talk about? Do what people usually do when they gossip about their neighbors—criticize yourself when you're alone; then you will get used to both speaking and hearing the truth. Above all, think about what you believe is your greatest weakness. Everyone knows their own body's flaws best. So, one person might ease their stomach by vomiting, another by eating often, and another by fasting regularly. Those whose feet hurt might avoid wine or baths. In general, people who are careless in other ways will go out of their way to treat the illness that frequently bothers them. It's the same with our souls; there are certain parts of us that are, so to speak, always sick, and those parts need the cure.

So, what am I doing with my free time? I'm trying to heal my own wounds. If I showed you a swollen foot, an inflamed hand, or some shriveled muscles in a withered leg, you would let me stay in one place and apply medicine to the affected part. But my problem is greater than any of these, and I can't show it to you. The abscess or ulcer is deep within my chest. Please, please, don't praise me or say, "What a great man! He has learned to despise everything and has escaped the madness of life!" I have condemned nothing except myself.

There's no reason why you should want to come to me to make progress. You're wrong if you think you'll get any help here; there's no doctor here, only a sick man. I'd rather have you leave saying, "I used to think he was a happy and wise man, and I was eager to hear him; but I was disappointed. I saw nothing and heard nothing that I wanted or came to hear." If you feel and speak this way, some progress has been made. I'd rather you forgive than envy my withdrawal.

Then you ask, "Seneca, are you really recommending withdrawal? Will you soon be quoting the teachings of Epicurus?" Yes, I do recommend withdrawal to you, but only so you can use it for better and more meaningful activities than those you've left behind. Knocking on the doors of the powerful, making lists of childless old men, or holding the highest offices in public life—these kinds of power make you hated, are short-lived, and, if you see them for what they are, are cheap. One person may be far ahead of me in public influence, another in their military salary and the position that comes with it, and another in the number of clients they have. But it's worth being outdone by all these people if I can outdo Fortune. And I can't compete with her in the crowd; she has more support.

I wish you had decided to follow this path earlier! I wish we weren't discussing the happy life while staring death in the face! But even now, let's not delay. Now we can rely on experience, which tells us that many things are unnecessary and harmful. For this, we should have listened to reason long ago.

Let's do what people do when they're late and want to make up for lost time—they speed up. Our stage of life is the best for these pursuits because the time of intense emotions has passed. The flaws that were uncontrolled in our youth are now weaker, and only a little more effort is needed to eliminate them.

You might ask, "When will it benefit you if you only learn this at the end of your life, and how will it benefit you?" It will benefit me by allowing me to die a better person. But don't think that any time in life is better suited to gaining wisdom than the time when you've overcome yourself through many trials, through long and repeated regret for past mistakes, and when your passions have calmed, and you've achieved a state of health. This is indeed the time to acquire this good; whoever has gained wisdom in old age has earned it through their years. Farewell.

Letter 69 - On rest and restlessness

I don't like it when you keep changing where you stay and moving from one place to another. My first reason is that such frequent moving shows an unsteady mind. And the mind cannot grow into unity through retreat unless it has stopped being curious and wandering. To control your mind, you must first stop the restless movement of your body.

My second reason is that the remedies that work best are those that are not interrupted. You should not let your peace or the forgetting of your former life be disturbed. Give your eyes time to forget what they have seen, and your ears time to get used to hearing healthier words. Whenever you move from one place to another, you will encounter things that will bring back your old desires.

Just as someone trying to get rid of an old love must avoid everything that reminds them of the person they once loved (because nothing grows back as easily as love), in the same way, someone who wants to give up all the things they used to crave so strongly must turn away both their eyes and ears from the things they have abandoned. Emotions quickly come back to challenge you; at every turn, they will notice something that catches their attention.

There is no temptation that does not offer some kind of reward. Greed promises money; luxury promises a variety of pleasures; ambition promises a purple robe, applause, and the power that comes from applause, and all that power can do. Vices tempt you with the rewards they offer, but in the life I am talking about, you must live without expecting to be rewarded. A whole lifetime may hardly be enough to bring our vices under control and to make them accept discipline, especially since they have been strengthened by long-term indulgence. And it is even harder if we shorten our brief time by any interruptions. Even constant effort and attention can hardly bring any one task to full completion.

If you listen to my advice, think about and practice this: how to welcome death, or even, if the situation calls for it, to invite it. It does not matter whether death comes to us or we go to death. Make yourself believe that all ignorant people are wrong when they say, "It is a beautiful thing to die one's own death." But no one dies except on their own day. You are not wasting any of your time because what you leave behind does not belong to you. Farewell.

Letter 70 - On the proper time to slip the cable

After a long time, I have seen your beloved Pompeii again. This brought me back to the days of my youth. It seemed to me that I could still do all the things I did there when I was young, as if I had only done them a short time ago. We have sailed through life, Lucilius, as if we were on a journey, and just like when we are at sea, as our poet Vergil says, "Lands and towns are left behind." In the same way, on this journey where time moves so quickly, we leave behind our childhood first, then our youth, and then the period that lies between young adulthood and middle age, which borders on both. Next, we leave behind the best years of old age itself. Last of all, we begin to see the final destination of the human race.

Foolish as we are, we believe this destination to be a dangerous reef; but it is the harbor where we must someday arrive, and we can never refuse to enter it. And if a man reaches this harbor in his early years, he has no more right to complain than a sailor who has made a quick voyage. For, as you know, some sailors are tricked and held back by sluggish winds and grow weary and sick of the slow-moving calm, while others are quickly carried home by steady winds.

You may think the same thing happens to us: life has carried some men very quickly to the harbor they were destined to reach, even if they delayed along the way, while others it has troubled and worn down. As you know, we should not always cling to such a life. For merely living is not a good thing, but living well is. So the wise man will live as long as he should, not as long as he can.

He will consider in what place, with whom, and how he is to live his life, and what he is about to do. He always reflects on the quality of his life, not the quantity. As soon as there are many events in his life that trouble him and disturb his peace of mind, he sets himself free. And this privilege is his, not only when the crisis is upon him, but as soon as Fortune seems to be turning against him. Then he carefully considers whether he should or should not end his life because of it. He believes it makes no difference to him whether his death is natural or self-inflicted, whether it comes sooner or later. He does not regard it with fear, as if it were a great loss, because no man can lose very much when there is little left.

It is not a question of dying sooner or later, but of dying well or badly. And dying well means escaping the danger of living badly. That is why I consider the words of the well-known Rhodian as most cowardly. This man was thrown into a cage by his tyrant and fed there like some wild animal. And when someone advised him to end his life by starving himself, he replied, "A man may hope for anything while he has life." This may be true, but life should not be bought at any price. No matter how great or well-assured certain rewards may be, I will not strive to gain them at the cost of a shameful admission of weakness. Should I think that Fortune has all power over someone who lives, rather than realize that she has no power over someone who knows how to die?

There are times, however, when a man, even though he knows that certain death and torture await him, will refrain from hastening his own death, although he would help another do so. It is foolish to die out of fear of dying. The executioner is upon you; wait for him. Why rush to meet him? Why take on the cruel task that belongs to someone else? Do you begrudge your executioner his job, or do you just want to relieve him of it?

Socrates could have ended his life by starving himself; he could have died from hunger rather than poison. But instead, he spent thirty days in prison awaiting death, not with the idea that "anything might happen" or that "there is hope in such a long wait," but to show that he respected the laws and to make the last moments of Socrates an example for his friends. What would have been more foolish than to scorn death, and yet fear poison?

Scribonia, a woman of the old-fashioned type, was the aunt of Drusus Libo. This young man was as foolish as he was well-born, with ambitions far greater than anyone could have expected for that time or for a man like him in any time at all. When Libo was carried away sick from the senate-house in his litter, with only a small group of followers—since all his relatives had deserted him when he was no longer a criminal but a corpse—he began to consider whether he should commit suicide or wait for death. Scribonia said to him, "What pleasure do you find in doing another man's job?" But he did not follow her advice; he took his own life. And he was right, after all, because when a man is doomed to die in a few days at his enemy's command, he is really "doing another man's job" if he continues to live.

Therefore, no general rule can be made about whether, when a power beyond our control threatens us with death, we should hasten death or wait for it. There are many arguments to pull us in either direction. If one death is accompanied by torture and the other is simple and easy, why not choose the latter? Just as I will choose my ship when I am about to go on a voyage or my house when I plan to live somewhere, I will choose my death when I am about to leave life.

Moreover, just as a long-drawn-out life does not necessarily mean a better one, a long-drawn-out death necessarily means a worse one. There is no time when the soul should be treated with more care than at the moment of death. Let the soul depart in the way it feels driven to go; whether it seeks the sword, the noose, or some poison, let it proceed and break the chains of its slavery. Every man ought to make his life acceptable to others as well as himself, but his death should be for himself alone. The best kind of death is the one we prefer.

It is foolish for men to think, "One person will say that my actions were not brave enough; another will say that I was too reckless; a third will say that a different kind of death would have shown more spirit." What you should really think is, "I am considering a purpose that has nothing to do with what others say!" Your only goal should be to escape from Fortune as quickly as possible; otherwise, there will be no shortage of people who will criticize what you have done.

You can find men who claim to be wise, but still say that one should not take their own life and that it is wrong for a man to cause his own death; they say we should wait for the end that nature has planned. But those who say this do not see that they are closing off the path to freedom. The best thing that eternal law has ever given us is that it allows us only one entrance into life, but many exits.

Must I wait for the cruelty of either disease or man when I can depart through the midst of torture and shake off my troubles? This is the one reason why we cannot complain about life: it keeps no one against their will. Humanity is well off because no one is unhappy unless it is their own fault. Live, if you want; if not, you may return to where you came from.

You have often had blood drawn to relieve headaches. You have had veins cut to reduce your weight. If you want to pierce your heart, you do not need a large wound; a small cut will open the way to that great freedom, and peace of mind can be bought at the cost of a pin-prick.

What, then, makes us lazy and sluggish? None of us thinks that one day he must leave this house of life; just like old tenants are kept from moving by fondness for a particular place and by habit, even when they are mistreated.

Do you want to be free from the chains of your body? Live in it as if you were about to leave it. Keep thinking that someday you will be deprived of it; then you will be braver when the time comes to leave. But how can a man think about his own end if he desires everything without end? And yet there is nothing more important for us to consider. Our training in other things may be unnecessary. Our souls have been prepared to face poverty, but our wealth has lasted. We have armed ourselves to scorn pain, but we have been fortunate enough to have healthy bodies, and so have never had to test this virtue. We have taught ourselves to endure bravely the loss of those we love, but Fortune has preserved to us all whom we loved.

It is in this one matter only that the day will come which will require us to test our training.

You need not think that only great men have had the strength to break free from the bonds of human life; do not believe that this can only be done by someone like Cato—Cato, who with his hand forced out the spirit he had not been able to free with the sword. No, even men of the lowest rank in life have escaped to safety through a powerful impulse, and when they were not allowed to die in a way that suited them or to choose their means of death, they have grabbed whatever was at hand and turned objects that were naturally harmless into weapons of their own.

For example, there was recently a German in a training school for gladiators who was preparing for the morning exhibition; he withdrew to relieve himself, the only thing he was allowed to do in private without a guard. While doing so, he grabbed the stick of wood, tipped with a sponge, that was used for the lowest purposes and stuffed it, just as it was, down his throat; in this way, he blocked his windpipe and choked himself to death. That was truly to insult death!

Yes, indeed; it was not a very elegant or dignified way to die, but what could be more foolish than to be overly concerned about dying? What a brave man! He certainly deserved to be allowed to choose his fate! How bravely he would have wielded a sword! With what courage he would have thrown himself into the depths of the sea or down a cliff! Cut off from every option, he still found a way to give himself death and a weapon to achieve it. So you can understand that nothing but the will needs to delay death. Let each person judge the actions of this determined man as they like, as long as we all agree on this point: that the worst kind of death is better than the best kind of slavery.

Since I started with an example from humble life, I will continue with that sort. For people will hold themselves to higher standards if they see that even the most despised people can despise death. We consider the Catos, the Scipios, and the others whose names we admire as beyond our ability to imitate, but I will now show you that the virtue I speak of is found as often in the gladiators' training school as among the leaders in a civil war.

Recently, a gladiator who had been sent out to the morning exhibition was being carried in a cart along with the other prisoners; pretending to be sleepy, he let his head fall so far over that it got caught in the spokes of the wheel; then he held his body in position long enough to break his neck as the wheel turned. So he made his escape using the very cart that was taking him to his punishment.

When a man wants to break free and leave, nothing can stop him. It is an open space in which Nature guards us. When our situation allows it, we may look around for an easy way out. If you have many opportunities available to free yourself, you can choose the best one; but if a good opportunity is hard to find, take the next best, even if it is something unheard of, something new. If you do not lack the courage, you will not lack the cleverness to die.

See how even the lowest class of slave, when driven by suffering, becomes resourceful and finds a way to outsmart even the most watchful guards! A man is truly great if he has not only ordered himself to die but has also found the means to do so.

I promised you more examples from the same games.

During the second event in a mock sea battle, one of the barbarians drove a spear deep into his own throat, a spear that had been given to him to fight his enemy. "Why, oh why," he said, "have I not escaped all this torture and mockery long ago? Why should I be armed and still wait for death to come?" This act was even more remarkable because it taught people that dying is more honorable than killing.

What, then? If such a spirit can be found in desperate and dangerous men, shouldn't it also be found in those who have trained themselves to face such situations through long meditation and by using reason, which rules over everything? Reason teaches us that fate has many paths but the same end and that it does not matter at what point the inevitable begins.

Reason also advises us to die, if we can, in a way that we choose; if this is not possible, she advises us to die in the best way we can and to seize whatever means are available to do so. It is wrong to "live by robbery," but, on the other hand, it is most noble to "die by robbery." Farewell.

Letter 71

On the supreme good

You keep asking me specific questions, forgetting that a great distance separates us. However, since the value of advice depends mostly on when it is given, by the time my opinion reaches you, the opposite opinion might be better. Advice needs to fit the situation, and our circumstances are constantly changing, or rather, being swept along. So, advice should be given quickly; even that might be too late—it should "grow while we work," as the saying goes. I want to show you how to find the right method.

Whenever you want to know what should be avoided or what should be pursued, think about how it relates to the Supreme Good, the purpose of your whole life. Everything we do should align with this; no one can put their life in order unless they have already set the main goal of their life. An artist may have all the colors prepared, but they can't create a picture unless they have already decided what they want to paint. The reason we make mistakes is that we all focus on the parts of life but never on life as a whole.

The archer must know what target he is aiming at; only then can he aim and control the weapon with his skill. Our plans fail because they have no aim. When a person doesn't know what harbor they're heading for, no wind is the right wind. Chance has a big influence on our lives because we live by chance.

Sometimes, however, people don't know that they already know certain things. Just as we often search for something that is right beside us, we often forget that the Supreme Good is near us. To understand the nature of this Supreme Good, you don't need many words or long discussions; it should be pointed out directly, like showing something with your finger, not broken down into too many parts. What good is there in breaking it up into small pieces when you can simply say: the Supreme Good is that which is honorable? Besides, and this might surprise you even more, that which is honorable is the only good; all other goods are mixed with impurities and are less valuable.

If you can convince yourself of this and come to love virtue with deep devotion (mere liking is not enough), anything touched by virtue will bring you blessings and prosperity, no matter how others see it. Torture—if, while suffering, you are calmer in mind than your torturer; illness—if you do not curse Fortune or give in to the disease; in short, all the things that others see as ills will become manageable and will turn out well if you can rise above them.

Once you understand that nothing is good except what is honorable, all hardships will earn the right to be called "goods," once virtue has made them honorable. Many people think that we Stoics have expectations beyond what human life can offer, and they have a right to think so. They only consider the body. But if they look back at the soul, they will soon measure a person by the standard of God. Wake up, my dear Lucilius, and stop getting caught up in the word games of philosophers who reduce a glorious subject to mere syllables and wear down the soul by teaching fragments. Then you will become like those who discovered these teachings, instead of those who make philosophy seem difficult rather than great.

Socrates, who brought all of philosophy back to rules for living and said that the highest wisdom was knowing the difference between good and evil, said: "Follow these rules if my words mean anything to you, so that you may be happy; and let some people even think you are a fool. Let anyone who wishes insult you and wrong you; but if only virtue stays with you, you will suffer nothing. If you want to be happy, if you truly want to be a good person, let someone despise you." No one can achieve this unless they come to see all goods as equal because no good exists without that which is honorable, and that which is honorable is always equal.

You might say, "What then? Is there no difference between Cato being elected praetor and his failure to be elected? Or whether Cato was conquered or victorious in the battle of Pharsalia? And when Cato couldn't be defeated, even though his side was defeated, wasn't his goodness equal to what it would have been if he had returned victorious to his homeland and arranged peace?" Of course, it was because it is by the same virtue that bad fortune is overcome and good fortune is managed. Virtue cannot be increased or decreased; it always stays the same.

"But," you might object, "Gnaeus Pompey will lose his army; the patricians, the noblest examples of the State, and the leading men of Pompey's party, a senate under arms, will be defeated in a single battle; the ruins of that great oligarchy will be scattered all over the world; one part will fall in Egypt, another in Africa, and another in Spain! And the poor State won't even be allowed the privilege of being ruined once and for all!" Yes, all this may happen; Juba's knowledge of every part of his own kingdom might be useless to him, and the brave resolve of his people fighting for their king might be in vain; even the men of Utica, overwhelmed by their troubles, might waver in their loyalty, and the good fortune that always followed men named Scipio might abandon Scipio in Africa. But long ago, destiny decided that Cato would not come to harm.

"He was conquered despite all that!" Well, you may count this among Cato's "failures"; Cato will bear with equal strength of heart whatever prevents his victory, just as he bore the loss of his praetorship. The day he lost the election, he spent in amusement; the night he intended to die, he spent reading. He viewed the loss of his praetorship and the loss of his life in the same light; he had convinced himself that he should endure anything that might happen.

Why shouldn't he suffer, bravely and calmly, a change in the government? What is free from the risk of change? Neither the earth nor the sky nor the whole fabric of our universe, though it is controlled by the hand of God. It won't always stay in its present order; it will be thrown off course in the future. All things move according to their appointed times; they are destined to be born, to grow, and to be destroyed. The stars you see moving above us, and this seemingly immovable earth we live on, will be consumed and cease to exist. There is nothing that doesn't have its old age; the intervals at which Nature sends all these things toward the same goal are simply unequal. Whatever exists will cease to exist, and yet it won't perish but will be broken down into its elements.

To our minds, this process means perishing because we only see what is closest to us; our sluggish mind, tied to the body, doesn't reach beyond the boundaries of what we can see. If it did, the mind would face its own end and the end of its possessions with greater courage, knowing that life and death, like the whole universe around us, go in cycles, that whatever has been put together will be broken up again, that whatever has been broken up will be put together again, and that the eternal craftsmanship of God, who controls everything, is working on this task.

Therefore, the wise man will say what Marcus Cato would say after reviewing his past life: "The whole human race, both those living now and those who will live in the future, is condemned to die. Of all the cities that have ruled the world at any time, and of all that have been the splendid ornaments of empires not their own, people will someday ask where they were, and they will be swept away by various kinds of destruction; some will be ruined by wars, others will waste away from inactivity and the kind of peace that leads to laziness, or by that vice that destroys even mighty empires—luxury. All these fertile plains will be buried out of sight by a sudden flooding of the sea, or the soil, settling to lower levels, will suddenly draw them into a gaping chasm. So why should I be angry or feel sorrow if I go before the general destruction by a tiny bit of time?"

Great souls should comply with God's will and accept whatever fate the law of the universe has ordained without hesitation; for the soul at death is either sent into a better life, destined to live with the divine in greater light and calm, or else, at least, without suffering any harm, it will be mingled with nature again and return to the universe.

Therefore, Cato's honorable death was no less good than his honorable life, since virtue cannot be stretched or increased. Socrates used to say that truth and virtue were the same. Just as truth doesn't grow, neither does virtue grow; it has its proper proportions and is complete.

You need not wonder, therefore, that all goods are equal, whether they are deliberately chosen or imposed by circumstances. For if you believe that they are unequal, thinking, for example, that bravely enduring torture is among the lesser goods, you will also consider it among the evils; you will say that Socrates was unhappy in his prison, Cato was unhappy when he reopened his wounds with more courage than when he first inflicted them, and Regulus was the most ill-fated of all when he paid the price for keeping his word, even with his enemies. And yet no one, even the most cowardly person, has ever dared to hold such an opinion. Even if they deny that a man like Regulus is happy, they do not say that he is wretched.

The earlier Academics did indeed admit that a man is happy even amid such tortures, but they didn't admit that he is completely or fully happy. We cannot agree with this view; for unless a man is happy, he has not attained the Supreme Good, and the Supreme Good admits no higher degree, as long as virtue exists within this man, and adversity does not weaken his virtue, and if, even though the body is injured, the virtue remains unharmed. And it does remain unharmed because I understand virtue to be strong and elevated, so that it is stirred by anything that challenges it.

This spirit, which noble young men often show when they are deeply moved by the beauty of something honorable, making them despise all the gifts of chance, is certainly infused in us and given to us by wisdom. Wisdom will bring the conviction that there is only one good—that which is honorable; that this good can neither be shortened nor extended, any more than a carpenter's rule, used to test straight lines, can be bent. Any change in the rule means spoiling the straight line.

So, using this same idea for virtue, we shall say: Virtue is also straight and does not bend. What can be made more straight than something already rigid? Such is virtue, which judges everything, but nothing judges virtue. And if this rule, virtue, cannot be made more straight, neither can the things created by virtue be more straight in one case and less straight in another. They must necessarily match virtue, so they are equal.

"What," you ask, "do you call reclining at a banquet and enduring torture equally good?" Does this seem surprising to you? You may be even more surprised by the following—that reclining at a banquet is evil, while reclining on the rack is good if the first act is done shamefully, and the latter honorably. It's not the action itself that makes something good or bad; it's the virtue. All acts in which virtue shows itself are of the same value.

At this moment, the person who measures all men's souls by his own is probably shaking his fist at me because I believe there is an equality between the goods of someone who passes judgment honorably and someone who suffers judgment honorably, or because I believe there is an equality between the goods of someone who celebrates a triumph and someone who, unconquered in spirit, is led before the victor's chariot. These critics think that whatever they cannot do themselves is impossible; they judge virtue based on their own weaknesses.

Why are you surprised if it helps a person, and even pleases them, to be burned, wounded, killed, or imprisoned? To a person who loves luxury, a simple life is a punishment; to a lazy person, work is torture; the dandy pities the hardworking man; to the slothful, studies are painful. Similarly, we regard those things in which we are all weak as hard and unbearable, forgetting that it's a torment for many people to abstain from wine or to be forced out of bed at dawn. These actions aren't naturally difficult; it's we who are soft and weak.

We must judge great matters with greatness of soul; otherwise, what is really our fault will seem to be their fault. It's like how perfectly straight objects, when placed in water, appear to be bent or broken to the viewer. It's not only what you see that matters, but also with what eyes you see it; our souls are too dull to perceive the truth.

But give me a strong-minded young person; they will say that the one who stands unbending under the weight of adversity, who remains superior to Fortune, is more fortunate. It's no wonder that someone isn't tossed about when the weather is calm; reserve your wonder for those who are lifted up when others sink and keep their footing when others fall.

What evil is there in torture and the other things we call hardships? It seems to me that the evil is that the mind sags, bends, and collapses. But none of these things can happen to the sage; he stands tall under any burden. Nothing can defeat him; nothing that must be endured bothers him. For he doesn't complain that he has been struck by what can strike any man. He knows his own strength; he knows that he was born to carry burdens.

I do not remove the wise man from the category of man, nor do I deny him the sense of pain as though he were a rock that has no feelings. I remember that he is made up of two parts: one part is irrational—it is this part that may be bitten, burned, or hurt; the other part is rational—it is this part that holds firmly to opinions, is courageous, and unconquerable. In the latter lies the Supreme Good of man. Before this is fully achieved, the mind wavers in uncertainty; only when it is fully attained is the mind steady and unshakable.

So when someone has just begun or is on their way to the heights and is cultivating virtue, or even if they are close to the perfect good but haven't yet completed it, they will sometimes backslide, and there will be a certain slackening of mental effort. For such a person has not yet crossed the uncertain ground; they are still standing in slippery places. But the happy person, whose virtue is complete, loves themselves most of all when their bravery is tested to the utmost, and when they not only endure but welcome what everyone else fears, if it's the price they must pay to fulfill a duty that honor demands, and they much prefer to have people say of them: "How much more noble!" rather than "How much more lucky!"

And now I have reached the point that your patient waiting calls me to. You must not think that our human virtue goes beyond nature; the wise person will tremble, feel pain, and turn pale. All these are sensations of the body. So where is the place of true distress, of what is really evil? In the other part of us, no doubt, if it's the mind that these trials drag down, force to confess its servitude, and cause to regret its existence.

The wise person overcomes Fortune by their virtue, but many who claim to be wise are sometimes frightened by the most trivial threats. At this stage, it's a mistake on our part to demand the same things from the wise person and the learner. I still urge myself to do what I recommend; but my urgings are not yet followed. Even if they were, I wouldn't have these principles so ready for action or so well-trained that they would come to my aid in every crisis.

Just as wool takes up certain colors at once, while others won't absorb unless soaked and steeped in them many times, so other teachings can be applied immediately by people's minds once accepted, but this teaching, unless it has gone deep and has sunk in for a long time, and has not just colored but thoroughly penetrated the soul, won't fulfill any of its promises.

The matter can be conveyed quickly and in very few words: "Virtue is the only good; there is no good without virtue; and virtue itself resides in our nobler part, that is, the rational part." And what will this virtue be? A true and unwavering judgment. From this will spring all mental impulses, and by its guidance, every external appearance that stirs our impulses will be clarified.

It will be in line with this judgment to see all things touched by virtue as good and as equally good. Bodily goods are, to be sure, good for the body, but they are not absolutely good. They will indeed have some value, but they will not possess true merit, for they will vary greatly; some will be less, others greater.

We must admit that there are great differences even among the followers of wisdom. One person has already made so much progress that they dare to raise their eyes and look Fortune in the face, but not consistently, for their eyes soon drop, dazzled by her overwhelming brightness; another has made so much progress that they can match glances with her—unless they have already reached the summit and are full of confidence.

That which is short of perfection must necessarily be unsteady, at times progressing, at other times slipping or weakening; and it will surely slip back unless it keeps pushing forward because if a person slackens even a little in effort and commitment, they must fall back. No one can resume their progress at the point where they left off.

So let us press on and persevere. There is still much more of the road ahead than we have put behind us, but the greatest part of progress is the desire to progress.

I fully understand what this task is. It is something I desire, and I desire it with all my heart. I see that you, too, have been awakened and are rushing with great eagerness toward infinite beauty. Let us, then, hurry; only on these terms will life be a blessing to us. Otherwise, there is delay, and indeed shameful delay while we busy ourselves with repulsive things. Let us ensure that all time belongs to us. But this cannot happen unless first of all, we ourselves begin to belong to us.

And when will we finally be able to despise both kinds of fortune? When will we finally, after subduing and controlling all our passions, be able to say, "I have conquered!" Do you ask me whom I have conquered? Not the Persians, nor the distant Medes, nor any warlike people beyond the Dahae; not these, but greed, ambition, and the fear of death—these have conquered the conquerors of the world. Farewell.

Letter 72

On business as the enemy of philosophy

The topic you asked me about used to be clear in my mind and required no thought because I had mastered it so well. But I haven't reviewed it in a while, so it doesn't come back to me easily. I feel like I'm in the same situation as a book whose pages have stuck together from not being used; my mind needs to be opened up, and the things stored there need to be examined from time to time so that they're ready when needed. So, let's put this topic off for now, because it requires a lot of effort and care. As soon as I can stay in one place for a while, I'll take up your question.

There are certain topics you can write about even while traveling, but there are also topics that require a study chair, quiet, and seclusion. Still, I should accomplish something even on days like these—days that are fully occupied from morning till night. There's never a moment when new tasks won't come up; we create them, and that's why one task leads to another. Also, we keep putting off our own plans, saying, "As soon as I finish this, I'll get down to serious work," or "If I can just get this troublesome matter settled, I'll focus on my studies."

But the study of philosophy should not be put off until you have free time; everything else should be set aside so that we can focus on philosophy, because even if our lives were extended from childhood to the very end of our days, there still wouldn't be enough time for it. It doesn't matter if you leave philosophy out entirely or study it only occasionally; either way, you won't make progress. Once you stop, it doesn't stay where it was, but instead, it goes back to the beginning, like something that flies apart when it's stretched too tight. We must resist the things that take up our time; we shouldn't try to untangle them, but rather push them out of the way. Indeed, there's never a bad time for meaningful study; yet many people fail to study in the very situations that make study most necessary.

They say, "Something will happen to prevent me from studying." No, that's not true for someone whose spirit is happy and alert, no matter what they're doing. It's those who haven't yet reached perfection whose happiness can be interrupted; the joy of a wise person, on the other hand, is a tightly woven fabric, torn by no random event or change of fortune. At all times and in all places, the wise person is at peace. Their joy depends on nothing external and seeks no gift from others or from fortune. Their happiness is something within themselves; it would leave their soul if it came from the outside, but it is born there.

Sometimes an external event may remind them of their mortality, but it's only a light touch and barely scratches the surface. Some trouble might, as I said, brush against them like a breath of wind, but that Supreme Good of theirs remains unshaken. This is what I mean: there are external problems, like pimples and boils that break out on a body that is usually strong and healthy; but there is no deep-seated illness.

The difference between a person of perfect wisdom and someone who is still progressing in wisdom is the same as the difference between a healthy person and one who is recovering from a long, serious illness, where "health" just means a milder attack of the disease. If the latter person isn't careful, they can immediately relapse and return to the same old problem; but the wise person cannot slip back or fall into any more illness at all. Health of the body is a temporary matter that even the best doctor can't guarantee, even if they've restored it; in fact, they're often called out of bed to visit the same patient they treated before. But the mind, once healed, is healed for good.

I'll tell you what I mean by health: if the mind is content with itself; if it has confidence in itself; if it understands that all the things people pray for, all the benefits that are given and sought, are not important for a happy life; under these conditions, the mind is healthy. Because anything that can be added to is incomplete; anything that can be lost is not lasting. But a person whose happiness is to be lasting should rejoice in what is truly their own. Now, all that the crowd chases after comes and goes. Fortune gives us nothing that we can really call our own. But even these gifts of Fortune can please us when reason has adjusted them to our liking; for it is reason that makes even external goods acceptable to us when they would be unpleasant if we took them in too greedily.

Attalus used to use the following comparison: "Have you ever seen a dog snapping at pieces of bread or meat that its master tosses to it? Whatever the dog catches, it swallows whole right away, and always opens its mouth in the hope of getting more. That's how we are; we stand expectantly, and whatever Fortune throws at us, we swallow immediately without really enjoying it, and then we're on edge, frantic for something else to grab." But it's not like that for the wise person; they are satisfied. Even if something comes to them, they accept it carelessly and set it aside.

The happiness they enjoy is extremely great, lasting, and truly their own. Assume that a person has good intentions and has made progress, but is still far from the heights; the result is a series of ups and downs—they are sometimes raised to the heavens, and sometimes brought down to the ground. For those who lack experience and training, there is no limit to how far they can fall; such a person falls into the Chaos of Epicurus—empty and boundless.

There is still a third group of people—those who toy with wisdom. They haven't truly grasped it, but they can see it, and they have it within reach, so to speak. They aren't tossed about, nor do they drift back; they aren't on dry land yet, but they're already in the harbor.

Therefore, considering the great difference between those on the heights and those in the depths, and seeing that even those in the middle are at risk of being pulled back into their old ways, we should not give ourselves over to things that occupy our time. They should be shut out because if they get in, they will bring in more distractions with them. Let's resist them from the start. It's better that they never begin than to have to make them stop. Farewell.

Letter 73

On philosophers and kings

It seems to me a mistake to think that those who have devoted themselves to philosophy are stubborn and rebellious, that they look down on rulers, kings, or those who manage public affairs. On the contrary, no group of people respects rulers more than philosophers do, and this is because rulers provide the greatest gift of all—the ability to enjoy peace and leisure.

So, those who benefit greatly from the security of the state, in terms of living a good life, should cherish the ruler like a father. They should do this even more than those restless people who are always in the public eye, who owe a lot to the ruler but also expect a lot from him, and are never satisfied with what they get because their desires grow every time they're fulfilled. When someone is always thinking about the benefits they want to get, they forget about the benefits they've already received. There's no greater flaw in greed than its ingratitude.

Besides, no one in public life thinks about the many people they've surpassed; instead, they think about those who have surpassed them. These people find it less satisfying to see many behind them than annoying to see anyone ahead of them. That's the problem with ambition—it doesn't look back. But it's not just ambition that is fickle; every kind of craving is, because it always starts where it should end.

But the other person, who is upright and pure, who has left the senate, the courtroom, and all public affairs to focus on nobler things, appreciates those who made it possible for him to do this in peace and security. He is the only one who gives them thanks voluntarily, the only one who owes them a great debt without them even knowing. Just as a person honors and respects their teachers, who helped them find their way out of early mistakes, the wise person also honors those under whose protection they can put their good ideas into practice.

But you might say, "Other people are also protected by the king's power." That's true. But just as, out of a group of people who have all benefited from the same calm weather, someone who had a more valuable cargo during that voyage feels a greater debt to Neptune, the god of the sea, so does the philosopher. The person with more valuable goods is more willing to pay his vow to Neptune than a simple passenger, and even among merchants, those dealing in spices, fine fabrics, and items worth their weight in gold feel more grateful than those carrying cheap merchandise that only serves as ballast for their ship. Similarly, the benefits of peace, which extend to everyone, are more deeply appreciated by those who make good use of it.

Many of our citizens find that peace brings them more trouble than war. Do you think that those who spend their peace in drunkenness, lust, or other vices owe as much for the peace they enjoy as we do? No, unless you think that the wise person is so unfair that they believe they owe nothing for the advantages they share with everyone else. I owe a great debt to the sun and the moon, even though they don't rise for me alone. I am personally grateful to the seasons and the god who controls them, even though they aren't specifically arranged for my benefit.

The foolish greed of people makes a distinction between what they possess and what they own, and they believe they don't truly own anything that the public shares. But our philosopher considers nothing more truly their own than what they share with all of humanity. These things wouldn't be common property, as they are, unless every individual had their share; even a small share makes one a partner. The greatest and truest goods are not divided so that each person has only a small part; they belong entirely to each individual.

When food is distributed, people receive only the amount promised to each person; the banquet, the meat distribution, or anything else a person can carry away is divided into parts. But goods like peace and freedom are indivisible—they belong entirely to all people just as much as they belong to each person.

Therefore, the philosopher thinks about the person who makes it possible for him to use and enjoy these things, the person who exempts him when the state calls for soldiers, guards, defenders of the city walls, and other demands of war. He gives thanks to the leader of the state. This is what philosophy teaches most of all—to honorably acknowledge the debt of benefits received and to honorably repay them; sometimes, the acknowledgment itself is the repayment.

Our philosopher will, therefore, acknowledge that he owes a large debt to the ruler who, through his management and foresight, makes it possible for him to enjoy rich leisure, control of his own time, and a peace that isn't interrupted by public duties. "Shepherd! A god gave me this leisure, and he shall be my god forever." If even the simple leisure of our poet owes a great debt to its giver, though its greatest benefit is this: "As you can see, he let me turn my cattle out to graze and play whatever tune I pleased on my rustic reed," then how much more should we value the leisure of the philosopher, which is spent among the gods and makes us like gods?

Yes, that's what I mean, Lucilius; and I invite you to reach heaven by a shortcut. Sextius used to say that Jupiter had no more power than the good person. Of course, Jupiter has more gifts to offer to people, but when you compare two good people, the one with more wealth isn't necessarily the better one, just as you wouldn't call one of two equally skilled pilots better simply because his ship is larger and more impressive.

In what way is Jupiter superior to our good person? His goodness lasts longer, but the wise person doesn't value himself any less just because his virtues are limited to a shorter time. Or take two wise people; the one who lived longer isn't happier than the one whose virtue was limited to fewer years. Similarly, a god has no advantage over a wise person in terms of happiness, even though he has an advantage in terms of years. Virtue doesn't become greater just because it lasts longer.

Jupiter possesses all things, but he has surely given over the possession of them to others; the only use of them which belongs to him is this: he is the cause of their use to all people. The wise person surveys and scorns all the possessions of others as calmly as Jupiter does and regards himself with greater esteem because, while Jupiter cannot make use of them, the wise person does not wish to do so.

Let us, therefore, believe Sextius when he shows us the path of perfect beauty and says, "This is the way to the stars; this is the way, by observing thrift, self-restraint, and courage!" The gods are not disdainful or envious; they open the door to you and lend a hand as you climb. Do you marvel that man goes to the gods? God comes to men; he comes even closer—he comes into men. No mind that doesn't have God in it is good. Divine seeds are scattered throughout our mortal bodies; if a good caretaker receives them, they grow up in the likeness of their source and equal those from which they came. If, however, the caretaker is bad, like barren or swampy soil, he kills the seeds and causes weeds to grow instead of wheat. Farewell.

Letter 74

On virtue as a refuge from worldly distractions

Your letter has given me joy and has stirred me from my laziness. It has also helped to revive my memory, which has been sluggish for some time. You are right, my dear Lucilius, in believing that the key to a happy life is understanding that the only true good is found in what is honorable. Anyone who thinks other things are good places themselves under the control of Fortune and becomes dependent on others. But the person who always defines what is good by what is honorable is happy with a happiness that comes from within.

One person is sad when their children die; another is anxious when their children become sick; a third is bitter when their children do something shameful or their reputation is damaged. Some people are tormented by desire for someone else's spouse, while others are tormented by desire for their own. You will find people who are completely upset by losing an election, and others who are troubled by the responsibilities of the offices they have won.

But the largest group of unhappy people are those who are driven to despair by the constant fear of death, which can come at any moment. Death can approach from any direction, so these people are like soldiers scouting in enemy territory—they are always looking around in fear and jumping at every sound. Unless someone gets rid of this fear, they live with a heart that is always racing.

You can easily remember those who have been exiled and lost their property. You can also remember those who are poor despite their great wealth, which is the most severe kind of poverty. You will recall people who have been shipwrecked or who have experienced something like a shipwreck—people who were calm and at ease until the anger or envy of the public, which is a deadly weapon against those in high positions, struck them like a sudden storm or a bolt of lightning. Just as anyone standing near a lightning strike is stunned and feels like they've been hit, so in these sudden disasters, even if only one person is directly affected, everyone else is overwhelmed by fear, and the possibility that they could be next makes them as miserable as the person who was actually hit.

Every person is troubled by the sudden misfortunes of others. Like birds that panic at the sound of an empty sling, we are frightened by noises as much as by actual blows. No one can be happy if they allow themselves to be ruled by such foolish fears. Nothing can bring happiness unless it also brings calm. A life spent in constant worry is a miserable life.

Anyone who has largely given themselves over to the power of Fortune has woven a huge web of worries from which they cannot escape. If someone wants to find safety, there is only one path—to despise external things and be content with what is honorable. Those who value anything more than virtue or believe that anything other than virtue is good are reaching out to grab whatever Fortune throws their way and are anxiously waiting for her favors.

Imagine that Fortune is hosting a festival and is throwing down honors, riches, and power to the crowd of people below. Some of these gifts are torn apart by those who try to snatch them, others are divided up by greedy partnerships, and still others are seized to the great harm of those who manage to grab them. Some people receive these gifts without even trying, while others lose out because they were too eager and, in their greed, let the gifts slip from their hands. But none of these people, even those who were lucky enough to grab some treasure, will find their joy lasting until the next day.

The wisest person, therefore, as soon as they see this distribution of goods beginning, leaves the scene because they know that the cost of small favors is high. No one will fight with them on their way out or hit them as they leave; the fighting happens where the prizes are being handed out.

The same goes for the gifts that Fortune throws to us. We, like fools, get excited, tear ourselves apart, and wish we had many hands to grab more. We look around frantically, eager to catch more of the gifts that seem to come too slowly. These gifts excite our desires because they can only reach a few, while everyone is waiting for them. We are eager to intercept them as they fall. We rejoice if we manage to grab something, and some of us are fooled by the empty hope of grabbing something. We either pay a high price for worthless plunder, which harms us in the process, or we are cheated and left empty-handed.

Let us, therefore, withdraw from this game and leave it to the greedy crowd. Let them chase after these "goods" that hang above them while they remain in suspense. Whoever wants to be happy should decide that the only true good is found in what is honorable. If they think anything else is good, they are, in the first place, unfairly judging Providence because good people often suffer misfortunes, and the time we have in life is short and fleeting compared to the eternity of the universe.

Because of complaints like these, we fail to appreciate the gifts of heaven. We complain that they are not always given to us, that they are few, uncertain, and fleeting. As a result, we lose the will to live and fear death. Our plans are in chaos, and no amount of success can satisfy us. The reason for this is that we have not yet reached the ultimate good, which is immeasurable and unsurpassable, where all our desires must end because there is no higher goal beyond it.

Do you ask why virtue needs nothing else? It is because virtue is content with what it has and does not crave what it lacks. Whatever is enough is abundant in the eyes of virtue. If you disagree with this view, then duty and loyalty will not endure. To show these qualities, we must endure many things that the world calls evil, and we must give up many things we are attached to because we mistakenly think they are good.

If we lose courage, which should always be testing itself, and lose greatness of soul, which can only shine if it scorns the things the crowd considers most important, then we also lose kindness and the ability to repay kindness if we fear hardship, if we think anything is more valuable than loyalty, or if we focus on anything other than the best.

But to set aside these questions: if these so-called goods are truly good, then man is more fortunate than God because God does not enjoy the things given to us. Lust, fine banquets, wealth, and all the things that attract people through degrading pleasure do not apply to God. Therefore, it is either not believable that these things are good if God does not possess them, or the fact that God does not have them proves that they are not good.

Furthermore, many things that are usually considered good are given to animals more abundantly than to humans. Animals enjoy their food with better appetite, are less weakened by sexual indulgence, and have greater and more consistent strength. So, they are much more fortunate than humans. For there is no wickedness, no self-harm in their way of living. They enjoy their pleasures more often and more easily, without any of the fear, shame, or regret that humans experience.

Given this, you should consider whether we can call anything good if God is outdone by man in having it. We should limit the Supreme Good to the soul; it loses its meaning if we take it away from the best part of us and apply it to the worst, that is, if we transfer it to the senses, which are more active in animals. The sum of our happiness should not be placed in the body; the true goods are those that reason gives us—they are substantial and eternal. They cannot fade, shrink, or be diminished.

Other things are goods only according to opinion, and though they are called by the same name as true goods, they do not have the essence of goodness. Let us, therefore, call them "advantages" or "preferred things." But let us also recognize that they are our possessions, not parts of ourselves, and let us have them without becoming attached to them, always remembering that they are outside us. Even if we have them, they should be considered as secondary and insignificant, the possession of which does not give anyone the right to feel proud. For what could be more foolish than being proud of something you did not achieve through your own efforts?

Let everything of this nature be added to us, but not become part of us, so that if it is taken away, it can leave without tearing anything away from us. Let us use these things, but not boast about them, and let us use them sparingly, as if they were given to us for safekeeping and could be taken away at any time. Anyone who does not use reason in managing their possessions will not keep them for long. For prosperity, if not controlled by reason, leads to its own downfall. If someone relies on the most fleeting goods, they will soon lose them, and to avoid losing them, they will suffer distress. Few people have been able to gently let go of prosperity. Most fall along with the things that made them famous, and they are weighed down by the very things that once lifted them up.

For this reason, we must use foresight to insist on limits and frugality in using these things, since excess leads to destruction. Anything without limits has never lasted unless reason, which sets limits, has kept it in check. The fate of many cities proves this— luxury has ruined all that was gained by virtue, and their power ended at its peak because they indulged in excess. We should protect ourselves against such disasters. But no wall can be built against Fortune that she cannot conquer; we must strengthen our inner defenses. If our inner self is secure, we can be attacked but never conquered.

Do you want to know what this weapon of defense is? It is the ability to remain calm no matter what happens, to understand that the very things that seem harmful are working for the preservation of the world and are part of the plan for the universe's order and function. Let man be pleased with whatever pleases God; let him marvel at himself and his own strength for the very reason that he cannot be overcome, that he has control over the powers of evil, and that he conquers chance, pain, and injustice with the greatest power of all—reason.

Love reason! The love of reason will arm you against the greatest hardships. Wild animals rush into the hunter's spear out of love for their young, and their wildness and unthinking charge prevent them from being tamed. Often, the desire for glory stirs the mind of youth to face both the sword and the stake without fear. The mere vision of virtue has driven some men to choose death. Reason, which is stronger and steadier than any of these emotions, will make its way through the greatest terrors and dangers even more forcefully.

People might say to us, "You are wrong if you think that nothing is good except what is honorable. This belief won't protect you from Fortune's attacks. You say that good children, a well-governed country, and good parents are goods, but you can't see these dear things in danger without being disturbed. Your calm will be shattered by a siege on your country, the death of your children, or the enslavement of your parents."

I will first tell you what we Stoics usually reply to these objections and then add my own thoughts. The situation is different when the loss of something good leads to something bad taking its place. For example, when health is lost, illness takes its place; when an eye is lost, blindness follows; when our leg muscles are damaged, we not only lose speed but are left with weakness. But there is no such danger with the goods I mentioned earlier. Why? If I lose a good friend, I don't have to endure a false friend in his place. If I bury a dutiful child, I don't have to deal with a disobedient one in return.

Moreover, the loss of a friend or child does not mean the loss of their goodness; it is only the loss of their bodies. A true good can only be lost by turning into something bad, which is impossible by nature's law because every virtue and every work of virtue remains uncorrupted. Even if friends or good children, who fulfilled their parents' hopes, have passed away, something remains to fill their place. Do you ask what that is? It is the virtue that made them good in the first place.

Virtue leaves no empty space within us; it fills the whole soul and removes all sense of loss. It is enough on its own because all good things begin with virtue. What does it matter if the stream of water is cut off and flows away as long as the source remains untouched? You would not say that a person's life is more just if their children are alive than if they have passed away, nor that it is better appointed, more intelligent, or more honorable—so it is not better either. The addition of friends does not make a person wiser, nor does their loss make them more foolish—so it does not make them happier or more wretched either. As long as your virtue remains unharmed, you will not feel the loss of anything that is taken from you.

You might say, "But isn't a person happier when surrounded by many friends and children?" Why should this be? The Supreme Good is neither diminished nor increased by such things. It remains within its own limits, no matter how Fortune behaves. Whether a long old age is granted or life ends early, the measure of the Supreme Good does not change, regardless of the number of years.

Whether you draw a larger or smaller circle, its size affects its area, not its shape. One circle may remain as it is for a long time, while the other may be immediately reduced or erased completely from the sand in which it was drawn; yet each circle has the same shape. The straightness of a line is not judged by its length, size, or duration; it cannot be made longer or shorter. Even if you shorten an honorable life from a hundred years to a single day, it remains equally honorable.

Sometimes, virtue spreads wide, governing kingdoms, cities, and provinces, creating laws, forming friendships, and managing the duties between relatives and children. Other times, it is confined by the narrow boundaries of poverty, exile, or loss. But it is no less when reduced from grand heights to a private station, from a royal palace to a humble dwelling, or from broad authority to a small, private space.

Virtue remains just as great, even when it retreats within itself and is confined on all sides. Its spirit is no less great and upright, its wisdom no less complete, its justice no less firm. Therefore, it is equally happy. For happiness resides in one place only, within the mind itself, and is noble, steadfast, and calm. This state cannot be achieved without knowledge of both divine and human things.

The other response, which I promised to give to your objection, follows this reasoning. The wise person is not distressed by the loss of children or friends. For they face their deaths with the same spirit in which they face their own. They fear the loss of others as little as they fear their own death. For the essence of virtue is harmony; all the works of virtue are in agreement with virtue itself. This harmony is lost if the soul, which should be uplifted, is cast down by grief or loss. It is always a dishonor for a person to be troubled and disturbed, to be numb when action is required. For what is honorable is free from worry, unafraid, and ready for action.

You might ask, "But won't the wise person feel some emotional disturbance? Won't their face change color, their expression show agitation, and their limbs grow cold? Aren't there things we do unconsciously, as a result of natural impulse?" I admit this is true, but the sage will hold firmly to the belief that none of these things is evil or important enough to break a healthy mind. Whatever remains to be done, virtue can accomplish with courage and readiness.

For anyone would agree that it is foolish to do something reluctantly and with resistance or to direct the body in one direction and the mind in another, being torn between conflicting emotions. Folly is despised precisely because of the things it prides itself on, and it does not do even those things willingly in which it takes pride. If folly fears some evil, it suffers from it even while waiting for it, just as if it had already happened—already suffering in anticipation of what it fears.

Just as in the body, symptoms of illness often appear before the disease itself—such as a certain sluggishness, a lack of energy, or a trembling and shivering that spreads through the limbs—the weak spirit is shaken by its troubles long before it is overcome by them. It anticipates them and stumbles before its time.

But what could be greater madness than to be tortured by the future and not save your strength for the actual suffering, but instead invite and bring on misery? If you cannot avoid it, you should at least postpone it. Don't you see that no one should be tormented by the future? A person who is told they will face torture fifty years from now is not disturbed by it unless they skip over the intervening years and throw themselves into the future suffering. In the same way, souls that enjoy being miserable and look for excuses to grieve are saddened by events long past, events that have been erased from the records. The past and future are both absent; we do not feel either of them. But there can be no pain except as a result of what you feel. Farewell.

Letter 75
On the diseases of the soul

You've mentioned that my letters seem a bit carelessly written. But who speaks carefully unless they want to sound overly polished? I prefer my letters to be just like our conversations would be if we were sitting together or walking—natural and relaxed. My letters aren't forced or artificial. If it were possible, I'd rather show you my feelings than just talk about them. Even when making an argument, I wouldn't raise my voice or wave my arms around—that's for orators. I'm content to share my thoughts with you without making them overly fancy or diminishing their seriousness. I want you to know that I truly feel what I'm saying. I not only feel it, but I'm committed to it. There's a difference between the way a man kisses his lover and the way he kisses his children, yet both kisses are full of affection. I do think our conversations on important matters should be thoughtful and not dry. Even philosophy doesn't reject cleverness, but we shouldn't focus too much on just the words. Here's my main point: we should say what we truly feel and feel what we say. Our words should match our lives. The person who keeps their word and acts the same way both in public and private is trustworthy. We will understand what kind of person someone truly is if they're consistent. Our words should aim to help, not just to sound good. If you can be eloquent without much effort and use it for good, then do so. But remember, eloquence should highlight the facts, not itself. Our concern here is the soul. When someone is sick, they don't look for a doctor who speaks well—they want one who can heal them. If the doctor happens to explain the treatment elegantly, the patient might appreciate it, but that's not why they sought the doctor in the first place. It's like having a skilled pilot who also happens to be handsome—that's not what matters. Why should you entertain me with words? I need treatment—whether it's surgery, cauterization, or a specific diet. That's why you're here, to heal my serious and chronic disease, which affects everyone. Are you worried about words? Be happy if you can deal with the real issues. When will you learn everything there is to know? When will you fully absorb and practice it? It's not enough to memorize these things; they must be lived out. A person isn't happy just because they know what's right, but because they do what's right. You might ask, "Is there no middle ground between a 'happy' person and a fool? Isn't there something in between?" I don't think so. Even though a person making progress is still technically among the fools, they are far removed from them. Among those making progress, there are also great differences. They fall into three groups, as some philosophers believe. First, there are those who haven't yet attained wisdom but are close. Even though they're near, they're still outside. These people, in my view, have already set aside all passions and vices and have learned what should be valued, but they haven't yet tested their newfound peace. They haven't put their understanding into practice, but they won't fall back into their old mistakes. They've reached a point where they can't slip back, but they don't realize it yet. They know what's right, but they're unaware of their knowledge. Some define this group—those who are making progress—as having overcome the mental diseases but not the passions and still standing on shaky ground. Because no one is safe from danger unless they've fully embraced wisdom. I've explained before the difference between the mind's diseases and passions, and I'll remind you again: diseases are deep-seated and chronic vices like greed and ambition. These have gripped the mind tightly and become permanent problems. To put it simply, a "disease" is a persistent wrong judgment, making us value things that aren't truly valuable. Or, we could say it's being overly zealous for things that aren't worth much or not worth anything at all. "Passions" are sudden and intense impulses of the spirit. They come often and, when ignored, they can lead to a state of disease, just like a mild cough can turn into a serious illness if it becomes chronic. So, those who've made significant progress have moved beyond the "diseases," but they still feel the "passions," even when they're near perfection. The second group consists of those who've laid aside the worst mental illnesses and passions, but they're not yet completely free. They could still slip back into their former state. The third group has escaped many, but not all, vices, especially the major ones. They've overcome greed, for example, but still feel anger; they're no longer troubled by lust but still struggle with ambition; they no longer have desires, but they still have fears. And because they still have fear, they're strong in some areas but weak in others. They may scorn death but still fear pain. Let's think about this for a moment. It's good if we can be counted in this third group. Reaching the second stage requires great natural gifts and constant dedication to study. But even the third type shouldn't be dismissed. Look around at the evils you see every day. See how crime is everywhere, how wickedness spreads daily, and how sins are common in both homes and public life. You'll realize that it's a significant gain if we're not among the worst. "But as for me," you say, "I hope I can rise to a higher level than that!" I would pray, rather than promise, that we may achieve this. We've been held back. We hurry toward virtue while still burdened by vices. I'm ashamed to admit it, but we only pursue what's honorable when we have spare time. But imagine the rich rewards that await us if we can just break free from the things that hold us back and cling to us so tightly! Then neither desire nor fear will disturb us. Untroubled by fears, unspoiled by pleasures, we won't fear death or the gods. We'll know that death isn't evil and that the gods aren't powers of evil. What harms us isn't stronger than what receives harm, and what's utterly good can't harm us at all. If we ever escape from these lowly conditions to that high and lofty place, we'll find peace of mind and perfect freedom when all error has been driven out. You ask what this freedom is? It means not fearing men or gods, not craving wickedness or excess, and having supreme control over yourself. And it's priceless to be the master of yourself. Farewell.

Letter 76

On learning wisdom in old age

You have been saying that you'll be mad at me if I don't keep you updated on everything I do each day. But look, you and I are very honest with each other, so I'll share even this with you: I've been attending lectures of a philosopher. It's already been four days since I started going to his school, where he gives speeches at two o'clock. You might say, "Isn't it too late in life for that?" But really, it's not too late at all! What's sillier than refusing to learn just because you haven't been learning for a long time? You might ask, "Do I really need to follow what the younger people do?" But if this is the only thing that makes my old age look foolish, then I'm doing okay. People of all ages can join these classes. You might argue, "Are we supposed to get old just to follow young people around?" But if I, an old man, can go to the theater, attend the races, and never miss a fight at the arena, should I be embarrassed to attend a philosopher's lecture?

You should keep learning as long as you don't know something—even if it takes your whole life. There's a saying that fits well here: "As long as you live, keep learning how to live." And guess what? There's even something I can teach in that school. You might ask, "What can I teach?" That even an old person should keep learning. But I feel sad about people whenever I enter the lecture hall. On my way to Metronax's house, I have to pass by the Neapolitan Theatre, which, as you know, is always packed with people. They're all very excited about deciding who's the best flute player; even the Greek piper and the announcer have their fans. But at the other place, where we're learning what it means to be a good person and how to become one, very few people show up. Most people even think those who do attend are wasting their time and are just a bunch of fools. Honestly, I'd love to be made fun of like that because when you're on the path to becoming honorable, you should ignore the insults of those who don't understand.

So, Lucilius, go ahead and hurry to learn, so you won't have to do it in your old age like I am now. In fact, you should hurry even more because you haven't studied this for a long time, and it's something that's hard to learn when you're old. You ask, "How much progress will I make?" As much as you try to make. So why wait? Wisdom doesn't just come to anyone by accident. Money might come on its own; titles might be given to you; power and influence might be handed to you, but virtue—the quality of being a good person—won't just fall into your lap. And you can't gain it with little effort or a small amount of work. But the hard work is worth it because you'll gain all the good things in life at once. There's only one true good, and that's being honorable. All the other things that people usually think are good aren't really certain or true.

Let me explain why there's only one true good, and that is honor, especially since you felt that I didn't explain it enough in my earlier letter. Everything is judged by its own special quality. For example, a vine is valued for its fruit and the taste of its wine, a deer for its speed. We look at work animals and judge them by how strong they are since they're used to carry loads. If a dog is supposed to track down a wild animal, the most important thing is its sense of smell; if it's supposed to catch the animal, it needs to be fast; if it's supposed to attack, it needs courage. Each thing should be best at what it's meant to do and by what we judge it for.

So, what quality is best in a person? It's reason—our ability to think—because that's what makes us better than animals and almost as great as the gods. Perfect reason is the special quality that makes us human. All other qualities, like strength, beauty, and speed, are things we share with animals and plants. A person is strong, but so is a lion. A person is beautiful, but so is a peacock. A person is fast, but so is a horse. I'm not saying that people aren't better than animals in some of these ways, but I'm looking for the thing that's only found in people. A person has a body, but so do trees. A person can move and act freely, but so can animals and even worms. A person has a voice, but a dog's bark is louder, an eagle's cry is sharper, a bull's roar is deeper, and a nightingale's song is sweeter. So, what makes a person special? It's reason. When our reason is correct and fully developed, we're truly happy. Therefore, if everything is praised for being the best at what it's meant to do, and if reason is what makes a person special, then when someone perfects their reason, they've achieved the best thing a human can achieve. This perfect reason is called virtue, and it's what we mean by being honorable.

So, the only thing that's truly good in a person is what's unique to them, and that's reason. We're not trying to find out what's good in general, but what's good in a person. If there's nothing else that's unique to people except reason, then reason is our only true good, and it's more valuable than anything else. If a person is bad, people will dislike them; if they're good, people will like them. So, the thing that makes a person good or bad is their main and only true good. You might not doubt that this is a good thing, but you might wonder if it's the only good thing. If a person has all sorts of other things like health, money, a noble family, and many visitors at their home but is known to be bad, you won't like them. On the other hand, if someone doesn't have those things—no money, no visitors, no rank or family history—but is known to be good, you will like them. So, this is the only true good in a person, and someone who has it should be praised even if they lack other things. But someone who doesn't have it, even if they have everything else, is condemned and rejected.

The same goes for things as it does for people. A ship is considered good not when it's decorated with fancy colors, or when its front is covered in silver or gold, or its figurehead is carved in ivory, or when it's loaded with treasure. It's good when it's strong, doesn't leak, can handle rough seas, obeys the helm, and sails quickly without worrying about the wind. You'd say a sword is good not because its hilt is gold or its sheath is covered in gems, but because it has a sharp edge and a point that can pierce armor. When we look at a carpenter's rule, we don't care how beautiful it is but how straight it is. Everything is judged based on the quality that defines it.

So, when it comes to people, it doesn't matter how much land someone owns, how much money they've loaned out, how many people visit their house, how expensive their couch is, or how fancy the cups they drink from are. What matters is how good they are. A person is good if their reason is well-ordered, correct, and in line with what nature intended. This is what we call virtue and what we mean by being honorable. It's the unique good of a person. Since reason is the only thing that can perfect a person, only reason can make a person happy. This is the only true good for people, the only thing that makes us happy. We might also say that things influenced by virtue, like all the actions of virtue, are good. But virtue itself is the only true good because there can't be any good without virtue. If all good things are in the soul, then whatever makes the soul stronger, better, and bigger is a good thing. Virtue does make the soul stronger, better, and bigger. Everything else we might desire just makes the soul weaker, and when we think these things are uplifting our soul, they're actually just inflating it with empty things. So, only that which improves the soul is good.

All the actions in life are controlled by what we think is honorable or shameful. These two things guide our decisions about what to do or not do. Let me explain: A good person will do what they believe is honorable, even if it's hard, harmful, or dangerous. They won't do something shameful, even if it brings them money, pleasure, or power. Nothing will stop them from doing what's honorable, and nothing will tempt them to do what's shameful. So, if someone is always determined to follow what's honorable, always avoids what's shameful, and in everything they do, they think about these two things, seeing nothing else as good except what's honorable and nothing else as bad except what's shameful—if virtue alone guides them and stays consistent—then virtue is that person's only good. Nothing can change that. Foolishness might try to climb up toward wisdom, but wisdom will never fall back into foolishness.

You might remember me saying that the things people usually want or fear have been overcome by many people in moments of strong emotion. There have been people who would put their hands in the fire, people who wouldn't stop smiling even under torture, people who wouldn't shed a tear at their child's funeral, and people who would face death without fear. Emotions like love, anger, and desire have driven people to face dangers. If a moment of stubbornness can achieve all this when someone is driven by a strong emotion, think how much more can be done by virtue, which acts not suddenly or impulsively but consistently and with lasting strength! This shows that the things often dismissed by people in moments of strong emotion and always dismissed by wise people are neither truly good nor truly bad. So, virtue is the only true good. It confidently stands between good and bad fortune, not caring much about either.

If you believe there's anything good besides being honorable, then all virtues will be weakened. Virtue could never be fully achieved if it had to consider anything outside of itself. If it had to, it would go against reason, from which all virtues come, and against truth, which can't exist without reason. Any opinion that goes against truth is wrong. A good person must, you'd agree, have a strong sense of duty toward the gods. This means they'll face whatever happens to them calmly, knowing that it's all part of the divine law that governs the universe. If this is true, then for them, there's only one good thing, and that's being honorable. This is because one of the rules of being honorable is to obey the gods and not get angry at sudden misfortunes or complain about their situation, but rather accept fate patiently and follow its orders. If anything other than being honorable is considered good, we'll be constantly driven by a desire for life and the things that make life comfortable—a never-ending, unstable state. So, the only true good is what's honorable and within limits.

I've said before that if things like money and high positions—things the gods don't even enjoy—are good, then a person's life would be better than that of the gods. There's another point to consider: if it's true that our souls continue to exist after leaving our bodies, then they'll be in a better state than when they were in the body. But if the things we use for our bodies are good, then our souls will be worse off after they're free. This goes against our belief that the soul is happier when it's free and part of the universe. I've also mentioned that if the things animals share with us, like instincts, are considered good, then animals would also live happy lives, which is impossible. We must be willing to endure anything to protect what's honorable, but this wouldn't be necessary if there were any other good besides being honorable.

Even though I've discussed this idea in a previous letter, I've tried to sum it up briefly here. But this idea will never seem true to you unless you raise your mind and ask yourself if, out of duty, you'd be willing to die for your country and give up your life to save everyone else. Would you offer your neck not just with patience but with joy? If you would do that, then you see no other good. Because you're willing to give up everything to gain this one good. Think about how powerful being honorable is: you'd die for your country without hesitation when you know it's the right thing to do.

Sometimes, noble actions bring great joy, even in a short amount of time. And even though you won't enjoy the benefits of your deeds after you're dead, just thinking about doing something great can bring happiness. A brave and good person, imagining the rewards of their death—like the freedom of their country and the safety of everyone they're sacrificing their life for—experiences the greatest joy and benefits from their own risk. But even if someone can't feel this joy, they'll still rush to their death without hesitation, content to do what's right and dutiful. You could tell them, "Your action will soon be forgotten," or "Your fellow citizens won't thank you much," but they'll reply, "That doesn't concern me. My focus is on the action itself. I know it's honorable. So, wherever honor leads and calls me, I will go."

This, then, is the only true good, and every perfect soul knows it. Even every naturally noble and rightly inclined soul knows it. All other so-called goods are minor and changeable. That's why they burden us if we have them. Even if Fortune generously gives them to us, they weigh us down and sometimes even crush us. None of the people you see dressed in fine clothes is truly happy, just like none of the actors on stage, who only pretend to be kings with their fake scepters and cloaks, are truly great. They play their part for a short time in front of a crowd, acting tall with their high shoes. But once they leave the stage, they take off the costume and return to their real height. The same goes for people who are raised to a higher status by wealth and honors—they're not truly great. So why do they seem great to you? Because you're including their fancy status in your judgment. A short person isn't tall just because they stand on a mountain, and a huge statue will still be huge even if you put it in a well.

This is the mistake we make, and it's why we're fooled. We don't value a person for who they truly are, but we add to them the decorations they wear. But if you want to know a person's true worth and what kind of person they really are, look at them when they're stripped of all these things—no inheritance, no titles, no tricks of fortune, not even their body. Look at their soul—its quality and size—and then decide if its greatness is real or just borrowed.

If someone can stare at the flash of a sword without fear, if they understand that it doesn't matter if their soul leaves through their mouth or a wound in their throat, you can call them happy. You can also call them happy if, when they're threatened with physical pain, whether by accident or by a more powerful person, they can calmly hear talk of chains, exile, and all the other silly fears that trouble people. They can say, "Oh, these hardships are nothing new to me; I've already faced them in my mind." Today, it's you who threatens me with these fears, but I've always been prepared for them and have trained myself to face them like a man facing human fate.

If you think about an evil thing before it happens, it hurts less when it comes. But for the fool and the person who trusts in luck, each event is new and surprising when it happens. Much of the pain they feel comes from the shock. This is proven by the fact that people endure things better once they've gotten used to them, even things they once thought were unbearable. That's why the wise person prepares themselves for coming trouble, making future hardships easier by thinking about them ahead of time, while others can only make them easier by enduring them for a long time. Sometimes you hear inexperienced people say, "I knew this was going to happen." But the wise person knows that anything could happen. Whatever comes their way, they say, "I knew it." Farewell.

Letter 77
On taking one's own life

Today, we suddenly saw the "Alexandrian" ships, the ones usually sent ahead to announce the arrival of the fleet; they're often called "mail-boats." The people of Campania are excited to see them; the crowds at the docks in Puteoli recognize these "Alexandrian" boats instantly, even among many other ships, just by the way their sails are set. These ships are the only ones allowed to keep their topsails raised, which are usually used when ships are far out at sea because they help the ship move faster. When the wind picks up and becomes too strong, ships lower their sails because the wind is less powerful closer to the water's surface. So, when the Alexandrian ships reach Capreae and the headland where tall Pallas watches from the stormy peak, all other ships lower their topsails, but the Alexandrian mail-boats keep theirs up.

While everyone was rushing around and hurrying to the waterfront, I felt pleased with my laziness. Even though I was expecting letters from my friends, I wasn't in a hurry to find out how things were going abroad or what news the letters might bring. I haven't had any big losses or gains lately. Even if I weren't an old man, I would still enjoy this feeling of contentment, but it's even greater now. No matter how small my possessions are, I still have more than enough for the rest of my journey through life, especially since this journey doesn't have to go all the way to the end.

In most journeys, stopping halfway would be incomplete, but life isn't incomplete if it's lived honorably. No matter when you stop living, as long as you stop with dignity, your life is complete. Sometimes, you must leave life bravely, and the reasons for doing so don't have to be huge; the reasons keeping us here aren't always huge either.

Tullius Marcellinus, a man you knew well, who was quiet in his youth and became old before his time, fell ill with a disease that wasn't hopeless but was long and bothersome, requiring a lot of care. He started thinking about dying. He called together many of his friends. Each one gave him advice – the timid friend encouraged him to do what he had decided; the flattering friend gave advice he thought Marcellinus would find pleasing later; but our Stoic friend, a rare and brave man, gave the best advice, I think. He said, "Don't torture yourself, my dear Marcellinus, as if this decision is a big deal. It's not important to live; even your slaves and animals live. But it is important to die honorably, wisely, and bravely. Think about how long you've been doing the same things: eating, sleeping, desires – this is your daily routine. The desire to die can come to the wise, the brave, the unhappy, or even someone who's just tired of it all."

Marcellinus didn't need someone to convince him, but someone to help him. His slaves refused to follow his orders. So, the Stoic friend eased their fears, showing them that there was no risk for them if it was clear that their master's death was his own choice. He also suggested to Marcellinus that it would be kind to give gifts to the people who had served him all his life, just as people share the leftovers after a banquet is over. Marcellinus, who was generous even with his own property, gave small sums to his sorrowful slaves and comforted them as well. He didn't need a sword or bloodshed; for three days, he fasted and set up a tent in his bedroom. Then, a tub was brought in, and he lay in it for a long time. As hot water was poured over him, he gradually passed away, not without a sense of peace, as he himself remarked – the kind of peace that comes with a slow fading away. Anyone who has fainted before knows what this feeling is like.

This little story, though a bit of a side note, will not be displeasing to you. You'll see that your friend left life without difficulty or suffering. Although he took his own life, he left it gently, almost slipping away. This story may also be helpful; sometimes, a crisis calls for such examples. There are times when we ought to die and are unwilling; sometimes we die and are unwilling. No one is so ignorant that they don't know we must all die at some point; yet, when death comes near, we try to flee, tremble, and cry. Wouldn't you think someone foolish if they cried because they weren't alive a thousand years ago? And isn't it just as foolish to cry because you won't be alive a thousand years from now? It's all the same; you won't be, and you weren't. Neither of those times belongs to you.

You've been placed in this moment of time; if you want to make it longer, how much longer would be enough? Why cry? Why pray? You're wasting your energy. Stop thinking that your prayers can change what the gods have already decided. These decisions are unchangeable and fixed; they're ruled by a powerful and eternal force. Your end will be the same as everything else. What's strange about that? You were born under this law; it happened to your father, your mother, your ancestors, and it will happen to all who come after you. An unbreakable sequence binds all things together and pulls everything along with it.

Think of the countless people destined to die after you, and the countless who will die with you! Would you die more bravely if you knew thousands were dying with you? And yet, there are thousands of people and animals dying right now, in their own ways, while you hesitate about death. Did you really think you wouldn't someday reach the end of the journey you've always been on? Every journey has its end.

You might think I should now give examples of great men, but instead, I'll tell you about a boy. There's a story about a young Spartan boy who was captured, but he kept shouting in his dialect, "I will not be a slave!" And he kept his word; the first time he was ordered to do a degrading task – to fetch a chamber pot – he smashed his head against the wall and died. Freedom is that close, and yet some people are still slaves. Wouldn't you rather have your son die like that than grow old by giving in weakly? Why, then, are you troubled when even a boy can die so bravely? Even if you refuse to follow him, you will be led. Take control of what is now controlled by another. Will you not borrow that boy's courage and say, "I am no slave!"? Unhappy person, you are a slave to men, to your work, to your life. For life, if you lack the courage to die, is slavery.

Do you have anything worth waiting for? The pleasures that hold you back have already been used up. None of them are new to you, and you've grown tired of them. You know the taste of wine and luxury. It doesn't matter if a hundred or a thousand drinks pass through your body; you're just a filter for the wine. You're an expert in the flavor of oysters and mullet; your indulgence has left you with nothing new to taste in the future, yet these are the things you're unwilling to leave behind. What else would you regret losing? Friends? But who can truly be your friend? Your country? What? Do you care enough about your country to be late for dinner? The sunlight? You'd snuff it out if you could, for what have you ever done that deserves to be seen in the light? Admit the truth: it's not because you long for the senate chamber, the forum, or even nature that you want to keep living; it's because you don't want to leave the fish market, even though you've exhausted its offerings.

You're afraid of death; but how can you despise it while having a feast? You want to live; well, do you even know how to live? You're afraid to die. But think about it: is this life of yours really living? Gaius Caesar was once walking along the Via Latina when a man with a grey beard hanging down to his chest stepped out from the crowd of prisoners and begged to be killed. "What!" Caesar said, "are you alive now?" That's the answer we should give to people for whom death would be a relief. "You're afraid to die; what! are you alive now?"

"But," someone says, "I want to live because I'm involved in many honorable pursuits. I don't want to leave the duties I'm fulfilling with loyalty and passion." But surely you know that dying is also one of life's duties? You're not abandoning any duty; there's no set number of tasks you're required to complete. No life is truly long. Compared to the natural world, even Nestor's life was short, or Sattia's, the woman who had "lived ninety-nine years" carved on her tombstone. Some people boast of their long lives, but who could have endured that old woman if she'd lived to be a hundred? Life is like a play – it doesn't matter how long it is, but how well it's acted. It doesn't matter when you stop. Stop whenever you choose, but just make sure that the final act is well done. Farewell.

☐

Letter 78 - On the healing power of the mind

I'm sorry to hear that you're often bothered by a stuffy nose and brief fevers that come after long, ongoing colds. I know what that's like because I've had the same kind of illness myself, and I ignored it when it first started. When I was younger, I could handle hardships and face illness bravely. But eventually, I got so sick that I was reduced to nothing but sniffles and became extremely thin. There were times I thought about ending my life right then and there, but the thought of my kind old father stopped me. I didn't think about how bravely I could die but about how little strength he had to endure losing me. So, I made myself keep living. Sometimes, just staying alive is an act of bravery.

Now, I'll tell you what helped me get through those tough days. Right from the start, I want to say that these things that brought me peace of mind were as effective as medicine. True comfort can lead to healing, and anything that lifts your spirit also helps your body. My studies saved me. I credit philosophy for helping me recover and regain my strength. I owe my life to philosophy, and that's just the smallest of the many ways it has helped me! My friends also played a big part in getting me healthy again. I found comfort in their encouraging words, the time they spent by my side, and their conversations. Nothing helps a sick person more than the love of their friends; nothing eases the fear of death as much. In fact, I couldn't even believe that I would die if they outlived me. It felt like I would go on living, not with them, but through them. I thought of it as not giving up my soul but passing it on to them.

All these things made me want to help myself and endure any suffering. Besides, it's a miserable state to lose your desire to die and have no enthusiasm for living. These are the things you should turn to. The doctor will prescribe walks and exercise; he'll warn you not to become lazy, which is often a problem for those who are sick and inactive. He'll tell you to read aloud and exercise your lungs because that's where the problem lies, or to sail and gently shake up your insides with some mild movement. He'll recommend the right food and the best time to strengthen yourself with wine or avoid it so your cough doesn't get worse. But my advice to you is this: and it's a cure, not just for this illness, but for your entire life—"Don't be afraid of death." There is no sadness in the world once we've escaped the fear of dying.

There are three serious parts of any illness: the fear of death, physical pain, and the interruption of pleasures. We've talked enough about death, but I'll add one more thing: this fear isn't a fear of illness but a fear of life itself. Illness has often delayed death, and many have been saved by the very thought of dying. You won't die because you're sick, but because you're alive; even when you get better, death is still waiting for you. When you recover, it's not death that you've escaped but just bad health.

Now let's think about the pain that comes with illness. It can be unbearable, but pain usually comes in waves, giving you some relief in between. No one can suffer severely for a long time; Nature, who cares for us tenderly, has made it so that pain is either endurable or short-lived. The worst pain comes from the smallest parts of our body—nerves, joints, and other narrow places hurt the most when something goes wrong in their small spaces. But these parts soon go numb, and the pain itself makes them lose their sensitivity. This happens because the body's energy, when blocked and turned inward, loses its strength and can't warn us as it should. Or because the harmful fluids in the body, when they can't flow freely, build up and make the painful parts numb. So, gout in the feet and hands, and pain in the spine and nerves, all have periods of rest when they've dulled the areas they once tortured. The first sharp pains are the most distressing, but over time, they lessen, and the pain fades when numbness sets in. Pain in the teeth, eyes, and ears is most intense because it starts in the narrowest spaces of the body, just like in the head. But if it gets worse than usual, it can lead to delirium and unconsciousness. So, there is some comfort in extreme pain—you can't keep feeling it if it becomes too much to bear.

The reason why people who aren't used to suffering get impatient when they're in pain is that they haven't learned to be content in their spirit. They're too attached to their body. So, a wise and brave person separates their soul from their body and spends more time with the better, divine part of themselves, only dealing with the weak and complaining body as much as necessary.

"But," people say, "it's hard to go without our usual pleasures—to fast, to feel thirsty and hungry." This is true when you first give them up. But later, the desire fades because the appetites that create the desire grow tired and leave us. Then, your stomach gets fussy, and the food you once craved becomes something you don't even want. Our very needs fade away. But there's no bitterness in doing without something you've stopped wanting. Besides, every pain eventually stops, or at least eases up; you can also take steps to prevent it from coming back, and when it does, you can manage it with remedies. Every kind of pain has warning signs, at least for pain that's chronic and recurring. You can handle the suffering that illness brings if you've learned to look down on its results.

But don't make your troubles worse by complaining. Pain is small if you don't add anything to it by your own thoughts. But if you tell yourself, "It's nothing—just a little thing at most; stay strong, and it will soon be over," then by thinking it's small, you'll make it small. Everything depends on your attitude; ambition, luxury, and greed all go back to attitude. We suffer according to our opinions. A person is as miserable as they've convinced themselves they are. I believe we should stop complaining about past sufferings and avoid saying things like: "No one has ever had it worse than I have. What hardships, what evils I've endured! No one thought I'd recover. How often has my family mourned me, and the doctors given up on me! People who are tortured aren't torn apart with such agony!" But even if all this is true, it's over and done with. What's the point of dwelling on past suffering and being unhappy just because you were once unhappy? Besides, everyone adds to their own troubles and exaggerates their suffering. What was bitter to endure is pleasant to remember. It's natural to be happy that your troubles are over.

So, we need to get rid of two things once and for all—the fear of future suffering and the memory of past suffering. The past no longer affects me, and the future hasn't arrived yet. But when you're in the middle of trouble, remind yourself: "Maybe one day this sorrow will even bring me joy." Fight against your troubles with all your strength. If you give in, you'll be defeated, but if you resist, you'll win. Most people, however, bring disaster on themselves by not supporting what's falling on them. If you start to back away from something that's pushing toward you and ready to collapse, it will follow you and lean on you even harder. But if you stand your ground and push back, it will be forced to retreat.

Look at what blows athletes take on their faces and all over their bodies! Yet, they endure every torture for the sake of fame, not just because they're fighting, but so they can keep fighting. Their training itself is torture. So, let's also aim for victory in all our struggles, because the reward isn't a garland, a palm branch, or a trumpeter who announces our name, but virtue, a steadfast soul, and a peace that lasts forever, if we've once defeated fortune in any battle.

You say, "I feel severe pain." What then? Will you be freed from it if you endure it like a coward? Just like an enemy is more dangerous to an army that's retreating, every trouble that fortune brings attacks us harder if we give in and run away. "But the trouble is serious." What? Is this why we're strong—so we can carry only light burdens? Would you rather have your illness drag on or have it be quick and short? If it's long, it gives you a break, time to rest, and plenty of time to recover. As it begins, so it must also end. A short and rapid illness will do one of two things: it will either put out your life or be put out itself. And what difference does it make whether it's gone or I am gone? In either case, the pain ends.

Another thing that will help is to distract your mind with other thoughts and move away from the pain. Think about the honorable or brave things you've done. Reflect on the good parts of your life. Remember the things you've admired the most. Then think of all the brave people who have conquered pain: like the man who kept reading his book while having varicose veins cut out, or the one who didn't stop smiling, even though his smile made his torturers so angry that they tried every cruel tool on him. If pain can be defeated by a smile, won't it be conquered by reason?

You can tell me about anything you like—colds, coughing fits that bring up parts of your insides, fevers that burn your very core, thirst, limbs twisted so badly that the joints stick out in different directions. Yet, worse than all of these are the stake, the rack, the red-hot plates, the tool that reopens wounds while they're still swollen and presses even deeper. But there have been people who didn't utter a single groan during these tortures. "More pain!" says the torturer, but the victim hasn't begged for mercy. "More pain!" he says again, but there's no answer. "More pain!" the victim has smiled, and not just a faint smile, but a hearty one. Can't you bring yourself, after seeing such an example, to laugh at pain?

"But," you might say, "my illness keeps me from doing anything; it has taken me away from all my duties." It's your body that's held back by illness, not your soul. That's why it hinders the feet of the runner and the work of the shoemaker or craftsman. But if your soul is trained, you can still plead and teach, listen and learn, investigate and think. What more do you need? Do you think you're doing nothing if you keep control of yourself in your illness? You're showing that disease can be beaten or at least endured.

There is, I assure you, a place for virtue even when you're lying sick in bed. It's not just in battle with swords that the soul shows itself as alert and unafraid. A person can show bravery even when wrapped in bedclothes. You have something to do: fight bravely against your illness. If it doesn't force you to do anything or trick you into anything, you're showing a great example. Oh, how much recognition you'd get if we could have an audience for our sickness! Be your own audience; seek your own applause.

There are two kinds of pleasures. Disease takes away the pleasures of the body but doesn't get rid of them entirely. Actually, if you think about it, it makes them more intense; the thirstier a person is, the more they enjoy a drink; the hungrier they are, the more they relish food. Anything you get after a period of doing without is welcomed with greater enthusiasm. The other kind, the pleasures of the mind, which are higher and more certain, can't be taken away by any illness. Whoever seeks these and knows what they are will look down on all the pleasures of the senses.

People say, "Poor sick fellow!" But why? Is it because he doesn't mix snow with his wine, or because he doesn't chill his drink—mixed in a big bowl—by adding ice? Or because he doesn't have fresh oysters from Lucrine Bay opened at his table? Or because there's no noise from cooks around his dining room, bringing in their cooking equipment along with the food? Because luxury has already come up with this idea—of having the kitchen brought to the dining room, so the food doesn't get lukewarm or isn't hot enough for a palate that's become dull. "Poor sick fellow!"—he'll eat only what he can digest. There won't be a boar lying in front of him, thrown off the table as if it were common meat, and his table won't be piled high with bird breast meat because it makes him sick to see birds served whole. But what harm has been done to you? You'll eat like a sick man, sometimes even like a healthy man.

All these things can easily be endured—gruel, warm water, and anything else that seems unbearable to a picky person, someone who's drowning in luxury, sick in spirit rather than in body—if only we stop fearing death. And we will stop, once we understand the limits of good and bad; then, and only then, life won't tire us out, and death won't scare us.

For being tired of life can never happen to someone who explores all the great and divine things around us; only useless idleness makes people hate their lives. To someone who travels through the universe, the truth will never become boring; it's the lies that will make you feel weary. And, on the other hand, if death comes near with its call, even if it comes too soon and cuts you off in your prime, a person who has tasted all that the longest life can offer has already had enough. Such a person understands the universe in a big way. They know that honorable things don't need time to grow; but any life will seem short to those who measure its length by empty pleasures that never end.

Refresh yourself with these thoughts, and save some time for our letters. There will come a time when we'll be together again, and however short that time may be, we'll make it long by knowing how to use it. As Posidonius says: "A single day among the wise lasts longer than the longest life of the ignorant." Meanwhile, hold on to this thought, and keep it close: don't give in to adversity; don't trust in prosperity; keep in mind the full range of Fortune's power, as if she will definitely do whatever she can. What has been expected for a long time comes more gently. Farewell.

Letter 79 - On the rewards of scientific discovery

I've been waiting for a letter from you so that you can tell me what new things you discovered during your trip around Sicily. I especially want to know more about Charybdis. I know that Scylla is just a rock, and not one that sailors fear much. But when it comes to Charybdis, I'd like a full description to see if it matches what the myths say. If you happened to investigate it, which I think you would find interesting, please explain this to me: Is it turned into a whirlpool by wind coming from only one direction, or do all storms stir it up? Is it true that objects pulled down by the whirlpool are carried underwater for many miles and then come up again on the beach near Tauromenium?

If you write me a full account of these things, I'll have the courage to ask you to do something else: to climb Mount Etna as a special favor to me. Some scientists think the mountain is slowly shrinking and sinking because sailors used to be able to see it from farther away. This might not be because the mountain is getting shorter, but because the flames have become weaker, and the eruptions are less strong and less frequent. Because of this, the smoke might also be less noticeable during the day. But either of these things could be true: the mountain might be getting smaller because it's being burned up every day, or it might be staying the same size because the mountain isn't consuming itself. Instead, the stuff that boils out collects in some underground valley and is fed by other material. The mountain itself isn't the fuel; it's just the way out for the flames.

There's a well-known place in Lycia, which the locals call "Hephaestion," where the ground is full of holes and surrounded by harmless fire that doesn't hurt the plants growing there. Because the flames don't burn but only give off a mild light, the place is fertile and full of growth.

But let's put off this discussion until you can describe how far the snow lies from the crater, especially the snow that doesn't melt even in summer, safely away from the nearby fire. But don't think you have to do this just because I asked; you were already going to indulge your love of fine writing without anyone asking you to. What should I offer you, not only to describe Etna in your poem, but also to give it the full attention it deserves, just as all poets are expected to do? Ovid didn't let the fact that Virgil had already covered this topic stop him from using it, and neither of them scared off Cornelius Severus. The topic has served them all well, and I think those who came before didn't say everything there is to say but just opened the way.

It makes a big difference whether you approach a subject that's been fully explored or one that's only been started. In the latter case, the topic grows every day, and what's already been discovered doesn't prevent new discoveries. Besides, the person who writes last has the advantage; they find words already at hand that, when arranged differently, reveal something new. And they're not stealing these words because they belong to everyone.

Now, if Etna doesn't excite you, then I'm mistaken about you. You've wanted for some time to write something in a grand style, like the older writers. Your modesty won't let you hope for more than that, and this modesty is so strong that it seems to me you might hold back your natural talent if you thought you might outdo others. You respect the old masters that much.

Wisdom has this benefit, among others: no one can surpass another, except while they're still learning. But when you've reached the top, everyone is equal; there's no more room to climb, and the competition is over. Can the sun grow any larger? Can the moon become fuller than usual? The seas don't get bigger. The universe stays the same, with the same boundaries. Things that have reached their full size can't grow any taller. So, people who've gained wisdom will be equal and on the same level. Each will have their own special talents: one might be more friendly, another more skilled, another more quick-witted, and another more eloquent. But when it comes to the quality that brings happiness, it's the same in all of them.

I don't know if your Etna can collapse and crumble, whether this tall peak, visible from miles away over the sea, is worn down by the constant power of the flames. But I do know that virtue can't be brought down by flames or destruction. Virtue is the only greatness that never diminishes; it can't rise any higher or sink any lower. Its stature, like the stars in the sky, is fixed. So let's strive to raise ourselves to this height.

We've already accomplished much of the task; or rather, if I'm honest, not much at all. Being good doesn't just mean being better than the worst. Who would brag about their eyesight if they could only catch a glimpse of daylight? Someone who sees the sun shining through the mist might be happy that they've escaped darkness, but they don't yet enjoy the full blessing of light.

Our souls won't have a reason to be truly happy until, freed from the darkness where they stumble, they've not only glimpsed the brightness but absorbed the full light of day and returned to their place in the sky—until they've regained the position they held at the beginning of their existence. The soul is called upward by its very origin. And it will reach that goal even before it's released from its earthly prison, as soon as it has cast off sin and, in purity and lightness, has risen into the celestial realms of thought.

I'm glad, dear Lucilius, that we're focused on this goal, that we're pursuing it with all our strength, even if only a few people know it, or even none at all. Fame is the shadow of virtue; it follows virtue even against its will. But just as a shadow sometimes comes before and sometimes follows behind or even lags, fame sometimes goes ahead of us and shows itself clearly, and sometimes it's behind, growing larger the longer it takes to arrive, especially once envy has retreated.

How long did people think Democritus was mad! Glory barely reached Socrates. And how long did it take our state to realize Cato's worth! They rejected him and didn't recognize his value until after they'd lost him. If Rutilius hadn't accepted the wrong done to him, his innocence and virtue might have gone unnoticed; the moment of his suffering was also the moment of his triumph. Didn't he give thanks for his fate and welcome his exile with open arms?

So far, I've mentioned those whose fame grew even in the face of persecution. But how many people's journey toward virtue was only recognized after they died? And how many were ruined, not saved, by their reputation?

Take Epicurus, for example. Look at how much he's admired, not just by the educated but also by the common people. Yet this man was unknown even in Athens, where he lived in seclusion. So, when he had already outlived his friend Metrodorus by many years, he wrote these last words in a letter, expressing gratitude for their friendship: "Metrodorus and I were so greatly blessed that it didn't matter to us that we were unknown and almost unheard of in this well-known land of Greece."

So, isn't it true that people didn't really discover him until after he was gone? Yet his fame still shone brightly. Metrodorus also admits this in one of his letters: that Epicurus and he weren't well-known to the public. But he says that after their time, anyone who wanted to follow in their footsteps would gain great and ready-made fame.

Virtue is never truly hidden, and even if it seems to be, it's not really lost. There will come a day when it's revealed, even if it's been kept out of sight or suppressed by the malice of the time. Anyone who only thinks of the people of their own generation is living for a very small audience. Many thousands of years and many thousands of people will come after you; it's for them that you should live. Malice might silence everyone in your time, but future generations will judge you fairly, without bias. If there's any reward that virtue gets from fame, even that won't disappear. We ourselves won't be affected by what people say in the future, but still, they will cherish and celebrate us even if we don't know it.

Virtue has always rewarded those who follow her faithfully, both in life and after death. This happens whether or not they've dressed themselves up or put on a show, and whether they appear suddenly or after being announced. Pretending doesn't achieve anything. Few are fooled by a mask that can easily be taken off. Truth is the same in every part. Things that deceive us don't have real substance. Lies are thin and see-through if you look at them closely. Farewell.

Letter 80 - On worldly deceptions

Today, I have some free time, thanks not so much to my own schedule but because of the games, which have drawn all the noisy people to the boxing match. No one will interrupt me or disturb my thoughts, which can now flow more freely because I feel confident that I won't be disturbed. My door hasn't been constantly creaking, and my curtain won't be pulled aside. My thoughts can continue safely, which is especially important for someone who thinks for themselves and follows their own path. Do I follow no one who came before me? I do, but I also allow myself to discover something new, to change things, or to reject ideas. I am not a slave to others, even though I respect their work.

Still, it was a bold statement when I said I would have some quiet and uninterrupted time. For now, I hear a loud cheer from the stadium, and while it doesn't distract me completely, it does make me think about the contrast it brings to mind. I think to myself, how many people train their bodies, and how few train their minds! Look at the crowds that flock to these games, even though they are just for entertainment, and see how empty the places are where good lessons are taught! How silly are the athletes whose muscles and broad shoulders we admire!

The question I think about the most is this: if the body can be trained to endure so much that it can take the hits and kicks from several opponents at once, and last the whole day under the scorching sun in the burning dust, drenched in its own blood—if this is possible, then how much easier should it be to toughen the mind so that it can take the blows of fortune and not be defeated, so that it can get back up after being knocked down and trampled on?

While the body needs many things to be strong, the mind grows from within, nourishing and training itself. Those athletes need lots of food, lots of drink, lots of oil, and long hours of training. But you can acquire virtue without any equipment or expense. Everything that makes you a good person is already inside you.

And what do you need to become good? You just need to want it. But what better thing could you wish for than to break free from this slavery—a slavery that weighs us all down, a slavery that even the lowest-born slaves, born in such lowly conditions, try in every way to escape? They spend their hard-earned savings, which they've collected by scrimping on their own needs, just to buy their freedom. Shouldn't you be just as eager to gain your liberty, especially since you consider it your birthright?

Why do you look at your money box? Freedom can't be bought. It's pointless to list "freedom" as an item in your ledger because freedom belongs neither to those who buy it nor to those who sell it. You have to give this gift to yourself and seek it from within yourself.

First, free yourself from the fear of death, because death is what puts the yoke around our necks. Then, free yourself from the fear of poverty. If you want to see how little evil there is in poverty, compare the faces of the poor with those of the rich. The poor smile more often and more sincerely; their troubles don't cut deep. Even if they feel anxious, it passes quickly, like a brief cloud. But the happiness of those who are called rich is fake, while their sadness is heavy and festering. It's even worse because they can't show their grief and must pretend to be happy, even when sorrow is eating away at their hearts.

I often feel the need to use the following example, and I think it's one of the best ways to explain this drama of human life, where we play our roles so poorly. Look at the man who struts on stage with a proud posture and head held high, saying: "Look, I am the one whom Argos hails as lord, the one whom Pelops left as the heir to lands that stretch from the Hellespont to the Ionian Sea and all the way to the

Isthmian straits." And who is this man? He is just a slave; his wage is five measures of grain and five denarii.

Another man, proud and arrogant, boasting of his power, declares: "Peace, Menelaus, or this hand shall slay you!" He receives a daily allowance and sleeps on rags. You could say the same about all those fancy people you see being carried in litters above the heads of men and above the crowd; in every case, their happiness is just an act, like the mask an actor wears. Tear it off, and you'll see how little they are worth.

When you buy a horse, you ask for its blanket to be removed; you pull off the clothes from slaves being sold so that no flaws on their bodies are hidden from you. So why would you judge a man when he is wrapped in a disguise? Slave dealers hide any defects under fine clothing that might otherwise turn you away, and for that reason, the very trappings make the buyer suspicious. If you see a leg or an arm wrapped in cloth, you demand that it be uncovered so you can see the body itself.

Do you see that Scythian or Sarmatian king over there, wearing his crown of office? If you want to see his true worth, take off his crown; you'll find much evil hidden beneath it. But why talk about others? If you want to know your own value, put away your money, your lands, your titles, and look into your own soul. Right now, you are relying on what others say about you. Farewell.

Letter 81 - On Favors

You complain that you've met someone who is ungrateful. If this is the first time you've experienced this, you should be thankful either for your good luck or your caution. But in this case, being cautious won't help much except to make you less generous. Because if you want to avoid the risk of someone being ungrateful, you might stop giving altogether; and then, instead of losing favors to others, you'll lose them to yourself.

It's better to receive nothing in return than to stop doing favors. Even after a bad harvest, one should plant seeds again because, often, years of poor crops can be made up for by one year of good growth. To find one grateful person, it's worth dealing with many ungrateful ones. No one is so perfect at giving that they aren't sometimes deceived; it's good for a traveler to wander off the path so that they can learn to find it again. After a shipwreck, sailors still go back to sea. A banker isn't scared away from the market by one cheater. If we gave up on everything that caused trouble, life would quickly become dull and lazy. But in your case, this situation might encourage you to be even more generous. When the outcome of an action is uncertain, you have to keep trying in order to eventually succeed.

I've already discussed this topic in detail in the volumes I've written called "On Favors." But I think we should explore another question that hasn't been made clear enough: "If someone who helped us later harms us, does that cancel out the help and free us from being grateful?" You could also ask, "What if the harm done later is greater than the help given before?"

If you're looking for a fair and strict judgment, you'll find that it balances one act against the other and says, "Even if the harm is greater than the favor, we should still give credit for any favor that remains after considering the harm." The harm might be greater, but the favor was given first, so the timing should also be taken into account.

There are some cases so clear that I don't need to remind you to consider things like: how willingly was the favor given, and how reluctantly was the harm done—since both favors and harms depend on the intention behind them. "I didn't really want to give the favor, but I was convinced by respect for the person, or because they insisted, or because I hoped for something in return."

Our feelings about any obligation depend on the spirit in which the favor was given; we don't measure the size of the gift but the quality of the goodwill behind it. So, let's be clear: the first action was a favor, and the later action, which outweighed the first, was an injury. A good person will look at both sides and choose to be generous by giving more weight to the favor and less to the harm.

But a more lenient judge, which is the kind I'd rather be, will tell us to forget the harm and remember the favor.

"But surely," you might say, "it's fair to give thanks for a favor and to seek retribution or at least feel resentment for a harm!" That's true when the harm and the favor come from two different people; but if it's the same person, the harm is lessened by the favor they provided. In fact, someone who should be forgiven even if they hadn't done any good deeds should receive more than just leniency if they made a mistake after doing something good.

I don't value favors and injuries equally. I think favors are worth more than injuries. Not everyone understands how much they owe for a favor; even a thoughtless person might know they owe something, especially right after receiving it, but they don't realize how much they're truly indebted. Only a wise person knows exactly how to value everything; because a fool, even with good intentions, either repays less than they owe or does it at the wrong time or in the wrong way. What they should have repaid, they waste or lose.

There's a wonderfully precise way of talking about these things, an old way of expressing certain actions with symbols that clearly outline what our duties are. We often say, "He has made a return for the favor." Making a return means voluntarily giving back what you owe. We don't say, "He has paid back the favor," because "pay back" is used when someone is demanded to pay, when they pay unwillingly, when they pay in any situation, or through someone else. We don't say, "He has restored the favor" or "settled it"; we've never used words that are really about repaying money.

Making a return means offering something to the person who gave you something. The phrase implies a voluntary act; the person who makes such a return has done so willingly.

The wise person will think carefully about all the circumstances: how much they received, from whom, when, where, and how. That's why we say only the wise person knows how to make a true return for a favor. Moreover, only the wise person knows how to give a favor—someone who enjoys giving more than the receiver enjoys getting.

Now, someone might think this is one of those surprising statements we Stoics like to make, the kind the Greeks call "paradoxes," and they might say, "Do you really believe only the wise person knows how to return a favor? Do you think no one else knows how to pay back a debt to a creditor? Or how to pay the full price when buying something?" To avoid any misunderstanding, let me tell you that even Epicurus says the same thing. Metrodorus, one of his followers, also said that only the wise person knows how to return a favor.

Again, the person who objected earlier might be surprised by our saying, "Only the wise person knows how to love; only the wise person is a true friend." And yet, part of love and friendship is returning favors, and it's something that happens more often than true friendship. That same person might also be surprised when we say, "There's no true loyalty except in the wise person," as if they don't believe the same thing! Or do you think someone who doesn't know how to return a favor can be truly loyal?

These critics should stop doubting us as if we're making impossible claims. They should understand that true honor resides in the wise person, while the general crowd only has a shadow or appearance of honor. Only the wise person knows how to return a favor. Even a fool can try to return it as best as they know how, but their fault is not in lacking the will but in lacking the knowledge. The desire to repay isn't something that can be taught.

The wise person will compare everything carefully because the same action can be more or less significant depending on the time, place, and reason. Sometimes, spending a fortune on a palace doesn't achieve as much as a small gift given at the right time. It makes a big difference whether you give freely or help someone in need, whether your generosity saves someone or helps them get started in life. Sometimes the gift itself is small, but the impact is great. And what do you think is the difference between taking something you lack when it's offered and receiving a favor to return the favor?

But let's not dive back into a topic we've already discussed enough. When balancing favors and injuries, the good person will judge as fairly as possible, but they will lean toward the side of the favor. They'll be more inclined to give more weight to the good.

Moreover, in these matters, the person involved is very important. People might say, "You helped me with that issue about my slave, but you hurt me in the case of my father," or "You saved my son but took away my father." In the same way, they'll compare other situations where differences can be found. If the difference is small, they'll pretend not to notice it. Even if the difference is big, if it doesn't affect their duty and loyalty, the good person will overlook it, as long as the injury only affects them personally.

To sum it up, the good person will be generous when striking a balance; they'll allow too much credit to go against the injury. They won't want to repay a favor by balancing it with an injury. They'll lean toward wanting to be indebted for the favor and wanting to repay it. Anyone who enjoys receiving a favor more than repaying it is mistaken. Just as someone who repays a loan feels lighter than someone who borrows, someone who frees themselves from the debt of a favor received should feel more joyful than someone who takes on a new obligation.

Ungrateful people make another mistake: they have to repay their creditors both the original amount and the interest, but they think favors are something they can use without paying interest. So, the debt grows with delay, and the longer they wait, the more they owe. A person is ungrateful if they repay a favor without interest. So, interest should also be considered when comparing what you've received and what you've given.

We should try in every way to be as grateful as possible. Gratitude is good for us, in a way that justice, which is usually thought of as something that concerns others, isn't. Gratitude benefits us directly. There isn't a person who, when they've helped their neighbor, hasn't also helped themselves. I don't mean just because the person you helped might want to help you back, or because someone you defended might want to protect you, or because a good example can come back around to benefit you, just as bad examples can come back to harm those who set them. The true reward for all virtues lies in the virtues themselves. Virtues aren't practiced for some reward; the reward of doing good is simply having done it.

I feel grateful not so that my neighbor, motivated by my kindness, might be more willing to help me in the future, but simply because it's a pleasant and beautiful act. I feel grateful not because it benefits me, but because it pleases me. And to prove this, I declare that even if I couldn't be grateful without seeming ungrateful, even if I could only return a favor by doing something that looks like harm, I would still strive calmly toward the goal that honor demands, even in the midst of disgrace. No one, I believe, values virtue more highly or is more dedicated to it than the person who loses their reputation for being good just to keep from losing the approval of their own conscience.

As I've said, being grateful is more beneficial to you than to your neighbor. While your neighbor has had an ordinary experience—receiving back the favor they gave—you've had a great experience that comes from a truly happy state of mind: the feeling of gratitude. If wickedness makes people unhappy and virtue makes them blessed, and if gratitude is a virtue, then the return you've made is just normal, but the feeling you've gained is priceless—the consciousness of gratitude, which belongs only to a divine and blessed soul. The opposite feeling, however, brings immediate misery. No ungrateful person will be unhappy in the future; I say they are unhappy right now.

So, let's avoid being ungrateful, not for the sake of others but for our own sake. When we do wrong, only the smallest and lightest part of it affects our neighbor; the worst and heaviest part stays with us and troubles us. My teacher Attalus used to say, "Evil itself drinks the largest portion of its own poison." The poison that snakes carry to harm others and secrete without harming themselves is not like this poison; this kind is ruinous to the one who possesses it.

The ungrateful person tortures and torments themselves; they hate the gifts they've accepted because they have to repay them, and they try to downplay their value, but they actually exaggerate the injuries they've received. And what's more miserable than someone who forgets the good done for them but clings to the wrongs?

Wisdom, on the other hand, adds grace to every favor and willingly remembers it, delighting in the continued memory of it. Evil people only enjoy favors for a short time, just while they're receiving them. But the wise person gets lasting and eternal joy from them. They find joy not so much in receiving the favor but in having received it, and this joy never fades; it stays with them always. They despise the wrongs done to them; they forget them, not by accident but on purpose.

They don't twist everything into something negative or look for someone to blame for every little thing; instead, they attribute even the wrongs of others to chance. They won't misinterpret a word or a look; they make light of all misfortunes by interpreting them generously. They don't remember an injury more than a favor. As much as possible, they let their memory focus on the earlier and better deeds, never changing their attitude toward those who have treated them well, except in cases where the bad deeds far outweigh the good, and the difference is so obvious that even someone who's trying to ignore it can see it. Even then, they'll only go as far as to try to return to the way they felt before they received the favor. When the injury is equal to the favor, some positive feeling remains.

Just as a defendant is acquitted when the votes are equal, and just as kindness always tries to interpret every doubtful case in the best possible way, the wise person's mind, when someone's merits equal their faults, will stop feeling an obligation, but won't stop wanting to feel it. They act like someone who pays their debts even after they've been legally canceled.

But no one can be truly grateful unless they've learned to scorn the things that drive most people crazy. If you want to return a favor, you must be willing to go into exile, to bleed, to face poverty, or—as often happens—even to let your innocence be stained and exposed to shameful slander. Being grateful isn't a cheap price to pay.

We value a favor highly when we're trying to get it; we value it cheaply after we've received it. Do you want to know why we forget favors we've received? It's because of our extreme greed for getting more. We don't think about what we've already obtained, but what we're going to seek next. We're led off course by riches, titles, power, and everything that seems valuable to us but is worthless when judged by its true value.

We don't know how to weigh things properly; we should judge them by their true nature, not by their reputation. These things don't have any real grandeur to capture our minds, except for the fact that we've gotten used to admiring them. They're not praised because they deserve to be desired, but they're desired because they've been praised. And when individuals' errors create public errors, the public error goes on creating more mistakes in individuals.

But just as we accept certain things based on others' opinions, let's also accept this truth that everyone agrees on: nothing is more honorable than a grateful heart. This idea will be echoed by all cities and races, even those from savage lands. On this point, good and bad people will agree.

Some people praise pleasure, some prefer hard work; some say pain is the greatest evil, while others say it's no evil at all; some include riches as part of the Supreme Good, while others say that finding wealth has harmed humanity and that no one is richer than the person who has nothing left for Fortune to give. Amid all this diversity of opinion, all people will agree that we should give thanks to those who have done well by us. On this question, even the rebellious common crowd will agree, but right now, we seem to repay injuries instead of favors. The main reason someone is ungrateful is that they feel they can't be grateful enough.

Our madness has gone so far that it's become dangerous to give great favors to someone; because the shame of not repaying them might make the person wish they didn't have to. "Keep what you've received; I don't ask for it back. I don't demand it. Let it be safe to have given a favor." There is no worse hatred than the kind that comes from the shame of not repaying a favor. Farewell.

Letter 82 - On the natural fear of death

I've already stopped being worried about you. "Which god," you ask, "have you found to be your guarantee?" Let me tell you, it's a god who deceives no one—a soul that loves what is right and good. The best part of you is on solid ground. Fortune can harm you; but more importantly, I don't worry that you'll harm yourself. Keep going as you've started, and settle into this way of living—not luxuriously, but calmly.

I'd rather be in hardship than in luxury, and you should understand "hardship" as most people do: living a "difficult," "rough," or "tough" life. We often hear people's lives praised like this when they're unpopular: "So-and-so lives in luxury," but by this, they mean, "He's softened by luxury." For the soul gradually becomes weak and lazy, matching the comfort in which it lives. Isn't it better for someone who is truly strong to become tough instead?

These same people who indulge in luxury end up fearing the very thing they've made their lives resemble. There's a big difference between lying around doing nothing and lying buried in a grave!

"But," you say, "isn't it better to lie idle than to be caught up in the chaos of busyness?" Both extremes should be avoided—both tension and laziness. I believe that someone who lies on a perfumed couch is no less dead than someone who is dragged along by the executioner's hook.

Leisure without purpose is death; it's like a tomb for someone who's still alive.

So, what's the point of retreating from life? As if the real causes of our worries didn't follow us wherever we go! Is there any place where the fear of death doesn't reach? Are there any peaceful spots so well-protected and far away that pain can't fill them with fear? Wherever you hide, human problems will surround you with noise. There are many external things that deceive us or weigh us down, and there are many internal things that trouble us even when we're alone.

So, shield yourself with philosophy, which is like an unbreakable wall. Even though many forces may attack it, Fortune can't find a way in. The soul stands on solid ground if it has let go of external things; it's independent in its own stronghold, and every weapon thrown at it falls short. Fortune doesn't have the long reach we think she does; she can only grab hold of those who cling to her.

Let's pull away from her as much as we can. We can only do this through understanding ourselves and the natural world. The soul should know where it's going and where it came from, what's good for it and what's bad, what it should seek and what it should avoid, and what Reason is—the thing that helps us tell the difference between what's desirable and undesirable, taming our wild desires and calming our fears.

Some people think they've overcome these fears by themselves, without the help of philosophy, but when something unexpected happens, they are forced to admit they were wrong. Their boastful words disappear when the torturer tells them to stretch out their hands, and when death gets closer! You might say to such a person: "It was easy for you to challenge troubles when they weren't close by; but now pain is here, the pain you said you could handle; now death is near, the death you spoke about so bravely! The whip cracks, the sword flashes: now, Aeneas, you must be strong and brave!"

However, this strength will only come from constant practice if you train not just your words but your soul, and if you prepare yourself to face death. But don't expect encouragement from those who try to convince you, with their tricky arguments, that death isn't bad. For I enjoy poking fun at the absurdities of the Greeks, which, to my surprise, I still haven't completely shaken off.

Our master Zeno uses a syllogism like this: "No evil is glorious; but death is glorious; therefore, death is no evil." Well done, Zeno! I'm cured of my fear; now I won't hesitate to offer my neck to the executioner. But shouldn't you be speaking more seriously instead of making a dying man laugh? Honestly, Lucilius, I couldn't tell you whether the person who thought he was quenching the fear of death with this argument was more foolish, or the one who tried to refute it, as if it had anything to do with the real issue!

For the refuter himself came up with a counter-syllogism, based on the idea that we consider death as "indifferent"—one of those things the Greeks call ἀδιάφορα. "Nothing," he says, "that is indifferent can be glorious; death is glorious; therefore, death is not indifferent." You see the tricky fallacy in this argument: mere death isn't glorious, but a brave death is glorious. And when you say, "Nothing that is indifferent is glorious," I agree, but I also say that nothing is glorious except in how it deals with indifferent things. I classify as "indifferent"—neither good nor bad—things like sickness, pain, poverty, exile, and death.

None of these things is glorious by itself, but nothing can be glorious without them. For we don't praise poverty, but the person who poverty can't break or bend. Nor do we praise exile, but the person who goes into exile with the same spirit he would have had if he were sending someone else into exile. We don't praise pain, but the person whom pain can't conquer. We don't praise death, but the person who dies without letting death overwhelm his soul.

All these things are not, in themselves, honorable or glorious, but any one of them, when touched by virtue, becomes honorable and glorious because of virtue. They are neutral, and what matters is whether wickedness or virtue takes hold of them. For example, the death that was glorious for Cato was disgraceful for Brutus. Brutus, who was sentenced to death, tried to get a delay; he took a moment to relieve himself, and when he was called to die and ordered to bare his throat, he said, "I'll bare my throat, but only if I can live!" What madness it is to try to escape when there's no way to turn back! "I'll bare my throat, but only if I can live!" He almost said, "Even under Antony!" This man indeed deserved to be condemned to life!

But as I was saying, you see that death itself is neither good nor bad; Cato faced death most honorably, while Brutus faced it most shamefully. Anything, when you add virtue to it, takes on a glory it didn't have before. We talk about a sunny room, even though the same room is pitch-dark at night. It's the day that fills it with light and the night that takes the light away; and it's the same with things we call indifferent or "neutral," like riches, strength, beauty, titles, kingship, and their opposites—death, exile, illness, pain, and all such evils that we fear to varying degrees. It's wickedness or virtue that gives these things the name of good or evil. An object isn't inherently hot or cold; it becomes hot when thrown into a furnace and cold when dropped into water. Death is honorable when connected to something honorable, like virtue and a soul that despises the worst hardships.

Furthermore, there are vast differences among these qualities we call "neutral." For example, death isn't as indifferent as whether your hair is worn evenly or unevenly. Death belongs among those things that aren't really evils but still seem like evils; because we have within us a love of self, a desire to live and to protect ourselves, and a fear of dissolution, because death seems to take away many goods and pull us away from the abundance we're used to. There's also another factor that makes us shy away from death: we're familiar with the present, but we don't know the future we're heading into, and we fear the unknown. Moreover, it's natural to fear the underworld, where death is thought to lead us.

So, although death is something indifferent, it's not something we can easily ignore. The soul must be toughened through long practice so that it can learn to face the sight and approach of death.

Death should be despised more than it usually is. We believe too many of the stories about death. Many thinkers have worked hard to make death seem more terrifying; they've described the prison of the underworld and the land covered in everlasting night, where

"Within his blood-stained cave Hell's huge guard
Sprawls his ugly length on half-crunched bones,
And terrifies the disembodied ghosts
With never-ceasing bark."

Even if you can prove that these are just stories and that the dead have nothing to fear, another fear sneaks in. The fear of going to the underworld is matched by the fear of going nowhere.

Given these beliefs, which have been drilled into us for so long, how could facing death bravely be anything other than glorious, and worthy of being considered one of the greatest accomplishments of the human mind? The mind will never rise to virtue if it believes that death is an evil; but it will rise if it believes that death is indifferent. It's not natural for someone to face a destiny with courage if they believe that destiny is evil; they'll approach it slowly and reluctantly. But nothing glorious can come from hesitation and cowardice; virtue does nothing under compulsion.

Moreover, no action is honorable unless the person doing it is fully committed to it and puts their whole heart into it, without any part of them rebelling. When someone faces something they believe to be evil, either out of fear of worse evils or in the hope of achieving something important enough to make the evil bearable, their judgment is pulled in two directions. On one side is the reason to act, and on the other is the reason to hold back because of fear or danger. As a result, they're torn between the two, and when this happens, the glory of the action is lost. Virtue carries out its plans only when the spirit is in full agreement with itself. There's no fear in any of its actions.

"Do not yield to evils, but go still braver
Wherever your fortune allows."

You can't "go still braver" if you believe those things are real evils. Remove this belief from your soul, or else your fears will keep holding you back, preventing you from moving forward like a soldier.

Some in our school would say that Zeno's argument is correct, but that the second argument I mentioned, which is set against his, is deceptive and wrong. But I refuse to reduce such important questions to mere logical rules or to the subtle tricks of an outdated system. Away with all that nonsense that makes someone feel trapped when asked a question, forcing them to agree to a premise and then making them say something they don't actually believe!

When truth is at stake, we must act more openly, and when we're combating fear, we must act more boldly. These questions, which the dialecticians twist into complexities, I prefer to solve and weigh rationally, with the goal of convincing rather than forcing agreement.

When a general is about to lead an army into battle, an army ready to face death for their wives and children, how will he inspire them? I remind you of the Fabii, who took on a war that concerned the whole state by themselves. I point out to you the Spartans standing in the pass at Thermopylae! They had no hope of victory, no hope of returning. The place where they stood was to be their grave.

What words would you use to encourage them to block the way with their bodies, to take on the destruction of their entire tribe, and to retreat from life rather than their post? Would you say, "That which is evil is not glorious; but death is glorious; therefore, death is not an evil"? What a powerful speech! After such words, who wouldn't throw themselves onto the enemy's spears and die where they stood? But take Leonidas: how bravely he addressed his men! He said, "Fellow soldiers, let us have breakfast, knowing that we shall dine in Hades!" The food didn't stick in their mouths, or catch in their throats, or slip from their fingers; they eagerly accepted the invitation to breakfast and to supper as well!

Think, too, of the famous Roman general; his soldiers had been sent to seize a position, and as they were about to make their way through a huge enemy army, he said to them: "You must go now, fellow soldiers, to that place, from which there's no 'must' about your returning!"

You see, then, how straightforward and commanding virtue is; but how can your tricky logic make anyone more courageous or upright? Rather, it weakens the spirit, which should never be more free and confident than when planning something great. It's not just the Three Hundred—it's all of humanity that needs to be freed from the fear of death.

But how can you prove to all those people that death isn't an evil? How can you overcome the beliefs we've held all our lives—beliefs we've had since we were born? What help can you offer for our human weakness? What can you say to make people rush eagerly into danger? What persuasive speech can you use to turn aside this universal fear, or what clever argument can you use to change the long-held conviction of the human race? Will you offer me catchy phrases or string together some tricky logic? It takes great weapons to strike down great monsters.

Remember the fierce serpent in Africa that terrified the Roman legions more than the war itself and couldn't be harmed by arrows or slings; it couldn't even be wounded by Pythius because its enormous size and toughness made spears and any weapon thrown by human hands bounce off. It was finally destroyed by rocks as big as millstones. So, are you throwing weak arguments like yours against death? Can you stop a charging lion with a tiny tool like an awl? Your arguments may be sharp, but there's nothing sharper than a stalk of grain. Some arguments are useless and ineffective because they're too subtle. Farewell.

Letter 83 - On drunkenness

You ask me to give you an account of each day and the whole day too, so you must think highly of me if you believe that there is nothing in my days that I need to hide. We should live in such a way that everyone could see how we live; and we should think as if there were someone who could look into our souls, because there is someone who can. What good does it do to hide something from people? Nothing is hidden from the sight of God. He sees everything in our souls, and He looks into our thoughts—just like someone who could leave at any moment.

So, I'll do as you asked and gladly tell you in a letter what I'm doing and in what order. I'll keep watching myself constantly, and—this is a very useful habit—I'll review each day. The reason we do wrong is that no one looks back over their own life. We only think about what we're going to do next. But our plans for the future always depend on what we've done in the past.

Today, no one took even the smallest part of my day from me. The whole time was divided between rest and reading. I spent a little time on physical exercise, and I have to thank old age for making exercise require very little effort; as soon as I start moving, I get tired. And getting tired is the goal of exercise, no matter how strong you are.

You ask who I exercise with? One person is enough for me—the slave Pharius, a pleasant fellow, as you know, but I will soon exchange him for someone else. At my age, I need someone even younger. Pharius says that he and I are at the same stage of life because we're both losing our teeth. Even now, I can barely keep up with him when he runs, and very soon, I won't be able to keep up at all. So, you see what little benefit we get from daily exercise. A wide gap quickly opens up between two people who travel at different speeds. My slave is climbing up just as I'm coming down, and you surely know how much faster coming down is. Actually, I was wrong; my life isn't just coming down—it's falling outright.

Do you still want to know how our race turned out today? We tied—something that rarely happens in a running contest. After wearing myself out this way (because I can't really call it exercise), I took a cold bath; but at my house, a cold bath is just short of hot. I used to be a fan of cold water, celebrating the New Year by plunging into the canal. Just as naturally as I would set out to do some reading, writing, or to compose a speech, I used to start the New Year with a plunge into the Virgo aqueduct. Now I've switched my loyalty first to the Tiber, and then to my favorite tank, which is only warmed by the sun, and only when I'm most robust and when my health is in perfect shape. I don't have much energy left for bathing.

After the bath, I had some stale bread and a breakfast that didn't require a table; no need to wash my hands after such a meal. Then came a very short nap. You know my habit: I only take a quick nap—like unhitching a horse for a short break. I'm satisfied if I can just stop staying awake. Sometimes I know I've slept; other times, I just suspect it.

Now, suddenly, I hear the noise of the races! The sound of cheering hits my ears all at once. But this doesn't disturb my thoughts or even break their flow. I can handle noise with complete calm. The mix of voices blending into one sound feels to me like waves crashing or like the wind whipping through the trees, or like any other sound that doesn't mean anything.

So, what have I been thinking about, you ask? I'll tell you. A thought has been sticking with me since yesterday—what did the greatest minds mean when they used the smallest and most complicated arguments to prove the most important problems— arguments that might be true, but still seem like tricks?

Zeno, the greatest of men and the founder of our noble and sacred school of philosophy, wants to discourage us from getting drunk. Listen to his argument proving that a good man won't get drunk: "No one trusts a secret to a drunk man, but people do trust secrets to a good man; therefore, a good man won't get drunk." Notice how silly Zeno's argument seems when we create a similar one to contrast with his. There are many examples, but here's one: "No one trusts a secret to a man who is asleep, but people do trust secrets to a good man; therefore, a good man doesn't go to sleep."

Posidonius defends our master Zeno in the only way possible, but I believe it can't be defended even this way. Posidonius argues that the word "drunken" can be used in two ways—one for a man who's drunk and out of control, and the other for a man who regularly gets drunk and is a slave to the habit. Zeno, he says, meant the latter—the man who is in the habit of getting drunk, not the one who is currently drunk. No one would trust a secret to this person because he might blurt it out when he's drunk.

This is a mistake. The first argument refers to someone who is actually drunk, not someone who is going to get drunk. You'll surely agree that there's a big difference between a man who is drunk and a drunkard. A person who is actually drunk might be drunk for the first time and might not have the habit, while a drunkard might often be sober. I interpret the word in its usual meaning, especially since the argument was made by someone who carefully chooses his words and weighs his language. Moreover, if this is what Zeno meant, and what he wanted us to understand, then he was trying to use a word with two meanings to create a trick, and no one should do this when the truth is the goal.

But let's admit that Zeno meant what Posidonius says he did; even so, the conclusion is false—that secrets aren't trusted to a habitual drunkard. Think about how many soldiers who aren't always sober have been trusted by a general, a captain, or a centurion with messages that must be kept secret! Regarding the famous plot to kill Gaius Caesar—the Caesar who defeated Pompey and took control of the state—Tillius Cimber was trusted with it just as much as Gaius Cassius was. Cassius drank only water his whole life, while Tillius Cimber was a drunk and a brawler. Cimber even joked about it, saying, "I carry a master? I can't even carry my liquor!"

So let everyone remember people they know who can't be trusted with wine but can be trusted with words. But one case comes to my mind that I'll share, so it's not forgotten. Life should be full of memorable examples. Let's not always look back to ancient history.

Lucius Piso, the Director of Public Safety in Rome, was drunk from the moment he was appointed. He spent most of the night at banquets and slept until noon. That's how he spent his mornings. Still, he was very diligent in his official duties, including protecting the city. Even the deified Augustus trusted him with secret orders when he made him governor of Thrace. Piso conquered that country. Tiberius also trusted him when he took a vacation in Campania, leaving behind many critical issues that stirred up both suspicion and hatred.

I think that since Piso's drunkenness worked out well for the Emperor, Tiberius then appointed Cossus, a man of authority and good sense, but so soaked in drink that once, at a Senate meeting after a banquet, he fell into a deep sleep that no one could wake him from, and he had to be carried home. It was to this man that Tiberius sent many orders, written in his own hand—orders he didn't trust even to his household officials. Cossus never let a single secret slip out, whether personal or public.

So let's get rid of speeches like this: "No man under the influence of alcohol has control over his soul. Just as new wine bursts the vats, and the dregs rise to the surface from the strength of fermentation, so when wine ferments in a person, whatever lies hidden inside is brought up and exposed. Just as a man overcome by drink can't keep his food down after drinking too much, he also can't keep a secret. He spills out both his own secrets and those of others."

This is what usually happens, but so does this—we discuss serious matters with people who we know drink heavily. So the argument made in defense of Zeno's logic is false—that secrets aren't trusted to habitual drunkards.

How much better it is to criticize drunkenness directly and expose its vices! Even the average good person avoids them, not to mention the perfect sage, who is satisfied with quenching his thirst. The sage, even if he occasionally gets carried away by good company, always stops short of getting drunk.

We'll talk later about whether a wise man's mind is affected by too much wine and if it leads him to act foolishly like a drunk. But for now, if you want to prove that a good man shouldn't get drunk, why use logic? Show how shameful it is to drink more than you can handle and not know your own limits. Show how often the drunkard does things that make him ashamed when he's sober. Say that drunkenness is just a state of insanity that we willingly bring on ourselves. Extend the drunkard's state for several days, and would you doubt his madness? Even as it is, the madness isn't any less—it just doesn't last as long.

Think of Alexander the Great, who stabbed Clitus, his dearest and most loyal friend, at a banquet. After realizing what he'd done, Alexander wanted to die, and he certainly should have.

Drunkenness brings out and reveals every kind of vice and removes the sense of shame that hides our evil actions. More people avoid doing wrong because they're ashamed of it than because they have good intentions. When the strength of wine takes over and controls the mind, every hidden evil comes out. Drunkenness doesn't create vice; it just brings it to light. The lustful man doesn't even wait for the privacy of a bedroom; without delay, he gives in to his desires. The unchaste man publicly shows his sickness. The ill-tempered person doesn't hold back his words or his hands. The arrogant man becomes more arrogant, the cruel man more ruthless, the slanderer more spiteful. Every vice is unleashed and comes to the forefront.

Besides, we forget who we are, our words become slurred and poorly spoken, our gaze becomes unsteady, our steps falter, our head spins, and the ceiling seems to move around as if a storm were shaking the whole house. Our stomachs ache when the wine causes gas, making our insides swell. At the time, these problems can be endured as long as the person still has some natural strength left. But what can he do when sleep weakens him and drunkenness turns into indigestion?

Think of the disasters caused by drunkenness in entire nations! This evil has betrayed the most spirited and warlike races to their enemies. It has breached walls defended by years of hard fighting. It has forced once unyielding and defiant people to submit to foreign rule. This evil has defeated in the wine cup those who were invincible on the battlefield.

Alexander, whom I just mentioned, survived many long marches, battles, and winter campaigns (which he endured by overcoming the disadvantages of time and place), crossing many rivers from unknown sources and many seas, all without harm. But excessive drinking took him down, along with the infamous death-dealing cup of Hercules.

What glory is there in holding your liquor? When you've won the prize, and the other drinkers are either passed out or vomiting, unable to keep up with your challenge to drink more; when you're the last one standing at the party; when you've outdrunk everyone else, proving yourself the most capable—yet you're defeated by the barrel itself.

Mark Antony was a great man, a man of remarkable ability. But what ruined him and drove him into foreign customs and un-Roman vices, if not drunkenness and—just as potent as wine—his love for Cleopatra? This made him an enemy of the state. This made him no match for his enemies. This made him cruel, as he sat at the table with the heads of state leaders brought in, identifying their faces and hands among the most elaborate feasts and royal luxuries after having proscribed them. Even though he was heavy with wine, he still thirsted for blood. It was bad enough that he got drunk while doing these things; how much worse that he did them while actually drunk!

Cruelty often follows drinking because a man's sound mind is corrupted and made savage. Just as a lingering illness makes people irritable and drives them wild at the slightest frustration, so frequent bouts of drunkenness brutalize the soul. When people often lose control of themselves, the habit of madness lingers, and the vices that alcohol stirs up remain even after the alcohol is gone.

So you should explain why the wise man shouldn't get drunk. Show the ugly truth and the haunting evils of drunkenness with facts, not just words. Do the simplest thing of all—show that what people call pleasures become punishments once they go beyond their limits. If you try to prove that the wise man can drink too much wine and still stay on course, even though he's drunk, you might as well try to prove with logic that he won't die if he swallows poison, that he won't sleep if he takes a sleeping pill, or that he won't vomit and expel what clogs his stomach when you give him hellebore. But when a man's feet stumble and his speech is slurred, what reason do you have to believe that he's half sober and half drunk? Farewell.

Letter 84 - On gathering ideas

The trips you mentioned—trips that shake the laziness out of me—I consider them good for both my health and my studies. You see how they benefit my health: because my love for reading makes me lazy and neglectful of my body, I can get some exercise while traveling.

As for my studies, I'll explain how these trips help them too, since I haven't let my reading slip even a little bit. And I believe reading is essential—not only to keep me from being too self-satisfied, but also to learn what others have discovered through their hard work, so I can judge their findings and think about the new discoveries still to be made. Reading feeds the mind and refreshes it when it gets tired from study; but remember, this refreshment isn't possible without studying.

We shouldn't focus only on writing or only on reading; if we only write, we'll wear ourselves out and become gloomy, and if we only read, we'll become weak and lack energy. It's better to switch between them and combine both, so the things we learn from reading can be solidified through writing.

People say we should follow the example of bees, who fly around and gather the flowers they need to make honey, and then store and organize everything they've collected. These bees, as our poet Vergil says, "pack the flowing honey tight, and fill their hives with sweet nectar."

It's not clear whether the juice they collect from flowers instantly turns into honey or if the bees change what they've gathered into honey by mixing it with something from themselves and with their breath's special quality. Some experts believe that bees don't actually make honey but just gather it; they say that in India, honey has been found on the leaves of certain reeds, created either by the unique dew in that region or by the reed's juice, which is unusually sweet and rich. They also say that a similar quality exists in our own grasses, though it's less obvious; a creature born to do this job could find and collect it. Others believe that the bees take what they've gathered from the delicate flowers and plants and turn it into honey through careful storing and preserving, helped by something like fermentation, where different parts come together to form one substance.

But I shouldn't get off-topic. I believe we should follow the bees' example too and carefully sift through everything we've gathered from a wide range of reading. These ideas are better preserved if they're kept separate at first; then, using the special abilities nature has given us—our natural talents—we should blend these different ideas into one delicious mixture. Even though it might show where it came from, it should still be clearly different from its original sources. This is what we see nature doing in our own bodies without us even trying. The food we eat, as long as it stays in its original form and floats in our stomachs as an undigested mass, is a burden; but it turns into tissue and blood only after it's changed from its original form.

It's the same with the food that nourishes our minds. We need to make sure that what we've absorbed doesn't stay the same, or it won't truly become a part of us. We must digest it; otherwise, it will just stay in our memory and won't reach our reasoning power. Let's fully absorb these ideas and make them our own so that something new and unified is created from many different elements, just like how a single number is formed from several smaller ones when we add them up. This is what our mind should do: it should hide away all the pieces that helped it, and reveal only what it has made from them.

Even if you end up resembling the person you admire deeply, I'd want you to resemble him as a child resembles his father, not as a picture resembles its original, because a picture is a lifeless thing.

You might ask, "Won't it be obvious whose style, reasoning, or clever sayings you're imitating?" I think that sometimes it's impossible to tell who's being imitated if the copy is truly accurate. A true copy leaves its own mark on all the features it takes from the original, blending them into one unified whole.

Don't you see how many voices there are in a choir? Yet, out of the many voices, we hear only one sound. In that choir, one voice sings the high notes, another the low, and another the middle range. There are women's voices too, mixed with the men's, and the flute plays along with them. In that choir, the individual singers' voices are hidden; what we hear is the combined voice of all. Of course, I'm talking about the kind of choir the old philosophers knew. In our modern performances, we have more singers than there used to be spectators in the theaters of old. The aisles are filled with rows of singers, brass instruments surround the auditorium, the stage echoes with flutes and other instruments of every kind, and yet, from all these different sounds, a harmony is produced.

I want my mind to be like this: equipped with many skills, many teachings, and examples of conduct taken from many periods in history, but all blending together harmoniously into one.

"How can this be done?" you ask. By constant effort and by doing nothing without the approval of reason. If you're willing to listen to reason, it will tell you: "Give up the pursuits that have made you run around aimlessly. Give up wealth, which is either a danger or a burden to those who have it. Give up the pleasures of the body and the mind; they only soften and weaken you. Give up your quest for power; it's an inflated, idle, and empty pursuit with no real goal, as worried about being overtaken as it is about having no one following. It's plagued by envy—actually, by double envy—and you see how miserable a person is when someone who is envied also feels envy himself."

Do you see those grand houses, with crowds of people making noise as they wait to pay their respects? They'll insult you as you enter the door and even more after you've entered. Avoid the steps that lead to rich men's homes and the porches made dangerous by the huge crowd, because there you'll be standing not just on the edge of a cliff but also on slippery ground. Instead, steer yourself toward wisdom and follow her ways, which offer true peace and abundance.

Whatever seems important in human affairs—no matter how small it really is and only prominent by comparison to the lowest things—can only be reached by a difficult and tiring path. It's a rough road that leads to the heights of greatness. But if you want to reach this peak, which lies far above the reach of Fortune, you'll look down on everything that people consider lofty, but even so, you can reach the top by traveling on level ground. Farewell.

Letter 85 - On some vain syllogisms

I was planning to go easy on you and avoid discussing some of the more difficult topics. I was satisfied just to give you a small sample of the views held by our Stoic school, which believes that virtue alone is enough to live a happy life. But now you ask me to include all of our logical arguments or those made by other schools that try to diminish us. If I were to do that, it would result in a book instead of a letter. And I must say again and again that I do not enjoy these kinds of debates. I feel embarrassed to step into the arena and defend such important ideas with such weak tools.

Here's an example: "A person who is wise is also self-controlled; a self-controlled person is steady; a steady person is untroubled; someone who is untroubled is free from sadness; someone who is free from sadness is happy. Therefore, a wise person is happy, and wisdom is enough to live a happy life."

Some of the Peripatetics (followers of Aristotle) respond to this argument by saying that words like "untroubled," "steady," and "free from sadness" should be understood to mean that someone is rarely troubled and only a little bit, not that they are never troubled. Similarly, they say that someone is called "free from sadness" if they don't often feel sad or if their sadness is not too strong. They argue that it's not natural for a person to be completely free from sadness or that the wise person is not overwhelmed by grief but only touched by it, and they present other arguments along these lines, all based on their school's teachings.

They do not eliminate the passions (emotions) this way; they only reduce them. But how insignificant is the advantage we give to the wise person if they are just a little braver than the most cowardly, a little happier than the most miserable, a little more self-controlled than the most out of control, and a little greater than the lowest? Would a runner boast about his speed by comparing himself to those who can barely walk?

This is what true speed looks like, not the kind that earns praise by being compared to what is slowest. Would you call a person healthy who only has a mild fever? No, because good health does not mean being just a little sick.

They say, "The wise person is called untroubled in the same way that ripe fruit is called mellow—not that there is no firmness at all, but that the firmness is less than before." That idea is incorrect because I am not talking about gradually reducing the bad feelings in a good person but about completely eliminating them; there should be no bad feelings at all, not even small ones. If there are any, they will grow, and as they grow, they will hinder the person. Just as a large and complete cataract (a cloudy area in the lens of the eye) can make someone completely blind, even a medium-sized cataract can dull their vision.

If, by your definition, the wise person has any passions at all, their reason will not be strong enough to control them, and they will be carried away as if by a strong current, especially if you give them not just one passion to wrestle with but all the passions. And a group of even moderate passions can affect the person more than a single powerful passion.

The person has a desire for money, although only a moderate amount. They have ambition, but it's not fully awakened. They have a temper, but it can be calmed down. They are inconsistent, but not extremely so. They have lust, but not in a strong way. We would rather deal with someone who has one fully developed vice than with someone who has all the vices but none of them in extreme form.

Again, it doesn't matter how strong the passion is; no matter its size, it doesn't listen to reason and doesn't welcome advice. Just like no animal, whether wild or tame, obeys reason since nature made it unable to understand advice, the passions don't follow or listen, no matter how small they are. Tigers and lions never lose their wildness; they might calm down for a while, but when you least expect it, their softened fierceness can turn into madness. Vices are never truly tamed.

Again, if reason prevails, the passions won't even start; but if they start against the will of reason, they will maintain themselves against the will of reason. It's easier to stop them in the beginning than to control them once they gain strength. This halfway approach is misleading and useless; it's like saying that we should be "moderately" insane or "moderately" sick. Only virtue has moderation; the evils that afflict the mind do not allow for moderation. It's easier to remove them entirely than to control them.

Can anyone doubt that the vices of the human mind, when they have become chronic and deeply rooted (which we call "diseases"), are beyond control, like greed, cruelty, and wantonness? The same applies to the passions because they lead to vices.

Again, if you allow sadness, fear, desire, and all other wrong impulses any room, they will no longer be within our control. And why? Simply because the causes that stir them up are beyond our control. They will increase in proportion to the size and closeness of the causes that trigger them. Fear will grow if the thing causing terror seems larger or closer, and desire will grow stronger if the hope of a greater gain arises.

If the existence of the passions is beyond our control, so is the extent of their power; once they start, they will grow with their causes and become as strong as they will grow to be. Moreover, no matter how small these vices are, they will grow larger. Anything harmful never stays within limits. No matter how small a disease is at the beginning, it can spread quickly, and sometimes even a slight worsening of a disease can bring down a weakened body.

But how foolish it is to believe that we can control the end of something when its beginnings are beyond our control! How can I bring something to an end if I didn't have the power to stop it from starting? It's easier to keep something out than to control it once it's inside.

Some people make a distinction like this: "If a person has self-control and wisdom, they are indeed at peace in their mind and habits, but not in terms of the outcomes. For as far as their mind is concerned, they are not troubled, sad, or afraid; but there are many external causes that can disturb them."

What they mean is this: "So-and-so is not naturally an angry person, but sometimes they do get angry," or "They are not naturally fearful, but sometimes they do experience fear"; in other words, they are free from the fault but not from the passion of fear. However, if fear is allowed to enter, it will eventually turn into a vice; and anger, once admitted into the mind, will change the previous habit of a mind that was once free from anger.

Besides, if the wise person, instead of ignoring all external causes, ever fears anything, then when the time comes for them to face a spear, flames, or other dangers for the sake of their country, laws, and freedom, they will do so reluctantly and with a weakened spirit. Such inconsistency of mind is not fitting for a wise person.

Then again, we should make sure that two ideas that should be tested separately are not confused. The conclusion that only what is honorable is truly good is reached independently of the conclusion that virtue alone is enough for a happy life. If only what is honorable is good, everyone agrees that virtue is enough for a happy life; but on the other hand, if virtue alone makes people happy, it does not necessarily follow that only what is honorable is good.

Philosophers like Xenocrates and Speusippus believe that a person can be happy through virtue alone, but they do not think that only what is honorable is good. Epicurus also says that a person with virtue is happy, but he argues that virtue alone is not enough for a happy life because it is the pleasure that comes from virtue, not virtue itself, that makes one happy. But this distinction is pointless because the same philosopher also says that virtue never exists without pleasure; therefore, if virtue always comes with pleasure and is inseparable from it, then virtue is enough on its own. For virtue brings pleasure with it and does not exist without it, even when it is by itself.

But it is absurd to say that a person will be happy through virtue alone, yet not completely happy. I cannot see how that can be since the happy life contains a good that is perfect and cannot be surpassed. If a person has this good, their life is fully happy.

Now, if the life of the gods contains nothing greater or better, and the happy life is divine, then there is no higher level to which a person can be elevated. Also, if the happy life lacks nothing, then every happy life is perfect; it is happy and at the same time the happiest. Do you have any doubt that the happy life is the Supreme Good?

Therefore, if it possesses the Supreme Good, it is supremely happy. Just as the Supreme Good cannot be increased (for what can be greater than what is supreme?), the happy life cannot be increased either; it is not without the Supreme Good. If you say that one person is happier than another, you are also saying that someone can be "much happier," which means making countless distinctions in the Supreme Good. But I understand the Supreme Good to be that which allows no degree above itself.

If one person is less happy than another, it follows that they would prefer the life of the other, happier person over their own. But the happy person prefers no other life to their own. Either of these two things is unbelievable: that there should be anything left for a happy person to wish for more than what they have or that they would not prefer what is better than what they already have. For certainly, the wiser a person is, the more they will strive for the best, and they will desire to achieve it by any means possible. But how can someone be happy if they still need, or rather are still bound, to crave something else?

I will tell you where this mistake comes from: people do not understand that the happy life is a single, unified thing. It is its quality, not its quantity, that makes such a life the highest form of existence. Therefore, there is complete equality between a long life and a short life, between a life that spreads out in many directions and one that is focused on a single goal. Those who measure life by number, size, or parts take away what makes it unique. Now, what is the unique feature of a happy life? It is its fullness.

I think that satiety, the feeling of being full, is the limit to our eating or drinking. A eats more, and B eats less; what difference does it make? Both are now satisfied. Or A drinks more, and B drinks less; what difference does it make? Both are no longer thirsty. Similarly, A lives for many years, and B for fewer; it does not matter, as long as A's many years bring as much happiness as B's few years. The person you claim is "less happy" is not happy at all; the word "happy" does not allow for degrees.

"He who is brave is fearless; he who is fearless is free from sadness; he who is free from sadness is happy." Our Stoic school created this argument, and those who try to refute it say that we Stoics assume a premise that is false and highly contested—that the brave person is fearless. "What!" they say, "Will the brave person have no fear of the dangers they face? That would be the condition of a madman, not a brave person. The brave person will, it's true, feel fear only a little, but they are not completely free from fear."

Now, those who argue this way are falling back on their old reasoning, treating vices in lesser degrees as if they were virtues. For indeed, the person who does feel fear, even if it is rare and slight, is not free from wickedness but is only troubled by it to a lesser extent. "Not so," they reply, "for I believe that a person is mad if they do not fear real dangers." What you say is true if the dangers are real evils; but if the person knows they are not evils and believes that the only evil is moral baseness, they will have to face dangers without anxiety and despise things that others cannot help fearing. Or, if it is characteristic of a fool or a madman not to fear evils, then the wiser a person is, the more they will fear such things!

"So," they argue, "the Stoics believe that a brave person will expose themselves to dangers." By no means; they will simply not fear them, although they will avoid them. It is right for them to be careful but not fearful. "What then? Should they not fear death, imprisonment, burning, and all the other threats of fortune?" Not at all, because they know that these are not evils but only seem to be. They consider all these things to be like nightmares that trouble the minds of people.

Paint a picture of slavery, whips, chains, poverty, mutilation by disease or torture, or any other fearsome thing; the brave person will see these as terrifying only to those who are afraid. Or do you think that something is truly evil if one day we might choose to face it willingly?

What then, you ask, is truly evil? It is yielding to those things that are falsely called evils; it is surrendering our freedom to them when we should suffer anything to keep our freedom. Freedom is lost unless we learn to despise those things that try to enslave us. If people understood what bravery is, they would have no doubts about how a brave person should behave. Bravery is not thoughtless rashness, love of danger, or seeking out frightening things; it is the knowledge that helps us distinguish between what is evil and what is not. Bravery takes the greatest care of itself and endures with the greatest patience all things that falsely appear to be evils.

"What then?" you ask, "If the sword is held over your brave man's neck, if he is continually wounded, if he sees his intestines in his lap, if he is tortured again after being given a break so that he feels the pain more intensely, and if the blood flows afresh from his wounds, has he no fear? Would you say he feels no pain either?" Yes, he feels pain because no human virtue can eliminate feelings. But he does not fear; he remains unconquered, looking down on his sufferings from a high place. Do you want to know what spirit animates him in these moments? It is the spirit of someone comforting a sick friend.

"That which is evil causes harm; that which causes harm makes a person worse. But pain and poverty do not make a person worse;

therefore, they are not evils." "Your argument," says the critic, "is wrong because not everything that causes harm necessarily makes someone worse. A storm and squall cause harm to a sailor, but they do not make him a worse sailor."

Some Stoics respond to this by saying: "The sailor does become worse because of the storm or squall, as he cannot accomplish his goal and hold his course; in terms of his skill, he is not worse, but in his work, he is worse." To this, the Peripatetics respond: "Therefore, poverty will make even the wise person worse, as will pain or any other similar thing. Although these things won't take away his virtue, they will hinder its work."

This would be correct if it weren't for the fact that the sailor and the wise person are different kinds of people. The wise person's goal in life is not to achieve everything at all costs but to do everything correctly; the sailor's goal is to bring the ship safely to port at all costs. The arts, like sailing, serve life; wisdom, however, commands life.

For myself, I think a different answer should be given: that the sailor's skill is never made worse by a storm, nor is his application of it. The sailor promised you not a successful voyage but the skilled practice of his art—that is, expert knowledge of steering the ship. And the more he is hindered by fortune, the more his skill becomes apparent. The sailor who could say, "Neptune, you will never sink this ship except on an even keel," has fulfilled the requirements of his art. The storm does not interfere with his skill, only with his success.

"What then," you ask, "isn't a sailor harmed by something that prevents him from reaching port, frustrates all his efforts, and either drives him out to sea or strands the ship?" No, it does not harm him as a sailor, only as a traveler; otherwise, he wouldn't be a sailor. In fact, it's so far from hindering his skill that it even showcases it. Anyone can steer a ship in calm seas; the proverb says so. These misfortunes disrupt the journey but not the skill of the sailor.

A sailor has two roles: one as a passenger, like everyone else on the ship, and one as a sailor, which is unique to him. The storm affects him as a passenger, not as a sailor. Likewise, external circumstances like poverty or pain don't make a wise person less wise. They might limit what he can do for others, but they don't stop him from living wisely.

A wise person is always active, even in difficult times. They're at their best when fortune challenges them. Their wisdom benefits both themselves and others, and they're prepared for whatever life throws at them.

Just as animal trainers can tame the fiercest creatures, a wise person can tame life's challenges like pain, poverty, and disgrace. These are things most people fear, but when these challenges meet a wise person, they become subdued.

Letter 86 - On Scipio's villa

I am resting at the country house that once belonged to Scipio Africanus himself, and I'm writing to you after paying my respects to his spirit and to what I believe might be the tomb of this great warrior. I believe his soul has returned to the skies, where it came from, not because he led large armies—since even a madman like Cambyses had large armies—but because he showed remarkable self-control and a strong sense of duty. I admire this quality in him even more after he left Rome than when he was defending it, because he faced a difficult choice: either Scipio should stay in Rome, or Rome should stay free.

Scipio said, "I don't want to break our laws or customs in any way. Let all Roman citizens have equal rights. My country, enjoy the good I've done for you, but do it without me. I've been the reason for your freedom, and I'll also be the proof of it; I'll go into exile if I've become more than what is good for you."

How can I not admire his greatness, which led him to leave voluntarily and relieve the state of its burden? Things had reached the point where either freedom would harm Scipio, or Scipio would harm freedom. Either of those outcomes would have been wrong in the eyes of the gods. So, Scipio stepped aside and moved to Liternum, making the state just as much in his debt for his exile as it was for the exile of Hannibal.

I've looked around the house, which is made of cut stone. There's a wall enclosing a forest, towers built outwards on both sides to defend the house, a well hidden among buildings and trees that's big enough to supply an entire army, and a small bath, buried in darkness, just like they used to be in the old days. Our ancestors didn't think you could have a hot bath unless it was dark. It was a great pleasure for me to compare Scipio's way of living with our own.

Imagine, in this tiny space, the "terror of Carthage," the man Rome should thank for not being captured more than once, used to bathe his body after working in the fields! Scipio was used to keeping himself busy and working the land with his own hands, just like the good old Romans used to do. Under this simple roof, he stood, and this plain floor supported his weight.

But who today could bear to bathe like that? We think we're poor and lowly if our walls aren't decorated with large, expensive mirrors; if our marble from Alexandria isn't surrounded by mosaics made from Numidian stone; if their borders aren't covered with intricate patterns, arranged in many colors like paintings; if our vaulted ceilings aren't covered in glass; if our swimming pools aren't lined with Thasian marble, which used to be a rare and wonderful sight in any temple—pools into which we lower ourselves after sweating heavily; and finally, if the water doesn't pour out from silver taps.

So far, I've been talking about ordinary baths; what should I say about those owned by freedmen? What a vast number of statues, of columns that don't support anything but are there just for decoration, just to spend money! And what huge amounts of water that crash down from one level to another! We've become so luxurious that we won't even walk on anything but precious stones.

In Scipio's bath, there are tiny slits—you can't really call them windows—cut out of the stone wall to let light in without weakening the structure. But nowadays, people think baths are only good enough for moths if they aren't arranged to get sunlight all day long through the widest windows, if men can't bathe and get a tan at the same time, and if they can't look out from their baths over stretches of land and sea. That's how it goes; baths that used to draw crowds and admiration when they were first opened are now avoided and considered old-fashioned as soon as luxury comes up with some new idea, which will eventually lead to its downfall.

In the early days, though, there were only a few baths, and they weren't decorated in any fancy way. Why would people decorate something that costs just a penny and was invented for use, not for pleasure? In those days, bathers didn't have water poured over them, and it didn't always run fresh as if from a hot spring. They didn't care if the water they washed their dirt off in was perfectly clean.

How delightful it is to enter that dark bath with a plain roof, knowing that your hero, Cato, as aedile, or Fabius Maximus, or one of the Cornelii, had heated the water with his own hands! For it used to be the duty of the highest-ranking aediles to enter these public baths and demand that they be cleaned and heated to the temperature needed for use and health, not the blazing heat that's fashionable today, so hot that a slave condemned for some crime ought to be boiled alive in it! It seems to me that nowadays, there's no difference between saying "the bath is on fire" and "the bath is warm."

Some people today might look down on Scipio as unsophisticated because he didn't let sunlight into his steam room through wide windows or didn't roast in the strong sunlight and lounge around until he could stew in the hot water. "Poor fool," they might say, "he didn't know how to live! He didn't bathe in filtered water; it was often cloudy, and after heavy rains, almost muddy!" But it didn't matter much to Scipio if he had to bathe like that; he went there to wash off sweat, not ointment.

And what do you think some people might say in response? They might say, "I don't envy Scipio; that was really an exile's life—to put up with baths like those!" Friend, if you were wiser, you'd know that Scipio didn't bathe every day. It's reported by those who have passed down the old ways of Rome that the Romans only washed their arms and legs daily—because those were the parts that got dirty during their daily work—and they bathed their whole bodies only once a week. Someone might respond, "Yeah, they must have been pretty dirty guys! How they must have smelled!" But they smelled of the camp, the farm, and heroism. Now that fancy baths have been invented, people are actually dirtier than they were before.

What does Horatius Flaccus say when he wants to describe a scoundrel, someone known for his extreme luxury? He says, "Buccillus smells of perfume." Show me a Buccillus these days, and he'd actually smell like a goat—he'd take the place of Gargonius, with whom Horace compared him in the same passage. Nowadays, it's not enough to use ointment unless you put on a fresh coat two or three times a day to keep it from evaporating on your skin. But why should a person brag about this perfume as if it were their own?

If what I'm saying seems too pessimistic to you, blame it on Scipio's country house, where I learned a lesson from Aegialus, a very careful landowner and now the owner of this estate; he taught me that a tree can be transplanted, no matter how old it is. We old men need to learn this lesson because none of us are planting an olive grove for ourselves; we're doing it for those who will come after us. I've seen them bear fruit in due time after three or four years of producing nothing.

And you too shall be shaded by a tree that grows slowly but brings comfort to your grandchildren in the years to come, as our poet Vergil says. But Vergil wasn't trying to be perfectly accurate; he wanted to write what sounded best, not what was closest to the truth.

For example, leaving aside all his other mistakes, I'll quote the passage where I noticed an error today: "In spring, sow beans, and then, O clover plant, you're welcomed by the crumbling soil; and millet calls for yearly care."

You can judge by this whether these plants should be set out at the same time, or whether they should both be planted in the spring. It's June as I write this, and we're well into July, and just today I've seen farmers harvesting beans and sowing millet.

But to get back to the olive grove, I saw it being planted in two ways. If the trees were large, Aegialus would take their trunks and cut off the branches, leaving only about a foot of each branch. He then transplanted them with the root ball after cutting off the roots, leaving only the thick part from which the roots hang. He smeared this with manure and placed it in the hole, not only heaping up the earth around it but also stamping and pressing it down.

He says there's nothing more effective than this packing process because it keeps out the cold and the wind. Besides, the trunk doesn't shake as much, and this packing helps the young roots to grow and take hold in the soil. These roots are still soft and have only a slight grip, so even a little shaking can uproot them. Aegialus also trims the root ball before covering it up because he believes that new roots will grow from all the trimmed parts. Also, the trunk should only stand about three or four feet above the ground. This way, there will be thick growth from the base, and there won't be a large, dry, withered stump like in old olive groves.

The second way he planted was similar; he set out branches that were strong and had soft bark, like those of young saplings. These grow a little more slowly, but since they come from a kind of cutting, they have a smoother and more attractive appearance.

Recently, I also saw an old vine transplanted from its original vineyard. In this case, you should gather the roots together, if possible, and then cover the vine-stem more generously so that roots can even grow from the trunk. I've seen these transplants done not only in February but even at the very end of March, and the vines took hold of and climbed up foreign elms.

But Aegialus says that all trees with thick trunks should be watered with tank water; if we have this resource, we can create our own rain.

I won't tell you any more of these tips because, as Aegialus did with me, I might be training you to become my competitor. Farewell.

Letter 87 - Some arguments in favour of the simple life

"I was shipwrecked before I even boarded the ship." I won't go into the details of how that happened right now, because you might think it's just another one of those strange Stoic sayings. But whenever you're ready to listen, or even if you're not, I'll prove to you that these words are true, and not as surprising as they first seem. In the meantime, my journey has taught me just how much we own that we don't really need, and how easy it is to give up things when we have to, without feeling their loss.

My friend Maximus and I spent two very happy days together, taking with us only a few slaves—just one carriage-load—and no extra stuff except what we were wearing. We slept on mattresses laid on the ground, with two simple rugs—one underneath us and one to cover us. Our meals were simple and took less than an hour to prepare, and we always had dried figs with us, as well as writing tablets. If I had bread, I ate the figs with it; if not, I ate the figs on their own. Every day felt like a feast to me, because I filled it with good thoughts and a peaceful mind. For the soul is never greater than when it lets go of unnecessary things, finds peace by fearing nothing, and becomes rich by not craving wealth.

The cart I rode in was a simple farmer's cart, and the mules pulling it only moved enough to show they were alive. The driver was barefoot, and not because it was summer, but because that's just how he lived. I have to admit, I was a bit embarrassed for others to think this cart was mine. I'm still a little ashamed to fully embrace the simple life in public. Whenever we met a more luxurious group of travelers, I couldn't help but blush. This proves that while I approve and applaud this way of living, it hasn't completely settled into my heart yet. If I'm embarrassed by riding in a simple cart, I'd probably boast if I were riding in something fancy.

So, I'm not quite there yet. I still care too much about what others think of me when I travel. But instead of worrying about that, I should be telling people, "You're mistaken, you're misled, you admire things that don't really matter! You don't judge people for who they really are. When it comes to money, you calculate very carefully who you should lend money to, or do favors for, as if giving a favor is just another transaction. You say things like, 'He has a lot of land, but he also has a lot of debt,' or 'He has a fancy house, but it's all on borrowed money,' or 'No one can show off a better entourage on short notice, but he can't pay his bills. If he pays his creditors, he'll have nothing left.' You should figure out the true worth of each person by eliminating all the extras they own.

You might call a man rich because he travels with gold dishes, owns land in every province, keeps large account books, and has estates so big that people would be envious if they were just wastelands. But after all that, he's still poor. Why? Because he's in debt. 'How much?' you ask. Everything he has. Or maybe you think it matters whether he owes money to another person or to fate.

What good are mules dressed up in fancy gear, or chariots decorated with gold and purple, with horses covered in gold and tapestries, chomping on golden bits? None of these things make the master or the mule any better.

Marcus Cato the Censor, who did as much for the state as Scipio did—because while Scipio fought our enemies, Cato fought against our bad habits—used to ride a simple donkey. This donkey carried not just Cato but also the saddle-bags with all his necessities. Imagine if he met one of today's fancy travelers on the road, with their escorts and luxury attendants. The dandy would probably seem more refined and well-attended compared to Cato, who, even with all his simple gear, would be wondering whether to reach for his sword or his hunting knife.

What a time it must have been when a general who had celebrated a triumph, a censor, and most importantly, a Cato, was content with just one simple horse, and not even the whole horse—because the saddle-bags took up some of the space! Wouldn't you rather have Cato's worn-out horse than a dandy's whole retinue of fat ponies, Spanish horses, and fast trotters?

I can see that this topic could go on forever unless I stop myself. So I'll end here on the topic of these unnecessary things; the man who first called them "hindrances" must have had a prophetic sense of how they would turn out to be exactly that. Now, I'd like to share with you a few logical arguments from our school that deal with the idea of virtue, which we believe is enough to live a happy life.

"That which is good makes people good. For example, what is good in music makes the musician. But random events don't make a person good, so they aren't goods." The Peripatetics (another school of thought) respond by saying that this statement is false; people don't always become good just because they have something good. In music, for instance, there are good things like a flute or a harp, but these instruments alone don't make a musician.

We would reply, "You misunderstand what we mean by 'what is good in music.' We're not talking about what equips the musician, but what makes the musician. You're talking about the instruments, not the art itself. If anything in music is truly good, it will always make a musician."

I'd like to make this even clearer. We define the good in music in two ways: first, by what helps the musician perform, and second, by what helps his art. Musical instruments, like flutes and harps, help the performance, but they don't create the musician's art. The musician is an artist even without them, though he might not be able to practice his art. But the good in a person is not twofold like this; for the good of a person and the good of life are the same.

"That which can fall to the lot of any person, no matter how base or despised, is not a good. But wealth can fall to the lot of a pander or a trainer of gladiators, so wealth is not a good." The Peripatetics say, "This statement is also wrong because we see that good things can fall to the lowest sorts of people, not just in scholarly pursuits but also in medicine or navigation."

However, these arts don't claim to have greatness of soul; they don't rise to any heights or look down on what fortune brings. Virtue, on the other hand, lifts people up and places them above what others value. Virtue doesn't crave too much or fear too much of what is considered good or bad. Chelidon, one of Cleopatra's eunuchs, had great wealth; and recently, Natalis—a man whose speech was as shameless as it was dirty, who did the vilest things with his mouth—was both the heir of many and made many his heirs. What then? Did his wealth make him unclean, or did he make his wealth unclean? Money sometimes falls into the hands of people like a coin falling into a sewer.

Virtue stands above all these things. It is valued on its own merits and doesn't consider these random windfalls to be good. But medicine and navigation don't prevent their practitioners from being impressed by such things. A person who isn't good can still be a doctor, a pilot, or a scholar—just like they can be a cook! If someone has something that is not random, that person cannot be called random. A person is worth what they possess.

A strongbox is only as valuable as what it holds, or rather, it's just an accessory to what it holds. Who values a full purse for anything other than the money inside? The same goes for owners of large estates; they are just accessories to their possessions.

Why, then, is the wise person great? Because they have a great soul. So, it's true that what falls to even the most despicable person is not a good. For this reason, I would never consider inactivity a good, because even a tree-frog or a flea has that quality. Nor would I consider rest and freedom from trouble a good because what is more at leisure than a worm? Do you ask what makes a person wise? The same thing that makes a god. You must agree that the wise person has something godlike, heavenly, and grand about them. The good doesn't come to everyone, nor does it let just anyone possess it.

Look at how each country has its own special produce. Here, corn grows best; there, the vine grows better. In another place, trees and grass grow naturally. See how Tmolus sends out its saffron, India its ivory, Sheba its incense, and the Chalybes their iron. These products are given to different countries so that people have to trade with each other, each seeking something from their neighbor in turn. In the same way, the Supreme Good has its own home. It doesn't grow where ivory grows or iron. Do you ask where the Supreme Good lives? In the soul. And unless the soul is pure and holy, there's no room in it for God.

"Good does not come from evil. But riches come from greed, so riches are not a good." The Peripatetics respond, "That's not true. Good can come from evil. Money can come from sacrilege and theft. So, although sacrilege and theft are evil, they are evil only because they cause more harm than good. They bring profit, but that profit comes with fear, anxiety, and suffering."

Anyone who says this must admit that sacrilege, though evil because it causes much harm, is partly good because it brings some benefit. But how can something so monstrous be true? We've actually convinced the world that sacrilege, theft, and adultery are among the goods. How many people don't blush at theft, and how many boast of committing adultery? Petty sacrilege is punished, but grand sacrilege is honored with a triumph. Besides, if sacrilege is partly good, it must also be honorable and considered right conduct because it concerns ourselves. But no thoughtful person can accept this idea.

Therefore, good cannot come from evil. Just as figs don't grow from olive trees, things produce according to their seed, and goods cannot come from evil. Just as what is honorable doesn't come from what is base, neither does good come from evil. For the honorable and the good are the same.

Some in our school argue against this, saying, "Let's suppose money from any source is a good. Even if it's gained through sacrilege, the money doesn't come from sacrilege itself. You can understand this through an example: In the same jar, there's a piece of gold and a serpent. If you take the gold from the jar, it's not because the serpent is there too, but despite the serpent. Similarly, profit comes from sacrilege, not because sacrilege is evil, but because it also contains profit. Just like the serpent in the jar is evil, but the gold is not."

But I disagree with this because the situations aren't the same. In one case, I can take the gold without touching the serpent. In the other, I can't get the profit without committing sacrilege. The profit isn't separate from the crime; it's mixed with it.

"That which causes many evils while we try to gain it is not a good. But while we seek riches, we get involved in many evils, so riches are not a good." The Peripatetics say, "Your first statement has two meanings. One is that we get involved in many evils while trying to gain riches. But we also get involved in many evils while seeking virtue. One person might suffer shipwreck while traveling to study, and another might be captured.

The second meaning is that if something causes us to get involved in evils, it is not a good. But this doesn't logically follow for riches or pleasure; otherwise, if riches cause us to get involved in many evils, then riches are not just not a good, but they're actually an evil. But you only argue that they're not a good. Moreover, you admit that riches have some use. You consider them advantages, but by your reasoning, they can't even be an advantage because we suffer many disadvantages while pursuing them."

Some people answer this by saying, "You're wrong to blame riches. Riches themselves don't harm anyone; it's people's own foolishness or the wickedness of others that causes harm, just as a sword by itself doesn't kill—it's the weapon used by the killer. Riches themselves don't harm you just because you suffer harm because of them."

I think Posidonius's reasoning is better. He says that riches cause evil, not because they do evil themselves, but because they drive people to do evil. The direct cause, which immediately causes harm, is one thing, and the indirect cause is another. The indirect cause lies in riches; they inflate the spirit and breed pride. They create unpopularity and unsettle the mind so much that even the mere reputation of having wealth, though it is bound to harm us, still brings delight.

All true goods should be free from blame; they are pure, they don't corrupt the spirit, and they don't tempt us. They uplift and broaden the spirit, but without puffing it up. Goods produce confidence, but riches produce shamelessness. Goods give us greatness of soul, but riches give us arrogance. And arrogance is nothing more than a false appearance of greatness.

"According to that argument," says the objector, "riches are not only not a good, but they're actually an evil." Now, riches would be an evil if they did harm themselves, and if, as I said before, the direct cause lay in them. But in reality, it's the indirect cause that lies in riches, and it not only stirs the spirit but actually drags it along. Yes, riches give us a false appearance of good, which looks real and convinces many people.

The indirect cause also exists in virtue; it brings envy—for many become unpopular because of their wisdom and their justice. But this cause, though it lies in virtue, doesn't come from virtue itself, nor is it a false appearance of the real thing. On the contrary, the vision that virtue gives to people's spirits is far more like reality, calling them to love and admire it.

Posidonius thinks the argument should be framed like this: "Things that don't give the soul greatness, confidence, or freedom from care are not goods. But riches, health, and similar things don't do these; therefore, riches and health are not goods." He goes further by saying, "Things that don't give the soul greatness, confidence, or freedom from care, but instead create arrogance, vanity, and insolence, are evils. But things that come from Fortune lead us into these evils. Therefore, these things are not goods."

"But," says the objector, "by this reasoning, things given by Fortune aren't even advantages." No, advantages and goods are different. An advantage is something with more usefulness than trouble. But a good should be pure and free from harm. A thing isn't good just because it has more benefit than harm, but only if it has no harm at all.

Besides, advantages can be found in animals, imperfect people, and fools. So, the advantageous can have some disadvantage mixed in, but it's called advantageous because the good part outweighs the bad. However, the good can only be found in the wise person; it must be pure.

Now, be of good cheer; there's only one more difficult argument to untangle, though it's a tough one: "Good doesn't come from evil. But riches come from many cases of poverty, so riches are not a good." Our school doesn't accept this argument, but the Peripatetics created it and offer a solution. Posidonius says that this fallacy, which has been debated in all schools of logic, was refuted by Antipater, who explained:

"The word 'poverty' doesn't mean possessing something, but rather not possessing, or as the ancients said, deprivation. 'Poverty' refers not to what a person has but what they lack. So, there can't be fullness from many voids; riches come from many things, not many lacks. You misunderstand what poverty means. Poverty isn't having little, but lacking much; it's about what a person doesn't have."

I could explain this more easily if there were a Latin word that could translate the Greek word for "not possessing." Antipater applies this quality to poverty, but I believe poverty is simply having little. If we ever have more time, we'll explore what wealth and poverty really mean. But for now, we should focus on reducing poverty and arrogance in wealth rather than getting caught up in words as if the issue were already settled.

Let's say we're called to a meeting to discuss getting rid of wealth. Will these arguments help us make the Roman people choose poverty and praise it—the poverty that was the foundation and cause of their empire—and fear their current wealth, realizing they took it from those they conquered? Will they understand that wealth brought office-seeking, bribery, and disorder into a city once known for its honesty and moderation? Will they see that whatever one nation took from others can be taken away even more easily from that one? It would be better to support this idea by our actions and confront our desires directly rather than try to outsmart them with logic. If we can, let's speak more boldly; if not, let's speak more honestly.

Letter 88 - On liberal and vocational studies

You wanted to know what I think about liberal studies. My answer is that I don't respect any study, and I don't consider any study good, if it is only about making money. These studies are just jobs that make money, and they are only useful because they get the mind ready for something bigger and don't keep it busy forever. We should spend time on them only until the mind can move on to something greater; they are like training, not the real work.

That's why they're called "liberal studies" because they are the kinds of studies that are supposed to be worthy of a free person. But there is really only one study that truly makes a person free, and that is the study of wisdom. Wisdom is noble, brave, and great-spirited. All other studies are small and childish. You wouldn't think there's anything good in the subjects taught by people who are, as you can see, often low and shameful? We shouldn't spend our time learning these things; we should be done with them.

Some people have decided that the real question about liberal studies is whether they make people good. But they don't even try to teach about this important topic. The scholar spends his time studying language, and if he wants to go further, he studies history, or if he wants to go as far as he can, he studies poetry. But how do any of these things help you become virtuous? Do they get rid of fear, stop desire, or control your emotions?

The question is, do these scholars teach virtue, or not? If they don't teach it, then they don't pass it on. If they do teach it, then they are philosophers. Do you want to know how you can tell that they don't teach virtue? Look at how different their subjects are. If they taught the same thing, their subjects would be more alike.

Maybe they try to make you believe that Homer was a philosopher, but they actually prove he wasn't by their own arguments. Sometimes they say Homer was a Stoic, who valued only virtue, rejected pleasure, and wouldn't give up his honor even for immortality. Other times they say he was an Epicurean, enjoying a peaceful life full of feasts and songs. Sometimes they claim he was a Peripatetic, dividing goodness into three parts. Other times they make him out to be an Academic, believing that nothing is certain. But it's clear that Homer wasn't any of these because these ideas all contradict each other. We might agree with them that Homer was wise, but surely he became wise before he knew anything about poetry. So let's learn what actually made Homer wise.

It doesn't really matter if we find out whether Homer or Hesiod was the older poet any more than it matters why Hecuba, even though she was younger than Helen, looked so much older and sadder. What's the point of figuring out the ages of Achilles and Patroclus?

Are you more interested in figuring out where Ulysses traveled than in figuring out how to keep yourself from going astray? We don't have time to listen to lectures about whether Ulysses wandered between Italy and Sicily or outside the known world (because such a long journey couldn't have happened in such a small area). We deal with storms in our minds that toss us around every day, and our bad behavior leads us into the same kinds of troubles that Ulysses faced. There's always something beautiful to tempt us, or an enemy to attack us. On one side, there are dangerous monsters that crave human blood, and on the other side, there are lies and false pleasures, and then there's shipwreck and all kinds of other disasters.

Show me, through the example of Ulysses, how to love my country, my wife, and my father, and how, even after facing shipwreck, I can still strive toward these noble goals. Why bother asking if Penelope was truly faithful or if she outsmarted her suitors, or whether she knew the man before her was Ulysses before she realized it was him? Instead, teach me what purity is, how valuable it is, and whether it comes from the body or the soul.

Now, let's move on to the musician. You're teaching me how different notes, like the high ones and the low ones, can work together in harmony, even though they come from different strings. But instead, help me bring my soul into harmony so that my goals aren't out of tune with each other. You're showing me what the sad notes sound like; instead, show me how to keep from singing a sad song even when life is hard.

The mathematician teaches me how to measure my land, but I'd rather learn how to figure out what's enough for a person to own. He teaches me to count and how to be greedy, but I'd prefer him to teach me that these calculations don't really matter and that being rich doesn't make you any happier, especially when you need so many people just to keep track of all your possessions.

What good is it to know how to divide up land if I don't know how to share it with my brother? What good is it to measure land down to the last inch and notice even the smallest mistake if I get angry when my bad-tempered neighbor takes a tiny piece of my land? The mathematician teaches me not to lose any of my boundaries; I want to learn how to give them all away without a second thought.

"But," someone says, "I'm being driven off the land that my father and grandfather owned!" So what? Who owned it before your grandfather? Do you even know who originally owned the land? You didn't start out as the master of the land, just a renter. And whose renter are you? If you win your case, you're just the renter of the heir. Lawyers say that public property can't be owned privately. What you hold and call your own actually belongs to everyone—it's public property.

Oh, what amazing skill! You know how to measure a circle, you can find the area of any shape, and you can calculate the distance between stars. There's nothing you can't measure. But if you're truly a master of your craft, measure the human mind for me! Tell me how big it is, or how small it is! You know what a straight line is, but what good does that do if you don't know what's straight in life?

Next, let's talk to the person who prides himself on knowing all about the stars and planets—who knows where the cold star of Saturn hides and the path Mercury takes. What good is it to know this? Will it just make me worry because Saturn and Mars are in opposition, or when Mercury sets at sunset in plain sight of Saturn, instead of learning that these stars, no matter where they are, are always favorable and unchanging?

These stars are driven by an unending cycle of destiny, on a path they can't change. They return at specific times; they either start the world's work or mark the times when it pauses. But if they control everything that happens, how will it help you to know the secrets of what can't be changed? Or if they only give signs of what will happen, what good is it to see what you can't avoid? Whether you know these things or not, they will happen anyway.

Look at the fleeting sun and the stars that follow it, and you'll never find the next day playing tricks on you, or a night that misleads you with clear skies. However, it's already been determined that I'm safe from being misled by anything.

"What?" you ask, "Does the 'morrow never play me false'? Anything that happens without my knowledge plays me false." For my part, I don't know what's going to happen, but I do know what could happen. I'm not worried about this; I'm ready for whatever the future brings. And if the future is less harsh than expected, I'll be grateful. If the future is kind to me, it might feel like I've been tricked, but it doesn't deceive me. Because just as I know that anything can happen, I also know that not everything will happen. I'm ready for good things to happen in every case, but I'm also prepared for bad things.

I must apologize if I don't follow the usual path in this discussion. I don't agree that painting belongs on the list of liberal arts, any more than sculpture, stone-cutting, and other skills meant for luxury. I also exclude from the liberal studies wrestling and any knowledge that involves oil and mud; otherwise, I'd have to include perfume-makers, cooks, and anyone else who uses their talents to satisfy our pleasures.

What's so "liberal" about these people who stuff themselves with food until they have to take something to make them vomit, whose bodies are fat but whose minds are thin and weak? Or do we really think that their training is "liberal" for the young men of Rome, who used to be taught by our ancestors to stand tall and throw a spear, to handle a pike, to guide a horse, and to use weapons? Our ancestors taught their children nothing that could be learned while lying down. But neither the old system nor the new one teaches or fosters virtue.

What good does it do to control a horse and guide its speed with the reins, but find that our own passions are running wild? Or to beat many opponents in wrestling or boxing, only to be beaten by our own anger?

"What then," you ask, "do the liberal studies offer nothing to our well-being?" They offer a lot in other ways, but nothing at all when it comes to virtue. Even these arts I've mentioned, which are clearly low-level because they rely on manual labor, contribute a lot to making life easier, but they have nothing to do with virtue. And if you ask, "Why do we educate our children in the liberal studies then?" it's not because they can give us virtue, but because they prepare the mind to accept virtue. Just like the "primary course," as the ancients called it, in grammar, which gave boys their first lessons, doesn't teach them the liberal arts, but gets them ready to learn them later, the liberal arts don't take the mind all the way to virtue, but they get it started in that direction.

Posidonius divides the arts into four groups: first, there are the common and lowly ones; then those meant for entertainment; next are those that involve teaching boys, and finally, the liberal arts. The common ones belong to workers and involve manual labor; they're about making life easier and don't pretend to have beauty or honor.

The arts meant for entertainment are those that try to please the eyes and ears. To this group, you can add stage-machinists, who create scaffolding that lifts itself up, floors that rise silently into the air, and many other amazing tricks, like things that fit together but then fall apart, or things that are separate but then join together automatically, or things that stand upright but then slowly collapse. People who haven't seen these things before are amazed by them because they don't understand how they work.

The arts that are somewhat like the liberal arts and are meant for teaching boys are the ones the Greeks call the "cycle of studies," but we Romans call the "liberal arts." However, the only truly liberal—actually, the only truly "free"—arts are those that deal with virtue.

"But," someone might say, "just like there's a part of philosophy that deals with nature, and a part that deals with ethics, and a part that deals with reasoning, this group of liberal arts also claims a place in philosophy. When we look at questions about nature, we rely on the mathematician to help us reach a decision. So, math is a branch of the philosophy it helps."

But lots of things help us without being a part of us. In fact, if they were part of us, they wouldn't be able to help us. Food helps the body, but it's not part of the body. We get help from math in the same way, and math is as important to philosophy as carpentry is to math. But carpentry isn't part of math, and math isn't part of philosophy.

Also, each has its own limits. The wise person studies and understands the causes of natural events, while the mathematician follows and calculates their numbers and measurements. The wise person knows the laws that govern the stars, their powers, and their qualities; the astronomer just notes when they rise and set, the rules for their movement, and the occasional times when they seem to stand still, even though no star can actually stand still. The wise person will know what causes a reflection in a mirror, but the mathematician can only tell you how far the object needs to be from the mirror and what shape the mirror should be to create a certain reflection.

The philosopher will prove that the sun is a large object, while the astronomer will calculate exactly how large it is, using trial and error to learn more; but to make progress, the astronomer must rely on certain principles. No art, though, can stand alone if it relies on borrowed principles.

Now, philosophy doesn't need anything from any other source; it builds everything on its own foundation. But math, so to speak, is like a structure built on someone else's land—it's based on outside principles. It accepts first principles and, with their help, draws more conclusions. If it could find the truth on its own, if it could understand the nature of the universe, I would say it could greatly benefit our minds. Because the mind grows when it engages with heavenly things and draws something down from above. There's only one thing that can perfect the soul—the unchangeable knowledge of good and evil. But there's no other art that studies good and evil.

I'd like to consider the different virtues. Bravery ignores things that inspire fear; it looks down on, challenges, and defeats the powers of terror and anything that would take away our freedom. But do the "liberal studies" make this virtue stronger? Loyalty is the most sacred good in a person's heart; it can't be forced into betrayal, and no reward can bribe it. Loyalty says, "Burn me, kill me! I won't betray my trust; and the more torture tries to find my secret, the deeper I'll bury it in my heart!" Can the "liberal arts" create this kind of spirit in us? Temperance controls our desires; some it hates and rejects, others it regulates and keeps in check, and it never pursues desires for their own sake. Temperance knows that the best measure of what we want isn't what we desire, but what we should desire.

Kindness stops you from being overbearing to others and stops you from being greedy. In words, deeds, and feelings, it shows itself gentle and courteous to everyone. It doesn't see any evil as someone else's problem alone. And the reason it loves its own good is mostly because it will someday be someone else's good. Do "liberal studies" teach a person this kind of character? No, just like they don't teach simplicity, moderation, self-restraint, thrift, or the kindness that values a neighbor's life as much as one's own and knows that it's not for humans to waste the lives of others.

"But," someone says, "since you say that virtue can't be attained without the 'liberal studies,' how can you deny that they help with virtue?" Because you can't reach virtue without food, either, but food has nothing to do with virtue. Wood doesn't help build a ship, even though a ship can't be built without wood. Just because something is necessary doesn't mean it contributes to the final product.

We might even say that it's possible to achieve wisdom without the "liberal studies" because even though virtue must be learned, it isn't learned through these studies.

Why should I think that someone who doesn't know letters will never be wise, since wisdom isn't found in letters? Wisdom teaches facts, not words; and it might be true that memory is more reliable when it doesn't depend on anything outside itself.

Wisdom is vast and spacious. It needs plenty of free space. We must learn about divine and human things, the past and the future, the temporary and the eternal, and we must learn about time. Just think of all the questions that come up about time alone: first, whether it exists by itself; second, whether anything existed before time or without time; and again, did time start with the universe, or, if something existed before the universe, did time exist then too?

There are countless questions about the soul alone: where does it come from, what is its nature, when does it begin to exist, and how long does it last? Does it move from one place to another and change forms, going from one animal shape to another, or is it enslaved only once, wandering the universe after being set free? Is it physical or not? What happens to it when it stops using us as its medium? How will it use its freedom when it escapes this current prison? Will it forget everything it knew before, and only start to understand itself when it's released from the body and returns to the skies?

So, whatever aspect of human and divine things you understand, you'll be overwhelmed by the huge number of questions and things to learn. And to make room in your mind for these vast and important subjects, you have to clear out all the unnecessary stuff. Virtue won't settle in our limited minds; a great subject needs a wide space to move. Get rid of everything else, and make room in your heart for virtue.

"But it's fun to know many different arts." Then let's keep only as much of them as is necessary. Would you criticize someone who fills their house with expensive but unnecessary items, but not criticize someone who fills their mind with unnecessary knowledge? This desire to know more than what's needed is a kind of excess.

Why? Because this excessive pursuit of the liberal arts makes people annoying, talkative, tactless, and self-satisfied bores who miss the important things because they're focused on unimportant things. Didymus the scholar wrote four thousand books. I would pity him if he had only read the same number of useless books. In these books, he explored questions like where Homer was born, who was really Aeneas's mother, whether Anacreon was more of a playboy or more of a drunk, whether Sappho was a bad person, and other questions that would be forgotten as soon as they were answered. Come on, don't tell me that life is long!

And when you consider our own countrymen, I can show you many works that should be cut down with an axe. We spend a huge amount of time and put others through a lot of discomfort just to earn praise like, "What a learned person you are!" Let's be content with a simpler compliment like, "What a good person you are!"

Do I mean this? Should I unroll the annals of world history and try to figure out who first wrote poetry? Or, without written records, should I estimate the years between Orpheus and Homer? Or should I study the silly writings of Aristarchus, who criticized other people's verses, and waste my life on syllables? Should I then wallow in the dust of geometry? Have I forgotten the useful saying, "Save your time"? Do I really need to know these things? And what should I choose not to know?

Apion, the scholar who attracted crowds all over Greece in the days of Gaius Caesar and was praised as a Homerid by every state, used to claim that Homer, after finishing the Iliad and the Odyssey, added a prologue to his work that covered the entire Trojan war. The argument Apion used to support this idea was that Homer had deliberately started his poem with two letters that contained a clue to the number of books he had written. A person who wants to know many things must know things like these and ignore all the time lost to illness, public duties, private duties, daily tasks, and sleep. Think about the years of your life; there isn't time for all of this.

I've been talking about liberal studies so far, but think about how much unnecessary and impractical material is in philosophy! Philosophers have even gone out of their way to make fine distinctions between syllables, to define the exact meaning of conjunctions and prepositions. They've been jealous of scholars and mathematicians. They've added all the unnecessary parts of these other arts to their own, so they know more about careful speaking than about careful living.

Let me tell you about the harm caused by excessive precision and how it's an enemy of the truth! Protagoras says you can argue either side of any question equally well—even the question of whether every topic can be debated from either side. Nausiphanes believes that in things that seem to exist, there's no difference between existing and not existing. Parmenides says that nothing exists of all that seems to exist, except for the universe alone. Zeno of Elea got rid of all the problems by getting rid of one; he says that nothing exists. The Pyrrhonian, Megarian, Eretrian, and Academic schools are all basically doing the same thing; they've come up with a new kind of knowledge—non-knowledge.

You can group all these theories with the unnecessary subjects of "liberal" studies; one group gives me knowledge that's useless, the other group takes away any hope of gaining knowledge. Of course, it's better to know useless things than to know nothing. One set of philosophers doesn't offer any light to help me find the truth; the other set blinds me completely. If I follow Protagoras, everything in nature is uncertain; if I agree with Nausiphanes, I'm sure only of this—that everything is uncertain; if I side with Parmenides, there's nothing except the One; if I go with Zeno, there's not even the One.

So what are we, then? What happens to all the things around us that support and sustain us? Is the whole universe just an empty or deceptive shadow? I don't know whether I'm more frustrated with those who say we know nothing or with those who won't even let us keep this one privilege. Farewell.

Letter 89 - On the parts of philosophy

It's good that you want to know this because it's important for someone who is seeking wisdom to understand the different parts of philosophy and how its vast subject is divided into separate sections. By studying these parts, we can more easily understand the whole. I only wish that we could see all of philosophy together as one whole thing, just as the whole sky is spread out before us to look at. It would be a view much like that of the sky. For then, surely, philosophy would captivate all people with a love for her. We would abandon all the things we mistakenly believe to be great, simply because we don't know what is truly great. However, since we can't have this, we must study philosophy as people gaze at the secrets of the sky.

A wise person's mind, of course, understands all the different parts of philosophy, looking at it as quickly as our eyes can take in the sky. But we, who must break through the darkness, and whose vision fails even for things close by, can be shown each part more easily, even if we can't yet understand the entire universe. So, I will fulfill your request and divide philosophy into parts, but I won't break it into tiny pieces. It's helpful to divide philosophy, but not to cut it into fragments. Just as it's hard to grasp something that is too large, it's also hard to understand something that is broken into too many small pieces.

People are divided into groups, and an army is divided into units. Anything that has grown too large is more easily understood if it's broken into parts, but these parts, as I said, shouldn't be too many or too small. Over-analyzing something is just as wrong as not analyzing it at all; anything that is cut so finely that it turns into dust is as good as being mixed into a single mass again.

First of all, if you agree, I'll explain the difference between wisdom and philosophy. Wisdom is the ultimate good of the human mind; philosophy is the love of wisdom and the effort to attain it. Philosophy strives toward the goal that wisdom has already reached. And it's clear why philosophy was given this name. The name itself shows the love for wisdom.

Some people have defined wisdom as the knowledge of divine things and human things. Others say, "Wisdom is knowing divine and human things, and also knowing their causes." This added phrase seems unnecessary to me because the causes of divine and human things are part of the divine system. Philosophy has also been defined in various ways; some have called it "the study of virtue," others have called it "a study of how to improve the mind," and some have named it "the search for right reason."

One thing is almost certain: there is a difference between philosophy and wisdom. It's not possible for the thing that is being sought and the thing that is doing the seeking to be the same. Just as there's a big difference between greed and wealth—where one is the desire and the other is the thing desired—there's a difference between philosophy and wisdom. Philosophy is the journey, and wisdom is the destination. Wisdom is what the Greeks call σοφία (sophia). The Romans also used this word in the same way that they now use the word "philosophy." This is proven by our old national plays, as well as by the inscription on the tomb of Dossennus, which says: "Pause, stranger, and read the wisdom of Dossennus."

However, some of our school, even though philosophy meant to them "the study of virtue," and even though virtue was the goal and philosophy was the path, still insisted that the two cannot be separated. Philosophy cannot exist without virtue, and virtue cannot exist without philosophy. Philosophy is the study of virtue, but it studies virtue by using virtue itself. Neither can virtue exist without the study of itself, nor can the study of virtue exist without virtue itself. It's not like trying to hit a target from a distance, where the shooter and the target are in different places. The way to reach virtue is through virtue itself; philosophy and virtue are tightly connected.

The greatest authors, and the most numerous ones, have said that philosophy is divided into three parts—moral, natural, and rational. The first part keeps the soul in order; the second studies the universe; the third works out the meanings of words, how they fit together, and the arguments that keep falsehood from replacing truth. But there have also been those who divided philosophy into fewer parts, and others who divided it into more parts. Some members of the Peripatetic school added a fourth division, "civil philosophy," because it deals with a special area of activity and focuses on different subject matter. Some added a department that they called "economics," which is the science of managing one's household. Still, others created a separate category for different ways of living. However, none of these subdivisions will be found outside the branch called "moral philosophy."

The Epicureans believed that philosophy was twofold—natural and moral; they did away with the rational part. But when they were forced by the facts themselves to distinguish between ambiguous ideas and to reveal fallacies that were hidden under the appearance of truth, they too introduced a category they called "forensic and regulative," which is really just "rational philosophy" under a different name, although they said that this section was secondary to "natural" philosophy.

The Cyrenaic school abolished both the natural and the rational departments and were satisfied with only the moral side; but even these philosophers included under a different name what they had rejected. They divided moral philosophy into five parts: (1) What to avoid and what to seek, (2) The Passions, (3) Actions, (4) Causes, (5) Proofs. But the causes of things really belong to the "natural" part of philosophy, and the proofs belong to the "rational" part.

Aristo of Chios argued that the natural and rational parts were not only unnecessary but also contradictory. He even limited the "moral" part, which was all that was left to him, by eliminating the category that included giving advice, saying that it was the job of a teacher, not a philosopher— as if the wise man were not the teacher of the human race!

Since philosophy is threefold, let's first set in order the moral side. It's agreed that this should be divided into three parts. First, we have the speculative part, which assigns each thing its proper function and measures the value of each; it is the most useful part. For what is more important than giving everything its proper value? The second part deals with impulse, and the third with actions. The first duty is to determine the value of things, the second is to form a controlled and ordered impulse about them, and the third is to make sure your impulse and your actions match, so that under all circumstances, you are consistent with yourself. If any of these three parts are lacking, the others will be confused as well. What good is it to know the value of things if you are excessive in your impulses? What good is it to control your impulses if, when it comes time to act, you don't know the right time, place, and way to carry out each action?

It is one thing to understand the merits and values of facts, another to know the precise moment for action, and still another to control impulses and proceed with care rather than rushing into what needs to be done. Life is in harmony only when action follows impulse, and when impulse towards an object arises in each case from the value of that object, being more or less intense depending on how much the object is worth pursuing.

The natural side of philosophy has two parts: bodily and non-bodily. Each is divided into its own levels of importance, so to speak. The study of bodily things is divided first into two categories: the creative and the created; the created things are the elements. Now, some writers say that the topic of the elements is complete in itself, while others say it is divided into matter, the cause that moves all things, and the elements themselves.

It remains for me to divide rational philosophy into its parts. All speech is either continuous, or it is divided between questioner and answerer. The first kind of speech is called rhetoric, and the second is called dialectic. Rhetoric deals with words, their meanings, and their arrangement. Dialectic is divided into two parts: words and their meanings—that is, into what is said and the words used to say it. Then each of these is further divided, and it is a vast subject. So, I will stop here and not go any further.

But let me address the main point; if I wanted to give you all the subdivisions, my letter would turn into a handbook for debate! I'm not trying to discourage you, my excellent Lucilius, from studying this subject, as long as you promptly apply everything you read to your actions. It's your actions that you must control; you must wake up what is lazy in you, strengthen what has become weak, conquer what is stubborn, and fight against your own desires and the desires of others as much as you can. And to those who say: "How long will this endless talk go on?" respond with the words: "I should be asking you, 'How long will these endless sins of yours go on?'" Do you really want my remedies to stop before your vices stop? But I will speak of my remedies even more, and just because you object, I will keep on talking. Medicine starts to work when it makes the sick body tingle with pain. I will speak words that will help people even if they don't want to hear them. At times, you should let words that aren't just compliments reach your ears, and since as individuals you don't want to hear the truth, hear it together.

How far will you extend the boundaries of your estates? An estate that once held a whole nation is now too small for a single lord. How much further will you push your plowed fields—you who aren't satisfied with farms even as large as provinces? You have noble rivers flowing through your private lands; you have mighty streams— boundaries of mighty nations—under your control from their source to their outlet. Even this is too little for you unless you can surround whole seas with your estates, unless your steward rules on the other side of the Adriatic, Ionian, and Aegean seas, unless the islands, once homes to famous leaders, are considered by you as the smallest of possessions! Spread your lands as wide as you want, as long as you have as a "farm" what was once called a kingdom; take whatever you can, as long as it is more than your neighbor's!

And now, a word to you, whose luxury is as wide as the greed of those I just mentioned. To you, I say: "Will this continue until there is no lake over which the rooftops of your country-houses don't tower? Until there is no river whose banks aren't bordered by your grand structures? Wherever hot springs gush forth in streams, there you will build new resorts of luxury. Wherever the shore bends into a bay, there you will immediately start laying foundations, and, not content with any land that hasn't been shaped by human hands, you will bring the sea within your boundaries. Let your rooftops shine in the sun on every side, now on mountain peaks where they command a wide view over sea and land, now lifted from the plain to the height of mountains; build your many structures, your huge buildings—yet you are still just individuals, and small ones at that! What good are all your many bedrooms? You sleep in just one. No place is truly yours where you yourself are not present."

"Next, I turn to you, you whose bottomless and insatiable hunger searches on the one hand the seas, and on the other the earth, with great effort, hunting down your prey, now with hook, now with snare, now with various kinds of nets; no animal has peace except when you are too full to eat it. And how small a portion of those feasts of yours, prepared by so many hands, do you actually taste with your worn-out palate? How small a portion of all that game, caught with such danger, does the master's sick and picky stomach actually enjoy? How small a portion of all those shellfish, brought from so far away, actually slides down your insatiable throat? Poor souls, don't you know that your appetites are bigger than your stomachs?"

Speak like this to other people, provided that while you speak, you also listen to yourself; write like this, provided that while you write, you also read, remembering that everything you hear or read should be applied to your actions and used to calm the fury of your passions. Study, not to add more to your knowledge, but to make your knowledge better. Farewell.

Letter 90 - On the part played by philosophy in the progress of man

Who could doubt, my dear Lucilius, that life is a gift from the immortal gods, but that living well is a gift from philosophy? That's why some people believe we owe more to philosophy than to the gods because living a good life is better than just living, though this wouldn't be true if philosophy itself weren't a gift from the gods. The gods haven't given the knowledge of philosophy to anyone, but they've given everyone the ability to acquire it. For if they had made philosophy a common gift, and if we were born with understanding, wisdom would lose its greatest quality—that it isn't one of the gifts of fortune. What is precious and noble about wisdom is that it doesn't come to us on its own; each person is responsible for finding it, and we don't need to seek it from others. What would make philosophy worthy of respect if it were simply given to us?

Philosophy's only purpose is to discover the truth about divine and human matters. Religion, duty, justice, and all the virtues are never separated from philosophy; they all stick together in close companionship. Philosophy has taught us to worship what is divine and to love what is human; it has shown us that the gods hold dominion and that fellowship exists among men. This fellowship remained unbroken for a long time until greed tore the community apart and became the cause of poverty, even for those it had made the richest. For people cease to possess everything the moment they desire everything for themselves.

But the first men, and those who came after them, still uncorrupted, followed nature, having one person as both their leader and their law, entrusting themselves to someone better than they were. For nature tends to make the weaker follow the stronger. Even among animals, the biggest or fiercest ones lead. It's not a weak bull that leads the herd; it's one that has beaten the other males with his strength. In the case of elephants, the tallest one leads; among people, the best is considered the highest. That's why a ruler was assigned to the mind; and that's why the greatest happiness was found among people where no one could be more powerful unless they were better. For the person who thinks they can't do anything except what they should do can safely accomplish what they want.

In that age, which is often called the golden age, Posidonius believed that the government was run by wise people. They controlled themselves and protected the weaker from the stronger. They gave advice on what to do and what not to do; they showed what was useful and what was useless. Their foresight ensured that their people lacked nothing; their bravery protected them from danger; their kindness enriched and adorned their people. For them, ruling was a service, not a display of power. No ruler tested their power against those who gave them their power in the first place, and no one had the desire or the excuse to do wrong, since the ruler ruled well and the people obeyed well, and the king couldn't threaten disobedient subjects with anything worse than making them leave the kingdom.

But when vice crept in and kingdoms turned into tyrannies, laws became necessary; and these laws were created by wise people. Solon, who established Athens on a firm foundation with just laws, was one of the seven men famous for their wisdom. If Lycurgus had lived in the same period, he would have been added as the eighth to that sacred group of seven. The laws of Zaleucus and Charondas are praised; they learned the principles of justice in the quiet, holy retreat of Pythagoras, not in the forum or the offices of skilled counselors. These principles were later established in Sicily (which was prosperous at that time) and throughout Grecian Italy.

I agree with Posidonius up to this point, but I do not agree that philosophy discovered the everyday arts that life uses. I won't give it credit for things that are more like a craftsman's achievements. Posidonius says, "When people were scattered over the earth, living in caves or shelters dug out of cliffs or the trunks of hollow trees, it was philosophy that taught them to build houses." But I don't believe philosophy came up with these clever buildings of ours, which rise story upon story, where city crowds against city, any more than I believe it invented fish-preserves, which keep people from having to risk storms just to satisfy their gluttony, and so that no matter how wildly the sea rages, luxury can have safe harbors where it can fatten up fancy breeds of fish.

What! Was it philosophy that taught us to use keys and locks? No, that was just a hint to greed! Was it philosophy that built all these towering buildings, so dangerous to the people living in them? Wasn't it enough for humans to provide themselves with a roof from whatever they could find and to create some natural shelter without art or trouble? Believe me, that was a happy age, before architects and builders existed!

All this came about when luxury was being born—this business of cutting timbers square and splitting a beam with a saw guided along a marked line. The first humans split their wood with wedges. They weren't preparing a roof for future banquet halls; they didn't haul pine trees or firs through trembling streets just to build panel ceilings heavy with gold.

Forked poles placed at either end held up their houses. They piled close-packed branches and leaves on top to make a roof that could drain even the heaviest rains. Under such homes, they lived, but they lived in peace. A thatched roof once covered free people; now, under marble and gold, slavery lives.

On another point, I also disagree with Posidonius when he says that mechanical tools were invented by wise people. If that were true, you could argue that those who taught the arts of trapping game, catching birds, and hunting with dogs were also wise. But these things were discovered by human ingenuity, not wisdom.

I also disagree with Posidonius when he says that wise people discovered our iron and copper mines when the earth, scorched by forest fires, melted the veins of ore near the surface and caused the metal to flow out. No, the people who discovered such things were the ones who were busy with them.

I also don't think this question is as tricky as Posidonius makes it seem, whether the hammer or the tongs came first. Both were invented by someone with a quick and clever mind, but not a great or exalted one; the same goes for any other invention that requires a bent body and a mind focused on the ground.

The wise man lived simply. And why not? Even today, he would prefer to be as free from burdens as possible. How can you admire both Diogenes and Daedalus at the same time? Which one seems wiser to you—the one who invented the saw, or the one who, when he saw a boy drinking water from his hand, immediately took his cup from his bag, broke it, and scolded himself by saying, "What a fool I've been, carrying around unnecessary baggage all this time!" and then curled up in his tub and lay down to sleep?

In our own times, which man do you think is wiser—the one who invents a way to spray saffron perfume high into the air from hidden pipes, who fills or empties canals with a sudden rush of water, who cleverly builds a dining room with a ceiling that changes patterns as often as the courses of the meal, or the one who proves to others, as well as to himself, that nature has not given us a harsh or difficult law when she tells us we can live without marble workers and engineers, that we can clothe ourselves without trading in silk, that we can have everything we need if we are content with what the earth provides on its surface? If people were willing to listen to this sage, they would realize that the cook is as unnecessary as the soldier.

Those were wise men, or at least like the wise, who found that taking care of the body was an easy problem to solve. The things that are necessary don't require a lot of work to obtain; only luxuries require effort. Follow nature, and you won't need skilled craftsmen. Nature didn't want us to be troubled. For whatever she forced upon us, she equipped us to handle. "But cold can't be endured by the naked body." What then? Aren't there the skins of wild animals that can protect us well enough from the cold? Don't many tribes cover their bodies with tree bark? Aren't the feathers of birds sewn together to make clothing? Even today, don't many Scythians wear clothes made from the skins of foxes and mice, soft to the touch and resistant to the wind?

"For all that, people must have something thicker than skin to protect them from the summer heat." What then? Didn't ancient times produce many shelters, hollowed out by time or other events, that became caverns? What then? Didn't the earliest people take twigs and weave them by hand into mats, cover them with mud, and then pile on stubble and wild grasses to make a roof, spending their winters safely with rain carried off by sloping gables? What then? Don't the people living near the Syrtes and other tribes with fierce sun live in dug-out houses because the dry ground is the only protection against the heat?

Nature wasn't so hostile to humans that, when she gave all other animals an easy life, she made it impossible for us to live without all these tricks. None of these things were forced upon us by nature; none had to be painfully sought out for our lives to continue. Everything was ready for us at birth; we're the ones who have made everything difficult for ourselves by rejecting what is easy. Houses, shelter, comfort, food, and all the things that are now sources of great trouble were ready at hand, free for everyone, and obtainable with little effort. Everywhere, the limit matched the need; we're the ones who made these things valuable, admired, and sought after with extensive and varied efforts.

Nature provides for what she demands. Luxury has turned her back on nature; she grows every day, gathering strength throughout the ages, using her wit to promote vices. At first, luxury desired what nature saw as unnecessary, then what was against nature; and finally, she made the soul a servant to the body, making it completely enslaved to the body's desires. All the crafts that keep the city running—or should I say in chaos—are just working to serve the body. There was a time when everything was offered to the body as to a slave, but now things are prepared for it as for a master.

That's where the workshops of weavers and carpenters come from; that's where the savory smells of professional cooks come from; that's where the wantonness of those who teach seductive poses and singing comes from. For that moderation that nature requires, which limits our desires to what we need, has been abandoned; it's gotten to the point where wanting only what is enough is seen as both crude and as a sign of utter poverty.

It's hard to believe, my dear Lucilius, how easily the charm of eloquence can lead even great people away from the truth. Take Posidonius, for example—who, in my opinion, has contributed greatly to philosophy—when he describes the art of weaving. He talks about how first, some threads are twisted and some are pulled from the soft, loose wool; next, how the upright warp keeps the threads stretched with weights; then, how the inserted thread of the weft softens the hard texture of the web, which holds it fast on either side, and is forced by the batten to join tightly with the warp. He claims that even the art of weaving was discovered by wise men, forgetting that the more complex art he describes was invented later.

Suppose he had seen the weaving of our own time, which produces clothing that will reveal everything—the kind of clothing that offers no protection to the body or even to modesty! Posidonius then moves on to farming. With no less eloquence, he describes the ground being broken up and crossed by the plow, so that the soil, now loosened, can better support the roots; then the seed is sown, and the weeds are pulled out by hand so that no wild plants grow up and spoil the crop. He claims that farming, too, was created by wise men, as if today's farmers weren't still discovering countless new ways to make the soil more fertile!

He doesn't stop at these arts; he even demeans the wise man by sending him to the mill. He tells us how the sage, by imitating nature, began to make bread. "The grain," he says, "once taken into the mouth, is crushed by the teeth, which grind against each other, and whatever grain slips out is pushed back by the tongue to the same teeth. Then it is mashed into a paste so that it can more easily pass down the throat. When this reaches the stomach, it is digested by the stomach's steady heat; then, and only then, is it absorbed by the body. Following this pattern," he continues, "someone placed two rough stones, one on top of the other, like teeth, with one set waiting for the other to move. Then, by rubbing one stone against the other, the grain is crushed and ground until it turns to powder. Then this person sprinkled water on the meal, kneaded the mass, and shaped the loaf. At first, this loaf was baked in hot ashes or a hot earthen vessel; later, ovens were gradually discovered along with other devices that follow the sage's will." Posidonius almost claimed that even cobbling was the invention of a wise man.

Reason did come up with all these things, but it wasn't right reason. It was a human, but not a wise person, who invented them, just as people invented ships to cross rivers and seas—ships with sails to catch the wind, and with rudders at the stern to steer the vessel in one direction or another. The model was the fish, which steers itself with its tail, bending its swift course with the slightest movement to one side or the other.

"But," says Posidonius, "the wise man did discover all these things; they were just too small for him to handle himself, so he gave them to his lesser assistants." Not so; these early inventions were thought up by the same kind of people who handle them today. We know that certain inventions have been made only within our own memory—like using windows made of transparent tiles to let in clear light, or the vaulted baths with pipes in their walls to spread heat evenly in all spaces. Why should I mention the marble that makes our temples and houses shine? Or the rounded, polished stones we use to build colonnades and buildings big enough for nations? Or the shorthand writing that allows us to take down a speech as quickly as it's spoken, matching the speed of the tongue with the speed of the hand? All these things have been devised by the lowest grade of slaves.

Wisdom's place is higher; she trains our minds, not our hands. Would you like to know what wisdom has brought to light, what she has accomplished? It's not the graceful movements of the body, or the varied notes of horn and flute, where breath is turned into sound. Wisdom doesn't create weapons, walls, or tools for war; no, her voice is for peace, and she calls all people to harmony.

It's not wisdom that is the creator of our everyday tools. Why do you give her credit for such small things? You should see her as the skilled master of life. It's true that wisdom controls other arts because the person whom life serves is also served by the things that support life. But wisdom's goal is to guide us toward happiness; that's where she leads us and opens the way for us.

She shows us what is truly bad and what only seems bad; she strips our minds of false illusions. She gives us true greatness, but she deflates the inflated, showy greatness that's full of emptiness. She teaches us to recognize the difference between what is truly great and what is just puffed up. She gives us knowledge of the whole of nature and her own nature. She reveals to us what the gods are like, what the spirits are, what the souls are that have been given lasting life and have been made part of the divine; where they live, what they do, their powers, and their will.

These are wisdom's sacred teachings, which unlock not just a village shrine but the vast temple of all the gods—the universe itself, whose true forms and true aspects she reveals to our minds. For our eyes are too dull to see such great sights. Then she goes back to the origins of things, to the eternal Reason that was given to the whole world, and to the force in all things that gives them the power to shape themselves according to their kind. Then wisdom begins to ask about the soul, where it comes from, where it lives, how long it stays, and into how many parts it divides. Finally, she turns her attention from the physical to the non-physical and carefully examines truth and the signs by which truth is known, asking next how to tell the difference between what is unclear and what is true, whether in life or in language; for in both, there are elements of falsehood mixed with the truth.

In my opinion, the wise man didn't withdraw from those arts we've been discussing, as Posidonius thinks, but rather he never took them up at all. For he would have decided that nothing was worth discovering that wasn't worth using all the time. He wouldn't take up things that would have to be set aside.

"But Anacharsis," says Posidonius, "invented the potter's wheel, which spins to shape vessels." Then because the potter's wheel is mentioned in Homer, people prefer to believe that Homer's verses are false rather than doubt Posidonius's story! But I don't believe Anacharsis invented this wheel; and even if he did, although he was wise when he invented it, he didn't invent it as a wise man—just as there are many things wise people do as ordinary humans, not as wise people. For example, suppose a wise man is very fast; he will win a race because he's fast, not because he's wise. I would like to show Posidonius a glassblower who shapes glass with his breath into forms that even the most skilled hands could hardly make. No, these discoveries have been made since people stopped discovering wisdom.

But Posidonius says, "Democritus is said to have discovered the arch, where stones lean toward each other in a curve and are held together by a keystone." I'm inclined to say this is false. There must have been bridges and gateways before Democritus where the curve didn't start until near the top.

It seems you've forgotten that this same Democritus discovered how to soften ivory and how, by boiling, a pebble could be turned into an emerald—the same method used today to color stones that can be treated this way! It may have been a wise man who discovered these things, but he didn't do it as a wise man; for he does many things just as well, or even better, as people who have no wisdom at all.

Do you ask what, then, the wise man has discovered and brought to light? First of all, there is truth and nature; and he doesn't follow nature blindly like other animals do, unable to see the divine in it. Second, there is the law of life, and he has made life conform to universal principles; and he has taught us not just to know the gods, but to follow them, and to accept the gifts of fate as if they were divine commands. He has told us not to pay attention to false opinions and has valued each thing by its true worth. He has rejected those pleasures that come with regret and has praised the good things that always satisfy. He has taught the world that the happiest person is the one who doesn't need happiness and that the most powerful person is the one who has power over themselves.

I'm not talking about the philosophy that places the citizen outside their country and the gods outside the universe, or that gives virtue to pleasure, but the philosophy that counts nothing as good except what is honorable—one that can't be bribed by the gifts of people or fortune, one whose value is that it can't be bought for any price. I don't believe this philosophy existed in such a rough age when the arts and crafts were still unknown and when useful things could only be learned by practice.

Next came the fortunate time when nature's gifts were open to everyone, before greed and luxury broke the bonds that held people together, and they, abandoning their communal life, separated and turned to plunder. The people of the second age were not wise, even though they acted like wise people.

Indeed, there is no other condition of humanity that anyone would admire more; and if God were to ask someone to create earthly beings and give laws to peoples, that person would approve of no other system than what existed among the people of that age, when no farmer tilled the soil, and it wasn't right to divide or mark off property. People shared their gains, and the earth freely gave her riches to her sons who didn't seek them.

What race of people was ever more blessed than that race? They enjoyed all of nature in partnership. Nature provided for them, first as their mother and now as their guardian; and her gift was the secure possession by each person of the common resources. Why shouldn't I call that race the richest among mortals since you couldn't find a poor person among them?

But greed broke into this happy state and, by its desire to take and use things for itself, made everything belong to others and reduced itself from limitless wealth to desperate need. It was greed that introduced poverty and, by craving more, lost everything. And so, even though greed now tries to make up for its loss, even though it adds one estate to another by buying out or wronging a neighbor, even though it extends its lands to the size of provinces and defines ownership as meaning extensive travel through one's property—in spite of all these efforts, no expansion of our boundaries will bring us back to the state we left behind.

When we can do no more, we will have much, but we once had the whole world! The very soil was more productive when it was untilled, and it provided more than enough for people who didn't plunder each other. Whatever nature produced, people found as much joy in showing it to others as in discovering it themselves. No one could surpass or fall short of another; what existed was shared among friends without quarrel. The stronger hadn't yet started to take from the weaker; the miser hadn't yet started to hoard what lay before him, cutting off his neighbor from even the necessities of life; each person cared as much for their neighbor as for themselves.

Weapons lay unused, and hands, unstained by human blood, turned all their hatred against wild animals. The people of that time, who had found shelter from the sun in dense groves and protection from the harshness of winter or rain in simple hiding places, lived their lives under the trees and spent peaceful nights without a sigh. Care troubles us in our purple beds and drives us from our sleep with sharp goads; but how soft was the sleep the hard earth gave to those people!

No ornate, paneled ceilings hung over them; instead, as they lay beneath the open sky, the stars quietly moved above them, and the firmament, the grand pageant of the night, passed swiftly by, carrying out its great task in silence. For them, by day as well as by night, the vision of this glorious world was open and free. It was their joy to watch the stars as they sank from the middle of the sky and others as they rose from their hidden places. What else but joy could it be to wander among the wonders spread across the heavens? But you, in the present day, shudder at every noise your houses make, and as you sit among your painted walls, the slightest creak makes you shrink in fear. They didn't have houses as big as cities. The air, the breezes blowing freely through the open spaces, the shifting shade of rocks or trees, clear springs, and streams not spoiled by human work, whether by pipes or by any confinement, but running freely, and meadows beautiful without the use of art—these were the settings of their simple homes, decorated with rustic hands. Such homes were in harmony with nature; it was a joy to live in them, fearing neither the home itself nor for its safety. Today, however, our houses are a large part of our fear.

But no matter how excellent and innocent the life of those people was, they were not wise; for that title is reserved for the highest achievement. Still, I wouldn't deny that they were people of great spirit and—if I can use the phrase—fresh from the gods. There's no doubt that the world produced a better generation before it became worn out. However, not all were blessed with the highest mental abilities, though in all cases their natural strength was greater than ours and more suited for hard work. For nature doesn't give us virtue; it is an art to become good.

At least, they didn't dig deep into the earth for gold, silver, or transparent stones; and they were still kind even to animals—so far removed was that time from the custom of people killing each other, not out of anger or fear, but just for show! They didn't have embroidered clothes, nor did they weave cloth of gold; gold wasn't even mined yet.

What, then, is the conclusion? It was because of their ignorance of things that those people were innocent, and it makes a big difference whether someone chooses not to sin or doesn't know how to sin. Justice was unknown to them, as were prudence, self-control, and bravery; but their simple life had qualities similar to all these virtues. Virtue isn't given to a soul unless that soul has been trained and taught, and brought to perfection by constant practice. We were born with the ability to achieve this, but not with it already in our possession; and even in the best people, before you refine them through instruction, there is only the potential for virtue, not virtue itself. Farewell.

Letter 91 - On the lesson to be drawn from the burning of Lyons

Our friend Liberalis is feeling down because he just heard about the fire that destroyed the city of Lyons. Such a disaster could upset anyone, especially someone who deeply loves his homeland. But this event has made him question the strength of his own character, which he has likely trained to face situations he thought might cause him fear. I'm not surprised, though, that he wasn't afraid of something so unexpected and almost unheard of because it's something that has never happened before. Fires have damaged many cities, but they've never completely destroyed one. Even when fire has been used as a weapon by enemies, the flames often die out in places, and although the fire is constantly rekindled, it rarely burns so completely that nothing is left for the sword. Even earthquakes have rarely been so violent and destructive that they've completely destroyed entire cities. Finally, no fire has ever burned so fiercely in any town that nothing was left for the future.

So many beautiful buildings, any one of which would make a single town famous, were destroyed in just one night. During a time of such deep peace, something worse than anything people might fear in wartime has happened. Who can believe it? When weapons are at rest everywhere, and when peace prevails across the world, Lyons, the pride of Gaul, is gone!

Usually, Fortune gives everyone a warning before they face the suffering they're destined to endure. Every great creation has had some time to prepare before it falls, but in this case, only a single night passed between the city at its peak and the city's complete destruction. In fact, it takes me longer to tell you it has perished than it took for the city to perish.

All of this has affected our friend Liberalis, shaking his will, which is usually so strong and steady in the face of his own troubles. And it's no wonder he's been shaken; it's the unexpected that hits us the hardest. The strangeness of such events makes calamities even worse, and every person feels more pain when something surprises them.

So, nothing should be unexpected for us. Our minds should be prepared in advance for all problems, and we should think not just about what usually happens, but what can happen. For what in existence can Fortune, when she decides to, not bring down from the height of its success? And what does she not attack more violently the more brightly it shines? What is difficult or challenging for her?

She doesn't always attack in the same way or even with her full strength; sometimes she uses our own hands against us, and other times, she relies only on her own power to create dangers for us. No time is safe; in the middle of our pleasures, causes of suffering arise. War comes in the middle of peace, and the things we depend on for protection turn into sources of fear; friends become enemies, allies become foes. The calm of summer is suddenly disrupted by storms, wilder than those of winter.

Even when no enemy is in sight, we suffer the same fates as if they were attacking us, and if other causes of disaster don't arise, excessive good fortune creates them for itself. The most temperate people are attacked by illness, the strongest by wasting disease, the most innocent by punishment, the most secluded by the noisy mob.

Chance finds some new way to bring her power against us, thinking we've forgotten her.

Whatever has been built up over many years, with great effort and the favor of the gods, can be scattered and destroyed in a single day. In fact, saying "a day" gives too much time to misfortune; an hour, a single moment, is enough to bring down empires! It would be some comfort for our weakness and the fragility of our works if things took as long to perish as they do to come into being; but as it is, growth is slow, but destruction is quick.

Nothing, whether public or private, is stable; the fates of people, just like those of cities, are in constant turmoil. Even in the greatest calm, terror arises, and even when no outside forces stir up trouble, evils burst forth from places where we least expect them. Thrones that have withstood civil and foreign wars collapse without anyone to push them. How few are the states that have carried their good fortune to the end!

We should, therefore, consider all possibilities and prepare our minds for the evils that may come. Exile, the pain of disease, wars, shipwreck—we must think of these things. Chance may take you from your country or your country from you or may banish you to the wilderness; this very place, now crowded with people, could become a desert. Let us fully understand the nature of human life, and if we don't want to be overwhelmed or shocked by unexpected evils, let us imagine not just the common misfortunes but the worst things that could possibly happen. We must fully consider what Fortune can do.

How often have cities in Asia, how often in Greece, been destroyed by a single earthquake? How many towns in Syria, how many in Macedonia, have been swallowed up? How often has this kind of destruction ruined Cyprus? How often has Paphos collapsed? We often hear news of entire cities being utterly destroyed; yet how small a part of the world are we, who often receive such news?

Let us, therefore, rise to face the actions of Fortune, and whatever happens, let us be sure that it's not as bad as rumor makes it out to be. A rich city has been burned to ashes, the jewel of the provinces, considered one of them yet not fully part of them; rich as it was, it was still built on a single hill, and not a very large one. But of all those cities whose magnificence and grandeur you hear of today, time will eventually erase every trace. Don't you see how in Greece, the foundations of the most famous cities have already crumbled to nothing, leaving no sign that they ever even existed?

Not only do things made by human hands collapse, not only are things created by human art and effort overthrown by time; no, even the peaks of mountains erode, whole regions sink, and places that were once far from the sea are now covered by its waves. The great power of fires has eaten away at the hills where they once glowed, and has leveled to the ground the peaks that once stood tall, serving as a guide and beacon for sailors. Even the works of nature itself are attacked; so we should bear the destruction of cities with calm minds.

They stand only to fall! This fate awaits them all; it may be that some internal force, or violent blasts trapped below, will break free and throw off the weight holding them down; or that a whirlpool of raging currents, stronger because they are hidden deep in the earth, will break through whatever resists them; or that the intensity of flames will shatter the earth's crust; or that time, from which nothing is safe, will slowly reduce them; or that a harmful climate will drive their people away and mold will eat away at their deserted walls. It would take too long to list all the ways fate may strike, but this one thing I know: all the works of mortal man are doomed to mortality, and in the middle of things destined to die, we live!

That's why I offer these thoughts as comfort to our friend Liberalis, who has an incredible love for his country. Maybe its destruction has happened only so it can be rebuilt to a better destiny. Often a setback makes room for better fortune. Many buildings have fallen only to rise higher.

Timagenes, who had a grudge against Rome and her success, used to say that the only reason he was upset when fires happened in Rome was that he knew better buildings would rise than those that had been destroyed. And probably in this city of Lyons, too, all its citizens will work hard to rebuild everything bigger and more secure than what they've lost. May it be built to last and, under happier circumstances, for a longer time! This city is only a hundred years old—not even the span of a single person's life. Founded by Plancus, the natural advantages of its location have helped it grow strong and reach the population it has today; and yet how many great disasters has it endured within the lifetime of an old man!

Therefore, let the mind be trained to understand and endure its own fate, and let it know that there is nothing Fortune doesn't dare— that she has the same power over empires as she does over emperors, the same power over cities as over the people who live in them. We must not complain about any of these disasters. This is the world we've entered, and these are the laws we live under. If you like it, obey; if not, leave for wherever you want. Complain in anger if any unfair measures are taken against you personally, but if this inevitable law applies to everyone, high and low alike, accept your fate, by which all things are dissolved.

You shouldn't judge our worth by our burial mounds or these monuments of different sizes that line the road; their ashes make everyone equal! We are unequal at birth, but equal in death. What I say about cities, I also say about their people: Ardea was captured just like Rome. The great creator of human law didn't make distinctions between us based on noble birth or famous names, except while we're alive. When, however, we reach the end that awaits all mortals, he says: "Let go of ambition! To all creatures that walk the earth, let one and the same law apply!" For enduring all things, we are equal; no one is more fragile than another, no one more certain of his life tomorrow.

Alexander, king of Macedon, began to study geometry; unhappy man, because he would learn how small that earth was of which he had only seized a part! Unhappy man, because he was bound to realize that his title of "great" was false. For who can be "great" in something so small? The lessons he was being taught were complicated and could only be learned through careful study; they weren't the kind of lessons to be understood by a madman whose thoughts were focused beyond the ocean. "Teach me something easy!" he cries; but his teacher replies: "These things are the same for everyone, just as hard for one as for another."

Imagine that nature is saying to us: "The things you complain about are the same for everyone. I can't give anything easier to anyone, but whoever wants to can make things easier for themselves." How? By having a calm mind. You must suffer pain, thirst, hunger, and old age if a longer stay among people is granted to you; you must be sick, and you must suffer loss and death. Nevertheless, you shouldn't believe those whose loud complaints surround you; none of these things is evil, none is beyond your ability to bear, or is too heavy. It is only by common belief that they seem frightening. Your fear of death is therefore like your fear of gossip. But what is more foolish than being afraid of words? Our friend Demetrius has a clever way of putting it when he says: "For me, the talk of ignorant people is like the noises that come from the stomach. For," he adds, "what difference does it make to me whether such noises come from above or from below?"

What madness it is to be afraid of disapproval from people who are themselves disreputable! Just as you've had no reason to shrink in fear from the talk of others, you have no reason now to shrink from these things, which you wouldn't fear if their talk hadn't made you afraid. Does it do any harm to a good person to be criticized by unjust gossip? Then let's not let this kind of thing make us think death is bad, either; death is also spoken of badly. But none of those who speak badly of death have experienced it. Meanwhile, it is foolish to condemn something you know nothing about. However, you do know this one thing—that death is helpful to many, that it frees many from pain, poverty, illness, suffering, and weariness. We are under the control of nothing once we have control over death. Farewell.

Letter 92 - On the happy life

You and I will probably agree that people seek out things in the world to satisfy their bodies, that we take care of our bodies because of our souls, and that in the soul, there are parts that help us move and stay alive, given to us for the sake of our most important part. In this most important part of us, there is something irrational and something rational. The irrational part listens to the rational part, and the rational part doesn't answer to anything else, but instead makes everything else answer to it. This is like how the divine reason is in charge of everything and isn't controlled by anything else; the reason we have is the same because it comes from the divine reason.

Now, if we agree on this, it makes sense that we will also agree on this next point: the happy life depends on this and only this—reaching perfect reason. It's this reason alone that keeps the soul from being crushed and helps it stand strong against Fortune; no matter what happens, it keeps people calm. And only that is truly good, which cannot be damaged. I say that the person is happy whom nothing can make weaker; he stays strong, relying only on himself because someone who relies on anything else might fall. If it's any other way, then things that don't really belong to us will start to have too much control over us. But who wants Fortune to be in control, or what sensible person takes pride in something that isn't truly theirs?

So, what is the happy life? It's peace of mind and lasting calm. You'll have this if you have greatness of soul; you'll have this if you have the strength that sticks to a good decision once it's made. How does someone reach this state? By gaining a full understanding of the truth, by keeping order, balance, and a sense of what's right in everything they do, and by having a will that is kind and focused on reason, and never strays from it—a will that commands both love and admiration. To sum it up briefly, the soul of a wise person should be like that of a god.

What more could someone want who already has all the honorable things? Because if dishonorable things can help someone live the best life, then it would be possible to have a happy life without an honorable one. And what could be more shameful or foolish than to link the good of a rational soul with irrational things?

Yet, some philosophers believe that the highest good can be made better because it's not complete when Fortune's gifts are against us. Even Antipater, one of the great leaders of this school of thought, admits that he gives some importance to external things, though only a very small amount. But you can see how absurd it is not to be content with daylight unless it's made brighter by a tiny fire. What difference can a small spark make in the middle of bright sunlight?

If you're not satisfied with what's honorable alone, it means you also want either the kind of peace that the Greeks call "undisturbedness" or pleasure. But the first can be achieved in any situation. Because the mind is free from disturbance when it's fully free to think about the universe, and nothing distracts it from thinking about nature. The second, pleasure, is simply the good of animals. We are just adding the irrational to the rational, the dishonorable to the honorable. A pleasant physical sensation affects our lives. So why do you hesitate to say that all is well with a person just because all is well with his appetite? And do you consider, I won't say a hero, but even a human, the person whose highest good is about flavors, colors, and sounds? No, let him step out of the ranks of the noblest class of living beings, second only to the gods; let him join the herd of dumb animals—an animal that finds joy in food!

The irrational part of the soul has two sides: one part is spirited, ambitious, and uncontrolled; it's driven by emotions. The other part is lowly, sluggish, and focused on pleasure. Philosophers have neglected the first part, which, although wild, is still better, and certainly more courageous and more fitting for a human. Instead, they have focused on the second part, which is weak and base, as if it were essential to the happy life.

They have commanded reason to serve this lower part; they have made the highest good of the noblest living being a low and shameful thing, and a strange mixture too, made up of different parts that don't fit together well. For as our Vergil describes Scylla, he says:

"Above, a human face and maiden's breast, –
A beauteous breast, – below, a monster huge
Of bulk and shapeless, with a dolphin's tail
Joined to a wolf-like belly."

And yet, to this Scylla, are added the forms of wild animals, dreadful and fast; but what monstrous shapes have these so-called wise people mixed together to create wisdom!

The main skill of humans is virtue itself; attached to this is the useless and temporary flesh, suited only for eating, as Posidonius says. This divine virtue ends in something filthy, and to the higher parts, which are worthy of worship and heavenly, is attached a sluggish and weak animal. As for the second desired thing—quiet—although it wouldn't really benefit the soul, it would remove obstacles from it; pleasure, on the other hand, actually harms the soul and weakens all its strength. What elements more incompatible than these can be found together? To the strongest thing is joined the weakest, to the most serious the most frivolous, to the most sacred the most unrestrained, even to the point of impurity.

Then comes the argument, "What, then, if good health, rest, and freedom from pain aren't likely to harm virtue, shouldn't you seek all these?" Of course, I'll seek them, but not because they are good—I'll seek them because they are natural and because I'll get them by making good decisions. So, what will be good in them? Only this— that it's good to choose them. For when I put on appropriate clothing, or walk as I should, or eat as I ought to eat, it's not my meal, my walk, or my clothes that are good, but the deliberate choice I make regarding them, as I keep, in everything I do, a balance that fits with reason.

Let me also add that choosing neat clothing is a worthy goal for a man because man is naturally a neat and well-groomed creature. So, the choice of neat clothing, not the neat clothing itself, is good since the good lies not in the thing chosen but in the quality of the choice. Our actions are honorable, but not necessarily the things we do.

And you can assume that what I've said about clothing also applies to the body. Because nature has surrounded our soul with the body as a kind of garment; the body is its cloak. But who has ever judged the value of clothing by the wardrobe that holds it? The scabbard doesn't make the sword good or bad. So, about the body, I'll give you the same answer—if I have a choice, I'll choose health and strength, but the good involved will be my judgment about these things, not the things themselves.

Another argument is: "Granted that the wise man is happy; nevertheless, he doesn't reach the highest good we've defined unless he also has the means that nature provides for reaching it. So, while someone who has virtue can't be unhappy, they also can't be perfectly happy if they lack natural gifts like health or physical wholeness."

But by saying this, you agree with the harder part to believe—that someone in constant, extreme pain is not miserable, in fact, is even happy—and you deny the much less serious idea that they are completely happy. And yet, if virtue can keep someone from being miserable, it will be an easier task for it to make them completely happy. Because the difference between happiness and complete happiness is less than the difference between misery and happiness. Can it be possible that something so powerful as to lift someone from disaster and place them among the happy can't also do what remains and make them supremely happy? Does its strength fail at the very top of the climb?

In life, there are things that are advantageous and disadvantageous—both beyond our control. If a good person, even when weighed down by all kinds of disadvantages, is not miserable, how are they not supremely happy, even if they lack some advantages?

Because just as they are not dragged down to misery by their disadvantages, they are also not pulled away from supreme happiness by the lack of any advantages; no, they are just as supremely happy without the advantages as they are free from misery despite their disadvantages. Otherwise, if their good can be weakened, it can be taken away from them altogether.

Earlier, I mentioned that a tiny fire doesn't add to the sun's light. Because of the sun's brightness, any light that shines apart from the sunlight is overshadowed. But someone might say, "There are certain objects that block even sunlight." The sun, however, is not weakened even when there are obstacles, and even if something comes between us and the sun, cutting off our view, the sun continues its work and stays on its course. Whenever it shines forth from behind the clouds, it's not smaller or less on time than when it's free from clouds; it makes a big difference whether something is merely in the way of its light or something interferes with its shining.

Similarly, obstacles don't take anything away from virtue; it's not smaller, but it just shines with less brilliance. In our eyes, it may seem less visible and less bright than before, but as far as it is concerned, it remains the same and, like the sun during an eclipse, it's still, though in secret, exerting its strength. So disasters, losses, and wrongs have only as much power over virtue as a cloud has over the sun.

We meet people who claim that a wise person who has suffered bodily misfortune is neither miserable nor happy. But they are also wrong because they are treating the results of chance as equal to virtues and are giving the same importance to things that are honorable as to things that are not. But what could be more detestable and unworthy than to put things that deserve no respect in the same class as things that deserve reverence? Because respect is due to justice, duty, loyalty, bravery, and wisdom; in contrast, those physical attributes are worthless, which even the most worthless people often have in greater measure—like strong legs, broad shoulders, good teeth, and healthy, solid muscles.

Again, if the wise person whose body is a burden to him is neither miserable nor happy but is left in a sort of middle ground, his life will also be neither desirable nor undesirable. But what could be more foolish than to say that the wise person's life is not desirable? And what could be more unbelievable than the idea that any life is neither desirable nor undesirable? Again, if physical problems don't make someone miserable, they also allow them to be happy. Because things that don't have the power to make their condition worse don't have the power either to disturb that condition when it's at its best.

"But," someone will say, "we know what is cold and what is hot; a lukewarm temperature is in between. Similarly, A is happy, and B is miserable, and C is neither happy nor miserable." I want to examine this comparison, which is used against us. If I add more cold water to your lukewarm water, the result will be cold water. But if I add more hot water, the water will eventually become hot. But with your person who is neither miserable nor happy, no matter how much I add to his troubles, he won't become miserable, according to your argument; so your comparison doesn't hold up.

Again, let's say I present to you a person who is neither miserable nor happy. I add blindness to his misfortunes; he's not made miserable. I cripple him; he's not made miserable. I add afflictions that are constant and severe; he's not made miserable. So, someone whose life isn't changed to misery by all these ills isn't dragged away from their happy life either.

Then if, as you say, the wise person can't fall from happiness to misery, they can't fall into non-happiness either. Because how, if someone has started to slip, can they stop at any particular place? What keeps them from falling to the bottom also keeps them at the top. Why, you ask, can't a happy life possibly be destroyed? It can't even be divided; and for that reason, virtue is, by itself, enough for the happy life.

"But," some say, "isn't the wise person happier if they've lived longer and haven't been troubled by pain than someone who has always had to fight against bad fortune?" Answer me this—are they any better or more honorable? If they're not, then they're not happier either. To live more happily, they must live more rightly; if they can't do that, then they can't live more happily either. Virtue can't be stretched further, and therefore neither can the happy life, which depends on virtue. Because virtue is so great a good that it isn't affected by such small attacks on it as a short life, pain, and various bodily troubles. Because pleasure doesn't deserve even a glance from virtue.

So, what is the main thing in virtue? It's the quality of not needing a single day beyond today, and not counting the days that are ours; in the smallest possible moment of time, virtue completes an eternity of good. These goods seem incredible to us and beyond human nature because we measure their greatness by the standard of our own weakness, and we call our vices by the name of virtue. Also, doesn't it seem just as incredible that anyone in extreme suffering could say, "I am happy"? And yet, this statement was heard in the very place where pleasure is supposed to reign, when Epicurus said: "Today and one other day have been the happiest of all!" even though on one of those days, he was tortured by kidney stones, and on the other by the incurable pain of an ulcerated stomach.

So why should the goods that virtue provides be unbelievable to us, who pursue virtue when they're found even in those who see pleasure as their master? These people too, base and low-minded as they are, say that even in the midst of great pain and misfortune, the wise person will be neither miserable nor happy. And yet this is also unbelievable—even more unbelievable than the other case. Because I don't understand how, if virtue falls from its heights, it can avoid being thrown all the way to the bottom. It either must keep us happy, or, if it's driven from that position, it won't stop us from becoming miserable. If virtue just stands its ground, it can't be driven off; it must either win or be defeated.

But some say: "Only the immortal gods have true virtue and the happy life; we can only reach for the shadow, so to speak, and the appearance of such goods as they have. We get close, but we never reach them." However, reason is something both gods and humans have in common; in the gods, it's already perfected, and in us, it can be perfected.

But it's our vices that make us lose hope; because the second type of rational being, man, is of a lower order—like a guardian who is too unstable to hold on to what's best, with judgment that's still wavering and uncertain. He might need sight and hearing, good health, a body that isn't ugly, and, on top of that, a longer life with an unbroken constitution.

Though through reason he can live a life without regrets, there's still in this imperfect being, man, a certain power that leads to badness because he has a mind that is easily swayed to do wrong. But suppose the badness that's visible and has already been stirred up is removed; the man is still not a good man, but he's on his way to goodness. However, someone who lacks any quality that leads to goodness is bad.

But the person in whose body virtue lives and a present spirit is equal to the gods; remembering his origin, he strives to return there. No one does wrong in trying to regain the heights from which he once descended. And why shouldn't you believe that something divine exists in someone who is part of God? This whole universe that surrounds us is one, and it is God; we are associates of God; we are his parts. Our soul has powers, and it's lifted there if vices don't hold it down. Just as it's in our body's nature to stand upright and look up at the sky, so the soul, which can reach as far as it wants, was made by nature to aim for equality with the gods. And if it uses its powers and stretches upward into its proper place, it's not by some foreign path that it climbs toward the heights.

It would be a great journey to travel to heaven; the soul just returns there. Once it has found the way, it boldly marches on, scornful of everything else. It doesn't look back at wealth; gold and silver—things that are fully worthy of the darkness where they once lay—it doesn't value by the shine that dazzles the ignorant, but by the dirt of ancient days, from which our greed first dug them out.

The soul knows that riches are stored elsewhere than in men's hoarded treasures; that it's the soul, not the strongbox, that should be filled. It's the soul that men can set in dominion over everything and can install as the owner of the universe so that it may limit its riches only by the boundaries of East and West, and, like the gods, may possess everything; and that it may, with its vast resources, look down from on high upon the wealthy, none of whom enjoys his wealth as much as he resents the wealth of others.

When the soul has lifted itself to this high place, it also sees the body, since it's a burden that must be carried, not as something to love, but as something to oversee; nor is it a servant to what it's set to rule over. Because no one is free who is a slave to his body. Indeed, leaving aside all the other masters created by too much concern for the body, the body's own rule is picky and demanding.

The soul leaves the body, sometimes calmly, sometimes with joy, and, once it has left, it doesn't care what happens to the empty shell left behind. No, just as we don't worry about what happens to hair or beard clippings, in the same way, that divine soul, when it's about to leave the mortal body, regards the fate of its earthly vessel—whether it's burned, buried, or torn apart by animals—as no more of a concern than the afterbirth is to a newborn baby. And whether this body is left out and torn apart by birds, or eaten when thrown to the sea creatures, how does that concern someone who no longer exists?

No, even while it's still alive, the soul fears nothing that might happen to the body after death; because even if such things were threats, they weren't enough to scare the soul before the moment of death. It says, "I'm not frightened by the executioner's hook, nor by the disgusting mutilation of the body exposed to the scorn of those who would witness the spectacle. I ask no one to perform the last rites for me; I don't entrust my remains to anyone. Nature has made sure that no one will go unburied. Time will bury those whom cruelty has cast out." Those were wise words that Maecenas said: "I want no tomb; for Nature provides for outcast bodies' burial." You would think this was the saying of a man with strict principles. He was indeed a man of noble and strong natural talents, but in prosperity, he weakened those gifts by becoming lax. Farewell.

Letter 93 - On the quality, as contrasted with the length, of life

While I was reading your letter where you were mourning the death of the philosopher Metronax, saying that he could have and should have lived longer, I noticed that you weren't being as fair as you usually are when you talk about people and things. But when it comes to this one subject, fairness seems to be missing, just like it is for all of us. I've noticed that many people are fair to others, but no one seems to be fair to the gods. Every day we complain about Fate, saying things like, "Why was A. taken away in the middle of his life? Why wasn't B. taken instead? Why should someone live so long when their old age is a burden to themselves and others?"

But tell me, do you think it's fairer for you to obey Nature or for Nature to obey you? And what difference does it make how soon you leave a place that you have to leave sooner or later anyway? We should focus on living rightly, not just living a long time. To live a long life, you only need Fate, but to live rightly, you need your soul. A life is truly long if it is full, but a full life is when the soul has achieved its proper good, meaning when it has taken control over itself.

What good does this old man get from the eighty years he spent doing nothing? A person like him hasn't really lived; he just stayed around in life for a while. He didn't die late in life; he just took a long time to die. Did he live eighty years? That depends on when you start counting his death! Your other friend, however, died in the prime of his life.

But he fulfilled all the duties of a good citizen, a good friend, a good son; in no way did he fall short. His age might not have been complete, but his life was. The other man lived eighty years, did he? No, he just existed for eighty years unless you mean "lived" the same way we say a tree "lives."

Let's make sure, my dear Lucilius, that our lives, like precious jewels, are valuable not because of their size but because of their weight. Let's measure them by what we achieve, not by how long they last. Do you want to know the difference between this strong person, who, despising Fortune, has gone through every battle of life and has reached life's highest good, and that other person who just let many years pass over his head? The first one still exists even after his death; the other died before he was even dead.

We should praise and count among the blessed that person who has made good use of the time, no matter how little, that was given to him; for such a person has seen the true light. He wasn't just another person in the crowd. He didn't just live; he thrived. Sometimes he enjoyed clear skies; sometimes, as often happens, the brightness of a great star flashed to him through the clouds.

Why do you ask, "How long did he live?" He still lives! In one leap, he has passed into the future and has entrusted himself to the care of memory.

And yet, I wouldn't turn down a few more years for myself; although, if my life is cut short, I won't say that I missed anything essential for a happy life. I didn't plan to live until the very last day my greedy hopes had promised me; no, I've looked at every day as if it were my last. Why ask when I was born, or if I'm still listed among the younger men? What I have is mine.

Just as a person who is short can still be a perfect person, a life that is short can still be a perfect life. Age is just an external thing.

How long I exist isn't up to me, but how long I keep living the way I am now is in my control. This is the only thing you have the right to expect from me—that I won't waste away in an inglorious old age as if I were in the dark, but that I will devote myself to truly living instead of just being carried along past life.

And what, you ask, is the fullest span of life? It's living until you have wisdom. The person who has gained wisdom has reached not the furthest point, but the most important one. Such a person can indeed boast boldly and thank the gods—and even themselves—and they can count themselves as having given Nature back more than they received. They will have the right to do so, for they have given back a better life than they were given. They have shown what a good person is like, showing the quality and greatness of a good person. If another year had been added, it would have just been more of the same.

And yet, how long should we keep living? We've had the joy of learning the truth about the universe. We know where Nature starts; how she controls the course of the heavens; how she brings back the year with its changing seasons; how she ends all things that ever existed and makes herself the only end of her own being. We know that the stars move by their own motion and that nothing except the Earth stands still, while all the other bodies move with uninterrupted speed. We know how the moon outpaces the sun; why the slower one leaves the faster one behind; how the moon gets her light or loses it again; what brings on the night and what brings back the day. You must go to that place where you can see all these things more closely.

And yet, the wise man says, "I don't leave life more bravely because of this hope—because I think the path to my own gods lies open before me. I've earned the right to be in their presence, and I've already been in their company; I've sent my soul to them just as they had sent theirs to me before. But suppose that I'm completely gone after death, and nothing of me remains; I am no less brave, even if, when I leave, my path leads—nowhere."

But you say, "He didn't live as long as he could have."

There are books with very few lines that are still wonderful and useful despite their small size; and then there are the Annals of Tanusius—you know how big that book is and what people say about it. This is like the long life of some people—a state that's like the Annals of Tanusius!

Do you think the fighter who is killed on the last day of the games is more fortunate than the one who dies in the middle of the festivities? Do you think anyone is so foolishly greedy for life that they would rather have their throat cut in the dressing room than in the amphitheater? We only precede each other by a short time. Death visits everyone; the killer soon follows the killed. It's a tiny matter, after all, that people worry about so much. And anyway, what does it matter how long you avoid something you can't escape? Farewell.

Letter 94 - On the value of advice

The part of philosophy that gives advice for specific situations—like how a husband should treat his wife, how a father should raise his children, or how a master should treat his slaves—this part of philosophy is seen by some as the only important part, while they dismiss other parts, saying those don't deal with practical needs. But how can someone give advice on just one part of life without first understanding life as a whole?

However, Aristo the Stoic thinks this part of philosophy isn't very important—he believes it doesn't really stick in the mind because it's full of old-fashioned rules. He thinks the greatest benefit comes from understanding the basic principles of philosophy and what the ultimate Good is. When someone has fully understood this and learned it well, they can figure out for themselves what to do in any situation. Just like a person learning to throw a javelin keeps aiming at a target to train their hand to aim properly, and once they've learned this through practice, they can aim at any target they want (having learned to hit exactly what they're aiming at). In the same way, someone who is prepared for all of life doesn't need advice for every little thing because they're already trained to handle the whole problem; they know not just how to live with their wife or son, but how to live rightly. And knowing how to live rightly includes knowing how to live with their wife and children.

Cleanthes thinks that this part of philosophy is useful but weak unless it comes from general principles—meaning it needs to be based on a knowledge of the main ideas of philosophy. So this subject has two sides: first, is it useful or not? And second, can it, by itself, make a person good? In other words, is it unnecessary, or does it make everything else unnecessary?

Those who argue that this part of philosophy is unnecessary say: "If something is blocking your vision, you need to remove it. As long as it's in the way, it's a waste of time to give advice like 'Walk this way' or 'Stretch out your hand in that direction.' Similarly, when something is blinding a person's soul and stopping them from seeing their duty clearly, it's useless to tell them 'Live this way with your father, or this way with your wife.' Giving advice won't help as long as their mind is clouded with error; only when the cloud is lifted will it be clear what their duty is in each case. Otherwise, you're just telling a sick person what they should do if they were healthy, instead of making them healthy.

Suppose you're trying to show a poor person how to act rich; how can that work if they're still poor? You're trying to show a starving person how to act like they've eaten well; but the first thing you need to do is take away the hunger that's gripping their stomach.

"The same thing applies to all faults; the faults themselves need to be removed, and you shouldn't give advice that can't be followed as long as the faults are there. Unless you get rid of the wrong ideas we suffer from, the miser will never learn how to use his money properly, and the coward won't learn how to stop fearing danger. You need to show the miser that money isn't really good or bad; show him rich people who are still miserable. You need to show the coward that the things that usually scare us out of our wits aren't as scary as we think they are, whether it's pain or death; that when death comes— which it will for all of us—it's often comforting to remember that it can never come again; that in the middle of suffering, having a strong soul is as good as a cure because the soul makes any burden lighter when it endures it with stubborn defiance. Remember that pain has this excellent quality: if it lasts a long time, it can't be very intense, and if it's intense, it can't last long; and that we should bravely accept whatever the inevitable laws of the universe lay upon us.

"When you've taught the person who was making mistakes to understand their own situation, when they've learned that the happy life isn't the one that follows pleasure, but the one that follows Nature, when they've fallen deeply in love with virtue as the only good for a person and have avoided baseness as the only evil, and when they know that everything else—riches, power, health, strength, control— falls somewhere in between and shouldn't be considered either good or bad, then they won't need someone to advise them on every little thing, to say to them: 'Walk this way, eat this way. This is how a man should behave, and that's how a woman should behave; this is how a married man should act, and that's how a bachelor should act.' In fact, the people who spend the most time giving this kind of advice often can't follow it themselves. It's like when a tutor advises a boy, or a grandmother advises her grandson; or when the angriest teacher says you should never lose your temper. Go into any elementary school, and you'll find that high-browed philosophers are giving the same advice as in a lesson book for kids!

"Should you give advice that's clear or advice that's unclear? Clear advice doesn't need a counselor, and unclear advice won't be believed; so giving advice is unnecessary. You should study the problem this way: if you're giving someone advice on something that's unclear and uncertain, you need to back up your advice with proof; and if you need proof, then your proof is more useful and satisfying on its own.

'This is how you should treat your friend, this is how you should treat your fellow citizen, this is how you should treat your partner.' And why? 'Because it's just.' But I can find all that under the heading of Justice. I find that fairness is desirable in itself, that we don't do it out of fear or for payment, and that no one is just if they're attracted to anything in this virtue except the virtue itself. After I've convinced myself of this and fully absorbed it, what good can I get from advice that only teaches someone who's already trained? For someone who knows, advice is unnecessary; for someone who doesn't know, it's not enough. Because they need to be told not only what to do but also why they should do it.

"I ask again, is this kind of advice useful to someone who has the right ideas about good and evil, or to someone who doesn't? The latter won't get any benefit from you; because some idea that conflicts with your advice has already taken over their mind. Someone who has carefully decided what to seek and what to avoid already knows what they should do, without any advice from you. Therefore, this whole part of philosophy can be abolished.

"There are two reasons why we go astray: either there's something wrong in the soul caused by false opinions, or, even if it doesn't have false ideas, the soul is easily led astray by some appearance that attracts it in the wrong direction. For this reason, we either need to carefully treat the sick mind and free it from faults, or take control of the mind when it's still uncorrupted but inclined to do wrong. Both of these can be done by the main teachings of philosophy; so giving advice is of no use.

"Besides, if we have to give advice to each person individually, the task is enormous. You'd need to give one kind of advice to a banker, another to a farmer, another to a businessperson, another to someone who's trying to win the favor of royalty, another to someone who wants to make friends with their equals, and another to someone who wants to get along with people of lower rank. When it comes to marriage, you'd give one person advice on how to treat a wife who was a virgin before marriage and another person advice on how to treat a wife who was previously married to someone else; you'd advise one man on how to deal with a rich wife, and another on how to deal with a wife without a dowry. Or do you think there's no difference between a woman who can't have children and one who can, between an older woman and a young girl, between a mother and a stepmother? We can't cover all the different types, and yet each type needs its own advice; but the rules of philosophy are simple and apply to all cases.

"Also, advice should be clear and certain: when things can't be clearly defined, they're outside the reach of wisdom; because wisdom knows the proper limits of things.

"So we should get rid of this part of philosophy that gives advice because it can't deliver what it promises to everyone; wisdom, however, helps everyone. There's no difference between the madness of the general public and the madness that needs medical treatment, except that one comes from disease and the other from false opinions. In one case, the symptoms of madness are due to bad health; the other is the bad health of the mind. If you try to give advice to a madman—on how to speak, how to walk, how to behave in public and private—you'd be crazier than the person you're advising. What's really needed is to treat the black bile and remove the cause of the madness. And this is what should be done in the other case—the case of a mind that's diseased. The madness itself needs to be cured; otherwise, your words of advice will vanish into thin air.

"This is what Aristo says, and I'll answer his arguments one by one. First, in response to what he says about removing something that blocks the eye and hinders vision: I agree that such a person doesn't need advice on how to see but needs treatment to cure their eyesight and remove the hindrance that's blocking them. Because it's Nature that gives us our eyesight; and the person who removes obstacles is restoring Nature's proper function. But Nature doesn't teach us our duty in every case.

"Also, if someone's cataract is cured, they can't immediately after their recovery give back eyesight to other people as well; but when we're freed from evil, we can free others too. There's no need for encouragement or even advice for the eye to distinguish different colors; black and white can be told apart without any prompting from another person. The mind, however, needs many pieces of advice to see what it should do in life; although in eye treatment too, the doctor not only cures but also gives advice.

"The doctor might say: 'Don't expose your weak vision to bright light right away; start with darkness, then go to half-light, and finally get used to the full light of day gradually. Don't study right after eating; don't strain your eyes when they're swollen and inflamed; avoid winds and cold air blowing directly on your face,' and other suggestions like these, which are just as valuable as medicine itself. The doctor's art combines treatments with advice.

"But," comes the reply, "error is the source of sin; advice doesn't remove error, nor does it get rid of our false beliefs about Good and Evil." I admit that advice alone doesn't overthrow mistaken beliefs in the mind, but it's still useful when combined with other measures. First, advice refreshes the memory; second, when organized into their proper categories, matters that seemed jumbled when considered as a whole can be examined more carefully.

According to Aristo's theory, you might even say that consolation and encouragement are unnecessary. But they aren't unnecessary, and neither is advice.

"It's foolish," they argue, "to tell a sick person what they should do as if they were healthy when you should really be restoring their health; because without health, advice is worthless." But don't sick people and healthy people have some things in common that they both need advice on? For example, not to eat too greedily and to avoid getting too tired.

The poor and the rich both have certain advice that fits them. "Cure their greed, then," people say, "and you won't need to lecture either the poor or the rich, as long as their craving has subsided." But isn't it one thing to be free from greed, and another thing to know how to use money properly? Misers don't know the proper limits when it comes to money, but even those who aren't misers don't always know how to use it well. Then the reply comes: "Get rid of error, and your advice becomes unnecessary." That's wrong because even if greed is lessened, if luxury is kept in check, if recklessness is restrained, and if laziness is spurred on, even after these vices are removed, we still need to learn what we ought to do and how to do it.

"Advice won't fix the more serious faults," they say. No, and neither can medicine cure incurable diseases; but it's still used sometimes as a remedy, sometimes as a relief. Even the power of universal philosophy, no matter how hard it tries, won't remove from the soul what has become a stubborn and chronic disease. But wisdom, even though it can't cure everything, can still make some cures.

"Why bother pointing out the obvious?" people ask. It does a lot of good because sometimes we know facts without paying attention to them. Advice isn't teaching; it just grabs our attention, wakes us up, and helps us focus our memory so we don't lose our grip. We often miss things that are right in front of us. Advice is like an encouragement. The mind often tries not to notice what's in plain sight; so we need to force it to see things that are already well known. You might repeat here what Calvus said about Vatinius: "You all know that bribery has been going on, and everyone knows that you know it."

You know that friendship should be honored, and yet you don't honor it. You know that it's wrong to expect your wife to be faithful while you're cheating with other men's wives; you know that just as your wife shouldn't have a lover, neither should you have a mistress; and yet you don't act accordingly. That's why you need to be constantly reminded of these things; they shouldn't just be stored away, but ready to use. And whatever is good for you should be talked about often and kept in mind so that it's not only familiar but also readily available. And remember, too, that what's clear can become even clearer.

"But if," they argue, "your advice isn't clear, you'll have to add proof; so the proof, not the advice, will be helpful." But can't the advice itself help, even without proof? It's like the opinions of a legal expert, which are valid even if the reasons behind them aren't explained. Moreover, the advice given has great value in itself, whether it's put into a song or condensed into a proverb, like the famous Wisdom of Cato: "Don't buy what you need, buy what you must have. What you don't need is expensive even if it's cheap." Or those sayings that sound like oracles: "Be thrifty with time!" "Know yourself!" Do you need to be told what they mean when someone repeats lines like these:

"Forgetting trouble is the way to cure it." "Fortune favors the brave, but the coward is defeated by their own fear."

These maxims don't need a special explanation; they go straight to our feelings and help us simply because they express a natural truth.

The soul has within it the seed of everything honorable, and advice helps that seed grow, like a spark that turns into a fire when fanned by a gentle breeze. Virtue is awakened by a touch, a shock. Also, there are some things that, though present in the mind, aren't immediately available but start to function easily once they're put into words. Some thoughts are scattered in different places, and it's hard for an untrained mind to organize them. So we should bring them together and connect them, making them more powerful and more uplifting to the soul.

Or, if advice isn't useful at all, then we should get rid of all methods of instruction and be content with Nature alone.

Those who believe this don't understand that some people are quick-witted and alert, while others are slow and dull, and some have more intelligence than others. The strength of the mind is nourished and grows through advice; it adds new perspectives to those that are inborn and corrects bad ideas.

"But suppose," people argue, "that someone doesn't have sound beliefs, how can advice help them when they're trapped by wrong beliefs?" In this way: that it frees them from those wrong beliefs because their natural disposition hasn't been destroyed, just overshadowed and held down. It's still trying to rise, struggling against the forces that pull it towards evil; but when it gets support and advice, it grows stronger, as long as the long-term trouble hasn't completely corrupted or destroyed the natural person. Because in such a case, not even all the strength of philosophy can restore the mind.

What's the difference between the principles of philosophy and advice? It's that principles are general, and advice is specific. Both deal with guidance—one through universal truths, the other through particular situations.

Some say: "If someone knows what's right, advice is unnecessary." Not true; because this person might know what they should do, but they might not see clearly what those things are. We're often stopped from doing what's right not only by our emotions but also by our lack of practice in figuring out what's needed in a particular situation. Our minds might be under control, but at the same time, they might not be trained to find the right path—and advice makes this clear.

Again, it's written: "Get rid of all false ideas about Good and Evil, but replace them with true ideas; then advice will have no function." Order in the soul can be established this way, but these aren't the only ways. Even though we can figure out by reasoning what Good and Evil are, advice still has its role. Wisdom and justice consist of certain duties, and duties are organized by advice. Moreover, judgment about Good and Evil is strengthened by following our duties, and advice helps us do this. Both work together; and advice usually comes first.

"Advice," it's said, "is endless." That's wrong! Important and essential advice isn't endless. Of course, there are small differences depending on time, place, or person; but even in these cases, general advice is given.

"No one," they say, "cures madness with advice, so they can't cure wickedness either." There's a difference; if you cure someone of insanity, they become sane again, but if you remove false ideas, insight into right conduct doesn't immediately follow. Even if it does follow, advice will still confirm the right opinion about Good and Evil. And it's also wrong to believe that advice is useless to madmen. Even though, by itself, it's not enough, it still helps towards the cure. Both scolding and correcting help rein in a lunatic. I'm talking about lunatics whose minds are disturbed but not completely lost.

"Still," it's argued, "laws don't always make us do the right thing; and what are laws but advice mixed with threats?" First of all, laws don't persuade because they threaten; advice, on the other hand, corrects people by reasoning with them. Also, laws prevent people from committing crimes out of fear, while advice urges them to do their duty. Besides, laws also help people do good, especially if they teach as well as command.

On this point, I disagree with Posidonius, who says: "I don't think Plato's laws should have preambles added to them. A law should be short, so that ordinary people can easily understand it. It should be like a voice from heaven, commanding, not discussing. Nothing seems more dull or foolish to me than a law with a preamble. Warn me, tell me what you want me to do; I'm not learning, I'm obeying." But laws framed this way are helpful; that's why you'll notice that a state with bad laws will have bad morals.

"But," it's said, "laws don't work in every case." Well, neither does philosophy; and yet philosophy isn't useless in training the soul. Furthermore, isn't philosophy the Law of Life? Even if we agree that laws don't always work, that doesn't mean advice is also useless. If that were true, you'd have to say that consolation, warning, encouragement, scolding, and praise are all useless since they're all forms of advice. But these are the methods we use to reach a perfect state of mind.

Nothing is more effective in bringing good influences to the mind or in straightening out the wavering spirit that's prone to evil than associating with good people. Just seeing or hearing wise people often sinks into the heart little by little and becomes as powerful as advice.

We are uplifted just by meeting wise people, and we can be helped by a great person even when they're silent.

I couldn't easily tell you how it helps, but I'm certain that I've received help this way. Phaedo says: "Some tiny animals don't cause pain when they sting us; their power is so subtle, and their harm is so deceptive. The sting is revealed by swelling, and even in the swelling, there's no visible wound." You'll have the same experience when dealing with wise people; you won't know how or when the benefit comes to you, but you'll know that you've received it.

"What's the point of this remark?" you ask. It's that good advice, often welcomed inside you, will benefit you just as much as good examples. Pythagoras says that our souls experience a change when we enter a temple and see the images of the gods face to face and wait for the words of an oracle.

Moreover, who can deny that even the most inexperienced are deeply affected by the force of certain advice? For example, by such brief but powerful sayings as: "Nothing in excess," "The greedy mind is never satisfied," "You must expect to be treated by others as you treat them." We're shocked when we hear these sayings; no one ever thinks of doubting them or asking "Why?" That's how strongly the simple truth attracts us, even without reason.

If reverence restrains the soul and checks vice, why can't advice do the same? Also, if a rebuke makes someone feel ashamed, why can't advice have the same power, even if it's just simple precepts? Advice that's backed up by reason—that adds the motive for doing something and the reward for carrying it out—is more effective and sticks deeper in the heart. If commands help, then so does advice. And if commands help, then advice also helps.

Virtue has two parts—understanding truth and right action. Training teaches understanding, and advice teaches action. And right action both practices and reveals virtue. So if advice helps someone act rightly, it also helps guide them. Therefore, if right action is necessary for virtue, and if advice clarifies right action, then advice is also necessary.

There are two strong supports for the soul—trust in the truth and confidence; both come from advice. People believe it, and when belief is established, the soul gets great inspiration and is filled with confidence. So advice is not unnecessary.

Marcus Agrippa, a great man, the only person among those who gained fame and power during the civil wars whose success helped the state, used to say that he owed a lot to the proverb "Harmony makes small things grow; lack of harmony makes great things decay."

He believed that he became the best of brothers and the best of friends because of this saying. And if proverbs like this, when welcomed into the soul, can shape the soul, why can't the part of philosophy that consists of such proverbs have the same power? Virtue depends partly on training and partly on practice; you must first learn, and then strengthen your learning through action. If this is true, then not only do the principles of wisdom help us, but also the advice that checks and controls our emotions.

It's said: "Philosophy is divided into knowledge and state of mind. Someone who has learned and understood what to do and what to avoid isn't wise until their mind is changed to match what they've learned. This third part—advice—is made up of both the principles of philosophy and the state of mind. So it's unnecessary for perfecting virtue; the other two parts are enough."

If that's true, then consolation would also be unnecessary, since it's also a combination of the other two, as are encouragement, persuasion, and even proof itself. Because proof also comes from a well-ordered and firm state of mind. But even though these things come from a sound mind, the sound mind also comes from them; it both creates them and is created by them.

Moreover, what you're talking about is the mark of someone who's already perfect, someone who's reached the height of human happiness. But the path to these qualities is slow, and in the meantime, in practical matters, the path should be pointed out for the benefit of someone who isn't yet perfect but is making progress. Wisdom, on its own, might be able to show the path without the help of advice; because it's brought the soul to a place where it can only move in the right direction. But weaker characters need someone to go ahead of them, to say: "Avoid this," or "Do that."

Also, if you wait until someone can know on their own what the best course of action is, they'll sometimes go astray, and by going astray, they'll be prevented from reaching the point where they can be content with themselves. The soul should be guided at the moment it's becoming able to guide itself. Boys learn by following direction. Their hands are held and guided by others so that they can trace the outlines of the letters; then they're told to imitate a copy and develop their own handwriting style based on that. In the same way, the mind is helped if it's taught with guidance.

All of this shows that this part of philosophy isn't unnecessary.

The next question is whether this part alone is enough to make people wise. This issue will be discussed at the right time; but for now, leaving out all arguments, isn't it clear that we need someone who can be our guide against the wrong advice we get from others?

There's no word that reaches our ears without doing us harm; we're hurt by both good wishes and curses. The angry prayers of our enemies fill us with false fears; and the affection of our friends spoils us with their kind wishes. This affection makes us chase after goods that are far away, uncertain, and unstable when we could be finding happiness close to home.

We aren't allowed to walk a straight path. Our parents and our servants lead us into error. No one keeps their mistakes to themselves; people spread their foolishness to their neighbors and receive it from them in return. That's why in an individual, you find the vices of nations because the nation has passed them on to the individual. Each person, in corrupting others, corrupts themselves; they take in and then pass on badness— the result is a huge mass of wickedness because the worst in every person is concentrated in one mass.

That's why we need a guardian, someone to constantly remind us and clear away rumors and protest against popular enthusiasms. Don't think that our faults are inborn; they come from outside and have been piled on us. That's why, by getting frequent advice, we can reject the false opinions that surround us.

Nature doesn't ally us with any vice; she created us in health and freedom. She didn't put before our eyes any object that would stir greed in us. She placed gold and silver beneath our feet and told us to crush everything that causes us to be crushed. Nature lifted our gaze to the sky and wanted us to look up at her glorious and wonderful works. She gave us the rising and setting sun, the whirling course of the world, which reveals earthly things by day and the heavenly bodies by night, the movements of the stars, which are slow compared to the universe but very fast if you think about the size of the orbits they travel at an unchanging speed; she showed us the regular eclipses of the sun and moon and other amazing phenomena that happen either regularly or suddenly, like fire trails at night or flashes in the sky without thunder, or columns and beams of light and other fiery sights.

She arranged for all these things to happen above our heads; but gold and silver, with the iron that never brings peace because of the gold and silver, she buried deep, as if they were dangerous things to trust to our care. It's we who have dug them up so that we could fight over them; it's we who have torn away the earth to dig out the causes and tools of our destruction; it's we who have blamed our own misdeeds on Fortune and aren't ashamed to value most highly the things that once lay in the depths of the earth.

Do you want to know how false the gleam is that has deceived your eyes? There's really nothing dirtier or more hidden in darkness than these earthly things, buried for so long in the mud where they belong. Of course, they're dirty; they've been hauled out through a long, dark mine-shaft. There's nothing uglier than these metals during the process of refinement and separation from the ore. And look at the workmen who have to handle and sift the worthless dirt, the kind that comes from the bottom; see how they're covered in soot! And yet the stuff they handle soils the soul more than the body, and there's more dirt in the owner than in the workman.

That's why we need to be advised, to have an advocate with an upright mind, and to hear one true voice amid all the noise and lies. But what voice should this be? Surely a voice that, amid all the commotion of self-seeking, whispers wholesome words into the deafened ear, saying: "You don't need to be envious of those whom people call great and fortunate; applause doesn't need to disturb your calm attitude and clear mind; you don't need to become dissatisfied with your peaceful spirit just because you see a powerful man, clothed in purple, protected by well-known symbols of authority; you don't need to think that the magistrate, for whom the road is cleared, is any happier than you, whom his officer pushes off the road. If you want to wield a power that benefits yourself and harms no one, clear your own faults out of the way.

"There are many who set cities on fire, who attack fortresses that have stood safe for generations, who build siege mounds as high as the walls they're attacking, who with battering rams and engines destroy towers that have been built to a great height. There are many who can send their soldiers ahead and crush the enemy from behind, who can reach the Great Sea dripping with the blood of nations; but before they could conquer their enemy, they were conquered by their own greed. No one could withstand their attack, but they couldn't withstand their desire for power and cruelty; when they seemed to be hunting others, they were being hunted themselves.

"Alexander was driven to misfortune and sent to unknown lands by a mad desire to destroy other people's territories. Do you think the man was in his right mind when he started by devastating Greece, the land where he was educated? A man who took away the dearest freedom of each nation, forcing Spartans to be slaves and Athenians to be silent? Not content with destroying all the states that Philip had either conquered or bribed into submission, he overthrew various commonwealths in various places and carried his weapons all over the world; his cruelty was exhausted, but it never stopped—like a wild beast that tears apart more than it needs to eat.

"He had already joined many kingdoms into one; already, Greeks and Persians feared the same ruler; already, nations that Darius had left free submitted to his rule; yet he went beyond the Ocean and the Sun, thinking it shameful to change his course of victory from the paths that Hercules and Bacchus had traveled; he threatened violence even to Nature herself. He didn't want to go, but he couldn't stay; he was like a weight that falls headlong, stopping only when it lies still.

"It wasn't virtue or reason that led Gnaeus Pompeius to take part in foreign and civil wars; it was his mad craving for false glory. He attacked Spain and the faction of Sertorius; then he set out to defeat the pirates and control the seas. These were just excuses to expand his power. What drove him into Africa, into the North, against Mithridates, into Armenia, and all over Asia? It was certainly his boundless desire to grow bigger because he didn't think he was great enough.

"And what led Gaius Caesar to his own ruin and the ruin of the state? Fame, self-seeking, and not being satisfied with being more powerful than everyone else. He couldn't let anyone outrank him, even though the state allowed two men to be its leaders.

"Do you think that Gaius Marius, who was once consul (he earned this office once and stole it all the other times) faced all his dangers out of virtue when he was slaughtering the Teutons and the Cimbri and chasing Jugurtha through the wilds of Africa? Marius commanded armies, but it was ambition that commanded Marius.

"When men like these were disturbing the world, they were disturbed themselves—like cyclones that whirl together everything they've seized, but are first whirled themselves and can rush on with greater force because they have no control over themselves. That's why, after causing such destruction to others, they felt in their own bodies the ruinous force that had enabled them to harm so many. You should never believe that a person can become happy through another person's unhappiness.

"We need to unravel all the cases that are forced before our eyes and crammed into our ears; we need to clear out our hearts because they're full of evil talk. Virtue must be brought into the place these have taken—a kind of virtue that can root out falsehood and ideas that go against the truth, that can separate us from the crowd in which we put too much trust, and can bring us back to holding sound opinions. Because this is wisdom—a return to Nature and a restoration of the state from which our errors have driven us.

"It's a big part of health to have left behind the advisors of madness and to have fled far from harmful company.

"To know the truth of my remark, see how different each person's life is in public compared to their private self. A quiet life doesn't automatically teach upright conduct; the countryside doesn't automatically teach simple living; no, but when witnesses and onlookers are removed, faults that grow in public and display sink into the background.

"Who puts on a purple robe just to show it off when no one's around? Who uses gold plates when they're dining alone? Who, lying down under the shadow of a rustic tree, displays their luxury when no one's there to see it? No one makes themselves elegant just for their own eyes, or even for the admiration of a few friends or relatives. They show off their well-dressed vices according to the size of the admiring crowd.

"It's true: admirers and witnesses are the fuel for all our foolish desires. You can stop us from craving if you only stop us from showing off. Ambition, luxury, and recklessness need a stage to act on; you'll cure all those ills if you seek solitude.

"Therefore, if our home is in the noisy city, we should have an advisor nearby. When people praise great wealth, he should praise the person who can be rich with a small estate and measures their wealth by how they use it. In the face of those who glorify influence and power, he should of his own accord recommend a life of study and a soul that has left the external world and found itself.

"He should point out people who are considered happy by the public but who are shaky on their envied heights of power, who are anxious and have a far different opinion of themselves than others have of them. What others think is high, to them is a steep cliff. That's why they're scared and anxious whenever they look down the sharp drop of their greatness. They think about the many ways they could fall and how the highest point is the slipperiest. Then they fear what they once strove for, and the good fortune that made them important in others' eyes weighs even more heavily on them. Then they praise simple leisure and independence; they hate the glamour and try to escape while they're still successful. Then at last you may see them studying philosophy out of fear and seeking good advice when their fortunes go wrong.

"These two things are at opposite poles—good fortune and good sense; that's why we're wiser in times of adversity. It's prosperity that takes away righteousness." Farewell.

Letter 95 - On the usefulness of basic principles

You keep asking me to explain right away a topic that I once said should wait until the proper time, and you want me to tell you by letter whether this part of philosophy, which the Greeks call "paraenetic" and we Romans call the "preceptorial," is enough to make us perfectly wise. I know that you'll understand if I refuse to do so, but I'm happy to accept your request and won't let the common saying lose its meaning: "Don't ask for something you might regret getting."

Sometimes we work hard to get something that we would turn down if it were offered freely. You can call that being fickle or stubborn, but we need to break that habit by going along with things. There are many things that we want others to think we wish for, but we don't really wish for them. A speaker might bring a huge book filled with tiny writing to the stage, and after reading a lot of it, he might say, "I'll stop if you want." Then people shout, "Read on, read on!" even though they really want him to stop right there. Often, we want one thing and pray for another, not telling the truth even to the gods, and the gods either don't listen or take pity on us.

But I won't take pity on you. I'll make you pay for asking by sending you a huge letter. If you read it reluctantly, you can say, "I brought this on myself," and put yourself in the same category as men who suffer because of their overly ambitious wives, or those who are worn out by the riches they earned with extreme effort, or those who are tormented by the titles they fought so hard to get, and all others who are responsible for their own misfortunes.

But enough of this introduction; let's get to the topic. People say, "The happy life comes from doing what's right; advice guides us to do what's right; therefore, advice is enough to achieve the happy life." But advice doesn't always lead us to do what's right; this only happens when the person is willing to listen. Sometimes, advice is useless if wrong beliefs control the mind.

Also, a person might do the right thing without knowing they're doing the right thing. Because no one, unless they've been trained from the start and equipped with complete reasoning, can grow into a person who fully understands when, how much, with whom, how, and why to do certain things. Without this kind of training, a person can't strive wholeheartedly after what's honorable, or even do so with consistency or joy, but will keep looking back and hesitating.

Some people also say, "If honorable actions result from advice, then advice is enough for a happy life; since honorable actions do result from advice, advice must be enough." But we'll reply that honorable actions do result from advice, but not from advice alone.

Then comes the reply, "If other skills can be learned through advice, then wisdom can too because wisdom is the art of living. And just like a sailor learns from advice how to steer the ship, set the sails, use the wind, and make the most of changing breezes—doing all these things in the right way—other craftsmen also learn their trades through advice. So advice should be able to achieve the same result for someone learning the art of living."

Now, all these skills are about the tools of life, not about life as a whole. That's why these skills can be hindered by outside things like hope, greed, or fear. But the skill that claims to teach the art of life can't be stopped by any circumstance from doing its job because it gets rid of complications and pushes through obstacles. Would you like to know how different it is from other skills? In those other skills, it's more forgivable to make a mistake on purpose than by accident, but in the art of living, the worst mistake is to sin on purpose.

I mean something like this: A scholar will be more ashamed of making a grammatical mistake unintentionally than of making it on purpose. If a doctor doesn't realize his patient is getting worse, he's a much worse doctor than if he realizes it but hides the fact. But in the art of living, a voluntary mistake is more shameful.

Furthermore, many skills, even the most respected ones, have their own teachings, not just advice—like the medical profession.

There are different schools of thought like those of Hippocrates, Asclepiades, and Themison. And besides, no skill that involves theories can exist without its own teachings. The Greeks call them "dogmas," while we Romans might call them "doctrines" or "principles"—like the ones you find in geometry or astronomy. But philosophy is both theoretical and practical; it thinks and acts at the same time. You're mistaken if you think philosophy only offers practical help; its goals are higher than that. It says, "I study the whole universe. I'm not content with just giving you good or bad advice. Great matters call me, things far above you."

In the words of Lucretius: "To you, I'll reveal the ways of the heavens and the gods, showing you the atoms from which everything is born, grows, and is nurtured by creative power, and also how they end when Nature casts them off."

So, since philosophy is theoretical, it must have its teachings. And why? Because no one can consistently do what's right unless they've been taught the reasoning that will enable them to fulfill all their duties in every situation. They can't follow these duties unless they receive advice for all occasions, not just for the present. Advice by itself is weak and, so to speak, rootless if it's only applied to specific parts and not to the whole. It's the doctrines that will strengthen and support us in peace and calm, covering the whole of life and the universe in its entirety. There's the same difference between philosophical doctrines and advice as there is between elements and parts; the latter depend on the former, while the former are the source of the latter and all things.

People say, "The wisdom of old times only advised on what one should do and avoid, and yet people were better back then. As scholars appeared, sages became rare. That straightforward, simple virtue has turned into hidden and crafty knowledge; we're taught how to debate, not how to live." Of course, as you say, the old-fashioned wisdom, especially in its early days, was simple. But so were other skills, which became more refined over time. And in those days, there wasn't as much need for carefully planned cures. Wickedness hadn't yet spread so far or become so strong. Simple vices could be treated with simple cures, but now we need stronger defenses because of the stronger powers attacking us.

Medicine used to be just about knowing a few simple remedies to stop bleeding or heal wounds. Over time, it developed into the complex field it is today. No wonder medicine had less to do in the early days! People's bodies were still strong and healthy; their food was simple and not ruined by art and luxury. But when people started seeking out food not to satisfy hunger but to stimulate their appetite and created countless sauces to feed their gluttony, then what used to be nourishment became a burden to a full stomach.

That's where the pale complexion, trembling muscles from too much wine, and a sickly thinness from indigestion come from. That's why people have weak, unsteady steps, and stagger as if they're drunk. That's why diseases like dropsy, where fluid builds up under the skin, and a bloated belly from taking in more than it can handle, happen. That's why people get jaundice, turning their skin yellow, and why their bodies rot from the inside, and their fingers become stiff and swollen, and why they feel numbness and have a pounding heart that never seems to stop.

Why do I need to mention dizziness? Or talk about the pain in the eyes and ears, the itching and aching in the fevered brain, and the internal ulcers throughout the digestive system? Besides these, there are countless kinds of fevers—some acute and deadly, others creeping in with subtle harm, and still others that hit with chills and severe shivering. Why should I mention the other endless diseases and the sufferings that come from high living?

People used to be free from these ills because they hadn't yet weakened themselves with indulgence, because they had self-control and provided for their own needs. They strengthened their bodies through work and real toil, tiring themselves out by running, hunting, or farming. They were refreshed by food that only a hungry person could enjoy. So, there was no need for all our complicated medical equipment, for so many instruments and medicine boxes. Because they lived simply, they enjoyed simple health; it took complicated habits to create complicated diseases.

Look at the number of things—everything that luxury mixes together—that all have to go down one person's throat, after plundering the land and sea. So many different dishes surely don't agree with each other; they're hard to swallow and hard to digest, each one clashing with the others. It's no wonder that the diseases caused by ill-matched foods are varied and numerous; there has to be an overflow when so many unnatural combinations are jumbled together. That's why there are as many ways to be sick as there are ways to live.

The famous founder of the medical profession noted that women never lost their hair or suffered from pain in their feet. But nowadays, they lose their hair and get gout. This doesn't mean that women's bodies have changed, but that they've been overwhelmed. By imitating men's indulgences, they've also imitated the illnesses men suffer. They stay up just as late and drink just as much. They compete with men in wrestling and drinking. They're just as prone to vomiting from their bloated stomachs and bringing up all the wine they drank again. They're also just as likely to chew on ice to cool their fevered stomachs. And they even match men in their passions, even though they were made to experience love passively (may the gods and goddesses curse them!). They invent the most unnatural forms of unchastity and, in the company of men, they act like men. So it's no surprise that we can prove the greatest and most skilled doctor wrong when so many women suffer from gout and baldness! Because of their vices, women have lost the privileges of their sex; they've abandoned their womanly nature and are now suffering from men's diseases.

Doctors of old didn't know about prescribing frequent nourishment or propping up a weak pulse with wine. They didn't understand how to let blood or ease chronic complaints with sweat baths. They didn't know how to wrap ankles and arms to draw out hidden strength that had retreated inward. They weren't forced to seek out many kinds of treatments because there weren't many kinds of suffering. But nowadays, how far have the evils of ill-health gone! This is the price we pay for pleasures that we've chased after beyond what's reasonable and right. Don't be surprised that diseases are countless; just count the number of cooks! All intellectual pursuits are neglected; those who teach culture lecture to empty rooms in out-of-the-way places. The halls of professors and philosophers are deserted, but the cafés are packed! How many young men crowd around the kitchens of their gluttonous friends!

I won't even mention the unlucky boys who have to endure other shameful treatment after the banquet is over. I won't mention the groups of boys, sorted by nation and skin color, who all have to have the same smooth skin, the same amount of youthful down on their cheeks, and the same way of doing their hair so that no boy with straight hair gets mixed in with the curly-haired ones. Nor will I mention the mix of bakers and the number of waiters who rush to bring in the dishes at a given signal. My goodness! How many people are kept busy to satisfy one belly!

What? Do you think those mushrooms, the gourmet's poison, don't cause hidden harm, even if they don't have an immediate effect? What? Do you suppose that your summer snow doesn't harden the liver? What? Do you think those oysters, a sluggish food fattened on slime, don't weigh you down with mud-begotten heaviness? What? Don't you think that the so-called "Sauce from the Provinces," the costly extract of poisonous fish, doesn't burn up the stomach with its salted rot? What? Do you think the overcooked dishes that a person swallows almost straight from the kitchen fire are quenched in the digestive system without doing harm? How repulsive, then, and how unhealthy are their belches, and how disgusted they are with themselves when they breathe out the fumes of yesterday's feast! You can be sure their food isn't being digested but is rotting.

I remember once hearing gossip about a notorious dish into which everything that gourmets love to indulge in was piled together by a restaurant that was fast going bankrupt. There were two kinds of mussels and oysters cut at the line where they're edible, with sea urchins added in for good measure. The whole thing was flanked by mullets cut up and served without the bones.

Nowadays, we're ashamed of eating simple foods; people mix many flavors into one. The dinner table does the work that the stomach should do. I expect the next step is for food to be served already chewed! And we're already close to it when we pick out shells and bones, with the cook doing the job of the teeth!

They say, "It's too much trouble to enjoy our luxuries one by one; let's have everything served at the same time and mixed into the same flavor. Why should I help myself to a single dish? Let's have many dishes on the table at once; the delicacies from various courses should be combined and confused."

Those who used to say this was done for show and notoriety should understand that it's not for show, but that it's an offering to our sense of duty! Let's have oysters, sea urchins, shellfish, and mullets all mixed together and cooked in the same dish." No food thrown up from the stomach could be more jumbled together.

And as the food itself is complicated, so are the diseases that result from it—complex, unpredictable, varied, and multifaceted. Medicine has begun to fight these diseases in many ways and with many treatment rules.

Now, I'm telling you that the same thing applies to philosophy. It used to be simpler because people's sins were smaller and could be cured with little trouble. But in the face of this moral chaos, we must try every remedy. And if only this plague might finally be overcome!

We're not just mad as individuals, but as a society. We punish murder and individual killings, but what about war and the much-praised crime of slaughtering entire nations? There are no limits to our greed, none to our cruelty. And as long as these crimes are committed secretly by individuals, they're less harmful and less terrifying. But now, cruelty is practiced with the approval of the government and the public is ordered to do what's forbidden to individuals.

Deeds that would be punished by death if done in secret are praised by us because they were carried out by generals in uniform. Humans, who are naturally the gentlest of beings, aren't ashamed to revel in others' blood, to wage war, and to send their sons to war, while even dumb animals and wild beasts live in peace with each other.

Against this overwhelming and widespread madness, philosophy has become more challenging and has grown stronger in proportion to the strength gained by the opposing forces. It used to be easy to scold men who were slaves to drink and sought out more luxurious food; it didn't take much effort to bring the spirit back to the simplicity from which it had only slightly strayed. But now,

Men seek pleasure from every source. No vice stays within its limits; luxury turns into greed. We've become so obsessed with what's attractive that we've forgotten what's honorable. Now, people, who should be respected by others, are slaughtered for entertainment. And those whom it used to be unthinkable to train to endure and inflict wounds are sent out, unarmed and defenseless, and it's considered a good show to see someone die.

Amid this moral chaos, we need something stronger than usual—something that can shake off these deep-seated ills. To root out a deeply ingrained belief in wrong ideas, we must guide our actions with doctrines. It's only when we add advice, consolation, and encouragement to these that they can be effective; on their own, they are not enough. If we want to hold people firmly and tear them away from the ills that grip them, they must learn what is truly evil and what is truly good. They must know that everything except virtue can change its nature and become good or bad depending on the situation. Just as a soldier's primary bond is his oath of allegiance, his love for his flag, and his horror of desertion, and just as, after taking the oath, other duties can easily be demanded of him and he can be trusted with responsibilities, so it is with those we want to lead to the happy life. We must first lay the foundations and work virtue into them. They should be bound by a kind of reverence for virtue, love it, desire to live with it, and refuse to live without it.

"But," people say, "haven't some people achieved excellence without complicated training? Haven't they made great progress by following simple advice alone?" Yes, that's true, but those people had favorable temperaments and found salvation almost by accident. Just as the gods didn't learn virtue—they were born with it, complete and perfect, containing the essence of goodness in their nature—some people are naturally gifted with extraordinary qualities and reach virtue quickly without much training, embracing honorable things as soon as they hear about them. These are the exceptional minds that quickly grasp virtue or even produce it from within themselves. But your average, sluggish person, weighed down by bad habits, needs constant work to scrape off the rust on their soul.

Just as those who are inclined toward good can be raised to greatness more quickly, so the weaker spirits will be helped and freed from their wrong beliefs if we teach them the accepted principles of philosophy. You can see how essential these principles are by considering this: Certain things make us sluggish in some ways and hasty in others. These two qualities—recklessness and laziness—can't be corrected unless we remove their causes, which are mistaken admiration and mistaken fear. As long as we're obsessed with these feelings, you might say to us, "You owe this duty to your father, this to your children, this to your friends, this to your guests," but greed will always hold us back, no matter how hard we try. A person may know that they should fight for their country, but fear will stop them. A person may know that they should work tirelessly for their friends, but luxury will forbid it. A person may know that keeping a mistress is the worst kind of insult to his wife, but lust will drive him in the opposite direction.

So it will do no good to give advice unless you first remove the obstacles that will get in the way of that advice. It will be like placing weapons by your side and approaching the enemy without having your hands free to use those weapons. The soul must first be freed in order to deal with the advice we offer.

Suppose someone is doing what they should; they can't keep it up continuously or consistently because they won't know the reason for their actions. Some of their actions may turn out right by luck or practice, but they won't have a rule to guide their actions and tell them if what they did was right. Someone who is good by mere chance won't stay good forever.

Furthermore, advice might help you do what should be done, but it won't help you do it in the right way; and if it doesn't help you do it in the right way, it doesn't lead you to virtue. I agree that if warned, a person might do what they should, but that's not enough because the credit lies not in the action itself but in the way it's done.

What is more shameful than an expensive meal that eats away at the income of even a wealthy person? Or what is more deserving of the censor's condemnation than always indulging oneself and one's "inner man," as the gluttons say? And yet, often an inaugural dinner has cost even the most careful person a fortune! The same amount that would be disgraceful if spent on food is acceptable if spent for official purposes! Because it's not considered luxury but an expense allowed by custom.

A giant mullet was presented to the Emperor Tiberius. They say it weighed four and a half pounds (and why shouldn't I please the gourmets by mentioning its weight?). Tiberius ordered it to be sent to the fish market and put up for sale, saying, "I'll be surprised if either Apicius or P. Octavius doesn't buy that mullet." His guess came true beyond expectation: the two men bid, and Octavius won, earning great admiration from his friends because he bought for five thousand sesterces a fish that the Emperor had sold and that even Apicius couldn't buy. Paying such a price was disgraceful for Octavius, but not for the person who bought the fish to present to Tiberius—though I'd still blame the latter as well, but at least he admired a gift he thought worthy of Caesar.

When people sit by the bedsides of their sick friends, we honor their motives. But when people do this to secure an inheritance, they're like vultures waiting for a carcass. The same act can be either shameful or honorable: the purpose and the manner make all the difference. Now, each of our actions will be honorable if we commit to honor and judge honor and its outcomes to be the only true good that can come to us; because everything else is only temporarily good.

I think, then, that there should be a deeply rooted belief that applies to life as a whole: this is what I call a "doctrine." And as this belief is, so will be our actions and thoughts. As our actions and thoughts are, so will our lives be. It's not enough, when a person is arranging their life as a whole, to give them advice about the details. Marcus Brutus, in his book "Concerning Duty," gives many pieces of advice to parents, children, and siblings; but no one will do their duty as they should unless they have some principle to guide their conduct. We must set before our eyes the goal of the Supreme Good, toward which we may strive, and to which all our actions and words may refer—just as sailors must guide their course according to a certain star.

Life without ideals is erratic: as soon as we decide on an ideal, doctrines become necessary. I'm sure you'll agree that there's nothing more shameful than uncertain and wavering behavior, than the habit of retreating timidly. This will be our experience in all cases unless we remove what holds back the spirit, clogs it, and keeps it from making an effort and trying with all its might.

Precepts are often given on how to worship the gods. But let's forbid lamps from being lit on the Sabbath because the gods don't need light, and people don't enjoy soot. Let's forbid people from offering morning greetings and crowding the doors of temples; these ceremonies attract human ambitions, but God is worshiped by those who truly know Him. Let's forbid bringing towels and flesh-scrapers to Jupiter and offering mirrors to Juno; for God seeks no servants. Of course not; He Himself serves mankind, always and everywhere, and is ready to help all.

Although a person may learn the limits they should observe in sacrifice and how far they should avoid burdensome superstitions, they'll never make enough progress until they have the right idea of God—seeing Him as one who possesses all things, gives all things, and bestows them freely. And why do the gods do good deeds? It's their nature. Anyone who thinks they're unwilling to do harm is wrong; they can't do harm. They can't receive or inflict injury; doing harm is in the same category as suffering harm. The universal nature, all-glorious and all-beautiful, has made those who it has removed from the danger of harm incapable of causing harm.

The first way to worship the gods is to believe in the gods; the next is to acknowledge their majesty and goodness because, without goodness, there's no majesty. Also, know that they are the supreme rulers of the universe, controlling everything with their power and acting as guardians of the human race, even though they may sometimes forget about individuals. They neither give nor have evil, but they do correct and restrain some people, impose penalties, and sometimes punish by giving what seems outwardly good. If you want to win the gods' favor, be a good person. Whoever imitates them is worshiping them sufficiently.

Then comes the second problem—how to deal with people. What's our goal? What advice do we give? Should we tell them not to shed blood? What a small thing it is not to harm someone you ought to help! It's truly worthy of great praise when people treat each other with kindness! Should we advise helping a shipwrecked sailor, showing the way to a lost traveler, or sharing bread with the hungry? Yes, but I'd rather tell you first everything that should be given or withheld; in the meantime, I can give humanity a simple rule for our duties in relationships: everything you see, everything that includes both God and humanity, is one—we are all parts of one great body. Nature made us related to each other since she created us from the same source and for the same purpose. She created us with mutual affection and made us prone to friendships. She established fairness and justice; according to her, it's worse to commit than to suffer injury. By her command, our hands should be ready to help all in need.

Let this verse be in your heart and on your lips: "I am a human being; and nothing in human experience is foreign to me." Let us share things in common; for we share a common birth. Our relationships with each other are like a stone arch, which would collapse if the stones didn't support each other and which is held up in this very way.

Next, after considering gods and people, let's see how we should use things. It's pointless for us to talk about advice unless we start by thinking about what opinion we should have about everything—about poverty, wealth, fame, disgrace, citizenship, exile. Let's reject rumors and set a value on each thing, asking what it really is, not what it's called.

Now let's turn to a consideration of the virtues. Some people will advise us to value prudence highly, to cherish bravery, and to cling more closely, if possible, to justice than to any other quality. But this won't do us any good if we don't know what virtue is, whether it's simple or complex, whether it's one thing or more than one, whether its parts are separate or interconnected; whether someone who has one virtue has all the virtues, and what exactly are the differences between them.

The carpenter doesn't need to question his craft in light of its origin or function any more than a dancer needs to question the art of dancing; if these crafts understand themselves, nothing is missing because they don't concern life as a whole. But virtue involves knowledge of other things besides itself; if we want to learn virtue, we must learn everything about virtue.

Conduct won't be right unless the will to act is right because that's the source of conduct. And the will can't be right without the right attitude of mind because that's the source of the will. Furthermore, such an attitude of mind won't be found even in the best people unless they've learned the laws of life as a whole, worked out proper judgment about everything, and reduced facts to a standard of truth. Peace of mind is enjoyed only by those who have attained a fixed and unchanging standard of judgment; the rest of humanity continually wavers in their decisions, floating in a state where they alternately reject things and seek them.

And what's the reason for this constant back-and-forth? It's because nothing is clear to them, because they rely on the most unreliable criterion—rumor. If you always want the same things, you must desire the truth. But you can't reach the truth without doctrines because doctrines cover the whole of life. Things that are good and evil, honorable and disgraceful, just and unjust, dutiful and undutiful, the virtues and their practice, the possession of comforts, worth and respect, health, strength, beauty, keenness of the senses—all these qualities need someone who can appraise them. Someone should be allowed to know the value of every object on the list. Because sometimes you're deceived and believe that certain things are worth more than they really are. In fact, you'll find that the things we value most—like riches, influence, and power—should be worth no more than a penny.

You'll never understand this unless you investigate the actual standard by which such conditions are relatively valued. Just as leaves can't flourish on their own but need a branch to cling to and draw sap from, so your advice, when taken alone, withers away; it must be grafted onto a school of philosophy.

Moreover, those who dismiss doctrines don't understand that these doctrines are proven by the very arguments they use to try to disprove them. Because what are these people saying? They're saying that advice is enough to develop life and that the doctrines of wisdom (in other words, dogmas) are unnecessary. And yet, this very statement of theirs is a doctrine—just like if I were to say that advice should be dismissed because it's unnecessary and that we should focus solely on doctrines, then I would be giving a piece of advice by saying that advice isn't to be taken seriously.

Certain matters in philosophy need admonition; others need proof, and a great deal of proof, too, because they're complex and can hardly be made clear even with the greatest care and skill. If proof is necessary, so are doctrines because doctrines lead to truth through reasoning. Some matters are clear, and others are vague: those that the senses and memory can grasp are clear; those that are beyond their reach are vague.

But reason isn't satisfied with obvious facts; its higher and nobler function is to deal with hidden things. Hidden things need proof; proof can't exist without doctrines, so doctrines are necessary.

That which leads to a general and perfect agreement is an assured belief in certain facts. But if, without this assurance, all things are in turmoil in our minds, then doctrines are essential because they give our minds the means to make firm decisions.

Furthermore, when we advise someone to value their friends as highly as themselves, to remember that an enemy may become a friend, to nurture love in a friend, and to restrain hatred in an enemy, we add, "This is just and honorable." Now, the just and honorable part of our doctrines is embraced by reason; so reason is necessary because, without it, the doctrines can't exist.

But let's combine the two. Because branches are useless without their roots, and the roots themselves are strengthened by the growth they produce. Everyone can understand how useful hands are; they obviously help us. But the heart, the source of the hands' growth, power, and motion, is hidden. And I can say the same thing about advice: it's visible, while the doctrines of wisdom are hidden. And just as only the initiated know the more sacred parts of the rites, so in philosophy, the hidden truths are revealed only to those who are members and have been admitted to the sacred rites. But advice and other such matters are familiar even to the uninitiated.

Posidonius believes that not only giving advice (there's nothing to stop me from using this word), but also persuasion, consolation, and encouragement, are necessary. To these, he adds the investigation of causes (but I don't see why I shouldn't call it "aetiology," since scholars who guard the Latin language use the term as if they have the right to). He notes that it will also be useful to describe each particular virtue. Posidonius calls this "ethology," while others call it "characterization." It provides the signs and marks that belong to each virtue and vice so that distinctions can be made between similar things. Its function is the same as that of advice. Because when someone gives advice, they say, "If you want to have self-control, act like this!" When someone illustrates, they say, "The person who acts like this and avoids certain other things possesses self-control." If you ask what the difference is here, I'd say that one gives the advice of virtue, the other its example. These illustrations, or, to use a business term, these samples, have, I admit, a certain usefulness. Just put them on display with good recommendations, and you'll find people who will copy them.

Would you, for example, consider it useful to have evidence that helps you recognize a purebred horse, so you're not cheated in your purchase or waste your time on a low-quality animal? But how much more useful is it to know the marks of an exceptionally fine soul— marks that you can take from someone else and make your own!

"Right away, the foal of the well-bred herd, raised in the pastures, walks with a spirited step and treads with a delicate motion; first on the dangerous path and into the threatening river, trusting itself to the unknown bridge without fear at its creaking, neck held high in the air, with a clear-cut head, a spare belly, a rounded back, and a chest full of courage and muscle. When the sound of clashing weapons is heard in the distance, it leaps from its place, pricks up its ears, and, trembling all over, releases the pent-up fire that was tightly shut in its nostrils."

Vergil's description, though referring to something else, could easily describe a brave person; at least, I wouldn't choose any other comparison for a hero. If I had to describe Cato, who wasn't afraid amid the noise of civil war, who was the first to challenge the armies already heading for the Alps, who threw himself into the civil conflict, this is exactly how I would describe him.

Surely no one could "march with more spirited steps" than someone who stood against Caesar and Pompey at the same time, and when some supported Caesar's side and others supported Pompey, challenged both leaders, showing that the republic also had its supporters. Because it's not enough to say of Cato, "without fear at its creaking." Of course, he isn't afraid! He doesn't flinch at real and immediate noises. In the face of ten legions, Gallic auxiliaries, and a mixed host of citizens and foreigners, he speaks words filled with freedom, encouraging the republic not to give up in the fight for freedom but to take all risks. He declares that it's more honorable to fall into slavery than to submit to it. What strength and energy he has! What confidence he shows amid the general panic! He knows he's the only one whose status isn't in question, and that people don't ask if Cato is free, but if he's still among the free. Hence his disregard for danger and the sword. What a pleasure it is to say, in admiration of the unshakable steadiness of a hero who didn't waver when the entire state was in ruins: "A chest full of courage and muscle!"

It will be helpful not only to state the usual quality of good people and to outline their figures and features but also to recount and set forth what kind of people have existed. We might imagine Cato's last and bravest wound, through which Freedom breathed her last; or the wise Laelius and his harmonious life with his friend Scipio; or the noble deeds of the Elder Cato at home and abroad; or the wooden couches of Tubero, set out at a public feast, goatskins instead of tapestries, and earthenware vessels laid out for the banquet before the very shrine of Jupiter! What else was this but consecrating poverty on the Capitol? Though I know of no other deed of his for which to rank him with the Catos, isn't this one enough? It was a censorship, not a banquet.

How pitifully those who seek glory fail to understand what glory is, or how it should be sought! On that day, the Roman people saw the furniture of many men; they only marveled at one! The gold and silver of all the others have been broken up and melted down many times, but Tubero's earthenware will last throughout eternity. Farewell.

Letter 96 - On facing hardships

Despite everything, do you still get upset and complain? You don't seem to understand that the only real problem is that you get upset and complain. If you ask me, I think that for a person, there is no misery unless they believe there is something miserable in the world. I will not endure anything on the day I find it unbearable.

I am sick, but that's part of life. My servants have also fallen ill, my income has dropped, my house is falling apart, and I've suffered losses, accidents, hard work, and fear. These are common things. No, actually, these are inevitable things. These events happen by order, not by accident. If you believe me, I'm sharing my deepest feelings with you: when everything seems difficult and like an uphill struggle, I have trained myself not just to obey God but to agree with His decisions. I follow Him because my soul wants to, not because I must. Nothing will ever happen to me that I will receive with bad temper or a sour face. I will pay all my dues willingly. All the things that make us groan or flinch are just part of the cost of living—things, my dear Lucilius, that you should never hope or try to escape.

You were worried because of your bladder disease. You sent me sad letters and were constantly getting worse. I'll be more direct and say that you feared for your life. But think about this: didn't you know when you prayed for a long life that this was what you were asking for? A long life includes all these troubles, just like a long journey includes dust, mud, and rain. "But," you say, "I wanted to live and not have to deal with any problems." Complaining like that doesn't suit a man. Think about how you should respond to this wish of mine (I say it not just with good intentions but with noble intentions): "May the gods and goddesses forbid that Fortune keeps you in luxury!"

Ask yourself which you would choose if some god offered you a choice: life in a café or life in a camp? And yet, life, Lucilius, is really a battle. That's why those who are tossed around at sea, who climb up and down difficult cliffs and heights, who go on dangerous campaigns, are heroes and front-line fighters. But those who live in rotten luxury and comfort while others work hard are like turtle-doves—safe only because others look down on them. Farewell.

Letter 97 - On the degeneracy of the age

You are wrong, my dear Lucilius, if you think that luxury, poor manners, and other bad habits that people blame on the time they live in are only typical of our own age. No, these are the faults of people, not just the time they live in. No period in history has ever been free from blame. Also, if you start looking at the problems of any specific era, you will find—shameful as it is to say—that sin has never been more open than it was during the time of Cato.

Would anyone believe that money was exchanged during the trial when Clodius was accused of secretly committing adultery with Caesar's wife and violating the ritual that is performed for the people, where all men are strictly kept away? And yet, money was given to the jury, and even worse, sexual favors were demanded from married women and noble youths as part of the bribe.

The accusation itself was less of a sin than what happened after it. The defendant, who was charged with adultery, spread the guilt around to make the jury criminals like him. All of this happened during the trial where Cato gave evidence, although that was his only involvement.

I will quote Cicero's exact words because the facts are so shocking they are hard to believe: "He made appointments, promises, pleas, and gifts. And even worse (good heavens, what a corrupt situation!), he even offered some of the jury the enjoyment of certain women and meetings with noble youths." The bribe itself is bad enough, but what was added to it was even worse. "Do you want the wife of that strict man, A.? Fine. Or of B., the millionaire? I guarantee you can have her. If you don't commit adultery, condemn Clodius. The beauty you desire will visit you. I promise you a night with that woman without delay, and I will make sure it happens within the legal postponement time." It's worse to arrange such crimes than to commit them; it's like blackmailing respected women.

These jurors in the Clodius trial asked the Senate for a guard—a request that would only make sense for a jury about to convict the accused, and their request was granted. So, Catulus joked after the defendant was acquitted: "Why did you ask for the guard? Were you afraid someone would steal your money?" And yet, despite jokes like these, Clodius, who was an adulterer before the trial and a pimp during it, got away unpunished and escaped conviction more disgracefully than he deserved.

Do you think anything could be more shameful than these morals—when lust couldn't even keep its hands off religious worship or the courts of law? When, during the very investigation ordered by the Senate, more crime was committed than was being investigated? The question was whether someone could be safe after committing adultery; it was shown that one couldn't be safe without committing adultery!

All of this bargaining happened in front of Pompey and Caesar, Cicero and Cato—yes, the same Cato whose presence is said to have kept the people from demanding the usual jokes and nudity of actresses at the Floralia, if you can believe that people behaved better at a festival than in a courtroom! Such things have happened in the past and will happen again in the future. The excesses of cities may sometimes decrease due to discipline and fear, but never on their own.

So, don't think that we have given in more to lust and less to the law than people in the past. The young men of today live simpler lives than those of a time when a defendant would deny adultery before his judges, and the judges would admit it before the defendant. When people used immorality to secure a verdict, Clodius, helped by the very vices he was guilty of, acted as a pimp during his trial. Could anyone believe this? The man who could have been condemned for one adultery was acquitted because of many.

Every age will produce people like Clodius, but not every age will produce people like Cato. We easily fall into corruption because we always have guides or companions in our wickedness, and wickedness continues even without guides or companions. The road to vice isn't just downhill; it's steep, and many people become hopeless because, unlike other skills where mistakes bring shame and regret, the mistakes of life actually bring pleasure.

A pilot isn't happy when his ship is thrown off course; a doctor isn't happy when his patient dies; a lawyer isn't happy when the defendant loses a case because of the lawyer's mistake. But on the other hand, everyone enjoys their own sins. Someone might take pleasure in an affair, attracted by its very difficulty. Another might take pleasure in forgery and theft, and only be upset when the crime doesn't succeed. All of this is the result of bad habits.

On the other hand, to show that people do have an idea of good behavior deep down, even those who have gone down the most corrupt paths, and that people aren't ignorant of evil but indifferent to it, I say that everyone hides their sins, and even when they succeed, they enjoy the results while hiding the sins themselves. A good conscience, however, wants to come out and be seen; wickedness fears even shadows.

That's why I find Epicurus's saying very fitting: "It's possible for the guilty to remain hidden, but it's not possible for them to be sure they'll remain hidden." Or, to make it clearer: "The reason it's no advantage to wrongdoers to stay hidden is that, even if they're lucky, they're not sure they'll stay hidden." This is what I mean: crimes can be well-guarded, but they can't be free from anxiety.

This view doesn't go against our school's principles if it's explained this way. Why? Because the first and worst punishment for sin is to have committed the sin. And crime, even if Fortune covers it with her favors and protects it, can never go unpunished because the punishment of crime lies in the crime itself. But these secondary punishments also follow closely behind the first—constant fear, constant terror, and distrust in one's own security.

So why should I free wickedness from such punishment? Why shouldn't I always leave it trembling in the balance? Let's disagree with Epicurus on one point, where he says there's no natural justice, and that crime should be avoided because one can't escape the fear that comes with it. But let's agree with him on the other—that bad deeds are whipped by the lash of conscience, and that conscience suffers the most because endless anxiety drives and whips it on, and it can't rely on its own peace of mind.

This, Epicurus, is the proof that we are naturally reluctant to commit crime, because even when we're safe, no one is without fear. Good luck might free many people from punishment, but no one from fear. And why should this be if we didn't have an ingrained hatred for what Nature has condemned? That's why even those who hide their sins can never be sure they'll stay hidden, because their conscience convicts them and reveals them to themselves. But it is the nature of guilt to be in fear. We would be in a bad situation, given the many crimes that escape the law's vengeance and prescribed punishments, if it weren't for the fact that those serious offenses against nature must pay the price in fear instead of suffering. Farewell.

Letter 98 - On the fickleness of fortune

You should never think that anyone who relies on happiness is truly happy. This happiness is weak and unstable. Any joy that comes from outside can easily leave in the same way it arrived. But the joy that comes entirely from within yourself is true and solid. It grows stronger and stays with you until the end, while all the other things that people admire are just temporary. You might ask, "Can't these things be both useful and enjoyable?" Yes, they can, but only if we control them, and not the other way around.

Everything that fortune gives us can be useful and pleasant, but only if we also control ourselves and are not controlled by the things we own. People make a mistake, my dear Lucilius, when they think that fortune gives us either good or bad things. What fortune really gives us is just the raw materials, which we then turn into either good or bad depending on how we use them. The soul is more powerful than fortune; it can direct its own life, making it either happy or miserable.

A bad person makes everything bad, even things that seem good at first. But a good and honest person can correct the wrongs of fortune. They can handle hardship and bitterness because they know how to deal with them. They also accept success with appreciation and moderation and face trouble with courage. Even if someone is wise, manages their life well, and doesn't take on more than they can handle, they won't reach true happiness unless they are prepared for the uncertainties of life.

Whether you look at others (which is often easier) or at yourself with an unbiased view, you will see that the things we desire and love are not truly useful unless we are ready for the unpredictability of life and its effects. You need to remind yourself often and calmly whenever something goes wrong, "This is what fate had planned for me." Or, to be even stronger and more truthful, say to yourself, "This is what fate had planned better for me!"

If you think like this, nothing will disturb you. A person will remain calm if they have already considered the ups and downs of life before they happen. They should look at their children, spouse, or possessions with the thought that they might not always have them and that losing them won't make them any more miserable. It's tragic for the soul to always worry about the future and fear losing what it enjoys. This kind of soul will never be at peace; in worrying about the future, it loses the present joys. There's really no difference between grieving over something lost and fearing that you might lose it.

But I'm not saying you should be indifferent. Instead, try to avoid anything that could cause fear. Be sure to foresee what can be foreseen by careful planning. Stay alert to anything that could harm you long before it happens. To do this, the best help is a confident mind, strongly determined to endure anything. A person who can handle the blows of fortune can also be on guard against them. There's no need to worry about waves when the sea is calm. And there's nothing more foolish or miserable than worrying before it's necessary. What madness it is to anticipate troubles!

To put it simply, those who are always busy worrying are just as unsteady when troubles come as they are before they arrive. They suffer more than necessary because they suffer before it's necessary. These people don't measure their suffering because they are just as unprepared for it as they are unrestrained in their hopes that their luck will last forever. They forget that life can change in an instant, and they foolishly expect that their good fortune will never end.

That's why I think Metrodorus's saying is so wise. He wrote in a letter to his sister after the loss of her promising son, "All the good things in life are mortal." He's talking about the things people rush after. True good doesn't perish; it's certain and lasting, made up of wisdom and virtue, the only immortal things that mortals can have.

But people are so forgetful of their ultimate goal that they are surprised when they lose something, even though they are bound to lose everything someday. Anything you own is in your possession, but it's not really yours because nothing weak is truly strong or lasting. We will lose our lives just as surely as we lose our property, and understanding this truth can be a comfort. Lose what you must with a calm mind, because you must also lose your life.

So, what can we do when faced with these losses? Simply this: remember the good times you've had and don't let the joy you got from them fade away along with the things themselves. You might lose the object, but you'll never lose the memory of having it. It's ungrateful to feel no gratitude after losing something, as if you never received it in the first place. Chance might take the thing away, but it can't take away the enjoyment and use you had from it unless you unfairly regret it.

Just tell yourself, "None of the things that seem so terrifying are unbeatable. Many have overcome separate trials: Mucius overcame fire, Regulus endured crucifixion, Socrates faced poison, Rutilius accepted exile, and Cato took his own life with a sword. So, let us also overcome something."

Moreover, the things that seem beautiful and desirable to most people have been scorned by many before us. Fabricius, when he was a general, refused riches, and when he was a censor, he condemned them. Tubero, by using earthenware dishes at a public festival on the Capitol, showed that man should be satisfied with what the gods themselves could still use. The elder Sextius rejected public office honors, even though he was expected to take part in public affairs. He wouldn't accept the rank offered to him by Julius Caesar because he understood that what can be given can also be taken away.

Let us also carry out some courageous act on our own. Let's be included among the heroes of history. Why have we been so hesitant? Why do we lose heart? What others have done, we can do too, if we purify our souls and follow nature. When we stray from nature, we are compelled to crave, fear, and be slaves to the whims of chance. But we can return to the right path and be restored to our true state. Let's do so, so that we can endure pain in whatever form it comes and say to Fortune, "You are dealing with a human being; find someone you can conquer!"

By these words, and others like them, the pain can be soothed, and I hope that it can be reduced, cured, or at least stopped so it ages along with the person suffering. I'm comfortable with how he's handling it. What we're really discussing is our own loss—the passing of an excellent old man. He himself has lived a full life, and any extra time he might wish for isn't for his own sake but for those who need him.

By continuing to live, he is being generous. Someone else might have ended their suffering, but our friend considers it just as wrong to flee from death as it is to rush towards it. "But," someone might say, "shouldn't he leave if the situation calls for it?" Of course, if he can no longer be of help to anyone and if all that's left for him is to deal with pain.

This, my dear Lucilius, is what we mean by practicing philosophy in real life. Observe the courage a wise person shows against death or pain when one approaches, and the other weighs heavily. We should learn what to do from those who actually do it.

So far, we've discussed whether anyone can resist pain or if the approach of death can shake even great souls. But why discuss it further? Here's an immediate example: death doesn't make our friend more willing to face pain, nor does pain make him more eager to face death. Instead, he trusts himself to face both. He doesn't endure pain just because he hopes for death, nor does he welcome death because he's tired of suffering. He endures pain and waits for death. Farewell.

Letter 99 - On consolation to the bereaved

I am including a copy of the letter I wrote to Marullus when he lost his young son and was said to be excessively emotional in his grief. Instead of following the usual form of expressing sympathy, I chose to take a different approach. I didn't think he should be treated gently because, in my view, he needed correction more than consolation. When someone is deeply hurt and struggling to cope with a severe loss, it's important to let them grieve for a while, to let them express their sorrow or at least work through the initial shock. But those who indulge excessively in their grief should be corrected immediately and taught that even in their tears, there can be a certain foolishness.

I wrote to him, "Are you looking for comfort? Well, let me give you a reality check instead! You are grieving like a woman over your son's death; what would you do if you had lost a close friend? Your son, a little child whose potential was still unknown, is gone; you have lost only a small amount of time. We often search for reasons to grieve and might even complain unfairly about Fortune, as if Fortune never gave us a real reason to complain! But I had thought you had enough strength to handle real problems, let alone the minor ones that people often mourn out of habit. If you had lost a friend, which is a much harder loss, you should focus on the happiness you shared rather than mourn because they are gone.

But many people fail to count up all the good things they have experienced and focus only on their losses. Grief like yours has many problems: it's not only pointless but also ungrateful. Has it all been for nothing that you had such a friend? After so many years of close companionship and shared experiences, has nothing been gained? Will you bury the friendship along with the friend? Why mourn their loss if having them in your life didn't matter? Believe me, a large part of those we've loved stays with us even after they're gone. The past belongs to us, and nothing is more secure than what has already happened.

We are ungrateful for the good things we've had because we're too focused on hoping for the future, as if the future, if it even comes, will not quickly become the past. We limit our enjoyment if we only take pleasure in the present; both the future and the past can bring us joy—the future with anticipation, and the past with memories. But the future is uncertain, while the past is definite and unchangeable.

So why let go of what is most certain? Let's be content with the pleasures we've already experienced, as long as, while we enjoyed them, our souls weren't like a sieve, losing everything they took in. Many people have buried sons in the prime of life without shedding tears—people who returned from the funeral to their duties and immediately busied themselves with other tasks. And rightly so, because, first of all, it's pointless to grieve if grief doesn't help. Secondly, it's unfair to complain about something that happens to everyone. And it's foolish to lament our losses when there's only a brief time separating us from those we've lost. We should be more accepting because we're not far behind those who have gone before us.

Notice how quickly time passes—the fastest thing there is. Consider the short journey we all make at top speed; think about the crowd of people all heading toward the same destination, with only the briefest intervals between them, even when they seem long. The person you're mourning has only gone ahead of you. And what could be more irrational than to mourn someone who has merely gone ahead of you on the same journey? Does a person lament something they knew was going to happen? Or if they didn't think of death as inevitable, they've only deceived themselves. If someone grieves over death, they're really grieving over the fact that the person was human. Everyone is bound by the same terms: those who are born are destined to die.

Time separates us, but death levels us all. The time between our first day and our last is uncertain and ever-changing: if you measure it by its hardships, it seems long even to a young person; if by its speed, it seems short even to an old one. Everything is uncertain, unreliable, and more changeable than the weather. All things are tossed around by Fortune and can change at any moment; in the midst of all this chaos, only death is certain. And yet, people complain about the one thing that is guaranteed not to deceive them.

"But he died as a child," you say. I'm not ready to claim that those who die young get the better deal; let's consider the case of someone who lives to old age. How much more does he really gain than a child? Look at the vast expanse of time and the universe, and then compare our so-called human life to infinity. You'll see how tiny is the thing we pray for and try to extend. How much of our time is spent weeping, worrying, and praying for death before it comes? How much time is consumed by our health concerns, fears, and inexperience or useless efforts? And half of all this time is spent sleeping. Add to this our labors, sorrows, and dangers, and you'll understand that in even the longest life, the time we truly live is the smallest part.

Even so, who would admit that a person isn't better off when they are allowed to return home quickly, when their journey is over before they're completely worn out? Life itself isn't good or bad; it's just the setting where good and bad things happen. So, this little boy has lost nothing except a gamble where loss was more certain than gain. He might have turned out to be temperate and wise; he might have been shaped by your guidance into a better person. But (and this fear is more realistic) he might have ended up just like most people.

Look at the young men from the noblest families whose extravagance has led them to ruin; look at those who indulge in their own and others' vices, who spend their days in drunkenness or shameful acts. You'll see that there was more to fear than to hope for.

So, don't look for excuses to grieve or make small burdens heavier by getting upset. I'm not asking you to summon all your strength and rise to great heights; I don't think you need to use every bit of your virtue to face this trouble. This isn't pain; it's just a small sting, and you're the one turning it into pain.

Philosophy has already helped you if you can bear the loss of a young child who was better known to his nurse than to his father! And what now? Am I telling you to be cold-hearted, to keep a straight face even at the funeral, and not let your soul feel any pain? Not at all. That would be more like lack of feeling than virtue—to watch the burial of those you love with the same expression as when they were alive, and to show no emotion over your first loss in the family. But even if I did tell you not to show emotion, there are some feelings that have their rights. Tears will fall, no matter how much we try to stop them, and when they do, they ease the soul.

So, what should we do? Let the tears fall, but don't force them. Let us cry as much as emotion demands, but not as much as imitation dictates. Let's not add anything to our natural grief or make it worse by following others' examples. The display of grief often demands more from us than grief itself does. How few people are truly sad when they're alone! They cry louder when others are around; people who are calm and quiet when they're alone are often stirred to new fits of tears when they see others nearby. That's when they start to tear at themselves, though they could have done it more easily if no one was there to stop them. That's when they start praying for death and throwing themselves around. But their grief lessens once the spectators leave.

In this, as in many other things, we make the mistake of following the crowd and focusing on what others think rather than on what is right. We abandon our natural feelings and give in to the mob, who are never good advisers and are always inconsistent. When people see someone handling their grief bravely, they call him unfeeling and heartless; when they see someone collapse and cling to their dead, they call him weak and womanish.

So, everything should be guided by reason. But there's nothing more foolish than trying to earn a reputation for sadness or to approve of tears. I believe that for a wise person, some tears fall by choice, others by force.

I'll explain it like this: When we first hear the news of a terrible loss, when we hold the form that will soon pass from our arms to the funeral pyre, tears are forced out by nature. The life force, struck by grief, shakes the whole body, including the eyes, from which it presses out the moisture that lies within. These tears fall against our will, but different tears come when we remember those we've lost. There's a certain sweet sadness in recalling the sound of a pleasant voice, a cheerful conversation, and the busy duties we once shared. At such times, our eyes are loosened by joy. We allow these tears; the first kind overwhelms us.

So, there's no need to hold back or force your tears just because others are around you. Whether restrained or let go, they're never as disgraceful as when they're fake. Let them flow naturally. But it's possible for tears to flow from those who are calm and at peace. They often flow without reducing the influence of a wise person—with such control that they show no lack of feeling or self-respect.

We can follow nature and still maintain our dignity. I've seen people who were worthy of respect during the burial of loved ones, with faces that still showed their love even after the mourning rituals were over, and who behaved only as true emotion allowed. There's a certain grace even in grief. This is something a wise person should cultivate; even in tears, just as in other matters, there's a certain limit. For the unwise, sorrows, like joys, overflow.

Accept what is inevitable with a calm spirit. What can happen that's beyond belief? Or what is truly new? How many people right now are making arrangements for funerals! How many are buying grave clothes! How many are mourning, just as you have finished mourning! Whenever you think about your child's passing, also think about humanity itself, which has no guaranteed future, and remember that Fortune doesn't always let us live to old age, but takes us whenever she chooses.

You may speak often about those who have passed and cherish their memory as much as possible. This memory will come back to you more often if you welcome it without bitterness. No one enjoys spending time with a sorrowful person, much less with sorrow itself. Whatever words or jokes your child made, no matter how small he was, that gave you joy—remember them again and again. Be confident that he might have fulfilled the hopes you, as his father, had for him.

To forget the beloved dead, to bury their memory along with their bodies, to mourn them greatly and then barely think of them afterward—this is the mark of a heart lacking humanity. That's how animals love their young; their affection is quickly roused, almost to the point of madness, but it fades entirely when the object of their love dies. This doesn't suit a person of reason; they should keep the memory alive but stop the mourning.

I don't approve of Metrodorus's idea that there's a certain pleasure mixed with sadness and that we should chase after it at times like these. I have no doubt about your feelings on this matter, for what could be worse than seeking pleasure in the midst of mourning—or even finding pleasure through mourning—and hunting for something enjoyable while still in tears? These are the people who accuse us Stoics of being too strict, criticizing our teachings for being too harsh because we say that grief should either not enter the soul at all or be driven out immediately. But which is more incredible or inhuman—to feel no grief at the loss of a friend, or to seek out pleasure in the middle of grief?

What we Stoics advise is honorable. When emotion has prompted a moderate flow of tears and has calmed down, the soul should not be given over to grief. But what do you mean, Metrodorus, by saying that we should mix pleasure with our very grief? That's like giving candy to children to stop their crying; it's how we soothe infants by pouring milk down their throats!

Even when your child's body is on the pyre, or your friend is taking his last breath, will you not stop seeking pleasure, rather than trying to mix it with grief? Which is more honorable—to remove grief from your soul, or to invite pleasure to join it in grief? Did I say "invite"? I mean "chase after" pleasure, and from the hands of grief itself. Metrodorus says, "There is a certain pleasure related to sadness." We Stoics might say that, but you cannot. For you, the only Good is pleasure, and the only Evil is pain. How can there be a relationship between Good and Evil? But even if there were such a relationship, now is the time to root it out.

Shall we examine grief and see what elements of delight and pleasure surround it? Certain remedies are good for some parts of the body but can't be applied to other parts because they're inappropriate. What might be helpful in some situations might be unsuitable in others. Aren't you ashamed to cure sorrow with pleasure? No, this sore spot must be treated more harshly. Here's what you should advise instead: that no harm can come to someone who is dead. If they can be harmed, they're not really dead. And I say that nothing can hurt someone who doesn't exist. If a person can be hurt, they're still alive. Do you think someone is badly off because they no longer exist or because they still exist in some way? No torment can come from the fact that someone no longer exists—because how can there be any feeling for someone who doesn't exist? Nor can torment come from the fact that they still exist because they've escaped the worst part of death—non-existence.

Let's say this to those who mourn and miss the young who have died: All of us, whether young or old, live such a short time compared to eternity that we're all on the same level. Out of all time, we get less than what anyone could call the least, because "least" still means something. But our life is almost nothing, yet we foolishly treat it as if it were so much more!

I wrote these words to you, not expecting to cure you at this late stage—for I'm sure you've already told yourself everything you'll read in my letter—but to rebuke you for the short time you strayed from your true self and to encourage you for the future, to strengthen your spirit against Fortune, and to be ready for all her blows—not as if they might come, but as if they are sure to come. Farewell.

Letter 100 - On the writings of Fabianus

You wrote to me saying that you eagerly read the work by Fabianus Papirius called The Duties of a Citizen, but it didn't meet your expectations. Then, forgetting that you're dealing with a philosopher, you started to criticize his style. Let's assume your critique is true—that he pours out his words rather than carefully placing them. I should tell you upfront that this trait you mention has its own unique charm and is actually fitting for a smooth-flowing style. I believe it matters a lot whether the words tumble out or flow along gently.

Fabianus's words don't just pour out; they flow in a way that's abundant but not confusing, fast but not chaotic. His style suggests that he didn't spend too much time perfecting every word and phrase. But even if your criticism is correct, remember that Fabianus was more focused on building character than crafting words. He was writing for the mind, not for the ear.

If he had been speaking these words directly to you, you wouldn't have had time to nitpick the details because his words would have carried you along. Often, what pleases us because of its speed and flow might seem less impressive when we sit down to read it carefully. However, the ability to attract attention at first glance is still a significant advantage, even if closer inspection reveals some flaws.

If you ask me, I'd say that someone who wins approval quickly is even more impressive than someone who earns it gradually, although I know the latter is safer and more reliable. A careful and overly meticulous style doesn't suit a philosopher. If he's timid with words, when will he ever be bold and steadfast in his thinking and actions?

Fabianus's style wasn't careless; it was confident. That's why you won't find anything sloppy in his work. His words are well-chosen, though not overly polished or forced into unnatural forms. They have a certain elegance, even though they're drawn from everyday language. His ideas are honorable and grand, expressed freely rather than locked into strict aphorisms. Sure, you might find some passages that aren't perfectly pruned or polished to today's standards, but when you look at the whole work, you'll see there are no shallow arguments or empty rhetoric.

There might not be any flashy decorations or fancy water fountains running from room to room, no luxurious additions that wealth often brings when simple elegance isn't enough. But, as the saying goes, it's still "a good house to live in."

People have different opinions about style. Some want it polished and free of any roughness, while others enjoy an abrupt style that intentionally breaks up smoother passages, surprising the reader with unexpected endings. If you read Cicero, for example, you'll notice his style is unified, moving at a measured pace, gentle but not weak. On the other hand, Asinius Pollio's style is more jarring and uneven, often ending unexpectedly. Cicero usually finishes his thoughts gradually, while Pollio tends to break off suddenly, except when he's sticking to a specific rhythm.

You also mentioned that Fabianus's work seems too ordinary and lacks elevation, but I disagree. His style isn't ordinary; it's calm and reflects his peaceful, well-ordered mind. It's not low or common but steady and consistent. You might be looking for the energy and sharpness of an orator, full of sudden, striking phrases. But take a look at the entire work—it's well-organized and distinguished. His style might not shout dignity, but it certainly suggests it.

Now, you might compare Fabianus to someone like Cicero, whose philosophical works are almost as numerous as Fabianus's. I'll concede that point; Cicero was great. But being less than the greatest is no small thing. Or you might compare him to Asinius Pollio. Again, I'll concede. It's an honor to be third in such a competitive field. You could also include Livy, who wrote both dialogues and philosophical works. I'll give way there, too. But think about how many writers Fabianus surpasses if only three of the greatest masters of eloquence rank above him!

Some might say that although Fabianus's style is elevated, it lacks strength and force. It might flow smoothly, but it doesn't have the power or clarity some might want. They may argue that it doesn't include any fierce condemnation of vice, bold words in the face of danger, or proud defiance of Fortune. They want to see luxury rebuked, lust condemned, and waywardness crushed. They're looking for the sharpness of oratory, the drama of tragedy, or the wit of comedy. But Fabianus didn't rely on such flashy rhetoric; he focused on the greatness of his subject, letting eloquence follow naturally, like a shadow.

Sure, he might not analyze every detail or emphasize every word. Sometimes, his phrases might fall short or seem to slip by too easily, but there's still plenty of insight throughout his work. There are long stretches that won't tire the reader. And most importantly, you'll see that he wrote with sincerity, aiming to share what he found important rather than just trying to impress you. His work is meant to help people grow and become better, not just to win applause.

I'm confident that Fabianus's writings are as I've described them, though I'm recalling them from memory rather than a recent reading. The overall tone of his work has stayed with me over the years, even if the details have faded. Whenever I heard him lecture, his work seemed to me not necessarily solid but full of substance—the kind of writing that would inspire young people with potential and encourage them to strive to be like him, without making them feel it's impossible to surpass him. I think this kind of encouragement is the most helpful. It's disheartening to inspire someone to reach for greatness only to make them feel it's out of their reach.

In any case, Fabianus's language was fluent, and while you might not agree with every detail, the overall effect was impressive. Farewell.

Letter 101 - On the futility of planning ahead

Every day and every hour shows us how insignificant we are and reminds us, with new evidence, that we forget our weakness. Yet, while we make plans as if we will live forever, life forces us to look back at death.

You may wonder why I'm saying this. It's about Cornelius Senecio, a respected and capable Roman knight whom you knew. He started from humble beginnings and worked his way up to fortune, and now the road ahead seemed easier. It's always easier to grow in status than to start from nothing. Making money when you're poor is slow and difficult until you can escape poverty. Senecio was already close to wealth, helped by two important skills—knowing how to make money and how to keep it. Either of these talents alone could have made him rich.

He lived simply, being careful about both his health and wealth. On that day, he visited me early in the morning, as usual, and then spent the whole day, even until nightfall, at the bedside of a friend who was very ill and unlikely to recover. After having a comfortable dinner, he was suddenly struck by a severe throat infection, and with his breath blocked by swelling, he barely made it through the night. Within just a few hours of being a healthy, active man, he passed away.

Senecio had been making investments on land and sea, engaging in public life, and trying all kinds of business ventures. Just as his financial success was becoming real and money was flowing in, he was suddenly taken from the world!

It's foolish to plan out your life when you don't even own tomorrow. What madness it is to make long-term plans! To say, "I will buy and build, loan money, collect debts, gain honors, and then, when I am old and full of years, I will enjoy a peaceful life." Believe me, everything is uncertain, even for those who seem to have it all. No one has the right to count on the future. The very things we hold onto can slip away, and chance can take away even the hour we are living in. Time does move along steadily, but it does so in the dark, and what good is it to me if Nature's course is certain when my own life is so uncertain?

We plan long journeys and dream of coming home after traveling to distant lands. We plan for military service and the slow rewards of hard work. We campaign for government positions and promotions—always thinking of what comes next—while death stands right beside us. We hardly ever think of death unless it happens to someone else. Death reminds us daily of how close it is, but we forget as soon as our shock wears off.

Yet what could be more foolish than being surprised by something that can happen every day? There is a limit set for each of us by Fate, but none of us knows how close we are to that limit. Therefore, we should live as if every day might be our last. Let us not put off anything. Let us make sure our lives are complete each day.

The biggest flaw in life is that it's always unfinished, always with something postponed. A person who makes sure every day is complete never lacks time. But from this lack of time comes fear and a craving for the future that eats away at our minds. Nothing is more miserable than worrying about what will happen. Our minds are troubled by fears we can't even explain.

How can we avoid this constant worry? There's only one way— by not reaching forward in life, by staying in the present. The only person who fears the future is the one who is unhappy with the present. But when my soul is content, when a well-balanced mind sees that a single day is just as good as eternity—no matter what the future brings—then the soul can stand tall, laughing at the endless march of time. For what can disturb us in the changing and uncertain world of chance if we are secure within ourselves?

So, my dear Lucilius, start living right now, and treat each day as a complete life. The person who is ready for this, who makes every day whole, is at peace. But those who live only for hope find that the future always slips away and that greed takes over, along with the fear of death, a fear that poisons everything else. That's how we end up with such sad prayers, like the one Maecenas made, where he was willing to suffer weakness, deformity, even the pain of crucifixion, just to keep living a little longer:

"Make me weak, crippled, hunched over, with rattling teeth, So long as I can keep living. Save my life, I pray, Even if I sit on the painful cross!"

There he is, praying for the very thing that would be the most miserable! He wants to extend his suffering, thinking it's the same as wanting life! I would think him despicable if he wanted to live right up until crucifixion. But he cries out, "You can weaken my body, just leave me alive in this broken and useless shell! You can deform me, but give me a little more time in the world! Nail me up, set me on the cross, just let me keep breathing!"

Is it worth it to endure all that, just to hold on to something that's supposed to bring relief from suffering and the end of pain? Is it worth staying alive only to give up that life in such a way? What would you ask for Maecenas except for the mercy of heaven? What does he mean by writing such shameful, cowardly verses? What does he mean by making a deal with his fears? Why does he beg so desperately to keep living? He can't have heard Virgil when he wrote:

"Tell me, is Death so terrible?"

Maecenas asks for the worst kind of suffering and, even worse, for that suffering to be prolonged, just so he can have a little more life. But what kind of life is it if it's just a drawn-out death? Is there anyone who would choose to waste away in pain, dying piece by piece, rather than dying all at once? Is there anyone who would choose to be nailed to that cursed tree, sick, deformed, swollen with horrible tumors, and breathe in agony? I think most people would find many reasons to die before they ever got to the cross!

Deny it if you can, but Nature is generous in making death unavoidable. Many people are willing to make even more shameful deals—betraying friends just to live longer, or willingly disgracing their own children to keep enjoying the sunlight that witnesses all their sins. We must let go of this desperate need to keep living and learn that it doesn't matter when our suffering comes because it will come eventually. What matters is not how long you live, but how nobly you live. And often, living nobly means you won't live long. Farewell.

Letter 102 - On the intimations of our immortality

Just like how it's irritating when someone wakes up a person who is having a pleasant dream (because even if the dream isn't real, it still feels like it is), your letter has done something similar to me. It abruptly brought me back to reality, just when I was deep in enjoyable thoughts and ready to keep going with them if I could. I was enjoying thinking about the idea of the immortality of souls, even believing in it. I was listening closely to the opinions of great authors who not only believe in but also promise this wonderful possibility. I was allowing myself to hope for this noble idea because I was already tired of my life, starting to despise the broken pieces of my existence, and feeling like I was destined to move on to that infinite time and the heritage of eternity. But then your letter suddenly woke me up and took away my lovely dream. But if I can deal with you quickly, I'll get back to it and reclaim it.

You mentioned at the beginning of your letter that I hadn't fully explained the whole problem, where I was trying to prove one of the beliefs of our school: that the fame we achieve after death is a good thing. I hadn't solved the problem we usually face: "No good can consist of things that are separate; yet fame consists of such things." What you're asking about, my dear Lucilius, belongs to another part of the same topic, which is why I had postponed the arguments, not just on this one topic but on other topics that also cover the same ground. As you know, some logical questions get mixed in with ethical ones. So, I dealt with the essential part of my subject, which has to do with conduct—whether it's foolish and useless to care about what happens after our last day, or whether our good deeds die with us and there's nothing left of us after we're gone, or whether any benefit can be gained or attempted from something that, when it happens, we won't be able to feel.

All these things relate to how we should behave, and that's why they were included under the right topic. But the arguments made by those who like to debate against this idea had to be set aside and were postponed. Now that you want answers to all of them, I will look at all their statements and then refute them one by one. However, before I do that, I need to make one thing clear, or it will be impossible to understand my responses. And what is that thing? Simply this: there are certain things that are continuous, like a person; there are certain things that are made up of separate parts, like ships, houses, and everything that is the result of joining different parts together into one whole; there are other things made up of distinct, separate parts, like an army, a crowd, or a senate. The people who make up these groups are connected by law or function, but by their nature, they are separate and individual. Now, what other preliminary remarks do I need to make? Simply this: we believe that nothing is good if it's made up of things that are separate. For a single good thing should be controlled by a single soul, and the essential quality of each single good thing should be singular. This can be proven on its own whenever you wish; for now, however, it had to be set aside because our own arguments are being used against us.

Opponents argue like this: "You say that no good can be made up of things that are separate? Yet this fame, which you speak of, is simply the good opinion of good people. Just like reputation doesn't come from just one person's remarks, and ill-repute doesn't come from just one person's disapproval, fame doesn't mean that we've only pleased one good person. To create fame, the agreement of many distinguished and praiseworthy people is necessary. But this comes from the decision of many people—in other words, people who are separate from each other. Therefore, it isn't a good thing. You also say that fame is the praise given to a good person by good people. Praise means words: and words, even from the mouths of good people, are not a good thing in themselves. For any action of a good person is not necessarily good; he might shout approval or hiss disapproval, but we wouldn't call the shouting or the hissing good— although his entire behavior may be admired and praised—any more than we would praise a sneeze or a cough. Therefore, fame isn't a good thing. Finally, tell us whether the good belongs to the person who praises or the person who is praised. If you say that the good belongs to the person who is praised, you are on as foolish a quest as if you were to claim that my neighbor's good health is my own. But to praise worthy people is an honorable action; thus the good belongs only to the person who does the praising, the person who performs the action, and not to us, who are being praised. And yet this was the question under discussion."

I shall now answer the separate objections quickly. The first question still is, whether any good thing can consist of things that are separate—and there are votes cast on both sides. Again, does fame need many votes? Fame can be satisfied with the decision of one good person: it is one good person who decides that we are good. Then the response is: "What! Would you define reputation as the respect of one individual, and ill-repute as the bad talk of one person? We believe that glory is more widespread because it demands the agreement of many people." But the position of the "many" is different from that of "the one." And why? Because if the good person thinks well of me, it's almost the same as being thought well of by all good people; for they will all think the same if they know me. Their judgment is alike and identical; the effect of truth on it is equal. They cannot disagree, which means they would all hold the same view, being unable to hold different views.

"You say one person's opinion is not enough to create glory or reputation." In the first case, one judgment is a universal judgment because all, if they were asked, would hold one opinion; in the other case, however, people of different character give different judgments. You will find confusing emotions—everything is doubtful, inconstant, and untrustworthy. And can you suppose that all people are able to hold one opinion? Even an individual does not always stick to a single opinion. With the good person, it's truth that causes belief, and truth has only one function and one form; while among the other group of people I spoke of, the ideas they agree on are wrong. Moreover, those who are false are never consistent: they are irregular and disagreeable.

"But praise," says the objector, "is nothing but words, and words are not a good thing." When they say that fame is praise given to the good by the good, what they refer to is not just words but a judgment. For a good person may remain silent; but if he decides that a certain person is worthy of praise, that person is the object of praise. Besides, praise is one thing, and the act of giving praise is another; the latter requires words as well. Hence, no one speaks of "a funeral praise," but says "praise-giving"—because its function depends on speech. And when we say that a person is worthy of praise, we assure human kindness to them, not in words, but in judgment. So the good opinion, even of someone who silently feels approval of a good person, is praise.

Again, as I have said, praise is more a matter of the mind than of words; because words express the praise that the mind has conceived, and they announce it to the attention of others. To judge a person worthy of praise is to praise them. And when our tragic poet says that it is wonderful "to be praised by a well-praised hero," he means "by one who is worthy of praise." Again, when another wise poet says: "Praise nurtures the arts," he does not mean the act of giving praise, because that ruins the arts. Nothing has corrupted speaking and all other studies that depend on hearing as much as popular approval. Reputation necessarily needs words, but fame can be satisfied with people's judgments and can exist without the spoken word. It's content not only with silent approval but even in the face of open protest. There is, in my opinion, this difference between fame and glory—the latter depends on the judgments of many; but fame depends on the judgments of good people.

The response comes: "But whose good is this fame, this praise given to a good person by good people? Is it the good of the one praised or the one who praises?" It is both, I say. It's my own good in that I am praised, because I am naturally born to love all people, and I rejoice in having done good deeds and congratulate myself on having found people who express their ideas of my virtues with gratitude; that they are grateful is a good to them, but it is a good to me too. For my spirit is so made that I can see the good of other people as my own—especially those whose good I have helped bring about. This good also belongs to those who give the praise, for it is given through virtue; and every act of virtue is a good. My friends could not have found this blessing if I had not been a good person. It is therefore a good thing for both sides—this being praised when one deserves it—just like a good decision is a good thing for both the person who makes the decision and the person in whose favor the decision is made. Do you doubt that justice is a blessing to its possessor, as well as to the person to whom justice was given? To praise the deserving is justice; therefore, the good belongs toboth sides.

This should be a sufficient answer to those who engage in these detailed arguments. But our goal should not be to discuss things in a clever way and drag philosophy down from its greatness to such small debates. How much better it is to follow the straightforward and direct path, rather than to create a complicated route for yourself that you must retrace with endless effort! For this kind of argument is nothing more than a game for people who are skillfully playing tricks on each other.

Instead, tell me how natural it is for the mind to reach out into the vast universe! The human soul is a great and noble thing; it does not accept any limits except those shared by the gods. First of all, it does not settle for a humble place of birth, like Ephesus or Alexandria, or any land that is even more crowded and full of homes. The soul's true homeland is the entire space that encircles the height and width of the firmament, the whole rounded dome within which land and sea lie, where the upper air separates humans from the divine but also connects them, and where all the stars keep watch.

Again, the soul will not tolerate a short life. "All the years," says the soul, "are mine; no period of time is closed to great minds; all of time is open for the growth of thought. When the day comes to separate the heavenly from its earthly blend, I shall leave the body here where I found it, and of my own will join the gods. I am not apart from them now, but am merely held in a heavy and earthly prison." These delays in mortal life are just a prelude to the longer and better life to come. Just as the mother's womb holds us for nine months, making us ready not for the womb itself, but for the life we are about to enter when we are ready to breathe and live in the open, so too, the years from infancy to old age prepare us for another birth. A new beginning and a new condition await us.

We cannot yet, except at rare times, bear the light of heaven; therefore, look forward without fear to that appointed hour—the last hour of the body but not of the soul. Look at everything around you as if it were luggage in a guest room; you must move on. Nature strips you as bare at your departure as at your entrance. You may take away no more than you brought in; what's more, you must leave behind most of what you brought with you into life: you will lose even the skin that covers you—the last layer of protection; you will lose the flesh and the blood that runs through your body; you will lose the bones and sinews, the framework of these temporary and fragile parts.

The day you fear as the end of everything is the birthday of your eternity. Lay aside your burden—why wait?—just as if you had not already left the body that was your first home! You cling to your burden, you struggle; at your birth, your mother also had to make a great effort to set you free. You weep and wail; yet this crying happened at birth too, but then it was understandable—you came into the world completely ignorant and inexperienced. When you left the warm and protective shelter of your mother's womb, you felt the fresh air on your face; you winced at the touch of a rough hand, and you looked in wonder at unfamiliar things, still delicate and unaware of everything.

But now it's nothing new for you to be separated from something of which you were once a part; let go of your already useless limbs with acceptance and part with the body you have lived in for so long. It will be torn apart, buried, and decay. Why be sad? This is what usually happens: when we are born, the afterbirth always perishes. Why love such a thing as if it were your own possession? It was merely your covering. The day will come that will tear you away and lead you out of the company of the foul and unpleasant womb. Withdraw from it now as much as you can, and turn away from pleasure, except for what is tied to essential and important things; distance yourself from it even now, and think about something nobler and higher. Someday the secrets of nature will be revealed to you, the fog will lift from your eyes, and bright light will shine in on you from all sides.

Imagine how great the glow will be when all the stars mix their fires; no shadows will darken the clear sky. The entire heavens will shine evenly, for day and night only alternate in the lowest atmosphere. Then you will say that you have lived in darkness, once you have seen, in your perfect state, the perfect light—the light which now you see dimly with your limited vision. And yet, even from far away, you already look at it in awe; what do you think the heavenly light will be like when you see it in its true form?

Such thoughts keep the soul from settling on anything mean, low, or cruel. They remind us that the gods are witnesses to everything. They tell us to live in a way that wins the gods' approval, to prepare ourselves to join them in the future, and to plan for immortality. Someone who has grasped this idea fears no attacking army, is not frightened by the sound of the trumpet, and is not intimidated by threats.

How could someone feel fear if they are looking forward to death? Even someone who believes that the soul lasts only as long as it's trapped in the body, and then scatters when the body dissolves, can still find a purpose in leaving something useful behind after death. For though a person may be taken from the sight of others, still:

"Often our thoughts return to the hero, and often the glory Won by his race recurs to the mind."

Think about how much we are helped by good examples; you will then understand that the presence of a noble person is just as valuable as their memory. Farewell.

Letter 103 - On the dangers of association with our fellow-men

Why are you worrying about problems that might happen but also might not? I'm talking about things like fires, buildings falling down, and other accidents that could happen to anyone, not things that are planned against us. Instead, be careful and look out for the dangers that come from other people, which follow us everywhere. Accidents, even if they're serious, don't happen often, like a shipwreck or falling out of a carriage. But the real danger comes from other people every day. Prepare yourself for that and pay close attention. There's no danger more common, more constant, or more sneaky than the harm that can come from other people.

Even storms give a warning before they hit; buildings make cracking sounds before they collapse, and smoke shows up before a fire starts. But when people are about to cause harm, it happens suddenly, and the closer it gets, the more it's hidden. You're wrong if you trust the faces of the people you meet. They may look like humans, but they might have the hearts of wild animals. The difference is that wild animals only hurt you when they first meet you;

they don't chase after you later. Animals only attack when they have to, like when they're hungry or scared. But people often enjoy hurting each other.

You should think about the danger that other people can bring so you can understand what your responsibility is as a person. Try not to hurt others in your interactions with them, so you don't get hurt yourself. Be happy for others when they're happy, and feel for them when they're in trouble. Always remember what you should offer and what you should keep to yourself.

And what can you achieve by living this way? You might not always be safe from harm, but at least you can avoid being tricked. As much as you can, turn to philosophy for help. Philosophy will protect you and keep you safer than you were before. People only clash when they're on the same path.

But don't go around bragging about how wise you are because of philosophy. If you use philosophy with arrogance and pride, it can be dangerous. Let philosophy help you fix your own mistakes instead of using it to criticize others. Don't separate yourself from the way most people live, and don't make it your mission to judge things you don't do yourself. A person can be wise without showing off or making enemies. Farewell.

Letter 104 - On care of health and peace of mind

I've gone to my villa at Nomentum. Why, you ask? Not to escape the city, but to shake off a fever that was starting to take hold of me. My doctor kept telling me that my circulation was out of balance, and that this was the start of an illness. So, I ordered my carriage to be ready immediately and insisted on leaving, even though my wife Paulina tried to stop me. I remembered what my teacher Gallio said when he began to feel sick in Achaia—he took a ship right away, saying that the sickness wasn't in his body, but in the place. I told this to my dear Paulina, who always urges me to take care of my health. I know she feels her life is tied to mine, and because I care so much for her, I'm starting to care more for myself too. Even though old age has made me braver in facing many things, I'm beginning to lose that bravery. I realize that inside this old man, there's still a bit of youth that needs care. So, since I can't convince her to worry less about me, she's convincing me to take better care of myself.

Sometimes, we must hold onto life, even when it's hard, for the sake of those we love. A good person shouldn't live only as long as they want, but as long as they should. Anyone who doesn't value their spouse or friend enough to stay alive a little longer for them, anyone who insists on dying just because they want to, is being selfish. The soul should tell itself to stay alive when the needs of loved ones require it, even if it's ready to die. It shows great character to come back to life for the sake of others, and many noble people have done this. Even though old age gives us the chance to be less careful about our health and live more boldly, we should be even more careful if we know it would make someone we care about happy. There's also a lot of joy in this because what's sweeter than being valued by your spouse so much that it makes you value yourself more?

So, you're curious about the result of this journey? As soon as I got away from the city's heavy air and the terrible smells from the kitchens, I started feeling better. How much stronger do you think I felt when I reached my vineyards? I felt so much better that I started to walk regularly. I'm now back to my old self, with no lingering tiredness or sluggishness. I'm starting to work with all my energy again.

But just changing location isn't enough unless your mind is fully in control and can find peace even in the middle of busyness. If you're always looking for new places and chasing after leisure, you'll find something distracting everywhere you go. Socrates is said to have replied when someone complained that they didn't feel better after traveling, "It's your own fault—you traveled with yourself!" Oh, how great it would be if some people could escape from themselves! But as it is, they bring trouble, worry, and fear with them wherever they go. What's the point of traveling from city to city if you're not really escaping your problems? You don't need a different place; you need a different attitude. Maybe you've reached Athens, or maybe Rhodes, but what does it matter where you are? You're bringing your own problems with you.

If you think wealth is a good thing, poverty will make you miserable—and it will be an imagined poverty at that. You might be rich, but because your neighbor is richer, you'll feel poor. If you think holding a high position is a good thing, you'll be upset if someone else is appointed to the job you wanted. Your ambition will drive you mad, making you feel like you're losing if anyone is ahead of you.

Or you might think death is the worst thing ever, even though there's nothing bad about it except the fear before it happens. You'll be terrified, not just by real dangers, but by imagined ones too, constantly tossed around by illusions. What good is it to have traveled to all the towns of Argolis as a fugitive if you're still worried about what might happen? Even peace will make you anxious if your mind is always in panic mode. Once your mind gets used to blind fear, it can't even keep itself safe. Instead of avoiding danger, it runs away from it, which actually puts you in more danger.

You might think it's the worst thing ever to lose someone you love, but that would be just as foolish as crying because the trees in your yard lose their leaves. Treat everything that makes you happy like a thriving plant. Enjoy it while it lasts because just like different plants lose their leaves in different seasons, so too will you lose the things you love. But just as the loss of leaves isn't a big deal because they grow back, the loss of loved ones is also something you can recover from, even though they can't come back to life.

"New friends won't be the same," you might say. No, and neither will you. You change with every day and every hour. You notice how time affects others more easily than you notice how it affects you. Others disappear before your eyes, while you are being slowly taken away from yourself. You won't think about these things or try to heal these wounds. You'll cause yourself more trouble by swinging between hope and despair. If you're wise, you'll mix the two: don't hope without some despair, and don't despair without some hope.

What good has travel ever done for anyone by itself? It doesn't stop you from indulging in pleasures, it doesn't curb your desires, it doesn't control your temper, and it doesn't calm your wild passions. Travel won't give you judgment or correct your mistakes; it only distracts you for a moment with something new, like how children are amused by unfamiliar things. In fact, it might even make your mind more restless because of the constant change. You might leave the place you wanted to see most just as eagerly as you arrived, like a bird flying away as soon as it lands.

Travel can show you the ways of other people. You might see mountains of strange shapes, unfamiliar plains, valleys with flowing springs, or learn about some river with special characteristics. You might notice how the Nile rises in the summer, how the Tigris disappears underground only to reappear later, or how the Maeander river winds back and forth, coming close to itself before continuing its journey. But none of this will make you a better or wiser person.

You should spend your time studying and learning from wise teachers, seeking answers to questions that have been explored but not settled. This is how you can free your mind from its most miserable state and bring it closer to freedom. As long as you don't know what to avoid or seek, what's necessary or unnecessary, what's right or wrong, you won't be traveling—you'll just be wandering.

There's no benefit to this constant movement because you're bringing your troubles with you. I wish they were just following you—then they'd be farther away. But instead, you're carrying them with you, and they're weighing you down. It's not new scenery that the sick person needs, but medicine. If someone breaks a leg or dislocates a joint, they don't travel somewhere else to get better—they call a doctor to fix the problem. So, when your spirit is broken, do you think a change of location will heal it? The problem is too deep to be fixed by a journey.

Travel doesn't make someone a doctor or an orator, and no art can be learned just by being in a certain place. The truth is that wisdom, the greatest of all arts, can't be found just by traveling. No matter how far you go, you won't escape desire, bad temper, or fear. If it were possible, people would have already found that place and moved there. As long as you carry the causes of these problems within you, they'll weigh you down and wear you out as you wander.

Do you wonder why running away doesn't help? The thing you're running from is inside you. So, change yourself—get rid of the burdens on your shoulders and control the desires that need to be removed. Cleanse your soul of all sin. If you want to enjoy your travels, make sure your traveling companion—yourself—is healthy. As long as you're greedy or selfish, greed and selfishness will stick to you. If you're proud and arrogant, those traits will follow you. If you're cruel, cruelty will stay with you. If your companion is an adulterer, they'll stir up your baser passions.

If you want to get rid of your faults, leave behind the things that cause them. The miser, the swindler, the bully, the cheat—they are all inside you and will do you harm just by being there.

So, change your company: live with people like Cato, Laelius, and Tubero. Or, if you like the Greeks, spend time with Socrates and Zeno. Socrates will show you how to die if necessary, and Zeno will show you how to die before it's necessary. Spend time with Chrysippus and Posidonius—they will teach you about earthly and heavenly things. They won't just teach you how to speak well, but how to be brave and rise above threats. The only safe harbor from the storms of life is to scorn the future, stand firm, and be ready to face whatever Fortune throws at you, without hiding or running away.

Nature has given us a brave spirit. Just as she has given some animals ferocity, others cunning, and others fear, she has given us a spirit that pushes us to seek a life of great honor, not just security.

This spirit is like the soul of the universe—it follows and imitates it as much as our mortal steps allow. It drives us forward, confident of praise and respect. It should be subservient to nothing, finding no task too heavy and nothing too strong to weigh it down.

Things that seem terrible in the dark are often laughable in the daylight. Our poet Vergil said that these terrifying shapes of toil or death are only "dread to look upon"—they seem terrible, but they're not. In these fears, what is there to be afraid of, my dear Lucilius, when we examine them closely? Why should we fear hard work or mortal death? Many people think that things they can't do are impossible, but I think more highly of those people—they could do them, but choose not to. Who has ever tried and found these tasks impossible? To whom did they not seem easier once they were done? The difficulty doesn't come from the task itself but from our lack of confidence.

If you want an example, look at Socrates, a long-suffering old man who endured every hardship and remained undefeated by poverty, the burden of family life, or the toil of military service. He was tested at home, whether by his rough and sharp-tongued wife or by his children who were more like their mother than their father. He lived through wars, tyrannies, and a democracy more cruel than both. The war lasted twenty-seven years, then the state fell to the Thirty Tyrants, many of whom were his personal enemies. In the end, he was condemned on the gravest charges—disturbing the state religion and corrupting the youth. They accused him of teaching young people to defy the gods, the council, and the state. He faced prison and drank poison, but none of these things changed Socrates. He remained calm and unshaken, no matter what happened.

If you want another example, look at Marcus Cato, who faced even greater hostility and more persistent misfortune. But he withstood it all and showed that a brave man can live and die despite Fortune's challenges. His whole life was marked by civil wars and political regimes that led to civil wars. Like Socrates, he stood for liberty in the midst of tyranny. Cato was never swayed by the state's changes—he remained the same in every situation, whether as a praetor, in defeat, under accusation, in his province, on the platform, in the army, or in death. When the republic was in crisis, with Caesar on one side with ten legions and Pompey on the other, Cato alone stood for the Republic.

In this struggle, you could say there were two parties—the people and the wealthy elite. But between them stood only the Republic and Cato. Like Achilles, he scorned and disarmed both factions. He decided that if Caesar won, he would take his own life; if Pompey won, he would go into exile. What was there for him to fear? He had already decided his fate, no matter who won. So, he died by his own choice.

You see that man can endure toil—Cato led an army on foot through the deserts of Africa. You see that man can endure thirst— he marched over sun-baked hills, dragging the remnants of a beaten army with no supplies, and always drank last from the few springs they found. You see that man can despise honor and dishonor—Cato played ball on the day he lost the election. You see that man can be free from fear of those above him—Cato attacked Caesar and Pompey simultaneously when no one else dared oppose either. You see that man can scorn death and exile—Cato chose exile and death for himself while war raged on.

So, if we are willing to cast off the yoke, we can face such terrors with a stout heart. But first and foremost, we must reject pleasures— they make us weak and dependent, causing us to rely too much on Fortune. Second, we must spurn wealth—wealth is the mark of slavery. Abandon gold, silver, and all other burdens that weigh down our homes. If you value freedom, you must value everything else less. Farewell.

Letter 105 - On facing the world with confidence

I will now tell you some things you should keep in mind to live more safely. You should listen to my advice as if I were telling you how to stay healthy at your country home in Ardea.

Think about what makes people harm each other: you will find that it is hope, envy, hatred, fear, and contempt. Of all these, contempt is the least harmful, so much so that many people have used it as a kind of protection. When someone despises you, they might hurt you, but then they move on; and no one keeps trying to harm someone they look down on. Even in battle, fallen soldiers are ignored: people fight with those who stand up and resist.

You can avoid making wicked people envious as long as you don't have anything that can stir up their evil desires, and as long as you don't own anything that stands out. People even desire small things if they catch attention or are rare.

You can escape envy if you don't push yourself into the public eye, if you don't show off what you have, and if you learn how to enjoy things privately. Hatred comes either from clashing with others, which you can avoid by not provoking anyone, or it is undeserved, which common sense will help you avoid. But still, it has been dangerous for many; some people have been hated even without having an enemy.

To avoid being feared, a modest fortune and a gentle nature will make sure of that; people should know that you are the kind of person who can be offended without it being dangerous to them, and your reconciliation should be easy and certain. Moreover, it's as troubling to be feared at home as it is abroad; it's as bad to be feared by a servant as by a gentleman. Everyone has enough strength to do you some harm. Besides, the person who is feared also fears others; no one has ever been able to inspire fear and live in peace of mind.

Contempt is the last thing to discuss. The person who has made contempt a part of their personality, who is despised because they choose to be despised and not because they have to be despised, has control over contempt. Any problems with this can be lessened by doing honorable activities and making friends with influential people; with these people, it will benefit you to form connections but not to become entangled, so that the solution doesn't end up costing more than the problem.

Nothing, however, will help you as much as staying quiet—talking very little with others, and as much as possible with yourself. There is something about conversation, a subtle and persuasive quality, which, like drunkenness or love, draws secrets out of us. No one will keep to themselves what they hear. No one will tell only as much as they were told. And the person who spreads tales will also name names. Everyone has someone they trust with exactly what was trusted to them. Even if they limit their own talkativeness and are content with one listener, they will soon spread the secret far and wide if what was a secret shortly before becomes common talk.

The most important thing for peace of mind is never to do wrong. Those who lack self-control live disturbed and chaotic lives; their crimes are balanced by their fears, and they are never at ease. They tremble after committing a deed, and they feel embarrassed; their consciences won't allow them to focus on other matters, and they are always forced to answer for what they've done. Whoever expects punishment, receives it, but whoever deserves it, expects it.

When someone has a guilty conscience, something may bring them safety, but nothing can bring them peace; they imagine that, even if they're not caught now, they might be caught soon. Their sleep is troubled; when they speak of someone else's crime, they think about their own, which seems to them not fully erased or hidden enough. A wrongdoer might sometimes be lucky enough to escape notice, but they can never be sure they will remain unnoticed. Farewell.

Letter 106 - On the corporeality of virtue

I was slow to answer your letter, but not because I was too busy. Don't believe that excuse; I have free time, and so does anyone who wants to be free. No one is forced to be busy. People get involved in things by choice and then convince themselves that being busy means they are happy. So, why didn't I answer your letter sooner? The topic you asked about was something I was already working on for my book.

I am planning to cover all of moral philosophy and address all the problems related to it. I wasn't sure whether to make you wait until I got to that part of my book or to give you an answer out of order. But I decided it was kinder not to make you wait, especially since you came from so far away. So, I'm going to take this topic out of the usual order and send you the answer right away, along with anything else related to similar questions.

Do you want to know what those are? They are questions where the knowledge is more interesting than useful, like your question about whether the good is physical. The good is something that acts because it benefits us, and anything that acts is physical. The good influences the mind and, in a way, shapes and connects with what is essential to the body. The good things of the body are physical, so the good things of the soul must be physical too, because the soul is also physical.

Therefore, a person's good must be physical since a person is physical. I would be very mistaken if the things that support a person and keep them healthy aren't physical, so their good is also physical. I'm sure you don't doubt that emotions are physical things, like anger, love, and sternness, because they change our facial expressions, wrinkle our foreheads, relax our faces, make us blush, or drain the blood from our faces. What else could cause such obvious physical signs except something physical?

And if emotions are physical, so are the diseases of the spirit, like greed, cruelty, and all the faults that harden in our souls until they become incurable. Therefore, evil is also physical, along with all its branches, like spite, hatred, and pride. And so are the good things, first because they are the opposite of the bad, and second because they show the same signs. Don't you see how bravery makes the eyes shine? How prudence leads to focus? How respect brings moderation and calmness? How joy creates peace? How sternness makes us stiff? How gentleness relaxes us? These qualities are physical because they change our bodies and have power over them.

All the virtues I mentioned are good things, and so are their effects. Do you doubt that anything that can touch is physical? Nothing but something physical can touch or be touched, as Lucretius says. Moreover, the changes I mentioned couldn't affect the body without touching it. So, they must be physical.

Furthermore, anything that has the power to move, force, restrain, or control is physical. Think about it! Doesn't fear hold us back? Doesn't boldness push us forward? Doesn't bravery give us momentum? Doesn't restraint pull us back? Doesn't joy lift our spirits? Doesn't sadness bring us down? In short, everything we do is driven by either wickedness or virtue. Only something physical can control or strongly affect another physical thing. The good of the body is physical, and a person's good is related to their bodily good, so it must be physical.

Now that I've answered your question, I know you might say, "What a trivial game this is!" We dull our sharp minds with these unnecessary pursuits; they make us clever but not good. Wisdom is a simpler thing than that; in fact, it's better to use our learning to improve our minds rather than wasting philosophy, just like we waste other efforts on unnecessary things. Just as we suffer from excess in all things, we also suffer from excess in learning; we end up studying not for life, but for the classroom. Farewell.

Letter 107 - On obedience to the universal will

Where is that common sense of yours? Where is that skill in examining things? Where is that greatness of soul? Are you really letting yourself be troubled by something so small? Your slaves took advantage of your being busy and ran away. Well, if your friends deceived you (for we might as well call them that, even if it's a name we mistakenly gave them), then yes, your affairs would be lacking something. But as it stands, you just lack people who were hindering your efforts and who saw you as a burden to those around you.

None of these things should be surprising or unexpected. It's as silly to be upset by such events as it is to complain about getting splashed with mud in the street. Life is like a bathhouse, a crowd, or a journey: sometimes things will be thrown at you, and sometimes you'll get hit by accident. Life isn't a gentle affair. You've embarked on a long journey; you're bound to slip, bump into things, fall, get tired, and cry out, "Oh, I wish I were dead!" – which is really just a way of lying to yourself. Along the way, you'll leave some friends behind, bury others, and face fears. It's through these stumbles that you must continue on this difficult journey.

Does someone wish to die? Let the mind be prepared for anything; let it understand that it has reached the heights where danger strikes. Let it know it has arrived in a place where sorrow, worry, sickness, and old age reside. These are the companions you must spend your days with. You can't avoid them, but you can learn to disregard them. And you will, if you often think ahead and prepare for what's to come.

Everyone faces danger more bravely if they've prepared for it ahead of time, and they can withstand even hardships if they've practiced dealing with them. But those who are unprepared get scared even by the smallest things. We need to make sure that nothing surprises us. And since things seem worse when they're unfamiliar, constant reflection will give you the power to stay calm, no matter what happens.

"My slaves have run away from me!" Yes, and others have been robbed, blackmailed, killed, betrayed, trampled, poisoned, or slandered; no matter what trouble you mention, it has happened to many people. There are many kinds of problems that can hit us. Some are already in us, some are coming at us right now, and some that were meant for others may still touch us.

We shouldn't be surprised by any condition we're born into or by anything that happens to us, because it's all part of the same human experience. We should remember that even those who escape certain hardships could have faced them. And fairness doesn't mean everyone experiences the same things, but that the same rules apply to all. Make sure your mind understands this fairness; we should accept without complaint the burdens of our mortality.

Winter brings cold weather, and we must shiver. Summer returns with heat, and we must sweat. Unusual weather can make us sick, and we must deal with illness. In certain places, we might encounter wild animals or people who are more dangerous than animals. Floods or fires may cause us loss. We can't change this order of things, but what we can do is strengthen our hearts, becoming brave enough to endure whatever chance brings, and live in harmony with Nature.

Nature manages this world we live in with her changing seasons: clear skies follow clouds; after calm, there is a storm; the winds take turns; day follows night; some stars rise while others set. Eternity is made up of opposites.

Our souls must adjust to this law, follow it, and obey it. Whatever happens, accept that it was bound to happen, and don't be angry at Nature. What you can't change, it's best to endure and to follow the God who guides everything without complaining, for it's a bad soldier who grumbles while following his leader.

For this reason, we should welcome our duties with energy and determination, and never stop following the natural course of this beautiful universe, where all our future challenges are intertwined. Let us speak to Jupiter, the ruler of this world, as Cleanthes did in his famous lines, which I'll now translate into Latin, following Cicero's example. If you like them, use them; if not, remember I'm just following Cicero's practice:

"Lead me, O Master of the lofty heavens,
My Father, wherever you wish.
I shall not hesitate, but obey quickly.
And even if I wouldn't, I would go and suffer,
In sin and sorrow, what I might have done
In noble virtue. Yes, the willing soul
Fate leads, but the unwilling drags along."

Let us live and speak in this way; let Fate find us ready and alert. Here is your great soul – the person who has surrendered to Fate; on the other hand, a weak and degenerate person fights against the order of the universe and would rather change the gods than change himself. Farewell.

Letter 108 - On the approaches to philosophy

The topic you're asking about is one of those where we seek knowledge just for the sake of knowing. However, since you're in such a rush to learn, you don't want to wait for the books I'm preparing for you, which cover all of moral philosophy.

I'll send you the books soon, but before that, I want to write to you about how this eagerness to learn, which I see in you, should be managed, so it doesn't become overwhelming. You shouldn't gather knowledge randomly or try to take it all in at once; it's better to learn piece by piece. The burden should match your strength, and you shouldn't take on more than you can handle. Absorb not everything you wish, but only what you can hold. If your mind is strong, it will be able to hold more as you grow.

I remember Attalus giving me this advice when I was always attending his classes, eager to learn, being the first to arrive and the last to leave. Even as he walked around, I would ask him different questions because he was always available to his students. He would say, "Both teacher and student should have the same goal – the teacher to guide and the student to improve."

When someone studies with a philosopher, they should leave with something good every day; they should go home each day a little better or at least on the path to becoming better. And they will, because philosophy helps not just those who study it but also those who are around it. Just like someone who walks in the sun will get sunburned, or someone who spends time in a perfumer's shop will carry the scent with them, anyone who follows a philosopher will gain something useful, even if they aren't trying very hard. But there's a difference between not trying hard and completely resisting.

You might ask, "Don't we know people who have studied under a philosopher for years and haven't gained any wisdom?" Yes, of course. Some people attend lectures without really wanting to learn, just like some go to the theater to enjoy a performance, not to learn anything. These people treat the philosopher's lecture room as just a place to pass the time. They don't go there to get rid of their faults or to find a rule to live by; they just want to enjoy listening.

Some even bring notebooks, but not to write down the ideas, only the words, so they can repeat them later to others without really understanding. Some people get excited by fancy words and change their mood to match the speaker's, just like those who get worked up by music. But a true listener is moved by the beauty of the ideas, not by empty words. When someone speaks boldly against death or Fortune, we are inspired to act on what we've heard. People are influenced by these words and want to become what they are told to be, as long as the inspiration lasts and they aren't discouraged by others.

It's easy to inspire someone to want to be good because nature has planted the seeds of virtue in all of us. We're all born with the potential for good, so when something stirs that potential, it's like freeing it from chains. Haven't you noticed how people in a theater cheer when they hear something true and universally understood?

The poor lack much; the greedy man lacks everything. A greedy person helps no one, and harms himself the most. Even a miser, the most selfish person, will clap and cheer when he hears his own vices condemned. How much more powerful it is when a philosopher speaks, mixing verses with wise advice to make the ideas stick better. Cleanthes used to say that just as our breath sounds louder when it passes through a trumpet, poetry makes ideas clearer. The same words are often ignored in prose but hit us harder when they're in verse.

We often talk about despising money, giving long speeches to convince people that true wealth is in the mind, not in the bank, and that the person who is happy with little is truly rich. But our minds are more moved when we hear a verse like, "He needs but little who desires but little," or, "He has his wish, whose wish includes only what is enough." When we hear these words, we are led to admit the truth. Even those who think nothing is enough are moved by these words and swear to hate money forever. When you see them feeling this way, keep encouraging them, pushing them towards this duty without clever tricks or complicated arguments. Preach against greed and luxury; when you see that you've made an impression, push even harder. You can't imagine how much progress you can make with this kind of talk when you truly care about helping your listeners.

When the mind is young, it's easier to be drawn to what's right and honorable; truth, if presented well, can strongly influence those who are still open to learning. When I used to listen to Attalus denouncing sin, error, and life's evils, I often felt sorry for humanity and saw Attalus as a noble and majestic figure, above mere mortals. He called himself a king, but I thought he was more than a king because he could judge kings.

When he praised poverty and showed how everything beyond our basic needs is a useless burden, I often wanted to leave his lecture room a poor man. Whenever he criticized our pleasure-seeking lives and praised personal purity, moderation in diet, and a mind free from unnecessary pleasures, I felt like limiting my food and drink. Some of these habits have stayed with me, Lucilius, because I made great resolutions in my life. Later, when I returned to being a citizen, I kept some of these good habits. That's why I've given up oysters and mushrooms forever since they aren't really food but just things to make an already full stomach eat more.

That's why I've avoided perfumes all my life because the best scent is no scent at all. That's why I've never gotten used to wine. That's why I've avoided the bath, believing that to sweat the body into thinness is both useless and effeminate. Other resolutions have been broken, but even then, I've kept them in a way that's almost like abstinence; maybe it's even harder because it's easier to give something up completely than to use it with restraint.

Since I've started explaining how much stronger my desire was to learn philosophy in my youth compared to now, I'll tell you how passionate Pythagoras made me. Sotion used to tell me why Pythagoras and later Sextius avoided eating animal food. Each had different reasons, but both were noble. Sextius believed that humans had enough food without eating meat and that cruelty was encouraged by killing animals for pleasure. He also thought that a varied diet was unhealthy and unnatural.

Pythagoras, on the other hand, believed that all living things are connected and that souls move from one body to another. If we believe him, no soul ever truly dies but only changes bodies. We might wonder when and how souls return to human form after passing through different creatures, but in the meantime, Pythagoras made people afraid of killing, as they might unknowingly harm the soul of a loved one living in an animal's body.

When Sotion explained this idea, he would add, "You don't believe that souls move from one body to another and that death is just a change of home? You don't believe that the soul of a man could be in a wild animal or a fish? You don't believe that nothing is destroyed, only changes where it lives? Great men have believed this. So while you hold your own opinion, keep this idea in your mind. If it's true, it's noble not to eat meat; if it's false, it's still wise. What harm does it do to believe this? I'm only asking you to give up food that lions and vultures eat."

I was so influenced by this teaching that I stopped eating animal food; after a year, it became as enjoyable as it was easy. I even started to feel my mind was sharper, though I'm not sure if it really was. You might ask why I gave up this practice. Well, I was young during the early days of Tiberius Caesar's reign. At that time, some foreign religions were being introduced, and avoiding certain animal foods was seen as part of these new cults. So, at my father's request, who wasn't afraid of being accused but hated philosophy, I went back to my old eating habits; and it wasn't hard to convince me to eat more comfortably.

Attalus used to recommend a hard pillow that wouldn't sink under your head; now, even in my old age, I use one so firm that it leaves no impression. I've shared all this to show how enthusiastic beginners can be about high ideals if someone encourages them and keeps their passion alive. Mistakes happen because some teachers focus on teaching how to debate rather than how to live; mistakes also happen because students come to learn not for wisdom but for cleverness. This is how the study of wisdom has become the study of words.

It really matters what your goal is when you approach a subject. If someone is studying literature and is reading Vergil, they don't focus on the deep meaning of "Time flies away, and cannot be restored." Instead of realizing that time moves quickly and we should act before it's too late, they just note how often Vergil uses the word "flies."

The best days of human life are the first to pass; disease and old age follow, and hard work until death takes us all. A philosopher would reflect on how fast time goes and how our best days are taken away first. Why do we hesitate to act so we can keep up with time? The best times go first, and the bad ones take their place.

Just as the purest wine rises to the top, and the thick dregs settle at the bottom, in human life, the best days are taken first, and the worst are left.

Shall we let others enjoy the best days while we are left with the worst? Keep this thought close to your heart: "Each best day of our short life flies by first." Why are these days the best? Because what's to come is uncertain. Why are these days the best? Because when we are young, we can learn and mold our minds to better purposes. This is the time for work, for study, and for strengthening our bodies with useful effort. What remains after youth is slower and less spirited, closer to the end.

Let us therefore strive with all our energy, avoiding distractions along the way. Let us keep our focus, so that we don't realize too late how quickly time is passing, a speed we cannot slow down. Every day that comes should be welcomed as the best and made our own.

We must catch what is slipping away. Someone who looks at these lines with a scholar's eye might miss the deep meaning of time's swiftness and instead focus on how Vergil often pairs disease and old age. And indeed, it's right to do so because old age is a sickness that cannot be cured.

But as I reflect on these thoughts, I remember that even in the same meadow, different animals find different things: the cow grazes, the dog hunts the hare, and the stork seeks out the lizard. When a philosopher opens Cicero's book On the State, he might be struck by how much is said against justice. A philologist, however, might notice details like the fact that there were two Roman kings—one without a father and one without a mother. The philologist will also observe that the official we call a dictator was originally called magister populi, as shown by the ancient records.

The scholar might even note that Romulus met his end during an eclipse and that there was an appeal to the people even during the time of the kings. These different observations show that everyone takes what they seek from the same source. The philosopher looks for wisdom, while the philologist and scholar seek linguistic or historical details.

But I advise that all study of philosophy and reading should be aimed at living a happy life. We shouldn't focus on obscure or complex words or fancy figures of speech, but rather on teachings that help us live better lives—words of courage and spirit that can be immediately turned into actions. We should learn them so well that words become deeds.

I believe that no one has harmed humanity more than those who treat philosophy as a trade, living in a way that contradicts their teachings. Those who fail to live up to the ideals they promote only show that their training is useless. A teacher like that can help no more than a seasick pilot in a storm. He must hold the tiller when the waves are tossing the ship; he must struggle with the sea, furling the sails when the storm rages. What good is a frightened and vomiting steersman to me? And how much greater, do you think, is the storm of life than any storm at sea! We must steer our lives, not just talk about it.

All the words these false teachers juggle before a crowd belong to others. They've been spoken by Plato, Zeno, Chrysippus, Posidonius, and a whole host of excellent Stoics. But I will show you how men can prove their words to be their own: by doing what they talk about.

Since I've shared this message with you, I'll now satisfy your craving for more and save a full response to your question for another letter. That way, you won't approach a difficult topic with a tired mind, but with full attention and care. Farewell.

Letter 109 - On the fellowship of wise men

You wanted to know if a wise person can help another wise person. We say that a wise person has everything they need and has reached perfection, so how could anyone help someone who already has everything?

Good people help each other because they practice their virtues together and keep their wisdom strong. Each one needs someone to compare ideas with. Just like skilled wrestlers need practice to stay strong, or a musician is inspired by another skilled musician, a wise person needs to keep their virtues active. They encourage themselves to do things, and another wise person can also encourage them.

How can a wise person help another wise person? They can inspire them and show them opportunities to do good things. They can also share their ideas and what they have learned. Even a wise person always has something new to discover, something that challenges their mind.

Evil people harm each other by stirring up anger, approving of bad behavior, and praising wrong pleasures. Bad people are at their worst when their faults mix together and their wickedness grows. On the other hand, good people help each other. How? Because they bring joy to each other, strengthen each other's faith, and find peace in their shared calmness. They also share knowledge because a wise person doesn't know everything. Even if they did know everything, another person might find shortcuts or better ways to understand things.

The wise help each other not just because they are strong, but because the other person is also strong. Yes, a wise person can grow on their own, but even someone running well can be helped by someone cheering them on.

Some might say, "The wise person doesn't really help another wise person; they only help themselves." But that's like saying sweetness isn't in the honey because it's the person eating it who tastes the sweetness. Both people need to be in good health for one to help and the other to be helped.

They might also say, "When something is as hot as it can get, adding more heat doesn't help; and when someone has the Supreme Good, they don't need help." But I say that when something is at its hottest, it needs to maintain that heat. And if someone objects that heat maintains itself, I'd say that's different from the help people give each other. Heat is just one thing, but help comes in many forms. Heat doesn't need more heat to stay hot, but a wise person needs others to keep their wisdom active and to share their goodness.

There's also a special kind of friendship among all virtues. When someone loves the virtues of another and shows their own virtues to be loved, they are helping each other. Similar things bring joy, especially when they are good and when people know they are appreciated by others. Also, only a wise person can inspire another wise person in a smart way, just as only a person can reason with another person. So, just as reason is needed to inspire reason, perfect reason is needed to inspire perfect reason.

Some say that we are helped even by people who give us things that aren't necessary, like money, influence, or security. If we think like this, then even the most foolish person could help a wise person. But true help means guiding the soul in line with Nature, both by the excellence of the helper and the excellence of the one being helped. And this benefits the helper too. By training another's excellence, a person also trains their own.

Even if we don't talk about the greatest goods, wise people can still help each other. Just discovering another wise person is a good thing because everything good is naturally dear to a good person, and that's why we feel connected to another good person just as we feel connected to ourselves.

Now, let me move on to another point to support my argument. Some people ask if a wise person will consider other opinions or seek advice from others. They will need to do this when dealing with practical matters, like duties at home or in the state—things that are part of mortal life. They will need outside advice, just like a doctor, a pilot, a lawyer, or someone pleading a case needs advice. That's why the wise sometimes help each other because they persuade each other.

In these important matters, which I've called divine, a wise person can also be helpful by discussing good things and sharing thoughts and ideas. It's natural to care for our friends and to celebrate their success as if it were our own. If we don't do this, even virtue, which grows strong by practicing our understanding, won't stay with us. Virtue tells us to manage the present well, to plan for the future, to think carefully, and to use our minds. A person who consults a friend can more easily focus and think things through.

So, they will look for either the perfect wise person or someone close to perfection. The perfect wise person will help us with good, practical advice. It's said that people see others' problems more clearly than their own. This happens because of flaws in character—people blinded by self-love and fear often can't see what's useful. A person is more likely to be wise when they are calm and free from fear. Still, even wise people sometimes see others' situations more clearly than their own.

Also, a wise person working with another wise person will confirm the truth of the old saying, "Always desiring and always refusing the same things." It's a noble result when they work together with equal effort.

I've answered your question, though it's part of a topic I cover in my writings on Moral Philosophy. Think about this, as I often remind you: there's nothing in these topics for us except mental exercise. I keep coming back to the thought: "What good does this do me? Make me braver, more just, more self-controlled! I don't yet have the chance to use my training; I still need the doctor. Why ask me for useless knowledge? You promised great things; now test me, watch me! You assured me I wouldn't be afraid even if swords were flashing around me, or if a blade were at my throat; you assured me I'd be calm even if fires were burning around me, or if a sudden storm tossed my ship across the sea. Now give me the training I need so I can scorn pleasure and fame. After that, you can teach me to solve complex problems, to settle doubts, to see clearly what's unclear. Teach me now what I really need to know!" Farewell.

Letter 110 - On true and false riches

I'm writing to you from my villa at Nomentum, and I want you to keep a strong and healthy spirit. This is the best way to gain the blessing of the gods, because when you are good to yourself, the gods will be good to you too. For now, forget the idea that each of us has a personal god who watches over us—a lower-ranked god like the ones Ovid calls "plebeian gods." Even though I suggest forgetting this idea, remember that our ancestors, who believed in such things, became Stoics and thought that every person had a Genius or a Juno as their personal guide. Later, we can talk about whether the gods really have time to care about each of us individually. For now, just know that whether we have special guardians or are left to Fortune, the worst curse you can wish on someone is that they are in conflict with themselves.

You don't need to ask the gods to be against someone you think deserves punishment; I believe the gods are already against such people, even if it seems like they are helping them. Look closely at how things really are, not just how people say they are, and you'll see that problems often help us more than they hurt us. How many times has something bad led to happiness? And how often have things we were thankful for led us into danger, lifting us up just to make us fall harder? But even falling isn't so bad if you think about the end, after which nature doesn't lower anyone any further. The ultimate limit is near; the point where the rich man falls and the poor man is set free is close to us. We make these limits longer with our hopes and fears.

If you're wise, measure everything by what is normal for humans, and keep both your happiness and fears under control. It's also a good idea not to celebrate too long, so you won't end up fearing for too long. But why stop here? There's no reason to fear anything. All the things that make us anxious and worried are just empty things. None of us has really tried to find out the truth; we've just passed our fears on to each other. No one has dared to face what scared them and understand their fear—and see the good behind it. That's why lies and false ideas still have power—they haven't been challenged.

Let's make it worth our time to really look at things; then it will become clear how short-lived, uncertain, and harmless the things we fear are. The disturbance in our minds is like what Lucretius described: like kids who are scared of the dark, adults are afraid even in broad daylight. But, Lucretius, we are even more foolish than kids because we "feel fear in the light of day." But you were wrong in one thing, Lucretius—we don't fear in daylight; we've turned everything into darkness. We don't see what harms us or what benefits us. We stumble through life, not stopping or being more careful because of this. But it's clear how foolish it is to rush ahead in the dark. In fact, we're so eager that we keep rushing forward, even when we don't know where we're going, yet we keep pushing on wildly.

However, light can start to shine if we're willing to see it. But this can only happen if we learn about divine and human things, if we really soak ourselves in it, if we go over the same principles, even when we understand them and keep applying them, if we investigate what is truly good, what is truly evil, and what has wrongly been labeled as such. And finally, if we explore what is honorable and what is shameful, and the idea of Providence. The human mind isn't limited by these things; it can explore beyond the universe—its beginning, its end, and the destruction that all nature is quickly heading toward. We've taken our minds away from thinking about these divine things and dragged them into lowly tasks, making them slaves to greed, turning away from the universe to follow the commands of masters who make us dig beneath the earth to find evil—unhappy with what was freely given to us.

Now, God, who is the Father of all of us, has given us what is good, without us even looking for it, and he gave it to us freely. But what would harm us, he buried deep in the earth. We can only blame ourselves; we've uncovered the materials for our destruction, against Nature's will, which hid them from us. We've tied our minds to pleasure, which is the source of all evil; we've surrendered to selfishness and the desire for reputation, and other pointless and useless goals.

So, what am I telling you to do now? Nothing new—we aren't trying to find cures for new problems. First of all, see clearly what is necessary and what isn't. What is necessary is easy to find; what isn't necessary has to be hunted down with great effort. But don't be too proud if you can ignore fancy couches and expensive furniture. What virtue is there in ignoring useless things? Be proud of yourself only when you've learned to ignore even the necessities. You aren't doing anything great if you can live without royal luxuries or don't crave enormous roasted boars or flamingo tongues or other ridiculous luxuries. I'll only admire you when you can despise even ordinary bread, when you can believe that grass grows just as much for humans as it does for cattle, and when you realize that food from treetops can fill your belly—which we stuff with valuable things as if it could keep what it receives. We should fill our stomachs without being too picky. What does it matter what the stomach gets, since it must lose whatever it has received?

You enjoy carefully prepared delicacies from land and sea; some are better when fresh, others when they've been fed and fattened until they can hardly hold their own fat. You like the subtle flavors of these dishes. But I assure you, once these carefully chosen and seasoned dishes enter the belly, they'll all rot the same way. Want to despise the pleasures of eating? Then think about its result! I remember some words of Attalus that everyone liked: "Riches fooled me for a long time. I used to be dazzled by their shine. I thought their hidden power matched their visible show. But once, at an elaborate feast, I saw silver and gold work worth as much as a whole city's wealth, and tapestries more valuable than gold or silver—not just from beyond our borders but from enemy lands. On one side were well-trained and beautiful slave boys; on the other, crowds of slave women and all the other things a rich and powerful empire could offer. What is this, I thought, but a stirring up of man's desires, which provoke greed? What does all this wealth mean? Did we come together just to learn what greed is? I left that place with less desire than when I entered. I came to despise riches, not because they're useless, but because they're small and petty. Have you noticed how, in just a few hours, that slow-moving and carefully planned event was over? Has something that couldn't fill up a whole day filled up our whole life?

"I also thought: these riches seemed as useless to their owners as they were to the onlookers. So I tell myself, whenever a show like that dazzles me, whenever I see a splendid palace with well-groomed servants and beautiful litter bearers: Why be amazed? It's all just for show; these things are displayed, not owned. While they please, they pass away. Turn instead to true riches. Learn to be content with little, and boldly say: 'We have water, we have porridge; let us compete in happiness with Jupiter himself.' And why not make this challenge even without porridge and water? It's wrong to make a happy life depend on silver and gold, and just as wrong to make it depend on water and porridge. But someone might say, 'What could I do without such things?' Do you ask what the cure for want is? It's making hunger satisfy hunger. If all else is equal, what difference does it make if the things that make you a slave are small or large? How little does it matter what Fortune can take from you? Even your porridge and water could fall under someone else's control. And remember, freedom comes not to the person over whom Fortune has little power, but to the person over whom she has no power at all. This is what I mean: you must crave nothing if you want to compete with Jupiter, for Jupiter craves nothing."

This is what Attalus told us. If you think about these things often, you'll strive not to seem happy but to be happy, and also to seem happy to yourself rather than to others. Farewell.

Letter 111 - On the vanity of mental gymnastics

You've asked me to find a Latin word for the Greek term sophismata. Many people have tried to define it, but no single name has stuck. This is understandable since the concept itself hasn't been widely accepted by us, and the name has faced some resistance. However, the word Cicero used seems to me the most fitting; he called them cavillationes.

If a person gives themselves over to these mental exercises, they can weave many clever and tricky arguments, but they won't make any progress toward real living. They won't become braver, more self-controlled, or nobler in spirit by doing this. On the other hand, someone who practices philosophy to heal their own soul becomes noble, full of confidence, unbeatable, and greater the closer you get to them.

This effect is similar to high mountains, which don't look as tall from a distance, but when you get close, you can clearly see how high the peaks are. This is how a true philosopher is, my dear Lucilius—true not because of tricks, but because of actions. He stands in a high place, worthy of admiration, lofty, and truly great. He doesn't stretch himself or stand on his tiptoes like those who try to appear taller than they are by deceit. He is content with his own greatness.

And why wouldn't he be content when he has grown so tall that Fortune can't reach him? He is above earthly things, steady and equal to himself in all situations, whether life flows smoothly or he is tossed around in troubled and desperate seas. But this kind of steadiness can't be gained through the kind of hair-splitting I mentioned earlier.

The mind might play with these exercises, but it doesn't gain anything from them; in fact, it just drags philosophy down from its heights to the ground level.

I wouldn't forbid you from practicing these exercises now and then, but only when you want to do nothing else. The worst thing about these exercises is that they can become attractive in a self-made way, occupying and holding the mind with their subtlety. But we have important matters that deserve our attention, and a whole lifetime doesn't seem enough to learn even the single principle of despising life.

"What? Didn't you mean 'control' instead of 'despise'?" No, "controlling" is the second step; because no one can control their life correctly unless they first learn to despise it. Farewell.

Letter 112 - On reforming hardened sinners

I am really eager for your friend to be shaped and trained, just like you want. But he is in a very tough spot because he has become set in his ways, or even worse, he's become really weak because of bad habits that he's had for a long time. Let me give you an example from something I know well. Not every vine can be grafted; if the vine is old and decayed, or if it is weak and thin, the vine either won't accept the new part, or it won't be able to grow it and make it a part of itself. The vine also might not adjust to the qualities and nature of the new part that's been added. That's why we usually cut off the vine above the ground. If it doesn't work the first time, we can try again and do the grafting below the ground on the second try.

Now, the person you wrote to me about has no strength because he has pampered himself with bad habits. He has become both weak and stubborn at the same time. He cannot accept reason, nor can he nurture it. But you might say, "He wants to learn and change on his own." Don't believe him. I don't mean that he is lying to you; he really thinks he wants to change. But his spoiled lifestyle has upset him for now, but soon he'll get used to it again. You might also say, "He's unhappy with the way he's been living." That could be true, but who isn't? People often both love and hate their bad habits at the same time. We should wait to judge him until he has shown us that he truly hates his luxurious lifestyle. Right now, he and luxury are just not getting along. Goodbye.

Letter 113 - On the vitality of the soul and its attributes

You want me to write my opinion about this question that our school has debated—whether justice, courage, foresight, and other virtues are living things. By focusing on details like this, my dear Lucilius, some people think that we waste our time sharpening our minds on useless ideas and that our discussions don't really help anyone. But I will do as you ask and explain the topic as our school views it. For myself, I admit I have a different belief: I think there are some topics better suited for people who care about fancy clothes and Greek styles. But I will tell you what the old philosophers believed and what ideas they debated.

People agree that the soul is a living thing because it is what makes us alive, and because living things get their name from the soul. Virtue is just the soul in a certain state, so it must also be a living thing. Virtue is active, and no action can happen without some kind of impulse. And if something has impulse, it must be a living thing, because only living things have impulses. But some people might say, "If virtue is a living thing, then virtue itself must have virtue." Of course, it has its own virtue! Just as a wise person does everything because of virtue, virtue does everything because of itself. "In that case," they might say, "all arts, thoughts, and everything the mind understands must also be living things. That means many thousands of living things live inside a person's tiny heart, and that each of us is made up of, or at least contains, many living beings."

Are you stuck on how to answer that? Each of these could be a living thing, but they wouldn't be many separate living things. And why is that? I'll explain if you focus on my words. Each living thing must have a separate substance, but since all these things share a single soul, they can be separate living things without being many. I am a living thing, and I am a person, but you wouldn't say there are two of me. Why? Because if that were true, there would have to be two separate beings. What I mean is that one would have to be separated from the other to make two. But whenever you have something that's made up of many parts but still one whole, it's considered a single thing and is therefore just one.

My soul is a living thing, and so am I, but we are not two separate beings. Why? Because the soul is part of me. It will only be considered a separate thing when it exists on its own. But as long as it's part of something else, it can't be considered different. Why? I'll tell you: because something that is different must be complete and whole by itself. I've already said that I have a different opinion: if you follow this belief, then not only virtues will be living things, but so will their opposite vices, and emotions like anger, fear, grief, and suspicion. The argument could go even further—all opinions and thoughts would also be living things. This doesn't make sense because not everything a person does is necessarily the person themselves.

People might ask, "What is justice?" Justice is a soul that holds itself in a certain way. So, if the soul is a living thing, then justice is a living thing too. But that's not true. Justice is really a state or a kind of power of the soul, and this same soul can change into different forms without becoming a different kind of living thing every time it acts differently. The result of soul-action isn't a living thing. If justice, bravery, and the other virtues were actually alive, would they stop being alive and then start again, or are they always living things?

But virtues can't stop being. So, there would be many, even countless, living things existing in this one soul. But no, they are not many because they are all part of the same thing, being pieces and members of a single whole. If we think of the soul like a many-headed hydra—each head fighting and acting on its own—still, there's not a separate living thing in each head; it's the head of a living thing, and the hydra itself is one single living thing. No one ever thought that the Chimaera had a living lion or a living serpent inside it; these were just parts of the whole Chimaera, and parts aren't living things.

So how can you say that justice is a living thing? People might say, "Justice is active and helpful, and something that acts and helps must have impulse, and something that has impulse is a living thing." That's true, but only if the impulse is its own. But in the case of justice, it's not its own; the impulse comes from the soul. Every living thing stays the way it started until it dies; a person stays a person until they die, a horse stays a horse, and a dog stays a dog. They can't change into anything else. Now, let's say that justice, which is defined as "a soul in a certain state," is a living thing. Let's suppose that's true. Then bravery is also alive, being "a soul in a certain state." But which soul? The one that was just defined as justice? The soul stays within the first being and can't move into another; it must live out its existence where it started.

Besides, there can't be one soul for two living things, much less for many living things. And if justice, bravery, restraint, and all the other virtues are living things, how can they all have one soul? They must have separate souls, or else they are not living things. Several living things can't share one body; even our opponents agree on this. Now, what is the "body" of justice? "The soul," they say. And of bravery? "The soul too." But one body can't belong to two living things.

They might say, "The same soul takes on the form of justice, or bravery, or restraint." This would be possible if bravery disappeared when justice was present, and if restraint disappeared when bravery was present, but as things stand, all the virtues exist at the same time. So how can the separate virtues be living things if there is one single soul that can't create more than one single living thing?

Again, no living thing is part of another living thing. But justice is part of the soul, so justice is not a living thing. It seems like I'm spending time on something that's already agreed upon; we should criticize such an idea rather than debate it. No two living things are exactly the same. Think about the bodies of all creatures: each one has its own color, shape, and size. One of the reasons I marvel at the genius of the Divine Creator is that with all this variety, there is no exact repetition; even things that seem similar are, when compared, different. God created all the countless leaves we see: each one has its own unique pattern. All the many animals: none looks exactly like another—there's always some difference! The Creator aimed to make things different and unequal. But according to your argument, all virtues are equal. Therefore, they are not living things.

Every living thing acts on its own, but virtue doesn't act on its own; it must act along with a person. All living things either have reason, like humans and gods, or are irrational, like animals and cattle. Virtues, in any case, are rational, but they are neither humans nor gods, so they are not living things. Every living thing with reason stays inactive unless it's first stirred by some external impression; then comes the impulse, and finally, the agreement that confirms the impulse. Now, I'll explain what agreement is. Suppose I should take a walk: I do walk, but only after telling myself to do it and agreeing with my own decision. Or suppose I should sit down; I do sit down, but only after the same process. This agreement is not part of virtue.

For example, if we say that prudence is a virtue, how will prudence agree with the idea, "I must take a walk"? Nature doesn't allow this. Prudence looks after the interests of its owner, not its own. Prudence can't walk or sit down. So, it doesn't have the power to agree, and it's not a living thing with reason. But if virtue is a living thing, it is rational. But it's not rational, therefore, it's not a living thing. If virtue is a living thing, and virtue is a Good—then isn't every Good a living thing? It is. Our school believes this.

Now, saving a father's life is a Good; it's also a Good to speak wisely in the senate, and it's a Good to make fair decisions; so, the act of saving a father's life is a living thing, and so is the act of speaking wisely. This argument has become so absurd that you can't help but laugh: wise silence is a Good, and so is a simple dinner; so, silence and dining are living things.

Indeed, I'll never stop amusing myself with this kind of nonsense. If justice and bravery are living things, they must be earthly. But every earthly living thing gets cold, hungry, or thirsty; so, justice gets cold, bravery gets hungry, and kindness needs a drink!

And what next? Should I not ask our honorable opponents what shape these living beings have? Is it like a person, a horse, or a wild animal? If they say it's round, like a god, I'll ask whether greed, luxury, and madness are also round. Because these are "living things" too. If they say these are round as well, I'll even ask whether a modest walk is a living thing; they must admit it, according to their argument, and say that a walk is a living thing, and a round living thing at that!

Now, don't think I'm the first one of our school to have my own opinion instead of following strict rules: Cleanthes and his student Chrysippus couldn't even agree on how to define the act of walking. Cleanthes thought it was the spirit being sent to the feet from the main life force, while Chrysippus believed it was the main life force itself. So why, following the example of Chrysippus himself, shouldn't everyone have their own freedom of thought, and laugh at the idea of so many "living things"—so many that even the universe can't hold them all?

One might say: "The virtues are not many living things, and yet they are living things. Just as one person can be both a poet and an orator, these virtues are living things, but they are not many. The soul is the same; it can be just, prudent, and brave all at the same time, maintaining itself in a certain state towards each virtue."

So, the dispute is settled, and we agree on this: I will admit, for now, that the soul is a living thing, but I deny that the actions of the soul are living beings. Otherwise, all words and verses would be alive; because if wise speech is a Good, and every Good is a living thing, then speech is a living thing. A wise line of poetry is a Good; everything alive is a Good, so the line of poetry is a living thing. And so, "Arms and the man I sing," would be a living thing; but they can't say it's round because it has six feet!

"This whole idea," you might say, "which we are discussing right now, is very confusing." I laugh every time I think that grammatical mistakes, foreign words, and logical arguments are living things, and, like an artist, I imagine what they would look like. Is this what we discuss with serious faces and deep thinking? I can't say now, like Caelius, "What pointless debates!" It's more than that; it's ridiculous. Why don't we discuss something useful and beneficial to ourselves, like how we can achieve virtues, and find the way to reach them?

Teach me, not whether bravery is a living thing, but show me that no living thing can be happy without bravery, that is, unless it has grown strong enough to face dangers and has overcome all the challenges of life by preparing and practicing for them. And what is bravery? It is the unbreakable defense for our human weaknesses; when someone has surrounded themselves with it, they can withstand life's challenges without fear, because they are using their own strength and their own weapons.

At this point, I would quote our philosopher Posidonius: "There are never any times when you should think you are safe just because you have the weapons of Fortune; fight with your own! Fortune does not provide weapons against herself, so men who are ready to fight their enemies are defenseless against Fortune herself."

Alexander the Great, for example, chased and defeated the Persians, the Hyrcanians, the Indians, and all the other nations in the East, even reaching the Ocean. But he himself, after killing one friend or losing another, would lie in the dark, sometimes crying over his crime, and sometimes mourning his loss; he, the conqueror of so many kings and nations, was brought down by anger and grief!

Because he had made it his goal to control everything except his emotions.

Oh, how mistaken are those who want to expand their empires beyond the seas, who think they are most successful when they occupy many provinces with their armies and add new territories to the old! They don't realize the greatest kingdom is as vast as the heavens! Self-Control is the greatest power of all. Let her teach me what a sacred thing justice is, which always looks out for the good of others and seeks nothing for itself except to be used. It should have nothing to do with ambition and fame; it should be satisfied on its own.

Let each person convince themselves of this above all: "I must be just without expecting a reward." And that's not enough; let them also convince themselves of this: "May I take joy in dedicating myself freely to practicing this greatest of virtues." Let all their thoughts be turned as far away as possible from personal gain. You don't need to look for the reward of a just deed; a just deed itself offers an even greater return.

Keep this deeply in mind, which I mentioned a little earlier: it doesn't matter how many people know about your righteousness. Those who want their virtue to be known aren't striving for virtue but for fame. Are you not willing to be just without being famous? In fact, you must often be just and still face disgrace. And then, if you are wise, let well-earned bad reputation be a pleasure. Farewell.

Letter 114 - On style as a mirror of character

You've asked me why, at certain times, people start speaking in a less refined way, and why their thoughts seem to decline into certain bad habits. Sometimes, speech becomes overblown and grand, while at other times, it becomes too delicate, like a soft piece of music. You wonder why bold ideas, sometimes bolder than we could imagine, have been popular, and why at other times, we hear phrases that are disjointed and full of hidden meanings, making us search for more than what was meant to be understood. Or why there were times when people thought it was acceptable to use extravagant metaphors. To answer, let me share a common saying: "A man's speech is just like his life."

Just as a person's actions reveal their character, the way people speak often reflects the general mood of the time. If the morals of society have weakened and people have given in to luxury, then extravagant speech shows that luxury has become popular and accepted, not just an isolated thing. A person's abilities and character can't be completely different. If someone's character is wholesome, disciplined, serious, and restrained, their abilities will also be sound and stable. But if their character deteriorates, their abilities will also suffer. Don't you see that if someone's spirit becomes sluggish, their body moves slowly and without energy? If a man is effeminate, you can tell by the way he walks. A sharp and confident spirit makes the body move quickly, while madness or anger, which is like madness, makes a person rush around.

This affects a person's abilities even more because abilities are deeply connected to the soul. They are shaped by it, follow its commands, and get their rules from it. How Maecenas lived is well-known. We know how he walked, how effeminate he was, and how he liked to show off. He didn't mind if people noticed his flaws. What about his speech? Wasn't it as loose as his unbelted tunic? His habits, his servants, his house, his wife—all of these things were as clearly reflected in his words as in his lifestyle. He could have been a great man if he had followed a straight path, if he had not avoided being understood, and if his speech had not been so loose. His eloquence was like that of a drunken man—twisting, turning, and endlessly rambling.

What could be more inappropriate than phrases like "a stream and a bank covered with long-haired woods"? Or "men plough the channel with boats and, turning up the shallows, leave gardens behind them"? Or "He curls his lady-locks, and sighs like a forest lord who prays with his head bent low"? Or "An unregenerate crew, they search out people at feasts, and attack households with the wine-cup, and, by hope, demand death"? Or "A Genius could hardly bear witness to his own festival"; or "threads of tiny tapers and crackling meal"; or "mothers or wives clothing the hearth"?

Can't you easily imagine that this was the man who always walked through the city in a flowing tunic? Even when he was taking care of the absent emperor's duties, he was always dressed casually when they asked him for the password. Or that this was the man who, as a judge, orator, or at any public event, appeared with his cloak wrapped around his head, leaving only his ears visible, like the millionaire's runaway slaves in a comedy? Or that this was the man who, when the state was in civil war, when the city was in trouble and under martial law, was attended in public by two eunuchs—both of whom were more manly than he was? Or that this was the man who had only one wife, yet was married countless times?

His words, poorly constructed, carelessly thrown together, and arranged in a way that went against common practice, show that the character of their writer was equally strange, unhealthy, and eccentric. Yes, we praise him highly for his kindness; he was sparing with the sword and avoided bloodshed, and he only displayed his power through his loose living. But he ruined this well-deserved praise with his overly fussy style. It's clear that he wasn't truly gentle, but effeminate, as shown by his confusing word order, his reversed expressions, and his surprising thoughts, which often contained something great but became weak in their expression. One might say that success went to his head. This fault is sometimes due to the person, and sometimes to the era.

When prosperity has spread luxury far and wide, people start by paying more attention to their appearance. Then they become obsessed with furniture. Next, they focus on their houses—making them bigger as if they were country homes, making the walls sparkle with marble imported from overseas, decorating the roof with gold to match the brightness of the inlaid floors. After that, they bring their refined taste to the dining table, trying to impress others with novelty and breaking the usual order of dishes, so that courses usually served last are served first, and departing guests eat food that was once served when they arrived.

When the mind gets used to looking down on the ordinary things of life and seeing what was once common as lowly, it starts searching for novelties in speech too. It uses outdated and old-fashioned words, coins new words, or distorts them. Bold and frequent metaphors become a key feature of style, following the latest trend. Some people cut their thoughts short, hoping to impress by leaving the meaning unclear and making the listener doubt their own understanding. Others stretch out their thoughts. Some even approach a fault—because a man must do this if he hopes to create an impressive effect—but actually enjoy the fault for its own sake.

In short, whenever you notice that a degenerate style pleases the critics, you can be sure that character has also strayed from the right path. Just as luxurious banquets and elaborate dress are signs of disease in society, a loose style, if popular, shows that the mind, which is the source of words, has lost its balance. You shouldn't be surprised that corrupt speech is accepted not just by the lower class but also by the more cultured crowd; for they differ only in their clothing, not in their judgments. You may be more surprised that not only the effects of vices, but even the vices themselves, are approved.

It has always been this way: no man's ability has ever been praised without something being forgiven. Show me any famous man; I can tell you what his era forgave him for, and what it purposely overlooked. I can show you many men whose vices didn't harm them, and some who were even helped by their vices. Yes, I will show you people of the highest reputation, held up as models for our admiration; but if you try to correct their errors, you destroy them because their vices are so intertwined with their virtues that they drag the virtues down with them.

Moreover, style has no fixed rules; it changes with the times and is never the same for long. Some orators look back to earlier times for their vocabulary, speaking like they did in the era of the Twelve Tables. For them, Gracchus, Crassus, and Curio are too refined and modern, so they go back to Appius and Coruncanius! On the other hand, some people, in trying to stick only to well-worn and common usages, fall into a boring style. These two groups, in their own ways, are both degenerate; and it's just as faulty to use only fancy, high-sounding, and poetic words while avoiding the familiar and ordinary.

Let's now talk about the arrangement of words. There are many kinds of faults here! Some people prefer abruptness and unevenness in their style, purposely disrupting anything that seems to flow smoothly. They think anything that sounds uneven is strong and manly. Others turn their words into music, so soft and sweet that their style glides along. And what can I say about those who delay their words, making them just barely arrive at the end of a sentence? Or of those who end their sentences in the same soft way, like Cicero, with a gradual and gentle descent, always the same and with the usual rhythm?

The fault isn't just in the structure of the sentences, whether they're too childish, degrading, more daring than modesty allows, too flowery and cloying, or if they end up being empty, achieving only sound and nothing more. Some individual makes these vices fashionable—someone who controls the eloquence of the time; others follow his lead and spread the habit to each other. When Sallust was popular, phrases were abruptly cut off, words ended unexpectedly, and obscure conciseness was considered elegant. L. Arruntius, a man of rare simplicity who wrote a history of the Punic War, was a strong supporter of the Sallust style. In one of Sallust's phrases, he says: "exercitum argento fecit," meaning "he recruited an army with money." Arruntius liked this idea and used the verb "facio" throughout his book. In one passage, he wrote: "fugam nostris fecere"; in another, "Hiero, rex Syracusanorum, bellum fecit"; and in another, "quae audita Panhormitanos dedere Romanis fecere."

I just wanted to give you a taste; his whole book is filled with this kind of writing. What Sallust used occasionally, Arruntius made a frequent habit—and there's a reason: Sallust used the words as they naturally came to him, while Arruntius went out of his way to find them. So you see what happens when you imitate another person's faults. Sallust also used the phrase "aquis hiemantibus," meaning "in the winter waters." Arruntius, in his first book on the Punic War, says "repente hiemavit tempestas," meaning "suddenly a storm wintered." And elsewhere, to describe an unusually cold year, he says, "totus hiemavit annus," meaning "the whole year wintered." And in another passage: "inde sexaginta onerarias leves praeter militem et necessarios nautarum hiemante aquilone misit," meaning "he sent sixty light cargo ships, besides soldiers and necessary sailors, in the winter north wind." He continues to use this metaphor in many passages. In one place, Sallust says: "inter arma civilia aequi bonique famas petiit," meaning "he sought a reputation for fairness and goodness amid civil war"; and Arruntius, in the first book, mentions "there were extensive 'reminders' concerning Regulus."

These and similar faults, which come from imitating another person's style, don't necessarily mean that someone's standards or mind are loose. They are usually personal and unique to the writer, showing their temperament. Just as an angry man will talk angrily, an excitable man will talk in a flustered way, and an effeminate man will speak in a soft and yielding style.

You can see this tendency in people who thin out their beards or closely shave their upper lip while letting the rest of the hair grow, or in those who wear brightly colored cloaks, transparent togas, and never do anything that won't be noticed. They try to attract attention and don't mind being criticized, as long as they get noticed. That was the style of Maecenas and others who strayed from the path, not by accident, but on purpose.

This is the result of deep trouble in the soul. Just like with drinking, the tongue doesn't slip until the mind is overwhelmed and gives in or reveals itself; this intoxication of style—what else can I call it?—only causes trouble when the soul begins to falter. So, I say, take care of your soul because our thoughts, words, dispositions, expressions, and even our walk come from the soul. When the soul is strong and healthy, the style is also vigorous, energetic, and strong; but if the soul loses its balance, everything else falls apart.

If the king is safe, the whole hive will live in harmony; but if the king dies, the bees will revolt. The soul is our king. If it is safe, all the other functions stay on duty and serve with obedience; but even a small imbalance in the soul causes them to waver along with it. When the soul has given in to pleasure, its functions and actions grow weak, and any task comes from a shaky and unstable source.

To continue with this metaphor—our soul is sometimes a king, and at other times a tyrant. The king respects honorable things, watches over the welfare of the body entrusted to him, and doesn't give the body any base or dishonorable commands. But an uncontrolled, passionate, and effeminate soul turns kingship into that most dreadful and detestable thing—tyranny. Then it becomes a victim of uncontrolled emotions, which follow it, feeling satisfied at first, like a crowd made lazy by too much indulgence, which will eventually lead to its downfall, spoiling what it cannot consume.

But when the disease gradually eats away its strength, and luxurious habits penetrate its core, the soul takes pleasure in seeing the limbs that, through its overindulgence, it has made useless. Instead of enjoying its own pleasures, it watches others indulge; it becomes the mediator and witness of passions that it can no longer feel due to self-gratification. The abundance of delights isn't as pleasing to that soul as it is painful because it can no longer swallow all the delicacies of the past through its overworked throat and stomach. It can no longer dance among eunuchs and mistresses, and it becomes sad because much of its happiness is cut off by the body's limitations.

Isn't it madness, Lucilius, that none of us thinks about the fact that we are mortal? Or fragile? Or that we are just one person? Look at our kitchens and the cooks, who bustle around so many fires; do you think all this activity and food preparation is for just one stomach? Look at the old brands of wine and storehouses filled with the vintages of many ages; do you think all that wine, sealed with the names of so many consuls and gathered from so many vineyards, is for just one stomach? Look at how many regions are plowed, and how many thousands of farmers are tilling and digging; do you think all those crops in Sicily and Africa are planted for just one stomach?

We would be more sensible and our desires more reasonable if each of us took stock of ourselves and measured our bodily needs, understanding how little we can consume and for how short a time! But nothing will help you practice moderation more than frequently thinking about how short and uncertain life is here on earth. Whatever you're doing, always remember death. Farewell.

Letter 115 - On the superficial blessings

I wish, my dear Lucilius, that you wouldn't be too concerned about the exact words and how they are arranged. I have more important things for you to focus on. You should think more about what you are writing rather than how you are writing it—and even then, not just for the sake of writing, but so that you truly feel it. When you feel it deeply, it becomes more your own, like stamping your own seal on it.

Whenever you notice writing that is too careful and polished, you can be sure that the mind is also caught up in unimportant things. A truly great person speaks naturally and easily; whatever they say, they speak confidently without having to try too hard. You've seen those young men who are always perfectly groomed, with their beards and hair neatly styled, looking like they've just come out of a shop. You can't expect them to have much strength or substance. Style is like clothing for your thoughts: if it's too trimmed, dyed, or overly treated, it shows that there are flaws in the mind. True elegance isn't about trying too hard.

If we had the chance to look into a good person's soul, oh, what a beautiful, holy, magnificent, gracious, and shining face we would see! It would be glowing with justice and self-control on one side, and with courage and wisdom on the other. And besides these, we would also see thriftiness, moderation, endurance, refinement, kindness, and—though it's hard to believe—love for others, a goodness that is so rare in people. All these qualities would shine brightly in that soul. There, too, we would find thoughtfulness combined with grace, leading to the most excellent greatness of soul, which is the noblest of all virtues. What charm, what authority, and dignity would they add! What a wonderful mix of sweetness and power! No one could call such a face lovable without also calling it worthy of worship.

If someone could see such a face, more exalted and more radiant than anything we usually see, wouldn't they pause in awe, as if struck by a divine presence, and silently pray, saying, "May it be allowed for me to have seen this!"? And then, drawn by the kindness in his expression, wouldn't we bow down and worship? Shouldn't we, after much thought about such a far superior face, more gentle and yet full of life, finally, with reverence and awe, say those famous lines of our poet Vergil: "O maiden, words are weak! Your face is more than mortal, and your voice rings sweeter than any human's. Blessed be you; and whoever you are, relieve our heavy burdens." And such a vision would indeed be a great help and relief to us if we were willing to worship it. But this worship doesn't involve sacrificing fattened bulls, offering gold or silver, or pouring money into a temple treasury; rather, it involves having a will that is respectful and upright.

There is none of us, I assure you, who wouldn't be filled with love for this vision of virtue if we had the chance to see it. But there are many things that block our vision, either blinding us with too much light or covering us with too much darkness. However, if we are willing to clear our mind's eye of these obstacles, just as certain medicines are used to sharpen and clear our eyesight, then we would be able to see virtue, even if it's hidden within a body—no matter if poverty stands in the way, or if lowliness and disgrace block the path. We would then see that true beauty, even if it's covered by ugliness. On the other hand, we would also be able to see evil and the deadening effects of a sorrowful soul, even if they are hidden by the gleam of riches or the false light of power and position.

Then it would be within our power to understand how worthless the things we admire really are—like children who think every toy is valuable, who cherish necklaces bought for a mere penny more than they cherish their parents or siblings. And what is the difference between us and these children, as Aristo says, except that we grown-ups go crazy over paintings and sculptures, and our foolishness costs us more? Children are happy with the smooth, colorful pebbles they find on the beach, while we take delight in tall columns of veined marble brought from faraway deserts to support a colonnade or a dining hall big enough to hold a crowd.

We admire walls covered with a thin layer of marble, even though we know what flaws the marble is hiding. We deceive ourselves, and when we cover our ceilings with gold, what else is it but a lie that we take pleasure in? Because we know that underneath all this gold there's just some ugly wood. And this superficial decoration doesn't just cover walls and ceilings; all the famous people you see walking around with their heads held high are just hiding behind a thin layer of gold. Look beneath the surface, and you'll see how much evil lies under that thin coating of titles.

Take a close look at the thing that occupies the attention of so many officials and judges, and which creates both officials and judges—money. Ever since money began to be respected, it has ruined the true honor of things. We've become both merchants and merchandise, and we ask not what something truly is, but what it costs. We fulfill our duties if it pays, or neglect them if it pays more. We follow an honorable path as long as it meets our expectations, ready to switch to a dishonest path if it promises more.

Our parents taught us to respect gold and silver; this craving was planted in us from an early age, settling deep within us and growing as we grew. The whole nation, even though it disagrees on everything else, agrees on this. This is what they value, this is what they want for their children, and this is what they offer to the gods when they want to show their gratitude—as if it were the greatest thing a person could have! And finally, public opinion has reached a point where poverty is seen as shameful and despised by both the rich and the poor.

Poets add to this problem by writing verses that fuel our passions, praising wealth as if it were the only credit and glory of mankind. People seem to think that the gods cannot give anything better than wealth—or even possess anything better themselves: "The Sun-god's palace, set with tall pillars, flashing bright with gold." Or they describe the chariot of the Sun: "Gold was the axle, golden too the pole, and gold the tires that bound the circling wheels, and silver all the spokes within the wheels." And finally, when they want to praise a time as the best, they call it the "Golden Age."

Even among the Greek tragic poets, some believe that wealth is better than purity, soundness, or a good reputation: "Call me a scoundrel, only call me rich! Everyone asks how much money I have, but no one asks whether my soul is good. No one cares where your money comes from, just how much you have. All men are worth as much as what they own. What is the most shameful thing for us to have? Nothing! If riches bless me, I'd love to live; but I'd rather die if I'm poor. A man dies nobly in pursuit of wealth. Money, that blessing to the race of man, cannot be matched by a mother's love, a child's lisp, or the honor due to one's father. And if the sweetness of a lover's glance is half as charming, then Love rightly stirs the hearts of gods and men to adoration."

When these lines were spoken at a performance of one of Euripides' tragedies, the whole audience rose together to hiss the actor and the play off the stage. But Euripides jumped to his feet, asked for a hearing, and told them to wait until the end to see what fate awaited this man who was obsessed with gold. In that particular play, Bellerophon was to face the penalty that everyone in life must face.

For everyone must pay the price for greedy acts, though the greed itself is punishment enough. What tears and hard work does money demand from us! Greed is miserable in what it desires and miserable in what it gets! Think about the daily worry that troubles every owner in proportion to their wealth! Having riches brings even more agony than getting them. And how we grieve over our losses—losses that weigh heavily on us, and yet seem even heavier! And finally, even if Fortune leaves our property intact, whatever we cannot gain on top of that feels like a loss!

But you might say to me, "People call that man over there happy and rich; they pray that one day they might have as much as he does." That's true. But what then? Do you think there is any more pitiful life than to have both misery and hatred? I wish that those who crave wealth could compare notes with the rich man! I wish that those who seek political office could talk to the ambitious men who have reached the highest honors! They would then surely change their prayers, seeing that these powerful men are always chasing after new gains and regretting what they've already achieved. Because there is no one in the world who is content with their success, even if it comes quickly. People complain about their plans and the results of their plans; they always want what they didn't get.

So philosophy can solve this problem for you, and give you, in my opinion, the greatest blessing that exists—freedom from regret over your own actions. This is true happiness; no storm can disturb it. But you can't achieve it through clever words or smooth language. Let your words flow naturally, as long as your soul keeps its own order, as long as your soul is great and stays true to its ideals, pleased with itself for the very things that displease others—a soul that uses life as a test of its progress, and believes that its knowledge is directly related to its freedom from desire and fear. Farewell.

Letter 116 - On self-control

The question has often come up whether it is better to have moderate emotions or none at all. Philosophers from our school reject emotions entirely, while the Peripatetics believe in keeping them under control. But I don't see how any halfway measure can be either healthy or helpful. Don't worry; I'm not taking away any of the things you're not willing to give up! I'll be kind and understanding toward the things you strive for—the things you believe are necessary, useful, or pleasant. I'm just going to remove the bad parts. After I've told you to avoid desires, I'll still let you want to do the same things without fear and with better judgment, and even enjoy pleasures more than before. And how can these pleasures not come more easily if you are their master instead of their servant?

"But," you might say, "it's natural for me to suffer when I lose a friend; give me some allowance to shed tears that deserve to flow! It's also natural to care about what others think and to feel upset when their opinions are unfavorable; so why shouldn't I be allowed to be bothered by a bad opinion?"

There isn't any vice that doesn't have some excuse; there isn't any vice that doesn't start off modestly and seem easy to accept, but then spreads and causes more trouble. If you let it start, you can't be sure it will stop. Every emotion is weak at first. But then it wakes up and gets stronger as it grows; it's easier to stop it before it starts than to give it up once it has taken hold. Who doesn't admit that all emotions seem to come from a natural place? We naturally care about our own well-being, but when this care is overindulged, it becomes a vice.

Nature has mixed pleasure with necessary things—not so that we would seek out pleasure, but so that the addition of pleasure makes the necessary things more attractive. If pleasure starts to demand its own rights, it becomes luxury.

So, let's resist these faults when they're just trying to get in, because, as I've said, it's easier to keep them out than to make them leave. And if you say, "We should be allowed a certain amount of grieving and a certain amount of fear," I reply that the "certain amount" can go on too long, and it might not stop when you want it to. The wise person can control themselves safely without becoming too worried; they can stop their tears and their pleasures whenever they want to. But for us, because it's not easy to turn back once we've started, it's better not to move forward at all.

I think Panaetius gave a very good answer to a young man who asked him whether a wise man should fall in love: "As for the wise man, we'll talk about that later; but you and I, who are still far from wisdom, shouldn't trust ourselves to fall into a state that is disordered, uncontrolled, and enslaved to another, and that makes us feel low about ourselves. If our love is returned, we get excited by the affection; if it's rejected, we are stirred up by our pride. A love that is easily won hurts us just as much as one that is hard to get; we are captured by what is easy and struggle with what is difficult. So, knowing our weakness, let's stay calm. Let's not expose this unstable spirit to the temptations of alcohol, beauty, flattery, or anything that entices and lures us."

What Panaetius said about love can be applied, I believe, to all emotions. As much as we can, let's step back from slippery places; even on solid ground, it's hard enough to stand firm. At this point, I know you might bring up the common complaint against the Stoics: "Your promises are too great, and your advice is too hard. We are just human beings, unable to deny ourselves everything. We will grieve, but not too much; we will feel desires, but in moderation; we will get angry, but we will calm down."

And do you know why we don't have the power to reach this Stoic ideal? It's because we refuse to believe we have that power. No, there's more to it: it's because we love our vices; we defend them and prefer to make excuses for them rather than get rid of them. We mortals have been given enough strength by nature if only we use this strength, if only we focus our powers and bring them all together to help us—or at least not to hinder us. The reason we don't succeed is because we are unwilling, not because we are unable. Farewell.

Letter 117 - On real ethics as superior to syllogistic subtleties

You're giving me a lot of trouble, and without realizing it, you're dragging me into a big discussion that's going to be quite a hassle if you ask me questions like these. Because when I try to answer them, I can't disagree with my fellow Stoics without losing my standing among them, and I can't agree with them without going against my conscience. Your question is whether the Stoic belief is true: that wisdom is a Good, but being wise is not a Good. I'll first explain the Stoic view and then I'll be brave enough to share my own opinion.

We Stoics believe that the Good is something physical because the Good is active, and anything active must be physical. Something that is good is helpful. But to be helpful, it has to be active; and if it's active, it must be physical. The Stoics say that wisdom is a Good, so it follows that wisdom must also be physical.

But they don't think that being wise can be considered the same way. Being wise is something non-physical and depends on something else, which is wisdom; so, it's not active or helpful in the same way.

"But why," you might ask, "do we not say that being wise is a Good?" We do say that, but only in relation to wisdom itself, which it depends on.

Let me tell you what other philosophers say before I start sharing my own view and taking a different stance. They argue, "If you think that way, then you must also say that living happily is not a Good, even though a happy life is a Good. But that doesn't make sense."

Another criticism against our school is this: "You want to be wise. Therefore, being wise is something desirable. And if it's something desirable, it must be a Good." So, our philosophers are forced to twist their words and add an extra syllable to the word "desired"—a syllable that doesn't normally belong in our language. But, with your permission, I'll add it here. "That which is good," they say, "is something to be desired; the desirable thing is what we get after we have attained the Good. The desirable isn't sought as a Good; it's an addition to the Good after we've achieved it."

I don't agree with this view, and I think our philosophers have been driven to this argument because they're stuck with their original definition and can't change it. People tend to give a lot of weight to things that everyone agrees on; we think that if everyone believes something, it must be true. For example, we believe that gods exist partly because everyone has some idea of a deity, and there's no group of people so far removed from laws and customs that they don't believe in some kind of gods. And when we talk about the immortality of the soul, we're influenced by the widespread belief in the spirits of the underworld, which people either fear or worship. I place a lot of value on this general belief: you won't find anyone who doesn't think that wisdom is a Good, and being wise is a Good too.

But let's not just go by popular opinion; let's dig into the details with our own reasoning. When something affects an object, is it inside or outside the object it affects? If it's inside, then it's as physical as the object it's affecting, because nothing can affect something else without touching it, and whatever touches something is physical. If it's outside, then it moves away after affecting the object, and movement means it's physical too.

Now, you might expect me to deny that there's a difference between "race" and "running," or "heat" and "being hot," or "light" and "giving light." I agree that these pairs are different but think they belong to the same category. If good health is a neutral quality, then so is being in good health; if beauty is a neutral quality, then so is being beautiful. If justice is a Good, then so is being just. And if being base is an evil, then it's evil to be base—just as if sore eyes are an evil, then having sore eyes is also an evil. Neither quality can exist without the other. A person who is wise has wisdom, and a person who has wisdom is wise. These two qualities are so closely linked that some people even consider them one and the same.

But here's a question I'd like to ask: if everything is either good, bad, or neutral, where does being wise fit in? People say it's not a Good; and since it's clearly not an evil, it must be neutral. But by "neutral," we mean something that can belong to both good and bad people, like money, beauty, or high social status. But being wise can only belong to a good person, so it's not neutral. And since it's not an evil either, it must be a Good. Whatever only a good person can have is a Good; and since only a good person can be wise, being wise must be a Good.

The objector might say, "Being wise is just something that comes along with wisdom." Okay, but does this quality of being wise create wisdom, or is it just something that goes along with it? It's physical in either case because both the thing that acts and the thing that is acted upon are physical, and if it's physical, it's a Good. The only thing that could keep it from being a Good is if it weren't physical.

The Peripatetics don't see a difference between wisdom and being wise because one implies the other. Now, do you think anyone can be wise without having wisdom? Or that anyone who is wise doesn't have wisdom?

The old masters of logic, however, made a distinction between these two ideas, and that distinction has been passed down to the Stoics. I'll explain what kind of distinction this is: A field is one thing, and owning a field is another thing; obviously, because "owning the field" refers to the owner, not the field itself. In the same way, wisdom is one thing and being wise is another. You'll agree, I suppose, that these are two different ideas—the possessed and the possessor: wisdom is what one possesses, and the wise person is the one who possesses it. Now, wisdom is the mind perfected and developed to the highest and best degree. It is the art of living. But what is being wise? I can't call it "the mind perfected," but rather what belongs to someone who has a "perfected mind." So, a good mind is one thing, and the possession of a good mind is another.

"There are," it's said, "certain natural classes of things; we say, 'This is a man,' 'this is a horse.' Then there are certain movements of the mind that describe something about the body. And these have a certain quality that is separate from the body; for example, 'I see Cato walking.' The senses show this, and the mind believes it. What I see is a body, and that's what I focus my eyes and mind on. Again, I say, 'Cato walks.' What I'm saying is not a body; it's a statement about a body—a statement, an utterance, a declaration. So, when we say 'wisdom,' we mean something related to the body; when we say 'he is wise,' we're talking about the body. And it makes a difference whether you mention the person directly or talk about the person."

Let's assume for now that these are two separate ideas (I'm not ready to give my own opinion yet); what's stopping there from being a third idea that's also a Good? I mentioned earlier that a "field" is one thing and "owning a field" is another; of course, because the owner and the thing owned are different—the land is the thing owned, and the person is the owner. But when it comes to wisdom, both the possessor and what's possessed are of the same nature.

Also, in the case of a field, the land and the owner are separate; but in the case of wisdom, the possessor and what's possessed belong to the same category. The field is owned by law, wisdom by nature. The field can change hands and have a new owner, but wisdom never leaves its owner. So, there's no reason to compare things that are so different from each other. I was about to say that these can be two separate ideas, but both can still be Goods—just like wisdom and the wise person are two separate things but are both considered Good. And just as there's no problem in seeing both wisdom and the possessor of wisdom as Goods, there's no problem in seeing both wisdom and the possession of wisdom—in other words, being wise—as Goods.

Because I only want to be a wise person in order to be wise. And what then? Isn't that a Good thing if you can't have one without the other? You would surely agree that wisdom, if given without the ability to use it, wouldn't be worth having! And what's the use of wisdom? It's being wise; that's its most valuable quality; if you take that away, wisdom becomes pointless. If torture is evil, then being tortured is evil too—with the understanding that if you take away the consequences, the former isn't evil. Wisdom is the state of "mind perfected," and being wise is the use of this "mind perfected." How can the use of something not be a Good if that thing itself isn't a Good without being used?

If I ask you whether wisdom is desirable, you admit that it is. If I ask you whether using wisdom is desirable, you also admit that it is; because you say that you wouldn't want wisdom without being able to use it. Now, whatever is desirable is a Good. Being wise is the use of wisdom, just like it is for eloquence to make a speech or for the eyes to see things. Therefore, being wise is the use of wisdom, and the use of wisdom is desirable. Therefore, being wise is something desirable; and if it is desirable, it is a Good.

For many years now, I've been blaming myself for copying these people while at the same time criticizing them, and for wasting words on something that is perfectly clear. Who could doubt that if heat is an evil, then being hot is also an evil? Or that if cold is an evil, then being cold is also an evil? Or that if life is a Good, then being alive is also a Good? All these matters are on the edge of wisdom, not at its core. But our focus should be on wisdom itself.

Even if someone likes to wander, wisdom has large and spacious places to explore: we can investigate the nature of the gods, the fuel that powers the stars, or the many paths of the planets. We can ask whether our lives move in harmony with the stars, whether the impulse for action comes from the heavens into the minds and bodies of everyone, and whether even the events we call random are bound by strict laws and nothing in this universe happens without order. These topics have been removed from discussions on ethics, but they uplift the mind and expand it to the size of the subject at hand; however, the things I was talking about earlier wear down the mind, not by sharpening it, but by weakening it.

And I ask you, are we to waste the time we should spend on greater and better subjects, on discussing a matter that might be wrong and is certainly useless? How will it help me to know whether wisdom is one thing and being wise another? How will it help me to know that one is a Good and the other is not? Suppose I take a chance and pray: "Wisdom for you, and being wise for me!" We'll end up in the same place.

Instead, show me the way to achieve those goals. Tell me what to avoid, what to seek, what studies will strengthen my weak mind, how I can resist the challenges that push me off course, how I can deal with all my troubles, and how I can get rid of the problems that have overwhelmed me and those I've brought on myself. Teach me how to bear the burden of sorrow without groaning and how to handle success without making others groan; also, how to avoid waiting for the inevitable end, and how to leave this life on my own terms, when it seems right to do so.

I think nothing is worse than praying for death. If you want to live, why pray for death? And if you don't want to live, why ask the gods for something they already gave you at birth? Just as it's settled that you must die someday, whether you like it or not, it's also up to you when you wish to die. The first fact is a necessity, the other is a privilege.

I recently read a very disgraceful statement made by a learned man (more shame on him!): "So may I die as soon as possible!" Fool, you're praying for something that's already yours! "So may I die as soon as possible!" Maybe you got old while saying those very words! At any rate, what's stopping you? No one is holding you back; you can leave whenever you want! Choose any part of Nature and ask it to provide you with a way out! These are the elements that keep the world going—water, earth, air. All of these are just as much the causes of death as they are of life.

"So may I die as soon as possible!" And what do you mean by "as soon as possible"? What day do you have in mind? It might come sooner than you wish. Words like this come from a weak mind, from someone looking for pity through self-cursing; the person who prays for death doesn't really want to die. Ask the gods for life and health; if you're determined to die, then stop praying altogether.

These are the kinds of problems, my dear Lucilius, that we should focus on, the kinds of problems that should shape our minds. This is wisdom, this is what it means to be wise—not to get caught up in empty subtleties in pointless and trivial discussions. Fortune has set so many problems before you—problems you haven't yet solved— and yet you're still splitting hairs? How foolish it is to practice your moves after the signal for the fight has already sounded! Forget these practice weapons; you need real armor for a fight to the finish. Tell me how to keep sadness and fear from disturbing my soul, how to get rid of this burden of hidden desires. Do something! "Wisdom is a Good, but being wise is not a Good;" such talk only makes us doubt that we can ever be wise, and it makes this whole field of study a joke—because it seems to waste its time on useless things. Imagine you heard that people were debating this question too: whether future wisdom is a Good? For heaven's sake, how could anyone doubt that barns don't feel the weight of the harvest that's yet to come, or that childhood doesn't sense the strength and power of approaching adulthood? A sick person, while still recovering, isn't helped by the health that's yet to come, any more than a runner or a wrestler is refreshed by the rest they'll get months later.

Who doesn't know that what is yet to be is not a Good, simply because it hasn't happened yet? For something to be good, it has to be helpful. And unless something is in the present, it can't be helpful; and if it's not helpful, it's not a Good; if it's helpful, it already exists. I will be a wise person someday; and this Good will be mine when I become wise, but for now, it doesn't exist. Something must exist first before it can have a certain quality. How can something that doesn't exist yet already be a Good? And what better proof do you need that something doesn't exist yet than to say, "It's yet to be"? Because if something is on the way, it's clear that it hasn't arrived yet. "Spring will follow:" I know that winter is here now. "Summer will follow:" I know that it's not summer yet. The best proof that something isn't here yet is that it's still on the way.

I hope someday to be wise, but right now I'm not wise. Because if I had that Good, I wouldn't be suffering from this Evil. Someday I'll be wise; and from this very fact, you can understand that I'm not wise yet. I can't be in a state of Good and in a state of Evil at the same time; the two ideas don't go together, and Evil and Good can't exist together in the same person.

Let's skip all this clever nonsense and move on to something that will actually help us. No one who's anxiously running to find a midwife for his daughter in labor will stop to read the judge's orders or the schedule of events at the games. No one rushing to save his burning house will pause to look at a checkerboard to figure out how to free a trapped piece. But good heavens!—in your case, all sorts of bad news is coming from all directions—your house is on fire, your children are in danger, your country is under siege, your property is being looted. Add to this shipwrecks, earthquakes, and all other things we fear; with all these troubles around you, are you really taking time to focus on things that are just mental entertainment? Do you ask what the difference is between wisdom and being wise? Are you tying and untying knots while disaster is hanging over your head?

Nature hasn't given us so much time that we can afford to waste any of it. Notice how much time is lost even when people are careful: some time is taken by illness, some by family problems; at one time private business demands attention, at another public duties do; and all the while sleep takes up a third of our lives. Out of this time, which is so short and passes so quickly, what's the point of spending most of it on useless things?

Besides, our minds are used to amusing themselves rather than healing themselves, to turning philosophy into something enjoyable when it should really be a remedy. I don't know what the difference is between wisdom and being wise, but I do know that it doesn't matter to me whether I know such things or not. Tell me: if I figure out the difference between wisdom and being wise, will I become wise? Why then do you waste my time with the words rather than with the actions of wisdom? Make me braver, make me calmer, make me equal to Fortune, make me stronger than her. And I can be stronger than her if I apply everything I learn to this goal. Farewell.

Letter 118 - On the vanity of place-seeking

You've been asking for more letters from me. But if we were to compare who owes whom, you'd actually owe more than I do. We agreed that you would write the first letters, and I would respond. But I won't be difficult about it; I trust you, so I'll write first. I won't just write whatever comes to mind, though, as Cicero once told Atticus to do. I'll always have something worth writing about, even if I skip all the gossip that Cicero included in his letters—like which candidate is in trouble, who is borrowing money to run for office, or who is trying to win the consulship by relying on Caesar, Pompey, or his own wealth, and who is being a ruthless moneylender.

But it's better to deal with our own problems than to focus on others'—to look at how many worthless things we are chasing after and decide not to chase them anymore. This, my dear Lucilius, is a noble thing that brings peace and freedom—to run for nothing, to ignore all the elections of Fortune. How can you find it enjoyable when the tribes are called together, and the candidates are offering gifts at their favorite temples—some promising money, others using agents to do business, or wearing out their hands by shaking the hands of people they will ignore once elected? How can you find it enjoyable, I ask, to stand there idly and watch this Vanity Fair without buying or selling anything?

How much greater joy does one feel who looks without concern, not just at the election of a praetor or a consul, but at the great struggle where some are seeking yearly honors, others permanent power, others a military triumph, others riches, marriage, or children, or the well-being of themselves and their relatives? What a noble act it is to be the only one seeking nothing, asking no favors from anyone, and saying, "Fortune, I have nothing to do with you. I don't need your help. I know that people like Cato are ignored by you, and people like Vatinius are made by you. I ask for nothing." This is the way to defeat Fortune.

These are the kinds of things we can write about in our letters, and this is the endless material we can draw from as we observe the restless crowds of people who, in their quest to attain something harmful, move from one evil to another, chasing after things they will soon have to avoid or that will overwhelm them. For who has ever been satisfied, after achieving what they prayed for, with the thing that once seemed so important? Happiness isn't a greedy thing like people think; it's humble; for that reason, it never fully satisfies a person's desire. You think the things you seek are lofty because you are so far below them, but they are insignificant to someone who has reached them. And I'm pretty sure that once he gets there, he will want to climb even higher; what you see as the top is just another step on the ladder.

Now, all people suffer from ignorance of the truth; deceived by popular opinion, they chase after these goals as if they were good, and then, after winning them and enduring much hardship, they find that they are either evil, empty, or less important than they thought. Most people admire what deceives them from a distance, and the crowd tends to think that big things are good things.

Now, to make sure this doesn't happen to us too, let's ask ourselves what the Good really is. It has been explained in different ways; various people have described it differently. Some say, "The Good is what attracts and draws the spirit to itself." But the problem with this is—what if it does attract, but only to lead to ruin? You know how seductive many evils are. What is true is different from what seems true; that's why the Good is connected with the truth, because it can't be good unless it's also true. But what attracts and lures is only like the truth; it steals your attention, demands your interest, and pulls you in.

Therefore, some have given this definition: "The Good is what inspires desire for itself or awakens the impulse of a struggling soul." But there's the same problem with this idea; many things stir up the soul's impulses, but seeking them can be harmful. A better definition is this: "The Good is what awakens the soul's impulse toward itself in accordance with nature and is worth seeking only when it's truly worth seeking." By now, it has become something honorable; because that is something fully worth seeking.

The topic at hand suggests that I explain the difference between the Good and the honorable. They have a certain quality that blends with both and can't be separated from either: nothing can be good unless it contains an element of the honorable, and the honorable is always good. So, what's the difference between these two qualities? The honorable is the perfect Good, and a happy life is fulfilled by it; through its influence, other things also become good.

I mean something like this: there are certain things that are neither good nor bad—like military or diplomatic service, or giving legal decisions. When these actions are done honorably, they start to become good, changing from being "neutral" to being Good. The Good comes from its partnership with the honorable, but the honorable is good by itself. The Good comes from the honorable, but the honorable comes from itself. What is good might have been bad; what is honorable could never be anything but good.

Some have defined it this way: "The Good is what is in accordance with nature." Now, pay attention to my own statement: the Good is what is in accordance with nature, but just because something is in accordance with nature doesn't mean it's immediately good; many things align with nature but are so insignificant that it's not right to call them good. They are unimportant and deserve to be ignored. But there's no such thing as a very small and insignificant Good, because as long as it's small, it's not good, and when it starts to be good, it's no longer small. So, how can we recognize the Good? Only if it is fully in accordance with nature.

People say: "You admit that the Good is in accordance with nature because that's its unique quality. You also admit that there are other things in accordance with nature that are not good. So how can one be good and the other not? How can the unique quality of something change when each shares the same attribute of being in accordance with nature?"

The answer is in its magnitude. It's not a new idea that some things change as they grow. A person who was once a child becomes a youth; their unique quality changes because the child couldn't reason, but the youth can. Some things not only grow in size as they develop but also grow into something else.

Some may argue, "But just because something becomes bigger doesn't mean it becomes different. It doesn't matter whether you pour wine into a small bottle or a large vat; the wine keeps its unique quality in both. Small and large amounts of honey don't taste different." But these are different cases you mention; wine and honey have a uniform quality; no matter how much the quantity increases, the quality stays the same.

For some things, their kind and unique qualities remain the same, even when they grow.

But there are other things that change their form as they develop and are transformed into something new. When the mind has developed some idea for a long time and has grown tired of trying to grasp its size, that thing begins to be called "infinite." At that point, it has become something very different from what it was when it seemed great but finite. In the same way, we may have thought of something as difficult to divide; but as it becomes harder and harder, we eventually find it to be "indivisible." Similarly, from something that could barely be moved, we have advanced to something "immovable." By the same reasoning, something was once in accordance with nature; its greatness has changed it into something else and made it a Good. Farewell.

Letter 119 - On nature as our best provider

Whenever I find something new, I don't wait for you to ask me to share it. I tell myself to share it with you right away. If you want to know what I've discovered, get ready to learn—it's a real treasure. What I'm going to teach you is how to get rich as quickly as possible. You're excited to hear this, and you should be! I'm going to show you a shortcut to the greatest wealth. But first, you'll need to borrow some money to get started in business. However, I don't want you to go through a middleman or have brokers gossiping about your credit. I'll give you a trustworthy lender, like the one Cato talked about when he said, "Borrow from yourself!" No matter how little you have, it will be enough if you can make up the difference from your own resources. My dear Lucilius, it doesn't matter if you want nothing or if you already have something. The key point is the same in both cases—freedom from worry. But I don't suggest you deny nature what it needs—nature is demanding and can't be ignored. She needs what she needs, but you should know that anything beyond what nature requires is just extra and not necessary.

If I'm hungry, I need to eat. Nature doesn't care if the bread is plain or made from the finest wheat; she just wants the stomach to be filled, not entertained. And if I'm thirsty, Nature doesn't care if I drink water from a nearby stream or if I chill it with ice. Nature only wants the thirst to be quenched, and it doesn't matter if the drink comes from a golden goblet, a crystal cup, or even just my hands. Focus on what really matters in everything, and you'll get rid of the unnecessary stuff. If I'm hungry, I'll grab whatever is closest; hunger makes anything seem appealing. A starving person won't reject anything.

So, what's the important thing I've found? It's this wise saying: "The wise person seeks the riches of nature the most eagerly." You might ask, "What? Are you giving me nothing? What do you mean? I was already planning how to fill my treasure chest, looking for new trade routes, or thinking about handling big businesses or acquiring more goods. This is a trick—you promised me riches, but now you're showing me poverty." But tell me, do you think someone is poor if they lack nothing? "Yes," you might say, "but that's because they're strong and determined, not because they're rich." Do you think someone isn't rich just because their wealth never runs out?

Would you rather have a lot or just enough? The person who has a lot always wants more—a sign that they don't have enough yet; but the person who has enough has reached a point that even the rich never achieve—a stopping point. Do you think this condition isn't wealth just because no one's ever been killed for it? Or because no one's family has poisoned them over it? Or because it's safe in times of war and brings peace in times of calm? Or because it's not dangerous to have or hard to manage?

"But isn't it too little if someone just avoids being cold, hungry, or thirsty?" you might ask. But even Jupiter himself isn't any better off. Enough is never too little, and not enough is never too much.

Alexander the Great was poor even after conquering Darius and the entire Indies. Am I wrong? He kept looking for something he could truly call his own, exploring unknown lands, sending new fleets across the ocean, and, so to speak, trying to break through the edges of the world. But what's enough for nature isn't enough for people.

Some people still crave more even after getting everything; their minds are so confused that they forget where they started once they've come so far. Someone who was recently the ruler of a small, unknown land feels disappointed when, after conquering the world, he has to walk back through lands he already owns. Money never made anyone rich; instead, it just makes people want more. Why? Because the more someone has, the more they can want.

To sum it up, you can bring forth any millionaire whose name is mentioned with the richest people. Let him show his wealth, his current possessions, and his future expectations, and add them all together: I'd consider such a person poor; you might think he's going to be poor someday. But the person who has organized his life according to nature's needs is free from both the fear and the feeling of poverty. And to show how hard it is to limit our wants to nature's needs—even this person, whom you might call poor, actually has more than they need.

Wealth blinds and attracts the crowd when they see large amounts of money coming out of a house, or when they see walls covered in gold, or a group of well-dressed servants. The wealth of these people is only for show; but the ideal person, whom we've freed from the control of the crowd and Fortune, is happy within.

For those people who think that restless poverty is actually wealth—those people don't own wealth; wealth owns them. Similarly, when someone is sick, we say, "The fever has them," rather than "They have a fever." In the same way, we should say, "Wealth owns them." So, here's my advice—and you can never have too much of this—measure everything by the needs of nature, because these needs can be met either without cost or very cheaply. Just don't mix in any bad habits with these needs.

Why worry about how your food is served, on what kind of table, with what kind of silver, or with what kind of well-dressed servants? Nature only requires food.

Do you, when you're thirsty, demand a golden cup? Do you refuse any food except peacock or fancy fish when you're hungry? Hunger isn't picky; it just wants to be satisfied, and it doesn't care much what food does the job. Those fancy things are just tools of luxury, which isn't happiness; luxury tries to keep hunger going even after you're full, to stuff the stomach rather than fill it, and to stir up a thirst that's already been quenched. Horace's words are excellent when he says that it doesn't matter to your thirst what kind of goblet the water is served in or how fancy the setting is. If you care about how curly your servant's hair is or how clear the cup is, then you're not really thirsty.

Among other things, Nature has given us this special gift: she frees us from being picky when it comes to basic needs. The extra things allow for choice; we say, "That's not good enough," or "This doesn't look right," or "That's uncomfortable." The Creator of the universe, who gave us the rules of life, made sure we can live in comfort, but not in luxury. Everything we need for comfort is ready and within reach; but what luxury requires can never be gathered without misery and anxiety.

Let's use this gift from Nature wisely, treating it as something very important; let's remember that Nature's greatest gift is that whatever we need for basic survival, we can accept without being picky. Farewell.

Letter 120 - More about virtue

Your letter touched on several small problems, but in the end, you focused on just one, asking how we can know what is good and what is honorable. Other schools of thought believe these two qualities are different, but in our philosophy, they are closely connected. Some people think that the Good is anything useful, like money, horses, wine, or shoes. They value the Good so little that they consider even these basic things to be Good. They believe that the honorable is whatever matches the principles of doing the right thing, such as caring for an elderly father, helping a friend in need, showing bravery in battle, or offering wise and balanced advice.

However, we believe that the Good and the honorable are not separate; they are the same thing. Only what is honorable can be considered truly Good, and what is honorable is always Good. I don't think it's necessary to explain this distinction again because I have mentioned it many times before. But I will say this: we do not consider anything to be good if it can be misused by anyone. You can see for yourself how many people misuse their wealth, power, or physical strength.

Now, to answer the question you asked: "How do we first learn what is good and what is honorable?" Nature did not teach us this directly. She gave us the seeds of knowledge, but not knowledge itself. Some people think we just stumbled upon this knowledge by chance, but it seems unlikely that anyone would accidentally discover the idea of virtue. We believe that understanding comes from observing and comparing things that happen often. Our school of thought holds that we understand the honorable and the good by drawing analogies. Since the word "analogy" has been accepted by Latin scholars, I think it should be allowed, and I will use it as a proper term.

Let me explain what this "analogy" is. We knew what physical health was, so from that, we figured out that there must be a similar kind of health for the mind. We also knew what physical strength was, so we reasoned that there must be mental strength too. Acts of kindness, humanity, and bravery have sometimes amazed us, and we began to admire them as if they were perfect. However, beneath these acts, there were often flaws, hidden by the appearance and brilliance of certain actions. Nature encourages us to praise things that seem good, and everyone tends to exaggerate the truth. From such deeds, we created the concept of some great Good.

For example, Fabricius refused the gold offered by King Pyrrhus because he thought it was greater to scorn a king's wealth than to wear a king's crown. Fabricius also warned King Pyrrhus when the royal doctor offered to poison him. This same man refused to be tempted by gold and refused to win through treachery. We admired the hero who could not be swayed by promises either for or against the king, who held firm to a noble ideal, and who – is anything more difficult? – remained innocent in war. He believed that it was possible to do wrong even to an enemy, and in his extreme poverty, which he had turned into a source of pride, he refused riches just as he refused to use poison. "Live, Pyrrhus," he said, "thanks to me, and rejoice that Fabricius cannot be bribed!"

Horatius Cocles blocked the narrow bridge alone and ordered it to be cut off so that the enemy couldn't cross. He fought off his attackers until the sound of the collapsing beams echoed in his ears. When he looked back and saw that his country was safe because of his own risk, he called out, "Whoever wants to follow me, come!" He then leaped into the river, taking as much care to emerge with his weapons intact as he did to come out unharmed. He returned with the glory of his victory as if he had walked back over the bridge.

These and other similar deeds have shown us what virtue looks like. I'll add something that might surprise you: sometimes even evil things can appear honorable, and the best can be revealed through its opposite. There are, as you know, vices that are close to virtues, and even what is lost and corrupt can resemble what is upright. For example, a spendthrift might look like a generous person, even though there's a big difference between knowing how to give and not knowing how to save. I assure you, many people don't give but just throw away their money, and I don't consider someone generous who is simply careless with their wealth. Carelessness can look like ease, and recklessness like bravery.

This resemblance forces us to be careful and to distinguish between things that appear similar on the surface but are actually very different. By watching those who have become famous for some noble effort, we have learned to observe who has done something with a noble spirit and lofty impulse, but only once. We've seen people who are brave in war but cowardly in civil matters, who face poverty courageously but are ashamed of disgrace. We've praised the deed but despised the person.

We've also seen others who are kind to their friends and restrained with their enemies, who conduct their public and private affairs with great care, enduring hardship where necessary and showing wisdom when action is needed. These people give generously when it's their duty, and when they must work hard, they do so with determination, lightening their physical exhaustion with their resolve. These people have always been consistent, sound in their judgment, and trained by habit so well that they not only act rightly but cannot help acting rightly. We have formed the idea that in such a person, perfect virtue exists.

We have broken down this perfect virtue into its parts. Desires had to be controlled, fear suppressed, proper actions organized, and debts paid. So, we included self-control, bravery, wisdom, and justice, giving each quality its specific role. How then did we come to understand virtue? Virtue was shown to us by this person's order, propriety, steadfastness, harmony of action, and greatness of soul that rises above everything. From this, we derived our concept of the happy life, which flows steadily and is completely under its own control.

How did we discover this truth? I'll tell you: the perfect person, who has attained virtue, never cursed their luck and never felt dejected by the results of chance. They believed they were a citizen and soldier of the universe, accepting their tasks as if they were orders.

Whatever happened, they did not reject it as if it were evil and the result of chance; they accepted it as if it were their duty. "Whatever this may be," they say, "it is my lot; it is rough and hard, but I must work diligently at it."

Therefore, the person has shown greatness by never grieving in hard times and never lamenting their fate. They have given many people a clear idea of themselves; they have shone like a light in the darkness and drawn the attention of everyone because they were gentle, calm, and equally obedient to the commands of both man and God. They possessed a soul so perfect, developed to its highest potential, that it was second only to the mind of God, from whom a part flows down into the heart of a mortal. But this heart is never more divine than when it reflects on its mortality and understands that humans were born to fulfill their lives, and that the body is not a permanent home, but a temporary place to stay, like an inn, which we leave when we become a burden to the host.

The greatest proof, I believe, my dear Lucilius, that the soul comes from a higher place, is that it looks down on its current situation and is not afraid to leave. For those who remember where they came from know where they are going. Don't we see how many discomforts drive us mad, and how ill-suited we are to the body? We complain about headaches, bad digestion, heartaches, and sore throats. Sometimes it's the nerves, sometimes the feet; now it's diarrhea, then it's a cold. We are at one time full of blood, then lacking it; now this thing troubles us, now that, and it makes us want to leave. It's like staying in someone else's house.

But we, who have been given such corruptible bodies, still set our sights on eternity and hope to live as long as possible, even though nothing will ever be enough for us. We know we will die someday, or rather, we are already dying; each day brings us closer to the edge, and every hour pushes us toward the cliff from which we must fall. How blind we are! What I speak of as happening in the future is happening right now, and a large part of it has already happened; it consists of our past lives. But we are mistaken in fearing the last day, seeing that each day counts just as much toward death. The failing step doesn't cause weariness, it just signals it. The last hour reaches death, but every hour brings it closer. Death slowly wears us away, but it doesn't suddenly snatch us away.

For this reason, the noble soul, knowing its higher nature, while taking care to live honorably and seriously at the post where it is placed, doesn't consider any of these external things as its own but uses them as if they were on loan, like a foreign visitor in a hurry to move on. When we see a person of such steadfastness, how can we help but recognize the image of such a rare nature? Especially if, as I mentioned, it shows true greatness through consistency. Consistency is what lasts; false things do not endure. Some people are like Vatinius or Cato at different times; sometimes they think even Curius isn't stern enough, or Fabricius isn't poor enough, or Tubero isn't frugal and content with simple things enough; while at other times they try to outdo Licinus in wealth, Apicius in feasting, or Maecenas in luxury.

The greatest proof of an evil mind is unsteadiness and constant wavering between pretending to be virtuous and loving vice.

There was a man who sometimes had two hundred slaves and sometimes only ten. He would talk of kings and grand rulers, but then he would say: "Give me a simple table and a tray of clean salt, and just a coarse-woven gown to keep warm." If you gave him a million, in five days, he'd be broke.

The people I'm talking about are like that. They're like the man Horace describes – never the same, never even like himself; he constantly swings between extremes. Did I say many are like this? It's true of almost everyone. Everyone changes their plans and desires day by day. Now he wants a wife, now a mistress; now he wants to be a king, then he wants to act like the most humble slave; now he puffs himself up until people dislike him, then he shrinks into greater humility than those who are truly modest; sometimes he throws money around, at other times he steals it.

That's how a foolish mind reveals itself: first in one shape, then in another, and never consistent – which, in my opinion, is the most shameful trait. Believe me, it's a great challenge to play the role of one person consistently. But only the wise man can be one person; the rest of us often change our masks. Sometimes you'll think us thrifty and serious, other times wasteful and idle. We keep changing our characters and acting in ways contrary to what we did before. You should, therefore, force yourself to maintain the character you assumed at the beginning of life to the very end. Make sure people can either praise you or at least recognize you. Indeed, regarding the person you saw just yesterday, the question may properly be asked: "Who is he?" because the change has been so great! Farewell.

Letter 121 - On instinct in animals

I'm sure you'll be upset with me when I tell you about today's topic, one we've already spent a lot of time on. You might say, "What does this have to do with character?" Complain if you want, but first, let me remind you that others like Posidonius and Archidemus have tackled similar issues, so take it up with them! Then I'll explain that not everything related to character directly makes a person better. We need different things for food, exercise, clothing, learning, and even enjoyment. Everything has to do with our needs, but not everything improves our character. Different things affect character in different ways: some help to correct and guide it, while others explore its nature and origins.

And when I try to figure out why Nature created humans and placed them above other animals, do you think I've stopped studying character? No, that's not right. How can you know what kind of character is good unless you understand what is best for humans? Or unless you've studied human nature? You can only learn what you should do and what you should avoid when you understand what you owe to your own nature.

You say, "I want to learn how to desire less and fear less. Help me get rid of my irrational beliefs. Prove to me that so-called happiness is unstable and empty, and that it's easy to lose." I'll meet your needs by encouraging your virtues and correcting your vices. Some people might think I'm too enthusiastic and reckless about this, but I'll never stop challenging wickedness, controlling wild emotions, easing the pull of pleasures that lead to pain, and urging people to reconsider their prayers. Of course, I'll do this because we often pray for the worst things, and from what we've been thankful for comes everything that requires consolation.

Meanwhile, let me discuss a few points that might seem unrelated right now. We once debated whether all animals have any awareness of their own bodies. This is proven by how naturally and skillfully they move, as if they've been trained for it. Every being is skilled in its own way. A skilled worker handles their tools with ease because of experience; a pilot steers a ship with expertise; an artist quickly applies colors to create a likeness on canvas. In the same way, an animal is agile in using its body.

We often marvel at how dancers move in perfect harmony with the music and emotions of a piece, matching the speed of the dialogue with their movements. But what art gives to the craftsman, nature gives to the animal. No animal struggles to use its limbs; they all know exactly how to use their bodies. They come into the world with this knowledge; they're born fully trained.

Some might say, "Animals move so well because if they don't, they'll feel pain. They're forced to move this way out of fear, not choice." This idea is wrong. Bodies moved by force are slow, but those that move on their own are quick. The proof that it's not fear of pain driving them is that even when they feel pain, they still try to move naturally. For example, a child learning to stand keeps trying, even if they fall and cry, until they can do it. And certain animals, like tortoises, when flipped on their backs, twist and turn until they're upright again. They don't feel pain from being on their backs, but they're restless because it's not their natural position, and they keep moving until they're back on their feet.

So, all animals have an awareness of their bodies, which is why they manage their limbs so well. We know this because no animal is unskilled in using its body. But some might argue, "If animals are aware of their bodies, they must understand the complex idea of 'constitution'—a principle that's hard even for humans to grasp!" Your objection would be valid if I were saying that animals understand a definition of their bodies. But I'm saying they understand their own bodies, not the definition. Nature is easier to understand than to explain. A child doesn't understand what "constitution" is but knows their own body. They don't know what a "living creature" is but feel that they are one. And this understanding is basic and unclear, like how we know we have souls but don't fully understand them.

Just as we are aware of our souls without fully understanding them, all animals have a basic awareness of their own bodies. They must feel this because it's the same awareness that lets them sense other things. They must feel the principle that guides and controls them. Everyone knows there's something that drives their actions, even if they don't know what it is. We know we have impulses, even if we don't understand them fully. So, even children and animals have a basic awareness of their bodies, though it's not very clear.

You might ask, "How can a child, who doesn't yet have reason, be adapted to a reasoning constitution?" But each age has its own constitution, different for a child, a boy, and an old man. They all fit their current constitution. A child is toothless, and they're adapted to that condition. Then their teeth grow, and they adapt to that too. Plants, which will grow into grains and fruits, also have different constitutions at different stages. No matter what stage the plant is in, it keeps its constitution and adapts to it. The stages of infancy, boyhood, youth, and old age are different, but I'm still the same person who has been through all these stages. So, even though our constitution changes at different times, our adaptation to it remains the same.

Nature doesn't give me boyhood, youth, or old age; she gives me to them. Therefore, a child is adapted to their current constitution, not the one they'll have in youth. Even if a higher phase is in store for them, the state they're born into is also natural.

First of all, every living being is adapted to itself because there has to be a standard to which all other things are compared. I seek pleasure—for whom? For myself. I avoid pain—on behalf of whom? Myself. So, I'm looking out for myself above all else. This quality is in all living beings—not added later, but born with them. Nature raises her own offspring and doesn't abandon them. Because the safest security is the one closest to us, every person is entrusted to themselves.

As I've mentioned before, even young animals, when they're born or hatch from eggs, know right away what's harmful to them and avoid things that could kill them. They even shrink back when they see the shadow of a bird of prey overhead. No animal enters life without a fear of death.

People might ask, "How can an animal at birth understand what's good or bad for it?" But the first question is whether it can understand, not how it understands. And it's clear they do because even with understanding, they wouldn't act any differently than they do naturally. Why does a hen show no fear of a peacock or a goose but run from a hawk, which is smaller and unfamiliar? Why do young chickens fear a cat and not a dog? These animals clearly have an instinct for what's harmful, even before they've experienced it.

Furthermore, to prove it's not just chance, these animals don't fear certain other things you might expect them to, and they never forget to be vigilant. They all equally avoid what's harmful. Their fear doesn't grow as they get older. This shows they haven't learned this through experience; it's an inborn instinct for self-preservation.

Experience teaches slowly and unevenly, but what Nature gives is shared by everyone immediately.

If you need an explanation, I'll tell you how every living thing understands what's harmful. It feels that it's made of flesh and knows how flesh can be cut, burned, or crushed, and what animals have the power to do this harm. It develops a hostile idea of such animals. These instincts are connected because every animal looks out for its own safety, seeking what helps it and avoiding what harms it. These impulses toward what's useful and away from what's harmful are natural. Without any prompting or advice, whatever Nature dictates is followed.

Don't you see how skilled bees are in building their hives? How they work together and endure their tasks in harmony? Don't you see how a spider weaves a web so delicate that a human hand can't imitate it? It carefully arranges the threads, some running straight for strength, others in circles to trap smaller insects. This skill is born with them, not taught. That's why no animal is more skilled than another. You'll notice that all spider webs are equally fine, and all honeycomb cells are the same shape. Whatever is taught by art is inconsistent, but what Nature gives is always the same. Nature has given nothing except the instinct to take care of themselves and the ability to do so. That's why living and learning start at the same time.

No wonder living beings are born with a gift that makes life possible. This is the first thing Nature gave them to maintain their existence—the ability to adapt and the instinct for self-preservation. They couldn't survive without wanting to. This desire alone wouldn't have made them thrive, but without it, nothing could thrive. In no animal can you see any lack of self-esteem or even carelessness for itself. Dumb animals, slow in other ways, are clever at staying alive. So you'll see that creatures that are useless to others are still alert for their own survival. Farewell.

Letter 122 - On darkness as a veil for wickedness

The day has already started to get shorter. It's gotten a lot shorter, but it still leaves enough time if you wake up early, as soon as the day begins. We are more hardworking, and we are better people if we get up early and greet the dawn, but we are lazy if we lie in bed until the sun is high in the sky, or if we wake up only at noon. For many people, even noon feels too early.

Some people have reversed the roles of light and darkness; they only open their eyes, still heavy from the previous day's partying, when night comes. It's similar to what Vergil describes about people who live in places directly opposite ours, where it's night when it's day for us. But it's not just their land that's opposite to ours, it's their whole way of living. There may even be people in our own city who, as Cato said, "have never seen the sun rise or set." Do you think these people know how to live if they don't even know when to live? Do they fear death if they've already buried themselves alive? They are like night birds. Although they spend their nights with wine and perfumes, although they spend their strange waking hours eating dinners with many different courses, they aren't really feasting; they are holding their own funeral ceremonies. And at least the dead have their banquets during the day.

But for someone who is active, no day feels too long. So let's make our lives longer by being active, because living means taking action. Let's shorten the night and use some of it to do the day's work. Birds that are kept in darkness so they can be easily fattened because they don't exercise are like people who don't move around; their idle bodies get overwhelmed with fat, and in their comfortable laziness, they grow fat from doing nothing. The bodies of those who have chosen to live during the night look terrible. Their complexions are more alarming than those of sick people; they are sluggish and swollen, like people with a disease called dropsy. Even though they're still alive, they're already like dead bodies. But to me, this would be one of their lesser problems. There's even more darkness in their souls. Such a person is confused inside; their vision is darkened, and they envy the blind. After all, who ever had eyes just to see in the dark?

You ask me how this bad habit affects the soul—this habit of switching day and night? All vices, or bad habits, go against Nature; they all abandon the natural order. Luxury is all about enjoying what is unusual, not just leaving what is right behind, but going as far from it as possible, and eventually even standing in opposition to it. Don't you think people live against Nature when they drink alcohol on an empty stomach, when they take wine into their empty veins, and go to eat while already drunk? And yet, this is one of the popular vices among young people—building up their strength so they can drink right before going into the bath, among other naked bathers; they even soak in wine and then immediately wipe off the sweat they've built up by drinking so much. To them, having a drink after lunch or dinner is too ordinary; it's what the country folk do, who aren't experts in pleasure. This unmixed wine excites them just because there's no food in their stomachs, so it enters their muscles more quickly; this kind of drinking pleases them just because their stomachs are empty.

Don't you think people live against Nature when they switch their clothes with women? Don't people live against Nature when they try to look young and fresh at an age when it no longer suits them? What could be more cruel or more pathetic? Can't time and the responsibilities of being an adult ever carry such a person beyond trying to stay like a boy? Don't people live against Nature when they crave roses in winter, or try to grow a spring flower like the lily using hot water and artificial heat? Don't people live against Nature when they grow fruit trees on top of a wall? Or when they raise forests on the roofs and battlements of their houses, where the tree roots start in places where even the treetops wouldn't normally reach? Don't people live against Nature when they build bathrooms in the sea and don't think they can enjoy their swim unless the heated pool is whipped by stormy waves?

When people start desiring everything against Nature, they end up completely abandoning Nature. They say, "It's daytime—let's go to sleep! It's time for people to rest—now it's time for us to exercise, go for a drive, and have lunch! Look, dawn is coming—it's time for dinner!" They don't want to do what everyone else does, because they think it's boring and too ordinary to live like other people. They want their days to be unique, special, and different from everyone else's.

In my opinion, these people are as good as dead. Aren't they basically at a funeral—before their time—when they live their lives in torchlight? I remember when this kind of life was very fashionable, among people like Acilius Buta, a person of high rank, who wasted a huge estate and, when he declared bankruptcy to Emperor Tiberius, received the reply: "You've woken up too late!" Julius Montanus, a poet who was only somewhat good, was known for his friendship with Tiberius as well as his fall from favor. He always filled his poems with lots of mentions of sunrise and sunset. Once, when someone complained that Montanus had read all day long and said no one should go to his readings, Natta Pinarius remarked, "I couldn't make a better deal: I'm ready to listen to him from sunrise to sunset!"

Montanus was reading and had reached the words: "The bright morning begins to spread its clear-burning flames; the red dawn scatters its light; and the sad-eyed swallow returns to her nestlings, bringing food to her chatterers and feeding them with her sweet beak." Then Varus, a Roman knight and hanger-on of Marcus Vinicius, who earned his place at fancy dinners with his low-brow humor, shouted, "Bedtime for Buta!" And later, when Montanus read, "Now the shepherds have folded their flocks, and the slow-moving darkness begins to spread silence over the land as it drifts into sleep," the same Varus remarked, "What? Night already? I'll go pay my morning call on Buta!" You see, nothing was more famous than Buta's upside-down way of living. But as I said, this kind of life was fashionable at one time.

Some people live this way not because they find anything particularly special about the night, but because they don't enjoy what's ordinary. Light, which costs nothing, is hated by a guilty conscience, and when people value things based on how much they cost, free light is despised. Also, people who love luxury want to be talked about their whole lives; if people aren't talking about them, they feel like they're wasting their time. So, they're unhappy whenever their actions don't make headlines.

Many people waste their wealth, and many people keep mistresses. If you want to stand out among such people, you have to not only live luxuriously but also be notorious; because in such a busy world, wickedness can't make a name for itself with ordinary scandals.

I once heard Pedo Albinovanus, a very entertaining storyteller, talking about living above the townhouse of Sextus Papinius. Papinius was one of those who avoided the light. "Around nine o'clock at night, I hear the sound of whips. I ask what's going on, and they tell me Papinius is going over his accounts. Around midnight, there's loud shouting; I ask what's the matter, and they say he's exercising his voice. Around two in the morning, I ask what the sound of wheels means; they tell me he's off for a drive. And at dawn, there's a huge commotion—slaves and butlers running around, cooks in a frenzy. I ask what this means, and they tell me he's called for his drink and snack after his bath. His dinner," said Pedo, "never lasted beyond the day, because he lived very frugally; he was generous with nothing but the night. So, if you believe those who say he was stingy and mean, you might also call him a 'slave of the lamp.'"

You shouldn't be surprised by how many different ways vices show up, because there are countless types, and they can't all be categorized. The way to stay righteous is simple; the way to be wicked is complicated and full of ways to go wrong. The same is true of character; if you follow Nature, character is easy to manage, free, and only has small differences. But the kind of person I've mentioned has a twisted character, out of harmony with everything, including himself.

The main cause of this disease seems to be a picky rejection of normal life. Just like these people stand out in their dress, or in the way they arrange their meals, or in the elegance of their carriages, they also want to be different in how they divide up the hours of their day. They don't want to be wicked in the usual way because their kind of wickedness seeks fame. Fame is what all such people seek—people who, in a way, are living their lives backward.

So, Lucilius, let's stick to the path that Nature has set for us, and let's not stray from it. If we follow Nature, everything is easy and straightforward; but if we fight against Nature, our lives become like those who row against the current. Farewell.

Letter 123 - On the conflict between pleasure and virtue

I was more tired from the discomfort of my journey than from its length, and I finally reached my Alban villa late at night. When I arrived, I found nothing prepared except for myself. So, I decided to sit at my writing table to shake off my fatigue. I realized that this delay by my cook and baker turned out to be a good thing because it gave me time to reflect. I thought about how nothing feels heavy if you face it with a light heart, and nothing needs to make you angry unless you choose to get angry.

My baker didn't have any bread ready, but I could get some from the overseer, the house-steward, or one of my tenants. You might think, "Bad bread!" But if you wait, even bad bread will taste good. Hunger will make it seem delicious and full of flavor. So, I decided not to eat until I was truly hungry. I would wait until I could get good bread or stop being picky about it.

It's important to get used to simple food because there are many times and places where even the richest person will face challenges.

No one can always get what they want, but it's in our power not to wish for what we don't have and to be happy with what we do have. A big step toward independence is having a good-humored stomach that can handle rough treatment.

You can't imagine how much pleasure I get from the fact that my weariness is starting to fade on its own. I'm not asking for slaves to rub me down, or a bath, or any other kind of relief except time. Whatever meal I have will give me more pleasure than a grand feast. I've tested my spirit suddenly, without any preparation, and this is a simpler and truer test. When a person prepares themselves to be patient, it's harder to see how strong their mind really is. The best proof of strength is when you handle your problems calmly and fairly, without losing your temper or arguing, and when you meet your own needs without craving something extra.

We often don't realize how many things are unnecessary until they are gone. We didn't use them because we needed them, but just because we had them. And we acquire many things simply because our neighbors have them, or because most people do. Many of our troubles come from living according to what others do, instead of living according to reason. There are things that, if only a few people did them, we wouldn't want to copy; but when the majority start doing them, we follow along, as if something becomes more honorable just because more people do it! Moreover, wrong ideas, once they become common, start to seem like the right way to think.

Nowadays, everyone travels with Numidian outriders ahead of them, and with a troop of slave-runners to clear the way. We think it's shameful not to have attendants who will push crowds aside, or not to have a great cloud of dust to show that an important person is coming. Everyone now has mules loaded with crystal and myrrhine cups carved by famous artists. We think it's disgraceful if our belongings don't make a grand noise as they're carried along. Everyone has servants who ride along with ointment-covered faces, so that the weather won't harm their delicate skin. We think it's disgraceful if none of our servant boys have healthy cheeks free of cosmetics.

You should avoid talking to people like this because they spread their bad habits from one person to another. We used to think the worst kind of these people were those who bragged about their words, but now there are those who even brag about their wickedness. Their talk is very harmful; even if it doesn't convince us right away, it leaves seeds of trouble in our souls. These seeds grow and gain strength, following us even after we've parted from them. Just like those who attend a concert carry the melodies and charm of the songs in their heads afterward, which interferes with their thinking and doesn't allow them to focus on serious subjects, so too the speech of flatterers and enthusiasts for what is depraved sticks in our minds long after we've heard them. It's not easy to get rid of a catchy tune; it stays with us, lingers on, and comes back from time to time.

So, you should close your ears against evil talk right from the start. If you let such talk in and the words get into your mind, they become bolder. Then, we start saying things like, "Virtue, Philosophy, Justice—these are just empty words. The only way to be happy is to enjoy yourself. Eating, drinking, and spending money is the only real life, the only way to remind yourself that you're mortal. Our days pass by, and life—which we can't get back—rushes away from us. Why wait to come to our senses? This life won't always allow pleasures; while it can, and while it demands them, what good is there in being frugal? So, let's get ahead of death, and spend now what death would take from us later. You don't have a mistress, no favorite slave to make your mistress jealous; you're sober when you appear in public each day; you eat as if you had to show your account-book to 'Papa'; but that's not really living, it's just sharing in someone else's existence. And how foolish it is to save up for your heir and deny yourself everything, only to turn your friends into enemies with the vast fortune you plan to leave! The more your heir is set to get from you, the more he'll be glad to see you go! All those stern people who criticize others' lives in a self-righteous way, while they're really enemies to their own lives, playing the teacher to the world—you shouldn't value them at all. Don't hesitate to prefer good living over a good reputation."

These are the voices you should avoid, just as Ulysses avoided the Sirens by tying himself to the mast. They are no less powerful; they lure people away from their country, their parents, their friends, and virtuous ways. By a hope that, even if it's not base, is ill-fated, they lead them into a life of disgrace. How much better it is to follow a straight path and reach a place where the words "pleasant" and "honorable" mean the same thing!

This goal will be possible for us if we understand that there are two kinds of things: those that attract us, like riches, pleasures, beauty, and ambition, and those that repel us, like toil, death, pain, disgrace, or frugality. We ought to train ourselves to avoid wanting the first group and fearing the second. Let's fight in the opposite way: let's move away from the things that tempt us and prepare ourselves to face the things that challenge us.

Don't you see how different it is to go down a mountain versus climbing up one? When coming down, people lean backward; when climbing up, they lean forward. For, my dear Lucilius, if you let your body lean forward when coming down, or backward when climbing up, you're giving in to vice. Pleasures pull us downhill, but we must work to climb up toward what is rough and hard. In one case, let's lean forward, and in the other, let's pull back.

Do you think I'm only saying that those who praise pleasure and make us fear pain are harmful? I believe that those who pretend to follow the Stoic school but still lead us into vice are just as dangerous. They boast that only the wise and learned know how to love. They say, "Only the wise man knows the art of love; the wise man also knows best how to drink and feast. Our study should be focused on how long the bloom of love can last!"

All this may be seen as a nod to the ways of Greece, but we should instead turn our attention to words like these: "No one is good by chance. Virtue must be learned. Pleasure is low and trivial, something to be ignored, and even the smallest animals seek it out. Glory is empty and fleeting, lighter than air. Poverty is no evil unless we resist it. Death is not an evil—why ask? Death is the one thing that's an equal privilege for all mankind. Superstition is the misguided idea of a fool; it fears those it should love and insults those it worships. What difference is there between denying the gods and dishonoring them?"

You should learn principles like these by heart. Philosophy shouldn't try to excuse vice. If a sick man's doctor tells him to live recklessly, he's beyond saving. Farewell.

Letter 124 - On the true good as attained by reason

There are many old teachings I could share with you if you weren't hesitant and ashamed to learn about simple duties. But you aren't hesitant, and you aren't put off by the complexities of study. Your educated mind doesn't take important topics lightly. I appreciate your approach because you make everything count toward some progress, and you only get frustrated when no amount of effort leads to success. I will work to show that this is also the case here. Our question is whether the Good is understood through our senses or our mind, and this also tells us that the Good doesn't exist in animals or young children.

Those who believe pleasure is the highest goal think that the Good is something we sense with our bodies. But we Stoics believe that the Good is understood with the mind, and we place it in our thoughts. If our senses were in charge of deciding what is good, we would never reject any pleasure because all pleasures attract us, and we would never willingly go through any pain because all pain is unpleasant to our senses.

Furthermore, those who love pleasure too much and those who fear pain greatly wouldn't deserve criticism if this were true. But we do criticize people who are controlled by their desires and cravings, and we look down on people who avoid doing anything brave because they fear pain. But what wrong would these people be doing if they only followed what their senses told them was good or bad? After all, you and others like you have put the senses in charge of deciding what to seek and what to avoid.

However, reason is clearly the deciding factor in matters like this. Just as reason has made decisions about the happy life, virtue, and honor, it has also decided what is good and what is bad. But for those who rely on their senses, the worst part of them is allowed to judge the better parts, so that the senses—dull and slow, and even less sharp in humans than in other animals—decide what is Good. Just imagine someone trying to tell tiny objects apart by touch instead of sight! There's no sense more delicate and sharp than sight to help us tell the difference between good and bad. So you can see how far from the truth a person is if they think the sense of touch can decide what the Supreme Good and Supreme Evil are.

He says, "Just as every science and every art must have something that can be touched and sensed, which is where they start and grow, the happy life also begins with things that we can touch and sense. Surely you agree that the happy life starts with things we can physically sense." But we define "happy" as things that are in line with Nature. And what is in line with Nature is clear and easy to see, just as easy as recognizing something that is complete. What is in line with Nature, what we are given as a gift at birth, is, I say, not the Good itself, but the beginning of the Good. But you place the highest Good, pleasure, in babies, so that a child at birth begins at the point where a fully developed adult arrives. You are placing the tree-top where the root should be.

If anyone were to say that a child, hidden in its mother's womb, with an unknown sex, delicate, unformed, and shapeless, is already in a state of goodness, they would clearly be mistaken. And yet how little difference there is between a newborn and a child still in the womb!

They are equally undeveloped when it comes to understanding good or bad, and a child is no more capable of grasping the Good than a tree or any dumb animal. But why doesn't the Good exist in a tree or an animal? Because they don't have reason either. For the same reason, the Good doesn't exist in a child, because the child also lacks reason; the child will only reach the Good when they reach reason.

There are animals without reason, animals that don't yet have reason, and animals that have reason but only partially. In none of these does the Good exist, because it is reason that brings the Good with it. What, then, is the difference between the groups I mentioned? In those without reason, the Good will never exist. In those that don't yet have reason, the Good can't exist at that time. And in those that have reason but only partially, the Good can exist, but it doesn't yet.

This is what I mean, Lucilius: the Good cannot be found in just anyone or at just any age. It is as far removed from infancy as the end is from the beginning, or as something complete is from something that has just started. So, it cannot exist in a fragile body, when the small frame has only just begun to grow. Of course not, no more than in a seed.

If this is true, we understand that there is a certain kind of Good in a tree or a plant. But this is not true during its first growth, when the plant has just started to sprout from the ground. There is a certain Good in wheat, but it doesn't yet exist in the growing stalk or when the soft ear is just starting to push out of the husk. It only exists when summer days and its full maturity have ripened the wheat. Just as Nature in general doesn't produce her Good until she is fully developed, in the same way, man's Good doesn't exist in him until both reason and man are fully developed.

And what is this Good? I'll tell you: it is a free mind, an upright mind, one that controls other things but is controlled by nothing. Infancy is so far from having this Good that even boyhood can't hope for it, and even young adulthood holds onto the hope without reason. Even our old age is very fortunate if it has reached this Good after long and focused study. If this, then, is the Good, the Good is a matter of the mind.

"But," someone might argue, "you admitted that there is a certain Good in trees and grass. Then surely there can be a certain Good in a child too." But the true Good is not found in trees or animals—the Good that exists in them is called "good" only as a matter of courtesy. "Then what is it?" you ask. It is simply what is in line with the nature of each. The real Good cannot be found in animals—not at all; its nature is more blessed and of a higher kind. And where there is no place for reason, the Good does not exist.

There are four kinds of nature we should mention here: tree, animal, human, and divine. The last two, having reason, are of the same nature, different only because one is immortal and the other is mortal. Of one of these, namely God, Nature perfects the Good. Of the other, namely man, effort and study do so. All other things are only perfect in their particular nature, and not truly perfect, since they lack reason.

To sum up, only that which is perfect according to nature as a whole is truly perfect, and nature as a whole possesses reason. Other things can be perfect according to their kind. That which cannot contain the happy life cannot contain what produces the happy life, and the happy life is produced by the Good alone. In animals, there isn't a trace of the happy life, nor of the things that produce it. In animals, the Good does not exist.

Animals understand the world around them only through their senses. They remember the past only when something reminds their senses. For example, a horse remembers the right road only when it is placed at the starting point. However, in its stall, the horse has no memory of the road, no matter how many times it has traveled it. The third state—the future—does not exist for animals.

How, then, can we consider the nature of beings who have no experience of time in its fullness as perfect? For time is threefold: past, present, and future. Animals only perceive the time that is most important to them—the present. They rarely remember the past, and only when there are present reminders. Therefore, the Good of a perfect nature cannot exist in an imperfect nature. Because if this type of nature could possess the Good, then so could mere plants. I don't deny that animals have strong and quick instincts toward actions that seem natural, but these instincts are confused and disordered. However, the Good is never confused or disordered.

"What!" you ask, "Do animals act in a disturbed and chaotic way?" I would say they act in a disturbed and chaotic way if their nature allowed for order. As it is, they act according to their nature. For something to be called "disturbed," it must also be able to be "not disturbed" at other times. In the same way, something is said to be troubled only if it can be at peace. No one is bad except someone who has the ability to be good. In the case of animals, their actions are just a result of their nature.

But, to not tire you out, a certain kind of good can be found in an animal, and a certain kind of virtue, and a certain kind of perfection. But not the true Good, nor true virtue, nor true perfection. Because these are the privilege of reasoning beings alone, who can understand the cause, the degree, and the method. Therefore, Good can only exist in those who have reason.

Do you ask now where our argument is leading, and what benefit it will have for your mind? I will tell you: it exercises and sharpens the mind and ensures, by occupying it honorably, that it will achieve some kind of good. And even that is beneficial, which holds people back when they are rushing into wickedness. However, I will also say this: I can be of no greater benefit to you than by revealing the Good that is rightfully yours, by taking you out of the class of animals, and by placing you on a level with God.

Why, then, do you focus on building physical strength? Nature has given greater strength to cattle and wild animals. Why cultivate beauty? Despite all your efforts, animals surpass you in attractiveness. Why do you spend so much time on your hair? Even if you style it in elaborate ways, you will see a mane that is thicker and more beautiful on any horse you choose, and a mane that is more stunning on the neck of any lion. And even after training yourself for speed, you won't be faster than a hare.

Are you not willing to give up all these pursuits—where you must admit defeat, striving as you are for something that is not your own—and return to the Good that truly belongs to you? And what is this Good? It is a clear and flawless mind, which rivals that of God, raised far above earthly concerns, and considering nothing outside itself to be its own.

You are a reasoning being. What Good, then, lies within you? Perfect reason. Are you willing to develop this to its fullest extent, to its greatest potential? Consider yourself happy only when all your joys come from reason, and when, having considered all the things people desire, pray for, or seek, you find nothing that you will desire. Mind you, I do not say prefer. Here is a simple rule by which to measure yourself, and by which you may feel that you have reached perfection: "You will have truly found yourself when you realize that those whom the world calls fortunate are actually the most unfortunate of all." Farewell.

On the Shortness of Life

Seneca

Letter 49: On The Shortness of Life

A person is indeed truly lazy and careless, my dear Lucilius, if he only remembers a friend when he sees a place that reminds him of that friend. But sometimes, familiar places bring back a feeling of loss that we've kept hidden inside. They don't just bring back dead memories but wake them up from where they've been sleeping, like how seeing a lost friend's favorite slave, cloak, or house can renew the sadness, even if time has made it softer.

Now, look at Campania, especially Naples and your beloved Pompeii. When I saw them, they made me miss you a lot. I can picture you clearly in my mind, like I'm about to say goodbye to you. I see you trying hard to hold back your tears but not being able to stop the emotions that rise up just when you try to control them. It feels like I lost you just a moment ago because, when we use our memory, everything feels like it happened just a short while ago.

It seems like just a moment ago that I was a young boy sitting in the philosopher Sotion's school, just a moment ago that I started working as a lawyer, just a moment ago that I lost the desire to practice law, and just a moment ago that I lost the ability to do it. Time flies incredibly fast, especially when we look back at it. When we're focused on what's happening now, we don't notice how fast time is passing because it moves so gently and quickly.

Do you wonder why? All the time that has passed is in the same place; it all looks the same to us, like it's all mixed together. Everything slips into the same emptiness. Also, something that is so short can't have long periods within it. The time we spend living is just a tiny point, or even smaller than a point. But this tiny bit of time, short as it is, nature has tricked us into thinking it's longer than it really is. She has divided it into parts like infancy, childhood, youth, the gradual slope from youth to old age, and old age itself is yet another part. How many steps there are for such a short climb!

It feels like just a moment ago that I saw you off on your journey, and yet this "moment ago" makes up a good part of our existence. This existence is so brief that we should remember it will soon end altogether. In other years, time didn't seem to go by so quickly; now, it seems to fly by faster than I can believe, maybe because I feel that the end is getting closer, or maybe because I've started to notice and count my losses.

For this reason, I'm even more upset that some people spend most of this short time on things that don't matter—time that, no matter how carefully we protect it, isn't enough even for the important things. Cicero said that even if he had twice as many days to live, he wouldn't have time to read the lyric poets. You could say the same thing about people who study complicated arguments, but they are foolish in a sadder way. The lyric poets admit that they are writing for fun, but these people think they're doing something serious.

I'm not saying you shouldn't look at these complex arguments, but you should only glance at them, like saying a quick hello at the door, just to avoid being tricked into thinking they're really valuable. Why stress yourself out and lose weight over some problem that it's smarter to ignore than to solve? When a soldier is relaxed and traveling at his own pace, he can stop to look at small things along the way, but when the enemy is close behind and the order is given to speed up, he has to throw away everything he picked up during peaceful times.

I don't have time to figure out the tricky details of words or to show off how clever I am with them. Look at the enemy gathering, the gates locked tight, and weapons ready for battle. I need a strong heart to listen to this noise of battle all around me without flinching.

Everyone would rightly think I was crazy if, while the older men and women were piling up rocks for the walls, and the young men in armor inside the gates were waiting or even asking for the order to attack, and the enemy's spears were shaking our gates, and the ground was trembling with mines and tunnels, I sat there doing nothing, asking silly questions like, "What you haven't lost, you still have. But you haven't lost any horns. So, you must have horns," or other nonsense like that.

And yet, you might think I'm just as crazy if I spend my energy on that kind of thing, because even now, I'm under siege. But in the first case, the danger would only be from the outside, with a wall between me and the enemy; but now, the danger of death is right here with me. I don't have time for such foolishness; I have a big task ahead of me. What should I do? Death is close behind me, and life is slipping away.

Teach me something to help me face these troubles. Help me stop trying to run away from death, and help me stop letting life slip through my fingers.

Give me the courage to face hardships; make me calm in the face of what I can't avoid. Help me make the most of the short time I have. Show me that the value of life doesn't depend on how long it is, but on how well I use it. Also, show me that it's possible, or even common, for someone who has lived a long life to have actually lived very little. Tell me when I lie down to sleep, "You might not wake up again!" And when I wake up, "You might not go to sleep again!" Tell me when I leave my house, "You might not come back!" And when I come back, "You might not leave again!"

You're wrong if you think that there's only a thin line between life and death on a sea voyage. No, that line is just as thin everywhere. It's just that we don't always see death so close by, but he's always just as near.

Take away these shadowy fears, and then it will be easier for you to teach me the lessons I'm ready to learn. When we were born, nature made us capable of learning, and she gave us reason, not perfect, but capable of being perfected.

Teach me about justice, duty, self-discipline, and the two types of purity—one that keeps us from harming others and one that keeps us true to ourselves. If you don't lead me down the wrong paths, I'll reach my goal more easily. As the tragic poet says: "The language of truth is simple." So we shouldn't make that language complicated; nothing is less suitable for a person with great goals than tricky cleverness. Farewell.

The End

As A Man Thinketh

James Allen

Introduction

"Mind is the Master power that moulds and makes,
And Man is Mind, and evermore he takes
The tool of Thought, and, shaping what he wills,
Brings forth a thousand joys, a thousand ills:—
He thinks in secret, and it comes to pass:
Environment is but his looking-glass."

~ James Allen

This little book, which is the result of meditation and experience, is not meant to be a complete work on the often-discussed topic of the power of thought. Instead, it aims to inspire rather than explain, with the goal of encouraging men and women to discover and understand the truth that—

"They themselves are makers of themselves."

This is because of the thoughts they choose and nurture. The mind is the master-weaver, shaping both the inner garment of character and the outer garment of circumstance. Although people may have woven their lives in ignorance and pain before, they can now weave in enlightenment and happiness.

James Allen
Broad Park Avenue,
Ilfracombe,

Chapter 1
Thought and Character

The saying "As a man thinks in his heart, so is he" describes not only a person's entire being but also covers every aspect of their life. A person is truly what they think, as their character is the sum total of all their thoughts.

Just as a plant grows from a seed and cannot exist without it, every action of a person comes from hidden seeds of thought and could not happen without them. This applies to actions that seem "spontaneous" and "unpremeditated" as much as it does to those that are planned.

Action is the blossom of thought, and joy and suffering are its fruits. Thus, a person harvests the sweet and bitter outcomes of their own cultivation.

"Thought in the mind has made us what we are. By thought was wrought and built. If a man's mind has evil thoughts, pain comes to him just as the wheel follows the ox. If one endures in purity of thought, joy follows him like his own shadow—sure."

A person grows by law, not by artificial means, and cause and effect are as absolute and unchanging in the hidden realm of thought as they are in the world of visible and material things. A noble and godlike character is not a gift or a result of chance but is the natural result of consistent right thinking and the effect of dwelling on godlike thoughts for a long time. In the same way, an ignoble and beastly character results from continually harboring lowly thoughts.

A person is made or unmade by themselves. In the workshop of thought, they create the weapons that can destroy themselves or the tools with which they build heavenly mansions of joy, strength, and peace. By choosing the right thoughts and applying them correctly, a person rises to divine perfection; by misusing and wrongly applying thoughts, they fall below the level of a beast. Between these two extremes are all the levels of character, and a person is their creator and master.

Of all the beautiful truths about the soul that have been discovered and brought to light in this age, none is more uplifting or full of divine promise and confidence than this: that a person is the master of their thoughts, the shaper of their character, and the creator of their conditions, environment, and destiny.

As a being of power, intelligence, and love, and the ruler of their own thoughts, a person holds the key to every situation and possesses within themselves the transformative and regenerative ability to become what they desire.

A person is always the master, even in their weakest and most abandoned state. However, in their weakness and degradation, they are a foolish master who mismanages their "household." When they begin to reflect on their condition and diligently search for the Law upon which their being is founded, they become the wise master, directing their energies with intelligence and shaping their thoughts to achieve positive outcomes. This is the conscious master, and a person can only become this by discovering within themselves the laws of thought. This discovery is entirely a matter of application, self-analysis, and experience.

Gold and diamonds are obtained only through much searching and mining, and a person can find every truth related to their being if they dig deep into the mine of their soul. They can prove that they are the maker of their character, the shaper of their life, and the builder of their destiny if they watch, control, and change their thoughts, observing their effects on themselves, on others, and on their life and circumstances. By linking cause and effect through patient practice and investigation, and using every experience, even the most trivial, everyday occurrences, as a means of gaining self-knowledge, they gain understanding, wisdom, and power. In this pursuit, like no other, the law is absolute that "He that seeks, finds; and to him that knocks, it shall be opened;" for only through patience, practice, and constant persistence can a person enter the Door of the Temple of Knowledge.

Chapter 2
Effect of Thought on Circumstances

A man's mind can be compared to a garden, which can be carefully tended or allowed to grow wild. But whether you take care of it or not, it will produce something. If you don't plant good seeds, weeds will grow in abundance.

Just as a gardener takes care of his garden, keeping it free from weeds and growing the flowers and fruits he wants, a person can tend the garden of their mind by removing wrong, useless, and impure thoughts and nurturing right, useful, and pure ones. By doing this, a person eventually realizes that they are the master gardener of their soul and the director of their life. They also discover the laws of thought within themselves and understand more clearly how thoughts shape their character, circumstances, and destiny.

Thought and character are connected, and since character shows itself through environment and circumstances, a person's outer conditions will always be related to their inner state. This doesn't mean that a person's circumstances at any moment fully reveal their entire character, but that these circumstances are deeply linked to some essential thought within them and are necessary for their growth at that time.

Every person is where they are because of the law of their being. The thoughts they have built into their character have brought them there, and nothing in their life happens by chance. Everything is the result of a law that cannot make mistakes. This is true for both those who feel out of harmony with their surroundings and those who are content.

As a growing and evolving being, a person is where they are to learn and grow. As they learn the spiritual lesson in any circumstance, it passes away and makes room for new ones.

People are affected by circumstances as long as they believe they are controlled by outside conditions. But when they realize they are a creative force and can control the inner seeds and soil from which circumstances grow, they become the true master of themselves.

Anyone who has practiced self-control and self-purification knows that circumstances arise from thought. They notice that changes in their circumstances occur in exact proportion to their mental changes. When someone sincerely works to fix their character's flaws and makes quick and noticeable progress, they often go through a series of changes.

The soul attracts what it secretly harbors, loves, and fears. It reaches the heights of its aspirations and falls to the level of its unrefined desires, and circumstances are how the soul receives its due.

Every thought planted in the mind takes root, grows into action, and bears fruit in the form of opportunity and circumstance. Good thoughts bring good fruit; bad thoughts bring bad fruit.

The external world shapes itself to the internal world of thought. Both pleasant and unpleasant conditions ultimately benefit the individual. As a harvester of his own crop, a person learns through both suffering and joy.

By following the desires, aspirations, and thoughts that dominate him—whether pursuing fleeting fantasies or steadfastly following the path of high endeavor—a person ultimately reaches their fulfillment in the outer conditions of their life. Everywhere, the laws of growth and adjustment apply.

A person does not end up in poverty or jail because of fate or circumstance but by following lowly thoughts and desires. Similarly, a pure-minded person does not suddenly commit a crime due to external forces; the criminal thought was nurtured in their heart long before, and opportunity revealed its power. Circumstance does not make the man; it reveals him to himself. One cannot fall into vice without vicious inclinations or rise into virtue without nurturing virtuous aspirations. As the lord of thought, a person makes himself, shaping his environment and destiny. Even at birth, the soul attracts the conditions that reflect its purity and impurity, strength and weakness.

People do not attract what they want but what they are. Their whims and ambitions are thwarted, but their innermost thoughts and desires are fulfilled, whether good or bad. The "divinity that shapes our ends" is within us; it is our very self. Only a person can chain themselves. Thought and action are the jailers of fate, imprisoning us when base and liberating us when noble. A person does not receive what they wish and pray for, but what they earn. Their wishes and prayers are fulfilled only when they align with their thoughts and actions.

In light of this truth, what does it mean to "fight against circumstances"? It means continually opposing an external effect while nurturing and maintaining its cause in one's heart. This cause may be a conscious vice or an unconscious weakness, but it hinders progress and calls for remedy.

People want to improve their circumstances but are unwilling to improve themselves, so they remain stuck. A person who does not shy away from self-sacrifice will always achieve their goals. This applies to both earthly and heavenly pursuits. Even someone who wants to become wealthy must be willing to make personal sacrifices to succeed. How much more must one do to achieve a balanced and strong life?

Consider a man who is desperately poor. He wants to improve his surroundings and comfort but shirks his work and thinks he is justified in deceiving his employer due to low wages. Such a man does not understand the basic principles of prosperity and is not only unable to rise out of poverty but attracts deeper misery by indulging in lazy and deceptive thoughts.

Or consider a wealthy man who suffers from a persistent disease caused by gluttony. He is willing to spend large sums to cure it but won't give up his excessive desires. He wants to enjoy rich food and good health, but he is unfit for health because he hasn't learned the basics of a healthy life.

Then there is the employer who cuts wages to increase profits, not realizing he is setting himself up for failure. When he faces bankruptcy in both reputation and wealth, he blames circumstances, not knowing he is the sole author of his condition.

These examples illustrate that a person often unconsciously creates their circumstances. While aiming for a good outcome, they undermine their success by nurturing thoughts and desires that don't align with their goals. Readers can trace the action of thought in their minds and lives and see how external circumstances cannot serve as the sole basis for reasoning.

Circumstances are complex, thought is deeply rooted, and the conditions of happiness vary greatly among individuals. A man's entire soul condition, though it may be known to himself, cannot be judged by another based solely on his external life. A man may be honest in some areas yet suffer privations; a man may be dishonest in some areas yet acquire wealth. The conclusion that one fails due to honesty and the other succeeds due to dishonesty results from superficial judgment, assuming the dishonest man is entirely corrupt and the honest man is entirely virtuous. Deeper knowledge and experience show such judgments to be false. The dishonest man may have virtues the other lacks, and the honest man may have vices the other is free from. The honest man reaps the rewards of his good thoughts and actions and suffers from his vices. The dishonest man similarly experiences his own suffering and happiness.

It's comforting to human vanity to believe one suffers due to virtue, but until a man removes every bitter and impure thought from his mind and cleanses his soul of sin, he cannot declare that his suffering is due to his good qualities. Before reaching supreme perfection, he will find the Great Law of Justice operating in his mind and life, which does not give good for evil or evil for good. With this knowledge, he will look back on his past ignorance and blindness and know that his life is and always has been justly ordered and that all his past experiences, good and bad, were the fair outcomes of his evolving self.

Good thoughts and actions never produce bad results, and bad thoughts and actions never produce good results. Just as corn cannot produce anything but corn and nettles nothing but nettles, this law is understood in the natural world. Still, few understand it in the mental and moral world, though it operates just as consistently there.

Suffering always results from wrong thoughts. It indicates that an individual is out of harmony with themselves and the law of their being. The sole purpose of suffering is to purify and remove all that is useless and impure. Suffering ceases for the pure. There is no reason to burn gold once the impurities have been removed, and a perfectly pure and enlightened being cannot suffer.

The circumstances a man encounters with suffering result from his own mental disharmony. The circumstances a man encounters with blessedness result from his own mental harmony. Blessedness, not material possessions, measures right thought; wretchedness, not a lack of material possessions, measures wrong thought. A man may be cursed and rich, or blessed and poor. Blessedness and riches only come together when riches are rightly and wisely used. A poor man only falls into wretchedness when he sees his situation as an unjust burden.

Poverty and indulgence are the two extremes of wretchedness, both equally unnatural and the result of mental disorder. A man is only rightly conditioned when he is happy, healthy, and prosperous, and happiness, health, and prosperity result from harmoniously aligning his inner self with his surroundings.

A person begins to truly live when they stop complaining and blaming others and start searching for the hidden justice that governs their life. As they align their mind with this justice, they stop blaming others for their condition and build themselves up with strong and noble thoughts. They stop fighting against circumstances and begin to use them to progress faster and discover their inner powers and possibilities.

Law, not chaos, is the dominant principle in the universe; justice, not injustice, is the soul of life; and righteousness, not corruption, is the force behind the spiritual governance of the world. This means that by aligning himself with righteousness, a man will find that the universe aligns with him. As he changes his thoughts towards things and people, things and people will change towards him.

The truth of this is in every person, allowing for easy investigation through introspection and self-analysis. Let a person radically change their thoughts, and they will be amazed at the rapid transformation it brings to their material conditions. People think thoughts can be kept secret, but they can't; thoughts quickly crystallize into habits, which solidify into circumstances. Bestial thoughts lead to habits of drunkenness and sensuality, which result in poverty and disease. Impure thoughts lead to habits of confusion and distraction, resulting in adverse circumstances. Fearful, doubtful, and indecisive thoughts lead to weak habits, resulting in failure and dependence. Lazy thoughts lead to habits of uncleanliness and dishonesty, resulting in poverty. Hateful and critical thoughts lead to habits of accusation and violence, resulting in injury and persecution. Selfish thoughts lead to self-seeking habits, resulting in distressing circumstances. Conversely, beautiful thoughts lead to habits of grace and kindness, resulting in pleasant circumstances. Pure thoughts lead to habits of self-control, resulting in peace. Courageous and self-reliant thoughts lead to successful and free circumstances. Energetic thoughts lead to habits of cleanliness and industry, resulting in pleasant circumstances. Gentle and forgiving thoughts lead to protective circumstances. Loving and selfless thoughts lead to self-forgetfulness habits, resulting in prosperity and true riches.

A particular train of thought, whether good or bad, will inevitably produce results on character and circumstances. While a person cannot directly choose their circumstances, they can choose their thoughts and, by doing so, indirectly shape their circumstances.

Nature helps everyone fulfill the thoughts they most encourage, and opportunities arise that will quickly bring good and evil thoughts to the surface.

Let a person abandon sinful thoughts, and the world will soften towards them and be ready to help. Let them discard weak thoughts, and opportunities will arise to aid their strong resolves. Let them nurture good thoughts, and no hard fate will bind them to wretchedness and shame. The world is your kaleidoscope, and its ever-changing patterns are the carefully adjusted pictures of your thoughts.

"So You will be what you will to be;
Let failure find its false content
In that poor word, 'environment,'
But spirit scorns it, and is free.
"It masters time, it conquers space;
It cowes that boastful trickster, Chance,
And bids the tyrant Circumstance
Uncrown, and fill a servant's place.
"The human Will, that force unseen,
The offspring of a deathless Soul,
Can hew a way to any goal,
Though walls of granite intervene.
"Be not impatient in delays
But wait as one who understands;
When spirit rises and commands
The gods are ready to obey."

Chapter 3
Effect of Thought on Health and the Body

The body serves the mind. It follows what the mind thinks, whether those thoughts are intentionally chosen or come automatically. When the mind is filled with negative or unlawful thoughts, the body quickly falls into sickness and decay. On the other hand, when the mind is full of happy and beautiful thoughts, the body becomes youthful and healthy.

Just like circumstances, disease and health are rooted in thought. Sickly thoughts show up in a sickly body. Fearful thoughts can kill a person as quickly as a bullet, and they are constantly affecting thousands of people, even if not as suddenly. Those who fear disease are the ones who often get it. Anxiety weakens the entire body and makes it susceptible to disease, while impure thoughts, even if not acted upon physically, will eventually harm the nervous system.

Strong, pure, and happy thoughts build up the body with strength and grace. The body is sensitive and responds to the thoughts it receives, and habitual thoughts will have their effects, whether good or bad.

People will continue to have impure and unhealthy bodies as long as they have unclean thoughts. A clean heart leads to a clean life and a healthy body. A polluted mind leads to a corrupt life and an unhealthy body. Thought is the source of action, life, and expression; make the source pure, and everything will be pure.

Changing one's diet won't help if a person doesn't change their thoughts. When a person purifies their thoughts, they no longer desire unhealthy food.

Pure thoughts lead to clean habits. A so-called saint who does not wash is not a saint. A person who strengthens and purifies their thoughts does not need to worry about harmful germs.

To protect your body, guard your mind. To renew your body, beautify your mind. Thoughts of malice, envy, disappointment, and despair rob the body of its health and beauty. A sour face is not an accident; it is created by sour thoughts. Wrinkles are caused by foolishness, passion, and pride.

I know a woman who is ninety-six with the bright, innocent face of a young girl. I know a man who is much younger, yet his face is distorted by passion and discontent. The difference is that the woman has a sweet and sunny disposition, while the man has been consumed by negative emotions.

Just as you cannot have a sweet and healthy home without letting in air and sunshine, you cannot have a strong body and a bright, happy face without letting thoughts of joy, goodwill, and calmness into your mind.

On the faces of the elderly, some wrinkles are made by sympathy, others by pure thought, and others by passion. Who cannot tell the difference? For those who have lived righteously, old age is calm, peaceful, and gently mellowed, like a setting sun. I recently saw a philosopher on his deathbed. He was not old, except in years. He died as sweetly and peacefully as he lived.

Cheerful thoughts are the best medicine for curing the body's ills, and goodwill is the best comfort for dispelling grief and sorrow. Living with thoughts of ill will, cynicism, suspicion, and envy is like being in a prison you've built yourself. But thinking well of others, being cheerful, and finding the good in everyone—such unselfish thoughts are like the gates to heaven. Living each day with thoughts of peace toward all creatures will bring peace to the person who has them.

Chapter 4
Thought and Purpose

Until thought is linked with purpose, there can be no intelligent accomplishment. Most people let their thoughts drift aimlessly through life. Aimlessness is a vice, and anyone who wants to avoid catastrophe and destruction must not let it continue.

Those who lack a central purpose in their lives are easily overwhelmed by worries, fears, troubles, and self-pity, all of which are signs of weakness. These lead to failure, unhappiness, and loss just as surely as deliberately planned sins, though by a different path, because weakness cannot survive in a universe where power is constantly growing.

A person should form a clear purpose in their heart and work towards achieving it. This purpose should become the center of their thoughts. It could be a spiritual ideal or a worldly goal, depending on their nature at the time, but whatever it is, they should consistently focus their mental energy on the goal they have set. This purpose should be their highest priority, and they should dedicate themselves to reaching it, not letting their thoughts wander off into temporary fancies, desires, and imaginings. This is the key to self-control and true concentration of thought. Even if they fail repeatedly to achieve their purpose (as they inevitably will until they overcome their weaknesses), the strength of character they gain will be a true measure of their success. This will become a new starting point for future power and triumph.

Those who are not ready to grasp a great purpose should focus their thoughts on performing their duties flawlessly, no matter how unimportant their tasks may seem. Only in this way can they gather and focus their thoughts, develop resolution and energy, and once this is achieved, there is nothing that cannot be accomplished.

Even the weakest soul, knowing its own weaknesses and believing the truth that strength can only be developed through effort and practice, will begin to exert itself. By adding effort to effort, patience to patience, and strength to strength, it will never stop growing and will eventually become divinely strong.

Just as a physically weak person can become strong through careful and patient training, so can a person with weak thoughts make them strong by practicing right thinking.

To get rid of aimlessness and weakness and to start thinking with purpose is to join the ranks of those strong individuals who only see failure as one of the paths to achievement, who make every condition serve them, and who think strongly, attempt fearlessly, and accomplish masterfully.

Once a person has conceived a purpose, they should mentally map out a direct path to its achievement, without looking to the right or the left. Doubts and fears should be strictly avoided; they are disruptive elements that break up the straight line of effort, making it crooked, ineffective, and useless. Thoughts of doubt and fear have never accomplished anything and never will. They always lead to failure. Purpose, energy, and the power to act disappear when doubt and fear creep in.

The will to act comes from knowing that we can act. Doubt and fear are the greatest enemies of knowledge, and anyone who encourages them or fails to eliminate them hinders themselves at every step.

A person who has conquered doubt and fear has conquered failure. Every thought they have is connected to power, and they face all difficulties bravely and overcome them wisely. Their purposes are planted at the right time, and they bloom and produce fruit, which does not fall prematurely to the ground.

Thought that is fearlessly linked to purpose becomes a creative force: anyone who knows this is ready to become something higher and stronger than a mere bundle of wavering thoughts and fluctuating sensations; anyone who does this has become the conscious and intelligent wielder of their mental powers.

Chapter 5

The Thought-Factor in Achievement

Everything a person achieves or fails to achieve is the direct result of their own thoughts. In a universe that is justly ordered, where any loss of balance would mean total destruction, individual responsibility must be absolute. A person's weaknesses and strengths, purity and impurity, are their own, not someone else's. They are created by themselves, not by others, and can only be changed by themselves, never by another person. Their condition is also their own, not someone else's. Their suffering and happiness come from within. As they think, so they are; as they continue to think, so they remain.

A strong person cannot help a weaker one unless that weaker person is willing to be helped, and even then, the weak person must become strong on their own; they must develop the strength they admire in another through their own efforts. No one but themselves can change their condition.

People have often thought and said, "Many people are slaves because one is an oppressor; let's hate the oppressor." However, there is now a growing tendency among some to reverse this judgment and say, "One person is an oppressor because many are slaves; let's despise the slaves."

The truth is that both oppressor and slave are cooperating in ignorance, and while they seem to harm each other, they are actually harming themselves. Perfect Knowledge understands the law at work in the weakness of the oppressed and the misused power of the oppressor; perfect Love, seeing the suffering that both states bring, condemns neither; perfect Compassion embraces both oppressor and oppressed.

Anyone who has conquered weakness and let go of all selfish thoughts belongs to neither oppressor nor oppressed. They are free.

A person can only rise, conquer, and achieve by lifting up their thoughts. They can only remain weak, miserable, and abject by refusing to lift their thoughts.

Before a person can achieve anything, even in worldly matters, they must raise their thoughts above base animal indulgence. To succeed, they may not need to give up all animality and selfishness, but they must at least sacrifice some of it. A person whose main focus is base indulgence cannot think clearly or plan methodically; they cannot find and develop their latent resources and will fail in any endeavor. Without beginning to control their thoughts, they are not ready to control affairs or take on serious responsibilities. They are not fit to act independently and stand alone. But they are limited only by the thoughts they choose.

There can be no progress, no achievement without sacrifice, and a person's worldly success will be proportional to how much they sacrifice their confused animal thoughts and focus their mind on developing their plans, strengthening their resolve, and becoming more self-reliant. The higher they lift their thoughts, the more manly, upright, and righteous they become, and the greater their success, the more blessed and enduring their achievements will be.

The universe does not favor the greedy, the dishonest, and the vicious, although it may sometimes appear to do so on the surface; it helps the honest, the generous, and the virtuous. All the great Teachers throughout history have declared this in various ways, and to prove and know it, a person has only to persist in making themselves more and more virtuous by raising their thoughts.

Intellectual achievements result from thought dedicated to the pursuit of knowledge or the beautiful and true in life and nature. Such achievements may sometimes be associated with vanity and ambition, but they are not caused by those traits; they naturally result from long and arduous effort and pure and unselfish thoughts.

Spiritual achievements are the culmination of holy aspirations. A person who constantly thinks noble and lofty thoughts and focuses on all that is pure and unselfish will, as surely as the sun reaches its peak and the moon becomes full, become wise and noble in character and rise to a position of influence and blessedness.

Achievement, of any kind, is the crown of effort and the diadem of thought. With self-control, resolution, purity, righteousness, and well-directed thought, a person rises; with animality, indolence, impurity, corruption, and confused thoughts, a person falls.

A person may rise to great success in the world and even reach high spiritual levels, but they can also fall back into weakness and misery by allowing arrogant, selfish, and corrupt thoughts to take over.

Victories achieved through right thinking can only be maintained with vigilance. Many people give up when success seems assured and quickly fall back into failure.

All achievements, whether in business, intellectual pursuits, or spiritual growth, result from well-directed thought, are governed by the same law, and follow the same method; the only difference is in the goal.

Someone who wants to achieve little must sacrifice little; someone who wants to achieve much must sacrifice much; someone who wants to reach great heights must make great sacrifices.

Chapter 6

Visions and Ideals

Dreamers are the saviors of the world. Just as the visible world is supported by the invisible, so people, through all their struggles, sins, and mundane tasks, are nourished by the beautiful visions of their solitary dreamers. Humanity cannot forget its dreamers or let their ideals fade away; it lives through them, recognizing them as the realities that it will one day see and know.

Composers, sculptors, painters, poets, prophets, sages—these are the creators of the future world, the architects of heaven. The world is beautiful because they have lived; without them, working humanity would perish.

Anyone who holds onto a beautiful vision, a lofty ideal in their heart, will one day realize it. Columbus had a vision of another world, and he discovered it. Copernicus imagined a universe full of worlds, and he revealed it. Buddha envisioned a spiritual world of pure beauty and perfect peace, and he entered it.

Cherish your visions; cherish your ideals; cherish the music that stirs in your heart, the beauty that forms in your mind, the loveliness that wraps around your purest thoughts. From them will grow all delightful conditions, all heavenly environments. If you stay true to them, your world will be built from them.

To desire is to obtain; to aspire is to achieve. Should man's basest desires be fully satisfied while his purest aspirations starve? This is not the Law: such a situation can never exist. "Ask and receive."

Dream big dreams, and as you dream, so shall you become. Your Vision is the promise of what you shall one day be; your Ideal is the prophecy of what you shall finally reveal.

The greatest achievement was once a dream. The oak sleeps in the acorn; the bird waits in the egg; and in the highest vision of the soul, an awakening angel stirs. Dreams are the seeds of reality.

Your circumstances may be unfavorable, but they will not remain so if you see an Ideal and strive to reach it. You cannot change within and remain unchanged without. Here is a young man struggling with poverty and labor; confined to long hours in an unhealthy workshop; uneducated and lacking refinement. But he dreams of better things: intelligence, refinement, grace, and beauty. He mentally builds an ideal life; the vision of greater freedom and opportunity fills him.

Unrest drives him to action, and he uses his spare time and resources, however small, to develop his latent powers. Soon, his mind changes so much that the workshop can no longer contain him. It becomes so out of tune with his mentality that it falls away like an old garment, and as new opportunities match his expanding abilities, he leaves it forever. Years later, this young man becomes a mature leader. He masters certain mental forces, wielding worldwide influence and nearly unmatched power. He holds great responsibilities, speaks, and changes lives. People hang on his words and reshape their characters. He becomes the central, luminous figure around which countless destinies revolve. He has realized his youthful Vision. He has become one with his Ideal.

And you, young reader, will realize the Vision of your heart, whether it is base or beautiful, or a mix of both, because you will always gravitate towards what you secretly love most. You will receive the exact results of your thoughts; you will earn exactly what you deserve. Whatever your current environment, you will fall, remain, or rise with your thoughts, Vision, and Ideal. You will become as small as your strongest desire or as great as your highest aspiration. In the beautiful words of Stanton Kirkham Davis, "You may be keeping accounts, and soon you will walk out of the door that seemed to be the barrier to your ideals, and find yourself before an audience—the pen still behind your ear, the ink stains on your fingers, and there and then you will pour out the torrent of your inspiration. You may be driving sheep, and you will wander into the city, wide-eyed; you will follow the spirit into the master's studio, and after a while, he will say, 'I have nothing more to teach you.' Now you have become the master, who dreamed of great things while driving sheep. You will set down the saw and the plane to take on the regeneration of the world."

The thoughtless, ignorant, and lazy see only the apparent effects and not the things themselves. They talk of luck, fortune, and chance. Seeing someone grow rich, they say, "How lucky he is!" Observing someone become intellectual, they exclaim, "How fortunate he is!" Noticing the saintly character and influence of another, they remark,

"How chance favors him!" They don't see the trials, failures, and struggles these people have voluntarily faced to gain their experience; they don't know the sacrifices made, the undaunted efforts, and the faith exercised to overcome the seemingly impossible and realize their heart's Vision. They don't know the darkness and heartaches; they only see the light and joy and call it "luck." They don't see the long, arduous journey but only the pleasant goal and call it "good fortune." They don't understand the process, only the result, and call it chance.

In all human affairs, there are efforts and results, and the strength of the effort measures the result. Chance does not exist. Gifts, powers, and material, intellectual, and spiritual possessions are the fruits of effort; they are thoughts completed, goals achieved, and visions realized.

The Vision you glorify in your mind, the Ideal you hold in your heart—this you will build your life upon; this you will become.

Chapter 7
Serenity

Calmness of mind is one of the beautiful jewels of wisdom. It is the result of long and patient effort in self-control. Its presence indicates matured experience and a deeper knowledge of the laws and operations of thought.

A person becomes calm as they understand themselves as a being shaped by thought. This knowledge requires understanding others as being shaped by thought, too. As someone gains the right understanding and sees more clearly the connections of things through cause and effect, they stop fussing, fuming, worrying, and grieving, and instead remain poised, steadfast, and serene.

The calm person, having learned to control themselves, knows how to adapt to others. Others, in turn, respect their spiritual strength and feel they can learn from and rely on them. The more tranquil a person becomes, the greater their success, influence, and power for good. Even a regular businessperson will find their business prospering as they develop greater self-control and calmness, because people always prefer to deal with someone whose demeanor is steady and balanced.

The strong, calm person is always loved and respected. They are like a shade-giving tree in a thirsty land or a sheltering rock in a storm. Who doesn't love a calm heart and a sweet-tempered, balanced life? It doesn't matter whether it rains or shines, or what changes come to those with these blessings, for they are always sweet, serene, and calm. That exquisite balance of character, which we call serenity, is the final lesson of growth, the fruit of the soul. It is as precious as wisdom and more desirable than gold—yes, even fine gold. How insignificant mere money-seeking looks compared to a serene life—a life that lives in the ocean of Truth, beneath the waves, beyond the reach of tempests, in Eternal Calm!

How many people do we know who sour their lives, ruin all that is sweet and beautiful with explosive tempers, destroy their balance of character, and create bad blood! It is a question whether the majority of people do not ruin their lives and mar their happiness by lack of self-control. How few people do we meet in life who are well-balanced, who have that exquisite poise that is the hallmark of a developed character!

Yes, humanity surges with uncontrolled passion, is tumultuous with ungoverned grief, and is blown about by anxiety and doubt. Only the wise person, only one whose thoughts are controlled and purified, makes the winds and storms of the soul obey them.

Storm-tossed souls, wherever you may be, under whatever conditions you may live, know this: in the ocean of life, the isles of blessedness are smiling, and the sunny shore of your ideal awaits your arrival. Keep your hand firmly on the helm of thought. In the vessel of your soul lies the commanding Master; He only sleeps—awaken Him. Self-control is strength; right thought is mastery; calmness is power. Say to your heart, "Peace, be still!"

Thank You for Reading

Dear Reader,

We hope this timeless classic has sparked your imagination and enriched your literary journey. Now that you've turned the final page, we want to share a vision for the future of reading—one where every classic you've ever wanted to explore is at your fingertips, in a format that best suits your life.

We'd like to invite you to gain immediate, unlimited digital & audiobook access to hundreds of the most treasured literary classics ever written—along with the option to secure deluxe paperback, hardcover & box set editions at printing cost. Together, we can spark a new global literary renaissance alongside our small, independent publishing house called "The Library of Alexandria."

Thousands of years ago, the Library of Alexandria stood as a beacon of knowledge—until it was lost to history. We aim to reignite that spirit of preservation and discovery right now, in the modern age— only this time, it's accessible to all, in every language and every format.

Picture a world where every timeless classic, novel, poem, or philosophical treatise is not only available to read but also updated for today's readers—modernized, translated into any language or dialect, and ready to enjoy in any format you choose, whether that is in an eBook, audiobook, paperback, or deluxe hardcover & box set version a printing cost.

By joining our movement to rebuild the modern Library of Alexandria, you become part of an unprecedented mission to offer:

- **Unlimited Audiobook & eBook Access to the Greatest Classics of All Time**

  Instantly explore thousands of legendary works, from Plato and Shakespeare to Jane Austen and Leo Tolstoy. All are instantly ready to read or listen to, giving you a complete literary universe at your fingertips.

- **Paperback & Deluxe Editions at Printing Costs:**

Purchase any title in a paperback, deluxe hardbound, or deluxe boxset edition at printing costs, shipped right to your doorstep. Curate your personal library of Alexandria with editions worthy of display—crafted to last, designed to captivate, and delivered straight to your door.

- **Modern translations for Contemporary Readers in all languages and dialects**

Discover a vast selection of classics reimagined in clear, current language—no more struggling with outdated phrases or obscure references. Next to the original versions, we aim to offer translations in as many languages and dialects as possible.

As we continue our translation efforts and add new languages, readers everywhere can connect with these works as if they were written today. By bridging linguistic divides, you're contributing to ensuring that these timeless stories become more meaningful, accessible, and inspiring for people across the globe.

- **Your Personal Library of Alexandria:**

Over the months and years, you'll curate a unique physical archive of classics—each volume a testament to your taste, curiosity, and love of knowledge. It's not just about owning books—it's about curating a cultural legacy you'll cherish and pass down for generations to come.

- **Join a Global Literary Renaissance:**

Your support fuels an ongoing mission: allowing us to reinvest in offering deluxe print editions (including special boxsets) at their true cost, broaden the range of available formats and translations, and extend the reach of these works to new audiences worldwide. By joining today, you're not just preserving a legacy of masterpieces; you set in motion a powerful wave of literary accessibility.

We are more than a publisher—we're a movement, and we can't do it alone. Your support lets us scale our mission, preserving and reimagining history's greatest works for tomorrow's readers.

Become a Torchbearer of knowledge.

Thank you for picking up this book and allowing us into your literary journey. As you turn the pages, know that you're part of something larger: a global effort to keep these stories alive, share their wisdom across borders and generations, and spark a true cultural revival for the modern era.

If this resonates with you—please consider taking the next step by visiting:

www.libraryofalexandria.com

With gratitude and a shared love of knowledge,

The Modern Library of Alexandria Team

Visit:

www.libraryofalexandria.com

Or scan the code below:

www.ingramcontent.com/pod-product-compliance
Lightning Source LLC
Chambersburg PA
CBHW011651010726
47499CB00010B/3214